the well of the dead

Clive Allan

Matador
9 Priory Business Park,
Wistow Road, Kibworth Beauchamp,
Leicestershire. LE8 0RX
Tel: 0116 279 2299
Email: books@troubador.co.uk
Web: www.troubador.co.uk/matador
Twitter: @matadorbooks

ISBN PB: 978 1788036 634
HB: 978 1788035 101

British Library Cataloguing in Publication Data.
A catalogue record for this book is available from the British Library.

Printed and bound by CPI Group (UK) Ltd, Croydon, CR0 4YY
Typeset in 11pt Aldine401 BT by Troubador Publishing Ltd, Leicester, UK

Matador is an imprint of Troubador Publishing Ltd

MIX
Paper from
responsible sources
FSC® C013604

For Rose

Where the graves of Clan Chattan are clustered together,
Where MacGillivray died by the Well of the Dead,
We stooped to the moorland and plucked the pale heather,
That blooms where the hope of the Stuart was sped.

Andrew Lang 1844 – 1912

2010

Prologue

Late afternoon sunlight plunged through the towering firs, hazy shafts of it, full of the dusty detritus of the forest. Its glow fell upon a small clearing, soft golden light that bathed the four men standing around the dome-shaped boulder at its centre. Long finger-like shadows reached out from them across the forest floor, sinister distorted cameos that failed to bespeak their mood.

Two of them were engaged in a heated conversation. The sound of their raised voices drifted upwards, to where the forest birds, disturbed by the din, were impelled to vacate their lofty perches in a frenzy of flapping wings.

The older of the two belligerents was incandescent. He spoke at a furious pace with a broad low-pitched accent, almost slurring his words.

'What on erth have ye got us out here fir?'

He spun around, arms outstretched as if to reinforce his point, then stood in silence, hands placed firmly on his narrow hips. He was well toned for a man past fifty, over six feet tall with lank swept-back hair that flowed down beyond the collar of his denim jacket. A greying goatee clung to his chin, like tangled wire wool, merging with the stubble that darkened his sunken cheeks. His eyes, like polished lignite, bore into the younger man, who now stood, arms folded, resting his foot nonchalantly on the boulder.

'You havenae answered me, son. What *is* this place all about?'

The conspicuous-looking figure facing him was even taller. He was a giant of a man, Neanderthal-like, with unruly red hair that hung about his scalp like a wet mop. Beneath his tousled locks, a ragged right ear was just visible, the result of a long-forgotten injury that had been inflicted during a vicious brawl.

Strangely enough, it was not the Neanderthal's features that made the older man wary. It was his apparel. For he was wearing old Highland dress, a *féileadh-mór* or great plaid of dull red tartan that extended to just beyond his bare white knees. From his shoulder, a thick leather strap supported the weight of a basket-hilted broadsword, and around his waist, a wide cowhide belt gathered up the folds of the heavy plaid. Hanging from it was a rudimentary sporran, worn in the old-fashioned way and a small dirk, a stabbing knife, concealed in a leather sheath.

The red-haired warrior slapped his leathery hand down upon the boulder, and glared at the older man. His accent was softer and of Highland origin, his voice hushed.

''Tis the Stone of the Massacre of the Officers. Nineteen of them, brought here on a cart by Cumberland's Royal Scots after the battle upon the moor, away yonder. Each one was murdered here, but for one of Lovat's men, who escaped with his life.'

The older man looked about him in puzzlement. His eyes focussed upon the tribute ribbons that danced on the breeze from the branches of a nearby birch tree.

'So why d'ye come here, son? Ah mean tae such a mingin' wee place as this?'

'To contemplate,' the Highlander replied curtly. 'I come here to reflect and pay my respects. No one disturbs me here, Mack.'

His voice then became raised, as if to make his point. 'Which means it's a good place to come and have a blether with the likes of you!'

He looked across at the other two men who were standing back beyond the sunlit boulder, close to the tree from which the tribute ribbons hung.

'Do yer friends there speak at all?'

There was no response from them. They stared back at him, expressionless. One, whose face remained darkened under the broad brim of a black fedora, sniffed the air and stuffed his hands into the pockets of his long beige trench coat. The other, a tall, broad-shouldered man with a prominent hooked nose and grey caterpillar-like eyebrows, preferred to look self-consciously down at his feet.

'They don't need tae speak, son. Ah can speak for them, y'see,' snapped the man he'd called Mack.

The Highlander cocked his head to one side. 'Well I'd like *you* to tell me then, why I got the call to meet after all this time, as if I'm suddenly very important, like.'

Mack sneered. 'You're no important to me, son... but you might be *useful*.'

The Highlander pointed back at him accusingly. 'You need to show me more respect, Mack...' He patted the intricate hilt of his sword. '... Or I might want to cut yer tongue out.' He leaned back against the boulder and grinned, the aggression suddenly gone. 'Tell me then, why the meeting with your chums here? What do you want from me, old pal?'

The man in the fedora pulled out a gold cigarette case and selected one of its contents. He tapped the cigarette repeatedly on the engraved lid before raising it to his mouth, then spoke, allowing it to jump around between his narrow lips.

'I've heard a lot about you my friend. Your *unusual* lifestyle fascinates me.'

Mack laughed. '*Fascinates you?* The fugly bastard gives *me* the friggin' creeps!'

The Highlander began to withdraw his sword from its scabbard. In response, the blade of a stiletto flashed in Mack's hand.

This undesirable escalation in hostilities prompted the man in the fedora to intervene.

'Don't be silly, gentlemen. Put the blades away and let's talk in a civilised manner.' He glared at the Highlander, who shrugged and reluctantly complied, his dark eyes still fixed on Mack.

'You're from Strathnairn, aren't you?' the man in the hat asked.

The Highlander flashed him a glance. 'Aye, that I am. What's it to you?'

'You must know of the Frasers at Cullaird Castle, then?'

'Sure I do. They Frasers, or their ancestors to be precise, still have the blood of my clan on their hands.'

'And why would that be, exactly?' His questioner finally lit his cigarette, and inhaled deeply.

The Highlander squinted back at him suspiciously and sidestepped the question. 'Who are you exactly?'

'It's not important who I am, really it isn't. But you may call me David if that would make you happier.' He flicked the excess ash from his cigarette. 'Now where were we? You were telling me about these awful Fraser people.'

The Highlander reluctantly returned to his story. 'They never turned up on the field at Culloden. Preferred to make themselves scarce, stealin' from folk, like common highwaymen, to line their own pockets. The story goes they returned to Cullaird with a great hoard of cash, whilst our Chattan brothers fell six deep before the redcoats' guns.'

'Oh, so you've heard about this so-called *hoard*, then?'

'Aye, of course I have. Some say it's still hidden somewhere inside the keep at Cullaird.'

'That's interesting, because *we*… that's my friends and I, are about to embark upon a project to locate that very hoard.'

The Highlander seemed interested now. Then he guffawed scornfully, and as his head jerked back, he squinted into the sunlight that flickered across his face. 'I suppose y'think I know where it is, eh? Well you're wrong, mister. I definitely cannae help you on that score.'

'No, no, of course I'm not suggesting that you have knowledge of where it is secreted, but I was wondering whether you'd like to *help* us find it. You've some experience of breaking into large country houses, I hear?'

The Highlander thought for a second before answering. 'How d'you know this hoard still exists after all this time? Surely the truth is the cash was all spent by the Frasers long ago?'

'You're absolutely right, my friend. I don't know for sure, but I have information that has recently come to light which may help us locate it… if it's still there… and I can assure you that if it *did* exist, the Frasers never located it.'

The Highlander wasn't convinced, his response almost mocking in its delivery. 'Och, I don't know. I'm finished with all that sort of thing. I prefer to live here quietly in the forest with the spirits of my long-dead brothers. Besides, you'd be lookin' for what? A sack of old coins worth a few grand… no, you and your pals can piss off. I think our wee chat has just ended, mister.'

David smiled, unperturbed by the Highlander's rebuff. He flicked the stub of his cigarette onto the ground. 'Seven million, to be exact. That would be its current value. Oh, and we're not just talking a sackful of coins here. There's a lot more than that!'

The Highlander stared at him wide-eyed, then laughed manically.

'Seven fucking million? Who are you kiddin' here, mister? Are you telling me that castle's stacked to the roof with gold bloody bars, then?'

David looked at him impassively. 'Not at all. There are possibly a few chestfuls, that's all. A dozen at the most: receptacles that could easily be secreted in a void behind a wall... something like that.'

'And how did you arrive at this incredibly large figure? Please do tell.'

'Simple. I have contacts, experts in their field. That's all you need to know.'

He stepped forward a couple of paces and placed a hand on the Highlander's shoulder. 'Let's you and me take a short walk, and I'll explain everything.'

The Highlander studied his new friend for a second, then grudgingly agreed to his proposal. The two men turned about and headed off up the grassy track, whilst Mack and his companion looked on dispassionately.

Ten minutes later they reappeared. The Highlander returned to his boulder, whilst David lit another cigarette and expelled a column of blue smoke up towards the cobalt sky.

'Our friend here has agreed to assist us, in return for a cut of twenty per cent, which I only consider to be fair. He *will* be taking all the risks after all. What do you say, gentlemen?'

The other two men nodded, Mack acting as their spokesman. 'Aye, so long as he doesnae do somethin' mental that'll drop us all in the shite.'

The Highlander looked from one man to the other, then a wide grin spread across his face.

'Then I'll do it, boys. The question is when, exactly?'

David pulled out his mobile phone and tapped the screen several times before looking up.

'How about the morning of Thursday, the fifteenth of April, earlyish? The Frasers will still be down in the Cayman Islands during that week, enjoying their usual spring holiday in the sun. The place should be completely empty, so you'll have it all to yourself for as long as you like.'

'You're sure? No doubts?' the Highlander challenged him. 'What about cleaners, alarms, things like that?'

'There is a cleaner who goes in on a Thursday when the Frasers are at home, but not until eleven. My source assures me she won't go in at all if they're away. But if, in the unlikely event she did turn up, I'm sure you could deal with her intrusion appropriately. As far as the alarm's concerned, there will be no problem deactivating it. Let's just leave it at that, shall we?'

'Okay. Thursday the fifteenth it is then, first thing, and let's hope the cleaner takes a day off!'

'Good. At last a chance to avenge your clan brothers, eh?'

David moved forward to shake hands with the Highlander and nodded towards Mack. 'Our mutual friend here will accompany you to the castle on the day in question, to help you carry anything you may find there.'

'If he must,' the Highlander grunted. 'As you say, we can take our time if no one's there, eh?'

David nodded in agreement. 'We'll leave you to enjoy your forest whilst we go away and have a little chat. Just need to make sure my colleagues here are in total agreement with the plan.'

'I thought they already were,' the Highlander protested.

'I believe it's only fair to canvas their views privately, especially when it comes to individual stakes in the project. I'm sure you get my gist?'

He turned and gestured to the other two men. The three of them then ambled off down the forestry track that led back to the road, leaving the Highlander standing alone amongst the creaking firs. He grimaced as he watched them go and stooped to rub his leg. The pain had come back again; a terrible burning that afflicted all his limbs from time to time. Seeking relief, he leaned back against the boulder, deep in thought, his ears full of the sounds of the forest. They were sounds that now morphed into agitated whispers, the unintelligible voices of the ragged Highlanders who'd stepped out from the gloomy plantation surrounding him. The whispering became louder and louder. He stood upright again, grasping the hilt of his sword, ostensibly surrounded by the bloodied apparitions of his ancestors, and then clamped his eyes shut as the whispering became unbearable. He shook his head violently from side to side, until the blood pulsed in his temples and he let out a long, mournful howl that echoed through the trees. Only then did the whispering finally fade, almost as quickly as it had begun. The lugubrious faces of the long-dead warriors had melted away into their woodland mausoleum once more.

Wings flapped somewhere up in the canopy of the forest, whilst the tribute ribbons danced in the breeze. All was as it should be… and the pain had gone.

David stood by the green Land Rover, gazing across the bonnet at his fellow conspirators.

'That boy's a true hothead, and as mad as a March hare. He tells me he has conversations with dead clansmen for God's sake.'

'That'll be the heather ale he brews up. The bloody stuff messes with his head!' Mack explained.

'Well, I believe he'll fit the bill perfectly,' David confirmed. Then he eyed each of his companions in turn. 'I think if we're all in agreement, we've found our man!'

Mack nodded, glancing across at the figure with the bushy

eyebrows who'd yet to contribute. 'So long as *he* can play his part.'

The self-effacing third man nodded uneasily, the distinctive eyebrows lifting slightly. 'Aye, it shouldn't be a problem.'

'Splendid, that's settled then,' said David, beaming. 'As long as you've both seen and heard enough. Then, Mack, I will leave you to do the honours with your Highland friend.'

Mack said nothing and headed off up the track to where the Highlander had been left waiting. The other two men climbed into the Land Rover and watched as Mack disappeared from view. David then turned on the radio and sat humming in accompaniment to a Righteous Brothers number that was playing. His nervous associate, by contrast, sat in silence, staring vacantly out through the windscreen, his pallid features reflecting the enormity of what he was about to embark upon.

Chapter One

Inverness
Monday 12th April

Neil Strachan trudged out of the dental surgery in Crown Drive feeling a little sorry for himself. There was rain in the air, and now he had a lengthy walk back to his beloved MG Midget. The tiny surgery car park had been full and the road outside was in the process of being dug up on the side that didn't have double yellow lines.

'Jesus,' he grumbled impiously, as the water board's jackhammer started up again, just yards from where he was standing. He rubbed his cheek and glared back at the innocuous-looking Victorian villa that apparently doubled as a torture chamber. Neil had had the nerve removed from a rear molar, and although the local anaesthetic was still providing much-needed pain relief, the vibratory effects of the drill had surged through his aching jaw. He made his way up the road, giving the workmen a wide birth. On seeing him, they stopped drilling and one of the yellow-clad labourers waved. 'Sorry, chum. Burst pipe, I'm afraid.'

Neil raised a hand in ungrateful thanks and produced a less than convincing smile. He'd left work early to undergo this violation of his tooth, and now he was going home to lie on the sofa and master the art of drinking tea with a half-numb mouth!

He drove slowly down Victoria Drive, past the youth hostel and out onto Milburn Road. A train startled him as it rushed by to his left, heading off down the lonely but dramatic line to Perth. Then, as he peered out from behind the windscreen wipers, it dawned upon him that tonight was Cat's gym night. He preferred calling his girlfriend Cat. Catriona seemed a bit of a mouthful! This meant she would be late in, and he'd have to cook... and in his condition too!

'Typical,' he mouthed as he sped down the slip road to the A9 and joined a queue of slow-moving traffic. Ten minutes later and he was passing the bus stop where Cat normally caught the bus into town each morning. Then it was a left into Stable Hollow, and up onto the driveway of the salmon-roofed new build they'd bought together just before Christmas.

With the MG secured in the garage, Neil fumbled for his front door key and pushed it into the lock. Frenzied barking erupted from inside the house, followed by a skidding of nails on the wooden floor of the porch. When he pushed the door open, a brown nose forced its way through the gap, sniffing and twitching as if wishing to confirm that the master was indeed home at last. Tam, his chocolate-coloured cocker spaniel, soon confirmed that this was indeed the case, and shot off on a celebratory lap of the house, his favourite pseudo-duck toy hanging limply from his mouth.

Neil's first stop was the bedroom, where he substituted his grey suit for a pair of old jeans and his favourite sweatshirt. Tam looked on from the centre of the bed, his eyes wild with delight.

'You'll be in deep shite wee laddie if the boss catches you on that bed throw,' he chuckled. Then, having chased the dog off the bed, he bounded down the stairs, playfully pursuing him but getting nowhere near. Next, he went out into the garden for a throw of Tam's tennis ball before finally sinking into the sofa, glass of water and two paracetamol in hand.

Drinking *any* form of liquid turned out to be a perilous business, so Neil had decided to forego the tea. He slid the Eric Bogle disc, *Plain and Simple*, into the CD player and, having carefully removed his new rimless glasses, sat back contentedly, one arm around his hound, eyes firmly closed. The gravelly voice of the Scottish folk singer soon did its work, and both man and dog were sound asleep.

It seemed that he'd only been quiescent for a matter of seconds when he woke suddenly to the sound of the front door closing. Tam had heard it too and scurried off to investigate. Daylight had faded to dusk, and the clock on the CD player said it was 8.05 pm.

His partner of nearly four years, Catriona Duncan, appeared in the doorway and turned on the light. She was wearing a clingy blue tracksuit and trainers, her long blonde hair tied tightly back.

'Have you been asleep all this time?' she enquired. 'I didn't know a dental filling was quite so tiring.' She smiled and headed on up the hallway, her work and gym bags in one hand, and two Tesco carrier bags containing groceries in the other.

Neil followed her into the kitchen, relishing how the tightness of the tracksuit accentuated the curves of her body. He rubbed his cheek and was pleasantly surprised that he could feel it again.

'Sorry,' he said, cautiously planting a kiss on her cheek. 'I took some painkillers, and put a CD on. Must have drifted off. How was work, anyway?'

'Aye, fine. Busy as usual. Jardine's cracking the whip as only he can!'

Her boss, Hugh Jardine, the area procurator fiscal for Inverness, could be a pain in the backside when he wanted to be. He was meticulous and sometimes aloof, but now that his wife Isla had declared her intention to retire from the solicitors' practice she worked for in Nairn, he'd become particularly tetchy. To cap it all, the kids had been off their hands for some time, and she was pressing him to downsize from their five-bedroomed house just outside the town.

'... And the gym? Good workout?'

She looked around at him suspiciously. 'Aye, fine. Why do you ask?'

'No reason... don't I always?'

'Umm, I suppose.'

'Were the usual faces there this evening?'

'Only Andrea and Kirsten.' She seemed eager to change the subject. 'How's your tooth, by the way?' she asked, returning to the task of emptying the contents of the Tesco bags onto the worktop.

'Fine, now that the paracetamol has taken effect.'

'Good,' she replied, sidling up to him and draping her arms around his neck. 'Then you can pop out and get a takeaway, seeing that tonight's *your* night to cook!'

Neil stepped back, a look of profound shock etched upon his youthful features. 'In my condition?'

Cat reached up and released her long hair from the hairband that had been holding it in place. She shook her head, allowing her flaxen locks to flow free, and stood glaring at him, hands on hips. 'What? You're looking at me like a goldfish!'

His look of surprise persisted, as if he'd just swallowed his damned tooth!

Then his expression melted into a grin, and he stooped to perform a flamboyant bow, worthy of any medieval servant. 'Your wish is my command, my sweet... Will it be Chinese or Indian?'

Cat punched him playfully on the arm. 'You old fool,' she giggled. 'Go and get the menu for that new Indian down on Ness Bank.'

Neil bowed again and headed off into the sitting room,

where he began ferreting around in the drawer of the oak wall unit for the all-important menu.

'I'm just going out to the freezer to put some of this cold stuff away,' she called out. 'Tam's coming with me.'

'Okay,' he replied, still searching. He heard the kitchen door slam and then there was silence. His hand finally emerged from the drawer clutching the menu. He'd promised himself that he'd clear that drawer out every weekend since they'd moved in! Then, as he stepped into the hallway, Cat's mobile phone began to ring from the small table by the stairs. Actually, it wasn't a ring at all; it was Il Divo blasting out 'Notte di Luce'... 'Nights in White Satin'!

He picked up the device, eager to put a stop to the racket, and pressed the 'accept call' button.

'Hi, Cat, hope you're okay. Missed you at the gym tonight.' It was Cat's good friend and ex-work colleague, Andrea MacLean.

Neil could feel his heart rate quicken. 'Hello, Andrea, actually it's me, Neil. Cat's just popped outside for a second.'

'Oh, hello, Neil. Sorry to disturb you. Obviously Cat's home, then. That's all I wanted to know. Unusual for her not to turn up at the gym. Must've been tied up at work this evening.'

'Aye, she's been a bit busy the last couple of weeks. I'll tell her you rang, Andrea. Thanks for the call.'

'Thanks Neil. Ta-ta for now.'

The phone line went dead. Neil lowered the device from his ear and gazed at the blank screen for several seconds before returning it to the table. His mind raced. *What was all that about? Where has Cat been, for Christ's sake... and why did she lie to me?*

He walked back into the kitchen just as Cat opened the back door.

'Did you find the menu?' she asked, oblivious to the frown now embedded upon his face.

'Aye, here it is. Let me know what you fancy.'

She grabbed the menu playfully and studied its contents, whilst Neil stooped to caress the top of Tam's head.

Her eyes then found his. 'Did I hear my phone go just now?'

He stood up, running a hand through his unruly chestnut-brown hair. 'Och aye, it was a cold call… something to do with home insulation.'

She returned to the menu. 'They're a pain in the arse. I wish they'd go and harass someone else. Right, this is what I'm having.'

She reeled off a list of dishes and handed him the menu. 'You happy to go and get it? Take my car if you want.'

'Will do, okay.'

He called the restaurant and made the order, then grabbed his jacket and disappeared through the front door. Once seated inside Cat's silver Renault Clio, he took a deep breath, still conscious of the thud of his heartbeat in his ears. *Why on earth would Cat lie about going to the gym? She's never done that before.* She even confessed to him that one of the trainee fiscals had given her an unwelcome kiss at her office Christmas party last year… 'Just in case you'd heard through the grapevine,' she'd said.

He turned onto Culloden Road and headed into town, still musing over his options. Should he just confront her? Surely she'd just give him an explanation and that would be that. But, no, this was a blatant lie. Why would she have said what she had, unless she had something to hide?

He needed to be sure before he said anything. But something was amiss… surely! He knew her too well.

The high walls of Porterfield Prison rushed past on his left. Then it was down along the riverbank to the bridge over the River Ness. But instead of turning down Ness Bank towards the Indian restaurant, he carried on along Glenurquhart Road towards the leisure centre.

The spacious glass-roofed reception area was quiet when he marched in. His eyes darted from left to right, urgently seeking out the manager, Martin Cumming. He spotted him behind the information desk, poring over a computer screen with a young woman, who, from her mode of dress, appeared to be a member of staff.

Cumming looked up, conscious of someone approaching the desk.

'Hello Neil, long time no see. No time for a game of squash these days, eh?'

Neil shrugged. 'You know how it is, Martin, what with work and everything.'

'Excuses, excuses. Anyway, what can I do for you? Is this business or pleasure?'

'Neither really, mate.' Neil's eyes sought out the door to the manager's office. 'Can we have a chat somewhere a little more private, like?'

Cumming immediately got the message, and ushered him into the tiny office. The young man in the polo shirt and shorts looked puzzled. 'This is all very intriguing, Neil.'

'Aye, aye, I suppose it must be. Look, can I have a quick look at your CCTV for earlier on tonight?'

'Yeah, I suppose. Who are you looking for exactly, Inverness's most wanted?'

Neil was in no mood for jokes. 'Cat, actually.'

'Cat! Why? Is she missing or something?'

Neil shook his head and smiled weakly. 'No, no, nothing like that. She came home without her work ID tonight, and now she's panicking. I was coming into town for a takeaway, so I said I'd drop in and ask. You know, to see if she was wearing it when she came in from work earlier on.'

'Oh, I see. Well we don't want anyone conning their way into the procurator fiscal's office, do we?' He gestured towards the CCTV monitor. 'Go on, fill your boots. What time did she get down here?'

'Would've been around five forty-five, usual time.'

'Okay, let's have a look-see. I was in the office around that time so wouldn't have seen her come in.'

He tapped busily on the grimy keyboard that sat in front of the monitor. 'Five forty-five, you say. Right, I've set it from five thirty. Just in case. You can fast-forward from then on.'

Having been given instructions on the workings of the CCTV software, Cumming left the office, promising that he would ask Mary on the front desk whether she'd seen Cat that evening.

Neil pushed his glasses back up his nose, then leaned forward to view the footage on the screen. He'd set it on fast forward, but not too fast, so that he might miss his partner strolling into the reception area. Five forty-five passed with no sighting of Cat breezing past the camera with her numerous bags and flowing blonde hair dancing upon her shoulders. At five forty-eight he spotted Andrea MacLean and Kirsten Graham, deep in conversation as they headed for the changing rooms. But Cat was nowhere to be seen.

In no time at all, the footage had reached six forty-five. Neil switched off the monitor and got up, exhaling deeply through pinched lips. His stomach growled, partly through hunger, and partly through nerves. There was no mistake, no communication failure, no missing each other. Cat had not gone to the centre that night. But he already knew that, if he was honest. The viewing of the CCTV was really just an excuse, a way of putting off the inevitable realisation that his beloved soulmate had lied to him. Just then his phone vibrated. He spoke, answering in monosyllables as Cat ranted at him to hurry up with the curry... 'Yep... yep... yep... will do. Fifteen minutes, okay?'

Cumming called over to him as he swept by, heading out to the car park.

'Did you find her?'

'Aye, I did, thanks. She didn't have it on, so must have left it at work. Thanks again, Martin. I didn't know where you'd got to. Better go and get that takeaway if I know what's good for me!'

'You know where to come, when you want to burn it off,' Cumming advised him with a broad grin.

Neil raised a hand in acknowledgement and then he was gone.

They sat in silence as they ate. Neil stroked Tam with his free hand, whilst the dog sat with his head resting on his master's knee, ever hopeful that a stray morsel of keema naan would fall his way.

Cat looked across at him as she took a sip from her wine glass.

'You're very thoughtful this evening. Penny for them.'

Neil swallowed a forkful of chicken bhuna. 'I was just thinking about something at work, that's all.'

'You know what they say: a problem shared…'

Neil smiled. 'Not unless you can think of a way to reduce my overtime budget by five per cent. When they've taken two DCs off the payroll to supplement a long-term drugs initiative…'

'Nope. I'll have to leave that one to you, my love. Surely Alex Brodie won't hold back when it comes to fighting the team's corner?'

She was right. Detective Chief Inspector Alex Brodie, Neil's abrasive, straight-talking boss was not one to mince his words when riled about something, whether it be crime detection targets, or the away record of his beloved Ross County FC!

Neil selected another poppadom. 'Alex hasn't been himself lately. Seems to have become very laid-back. I think he must be sickening for something.'

'Perhaps you should take a leaf out of his book, then. If you don't stop worrying, you're going to get indigestion.'

'If anything's going to give me indigestion, it'll be this stuff!' he joked, momentarily distracted from what was really worrying him. They both laughed.

'What about you?' he asked. 'Everything okay at the office? Jardine's not putting too much on you, work wise?'

Cat shook her head. 'It's pretty busy at present, what with all the referrals coming in and all the new kids they've taken on. Hugh does lean on me a bit, but I can cope. If I can't, I'll tell the stroppy old sod in no uncertain terms, believe me.'

'I bet you will,' Neil replied, rewarding Tam with his long-awaited treat. 'Still, getting into the gym must release some of that pent-up tension, eh?'

They gazed silently into each other's eyes, both probing the other for any affective signs that would confirm the emotions they inwardly harboured. In him it was suspicion and, in her, guilt. The signs were painfully apparent on both their faces, but neither of them were prepared to speak openly about their respective fears.

'Yes, it does,' Cat responded, with no hint of humour.

'Good,' said Neil, as he replenished their wine glasses.

Cat had filled the dishwasher after their meal, then gone off to bed, complaining that she had a headache. Neil had retreated to the sofa with another glass of red wine, but his mind was not on the debate raging between local politicians on the TV ahead of the forthcoming general election. It was on Cat and her now proven prevarication.

The more he thought, the more he was sure that she'd met someone else. Someone at work probably, or perhaps in a bar on one of the occasions she'd had a night out with the girls. His mind strayed back to the time he'd first met her, at school, when they both lived out on the Black Isle. She'd never been short of admirers, and had frequently been referred to as 'eye candy' by his peers! He'd readily agreed with them back in those days, but now the phrase really annoyed him. Then there was her personality. She'd always been a genial, larger-than-life character. It was one of her many strengths, perhaps the one that attracted him most. Now he feared it was working its magic on someone else.

But then, just as he'd convinced himself of her infidelity, his sense of reasoning swung in the opposite direction. This was Cat, for heaven's sake, the woman who ranted about anyone who cheated on their partner... male or female! 'If he wants to go off with someone, why doesn't he just bloody say so?' he recalled her saying, upon learning of her cousin's affair with his secretary after twenty years of marriage. No, there was a reason for this, and he needed somehow to get it out into the open. Yes, that was the only course of action to be had. He would bring it up in the morning. Decision made.

He drained his glass and let Tam out into the garden, then headed off to bed, spaniel in tow. But by the time he'd reached the bottom stair, the doubts had begun to surge through him again. The image of Cat, laughing and drinking with a man in a bar, now filled his subconscious. Her companion was a faceless, murky figure, the average man... no one he knew, or so he hoped! More concerning, the imagery wouldn't fade, playing out like a cine film on an ever-repeating reel. To make things worse, he kept hearing a voice deep within him, advising him... *Best not to know, eh? Leave it well alone for now. It'll all sort itself out. Remember, you could do untold damage if you interrogate her... and you discover your fears are unwarranted!*

But his wariness remained, born out of his mother's traumatic experience with his wayward father.

He switched off the hall light and began to climb the stairs, more inclined at that stage to accept the advice of his alter ego!

Chapter Two

Wednesday had dawned grey, with the prospect of more spring rain. The weather matched Neil's mood as he trudged across the car park at the force headquarters just off the Old Perth Road. He'd hardly slept the previous night, and to add to that, Cat had seemed particularly glum whilst she prepared to leave for work. In fact they'd hardly spoken, so it hadn't really been a good time to suggest to her that she was over the side!

Once through the doors of the airy office complex, he climbed the stairs to the Crime Services Wing and strolled along the corridor that led eventually his office. Approaching him from the opposite direction was the scrawny figure of Detective Inspector Ross Haggarty, a colleague of Neil's in the Major Enquiry Unit, and manager of the force's HOLMES Unit.

HOLMES, a backronym of Conan Doyle's famous detective, was the shortened title for Home Office Large Major Enquiry System. It had been updated post-2000 to HOLMES Two, and was now used by police forces across the country as an essential tool in the investigation of complex serious crime. If the MIR or major incident room was the engine room of a murder enquiry, then the HOLMES system was its engine!

Haggarty was forty-five years old, balding, and the possessor of a long, pointed nose. Perched either side of that prominent nose was a pair of languid brown eyes, earning him the sobriquet of Dozy, which he hated!

'Morning, sir,' he chirped as Neil passed by.

'Morning, Ross,' Neil responded, and continued on towards his office. Then he pulled up abruptly and turned to look back at Haggarty's macilent form as it retreated up the corridor.

'Oy, what's with the "sir"? Have Professional Standards finally caught up with you and demoted you or something?'

Haggarty glanced back at him, the corner of his mouth turned up to form a semi-smile. It was the most anyone had ever achieved when sharing a joke with him.

'Sorry, *sir*. Slip of the tongue, that's all.'

Neil shook his head, puzzled by his colleague's strange behaviour. The geek had finally lost the plot completely!

He threw open the door to his office, the little sanctuary that Alex Brodie had offered him following his success on the Glendaig enquiry the year before.

'Any detective who can clear up a murder that's seventy years old should be entitled to his own bolthole,' Brodie had proclaimed in the general office one afternoon... 'A place where he can think and work, untroubled by you lot rabbiting, whinging and farting all day long.'

There had been a lot of mumbling, but no one had dared raise an objection!

Neil stopped in his tracks, still halfway through the doorway. Standing by the window, busily tapping away on the keypad of his BlackBerry was the head of the Crime Services Unit, Detective Superintendent Angus Hardie BA (Hons), QPM... according to the polished wooden plaque on his own office door further along the corridor.

'Oh, good morning, sir. Hope you've not been waiting long.'

Hardie returned the device to his pocket and smiled. 'Och no, Neil. I popped in just before you arrived. Just wanted a quick word.'

Hardie was a dapper individual in his late forties, a little short in stature, but nevertheless a commanding character who was approachable, yet no pushover. He hailed from the Corstorphine area of Edinburgh, was the son of an eye surgeon and had commenced his police career in that hallowed city some twenty-five years previously. Since then, he'd worked his way up through the ranks, recently having returned from an attachment to Europol, and was now the most senior detective employed north of the River Dee.

Hardie eased himself into the chair next to Neil's desk and gestured to him to sit down.

'I've received some rather unpleasant news this morning, Neil. Alex Brodie had a heart attack at home last night. He was lifting furniture into his loft at the time, and had a nasty fall too, apparently.'

Neil's mouth dropped open, concern graven upon his face. 'Oh my God, is he okay? I mean…'

Hardie nodded. 'Aye, the paramedics got to him very quickly. Jill was helping him at the time, thank God. He's been taken to the cardiac unit at Aberdeen Royal Infirmary. Looks like he's going to need an urgent bypass, so may be off for some while.'

Neil sat back, relieved that the news wasn't as bad as it could've been. As it happened, he'd often thought Brodie was a candidate for heart problems, what with his expanding waistline and unquiet temperament.

'I'll call in and see Jill, offer any support I can.'

'Aye, that would be great, Neil. I know you've spent time with the family previously. I'll keep in touch too, of course, and get over and see him in hospital when we get the green light. I called Jill just now and have asked her to let me know if she needs anything help-wise, transport, anything at all.'

'Okay, sir, I'll do the same. Just let her know we're thinking of them. Thanks for letting me know.'

'That brings me to the other issue I've dropped in to discuss... *SIO cover*.' Hardie sat back and draped one leg over the other. 'You've attended the SIO course at Tulliallan, I believe? Just before I arrived here.'

'Aye, that's right, back in January, sir.'

'Good. Well I find myself in something of a predicament, now that poor old Alex is off sick and David Chisholm is over in Canada for more than a month, visiting his brother. That means two of the regular SIOs on this unit are unavailable. Helen Lindsay's tied up long-term on the force crime management review. That, as you know, just leaves me, this being such a small force. So I'm hoping you can help me out.'

Neil was all ears now. He knew what was coming, or at least he thought he did. 'If I can, sir, just name it.' *Oh God, how corny was that response!*

'Excellent. I'd like you to run the MEU and cover the on call SIO role for the time being, Neil... as acting DCI, of course. What do you say?'

'I'd be delighted.' Neil's response was immediate. Far too immediate, he reflected later! He knew that Hardie had other options within the force. There were several senior officers qualified for the role of senior investigating officer he could call upon, colleagues now attached to other departments. So his boss was sending out a message, and he had received it loud and clear! This was a career development offer that he wasn't going to let slip from his grasp!

'Good, that's settled then,' said Hardie, patting his thigh as if in celebration of his own plan. 'We'll have a longer chat later on. Is there anything going on in your world that could be an obstacle, cover-wise? You know, court, annual leave, anything like that?'

'No, nothing of any significance at present, sir.'

'Even better. Well, let's hope things don't get too hectic for you! I can always stand in if needed, but I doubt that will be necessary. I have every confidence in you!'

Neil grinned. 'I bet it'll be as quiet as the grave, now you've asked me to provide cover.' Then he shook his head as if some sudden realisation had just flared within him. He grinned, prompting Hardie to look back at him quizzically.

'Something I've missed?' the detective superintendent enquired.

'No, not at all. It's just dawned on me why Ross Haggarty called me "sir" in the corridor just now… did he know about this?'

Hardie laughed. 'No, he hasn't heard anything from me. But Dozy's no fool. He knew about Alex's situation and he knew I was looking for you just now. He also knows you've done the SIO course. Two and two comes to mind!'

'Ah, right. I suppose that explains it, then,' Neil sighed.

Hardie got up and made his way to the door. Then he stopped abruptly and raised a finger, as if he'd forgotten something. 'I know you've lost two DCs to the drugs initiative that starts tomorrow. Not a lot I can do about that, seeing that we're not exactly overwhelmed with work at present. But I have managed to secure a new DS from uniform. I took the decision to bring forward her move into MEU… her name's Holly Anderson… know her?'

Neil sat back and folded his arms. 'Aye, I met her over on the west coast last year. She was duty DC at Fort William when those bones were found on the beach over at Glendaig. She's dead keen, but a wee bit up herself, I'm afraid. The boys call her "Pepper" after that American TV cop from the seventies.'

'Och, aye… who was that actress who played her? I remember watching the show when I was a laddie.'

'Angie Dickinson; *Police Woman* was the show,' Neil

prompted, recalling Brodie's response when the same subject had been raised in conversation the year before.

'Aye, that was it. Best you don't let on that I watched stuff like that; could damage my career… and my reputation if it gets out! Anyway, Holly starts today. I've heard great things about her from the DI over at Fort William and I'm sure you'll find a way to temper any undue self-regard on her part! I'll get her to seek you out once I've spoken to her and given her the usual welcoming speech! She's a trained FLO, by the way. Could be a bonus.'

'Useful to know,' Neil acknowledged. Trained family liaison officers were invaluable when it came to murder enquiries. But, with his track record, it was unlikely he'd need her services, though. His only previous homicide investigation was a case dating back to the Second World War, when any family liaison could only have been conducted through a medium!

Hardie pulled the door open, but then as a parting shot asked, 'You went to Stirling University, didn't you, Neil?'

'Aye, I did, back in '98. Had a good time there, both academically and socially. Why do you ask?'

'My daughter's got a placement there, studying law. Your BA was in history, if I'm not mistaken?'

'That's right. History and politics, to be exact.'

Hardie nodded. 'Umm, good for you. As long as she commits as much time to studying as she does to socialising, I'll be content my investment is worthwhile!' With that he closed the door, and his footsteps faded along the corridor.

Neil had taken himself off to the canteen following his meeting with Hardie. He needed a caffeine fix accompanied by a cheese scone, and the lovely Cynthia, resplendent in her white catering garb, could supply both in considerable quantities!

He sat down with his tray at a table by the window, prompting several junior officers who were chatting nearby to get up and leave. It wasn't that they disliked him. The guilty looks on their faces suggested that they'd merely overstayed their coffee break. He smiled as he watched them leave. As if chasing *their* arses was uppermost in his mind right now!

He tapped the screen on his mobile. The envelope icon informing him that he'd received a text appeared on the wallpaper image of Cat hugging Tam on a walk in Glen Affric. On further inspection, he was relieved to see that she was in fact the sender...

Hi, Sorry about this morning. Didn't sleep very well either, and wasn't feeling my best. Shouldn't have taken it out on u. Will make it up to u tonight. Luv u Cat xx

Neil tapped out a brief acknowledgement, at the same time experiencing a welcome surge of relief. Surely these weren't the words of someone having an affair behind his back.

He took a sip of his coffee, then commenced cleaning the lenses of his glasses, whilst brooding over his predicament. Cat's next opportunity to meet someone, or do whatever she was doing instead of visiting the gym, would be the Monday after next. She only ever attended the gym at the leisure centre on Mondays, always remarking that the desire to abuse her body lessened as the week progressed. The following Monday, she was babysitting her eldest sister's two kids, so was giving the gym session a miss. But the Monday after that, the 26th April, she'd be back to her normal schedule. He decided then and there that he'd follow her from work that night. It really went against the grain, and he hated himself for considering such a furtive response... but if she couldn't be honest with him, then needs must!

'Hello sir, long time no see. You should think about getting yourself some contact lenses, you know.'

The soft, confident Highland accent was somehow familiar. He looked up to see Holly Anderson beaming down at him. 'Just popped in to get a bottle of water before my meeting with Mr Hardie. Saw you sitting here all alone and thought I'd come over and say hi.'

Neil got up and shook hands with her. 'Good to see you again, Holly. My partner says I should wear bloody contact lenses. The truth is, I can't bear the thought of having them anywhere near my eyeballs.'

She grinned. 'Coward. Still, the specs suit you, I suppose.'

'I'm flattered. So… I hear you're joining us on MEU.' He sat down again, prompting her to do the same. 'Have you got a minute?'

'Of course, sir. You're the boss, literally!'

Holly settled into the chair opposite him and twisted the cap off the plastic bottle. She took a mouthful of water, then looked across at him suspiciously.

'I hope the big boss hasn't changed his mind. Only I wasn't due to start for a couple of weeks.'

Neil grinned. 'No, he's keen to have you on board as soon as possible. We have a few personnel issues currently, and urgently need a pair of helping hands.'

'Really, sir? Tell me more.' Her cornflower blue eyes were eager for gossip and Neil found himself gazing into them, momentarily struck dumb. They had the enduring appeal of sunlight after a storm, and in some strange way lifted his mood more than a little! Holly was more attractive than he remembered. Her long barley-coloured hair had been tightly gathered up, with all but a few strands out of place, seductively exposing her prominently high cheekbones and alabaster skin.

'Hello, anyone there?' She looked back at him, her glossy lips seeking out the neck of the bottle once again.

19

'Sorry, I was miles away.' He cleared his throat. 'We've lost two DCs to Operation Lapwing, the force drugs initiative, and now DCI Brodie's had a heart attack, so I'll be acting up in his place for the time being.'

'Whoa, poor Mr Brodie. So you'll be my first- *and* second-line boss, then, at least for the short term?'

'Aye, looks like it, so don't even think about pissing me off, eh?'

Holly raised her hand in mock salute, grinning from ear to ear so that deep dimples formed either side of her mouth. She was, without doubt, a cocky wee besom, but there was something truly endearing about her... not to mention the bonus of her youthful beauty.

'So, Holly, what have you been up to since I last saw you out on that beach in the middle of nowhere?'

'Well, I passed my sergeant's exam at the end of 2008, but wanted to spend some time in the CID, gaining some experience before going for promotion. As you know, I got the job at Fort William and loved it... apart from persistently being called "Pepper", that is.'

She tilted her head to one side. 'Please tell me you're not going to call me that... are you?'

'No, Holly, I won't, but I can't talk for Angus Hardie. He was a great fan of the show, I believe.'

'Oh, God, no. I thought I'd left that label back the other side of Ben Nevis!'

'You were saying, Holly... about the job at Fort William.'

'Ah, yes. Well the sergeants' promotion board came up not long after my move there and my DI advised that I have a go, even if it was just for experience. So I did, and to my amazement, I got myself promoted... how cool was that? It was back to uniform patrol here at Inverness, though. That was just before last Christmas. Could've killed that DI when he broke the news to me. I only ended up doing seven months on CID proper, as it turned out. Anyway, I did the FLO course down at the police college and put my name forward for this unit, not holding my breath, like… but here I am!'

Neil looked impressed, and he was. She'd done well, and she was still only twenty-six. But then again, he couldn't talk, having just turned thirty-one!

'Good for you, Holly, but be prepared for some ribbing from the oldies around here, though. They still believe you should have one foot in the grave before you get promoted at all. We'll just have to prove them wrong, eh?'

Holly got up. 'Aye, we will, sir.'

She picked up her bottle. 'Better not be late for the big boss on my first day. I'll catch up with you later, sir, and we can discuss how best we can foster a positive working relationship with the walking dead!'

She marched off, dangling the bottle from her right hand, leaving Neil shaking his head in amused disbelief.

On his way back to the MEU suite, he stopped and tapped on the door, upon which the name panel read – 'Detective Inspector Ross Haggarty – HOLMES UNIT'.

He heard muffled voices from behind the clouded glass.

'Come in, if you must,' came the response.

Neil entered to see Senior Scene Investigator Fraser Gunn lounging in a chair in front of Ross's desk, sipping coffee from the largest mug he had ever seen. Ross wheeled his chair backwards, mock surprise imprinted upon his bony features.

'All rise for our new *führer*,' he joked, and both men leapt to their feet, clicking their heels as they did so.

Neil slumped into Gunn's chair, prompting a savage response from the veteran Scenes of Crime Officer.

'Hey, who do you think you are, the DCI?' They both chuckled, pleased with their respective gibes.

Neil casually rotated the chair from side to side. 'It's amazing who you find hiding away in the offices along this corridor. I can see I'm going to need to make more impromptu visits, keep you on your toes.'

He looked from one man to the other. 'You know, I was just talking to our new DS, Holly Anderson. We were discussing how best to resurrect the "walking dead" in this unit... her words, I hasten to add! I can see I've got a serious challenge on my hands when it comes to you two.'

He got up, straight-faced, leaving the other two men lost for words. 'I'll see myself out. Oh, and by the way, Ross, I quite like the idea of you calling me *sir*, so you can carry on doing so from now on... that's an order.'

He walked out, pulling the door closed behind him, the smug look on his face persisting at least until he reached his own office door. Ironically, both of the cadaverous-looking jokers he'd just dropped in on could well be mistaken for the walking dead! They hadn't earned the nicknames 'Dozy' and 'the Skull' for nothing!

Several minutes later, a grinning Fraser Gunn poked his head around the half-open door to his office. His wispy auburn hair glowed in the sunlight from the nearby window. There was a devilish smirk present upon his narrow lips, as if he had to have the last word.

'Best you get comfy in that big leather chair of yours, Neil. You'll be spending more time sitting on your arse pushing paper over the next few weeks than you will playing Sherlock bloody Holmes, believe me!'

How wrong he would be!

Chapter Three

The call had come in just before eleven o'clock. The communications assistant in the force control room initially had difficulty understanding what the young woman was saying. She'd been almost hysterical, sobbing, sniffing and then screaming, making no sense at all. The only word she'd picked up for sure was 'murdered'. The call had originated from the landline phone at Cullaird Castle. Cullaird was an imposing sixteenth-century keep located at the eastern end of Loch Ruthven, a small inland loch nestling deep within the gently undulating countryside of Strathnairn. The topography of this region, located to the east of the Great Glen, some thirteen miles from Inverness, was wild and remote, there being few settlements of any substantial size.

A traffic patrol unit had initially been dispatched from the A9 at Moy to investigate. When the two constables arrived at Cullaird fifteen minutes later, they found a young woman, Ruth Morton, in a state of collapse on the long gravel driveway that led up to the castle. One of the constables had tended to her, whilst the other, baton in hand, had made his way up the driveway towards the one and only means of ingress to the property. The low stone doorway still bore the distinctive scars of clan feuding and medieval siege. But today its heavy oak door had stood enticingly ajar, as if welcoming the wary visitor into a preset trap. The constable had ducked under the lintel and cautiously edged his way into the property with a stolidity befitting his twenty-two years of police service. What he had discovered inside had brought him staggering out again, pale and staring, the sweet taste of vomit rising in his throat.

Forty-five minutes had passed since then. The world and his wife were now en route to Cullaird, including Neil Strachan and Holly Anderson in one of the team's newer Ford Focus unmarked cars.

Holly had broken the news to Neil, who'd been ensconced in a meeting with Hardie and dreaming of extrication! The detective superintendent had been quick to suggest that Holly attend with him, there being no doubt that there would be an imminent requirement for a family liaison officer. Neil, not surprisingly, had heeded Hardie's advice, and they were now hurtling along the B851, travelling west alongside the River Nairn. Holly sat behind the wheel, whilst Neil stared out through the windscreen, his phone pressed to his ear, responding to a distant retinue of senior officers offering their assistance and support.

During a moment of downtime, whilst he checked his phone for texts from Cat, Holly said, 'You know there should be two of us assigned to this... FLOs, I mean... and a risk assessment done before we're deployed. There's ACPO guidance on the use of FLOs, you know.'

Neil squinted across at her and gave her a perfunctory nod. He was well acquainted with the guidance manual published by the Association of Chief Police Officers. Before he could reply, she jumped in again.

'I was just saying... being helpful, like.'

He waited for a couple of seconds, just in case she had anything further to add.

'Finished?' he asked.

'Aye,' she murmured, her eyes now fixed on the road ahead.

'Actually, I'd had second thoughts about deploying you as an FLO on this enquiry. That was Hardie's idea. I thought you might want to work *with* me on this one. You know, act as SIOs assistant.'

'You make it sound like I'd be some sort of magician's sidekick, sir. Will there be a requirement to wear a sequinned costume and top hat, and perhaps dance around you with a wand?'

Neil grinned. 'Whatever floats your boat, Holly. You'd certainly keep the other boys on the team entertained, dressed like that. My advice, though, would be to retain your current mode of attire, which would very much enhance your credibility… as would getting to the scene of this crime with the SIO still in one piece… There's a sharp bend coming up!'

'Sorry. And yes, of course I'd really like to be your assistant, bagperson, whatever.' She slammed on the brakes, a little too late for Neil's liking, and opted for a period of reflective silence.

They soon reached a small group of modern dwellings clustered around a minor junction and turned right along another, even narrower road, which would take them down towards Loch Ruthven. The fields gave way to wild, heather-strewn moorland, over which the road twisted and turned until the silvery glint of the loch came into view through the low trees that grew along its shoreline.

At the very end of the loch, opposite a field in which grazed a herd of torpid-looking Highland cattle, were two imposing stone pillars. Set into one was a plaque, inlaid in gold, informing visitors that they'd arrived at Cullaird Castle. Next to the post stood a police Land Rover, its single occupant straining to recognise the new arrivals before raising a hand in greeting. Holly manoeuvred the car between the posts and headed up the gravel track.

The driveway meandered gently uphill through a plantation of black-budded mountain ash, beyond which stood the forbidding stone keep. Parked along one verge, adjacent to another smaller gateway, were several yellow and blue Battenburg-liveried police cars. Amongst them were two white Scientific Support Unit vans and a couple of unmarked SUVs. On the opposite verge stood a paramedic ambulance. Its rear doors had been left open and inside, a green-suited figure was attending to a young woman.

A uniformed constable stood guard in the open gateway, a clipboard tucked firmly under his arm. Behind him, spanning the narrow opening, fluttered a length of blue and white barrier tape, above which towered the honey stone edifice that was Cullaird Castle.

Holly and Neil struggled into their white forensic suits with the usual degree of indignity, then shuffled up to the log keeper like a couple of snowmen.

'Morning. Acting DCI Strachan and DS Anderson,' Neil announced authoritatively, whilst running a hand through his wind-tussled hair.

'Thank you, sir,' the young man replied as he noted down their names and arrival time. 'Doctor Carnie's just arrived. He's inside with the boys from SIU.'

Neil acknowledged the information with a polite nod whilst he checked his own watch. It was just coming up to midday.

They ducked under the tape and stepped inside the gateway, pausing briefly to take in the general scene. The castle was environed by a wide expanse of gravel that bordered it on two sides. In contrast, the rear elevations of the building were fringed by neatly tended lawns, the whole being enclosed within newly renovated dry stone walls. The walls themselves were constructed from recently hewn rock with a pleasing pale hue that matched those of the castle.

'I love the way the darker stones in the walls contrast with the sand-coloured ones,' Holly observed as she contemplated the building, admiring its stepped gables and corner turrets. 'And those tiny little windows must be so old.'

'Have you ever thought of becoming a presenter on *Grand Designs*?' Neil propounded as he made for the low doorway ahead of him. He pointed to the shiny black Range Rover and the brand new Audi A3 parked nearby.

'Nice cars. Obviously not short of a bob or two.' Then he nodded towards the elderly Ford Fiesta a few yards away. 'Bet that's the cleaner's,' he continued.

'Snob… sir!' Holly retorted, shaking her head.

Having ducked to step inside, avoiding the low sloping lintel, they came across Fraser Gunn, tripping down the flight of grey stone steps in front of them. More police barrier tape extended up the staircase, effectively halving its breadth. On the third step, closest to the wall, was a yellow plastic evidence marker, positioned next to a partial bloody footprint.

'Just popping out to get another lens for the camera,' Gunn announced. 'Adam's up in the great hall examining the body. Keep to this side of the tape as you go up the stairs and onto the landing. The red stuff's everywhere, and I don't really want you plodding through my scene!'

Neil smiled, acknowledging the warning. 'Was that the cleaner who discovered the body, the female in the back of the ambulance?'

'Yep, the very same. She's in a right state, poor girl. Not surprising when you see what's gone on upstairs!'

Neil turned to Holly. 'Can you go and have a word with her? See what you can find out background-wise.'

'Aye, sure I can, sir. On my way.'

She immediately turned and swished back through the open door.

Neil focussed his attention back on Gunn. 'What's the situation with the family, Fraser? Have you picked up anything?'

'Seems like the victim may have been here alone when she was attacked. There's a husband somewhere, don't know where, and there's extended family all over the place, apparently.'

'Okay, thanks, I'll let you get on.'

Neil took a slow deep breath and commenced his ascent of the staircase, preparing himself mentally for the scene that awaited him. After a dozen or so steps, it turned back on itself. Other yellow markers came into view, drawing his attention to a further series of macabre-looking footprints. Also, where the steps turned the corner, a long smear of blood defaced an otherwise pristinely painted white wall.

A further turn and he found himself on a small landing facing a tiny leaded glass window. The tape extended through a doorway to his right, past the opening to a spiral staircase that presumably led to the upper floors.

Neil warily entered the great hall, a cavernous space under a vaulted oak ceiling from which two massive circular iron chandeliers were suspended. On one side of the room was a vast stone fireplace, above which hung a faded heraldic crest, flanked on either side by studded leather *targes* (small calfskin shields) and crossed broadswords. Around the room, gilt-framed portraits, presumably of family ancestors, gazed down austerely from their lofty stations, high on the uneven walls.

A cluster of battered leather sofas stood around a large coffee table in front of the fireplace, and along the opposite wall a highly polished cherrywood table extended almost the entire length of the room, its fourteen matching chairs upholstered in a red, green and blue tartan. Other than occasional tables cluttered with ornaments and family photos, the only other large item of furniture present was a heavy oak bookcase, built in the Jacobean style, and crammed with ancient leather-bound works. An overturned lamp table and a spotlight on a tripod (clearly not in keeping with the furnishings) were the only signs of anything appearing amiss upon first inspection. Then a white-suited figure popped up suddenly from behind one of the leather sofas. Neil, briefly startled by the masked apparition, recognised the gleaming eyes immediately. It was none other than the slightly eccentric Doctor Adam Carnie, local Home Office pathologist.

'Good day to you, Neil. Found the old place, then?'

The doctor dragged his mask down to reveal his rubicund face and spread his arms about him. 'What magnificent surroundings, eh? Come here, dear boy. You need to see this.' Then he pointed to the shiny blue and white tape that ran around behind the table. 'Do keep behind that tape, Neil, or the pugnacious Mr Gunn will be on your case in a trice!'

'I've already had the gypsy's warning,' Neil acknowledged, edging his way between the dining chairs and the wall. Then, when he reached the end of the table, the scene that greeted him instantly numbed his senses to the core. A surge of shock followed, jolting him like a well-placed punch to the abdomen. Involuntarily, he raised a hand to his already masked mouth as he struggled to take it in.

Lying on her back behind the sofa was a small woman, aged between sixty and seventy years, there being a look of stupefaction present in her glazed blue eyes. Her short white hair was compressed to the side of her forehead, and encrusted with semi-clotted dark red blood. Beneath her, and pooled about her on the ancient floorboards, there was more blood, so much in fact that Neil doubted whether any still remained within the veins and arteries of her body. She wore a dark blue corduroy skirt and moccasin shoes, which, apart from the odd spot of blood, appeared unsoiled, certainly from the front.

It was the savagery that had been inflicted upon her above the waist that would cause the uninitiated in such a situation to boak. Her white cotton blouse, now drenched in blood, had been ripped open, exposing her pale abdomen beneath a white bra. Neil gaped in disbelief as he counted the numerous tell-tale stab wounds that scarred her torso from the waistband of her skirt up to the prominent strut of her collarbone. Above this, one deep incision had opened up her throat, exposing the remnants of her windpipe.

'For God's sake,' were the only words that Neil could summon initially. He stood for a second, whilst his brain attempted to process the level of carnage before him. He'd dealt with a few domestic stabbings in his time, and on one occasion, the particularly nasty aftermath of a bar fight, but nothing, nothing like this.

He stooped to inspect the wounds to the woman's abdomen, but more particularly, the crudely incised symbols carved above her navel. If he wasn't mistaken, the larger of the two resembled an image of a cat crouching within a circle, and above that, a deep vertical scratch intersected by three similar parallel scratches. He rested his clenched fist against his mask whilst he considered the symbols.

Carnie could see that the young detective was deeply shocked.

'Seems we've got a right nutcase on the loose here, Neil. Not something to be cutting your teeth on as a new DCI, perhaps?'

'I have to take what comes, Adam… do you suppose this symbol here could be a *cat*?' He pointed a latex-gloved finger at the ghoulish tattoos.

'That's the impression I got,' Carnie agreed. 'The one above it looks to me like it's Chinese. Very bizarre!'

Neil gestured towards the large crest that surmounted the fireplace.

'Bit of a coincidence, having a cat on your family crest, and then getting one carved into your abdomen when you're murdered, eh?'

Carnie looked up and nodded in agreement. The animal depicted on the crest was indeed a cat – not a domestic one, more of a wildcat. The image was circumscribed by a representation of a belt, upon which the words 'Touch Not This Cat' were clearly visible.

'Yes, I noticed that earlier. Heraldic crest of the Frasers hereabouts, I suppose.'

Neil was back on his feet, flicking through the pages of his notebook. He looked down at the corpse.

'So this is Laura Fraser, aged sixty-seven years, who lived here with her husband, Duncan Fraser?'

'Aye, according to the cleaner. Obviously a very wealthy couple. The husband is chairman of the Lochmhor Distillery, a couple of miles to the west of here.'

'Is that right? Neil replied. 'I rather like a nip of the Lochmhor malt. Got a couple of bottles of their twelve-year-old stuff at home.'

He motioned towards the bloody lesions present on the corpse.

'Don't suppose I need to be a rocket scientist to deduce cause of death?'

'Not at all, Neil. Multiple stab wounds. A couple into the heart if I'm not mistaken. Looks like the jugular vein was severed here, so massive and rapid loss of blood. I'm pretty sure the action started up in the master bedroom on the next floor. There's evidence of a disturbance up there and a few spots of blood present, but nothing significant. It certainly ended down here. There are blood pattern traces all over this corner of the room. My guess is, the offender may have been disturbed upstairs initially, having broken in, I assume. Fraser mentioned there's been a search made of most of the upstairs rooms.'

Neil inclined to examine a photo of the couple in a silver frame.

'Umm, there's also the husband to consider. Where has he mysteriously disappeared to, I wonder? Wherever he's gone, his Range Rover's still parked outside. Can't rule anything out at this stage, I suppose.'

'Very true,' Carnie agreed. 'I'm not aware of any domestic strife between the two of them, though… not according to the cleaner.'

Neil looked about him, taking in the rest of the room. 'I need to make sure this building and its grounds are searched down to the last inch, just in case he's lying undiscovered somewhere nearby, which is a distinct possibility. You could lose yourself around this place very easily!'

'Good plan, Neil. Not finding him would certainly be an embarrassing start to your career as an SIO!'

'So what can you impart thus far, Adam? Tell me something I haven't worked out for myself.'

Carnie knelt by the side of the body, gloved hands resting on the tops of his thighs.

'Well, like I said, I believe she sustained her fatal wound, if not *all* her injuries, in here. Otherwise there would've been much more evidence of bloodstaining elsewhere in the property.'

He selected one of the many wounds present on her abdomen. 'Note that both the edges of the wound here are v-shaped, even when I do this.'

He compressed the two sides of the wound to re-approximate the original point of entry of the weapon.

'You see, the actual configuration of the wound is affected by the alignment of the collagen fibres of the skin. We call them Langer's lines. This one is parallel to this alignment, and doesn't gape so much. By pushing the edges together, though, I can get a better idea of the type of blade used. From what I can see here, I would say the blade may well have been double-edged. A dagger-like weapon, perhaps. A word of warning, though. This isn't conclusive by any means, as skin tears can sometimes give the same outward appearance. As to how long the blade was... well that's something for the PM. I can't see any abrasion of the skin around these wounds either, which suggests insertion of the blade was not to the hilt, or that the weapon had no discernible hilt or cross guard.'

'Okay. What about time of death?'

'From the look of all this blood and how it has clotted and separated... you see this yellowing here? I'd say several hours, no more. I've taken her temperature and it's only down a couple of degrees, but again, a number of factors can affect this. There's also some evidence of lividity on her back and legs... this red patchy appearance where the blood, what's left of it, sinks to the lower extremities.'

'What about rigor mortis?'

'Signs of it around the jaw and face, that's all, which supports my theory that we're talking less than four hours.'

Gunn then appeared behind them and started setting up his camera.

'Hell of a mess, eh, Neil? I take back what I said about you spending too much time in that nice leather chair of yours!'

Neil managed a half-smile. 'Okay if I have a look upstairs?'

'Aye, go ahead,' said Gunn. 'Lynn's up there. Just follow the taped route I've set up and don't touch anything.'

'As if...' Neil replied. 'See you later.'

The master bedroom was almost as grand as the great hall, with its enormous four-poster bed, antique furnishings, and free-standing bath. At each corner of the room, steps led up into the turret rooms, one with a dressing table, and another containing a walk-in shower. Several pieces of furniture had been turned over, and the remnants of ornaments lay smashed on the floor. More surprisingly though, some of the floorboards had been levered up.

Lynn Cowan, Gunn's junior colleague, was busy dusting an upturned bedside table for fingerprints. She greeted him in her soft, mellifluous Highland accent.

'Hello, Mr Strachan. If you could stay by the doorway that would be great. I've only just started in here.'

'Will do, Lynn. I've got a feeling you're going to be working here for some time!'

'It's certainly going to take a good while. We've got reinforcements coming over from Aberdeen, though.'

'Excellent. Seems like there's been one hell of a fight in this room.'

'Aye, there has that. Not much blood, though, and it looks like someone defended themselves with this golf club... unsuccessfully.'

Lying on the wooden floor was a shiny-headed club that Neil recognised as a five iron.

'Got anything off any of those surfaces?'

'Well, yes and no. I've lifted some marks, but they're not prints. Looks like our offender was wearing Marigold kitchen gloves.'

'I see. So he came prepared, then?'

'Without a doubt. It's not unheard of for Marigolds to be worn by housebreakers.'

'Aye, I know. It's looking less like a domestically motivated incident, then? Don't suppose there's any indication as to how many offenders we're looking for?'

Cowan looked up and frowned.

'That'll be a no, then... okay if I check out the upper rooms?'

'If you can look in from the outside, no problem.'

Neil thanked Cowan and moved on up the spiral staircase. There were five further bedrooms leading off the twisting stone stairs. All were lavishly furnished with antiques, and some with four-poster beds. Like the great hall, the undulating plastered walls of the upper rooms were liberally bestrewed with dusty oil paintings, some large, some small, whilst the soft furnishings in these rooms were themed in tartan, each featuring a different sett.

There was evidence in each room of a hasty and frenzied search. Drawers lay upturned on the floors. Cupboard doors were left open, some having been forced with an instrument of sorts. Remarkably, the tartan carpets in some rooms were littered with personal items, jewellery, watches, and even some cash. The person responsible for this was after something far more significant than the usual booty sought by the average housebreaking drug addict!

Neil made his way back down the stairs to the ground floor and turned right towards the kitchen. The passageway took him past the doorway of a small chapel, before hooking left towards the large basement kitchen and an incapacious little dining room with a low, barrel-vaulted ceiling. The long rustic oak table that ran the length of this room was set for breakfast. Two half-full cups of tea, two bowls of cereal, one empty and one still full, together with a basket of uneaten toast remained *in situ*. A copy of the *Financial Times* lay open next to the seemingly untouched bowl. There was no evidence of disruption or violence in this area, and Neil did not wish to linger too long whilst the SOCOs were still in play. He retreated along the corridor, pausing to poke his head around the door of the chapel. Again everything was in its place. A tiny altar stood at one end, onto which faced several rows of battered wooden pews. Silver candlesticks stood on the heavily embroidered altar cloth, together with a wooden cross in the Celtic style.

I can't believe those candlesticks are still here, Neil mused as he stooped again to pass through the external doorway.

Once out into the warm spring sunshine, he paused to examine the heavy oak front door. 'No evidence of forced entry here,' he muttered to himself. 'Not in this century anyway!'

He then walked slowly around the base of the castle, all the while gazing up at the lofty walls. *Little opportunity of getting in, other than through the low threshold I've just exited from*, he concluded. There was, after all, only the one door, and the nearest window, which was securely fastened, was well out of reach above him. No, whoever committed this crime walked in through the front door, just as he had done.

'Ah, there you are, sir.' Holly bustled along towards him. 'I hear it's pretty grim in there.'

'Aye, Holly, it is. There's a monster… or possibly *monsters* at large out there somewhere. The only consolation is… I think this family has been targeted specifically, and for something particular. Thousands of pounds worth of jewellery and cash have been left on the floor upstairs!'

'Wow, so no opportunist druggie, then?'

'I think not. So what have you gleaned from the cleaner, what's her name?'

'Ruth Morton, sir. She's still pretty shaken up. She lives a mile or so away, back along the B851. Husband runs a local trout farm, and she has a young baby. She's been cleaning here for three years. Loves the Frasers. They've been very good to her, apparently. They pay her well, overtime when she wants it, stuff like that. She arrived here this morning just before eleven… as she always does every Tuesday and Thursday. Sometimes works on a Saturday morning too. Today, it seems, she pulled up outside the castle, where her car, the Fiesta, is now. She saw the front door ajar and knocked… She has a key, but never just walks in…'

'Go on,' Neil prompted, as he leaned back against the boundary wall.

'When she got no response, she went in and called out. She was expecting Laura, the victim, and Duncan, that's her husband, both to be in. Anyway, there was no answer, so she checked the kitchen on the ground floor, round to the left from the entrance hall, apparently. That's where the couple normally hang out in the mornings. When she couldn't find them down there, she went up to the great hall… and the rest is history, so to speak. She ran out screaming, having called us on the landline in the kitchen.'

'So she saw no one in or around the place, then?'

'Not a thing.'

'What about the cars? They both belong to the Frasers, I'm told.'

'Aye, the Range Rover's his, and the Audi is hers. No other vehicles are owned by the couple.'

'Did you ask her about the Frasers' relationship at all? Adam Carnie tells me she believed they were getting along fine.'

'Aye, she said they were all loved-up. Like teenagers, apparently. No way would he have attacked his wife, according to her.'

'What about the rest of the family?'

'They live all over the place, apparently. There's a daughter down in Wiltshire, and a son who owns a vineyard in France, well, his wife does. There was another younger son, but he was killed in a skiing accident a few years ago.'

'Anything else?'

'Not really. The local PC is going to take Ruth home. We'll get a statement from her tomorrow, when she's got over the shock. As I said, according to her, the Frasers were devoted to each other and well liked by all…'

'Certainly not by all!' Neil interjected cynically. 'So where is Mr Fraser? What was so urgent that he had to abandon his breakfast and disappear... and without his car? I'm sure the urge for a walk wasn't so strong he couldn't finish his cereal.'

'How do you know it was his bowl that was still full?' Holly enquired. 'You're not suggesting that it must've been him who was reading the paper? We women can read too, you know.'

'No, but only a man would fill his bowl that full of cereal, Holly! Cat's always telling me she can't afford me because I do the same... and besides, the *FT* must've been his. Only a businessman could stomach all that stocks and shares shit at breakfast time.'

She nodded. 'Fair point, I suppose.'

He looked at her enquiringly. 'I assume this building has been properly searched by the uniforms prior to our arrival? I'm not at all convinced that he hasn't become a victim too and I don't want anything, least of all *him*, missed!'

Holly nodded attentively. 'Aye, it has, sir, within reason. The place is like a maze, though; it'll be a considerable undertaking to search the castle and grounds properly.'

Neil marched away along the wall line, not bothering to look back at her.

'When we get back to the office, that's your first task, then. Get hold of a PolSA and arrange exactly that: a thorough search of this place *and* its environs, all the way back to the loch.' Then he glanced over his shoulder. 'And if by waving that bloody magician's wand of yours, you can locate Mr Duncan Fraser... then so much the better!'

Holly looked down at her feet and grinned, amused at Neil's wry sense of humour.

He wasn't finished though. 'Oh, and Holly...'

Her head jerked up in response. 'Yes, sir?'

'I need an operational name.'

'Yes, sir. I'll get one allocated.'

Neil stopped in his tracks and rested his back against the dry stone wall once more. He watched as Holly hurried away across the weedless lawn and found himself admiring her perfectly formed rear for a second or two. Guilt quickly got the better of him and he turned to take in the panorama. It was an altogether safer option!

He'd been admiring the view for no more than a minute or two when he sensed the presence of someone approaching from the direction of the keep. He turned about to find Adam Carnie meandering towards him, apparently having some difficulty lighting his pipe.

'Ruddy lighter. I need to get a new one,' Carnie muttered as he joined Neil by the wall. He sucked hard on the stem of the highly polished device, causing the tobacco in the bowl to glow red.

'Ah, at last,' he sighed between clenched teeth. 'Impressive view, what?'

'Aye, you're not wrong there,' Neil agreed. 'Makes you appreciate the land we call home.'

Carnie removed the pipe from his mouth and gestured with it at arm's length. 'Two hundred and sixty-odd years ago to the day, that strath out there would've been teeming with men, heading east towards Drumossie Moor for the final showdown with "German Geordie's" royal army.'

Neil gave the pathologist a brief sideways glance. 'Of course. Tomorrow's the 16th April... the anniversary of the Battle of Culloden!'

1746

Chapter Four

From the small leaded windows that faced out along the southern aspect of Culloden House, the ridge that marked the highest point on Drumossie Moor could just be seen through the screen of pines beyond the fortified barmkin wall. The moor was a windswept wilderness, criss-crossed by cart tracks that linked a number of isolated farmsteads. At times, cattle would graze upon this depressingly bleak landscape, foraging amongst the dead brown heather for what little fodder they could find. The scene had remained unchanged for centuries, there being little to stimulate the interest of a roving eye. But that was not the case today. Beneath the leaden sky, and through the icy swirling sleet, any casual observer watching from the southern tree line of Lord President Duncan Forbes's lavish estate would certainly be entertained.

Less than a mile to the south-east, and formed up in line of battle across the ridge, stood a ragtag Highland army. Their ranks were permeated by wide gaps, spaces where their comrades should have been standing with them shoulder to shoulder. Those comrades were still away, raiding their neighbours' lands for their cattle, or protecting their homes from the marauding Campbells who were loose in the hills.

Keppoch's Macdonalds had not arrived, nor had the men pledged to reinforce Glengarry's regiment. The MacGregors were still occupied in Cromarty, and although Cluny Macpherson and his men were on the march, they still hadn't arrived from Badenoch. Many of the Frasers were missing too, and it was thought they would not arrive in time for the final showdown.

Nevertheless, those present were ready to fight. Wrapped in their drab shawl-like plaids, and sheltering behind targes, their reddened eyes anxiously scanned the moor to the east, awaiting the arrival of the Duke of Cumberland's red-coated infantry. Behind them, their colourful banners flapped noisily in the stiffening breeze. To the front, pipers stood proudly by the clan chiefs or their nominated colonels. Chilled fingers tapped busily upon laburnum or hollywood chanters, whilst the wind tugged at the drones spread across the musicians' shoulders. The air resounded with stirring laments. They were tunes that had long inspired valour within their ancestors, the haunting music of the mountain men.

It was a scene that would have filled any Highlander with pride, but Lord George Murray had other things on his mind. He stood pensively behind the sleet-spattered glass, gazing out towards the moor, his ears just detecting the distant skirl of the pipes. George Murray was forty-six years old, the sixth son of the First Duke of Atholl. He'd been a soldier from the age of eighteen, initially with the British forces of Queen Anne in Flanders, but latterly, he'd pledged his affiliation to the Jacobite cause and had fought with the Earl of Mar during the 1715 rebellion. He was now an experienced, battle-hardened commander and lieutenant general in the Highland army led by the flamboyant Prince Charles Edward Stuart.

Murray's relationship with the young prince had become increasingly fractious over recent weeks, and he'd become something of an isolated figure when it came to making strategic and tactical decisions. The 'Young Pretender', as Charles was now known, had become more and more influenced by his Irish advisors, namely the aged Thomas Sheridan, and more dangerously – in Murray's opinion – his quartermaster general, John William O'Sullivan.

It had been O'Sullivan's decision to muster the army on Drumossie Moor that morning, a decision that Murray had deemed to be entirely flawed. In his view, it was an invitation to the Prince's equally youthful Hanoverian cousin, William Augustus, Duke of Cumberland, to slaughter his beloved clansmen on a field of battle entirely unsuited to the tactics of the Highland army.

Murray leaned forward into the window aperture and produced a pewter snuffbox from beneath the folds of his flowing cloak. He busied himself, opening the small lid with numb fingers and applying a pinch of snuff to each nostril, all the while keeping one eye on the scene outside. He was a tall man, robust in stature with dark, thoughtful eyes. He never wore his formal bag wig when on campaign, and today his thick brown hair curled around the collar of his cloak. Beneath it, he wore a tunic of the same prominent weave, the distinctive red, green and blue Tullibardine tartan, his family sett.

Upon hearing footsteps on the old oak floorboards behind him, he turned back from the window, allowing his cloak to fall open to one side. He returned the snuffbox to the pocket of his tunic and adjusted the shoulder-borne leather strap that supported his basket-hilted broadsword. The sword, his constant companion, was a formidable weapon measuring at least a yard in length and two inches wide. As such, its weight played heavily upon his shoulder when carrying it for long periods, and this was certainly one of those periods!

Murray's preoccupation with his personal comfort was promptly curtailed when his aide-de-camp, James Johnstone, approached with considerable haste through the doorway to his chamber. Content as to the identity of his visitor, he turned back to the window without uttering a greeting, preferring to peer out towards the mottled greenery that punctuated the backdrop of fast-moving grey cloud.

Johnstone halted several feet behind him and waited. He was twenty-six years old, born to the wife of an Edinburgh merchant and indulged from an early age by his mother, who'd belonged to a lesser sept of the Clan Douglas. A short, wiry young man, diffident by nature, his presence and stature belied his courage as a warrior and his enthusiasm for the Jacobite cause. Johnstone would become known as the Chevalier de Johnstone, and would eventually go on to serve in the colonial French forces in Canada.

Murray finally turned back to face him, prompting Johnstone to tip his head respectfully.

'I bid you good morning, my lord. There's certainly a nip in the air once more.' He looked past Murray towards the window. 'My sympathies are surely with those gallant boys out there on the field.'

Murray had no time for small talk. 'What news is there of Cumberland this hour? Does he show signs at all of moving his forces from Balblair?'

The portly Duke had marched his 8,000-strong army from Aberdeen in the east, crossing the Spey on the 12th April, and had now set up camp around the small Morayshire town of Nairn.

Johnstone shook his head. 'No, my lord. Intelligence has been received but a short time ago from a rider sent by the Mackintoshes. There is no movement at all, only the deployment of patrols along the Inverness road.'

Murray rubbed his stubbly chin. He'd not been sleeping well of late and was struggling to make sense of Cumberland's tactics. He responded after a few seconds' reflection. 'I suppose the Duke's actions do not cause me surprise; he has marched his men hard from Aberdeen, and today is his birthday, of course. It is my reckoning that he will rest his army for the remainder of the day and celebrate as I would expect of a man such as him. Is the Prince aware of this news?'

'Aye, my lord, he's of a mind to retire our regiments soon, and allow them to refresh themselves.'

Murray frowned. '*Refresh themselves*? If it's food he speaks of, then he must possess knowledge of which I am unaware. That detestable man Hay has made no attempt to bring up the supply carts from Inverness. All he tells me is "everything will be got", but he singularly fails on each and every occasion to do so!'

Johnstone allowed himself a muted grin. John Hay, the Prince's secretary was a weak and deeply unpopular man, despised by Murray to the same degree as O'Sullivan.

'Go to the Prince, and pay him my compliments. Tell him that I advise he retires our men without delay... before they freeze out there on the moor. I assume O'Sullivan has taken to his bed again for one of his bleedings. Am I correct?'

Johnstone grinned. 'You are indeed correct, my lord. He has retired to Inverness, I'm told.'

'That is indeed fortunate, James. Perhaps His Royal Highness will accept my advice on this occasion, without the prospect of that Irish fool meddling in our transactions!'

He searched under his cloak for the snuffbox again.

Johnstone turned, and grasped his sword. 'Will there be anything else, my lord?'

'Yes, James. Which officers are currently present in the house, who may ride out on an errand for me?'

The little man thought for a second. 'Brigadier Stapleton, of the Irish Picquets, and Colonel Ker of Graydyne are presently resting in the parlour and have their mounts outside, my lord.'

'Good. Tell them I desire that they ride out to the far banks of the Water of Nairn and review the ground there. I do not like this moor, James; it is certainly not proper for Highlanders to fight upon. There must be a better location where we may engage the enemy to greater effect.'

Johnstone nodded politely and scurried away through the doorway, leaving Murray to his own thoughts and another pinch of snuff.

The grandfather clock in the hallway was yet to strike two o'clock when Stapleton and Ker strode into the high-vaulted drawing room of Culloden House. Murray was standing next to the majestic stone fireplace, in which several flaming logs crackled and spat onto the hearth. By his side was Prince Charles Edward Stuart, with whom he was enjoying a glass of claret. The ruby red liquor that filled their glasses had been pilfered from the cellars of the property's owner, Duncan Forbes, who at that time was Lord Chief Justice of Scotland. As staunch Presbyterians, the Forbes family had suffered during earlier Jacobite uprisings, the house having been occupied and plundered by Viscount Dundee in 1688. And now, once again, its grand rooms were filled with the chatter of Jacobite voices.

The two officers, their tartan trews spattered with mud, and soaked from their ride through the icy water of the River Nairn, bowed graciously, having first removed their bonnets. Prince Charles returned their gesture with a nod of the head.

'Please, gentlemen, take a glass of claret with us. From the look of you, it would seem that you could do with it.'

He gestured to his steward, who took up the hogshead from the large polished table by the door and poured out two generous glassfuls. Stapleton and Ker stepped forward, sweeping back their cloaks, and accepted a glass each.

'For what do we owe this pleasure?' the Young Pretender

asked, settling himself into a large rosewood chair by the window. The Prince was twenty-five years old, son of James, the one-time Prince of Wales who'd claimed the throne of England and Scotland upon the death of his own father, King James the Second. He was a headstrong and stubborn young man, boyishly handsome and almost effeminate-looking in his white powdered wig, gathered in black silk behind his slender neck. He was possessed of his mother's weak chin and slightly bulging eyes, which now studied his two guests intently. He wore a buff waistcoat, edged in silver, and a tartan jacket, upon which was suspended the blue silk sash and breast star of the Order of the Garter. His trews were woven in the bright Royal Stuart tartan, and his black brogues shone in the light of the fire. No one would disagree that his stature and bearing were most certainly that of a prince.

Stapleton placed his glass on the table before approaching Charles and his second in command.

'My Lord Murray was seeking confirmation of the terrain to the south of the Water of Nairn, sir. I now have the news he requested.'

Charles regarded Murray with a degree of consternation. 'I was not aware of this instruction, sir'

Murray cleared his throat. 'I am greatly concerned, my Prince, that the field of battle selected today by General O'Sullivan is in nature unsuited to the tactics of our army. I am more disposed to the ground across the Water of Nairn. It is my view that this location would provide us with a much-needed advantage over Duke William's army.'

Charles turned back to Stapleton. 'And what is your view, Brigadier?'

Stapleton flushed slightly, a little uneasy as to the situation in which he now found himself. In essence, he was fully supportive of Murray's standpoint on the issue, but he was not of a mind to rile the Prince. Charles had, after all, made it clear that he would remain in overall command of the army for the forthcoming clash with his Hanoverian cousin.

'Well?' the Prince enquired, craning his neck. 'Do speak up, man.'

Stapleton always had a stern disposition, but in this instance his displeasure was clear to see. 'If I may speak candidly, sir?'

'Yes, yes, please do,' the Prince urged with a flamboyant gesture of his free arm.

'I am of the view, sir, that the ground to the south of the water is indeed more suitable for the deployment of our army. It is rugged ground, mossy and soft, so that no horse could be of use there. The land would also be unfit for the siting of cannon, especially guns of a heavy calibre, such as those being drawn by the royal army.'

'I see,' hissed the Prince, his bulbous eyes swivelling around to glare at Murray. 'Well, thank you, gentlemen, for your good counsel. You may now take your leave whilst we confer upon this subject.'

Stapleton and Ker both stooped in a synchronised gesture of reverence, holding the bow for a few seconds before strutting out through the open doorway and leaving their half-full glasses on the table.

Charles ushered his steward away, then looked up at Murray, his mouth tight, his blazing eyes boring into those of the man from Perthshire.

'I am sorely disappointed, sir, that you find it necessary to act alone and to seek your own intelligence as to the best suited field of battle for our forthcoming engagement with Duke William. Having said this, it is clear that I must take account of your view, for I am certain in the knowledge that your concerns will be shared by those who shall fight alongside us.'

He rose to his feet and drained his glass. 'I shall not waste time discussing this with you now, but will wait upon the hour of four, when we are assembled for a council of war. Until such time, I shall bid you adieu, sir, whilst I sit alone and consider my position on this subject.'

Murray nodded obediently and retrieved his bonnet from the nearby table. He bowed, a brief, stiff little gesture, offering the minimum of deference. 'Your servant, sir,' and he too left the room.

The Prince ambled over to the window and peered out into the murk. Sleet still tapped against the glass, whilst the wind sought to exploit any tiny chink in its ageing frame.

Murray could be troublesome at times. The two men rarely saw eye to eye these days, and the Prince was of the opinion that his lieutenant general was no longer the staunch ally he once believed him to be. Indeed, treachery was a word not far from his lips when he reflected upon the fragility of their current relationship. But, on the other hand, Murray might be right. Facing an army of well-trained redcoats on that wild sloping moor might, just might, be his undoing.

Four o'clock, and the council of war had once more convened at Culloden House. The Prince stood at the head of the long, highly polished table in the same room he'd confined himself to for most of the day. Around him were clustered a large group of men. They varied in age and stature. Some wore the kilt, some the belted plaid, and others wore more conventional soldiering attire. There were men of substance, educated men, clearly distinguishable by their fine clothes. The statutes of Iona in 1609 had required clan chiefs to send their heirs to Lowland Scotland to be educated in English-speaking Protestant schools. As such, they no longer subscribed to the ancient traditions of their forebears, but were gentlemen, highly status-conscious, preferring the trappings of gentility to the traditional lifestyle that had endured for centuries.

It was a colourful assemblage, comprising the muted ancient setts of the numerous clans represented: scarlets, greens and blues. Some even wore garments of differing setts. Then there were the red-faced uniforms of blue, worn by the Scots Royal, raised for King Louis of France by the house of Drummond. Upon many a head sat the blue bonnet, adorned with a clan badge or the white silk cockade of the Stuarts. To the casual observer it was a memorable scene, a final coming together of the Jacobite army's high and mighty. At the Prince's shoulder were men whose names would become legendary, names such as Donald Cameron of Lochiel, known as 'The Gentle Lochiel', due to his reputation for humanity; James Drummond, the Third Duke of Perth and Lord John Drummond, his brother. At the opposite end of the table to the Prince stood William Boyd, Earl of Kilmarnock; John Roy Stewart and John Gordon of Glenbucket, a craggy old man of seventy years. These were but a few of the assembled throng, huddled close to the table to hear what the Prince had to say. To the rear, standing by the doorway was Colonel Alexander MacGillivray of Dunmaglass, 6 feet 5 inches tall and known affectionately amongst his peers as Alasdair-Ruadh-na-Feille, 'generous red-headed Alexander', on account of his mop of fiery red hair. He'd been quoted as being the 'handsomest' youth in the Highlands and was now colonel of the Clan Chattan Regiment (raised by Lady Anne Mackintosh in defiance of her husband, who'd taken a commission in the royal army).

Clan Chattan had once been a conventional Highland Clan, but in recent times it had become a confederation of smaller septs; groups made up of the descendants of the original clan, predominantly the Mackintoshes and other non-blood-related families, such as the MacGillivrays and the Davidsons.

Standing next to the charismatic and youthful Lord Lewis

Gordon was a young captain in the Clan Chattan Regiment. His name was Simon MacGillivray, aide-de-camp to his second cousin Alexander. Simon, the son of Alisdair MacGillivray of Cullaird, had raised a small company of men from his father's estate in Strathnairn, some nineteen miles to the west of where they now stood.

If there was ever an example of the new breed of Highland gentry, Simon was it. He'd been brought up in affluent surroundings at the family's imposing seat, Cullaird Castle. Having been well educated, he now managed the lands originally granted to his grandfather, Lachlan, under 'tack' or lease by the clan's sixth chief, Farquhar 'Fladaigh' MacGillivray.

Simon was thirty-one years old, of slight build and fine-featured. Today, his thick tawny-coloured hair had been tied back with black ribbon. He wore a tunic, waistcoat and trews from the ancient MacGillivray tartan, a distinctive aggregation of dark and pale blues against a background of orange. It was without doubt one of the more vivid setts on display that day. On his left hip hung a newly forged broadsword of the latest military pattern, its blade bearing the mark of the celebrated swordsmith Andrea Ferrara. On his right, a dirk hung in its sheath, together with his eating knife and fork. The richly carved, triangular-bladed weapon had been handed down through the generations, having last been used by his father during the 1715 rebellion.

Simon was well liked and respected by his men. He was a gregarious character, who'd always led from the front: an experienced soldier, if somewhat unorthodox on occasions. He loved nothing more than to lead his men on raids, surprising the redcoats on their own ground, a tactic that had worked to great effect during the long march to Derby. Today, his usual crooked smile was missing. Like many of the others in the room, his face was etched with fatigue and also concern. There were few present who were comfortable with Prince Charles's choice of battlefield, and they knew O'Sullivan was behind this controversial decision. If Simon could have had his way, the army would have withdrawn to the mountains over in the west, where they would have embarked upon a guerrilla campaign to degrade the government forces over time. Then, when the best opportunity had arisen, they could've finished them off once and for all. But that wasn't going to happen. Charles was adamant that they form up across that wretched moor and slaughter each other like gentlemen. Only, it wouldn't be the redcoats who would be slaughtered on that ground; it would be him, and his fellow clansmen!

Charles, now content that all were present, raised an arm, signalling an end to the loud chatter that filled the room.

'Gentlemen, gentlemen... I thank you for your attendance. We meet here, perhaps for the last time, on the eve of what must surely be the decisive action of our short adventure. In God, I trust that we will be blessed with one final glorious victory.' He spoke English with a subtle lisp, heavily accented from his early days in Rome.

Seeking out Alexander MacGillivray, he asked, 'Colonel, can you give us news of the disposition of my cousin's army?'

'Aye, my Prince. Our picquets posted by the Nairn road report no movement of his infantry or horse. We have spies in and around the town who speak of much merriment and drinking around the fires at Balblair, and within the Burgh itself.'

The Prince smiled. 'It is my guess that the Duke will be amongst them, celebrating his special day with great fervour, and will sleep soundly upon that growing belly of his this night.'

Laughter rippled around the room, and a voice called out from the crowd. 'There'll be no growing of bellies in our camp tonight, not with only one biscuit inside them.'

The Prince flushed. 'Your voice is heard, sir, and I give you my word that I will ensure sufficient supplies are hastened from Inverness to provide suitable refreshment.'

Simon leaned across to Alexander and whispered, 'I'll believe that when I see it. The boys will boil up wee John Hay himself if they don't eat soon.'

The Prince clearly wished the subject changed. He tapped on the sepia-coloured map that lay unravelled upon the table before him.

'Gentlemen, I propose we remain within the parks of this house, and meet the Duke upon the moor yonder, when he is sober enough to climb upon his mount.'

There was more polite laughter. He went on. 'It is my view, and that of my advisors,' nodding in O'Sullivan's direction, 'that we are best placed to meet our enemy here, as the moor is large and plain, and though interspersed with moss and deep ground, it is a fair field and suitable for horse. I am concerned that we do not stray from our intention to defend Inverness, where a great deal of our baggage and ammunition is kept.'

He then turned to Lord George Murray, who was standing by his shoulder. 'Yet I am minded to reveal that my Lord Murray here is not fully of my persuasion.'

He gestured to Lord George. 'Please share your concerns with these gentlemen, sir. We should of course contemplate every proposal.'

Lord George bowed briefly and then scanned the room. All eyes rested anxiously upon him. He leaned across the map and tapped his finger on the south bank of the River Nairn.

'Here, gentlemen. This is where our Highland army should be drawn up in line of battle. The ground is rugged, mossy and soft, so that no horse or cannon will be of use there. The ascent from the water side is steep and inaccessible, there being only a few places in four or so miles where horses may cross. So, gentlemen: no cavalry and no cannon. The odds are therefore tipped in our favour. An infantry action alone upon such ground will see us victorious, regardless of any numerical superiority on the side of the enemy.'

He looked up, passion flaring in his eyes. 'This is where we must fight. If we stand upon the moor beyond these parks, we will be cut down by their grapeshot and finished off by their dragoons. Is this how you want our adventure to end?'

O'Sullivan shook his head. 'Surely my lord, an action upon the ground to the south will be a futile gesture. We would be but a mile further from here... and indeed, Inverness, which we have resolved not to abandon! I fear too, that Cumberland may well outflank us and leave us standing like fools in that wretched field. No, we must not shun the enemy, but face them like gentlemen.'

Lord George sighed. The silence in the room was broken, as those present debated the options in low voices. Deep concern was present on many of their tired faces.

He addressed the council once more. 'Fear not, gentlemen, that the Duke will pass us by. He will wish to finish us, and I pledge he will not leave us standing in any wretched field. The general is mistaken.'

Prince Charles intervened. 'I am minded to follow General O'Sullivan's reasoning. It is not my desire that the Duke be *shunned!*'

Another ripple of laughter emerged from the crowd. Yet their solemn features did not reflect such a jovial response. The Prince raised his arms and spread them in a priest like gesture.

'What say you, my friends and brothers?'

A voice from the rear called out. 'We will fight and die wherever you entreat upon us to do so, my Prince.'

Lord George could read their faces. Many were silent. Their desire to be heard, and for good sense to prevail, extirpated by an even greater sense of loyalty.

Lord John Drummond eventually spoke up. 'What if we

fell upon the enemy whilst they marched to confront us; surprise them when they are not formed up to repel us? Such tactics were of value at Prestonpans.'

He had hardly finished speaking when Lord George, his eyes suddenly gleaming, took up the argument.

'I am certainly minded to agree with you, sir, but my proposal is perhaps a more radical one.'

All eyes were once more upon him, willing him to contrive a plan that would provide them with some hope of returning to their lands and families, still with breath in their bodies.

Lord George leaned forward, supporting himself upon his knuckles. He smiled, and someone coughed, as if in response.

'We will march upon them tonight, gentlemen. Encircle their positions at Balblair and catch them in their beds, still full of piss.'

The young Lord Elcho called out. 'Surely their patrols will provide intelligence of our approach, long before we see the glow of their fires?'

Murray shook his head. 'Not if we march upon a route that does not take us from the moor, so that we may avoid any dwelling houses and remain hidden from the high road between Inverness and Nairn.'

He looked towards the Mackintoshes, and addressed them collectively. 'What say you, my friends? These are your lands, after all.'

Heads nodded and gruff voices muttered, 'Aye, it could be done, true enough.'

The debate continued for a time. Some had reservations about their numbers, there being several clans not present. Others feared what would happen if they were beaten off and were forced to retreat. Then there were those who were hungry and had concerns as to their ability to fight in such a state. The Prince listened attentively to the arguments, and to the solutions offered by Murray and his henchmen, Lochiel and the Duke of Perth. In the end he raised his hand and bellowed, 'Gentlemen, I have heard enough. I am confident that we have sufficient numbers to defeat a dispirited enemy, and you are all aware that I am resolved to fight the enemy without further delay or complication.'

He turned to Murray. 'Is it not ironic, that I too had considered such a move as you now propose? Yet I feared it would not find favour with these gentlemen. But now my mind is changed. I see this as our opportunity to finish this campaign decisively and send my bloated cousin back to his father in London.'

He looked around him, then grinned. 'We march tonight, my brave fellows, and tomorrow we will celebrate, by filling our bellies with mutton and good wine.'

Muted cheers erupted from the tartan-clad warriors crowded around the table. The decision had been made.

2010

Chapter Five

Culloden Battlefield
16th April

Silence greeted him as he climbed out of the Land Rover. Then the distant warbling of a solitary skylark filled his ears. It sang for nearly a minute, before parachuting back to the rusty-coloured heather and falling silent. The moor was his again, its pale, wispy grass swaying gently alongside the green-edged footpath that snaked away before him. Beyond was the battlefield itself, its quiescence disturbed by the pre-dawn light. It lay waiting; an inhospitable wilderness of peat and coarse-clumped heather, amongst which spidery veins of putrid water stood dark and motionless.

In contrast to this hallowed and minacious field, the dawn sky outwith the gentle undulations of Saddle Hill and Beinn Bhuidhe Bheag was anything but foreboding. A collage of plump stationary cloud had formed over these eastern hills, its underbelly burned red by the rising sun. Further west, above the battlefield itself, the sky was streaked blue and purple and still verging upon night.

He had to act now... before the sun had fully risen on this, the 264th anniversary of the last pitched battle on British soil.

The visitor centre car park was, not surprisingly, completely empty at this early hour. He'd parked close to the approach road, in what amounted to a lay-by just inside the entrance to the site. His eyes panned across to the B9006 that ran along the northern boundary of the battlefield. Nothing moved, not even an early morning commuter hurrying to work. He stood for a second or two preparing himself for the task ahead, then opened the rear door of the battered green vehicle. It squeaked, and he paused, as if the sound would wake the entire world from its slumbers. A fox halted nearby and looked across inquisitively, before continuing its journey across the car park. Reassured, he resumed his undertaking, holding the door wide open whilst he peered in at the cargo stored between the bench seats. It was wrapped in an old dustsheet; one of those cream-coloured linen throws that annoyingly always shed fibres when unravelled.

As it happened, this expanse of cloth had taken on a role for which it was never initially intended. It now formed a shroud, a bloody one at that, wrapped tightly around the human-shaped contours of a stocky figure measuring around 5 feet 10 in height. At the head end, the cloth was heavily soaked in the occupant's blood, still wet and bright red in places. Across the chest area too, maculation was present in the form of ragged streaks, where the blood beneath had run away from the centre of the chest and down the sides of the torso. Then, at equidistant intervals, nylon string had been tied tightly around the corpse to hold the sheet firmly in place.

He took a firm grip on the feet, and slid the corpse towards him across the grubby rubber matting that formed the floor of the vehicle's load area. It moved easily, and he guided the feet towards the ground, before placing an old towel across his right shoulder. He then unceremoniously heaved the torso up and over that shoulder, before straightening up and stumbling slightly as the weight affected his balance. But he was a strong, fit man, and the burden was no real challenge for him.

Leaving the Land Rover's door open, he took his first steps

onto the unmade path and headed out onto the moor. The corpse sighed as the last remaining air escaped from its lungs, but he was unperturbed by these occasional unsettling sounds, focussing on the route ahead.

He marched purposefully, past the old thatched Leanach Cottage to his left, towards the fluttering red flags that marked the government front line ahead of him. He could feel his shoulder begin to ache now, and his breathing became more laboured. Then, at last, he reached the well-trodden path that the tourists followed to walk from the visitor centre to the heart of the marshy battlefield. Above the gentle rush of the wind, he could hear his footfall on the pale, crushed stone as he walked between the random clumps of windswept daffodils that bordered the route. He then came across the pointed stone marker declaring that this was the... *Field of the English. They were buried here.* He halted by the grim little Victorian monument to catch his breath. It was a fixture that merely theorised as to the location of the fifty or so government soldiers who had perished during the iconic battle. Historians had yet to locate the bones of these men; ironically not all Englishmen as the stone pronounced, but in all probability Lowland Scots too.

He was now approaching a crossing in the path. To his left stood a panel explaining to the tourist that this point marked the government front line. Directly above it, one of the red flags thrashed about, straining against its white nylon halyard. He continued on, down a slight gradient, whereupon his route threaded its way between dry stone walls. To his right, ecru-coloured grassland dotted with dark green gorse rose to a slight ridge, upon which another red flag flapped in the distance through the morning gloom.

Twenty yards to the west, the path turned sharply to the right. Sheltered by another rising dry stone wall, and partially overgrown by grass, was an arc of small, randomly shaped stones. Enclosed within the arc was a small pool of still, green water, the remnants of an ancient well that had graced this spot for centuries. Next to this ostensibly insignificant location stood another arrow-headed memorial marker, embedded into the grassy bank that skirted the route. This old grey stone bore the scars of a century of weathering, mottled and pitted, rough to the touch, and adorned with green and white lichen. The words though, carved deeply into its gnarled face, were still clear to see. They read: *Well of the Dead. Here the chief of the MacGillivrays fell…* and here, he stopped. It was journey's end.

With bended knees, he stooped to offload his limp cargo. Still grasping the legs, he leaned forward slightly, until the head and torso slumped heavily onto the grass beside the marker stone. He then produced a lock knife and proceeded to cut the bindings around the blood-soaked cloth. Once free of its bonds, he began to unravel the makeshift shroud. From within it, the body of a distinguished-looking man emerged, naked and pale as ivory. His torso and head were smirched in his own (now semi-coagulated) blood. Deeply incised wounds crisscrossed his abdomen, exposing the underlying tissue, and in places his intestines. Similar incisions adorned his balding scalp, at least four of them, like bloody furrows, tracking from front to rear. Then one massive fissure, shorter than the others, but more devastating than the rest, ran at an angle across the very top of his head. This cloven trauma extended deep beyond the skull casing, exposing the distinctive grey brain matter beneath.

Much of the face was swollen and purple with bruising, to such an extent that not even his closest kith and kin would now have recognised him with ease. For most, this would have been the most shocking of sights, but the face of his carrier displayed no flicker of emotion. His features remained expressionless, business like… undaunted. He knelt down next to the corpse and tied a grubby white handkerchief around its upper left arm, all the while looking about him for signs of life nearby. He stood again, gathering up the bloodied dust sheet as he did so. Gazing down at the symbolic carvings etched into the pale chest with the very knife he now held in his right hand, he half whispered his farewell, as if conversing with the lifeless form beneath him.

'*Beannachd leat*, old man!'

He turned and walked away, retracing the route he had taken from the lay-by. A gentle heat played on his cheek as the morning sun broke cover in the east, and he quickened his pace a little.

Less than five minutes later, he was back where he started. He threw the dust sheet into the rear of the Land Rover and closed the door, then hastily made his way along the side of the vehicle, keys in hand. He again surveyed the scene before him, across towards the junction with the B9006. On this occasion, to his surprise, he caught sight of a solitary cyclist heading in the direction of Croy.

'Damn it,' he growled under his breath, and for a second wondered whether he should move to eliminate this unexpected interloper. But no, he was some distance off and the sun must have been in the rider's eyes; he wouldn't have got a good view of him or his vehicle. *Leave it*, he thought. *Why make things complicated?* So he climbed into the driver's seat and sat motionless behind the wheel for a moment or two, waiting for the cyclist to clear the area. Then, with a twist of the key, the engine burst into life, emitting a momentary puff of grey exhaust vapour from the rear. He eased out the clutch and turned the Land Rover 180 degrees, before straightening up and heading out to the main road. At the junction, all was now clear, so he swung the wheel, turned right and sped away to the east.

Eddie Craig had by now reached the railway bridge beyond Newlands. He cycled this way every day from his home in Westhill, on the edge of Inverness, to the farm near Croy where he worked for his brother-in-law. He'd done it for twenty years, rain or shine, summer and winter, and was always mindful of the teasing his mates dished out in the pub about the battlefield. They had warned him on many occasions that he should be very wary of the ghosts of the slaughtered combatants who were known to roam the area in the wee small hours! He'd always laughed at them... and still did of course, but what he'd just seen had certainly reminded him of their jovial prophecies. He replayed in his mind's eye the moment when he'd just passed the entrance to the approach road that led up to the battlefield visitor centre. He could see the wide mouth of the junction, the white, slightly faded markings on the road surface and the small boulders that lined the verge just inside the entrance. There were the red boards, welcoming people to Àrach Blàr Chùil Lodair... Culloden Battlefield in the Gaelic. Behind them were the flagpoles from which the saltires proudly fluttered. He could even see away up the driveway, beyond the lay-bys to the strangely located red postbox (in his opinion), secured on its post and sited on a patch of grass some way from the pathway. In the distance was the unconventional profile of the new visitor centre. All was as it should have been on this early spring morning, when the sun rose over the distant hills beyond the River Nairn.

Eddie was no historian, but he knew what he'd seen, and the sight had definitely spooked him! He tried hard to firm up the image in his subconscious. Yes, there it was. The glare of the sun had prevented him from registering some of the detail, but he *was* sure. There was a tall man standing alone by what he recognised to be a long wheelbase Land Rover... a man dressed in full Highland garb! Not the usual kilt that most people would've expected, but the *breacan-*

an-feileadh, the ancient belted plaid or great kilt, woven in a predominantly red tartan with a lighter inlay. It was gathered in around the waist and suspended over the shoulder in the traditional fashion and consisted of yards of loose cloth, once used by Highlanders as their bedding and clothing combined. The figure also wore a dark-coloured bonnet, to which a white ribboned cockade was attached. He remembered that because it really stood out against the darker-coloured material of the headwear. He also thought he saw something pointed, suspended from somewhere under the folds of cloth that were draped over his shoulder. He wasn't sure, but could have sworn it was a *sword*!

The glimpse was momentary, but it was real, very real indeed. Eddie had seen re-enactors at the battlefield on several occasions, but not at this time of day. Had he realised the significance of the date, then he may well have been a little less suspicious, but today was just another working day for him. There were, after all, a world full of eccentrics and nutters out there who'd do something like this on 16th April! But he'd *not* remembered what date it was, and so he'd taken more notice of the figure. He didn't believe in ghosts, especially those who climbed into Land Rovers! However, this was out of the ordinary, really weird, if he was honest... something to tell the boys in the pub that night.

He chuckled to himself, shaking his head in disbelief as he rode on along the lonely road to Croy... blissfully unaware that Duncan Fraser, a man completely unknown to him, lay alone, waxen and lifeless at the Well of the Dead...

Mack and the man known as David were waiting for him when he returned to the small cedar-clad cabin that stood silently in the forest's shadow. It was a shabby affair, its wooden walls bearing the green hue of extensive mould, whilst its once-black iron guttering sagged under dripping eaves, oxidisation now claiming much of its surface.

Around the structure lay an assortment of discarded woodsman's tools, rusted and unused for years, and testament to the labours of a previous occupant. To the right of the cabin stood a small hut, a tool store, once used by the forester who had resided at this lonely spot. Its wooden door sagged on ageing hinges, remaining closed only because of the large rusting cross-saw that stood propped against it.

David sat casually on the pile of old logs that had been discarded by the front door. He was puffing on a cigarette when the Land Rover pulled up. His companion had recognised the high-pitched drone of the approaching engine and appeared in the doorway, leaning with arms folded against its discoloured frame.

The driver of the Land Rover slid silently out from behind the steering wheel, making no effort to acknowledge the presence of the other men. He opened the back door and pulled out the dust sheet, rolling it up and then dumping it some twenty feet away from the vehicle. He then stood for a while staring down at the bloody shroud, panting heavily.

Mack appeared at his shoulder. 'Everything go tae plan, then?' He produced a box of matches from the pocket of his leather jacket and handed them to the figure draped in tartan.

'Aye, it's done,' the new arrival confirmed, squatting next to the bloodied sheet. He struck a match, applying it to the fabric, then stood up as the flames engulfed the material.

'Did anyone see you up on the battlefield?'

'Only a laddie on a bike. He passed by at a distance when I was returning to the Land Rover. He wouldn't have seen the number plate, though. He was too far away.'

'Seein' it wouldnae help the polis much,' Mack added with a smirk.

'A sighting from a distance would be somewhat fortuitous, though,' David submitted nonchalantly. 'It all helps to build a picture of their prime suspect!'

The so-called 'prime suspect' made no reply. He removed the blue bonnet from his head and ruffled the ragged red hair that lay beneath, before hurrying off towards the cabin and leaving Mack to stare into the dying flames.

He reappeared several minutes later wearing blue jeans and a hacking jacket.

'Feeling better, now you've got shot of all that garb?' David enquired with a grin.

The two men gazed into each other's eyes.

'I'm never going to feel better about what I've just done. It shouldn't have happened. They were supposed to have been away, for God's sake. There was no talk of killing anyone when I agreed to this. Things have got out of hand.'

David sighed. 'Well, what can I say? Shit happens, my friend. Just think of it as getting your own back, and put it behind you.'

He walked across to the Land Rover, not wishing to reveal the sense of unease that he too was feeling since the inadvertent murders of the old couple. Standing by the passenger door, he looked back.

'Don't you think we should be getting along?'

They drove away along the forestry track, leaving a cloud of dust in their wake. No one was speaking. The man in the hacking jacket was once again behind the wheel, staring out through the fly-spattered windscreen. David sat next to him, humming to the song on the radio, whilst Mack, who was sitting in the rear, seemed mesmerised by the passing trees.

When they emerged onto the main road some ten minutes later, David eyed the driver apprehensively and said, 'You know we're going to have to have another go... when the dust has settled, of course?'

His ashen-faced companion glared back. 'In yer dreams, my friend. You're going to have to find some other wee mug to do yer dirty work for you next time.'

'You'll come around to the idea,' David retorted, unfazed by the driver's reaction. 'You have, after all, got everything to lose and very little to gain, should you wish to pull out of our little arrangement now.'

They sped on towards Inverness, their conversation non-existent again until the driver finally asked, 'Where do you want dropping?'

'The railway station will be fine,' David informed him. 'I'll pick up my car from there.'

'Right you are, then.'

'Keep your head down for a while,' David went on to advise him. 'Whilst the boys in blue go about their usual business. Then I'll get in touch again and we can discuss our next move.' He sensed an imminent and less than positive reply from the man sitting next to him, prompting him to raise his finger to his lips.

'Hush,' he whispered. '*No* is not an option.'

Chapter Six

Neil sat in his high-backed leather chair gazing searchingly at the screen of his PC. The website of the Lochmhor Distillery was displayed in front of him. It was a professional creation, well designed, with some swanky photography to boot. The home screen linked in to all that you'd expect from a distillery site. It included stuff about the range of products, the history of the plant and the distilling process, and all the tourist bumph about tastings. There was also some useful information about whisky trail tours and the like.

He raised his coffee mug to his lips just as Holly walked in with a uniformed sergeant, who Neil recognised as one of the force's police search advisors, affectionately known as PolSAs.

'Your operational name is Cawdor,' were Holly's first words.

'Umm, Operation Cawdor. That'll do. At least it's locally relevant, and not one of the other weird concoctions they push out these days. Thanks Holly.'

Neil turned his attention to her companion. 'Morning, Stevie. How's the search going?'

Steve Armsley was an Englishman and ex-Royal Marine

who'd transferred to the Scottish force from the Metropolitan Police in London. He squinted up at the wall clock and checked the time against his own watch.

'Eight o'clock. They should be just starting. One team is still doing the track up to the castle. They finished the search of the immediate grounds last night, just as the light was going, but found nothing of interest. Another team has been tasked to the interior of the property, following the SOCOs as they vacate each floor. Nothing there so far, either... not that we'd expect to find anything obvious if Fraser Gunn and his team have done their job properly.'

He was a no-nonsense sort of a guy, Steve. A man whose lugubrious expression rarely strayed far from his weather-beaten features... unless of course the English rugby team was having a good run! Then you'd just about raise a smile from him if you said something exceedingly witty.

'Thanks, Stevie. I'll get out and see the boys later; pass on my gratitude to them personally.'

'Thanks, they'd appreciate that Boss, cheers!'

Just then, one of the unit's older DCs, a stocky Glaswegian called Bryan Findlay, stuck his head around the doorframe.

'Thought you shud know, sur. A man's body has been found oot on the battlefield at Culloden. Sounds like he's been murdered. Old guy, apparently. Nasty injuries, I'm told.'

'Where exactly on the battlefield, Fin? It's a big place.'

Neil was already rising from his chair and donning his jacket.

'Just on the battlefield, sur. A place called the Well of the Dead.'

'Okay, tell the ops room I'm on my way. Come on, Holly, grab the car keys.'

He picked up his phone. 'Looks like your team will be much in demand over the coming days, Stevie.'

They hurried out and headed off down the corridor, leaving

Armsley looking gloomier than ever and Findlay calling after them that uniform were already well on their way.

The B9006 to Culloden was still busy with rush hour traffic when they joined it at the Inshes roundabout. Luckily, a distinctively marked patrol car overtook them, having hurried up from the A9 slip road. It manoeuvred its way steadily along the centre line with its siren wailing and blue strobe lights pulsing, thereby inducing the crawling traffic ahead of it to part, as the Red Sea had done for Moses. Neil followed in its wake, akin to a grateful Israelite, threading his way through a corridor of flashing indicators and flickering brake lights.

They were soon speeding out of the urban sprawl of Inverness and had left its traffic behind them. The landscape opened out into a tapestry of fields, bordered on one side of the road by a low dry stone wall, and on the other, by a ragged hedgerow of early-flowering yellow broom. In the distance, the broad melancholic heath that was Culloden Battlefield basked in the early morning sun. Above its carpet of hardy grass and copper-hued heather, the red and blue flags marking the opposing front lines, confronted each other across the moor.

Neil followed the patrol car up the approach road to the visitor centre and parked next to several distinctive yellow and blue liveried police cars in the disabled bays close to the entrance.

A young constable hurried over, waiting anxiously whilst the two detectives climbed out of the CID car.

'Constable Ewan Sinclair, sir. I've been sent by Sergeant Crerar to escort you to the scene.'

'Lead the way then, Ewan,' Neil directed, trying hard not to show his amusement at the young man's sense of formality. 'SIU on their way?'

'Aye, sir. Mr Gunn. ETA twenty minutes.'

The three officers followed the paved route that skirted the side of the visitor centre, and then along a pathway that snaked its way out across the battlefield. To their right, the stonework of Leanach Cottage glowed in the spring sunshine. Neil pointed across to it as they hurried past.

'Amazing that the old place ever survived with the battle raging around it...' Then he stopped abruptly, remembering Adam Carnie's comment the day before. 'I didn't mention to you, did I, that today's the anniversary of the battle? The 16th April 1746. Did you know that, Holly?'

'No, I'm terrible with dates, especially historical ones!' Holly contributed as they resumed their march. 'But the monster who's responsible for this probably did.'

'No "probably" about it, Holly. Too much of a coincidence, surely.'

They arrived at a junction in the path, where their young guide took a right turn. A short distance ahead, their route was barred by blue and white barrier tape, where another constable was keeping a scene log. Following a brief conversation with the log keeper and words of encouragement from Neil, they left Sinclair with his colleague and ducked under the tape.

At a crossing of two paths, next to a pole from which a red flag snapped above them, they turned left, down a gentle slope between banks of tufted brown grass. There, next to the path, stood a low, pointed stone that inclined at an angle. Behind it, on a small knoll, lay the naked body of an elderly male, the pallid colour of his skin exacerbated by the vivid green grass upon which he lay. Standing some distance from the corpse was Sergeant John Crerar, who was busily unravelling more blue and white tape across the path beyond the crime scene. He turned when he heard the approaching footsteps and joined Neil by the leaning stone.

'Morning sir... Holly. Bloody shocking, this, eh? And the second in two days.'

Neil nodded in agreement, staring down incredulously at the locus before him. Holly, shocked to the core, turned away, covering her mouth with her gloved hand.

'That's Duncan Fraser, all right,' Neil confirmed.

Holly turned back. 'How on earth can you tell, with head injuries like that?'

He pointed at the corpse. 'Same symbols carved into the chest there. A cat in a circle, and the three horizontal lines across a vertical just above it.'

He continued to study the body, still trying to absorb the level of brutality involved.

'He's also wearing the pinky ring I saw in a photo at Cullaird Castle yesterday, and his hair, what I can see of it, has the same colour and degree of regression across his scalp. No, that's definitely him. Christ knows how the family are going to deal with this.'

An inspector from Wiltshire Police had finally broken the news of Laura's murder to the couple's daughter Selina at their home in Winterbourne Compton the previous afternoon. Now it seemed the whole solemn ritual would have to be repeated.

Duncan Fraser's swollen eyes stared vacantly up at the slow-moving clumps of cloud that had all but stalled above the battlefield, as if to gawp at the scene below. The deep wound across the top of his head appeared almost surreal. Clumps of grey cerebral matter had oozed through a fissure in the skull, like excess glue when two surfaces being repaired had been pushed together. As if that wasn't shocking enough, a dozen or so deep incisions tracked across the abdomen, exposing glimpses of intestine that were now partially obscured by dried blood.

'Who found him, John?'

Crerar thumbed through his pocket book. 'One of the staff working here. A boffin by the name of Dr Malcolm

Breckenridge. Big guy; a bit geekish. I sent him up to the centre with one of my lads. I think he needed some hot sweet tea.'

'So do I. Good idea,' Holly agreed. 'What's the story with that handkerchief around his arm?'

Neil rubbed his chin thoughtfully. 'Umm, I'd wager it's symbolic, like the cat and the other scratches.'

They turned as the swish of plastic reached their ears. Fraser Gunn was approaching, clad in his white coveralls, his trademark steel cases in both hands. He stopped by the stone that was inscribed: *Well of the Dead. Here the Chief of the MacGillivrays fell.*

'My God. Is this Mr Fraser, then?'

'Looks like it,' said Holly. 'The boss reckons so.'

'Aye, it's him,' Neil murmured, as if to reinforce his earlier deduction.

'Strange leaving a Fraser here,' Gunn mused. 'At an iconic memorial to the MacGillivrays. What was his name? Colonel Alexander MacGillivray of Dunmaglass. They moved his body from here after the Battle of Culloden and reinterred him over at Old Petty Church.'

He pointed over towards the blue waters of the Moray Firth that glittered in the distance. 'Over there, beyond Castle Stuart. They say his sweetheart, Elizabeth Campbell of Clunas, died of a broken heart, four months after the battle. Sad tale, eh?'

Holly smiled perfunctorily. 'Thanks for the history lesson, Fraser. Ever thought of writing chick lit for a living?'

'Hey lassie, Neil Strachan's not the only bloody historian around here, I'll have you know. I came here many times as a wee boy. Fascinating place, this… spiritual, almost.'

He gestured towards Neil. 'The historian we call "boss" has got his work cut out now… double murder, and he's only been in the job for two days. Still, he's the best man for it, probably, having solved the mystery of that missing submariner last year.'

Gunn stooped to open his cases. 'Best I get to work, then. I've got two more SOCOs on their way, and Adam Carnie should be here shortly.'

'Good stuff,' Neil acknowledged, as he walked over to the green pool of water that was ostensibly the Well of the Dead. The tiny pool, enclosed within a horseshoe of small boulders, was anything but spectacular. His eyes scanned the straggly clumps of drooping grass that grew around the site, eagerly seeking the tiniest of clues. A weapon perhaps, discarded clothing, anything at all. But there was nothing. Just the naked, butchered corpse of an old man. The killer had certainly been conscientious in his work.

Neil turned again to Crerar. 'Can you speak with the duty inspector at Inverness and get some more boots on the ground out here? I need this entire complex closed off until we've examined it in detail. Let me know if there's a problem with that, will you?'

Crerar responded with a wave and searched his pocket for his mobile phone. Neil called to Holly, who was looking out wistfully towards the memorial cairn at the centre of the battlefield... and still looking a little green.

'Come on, Holly, let's go and have a chat with Mr Breckenridge. Leave these boys to do their work.'

Minutes later they were sitting in the warmth of one of the offices in the visitor centre, a rosy glow now restored to Holly's cheeks. They were sipping cups of steaming tea and waiting patiently whilst Dr Malcolm Breckenridge fielded an urgent phone call. Neil studied him, whilst he drank. He was indeed tall, well over six feet in fact, and more than a little way into his forties. Having said that, he had successfully retained the persona of his university days, sporting a full ragged beard, grey for the most part, but with a distinctive crescent of rusty brown that framed his chin. An inconspicuous jewelled stud adorned his right earlobe, and sizable circular framed tinted spectacles completed the image of youthful academia.

The phone call concluded, Breckenridge smiled, or at least the corners of his mouth turned upward momentarily. 'Sorry about that, folks. What an awful start to the morning.'

He blew through pouted lips, then took a hurried sip of his tea, as if he were expecting the cops' questions to batter him in rapid succession.

'Do you normally walk the battlefield this early in the morning, Doctor?' was Neil's opener.

'Not as it happens, no. But today I went out to inspect some trenches we'd dug yesterday, out beyond the Jacobite line. You know, the area marked by the blue flags. We're doing some excavations in the vicinity of where we believe Prince Charles was stationed during the battle. I was afraid they may have become waterlogged, preventing any further work today.'

'I see,' said Neil, his gaze fixed involuntarily upon the ear stud. 'And were they… waterlogged, I mean?'

'I never got that far. When I approached the Well of the Dead, I saw that poor man lying there. Naturally, I didn't hang about, and ran back here to call yourselves.'

'Did you see anyone on the battlefield whilst you were out there, anyone at all?' Holly was the questioner this time, giving Neil the opportunity to drink some of his tea.

'No, no one. I was one of the first staff to get in this morning. There were no other cars parked in the car park. The place was completely deserted.'

'So to confirm, then, did *anyone*, staff I mean, get here before you?'

'I don't think so, although Maggie, one of the ladies who works on the ticket desk was here when I ran in to make the phone call.'

'Okay, we'll speak to her too. Tell me, when do you open to the public at this time of year?'

Breckenridge tugged at his beard. 'During April, they open at nine and close at five thirty.'

Neil placed his mug on the tea-stained mat that had been supplied with the drink. 'You say "they", as if you're not actually a member of staff here. What exactly is your role at the centre, Dr Breckenridge?'

Breckenridge sat back in his chair and mused over his response. 'I'm actually on long-term secondment to the NTS, the National Trust for Scotland, from the Centre for Battlefield Archaeology at Strathclyde University. You see, there's still much work to be done on and around this site. By basing myself at the battlefield, I can carry on that work, whilst assisting the staff here to catalogue and identify the artefacts that keep on coming up out of the ground. We're also trying to return the moor to exactly how it would've been, topographically on this very day in 1746, and that's going to be quite a long job.' He removed his glasses and cleaned the lenses on his jumper.

'Did you know it was in fact the anniversary of the battle today, Chief Inspector?'

Neil got up. 'Yes, it hadn't passed me by, Doctor. Thank you for your time. I'll need to get back and speak to you again at some stage. Perhaps you can talk me through the historical factors that may be significant here.'

'Most definitely, Chief Inspector. Any time, I'm here most days.'

'Good. DS Anderson will take a statement from you now, if that's okay, and then perhaps you could introduce her to your colleague Maggie?'

'Of course,' Breckenridge replied, nodding with alacrity.

Neil placed a friendly hand on Holly's shoulder. 'I'm going down to the scene to speak with Adam Carnie. Then I'll head back to the office. When you've finished here, grab a lift with the uniform boys, okay?'

'Aye, sir. See you later.'

Neil sauntered out across the moor, hands stuffed snugly in his pockets. He was deep in thought, but it wasn't the brutal murder of Duncan Fraser, or the Battle of Culloden that now occupied his mind. It was that damned business with Cat, and his own personal battle, the one that was still raging inside him: whether to confront her about her whereabouts on the previous Monday, or to bide his time. She had been acting normally all week, and there'd been no signs of any detachment or coolness on her part. That had to be a good thing, he concluded. The appearance before him of the constable with the scene log prompted him to snap back to the task in hand.

'Is Dr Carnie here yet?' he enquired of the officer.

The young man checked his log. 'Aye, he is, sir. He arrived ten minutes ago.'

Neil found the pathologist suited up and squatting next to Duncan Fraser's body. He looked up when Neil approached and clambered to his feet, groaning in the process.

'Age is not a pretty thing, Neil,' he grumbled, tucking his chin into the wings of the vibrant bow tie that peeked out above the collar of his green coveralls. 'My, you are being challenged early into your new role, my boy.'

Carnie stepped back and rested his gloved hands on his hips. He studied the corpse mirthlessly, tilting his head to one side. 'Looks like you have a double murderer on the loose here, Neil.'

'I'd gathered that, Adam,' Neil replied. 'How long do you think he's been here?'

'Difficult to say. There's little or no bloodstaining and no other disturbance on the grass, so it seems that he's merely been dumped here. His temperature is down about four degrees, but we need to take into account his weight, state of undress and of course the ambient temperature out here this morning. Then we need to include some precalculated corrective factors.'

The pathologist hesitated whilst he ran some mental calculations.

'What about rigor?' Neil enquired impatiently.

'There's some evidence of it around the face and upper body, but that's all...'

'Which means... taking everything into account?'

'Probably two to six hours. There is some lividity present. The discolouration isn't fixed yet, so yes, we're looking at less than six hours. That would tally with my estimation in terms of post-mortem cooling.'

'So, in short, he hasn't been dead that long?' Neil stamped his feet several times, primarily because they were cold, but also through frustration, and the need for a pee!

'There are many variables at play here, dear boy: temperature and age, to name but two. But your assumption is correct: *not that long*. Like I said, my best guess is no more than six hours.'

'Anything else immediately apparent, would you say?'

'Well, as you can see, he has the same symbols carved into his torso as those that were present on his wife. These symbols appear to be our offender's preferred signature. Then there's the handkerchief, tied around the upper arm here. I doubt that it's an attempt at first aid! Another bizarre calling card, I'd wager.'

The pathologist gathered his thoughts for a second or two before continuing his assessment. 'From first impression, I'd say there was more than one weapon used. A dagger-type knife: double edged, possibly, as before. Very likely to be the same one that was used on his wife. Also some sort of axe inflicted that head wound, apparent from the wedge shape of this gash and the fractures of the skull.'

He dropped to his haunches again and pointed at the deep slash wounds across the torso.

'There's no sign of haemorrhage in some of these slashes. Seems that they were caused post-mortem. Only a psycho could be responsible for this, Neil.'

He then waved a finger across the corpse. 'And this blood is fully clotted, so again, a good few hours since the wounds were caused.'

'Okay. Thanks, Adam, I'll wait for the PM results. Hopefully you can tell me more then.'

Having said his goodbyes, Neil strutted off towards the car park deep in thought. He made a short detour to the toilets in the visitor centre then returned to the car, glad of the silence and relative warmth inside the vehicle. As he probed beneath the steering wheel for the ignition lock, his phone began to chirp.

'Hello, DI Strachan.' He couldn't be doing with the mouthful of 'Acting DCI Strachan'!

'Hello, Mr Strachan. It's Selina Cope here, Laura Fraser's daughter.'

The sound of her voice penetrated his soul like a stake being plunged through his chest. He took a long silent breath. 'Hello Mrs Cope, I'm sorry I didn't get to speak to you last night.'

'That's okay. We were out in Salisbury until early afternoon, so the very nice lady inspector from Devizes didn't get here until after four o'clock. I'm sure you've been very busy.' She paused to cough. 'Oh, and please call me Selina.'

'Thank you, Selina. Please accept my deepest condolences. I can assure you that we will do all in our power to discover who did this.'

His mind raced. *What the hell do I tell her now? Is it the right time?* The decision was taken out of his hands though.

'I just wanted to let you know that my husband and I are travelling up as we speak. My brother will also be arriving from France, so we will be at my parents' home sometime this evening.'

There was a pause, then a discernible sob. 'Is there any news of my father yet? I am so terribly worried about him.'

Neil was just about to respond when her soft voice flowed through the earpiece again. It was preceded by another muffled sob, like that of a lost child.

'I fear the worst, Inspector. Daddy would never just disappear like this. He's been taken, I know he has, and it's just going to be a matter of time before you find him too.'

Neil's eyes found the vanity light on the car's roof, and he sighed resignedly. 'Is there someone there with you, Selina?'

'Yes, Inspector, my husband and daughter.' Then, after a pause. 'You do know something, don't you? Please tell me. You must.'

'Selina, I believe we *have* found your father. We do need to confirm this, but I'm confident it is him.'

He heard a gasp at the other end of the line.

'He's dead, isn't he? That murdering bastard, whoever it is, has killed him too.' His ear was filled with the sound of high-pitched wailing. Then he heard comforting voices, and a man with an educated English accent spoke. 'Nathaniel Cope here, Inspector. What on earth has happened?'

'Hello, Mr Cope. I'm so sorry to be the bearer of more terrible news, but I believe we've found your father-in-law's body. It seems that he has been murdered too.'

'Oh, my God. Where exactly?' he responded curtly.

'Out on Culloden Moor. The site of the battlefield, to be exact. We were called here only an hour or so ago. I'm still here now.'

'I can't believe it. Are you sure it's him, Inspector?'

'Almost certain, I'm afraid.'

'Surely you've seen a photograph of him by now... you must be able to recognise him for heaven's sake?' came the irascible reply.

'He has suffered some significant facial injuries, Mr Cope, so it's not that straightforward, I'm afraid. Look, I wouldn't be giving you this news if I wasn't entirely confident. But a formal identification will need to be made in due course. I'll come out to see you when you arrive: probably best first thing tomorrow. I'll know more by then.'

'All right, Inspector. I understand. Sorry if I seemed a bit touchy. I don't know when we will get there tonight, so we'll see you tomorrow. I'll call you when we get to Cullaird. Just so you know.'

'I understand, Mr Cope. Thank you. Please pass on my apologies to your wife for having to give her this news over the phone like this. It was unfortunate timing, I'm afraid.'

'Fully understood, Inspector. We'd have been pretty miffed if you hadn't been up front with us. Calling you when we did obviously put you in an awkward position. Speak later.'

'Before you go, Mr Cope... Do you know whether your father-in-law had any connections with Culloden Battlefield? You know... ancestral links, perhaps?'

Nathaniel paused to think. 'I don't know of any, Inspector. Let me ask Selina.'

The sound of muted voices could be heard beyond the hand that had been applied to the receiver. Then Cope's shaky voice emerged once more.

'Selina says that as far as she's aware, none of her immediate ancestors fought at Culloden. In fact there's a humorous story that still circulates around the family that tells of some of them missing the battle altogether! She says she can't think of any other link her father had with the battlefield. Other than visiting it... and he hadn't done that for years.'

'Thanks for that, Mr Cope. I'll be in touch.'

Neil heard Nathaniel comforting his wife in the background before the line went dead. He threw his phone onto the passenger's seat, and stared out through the windscreen. What a shit week it had been, and he was fearful that it would get far worse before it got better!

Chapter Seven

The Copes had just arrived at Cullaird when Selina called Neil late on the Friday night to tell him that they'd be available at the East Lodge any time the following morning. The castle itself was still being treated as a crime scene and the family were, in the circumstances, more than happy to stay out of the forensic investigators' way.

It was just after ten when Neil and Holly turned in between the stone pillars at the entrance to the driveway up to the castle. They were travelling in the CID Ford Focus they'd been using for several days and Holly was once again behind the wheel. Neil, meanwhile, briefed the two young female officers who were sitting in the rear. Both had been nominated to act as family liaison officers to the Copes.

Lorna McKirdy and Aili Hughes sat in silence, whilst he apprised them fully as to the progress of the enquiry overnight. Not that there was much to impart! He'd covered all the usual administrative stuff at the office the night before; risk assessment, deployment objectives and reporting chain. They'd absorbed everything he'd said, whilst taking notes and nodding attentively, knowing it was a formal requirement that the senior investigating officer thoroughly briefed his FLOs.

During their training, the lengthy manual relating to the deployment of FLOs prepared by the Association of Chief Police Officers had become their bible. They could almost quote it word for word, but always listened attentively all the same. Now their interest had once more been heightened as he provided them with more details of what was known about the family... which wasn't very much at that stage, but vital nonetheless.

'Will the Copes be up here for long, sir?' Hughes asked, as she scrawled in her notebook.

'I have no idea at present, Aili. We'll get a better steer when we've spoken to them. Once I've introduced you both and have had a chat, I would like you to deal with the victimology, and get a detailed statement about the family background. Feed it into the incident room soon as, okay?'

'Yes, of course, sir. Will do.'

Neil pressed the point. 'If I'm not mistaken, family background is going to play a significant part in this investigation.'

'Your average housebreaker doesn't normally kill two members of the same family, carve symbols on their bodies and dump one of them at a MacGillivray shrine for nothing,' Holly contributed.

'Exactly,' Neil agreed. 'So take your time and don't miss a thing, or I'll have you both issuing parking tickets on St Kilda.'

'But there are no cars on St Kilda,' Lorna replied naively. 'In fact there's no one on St Kilda, other than seabirds. The island's been abandoned for years.'

'Exactly, so it'll be a shit of a job,' said Neil, straight-faced, but sneaking a sideways glance in Holly's direction. His sergeant responded with a grin, one that the petite redhead in the back immediately picked up on.

'Oh ha ha, very funny... sir!' she riposted, and snapped her notebook shut.

A hundred yards beyond the entrance to the castle, another unmade track diverged from the main driveway and led away across open moorland to a sturdy-looking Victorian hunting lodge. The building was constructed of random grey stone under a dark slate roof. It was not a small house by any means, with its pinnacled dormer gables that capped the numerous small windows providing views from at least five bedrooms.

A shiny black Mercedes estate stood outside, together with a silver BMW 3 series, in which the Avis car hire tag still hung from the rear-view mirror.

Nathaniel Cope opened the white panelled front door. He was a tall, handsome man in his late forties with cropped grey hair that stood up from his scalp like the spines on a hedgehog. He was dressed casually, in a denim shirt and expensive jeans.

'Come on in, Chief Inspector. Thank you for coming.' He shook Neil's hand firmly, whilst the latter introduced him to Holly and the two FLOs.

Inside, the lodge appeared cosy and deceivingly compact compared to the pretentious facade that greeted the visitor on the outside. The interior had recently, and expensively, been renovated to a high standard, most probably with the help of an interior designer.

'Come in and meet the family,' said Nathaniel in a loud, opulent voice, more suited to the stage. The officers followed him into the sitting room, where five solemn faces turned to look at them in concurrence. Nathaniel introduced them one by one as they rose from their seats. Selina shook hands first. She was an attractive woman of diminutive proportions with short, unruly blonde hair that swept down either side of deepset grey eyes. She reminded Neil of the actress Meg Ryan in *Sleepless in Seattle*, a movie Cat had forced him to endure on at least four occasions!

'We meet at last, Chief Inspector. I'm sorry we couldn't

get here quicker.' She turned and gestured to the teenage girl who'd been sitting next to her. 'This is my daughter Emily.'

The girl looked up coyly, her eyes red from sobbing, and smiled briefly. Her resemblance to Selina was uncanny, so there was really no need for introductions.

Also present was Selina's brother, Alisdair, a couple of years older than his sister, and totally bald. But, as Holly commented later, it was a look that nevertheless suited him. His tall, slim French wife, Simone, stood behind him, a true Gallic beauty in every sense of the word. She peered dreamily out from behind her dark fringe and nodded her greeting. '*Bonjour Monsieur*,' she purred, offering Neil a warm, slender hand.

The last family member to be introduced was Alban Fraser, also bald and heavily tanned, the sixty-nine-year-old second cousin of Selina, who'd flown in from his home in the Spanish city of San Sebastián.

With the formalities out of the way, tea was offered and accepted. Nathaniel and Emily volunteered to provide the refreshments and hastily left the room, leaving Neil to offer his condolences once more, and those of his team as a whole. He then provided an update on the investigation as it stood, impressing upon the assembled family members that these were early days. He mentioned that the forensic teams were working hard at both scenes; that an incident room had been set up and that there were several distinct lines of enquiry they would be working on during the coming days. It was all frustratingly vague! The family listened with intense interest, until he asked them whether they had any questions. He knew things would get difficult from then on… and he was right.

'Where are our parents now?' Alisdair asked in a strange accent that appeared to be a collaboration of Scottish and French.

'They have been taken to the mortuary at Raigmore Hospital for the time being,' Neil explained softly.

'No doubt there will be post-mortems carried out on them, I suppose?'

Neil sighed. 'Aye, I'm afraid so, Alisdair. We need to find out all that we can about what happened to them.'

'And I expect you will be wanting someone to officially identify them, then?'

Neil had dreaded this question. 'Your mother, yes. But it may be best if we complete the identification formalities in respect of your father in a different way, through dental records, perhaps.' He frowned. 'There's no easy way of saying this, but you see, he sustained injuries to his head, and that may make normal identification difficult.'

Selina sobbed, whilst Alisdair dropped his head into his hands. Simone's dark eyes found Neil's. 'You *are* going to find ze monster who did zis, aren't you? Tell me you are, Inspecteur?'

Neil nodded glumly. 'We will do all that we possibly can Simone, believe me.'

Selina looked up, tear tracks glistening on her flawless cheeks. She'd picked up on Simone's reference to 'monsters'.

'How many suspects are there? Do you have any idea, Chief Inspector, any at all? It must've been a bungled robbery. Nothing else makes sense. Mummy and Daddy had no enemies. Everyone loved them.'

'Well, that's what we need to find out,' Neil affirmed, his tone still hushed. 'We're not sure how many offenders were involved at this stage.'

He scanned the room. 'Can any of you think of *anyone* who may have wished to harm Laura and Duncan? An ex-employee, perhaps? I have to ask, I'm afraid.'

There was much shaking of bowed heads.

'Absolutely not,' Selina protested, looking at each member of her family in turn.

'Okay, thank you. To answer your question about suspects,

hopefully our forensic experts will be able to help us with that. But, for now, we're going to have to ask a lot of questions, starting with your family background. Aili and Lorna will need to obtain a detailed statement from each of you, covering everything, from who is related to who, who's fallen out with who over the years and any other possibly relevant information that may give us a lead.'

He focussed on Selina. 'It may not be easy for you. I understand that, Selina.'

'She'll be fine,' Alban grunted from behind his handkerchief. Then came the expected trumpet-like blow of the nose.

Selina ignored him. 'Of course I'll help all I can. Just tell me what you need to know,' she confirmed between sniffs.

'We will,' said Neil. 'Perhaps we can start with a few questions from me, things I'd like to know from the outset.'

'Fire away,' said Alisdair, his head nuzzling against that of his wife.

'Okay. Let's turn to you first, Selina.'

Neil referred briefly to the open page of his A4 notebook.

'You and your brother here are the only surviving children of your parents, yes?'

Selina nodded. 'That's correct. We had a younger brother called Jamie who died in 2002, following a skiing accident in Chamonix.'

She looked across at Alisdair and smiled. 'It would've been his forty-first birthday tomorrow, as it happens.'

'No stepchildren, half-siblings... Anything like that?'

'No,' Selina confirmed, shaking her head. 'We three were the only children our parents had. There were no previous marriages or anything like that. Our parents were happily married for... must be coming up for forty-eight years.'

She grinned weakly. 'And I'm not aware of there being any love children... before you ask!'

'Okay,' said Neil. 'Did your parents have any living siblings?'

'Daddy was an only child. Mummy had one brother, Myles, who died a couple of weeks ago. He'd been ill for some time. My parents had returned early from their place in the Caymans to attend his funeral. They usually spend the whole of April out there.'

'When did your parents return home, exactly?' Neil asked, sitting forward. This was interesting. Shame Ruth Morton hadn't mentioned it!

'The day before the break-in,' Selina replied. 'I don't recall the exact time.'

'So anyone not in the know would've expected them to be away during the whole month of April, then?' Neil suggested.

'I suppose so, but it was no secret that they were returning early... not amongst the immediate family,' said Selina.

'How about other extended family? Do you keep in touch?' Holly asked, observing Nathaniel as he carried in a tray of tea.

'My mother has... or should I say *had*... two nieces, daughters of my Uncle Myles. One is in Canada. She has little to do with this side of the family... and her father too, so I hear. She married a chap whose family own most of Alberta. The other niece, Jane, lives not far from us, down in Somerset. She knew my parents were returning early. We see her quite regularly. She proofreads my books.'

'I didn't know you were a writer,' Neil interjected, in an attempt to lighten the mood of the meeting.

'I write children's books, Chief Inspector. Have done for a few years now. It's a living, and I can work from home, so it's really convenient for me.'

Alban then saw his chance when the conversation died temporarily. 'There are cousins on our side of the Frasers too,' he declared, as if his branch of the family had been forgotten.

Neil adjusted his position on the sofa so that he was facing Alban. 'Go on,' he prompted.

Alban cleared his throat. 'My father, Farquhar, was brother to Alisdair, Selina's grandfather. He ran the distillery and estate before poor old Duncan did. I also have a sister, Miriam, who lives down in London. There was another sister, Shona, but she's dead, I'm afraid.'

Selina returned her cup to its saucer and smiled again.

'Miriam and I are really close. We used to visit her for holidays when we were children. She lived in South Africa then. We always had such a great time with her. I remember her teaching me to ride out there when I was small. Then, when she came back to London, she visited us at Winterbourne all the time. She loved babysitting our kids when we had to go up to London for Nat's work dos.'

'Why did she come back, then?' Holly asked.

'Oh, she got divorced back in 1985,' said Alban, accepting a biscuit from Emily. 'She was married to a frightful chap, fat little diamond merchant from Cape Town. Never liked him. He was exceedingly rich. Thought he could get away with anything, including bedding his PA. But Miriam found out and took him for millions of rand. He set her up in an apartment in Kensington, and that was it. They rarely see each other these days, unless of course there's something going on with their kids.'

Holly eyed Alban with interest. 'So is Miriam down in London as we speak…? Does she know what has happened up here?'

Alban shook his head. 'No, not yet. She's currently on a Caribbean cruise. Not back until the beginning of May. So we decided to leave telling her until then. No point in spoiling her holiday for the sake of a few days.'

'I see,' said Neil. 'Fair enough, I suppose.'

'She'll be mortified that we didn't tell her,' said Selina, 'but I do tend to agree with Alban's stance, though.'

'Was she close to your parents, Selina?' Neil enquired, probing further.

'Oh yes, very much so. She and Mummy were like best friends. She was always up here for weekends.'

Neil turned his attention to Alban once again. 'What about you, Alban? You must've been close to Laura and Duncan too, certainly enough to drop everything and fly over here when you heard the news.'

Alban scratched his ear, slightly embarrassed by the question's implication.

'I was close to Duncan and Laura, yes, of course I was.'

He rocked his head slightly, as one would if they were suffering from a stiff neck. Neil detected unease.

'I fell out with my parents some years back, when I completed my studies at Grays School of Art in Aberdeen. I wasn't doing anything with my life, according to them, so our relationship became somewhat fractious. Then, to add insult to injury, I finally came out to them, told them I'd been having a gay relationship with a fellow student at Grays. I had to. Oliver, that was his name, Oliver Ruskin, hanged himself in my flat. Our relationship had become too intense. He'd become jealous of my friendship with other students, paranoid in fact. I turned to my parents for support, but they just shut me out. So I came to stay here at Cullaird until I could get the money together to go to Spain.'

The fact that Alban was gay had not come as a shock to Neil. He'd noticed the telltale signs of epicenism the moment he'd walked into the room.

'I'm sorry to hear that,' said Neil wondering how his parents could've been shocked by the revelation. 'It must've suited you. Spain, I mean. I understand you've lived there for a number of years?'

'It did. I had friends there, you see. I went out to San Sebastián at the end of 1965. My friends introduced me the artisan community there and I never looked back.'

He hesitated, then went on. 'I met my partner, Aldo, twenty-five years ago. He's an art dealer, a native of the city. We have a good life out there now.'

'I'm pleased for you,' Neil said, happy that the biographical speech had concluded. 'Have you kept in touch with the Frasers over the years?'

'Oh yes, we've been to them for holidays and *al revés*, I mean "vice versa", sorry!'

Neil's next target was Alisdair, who'd remained distinctly taciturn up until now. 'How about you, Alisdair? Do you come back often?'

Alisdair looked at his wife, as if to check that it was all right for him to answer. She must've provided him with the coded consent he required.

'Several times a year, yes.' He swallowed hard. 'I run a small restaurant called *La Vielle Alliance* in our little town in France, and also help run Simone's family vineyard. So we don't get much time to ourselves, I'm afraid.'

'Where in France exactly?' Neil asked. He'd spent a good deal of time in the country as a youth and felt he knew it reasonably well.

'A small place called Valcourt St Jacques, down in the south, in the Languedoc region near Montpellier. Do you know it, Inspector?'

'I know Montpellier. The taxi drivers are nuts there,' Neil joked. His gibe proved to be a big mistake. He could feel Simone's glare burn into the side of his face.

Holly sensed his embarrassment and came to the rescue. 'Any kids?' she asked Simone, smiling politely.

Simone's features softened. '*Ah, oui*, two girls, Lucie and Gabrielle. Lucie's studying economics at the Sorbonne in

Paris, and Gabrielle works for a fashion magazine in Nice.'

'You must be very proud of them,' Neil suggested, trying to recover the situation.

'We certainly are, of course,' Simone snapped, her expression saturnine once again.

Neil was now losing patience with the Frenchwoman's petulance and decided to change the subject.

'Tell me a bit about the family distillery, Selina.'

She had been gazing dreamily out towards the window and seemed a little startled that she was centre of attention again.

'Lochmhor's been in the family for years, Chief Inspector. Since 1872 in fact, when it was founded by my great-great-great-grandfather, Simon Donald Fraser. He initially worked for his father as estate factor, but became concerned about the health of his workers, who were drinking the very potent liquor they produced in their own illicit stills. So he branched out into whisky production, and the rest is history, as they say!'

She paused, but seeing that Neil was expecting more, she was impelled to continue. 'Part of the original complex was rebuilt after a fire in 1952. Its been further extended since then. My father held the position of non-executive chairman, whilst most of the day-to-day management of the plant has been the responsibility of Sandy Blair, the CEO and plant manager.'

'Were there any relationship problems between your father and Mr Blair, or any other members of the board?'

Selina laughed. 'No, nothing like that. Sandy's been with us since 1980. He's almost family. All the board members are family friends, and the staff at the plant were well looked after by my father. They would've done anything for my parents.'

'Sounds like a tight-knit little team,' Neil propounded.

'Not so little, actually. We employ over a hundred people.'

'Definitely no disgruntled staff, then? I wish the police force was like that!'

The joke passed her by. 'No, not that I'm aware of. Did you know of any problems, Alisdair?'

Alisdair shook his head. 'I wouldn't have been told if there were.'

Selina looked a little embarrassed. 'Alisdair and Daddy didn't always see eye to eye on things. Daddy wanted him to take on the running of the business when he retired. He was a little miffed when Alisdair went off to London to train as a chef and then buggered off to France.'

'He was more than a little miffed.' Alisdair looked directly at Neil, a look of hurt upon his tanned face. 'Do you know what? When I told him I'd received my Cordon Bleu diploma, he hardly cracked his damned face.'

Holly folded her arms. 'Did the relationship always remain strained, Alisdair?'

'We worked at it, for the kids' sake. Let's put it this way, we spoke!'

He turned to Alban. 'I should've come out like you, Cuz. Then he may have taken more interest. Like he did in you.'

Alban remained silent, responding only with an affected flick of the head.

'Alisdair!' Selina growled reprovingly.

'Well, it's true,' he sulked.

Holly smiled at Emily, who'd been sitting quietly, her hands clasped upon her lap. 'So what do you get up to when you're at home, Emily?'

The teenager looked across at her, the sullen expression still present upon her pale face.

'I'm studying at Marlborough College for my GCSEs.'

Selina squeezed her shoulder. 'She wants to be a vet. She adores animals.'

Holly again focussed on Emily. 'What about your brother, Fergus? Are you both close?'

'He's a sixth-former at Marlborough. Then he wants to be

a lawyer like Dad.' She looked at her mother for reassurance. 'I s'pose we're kind of close… most of the time.'

'Of course you are, my love, *most* of the time!' Nathaniel leaned across and patted her affectionately on her knee.

'So you're a lawyer, Mr Cope?' Neil shifted his position again to make eye contact with him.

'Yes, I'm a company lawyer for a merchant bank in the city: Paxton and Fortescue.'

In a change of tack, Neil said, 'I see, and did you both get up here very often?'

'Selina came up more than I did. We managed a joint visit two or three times a year at most.'

'I usually got up every two months or so,' Selina confirmed. 'I last saw Mummy and Daddy in mid March. In fact Mummy was due to come down to us for a few days at the beginning of May.'

Neil drained his cup, prompting Holly to do likewise. 'Right, we'll leave it at that for now. Thanks for the tea, and for answering all our questions. I'll leave you with Aili and Lorna so that you can get to know each other. They will be your first line of contact with us, so feel free to give either of them a call any time of the day or night.'

He distributed small business cards to each of the family. 'You can get hold of me on these numbers at any time too, but I'll be in regular touch from now on. Just quote the name Operation Cawdor if you need to call our switchboard.'

'Are we all suspects now, then?' Alban asked acrimoniously whilst studying the business card.

'Not at all, Alban,' Neil reassured him whilst he shook hands with Selina. Then he smiled. 'Unless of course, I discover something to make me change my mind!'

Alban scowled briefly, and reached for the newspaper he'd been reading.

Neil turned his attention the FLOs, promising them that

he'd arrange a car for them when he returned to the office. Then he and Holly excused themselves and headed for the front door, escorted by Selina.

He looked back at her as he stepped out onto the pathway. 'I saw a crest above the fireplace up at the castle, Selina. A wildcat crouching within a belt bearing a motto. I assume that is something to do with your family?'

Selina nodded. 'Yes, it dates back hundreds of years. I don't recall the origins of it, I'm afraid. I'm not much of a history buff really. Personally, I prefer to live in the present, but I'll certainly find out if you need to know.'

Neil smiled. 'That would be very helpful... and you've had no further thoughts as to any links your family, or your father specifically, had to the battlefield at Culloden?'

Selina shook her head. 'We can't think of any. Sorry.'

'Okay, that's fine. One last question. Do you know who has keys to the castle? Perhaps there is a list available somewhere.'

'I certainly have a key,' Selina confirmed. 'As far as I know, no other members of the family have one. The cleaner, Ruth Morton, has one, and I believe there is a spare down at the estate office. I'm going to have to do some research, I'm afraid.'

'If you could let me have a list as soon as you can, that would be helpful too.'

'Leave it with me, Chief Inspector.'

Neil smiled politely. 'Thank you again for the tea. We'll speak later.'

Both detectives said their goodbyes and meandered slowly back to their car. As he walked away, Neil sensed Selina's eyes following their progress. He was right. She had remained in the doorway, proffering a wave, and an alluring smile, unseen by the two detectives.

'What do you think, sir?' Holly asked as she climbed into the car.

'About the family, you mean?' he responded, as his head

disappeared beneath the roof. Once inside the vehicle, he pursed his lips as he considered her question.

'Who knows? But as of now we keep an open mind on all of them.'

'Right,' said Holly. 'That's what I thought you'd say,' and she turned the ignition key.

Chapter Eight

Sunday had dawned grey, and heavy rolling cloud had all but blotted out the few glimpses they'd had of the sun during their drive along the B851.

Neil and Holly were back in Strathnairn, driving slowly down the narrowest of lanes. The route, according to the map on Holly's lap, led to Tordarroch Lochs Trout Farm, the home of Ruth Morton.

Neil had wanted to drop in the previous day, after visiting the Copes, but there had been no reply when he called. He had since made contact with the Frasers' cleaner, and had been assured that on this occasion she would be expecting them.

A freshly painted fingerpost heralded their imminent arrival at the little cluster of farm buildings that now appeared before them atop a low, barren hill. The location had no doubt been carefully selected to provide wide-ranging views across the strath, and in particular, the shimmering waters of the River Nairn that meandered nearby. It was not a complex of any notable age and consisted mainly of a substantially sized dwelling, no more than ten years old and painted white under a shallow pitched slate roof. Behind the house stood a series of outbuildings, adjoined to it so as to form a quadrangle. To the side of the property, the driveway divided. A farm gate, fixed to the house itself, stood open, thereby providing access to the courtyard, whilst a continuation of the track curved away to the right and up the hill. Another fingerpost informed visitors that this track was private and led up to the trout lochs.

Neil pulled in through the gate and swung the car around so that it came to rest outside the porched entrance to the main house. A dog barked somewhere behind them and a door opened in one of the outbuildings. A black Labrador squeezed past the youngish man who was emerging from the opening and ran full pelt towards the two detectives, still barking gleefully. Neil stooped to stroke the dog, whilst Holly retrieved her paperwork from the back seat of the car.

'You must be Chief Inspector Strachan, then?' the man surmised as he approached them.

Neil broke away from the excited dog. 'That's right. We've come to see Ruth, if that's okay.'

'Aye, she's in the kitchen. Sorry we weren't about yesterday. Family commitment up north, I'm afraid.' He raised an apologetic hand. 'I'm Rodaidh, by the way. Her husband.'

'Pleased to meet you, Rodaidh. Don't worry about yesterday. This is my colleague, DS Holly Anderson.'

They shook hands and followed Rodaidh to the house, whereupon he breezed through the front door and called out, 'Ruth, the police are here to see you lassie.'

The kitchen was extremely tidy: everything in its place and the worktops devoid of any clutter. It was not what Neil was used to, having visited numerous farms and small holdings in the rural hinterland that surrounded Inverness. In his experience, the kitchens of Highland farmhouses were cluttered spaces, extensions almost of the workplace! Unlike this one, they often appeared tired due to years of decorative neglect and the constant traffic that passed through them.

Ruth appeared from a doorway to their right, carrying a

tiny baby. She was petite, plain-featured and no more than 5 feet 3 inches tall, with short, almost black hair, fashioned around her button-like ears.

'Hello, Mr Strachan… Sergeant Anderson. You found us, then?'

'Aye, no problem at all. The fingerpost at the top of the lane gave us a clue.' Neil looked around him. 'Nice place you have here, Ruth.'

'Thank you. We moved down from Ullapool four years ago, so that Rodaidh could take on the trout farm. He's always been in that line of work.'

Holly turned to Rodaidh. 'I love it up there. Is that where you're from?'

Rodaidh nodded. 'Aye, Rhue to be exact. My family had a fish farm out on Loch Broom.'

Rodaidh Morton was squatting on his haunches, holding the Labrador's collar with an enormous freckled hand. He was a big, strapping individual with curly auburn hair and a full beard, and uncharacteristically shy for a man of that stature, Holly thought.

'What about you, Ruth? Do you hail from the wild north as well?'

'Och, no, Sergeant, I'm from down here in Strathnairn. My parents both work at the distillery up the road. My mother's a MacGillivray, of which there are many still living hereabouts!'

Neil was listening to the conversation, whilst trying to estimate the couple's age. He concluded that Ruth could not have been more than twenty-five and her husband a couple of years older, say twenty-seven or eight.

'Business doing well?' he asked.

Rodaidh nodded his head vigorously. 'We're getting there. It's taken a while for us to get known, but the old word of mouth trick finally seems to be working well for us. The lochs are well stocked, and we have a few local restaurants on side just now.'

'Good. Pleased to hear it.'

'Rodaidh's also a wood carver, Mr Strachan. He specialises in Celtic knotwork, stuff like that. We supply to various craft shops and tourist outlets across the Highlands.'

'Irons in a few fires, then,' said Neil, impressed by their entrepreneurial spirit.

Ruth gestured to her husband to take the baby, who was now sound asleep. Then she nodded towards the dog.

'Can you put Oscar out while we talk?'

The young Labrador was duly ejected from the house, followed by Rodaidh, who was now carrying the baby.

Ruth invited the two detectives to sit down at the kitchen table.

'Tea or coffee, anyone?' she enquired whilst filling the kettle.

They both accepted her offer and settled themselves down either side of the table.

'Must've been a terrible shock for you the other day,' said Neil, having sensed an awkward silence.

Ruth turned and faced him, folding her arms in the process. 'Aye, shock's an understatement. Such a nice couple, they were.'

Holly checked her notes. 'I understand you've been working for them for three years?'

'Aye, about that. My father mentioned to Duncan that I was looking for a job locally, so they kindly took me on. Their previous cleaner was messing them about a wee bit. Not turning up… that sort of thing.'

She turned away to pour water into the mugs that were standing on the worktop, but carried on with her explanation.

'It's a big job for one person, keeping that place clean, so I went in twice a week, and often on Saturdays. Then, if I needed to go in and do anything specific, such as cleaning all the silverware, stuff like that, they'd happily pay me overtime.'

She delivered the mugs to the table and sat down next to Holly.

'They were very good when the baby was born too. Bought him presents, clothes… you name it.'

'So the perfect employers, then?'

'Pretty much, yes. Duncan could be a bit grouchy sometimes, but Laura was lovely: never any different.'

Holly looked up from her note taking. 'Tell us again, in as much detail as you can, what happened the other day, from when you left home.'

Ruth exhaled audibly, not relishing the prospect of reliving the tragic episode yet again.

'I left here about ten forty-five as normal, drove along to Cullaird via the 851 and arrived there just before eleven. I did stop briefly to talk to my neighbour at the end of our drive, so that delayed me for several minutes, I suppose.'

She thought for a second or two. 'When I parked outside the castle, I noticed that the door was ajar. That wasn't unusual, though. The Frasers often left it open in good weather. So I left my house key in the car and went across and knocked on the door. There was no reply, so I called out to say I'd arrived. Then, having got no response after several attempts, I decided to go in and look for them. Again, the place is so big, I wasn't in any way surprised that they hadn't heard me.'

Neil decided to interject. 'From what you're saying, you clearly knew that they had come home early from their holiday.'

Ruth raised her hand to her mouth, realising her oversight.

'Oh dear. Sorry. I should've mentioned that before, shouldn't I? Yes, they left a message on our answerphone. That would've been on the Tuesday. Laura explained that her brother had died suddenly, and that they'd arranged their flights home. They expected to arrive back at Cullaird on the Wednesday evening. Laura wanted me to go in on the Thursday as normal, even though I'd suggested that I leave it.'

'Do you know whether they called anyone else to tell them they were coming home early?'

'Sorry, I don't. They sounded as if they were in a rush, but I assume they found time to call their kids.'

'Any reason why you didn't mention they'd been away, when I spoke to you at Cullaird, Ruth?' Holly stopped writing and took a sip of coffee.

'I just forgot, that's all. I had a lot on my mind at that point, I suppose.'

She looked out of the window reflectively, then back towards her interviewers. 'No, it went right out of my mind. That's shock for you.'

Neil nodded. 'Okay, Ruth, carry on. Sorry to interrupt you.'

Ruth went on to explain that she'd checked the kitchen first and had noticed the breakfast things on the table, then had gone up to the great hall.

'It was at that stage I saw the blood on the stairs, the footprint and the smears on the wall.'

She raised her trembling fingers to her mouth once more. 'That's when I realised something was seriously amiss.' Her words tailed off into a sob, prompting Holly to place a comforting hand on her arm.

'Just take your time, Ruth. We know how difficult this is.'

'There's nothing much more to tell. I made my way into the great hall, and looked around. The silence about the place was frightening me. Then I found Laura lying there in that state, covered in blood.' She gulped as she tried to suppress the sobs. 'I just screamed and ran back downstairs and out to the car. Then I realised that the battery on my mobile was dead, so I ran back into the kitchen. There's a phone on the wall in there, you see. Then I called you people, and waited by the gates until the first police car arrived.'

'So, to confirm. You only went up to the great hall, having checked the kitchen. You didn't check the upper floors?'

'You mean the bedrooms?'

'Yes.'

'No way. I needed to get out. I can't quite believe I found the courage to go back in and make that 999 call, but I had no option.'

Neil nodded pensively. 'Understandable and very brave of you. So you saw and heard nothing when you were in the castle to suggest that anyone else was still present in the building? Noises upstairs, that sort of thing.'

'No, nothing. Neither did I see anyone leaving the area when I initially drove along the road towards the castle.'

'Okay, let's move on. Did you ever come across anyone locally who disliked the Frasers?'

Ruth shrugged. 'Never. They were much liked and respected locally. They were certainly no pushover and called a spade a spade, Duncan especially, but I never heard anyone utter a bad word about them. Nor did my parents over at the distillery.'

'What about the wider family? Did you ever detect any feelings of animosity between family members when they were present at Cullaird?'

'I never saw that much of them. I got to know Selina quite well, and Miriam, Duncan's cousin. The others only visited on high days and holidays, even Alisdair, their son. I did detect a coldness between Alisdair and his father, but I'd hate you to read too much into that. I may be entirely wrong.'

Neil smiled. 'Don't worry, we won't, but your views are helpful when it comes to building up a picture.'

He got up and peered out of the kitchen window, then stuffed his hands in his pockets before spinning around and asking, 'Do you have any idea who else has a key to the property, other than you and the Frasers themselves? We've asked Selina for a list, but I was hoping you may be able to help on that score.'

'I know Selina had one. Apart from her, we were the main keyholders. I believe there was a spare kept at the estate office, down behind the East Lodge. It's kept in the key safe in the factor's office. Funny thing is, it's never locked, so anyone could've had access to it.'

Holly checked her notebook. 'That would be John MacKeith's office?'

'Aye, he's the current factor. But he's away on his holidays at present. He's not due back for another four weeks.'

'Sounds like he's gone somewhere exotic?' Neil suggested.

'You could say that. He's gone down to see his daughter in New Zealand. He went off a couple of days before the murders.'

'How well do you get on with John, Ruth?'

'I like him very much. He's been a loyal servant to the Cullaird Estate for many years. He's the second keyholder. The thing is, he lives some way off, down near Moy. We are closer, so agreed to be the first point of contact.'

'Do you know all the estate staff?' Holly asked.

'Most of them. The numbers have dwindled of late. Much of the estate management work is outsourced these days.'

'Tell us about the ones you know.'

Ruth hesitated. 'None of them are responsible for this. They're good people; well liked within the local community.'

Neil smiled. 'All the same, it's useful for us to know what you think.'

'Okay. Well, there's Ann, who does the estate admin. She's in her sixties, and is married to the estate stalker Ken Howie, another long-serving employee. Then there are a couple of young ghillies who work with John: Seth Gordon and Aulay

Sinclair. That's about it. There are several tenant farmers, but I'm afraid I don't know them that well. They seem okay, though.'

'That's really helpful, Ruth. We'll be speaking to them all, and as I said, we're expecting a list of keyholders from Selina Cope too, so we'll leave it at that for now.'

Neil gestured towards the door. 'I think I'll go and speak to your husband now. Holly will get down on paper what we've just been talking about, if you don't mind.' With that he skirted around the table and disappeared through the door.

'A perk of seniority, disappearing when there's any writing to be done,' Holly joked as she pulled some statement forms out of her folder.

Neil found Rodaidh in his workshop, perched upon a rotating stool with the baby supported on his knee. Oscar the dog sat at his feet chewing an old offcut from the pile of wood that had accumulated beneath the nearby workbench.

Around the walls hung examples of Rodaidh's creations, beautiful specimens of Celtic artwork, translated into a variety of objects, such as ornate crosses, plaques and paddles.

'They're very impressive,' said Neil, moving from one object to the next. 'You call this knotwork, yes?'

Rodaidh's eyes followed Neil's progress around the workshop. 'Aye, that's right. It's an ancient decorative and religious art form, born from the traditions of the ancient Celtic people who settled in Britain during the seventh century BC. The story goes that the never-ending path of a strand of knotwork represents the permanence and continuum of life, love, and faith. To the ancient Celts, interlacing knotwork in one continuous line symbolises eternity.'

'Interesting,' said Neil, finally turning to face the young

man. 'I've often admired examples of this work on both wood and on standing stones.'

'They used it to decorate the pages of books too. Probably the best example is the Book of Kells at Trinity College in Dublin.'

'Ah, yes, I had the pleasure of seeing the Book of Kells many years ago. So how did you get interested in carving, Rodaidh?'

'Some of the old crofters who lived near us up north were carvers. They instilled in me the urgency of preserving these ancient skills, so I took it up, as a hobby initially. I was surprised to discover that I was actually quite good at it!'

'You're very modest. These are far beyond "quite good", my friend!'

'Thank you, Chief Inspector. It's good to know my work is appreciated.'

Neil pulled up another stool and sat down next to the bench.

'What do you make of this awful business over at Cullaird, Rodaidh?'

The big man fidgeted on his chair, a little uncomfortable with the question.

'What can I say? They were lovely people. I didn't know them as well as Ruth did, though.'

He squinted as the sun broke through the cloud and streamed through the dusty window, directly onto his face. 'The manner of their dying was truly shocking. I heard Mr and Mrs Fraser were both... how I shall put it... *mutilated*. Please tell me that's not true.'

Neil frowned. 'What do you mean... *mutilated*?'

Rodaidh flushed noticeably. 'I heard the killer had carved stuff on their bodies.'

Neil sat back. 'And who gave you that impression, Rodaidh?'

Now Rodaidh regretted saying anything. 'Oh, you know how rumours go around after an event like this. Word travels fast.' He smiled nervously.

'Did your wife tell you that?'

'Och, no. She told me she never got close enough to Mrs Fraser's body to see her injuries in any detail, just a lot of blood. That was bad enough.'

'Then who exactly? You must remember, surely.'

'I really don't recall, Chief Inspector. I must've heard someone talking about it somewhere around here, away down on the estate, perhaps. I just remember some mention of weird symbols being found on their bodies, that's all.'

Neil looked deeply into Rodaidh's eyes, the dark pupils of which were now fully dilated, like those of a wild animal caught in a trap.

'Are you sure you can't recall who mentioned this?' he asked a second time, this time with attitude.

'No, no, not at all,' Rodaidh whimpered.

'Well, it would be very helpful if such rumours were not passed around by members of the local community, Rodaidh. Or they may find themselves under a very bright spotlight.'

Rodaidh knew that meant him!

'Yes, yes, of course. Leave it with me. I'll quash any stories I hear, mark my words.'

Neil picked up a pencil and an offcut of wood that were lying on the bench and drew the symbol that had been found on the Frasers' bodies.

'As we're on the subject of weird symbols, do you recognise this one, Rodaidh?' he asked.

Rodaidh studied the drawing, then shook his head. 'No. Should I?'

'I just thought you may have come across it, in connection with your carving, that's all.'

'It's not something I've seen when I've been researching

knotwork patterns. It may be much older than that: pagan language or symbolism, perhaps. I've seen something similar in the Wemyss caves in Fife. Have you heard of them?'

'Yes, but I've never been there.'

'Incredible place. It's been said that there are more ancient markings in those caves than all the other caves in Britain put together!'

'Really, that many?'

Their conversation was cut short when Holly walked into the workshop.

'All done,' she announced. 'Ruth says you're allowed back in the house now, Rodaidh!'

She looked around at the carvings on the walls. 'Nice stuff,' she uttered.

'Thank you,' said Rodaidh, standing up and adjusting the now sleeping baby's position in his arms.

The two detectives walked through the door, but not before Neil turned and said, 'If you miraculously recall who was responsible for the mutilation rumour, please let me know, eh?'

Rodaidh swallowed hard. 'Will do, Chief Inspector. Will do.'

As they drove out of the courtyard, Holly glanced across at her boss, a visage of puzzlement on her face.

'What's all this about mutilation?' she enquired. He glanced back at her, straight-faced. 'He asked me whether it was true that the Frasers' bodies had been mutilated! When I asked him who'd told him that, he conveniently couldn't remember and looked very uncomfortable.'

'Well, there's not too many people who know about that. I hope to God someone on our team hasn't been blabbing.'

Neil nodded. 'I hope so too. Unlikely, though. But you're right. Not many people outside our organisation have knowledge of that fact, but someone certainly does... and that's the killer himself!'

Chapter Nine

Cat stood stiffly behind the clouded Perspex of the bus shelter on Woodside Farm Drive. She was watching a young boy throwing a Frisbee for the boisterous puppy that wheeled around his legs. The mornings had been distinctly chilly of late, more suited to winter than mid spring, and today was no exception. A keen breeze ruffled the unruly patch of long grass behind the bus shelter where the boy and his dog were playing, causing it to shimmer in the morning sunshine.

She turned away and focussed on the road junction down the hill to her right. Her bus would appear from this direction any second now… she hoped!

Several cars climbed the hill, highlighted against the backdrop of salmon-coloured roofs that bordered the skyline. In the distance, legions of white-capped wavelets hurried across the dull grey tract of the Moray Firth, as if racing the fast-moving shadows of the plump, hoary cloud that floated above. Her fixation on the distant vista had diverted her attention from the road, so she was relieved when she saw that her bus was now lumbering up the hill. The whine of its engine became steadily louder, and she sighed contentedly as the vehicle drew up in front of her.

The doors hissed and swung open, revealing the warm interior and the boyish grin of the young driver. Cat stepped aboard and presented her travel pass.

'Sorry to keep you waiting. Traffic's been heavier than usual today.' The hawkish young man with the dark spikey hair beamed at her, waving her through to the main cabin.

'Don't worry, the fresh air did me a power of good,' she lied, unconvincingly!

'Sounds like you had a big night last night,' the driver suggested as he closed the doors behind her.

'Och no, never on a Sunday!' She smiled and headed towards the back of the bus, trying not to make visual contact with the dour-looking souls whose Monday morning eyes had swivelled nonchalantly in her direction.

Three rows from the back of the bus, she found herself looking down into the smiling face of Maureen Cameron. The slightly plump redhead lived a short distance away from Cat and Neil. She worked for one of the long-established estate agencies in Inverness and had recently sold Cat's flat in the city centre.

Cat lowered herself into the seat next to Maureen, and unravelled the scarf from around her neck. 'He's a cheeky wee devil, that young laddie behind the wheel.'

Maureen grinned back at her. 'Aye, he's always the same. I don't know what he takes with his porridge, but whatever it is, I could do with some of it on a Monday morning!'

The two women giggled as the bus looped its way back onto Tower Road, and headed down the hill towards the A9.

'Isn't the news about that poor couple over at Cullaird Castle shocking? Such brutal murders too, the sort of thing you only hear about down south in the big cities.'

Maureen's eyes studied Cat, hoping for a snippet of gossip or two from the horse's mouth.

'Aye, Neil's working all hours at the moment. In fact I've

hardly seen him for the past couple of days. He doesn't tell me much, I'm afraid; keeps things very close to his chest.' No way was she going to divulge any of the horrific detail that Neil had in fact shared with her over a glass of wine the previous evening.

'Got many viewings today?' she asked in an attempt to change the subject.

'Och, the diary's full, but I've got meetings all day, so I'll be stuck in the office.'

Maureen knew that her enquiry was not going to bear fruit, but nothing ventured, nothing gained.

Their conversation turned to more trivial matters as the bus threaded its way into town, eventually disgorging its sullen-faced cargo in Academy Street, outside Marks & Spencer. The two women said their goodbyes, and Cat headed off towards Baron Taylor's Street. She was weaving her way forcefully through the plethora of city centre workers, hurrying to their respective offices and shops, when a hand grabbed her arm. She spun around, taken aback.

'Oh, it's you, Jack. Where on earth did you appear from?'

Jack Guthrie worked as a clerk at the area procurator fiscal's office. He hailed from Fortrose, Cat's home town, and lived just a couple of streets away from her parents.

'My, Cat, you don't hang about. I could hardly catch up with you!'

The twenty-one-year-old peered intently into his colleague's eyes, probing for any response bespeaking her pleasure at seeing him. All the while, he himself presented a blank countenance, one that she found unsettling. She looked back at him, searching for his eyes under the dark strands of lank hair that flopped across his forehead, a little like seaweed clinging to a rock.

'I'm running a wee bit late this morning, Jack. Sorry I didn't see you.' *As if she'd ever wanted to!*

Guthrie hurried after her as she crossed Inglis Street and made her way down the narrow alleyway that was Baron Taylor's Street.

'Josh said to say hello,' he panted, still struggling to keep up.

Cat frowned. There was definitely something about the young man that made her skin crawl. Josh Guthrie, Jack's vacuous older brother, had gone to school with her. *He* made her skin crawl too!

At least Jack was holding down a full-time job, she supposed, but his prospects seemed limited as he lacked any ambition, and his personality left a lot to be desired!

She remembered him announcing during the last office Christmas party that 'Some people are just born to live dead-end lives, and there is nothing they can do about it.' He'd been drunk of course, breathing fumes over her when he'd slurred, 'It's luck that gets you ahead, Cat. Pure luck.' She'd just walked away, having told him in no uncertain terms to take a long hard look at himself, but however hard she tried, and however blunt she was with him, he still came back for more… just like a bad penny.

'What's Josh doing with himself these days?' she asked impassively, as they reached the door to the office.

'He's still unemployed. Pop's tried to get him into the building trade, as an apprentice, like, but he's no interested.'

'There's a surprise,' Cat mumbled under her breath as she scurried up the stairs.

'What was that you said, Cat?' Guthrie's panting had now given way to wheezing.

'Oh, nothing,' Cat lied for the second time that morning!

Neil's morning had flown by. He'd briefed his enquiry team first thing and had then spent an hour with the FLOs, going through the lengthy witness statements they'd taken from Selina Cope and her family. Angus Hardie had also wanted an update, and so too the force press officer. Neil wondered why senior managers seemed incapable of attending scheduled briefings, often preferring their own private audience with the SIO and always at their convenience! Now he was late for an appointment with the area procurator fiscal, Hugh Jardine, and Jardine hated latecomers.

The glass doors to Number Two, Baron Taylor's Street swung back behind him as he ran up the stairs, two at a time. He checked his watch when he reached the inner door welcoming visitors to the 'Crown Office and Procurator Fiscal Service – Inverness Area Office'.

It was 11.10 am. He was ten minutes late. Damn! Instinctively, he scanned the office for any sign of Cat and located her sitting at her cluttered desk. She was looking up and beaming at a young man who stood next to her. He had a smudge of a goatee beard and long, lank hair that seemed to have a life of its own. *Ridiculous*, he thought. *Bloody silly hairstyles these kids go for these days* – and he immediately felt very old.

Cat's colleague placed a mug on her desk, and she in turn squeezed his forearm in obvious appreciation. The young man responded by massaging her shoulder as he gazed down at her. At that point Cat looked up and saw Neil standing by the door. She beamed and waved, before beckoning him over. The bearded youth remained by her side, his protective stance obvious to any onlooker. Neil could feel his hackles rising. It was not an emotion he'd normally experience, but the recent events surrounding Cat's supposed visit to the gym had made him unusually wary. So much so that his interpretation of interactions between his partner and any other man, young or old, were now infused with a hint of paranoia.

'Hi there,' Cat greeted him. 'What brings you in here?'

'Och, I've just popped in to see Hugh Jardine. He wanted an update on progress with the Cullaird enquiry.'

'Oh, I see. Well come and find me when you're done, and I'll make you a coffee. I think the big boss is on the phone at the moment.'

Cat's overly attentive cohort had been studying Neil all the while, and now that the conversation between him and Cat had naturally lapsed, he stuck out his hand.

'Jack Guthrie. Pleased to meet you, Neil. I've heard a lot about you.'

Neil took his hand, applying considerably more pressure than Guthrie had done.

'Hello, Jack. What do you do here... apart from making tea for the lassies, that is?'

Neil smiled provocatively, his eyes fixed on Guthrie's. Cat glared back at him, then interjected. 'Jack's brother went to school with me, Neil. His parents live down the road from mine. We've known each other for years.'

Neil's eyes never strayed from the young man. He smiled again. 'Ah, right. I thought I recognised the name.'

'I'm just a lowly clerk here, Neil. Bottom of the pile, I'm afraid.' Guthrie's expression, as always, appeared lifeless, like that of a mask.

'We all have to start somewhere, Jack,' Neil riposted. 'Pleased to meet you, anyway.'

The message was well and truly received, prompting Guthrie to nod and turn away. 'See you later, Cat,' he murmured as a parting shot.

'What was all that about, Neil?' Cat was tight lipped and speaking in a semi-whisper.

'What do you mean?' Neil looked puzzled.

'You know bloody well what I mean... the comment about making the tea. He's only a kid, for Christ's sake.' She raised the palm of her hand, acknowledging that his first impression of Guthrie was not a good one. 'I know he's a wee bit freakish, but I thought you were going to punch him.'

'Rubbish, 'Neil protested. 'I just don't like surly-lookin' youths coming on to my woman, that's all!'

Cat's icy glare crumbled into a coy smile. 'I never took you to be the jealous type, Neil Strachan, and for the record, I'm not some kind of cave girl... "My woman" indeed!'

Neil seemed amused by her comment, but behind the friendly face, angst still lingered. The events of the previous Monday were constantly playing on his mind. He still hadn't found the courage to confront her and so work had become his saviour during the past week.

'Ah, Acting DCI Strachan, welcome. Sorry to keep you waiting. Important phone call, I'm afraid.' Hugh Jardine's dulcet Highland brogue boomed across the office. Cat and Neil exchanged grins, and the detective headed for the fiscal's open door.

'So, Neil, what's it like to be heading up a double murder enquiry, eh? All eyes will be on you now, you know?'

Jardine sank back into his leather chair, interlocking the fingers of both his hands and resting them on his stomach. Expensive-looking cufflinks glinted from his shirtsleeves, sleeves that bore the sharpest creases Neil had ever seen. His grooming was impeccable, as always.

'I'm just pleased that Angus Hardie has the confidence in me to let me run with it. I wouldn't have been entirely surprised if he'd wanted to head up the enquiry himself, taking account of my lack of experience.'

'Och, you're far too modest, Neil. You proved yourself on that Friedmann case over in the west last year, and no one expected a result from that one.'

He chortled to himself. 'I remember Alex Brodie speaking

to me at the golf club shortly after the court hearing. Told me he thought the result you'd achieved there was nothing short of miraculous! Praise indeed from one so inclined to find fault with all things connected to policing! How is the old moaner, anyway? Hope he hasn't rubbed his cardiologist up the wrong way!'

'Aye, he's coming on. The doctors are happy with his progress, but he won't be back at work for some time.'

'Excellent news… That he's improving, that is. I'll have to drop by with a bottle of malt. That'll get his blood flowing again!'

'I'm sure he'd appreciate that,' said Neil, grinning, and knowing that a session of drinking whisky with Hugh Jardine would probably put Brodie back at least a month!

'Umm, I'll do that, then.' Jardine leaned forward. 'Now, onto business. How's the Fraser enquiry coming along?'

Neil laid a box file on the desk and removed the contents. He passed a selection of photographs across to Jardine.

'As you know, the Fraser family have had connections with Strathnairn for generations. The male line have long been gentlemen farmers, until the late Victorian period, when one of the family, a guy by the name of Simon Fraser, diversified into the distilling business. Seems to have been a success, because the Lochmhor Distillery is still going strong today, producing over three million litres of malt each year.'

Jardine raised a knowing finger. 'I am very well acquainted with their excellent product and have a much coveted bottle of the twelve-year-old malt at home!'

'Have you, indeed? Me too!' Neil wished to return to the matter in hand. 'Well, as far as we can tell, the Cullaird Castle estate and the distillery are efficiently run family businesses, and the murdered couple seemed to have been well liked by all those who worked for them. It's still early days, though, and there's much to do.'

'What about the family themselves? Any thoughts on them?'

'The daughter Selina and her husband are staying on the estate as we speak. The son, Alisdair, is also over with his French wife. They run a vineyard in the south of France. One of the cousins has also turned up, a chap called Alban Fraser. He lives in Spain with his male partner.'

'Oh, I see. Any other children?'

'There was another son, Jamie, who was killed in a skiing accident some years back. We're also looking into the wider family: several distant cousins who seem to be dispersed far and wide.'

'No evidence yet of any rifts in the family, then?'

'I think they've had their moments. Alban seems to be a rather complex character, and Alisdair didn't always get on with his father, who apparently wanted him to get involved with the running of the distillery.'

'Nothing glaringly obvious, then?'

'Like I say, it's early days.' Neil gestured towards the photos. 'The victims had both been attacked with bladed instruments, one thought to be a dagger-type weapon, and in Duncan Fraser's case, a hatchet or axe… something like that. What's interesting is that both bodies were crudely tattooed with those symbols you see there.'

Jardine picked up his glasses and perched them on the end of his nose before examining the photos closely. 'Is that a cat?'

'Aye, that's what it seems to be. There's a similar emblem… inscription, whatever you want to call it, over the fireplace at the castle, and I'm told it's an ancient family crest.'

'Any ideas what the connection with Culloden Battlefield is Neil, or are you going to say that it's "early days"?'

Neil coloured slightly.

'I thought so,' Jardine smiled. 'Forgive me. I don't wish to pressurise you, even though this is probably the most high-profile murder enquiry running in the UK at present!'

Neil returned the photos to the box file. 'I appreciate that, Hugh. I've got an appointment with one of the curators at the battlefield tomorrow, so should know more then. All I can tell you is that Duncan Fraser's body was dumped at a location on the battlefield called the Well of the Dead. He wasn't murdered there. The well is the site of—'

'Yes, I know, it's the place where Alexander MacGillivray was killed during the battle. I recall he was colonel of the Mackintoshes, something like that. Is it at all possible that some sort of clan feud has resurfaced here, then?'

Neil shifted in his seat. 'These clan affiliations can be quite complex. Hopefully I'll be able to gain a better understanding tomorrow.' Then, out of deference he added, 'But I think you're probably on the right track.'

Jardine sat back again. 'Okay, and the post-mortems?'

'This afternoon,' Neil confirmed.

'And how are the press behaving?'

'They're all over this like a rash, understandably. Our press officer's been keeping them briefed, and we're doing an appeal tonight, now the family have had some time to come to terms with things. They've got two good FLOs and seem content we're doing what we can in terms of progressing the enquiry.'

'Good. Well, keep things sweet with our press friends. They might just help you get a breakthrough!'

'I know,' Neil agreed, not particularly grateful for the advice.

Jardine got up. 'Well, I won't take up any more of your valuable time. I'd hate you to be late for Adam Carnie, eh?'

With a shake of the hand, they parted company in the doorway, Jardine heading back into his office and Neil making for Cat's desk.

'How was he?' she asked, still tapping away on her keyboard.

'I think I got off lightly. He seemed quite happy with things. Got the usual patronising lecture about the press.'

'Time for a coffee?'

'Aye, a quick one. Where's your wee admirer?'

Cat shook her head as she led him over to the kitchenette. 'You never give up, do you? For your information he's gone over to the Sherriff Court with some paperwork.'

'Good,' he said, wrapping his arms around her waist whilst she spooned coffee into two mugs. She turned to free herself. 'Not in here,' she mouthed softly.

'Sorry,' he whispered back, before adding, 'are you going to the gym tonight?'

'No,' she replied, handing him a mug. 'I'm babysitting for Eve tonight, remember?'

He nodded, knowing full well that Cat had told him that her eldest sister and her husband were going out for a wedding anniversary meal.

'Looks like it'll be just Tam and me on the sofa tonight then?'

'Unless you want to come and babysit too?'

'I think not on this occasion, the footie's on.'

He finished his coffee and placed the mug on the drainer. 'You don't mind do you?'

'Course not, I'll be able to watch some trash telly too!'

He gave her a playful poke, and picked up his box file. 'Best be off, got a hot date at the mortuary.'

'Charming.' She kissed him on the cheek. 'I'll bus it to Eve's, but can you collect me when I call?'

'Of course I can.'

'Good, then you may well be rewarded… in a cave-girl sort of a way!'

Neil ambled out of the office with a smile on his face, but it had faded by the time he'd reached the stairs. At least tonight, he knew where she'd be, and she'd expect him to call her at her sister's place during the evening. But this arrangement was akin to a plaster being applied to a festering wound. He knew that at some stage he was going to have to confront Cat head-on.

Chapter Ten

Raigmore Hospital, Inverness
2.00 pm, Monday 19th April

Neil maintained a respectable distance from Adam Carnie's area of operations. To his left stood Holly Anderson, arms tightly folded across her green-aproned chest and a solicitous expression etched upon her attractive features. It was a countenance that betrayed her innermost thoughts, namely how long could she endure this scene of butchery before succumbing to the embarrassing need to rush to the nearest sink, or worse, having to be picked up from the cold, tiled floor?

Neil shot her an enquiring glance. 'You all right, Holly?'

'Of course,' came the insouciant reply.

Neil grinned. 'If you need to go, just go.'

'Everything okay?' asked the incurious-looking assistant fiscal, standing to his right.

'Aye, she'll get used to it,' Neil assured him. But his confidence was short-lived. When Adam Carnie approached the little group with the dissected remnants of Laura Fraser's heart in a large steel dish, Holly had clearly decided that this was the time for her to make her escape. She scurried through the swing doors, hand clamped tightly to her mouth as she retched repeatedly.

'Oh dear,' Carnie remarked, 'I do hope she's all right. Nothing a strong cup of sweet tea won't put right.'

'Have you found something interesting?' Neil asked, not wishing to dwell too long on the subject of his colleague's welfare.

'Well, estimating the type and size of a weapon in these circumstances is never an exact science, but Henry and I have managed to delineate the track of one of the deeper wounds to Mrs Fraser's chest. You may recall at the scene, I didn't initially notice any hilt marks at the wound sites.'

'Aye, I recall you saying that.'

'Well, it seems I was wrong. There is some faint evidence of hilt abrasion on this particular wound, which tells us the blade was inserted to full length, and with some force, I have to say. It entered under the left nipple, and dissection has revealed a defect to the chest wall in the sixth intercostal space. Once inside the thorax, the blade has fully transfixed the right ventricle of the heart. See here.'

He offered up the steel dish, and pointed at the blood-soaked organ that lay in sections within it. Neil could just make out the incised track of the blade through the tissue. He winced. 'Yes, I see what you mean, so did this kill her?'

'Could well have done, dear boy. So could the second thrust to the chest. Personally, though, I still think it was the wound to the throat that finished her off. Difficult to be sure, though.'

He gestured towards the dish again, prompting Neil to take a further look. 'The blade continued from the cardiac muscle, through the diaphragm, eventually terminating in the liver, to the right of the midline.'

'So what does that tell us?' asked the assistant fiscal.

'Quite a lot actually,' the pathologist replied with a smile. 'Firstly, it tells us the knife thrust was downward from left to right. Secondly, the presence of the hilt abrasion allows us to estimate the length of the blade to around 13.5 inches, but with certain caveats, which I won't burden you with. Also, interestingly, I can tell you that the blade was most probably double-edged and tapered to a point from a top-end width of 1.75 inches. So, gentlemen, my guess is that you are looking for someone left-handed who carries a stabbing knife such as the Highland dirk.'

Neil let out a low whistle. 'It kind of makes sense, I suppose, taking into account the symbols tattooed onto the bodies, and the location where Duncan Fraser was found. The offender clearly has some obsession with the past, so why not use an antique weapon like a Highland fighting knife to do your dirty work? Anything else to report, Adam?'

Carnie gestured towards the inert body of Duncan Fraser, which was lying on the next table, his chest cavity opened up like the bomb bay doors of an old wartime aircraft.

'The stab wounds to Duncan's torso vary in depth and angle of entry, but there's one that suggests a similar length of blade to that used on Laura. The facial injuries appear to be the result of a severe beating, but I would say the wound to the top of his head was the cause of death. The damage was probably inflicted with an axe, or something similar.'

Neil frowned. 'You're not going to tell me he was the victim of a Lochaber axe, are you? Surely not.'

Carnie raised both latex-gloved hands. 'It's certainly not beyond the realm of possibility,' he replied.

Neil shook his head in disbelief. He recalled the examples of the Lochaber axe he'd seen in museums. It was a type of halberd, a two-handed pole-mounted weapon employed by the old Highlanders since time immemorial. The axe itself was similar to tools used when harvesting crops, such as the scythe, but in times of war, its eighteen-inch pointed blade became a formidable weapon.

Holly had now reappeared through the swing doors, still looking sickly pale, prompting the four men to look around.

'Feeling better, lassie?' Henry, the assisting pathologist asked.

'Marginally,' came the hesitant response.

Carnie punched the air. 'Splendid! So, what else have I discovered that will be of interest to you?' He returned to the table where Duncan Fraser lay.

'We found traces of fine sawdust in Duncan's hair. They'll be sent off for analysis, but I'd say the body had been lying in a location where some sort of woodworking had been taking place. A workshop, perhaps.'

Holly's eyes remained focussed on the tiled floor, in fearful anticipation of what Carnie was about to say next. But the fact that sawdust was now the sole topic of conversation allowed for some degree of recovery from her parchment-like pallor.

Neil scrawled in his notebook. 'Interesting. Anything else?'

Carnie returned to the table where Laura Fraser's body was lying. He returned with another kidney dish.

'We checked out the contents of their stomachs. Laura's still contained a quantity of cereal and tea, so…' He paused, as he watched Holly scurry back through the swing doors. 'I do feel for that poor girl, you know. I'm sure she'll cope better in time.'

'I'm sure she will,' said Neil dismissively. 'You were saying Adam?'

'Ah, yes. Well, the fact that partially digested food traces are still present in the stomach tells me that Laura died shortly after breakfast. In Duncan's case, the stomach and small intestine are empty, so death occurred twelve or more hours after the last meal.'

Neil made a quick mental calculation. 'We know he drank some tea at breakfast time, so the fact that there's no trace of it in his system suggests that he died during the evening of the fifteenth or early on the sixteenth?'

'In essence, yes.'

'Okay, what about the tattoos? Any thoughts on them?'

Carnie led the men back to the table supporting Laura Fraser's body.

'All I can say is they were carved with a small sharp knife, and the artist, if you can call him that, took his time over it.'

He pointed to the cat emblem carved on the abdomen. 'That's not easy to do, and in such detail. Especially if you're in a hurry.'

'We're pretty sure that in both cases, the carvings were done post-mortem,' Henry interposed.

'That's right,' Carnie confirmed. 'Hardly any blood loss. I'd bet the cat is connected to the family crest, but this symbol here… Well, that's going to need some research.'

'Looks oriental to me,' suggested the fiscal.

'Umm, we'll look into it,' Neil murmured, unconvinced. He pointed at the deeply flapped incisions at the base of the fingers on Laura's right hand. 'Defence wounds, I assume?'

'Exactly,' Carnie confirmed. 'Typical of a knife attack. The fingers are closed around the blade, so that when it's withdrawn, it cuts across the flexures of the phalanges, slicing the skin, and in this case the tendons. She was a gutsy lady, Mrs Fraser. Put up one hell of a fight.'

'Have you found any traces from the offender on her? No DNA, I suppose?'

'Sadly not, but there were a couple of red-coloured fibres under her nails.'

'What about Duncan?'

'Nothing. He's as clean as a whistle, and no significant defence wounds either, other than some faint bruises on the forearms and back of the hands. Probably from the initial assault at the castle.'

'Okay, you've at least given us something to work with

Adam. You'll let me know when the toxicology and other results come back, yes?'

'Of course I will, Neil. We've still got some other tests to do, but I stand by my initial assessments regarding time of death, et cetera.'

Relieved that the experience was over, Neil said his goodbyes and accompanied the assistant fiscal out of the mortuary suite.

'I hate those places,' he remarked. 'Would you believe it? First time I attended a PM, my sadist of a bloody sergeant treated me to a fried breakfast afterwards.'

The fiscal smiled. 'Did you eat it?'

'Too right, I did! He was paying, wasn't he?'

The two men continued to chuckle as the echoes of their footsteps faded along the corridor.

'What are you two laughing at?' Holly was standing by the car, drinking from a bottle of mineral water. 'Believe me, there's nothing funny about being in there!'

'Get used to it, DS Anderson,' Neil growled in a less than avuncular tone. 'You've been to a PM before, haven't you?'

'Actually, no,' Holly replied dismissively. 'Never got round to it, if I'm honest.'

Neil shook his head in disbelief and climbed into the car. He wound down the window and raised a parting hand to the fiscal.

'Tell Hugh I'll be in touch.'

The mental link to Jardine's office momentarily invaded his subconsciousness, resurrecting the image of Guthrie flirting with Cat earlier that day.

'Let's go back to the office,' he snapped fractiously.

'Yes, Boss,' Holly murmured under her breath as she secured her seat belt.

The late afternoon sun permeated the gaps in the vertical blinds, projecting dust-laden shafts of light onto the pile of paperwork that had accumulated on Neil's desk. He was sure the pile had grown whilst he'd been out at the post-mortem, but on checking the uppermost item, he realised it hadn't!

He hung his jacket on the back of the door and glowered at the heap of files until the sun passed behind a cloud and the lightshow faded to gloom. He slumped into his chair and sighed, thankful for the brief period of solitude.

But it wasn't to be. His quiet interlude was promptly interrupted when there was a sharp knock on the door and Holly entered with a mug of coffee.

'Thought you could do with this,' she announced, before turning tail and heading for the corridor.

'Sorry about before, Holly,' Neil called after her. 'Had a lot on my mind, but I shouldn't have snapped at you.'

'That's okay,' she grinned. 'We all have our off days. I've just had a particularly bad one too!'

'The PMs, you mean?'

'Ah ha. My stomach's still not right, but to use your words, I'll have to get used to it. I just find the clinical nature of the process hard to come to terms with.'

Neil smiled. 'I know what you mean. Luckily we don't have to spend our lives attending such things, unlike that sad bugger Carnie.' He paused before adding, 'But I s'pose we need people like him, don't we?'

'Let's hope we don't get into a habit of meeting up with him, now we've got this monster on the loose,' said Holly, glum-faced.

Neil was just about to reply, when Fraser Gunn's gangly frame filled the doorway behind her.

'Hi, Neil. Thought you'd like to know we've completed the examinations of the two scenes at last.'

Both he and Holly perched on the two available chairs.

'Found anything exciting?' Neil asked whilst sipping his coffee.

'Lots of blood. The victims' blood, that is. Nothing from the offenders, though. Also lots of Marigold glove marks, and a fair amount of damage to the fabric of the castle.'

'Any idea yet whether there was more than one offender?'

'Evidence at the first scene suggests only one, and he was definitely looking for something specific. This wasn't just any old break-in. As you saw for yourself, there was jewellery and cash lying everywhere in those upper rooms, but none of it was taken. He's used a jemmy on some of the locked doors, and has even pulled up the floorboards in some rooms.'

'Is there any pattern to the search, or is it just random, do you think?' Neil looked thoughtful.

'Funny you should say that,' Gunn mused. 'The worst damage seemed to be done in areas where examples of this crest were present.'

He pushed a photo across the desk towards Neil. Holly got up and positioned herself at Neil's shoulder, so that she could see too. The photo showed the bottom left-hand corner of a gilt-framed oil painting. A tartan-clad leg wearing a shiny buckled shoe was clearly visible, but the subject of the photo was an emblem carved into the frame itself. It depicted a crouched wildcat nestling within the fronds of a red-berried plant, beneath which were the words 'Touch not the cat bot a glove'.

'I've seen this emblem before,' Neil remarked, 'above the fireplace in the great hall at the castle.'

'Ah, not quite,' Gunn corrected him. He offered Neil another photo. 'This is an enlargement of the top right-hand corner of the frame, into which another emblem has been carved. You will note there is a subtle difference in the two examples.'

Neil and Holly looked closely. Sure enough, the emblem

they were now studying also showed a wildcat, but this one was sitting within the confines of a sturdy buckled belt, upon which was the motto 'Touch not this cat'.

'I remember now,' said Neil. 'Yes, this was the emblem above the fireplace.'

'Correct,' said Gunn. 'Which leads me to believe that these are two distinctly different clan crests. Now have a look at the whole painting.'

Another A4 photo glided across the desk towards Neil. The subject of the painting was a tall, youthful gentleman clad in red tartan trews and wrapped in a voluminous plaid of a matching sett. At his throat was a ruffle of white lace, and upon his head he wore a powdered wig. Neil looked closely at the face that smiled out at him from the cracked varnish.

'Who's this then, Fraser?'

'This, Neil, is Major Alisdair MacGillivray of Cullaird, a former resident of the castle. He was born in 1685, and died in 1742.'

'How do you know that?' Holly asked.

'Because it says so on the little plaque at the foot of the painting. Call yourselves detectives!' came the smug reply.

Holly nodded in defeat and coloured slightly. Her day was getting worse.

'You will see the two cat emblems carved into the frame at opposing corners, and the colourful family crests on the opposite corners. They are different but both include the same blue sea galley, reinforcing my assumption that there are *two* connected families or clans, whatever you wish to call them, referred to here.'

'... Just as you alluded to in relation to the clan crests. Makes sense,' Neil agreed. 'And your point is?'

Gunn folded his arms. 'My point is, Neil, that these two cat emblems can be found all over the castle. Paintings, carvings, even embroidery and soft furnishings. But the offender's search, and the damage done consequential to that search, was mainly apparent in the vicinity of only one of them: the one with the motto that mentioned the glove.'

'Couldn't that just be a coincidence?' Holly suggested.

'Lassie, I've been doing this job for many years. Believe me, this is more than a coincidence.'

'Where did you find the painting, Fraser?' Neil was still studying the photos closely.

'On the floor of the master bedroom, next to a locked door to what I understand was once the laird's spying chamber, apparently somewhere he could look down unnoticed on his guests in the great hall. The door had been jemmied and the floorboards nearby had been pulled up. Even the lining of the painting itself had been torn off. But, for all his efforts, the offender failed to get into the little room.'

'Have you been in since?'

'Oh, yes. It's completely empty. Nothing of interest in there.'

'Okay, and what about the scene at Culloden? Anything there?'

Gunn shrugged. 'Not much. You know we've found some traces of sawdust on and around the victim's head?'

'Aye, Adam Carnie mentioned that earlier.'

'I also managed to recover some fibres from the grass under the body. Looks like some sort of light-coloured linen. I'll know more when the lab have had a look. Other than that, nothing at the scene. The killer has been very thorough. He delivered the corpse to the site naked and probably wrapped in some sort of covering. My guess is, he dumped it there and then removed the covering. I agree with Adam; Duncan Fraser was definitely murdered elsewhere.'

'And that's it? Nothing else?'

'Yep, that's it for now.' Then he raised a finger. 'Oh, we did find some partial tyre tracks. Fresh ones, in the mud next to the lay-by, halfway up the approach road to the visitor centre. They may not be connected, though. Anyone can access that lay-by any time of the day and night. Could be a courting couple, or a dog walker, perhaps.'

'What type of tyre tracks?'

'Biggish. Could be a four-wheel drive; something like that.'

Gunn picked up his photographs. 'I'll be in touch,' he assured the two detectives and disappeared through the open doorway.

When he'd gone, Holly shook her head. 'I'm still not sure this cat emblem theory isn't just a coincidence,' she remarked. 'What do you think?'

'No, I rate Fraser's judgment. We certainly need to look closely at the origins of these emblems or crests, whatever you like to call them.'

He drained the remnants of coffee from his mug and placed it on the desk. 'I'm certain of one thing – it's no coincidence that Duncan Fraser was dumped at the Well of the Dead. The chief of the MacGillivrays died there in 1746, and now 264 years to the day, another corpse, apparently with MacGillivray connections, is laid out there. What's the betting they share the same blood?'

'You really believe that?' Holly asked, easing herself out of the chair.

Neil nodded. 'I'd stake money on it!'

1746

1746

Chapter Eleven

Drumossie Moor
7.45 pm, Tuesday 15th April

Darkness had settled over the moor, a dank, foggy darkness
that consumed the long column of men and horses filing past
the dry stone walls enclosing Duncan Forbes's estate. Away to
the north, candlelight glimmered through the sleet-splattered
windows of Culloden House, whilst the faint smell of peat
smoke hung in the air from the numerous fires that burned
within the Highlanders' encampment. They were fires that
would be kept alight whilst the army were away, so as not to
arouse suspicion amongst the lookouts on the Royal Navy
ships anchored out in the Moray Firth.

Lord George Murray stood impassively, watching the
column of weary men amble by. By his side was the Prince
and an aggregation of his senior officers. Charles was in
jubilant mood and draped a comforting arm around Murray's
shoulder. He leaned across until the two men were almost
cheek to cheek.

'This will crown all!' he declared. 'You'll restore the King
by it. You'll have all the honour and glory of it. It is your work!'

Murray backed away, removed his bonnet and bowed. Yet
there was no warmth in the gesture and he chose to say nothing.

By now, Murray's Athollmen were passing the little group

of onlookers, and so he mounted his horse with the intention of riding up to the head of the van. With a nod of the head to James Johnstone, who'd already swung into his saddle, the two men galloped away into the fog and incertitude.

Simon MacGillivray had started out early with his small company of men from Cullaird. They marched with other elements of the Clan Chattan, at the head of a column of over 3,000 ragged clansmen. Scouting ahead were officers from the Mackintoshes, whose lands the Jacobite army were now marching upon. They were men who knew this wild country intimately; every bothy, burn and cattle track.

After an hour the rain began to fall. It was a fine, sleety drizzle that percolated the fog, soaking through the clansmen's plaids to their chilled skin beneath. For many, a sense of desperation had now begun to claw at their very souls. So much so that they maintained only a conservative pace across the drenched moorland, mostly avoiding the numerous quagmires and pools of rancid water that lay before them. To the rear, the whinnying of horses could be heard above the muffled sounds of their sluggish footfall and the occasional clank of broadsword against targe.

Murray and Johnstone rode up at the trot and halted to confer with Alexander MacGillivray, their voices sometimes lost on the relentless, prowling wind. Simon could still just about hear the conversation from several yards distant. Murray planned to have the right wing of the front line attack Cumberland's rear, having crossed the river and encircled the town of Nairn. Meanwhile the Duke of Perth, with the left wing, would attack the government's front. In support of Perth, the Prince himself would bring up the second line. As they talked, another rider galloped up and raised his bonnet to Lord George.

'I come with the compliments of his Grace, the Duke, my lord. He requests that you halt your progress so that the men to the rear may catch up. There are gaps opening within the van and some are falling by the wayside, citing hunger and fatigue as their reason.'

Murray glanced down at Alexander, and saw the look of concern upon his face. 'Let us halt, then, but only for a short while, until we are assured the van is once again as one.'

The rider nodded. 'Thank you, my lord,' and then retreated hastily, back into the fog.

Word of the decision was duly passed back from man to man, and each and every one of them sank down onto the wet ground, thankful of a rest. There was little desire to talk, and once more the sound of the wind presided over the uneasy silence.

Simon sat with his men, shivering a little, now that the flow of blood through his limbs had slowed. He pulled his cloak a little closer to his chin, all the while studying their long, tired faces.

'Hunger is indeed a man's greatest foe,' he joked, when his stomach groaned for the umpteenth time since they'd set out on the march. 'Still, I beg of you boys, keep up the pace and see this through, and I give you my word your families will get ample venison to feed yourselves for a year.'

There was a rumble of approval from the Cullaird men. They trusted Simon and knew he would deliver on whatever he promised. Old John Shaw, now fifty-six years old, massaged his nose against the cold. He'd been a loyal servant of the MacGillivrays for years, and had followed Simon's father in the last rebellion.

'You need not offer up such promises to us, Master Simon,' he proclaimed in his distinctive gravelly voice. 'You know we will follow you until we fall.'

Simon was visibly moved. 'Of that I have no doubt, John.

I merely wish to provide you with a focus upon which we may look forward to better days ahead.'

'Do you truly believe we can be victorious, against these redcoats, sir?' Angus Mackintosh, another ageing stalwart, enquired.

'Aye, Angus, I do, with a little luck. Duke William is said to have delivered two gallons of brandy to each of his regiments, so that they may celebrate his birthday. If we can reach their camp in good time and before daybreak, then we will fall upon them whilst they sleep... deeply, like drunks always sleep. I wager they will be in disarray, and won't know their bayonets from their backsides.'

Laughter broke out, prompting the other men sitting nearby to turn their heads and look on inquisitively.

'Look lively, boys. Get yourselves up. Let's be getting along now.' One of the Clan Chattan's lieutenants marched up the line with news that the van had rejoined, and the trek to Nairn could resume once more.

The men from Strathnairn hauled themselves onto their aching feet and formed up. They'd only covered a mile so far that night, and there were nine to go before they could finally do battle with Cumberland's befuddled troops.

Simon's cheerful disposition in the presence of his men belied his inner torment. His true assessment of what the coming hours would bring was anything but optimistic. It was more a sense of foreboding that left him fearful he'd not have to honour his promise to the majority of those brave boys trudging along before him.

They had marched no more than half a mile, when the same aide-de-camp from the Duke of Perth's column at the rear thundered up to the head of the van, requesting yet another pause. Apparently the main body of the army had fallen behind yet again. So they stopped and waited, until once more the word came to move on. And so the night wore on, with frequent stops and word of desertions, whilst clansmen literally collapsed by the wayside from hunger and fatigue.

Just before two in the morning, Cameron of Lochiel rode up to confer with Murray. He was joined shortly after by Lord John Drummond and the Duke of Perth himself. They sat upon their mud-spattered mounts, engaged in lively debate, a discussion that Simon MacGillivray once again could discern with some ease. Lochiel and Perth were expressing their concern that the army would never reach the government camp before daylight. They had only just reached the walls that surrounded the wood of Culraick, four miles south-west of the redcoats' tents at Balblair. Lord Drummond now proposed an ordered retreat back to the Culloden Parks, a sentiment that his fellow officers clearly shared. At this point, General O'Sullivan appeared out of the fog and reported that the Prince was keen for the march to continue and the attack pressed home. There was much shaking of heads and dissent, one chief calling out above the wind, 'If we are to be killed, sir, then surely it would be better in daylight, so we can see how our neighbours behave?'

Simon too, shook his head in disbelief, and returned to his men who were resting in the heather a few yards away. 'I fear we shall be asked to turn about, boys,' he announced, and slumped down amongst them to recount what he'd heard.

It was not long before Lochiel galloped past, followed by the other parties to the recent conference. Johnstone made his way up to where the Cullaird men were sitting. He looked glum-faced.

'Lord Murray has decided to return to the parks at Culloden, so that the army may refresh itself and be ready to meet our enemy when they deem to engage us. Our progress this night has not been sufficiently swift to meet our objectives before daybreak.'

He rode on back along the line to announce the decision to those who were still awaiting orders.

Within fifteen minutes, they were on the move again, initially marching ahead, before looping around to the north and heading for the high road from Inverness to Nairn. The sleet flurries had now become heavier and the biting north-easterly wind keener, as they wheeled about so that the icy precipitation now stung their wet faces like needles. Distinct gaps had opened up within the column, and the huddled groups of exhausted men marching ahead of the Cullaird contingent now faded into the swirling fog, eventually being swallowed completely. There was no path, just clumps of sodden heather and peat, into which already soaked feet and legs were being sucked. Simon walked beside his men, urging them on as best he could, until he heard a dull thud accompanied by a muffled splash. He hurried back to the end of the line, seeking clarification as to what had happened. There, he found John Shaw lying on his side in the heather, being tended to by Angus Mackintosh and his younger brother Conal.

Simon dropped to his knees, genuine concern present upon his grubby features.

'What has happened here?' he asked softly. 'Have you injured yourself, John?'

The older man shook his head, barely conscious. His mouth opened in an attempt to form words, but no sound came forth.

'He's exhausted,' said Conal, half whispering. 'Not a morsel has passed his lips since the morn.'

Angus looked up at his captain. 'What shall we do? We cannae leave him here.'

Simon surveyed their surroundings, anger now rising within him. *What a darned mess. Did these so-called lords and princes have any idea what they were doing? At this rate there would be no army left to confront the redcoats on that wretched moor.*

To his right, he could make out a slight rise in the ground, upon which a dense cluster of firs was just visible through the fog. Enclosing the wood was a partially collapsed dry stone wall.

'Take him up there to rest, Angus. Of course we'll not leave him behind. I'll muster the rest of our men and we will shelter amongst the trees for a while. Then we'll head back to the army when we are sufficiently recovered.'

Angus and Conal nodded in agreement and heaved the inert body of John Shaw up from the wet ground. Simon scurried away, back to the other men to inform them of his decision.

They were soon lodged deep within the small wood. All twelve Cullaird men huddled together amongst the creaking firs, their plaids pulled up around them so that any body heat they could raise would be trapped within the cloth. John had been given a drink of water from a nearby burn and was now sandwiched between his two giant Mackintosh minders, sleeping like a baby. And so they all slept, soothed by the nocturnal rhythms emanating from the boughs above their heads, and the repetitive hooting of a distant owl.

Simon awoke suddenly from beneath his heavy cloak. It was still dark, or so it seemed, but as his level of consciousness grew, the realisation dawned upon him that this was due to the folds of dense cloth that lay draped about his head. He could clearly hear the shrill call of the moorland finches, as they darted amongst the clumps of broom that carpeted the austere landscape. But more importantly he could hear drums; the incessant regular beat of drums in the distance. He sat up, pulling the cloak away from his head, and ran his hands across his face, rubbing the sleep from his eyes. Some of his men were stirring too, having also heard the cadence of the drums.

The new day had dawned some time ago, but it remained gloomy beneath the canopy of firs. Simon could just make out the grey sky through the treetops and he cursed himself for not having wakened earlier. He ordered young William MacGillivray to reconnoitre the south and east sides of the wood, whilst he and Angus Mackintosh set out to investigate the source of the drumming. They had entered the wood from its southern edge, and were now surprised by its overall size. So, clutching his broadsword with his left hand, so as to ease his movement between the trees, he ran to its northern boundary, where he came across more remnants of the old wall. The piles of stones that now remained fortunately provided some cover from view, so they crouched behind them and surveyed the landscape beyond.

The fog had cleared to leave a few pockets of mist clutching at the moorland below, but visibility was now much improved, allowing for wide-ranging views across to the Moray Firth towards the blue-tinted peninsula of the Black Isle. In the middle distance, Rear Admiral Byng's supply ships rode lazily at anchor, their mainsheets securely furled and their naval ensigns flapping proudly in the wind. It was a blustery wind too, still blowing through the trees from the north-east, a cold blast from which any form of precipitation was likely to fall as sleet or snow.

Below them in the foreground ran the high road from Nairn to Inverness. It was the only prominent feature in an otherwise uninteresting landscape, punctuated by the odd glistening burn and carpeted with dead brown heather. There was no sign of any remnants of the Highland army, no tartan in sight at all. Undoubtedly, they had long dispersed before daybreak, back to their fires beyond Culloden House.

What they could see from their vantage point above the road were three long columns of red approaching at a steady pace along the dirt road from the east. Cumberland's army was on the march, heading for its final showdown with the exhausted and depleted forces of the Young Pretender.

'God help us,' Angus whispered. 'There are thousands of them.'

Indeed there were: sixteen battalions of foot and three of horse. There were 8,000 men in all, advancing steadily at seventy-five paces to the minute to the thunderous beat of the grenadier drummers of the Royal Scots. It was 8 am on Wednesday 16th April, five hours before the first shots would be fired on the field at Culloden.

Young William joined them behind the wall, and let out a low whistle on seeing the royal army.

'What did you see from yonder side of the wood, William?'

'Troopers sir, dressed in blue with red facings, thirty or more, and redcoats attired in plaid and bonnet. They are close to Croy. I could fair see the smoke from the cottages there, and from Kilravock House beyond.'

'Umm,' Simon muttered. 'They'll be the vedette, marching forward of the main force. From what you say, boy, there must be Campbells in their midst.'

Just then, they were disturbed by rustling amongst the bracken behind their position, prompting them to leap up and seek the hilts of their swords. A group of clansmen emerged from the trees, their plaids soiled with mud, their faces pale through lack of sleep. At their head was a tall, powerfully built man with flowing sandy-coloured hair and eyes as dark as a mountain lochan. Simon stepped forward and embraced him. 'Fionn MacBean! Well, well, and where did you come from?'

MacBean stepped back from him. 'We lost our way during the night... as did you, it would seem. We passed to the east of here and sought shelter amongst the trees away yonder just before dawn.'

MacBean was in his late thirties, an ardent supporter of the Jacobite cause. He farmed land near Torness, not far from

Cullaird, and the two men had met at livestock fairs on many occasions.

'Have you seen what approaches?' Simon pointed to the oncoming snake of crimson that had now reached a point not half a mile from where they stood.

MacBean nodded. 'Aye. We almost ran into them earlier, whilst we were seeking the high road back to Culloden, so we concealed ourselves in this here wood.'

'Will you stay with us a while, Fionn, until the army passes?'

'Is that your intention, MacGillivray, to remain here?' MacBean's eyes narrowed in disbelief.

'What other plan is there?' Simon enquired.

MacBean shrugged. 'Surely we must endeavour to return to our lines before the fighting begins?'

'I agree, Fionn, but I have other concerns. We have older men amongst us. Some are exhausted and have not eaten for a day or more. I am not sure we can outrun an army marching to the drum. Besides, there are government dragoons and Campbell's Highlanders scouting to the west of here.'

MacBean adjusted his bonnet. 'Well, MacGillivray, that must be a matter for you and your conscience, but we intend to seek a way to join up with our neighbours. So I bid you good morning and good luck.' To Simon's surprise, the MacBeans turned and headed off into the wood.

'Perhaps he's right, sir. Perhaps we should go with them?' Angus suggested with a hint of angst.

Simon gestured towards the advancing redcoats. 'Do you see that, Angus? I estimate there to be upwards of 10,000 men and horse out there, with artillery behind them. What chance do we have against them on that wretched moor? No, if we follow the orders of that misguided Italian youth they call The Pretender, then we'll not live to see the next winter snow… just as Lord Murray and the other chiefs have warned. They will mow us down in our hundreds. Besides, we must carry old John with us, and I fear that we shall be overrun at such a slow pace. No, we'll wait for the army to pass, then skirt around to the north, along the high road back to Inverness and join the garrison there. Perhaps then we can do our duty, but also return to our homes alive when the day is done.'

He turned to observe the government army again and could see individual soldiers now; their faces shaded beneath the brims of tricornes and tall mitre caps. To the front of each battalion, standards strained against the chill breeze. An ensign carried the Union flag, and another the regimental colours, green, blue, yellow and buff, like the facings on the bright red frock coats behind them.

To the right of the infantry, the artillery train rumbled along behind, hauled by giant shire horses, the clanking of their bridle chains and the screech of their wooden wheels carried along on the wind. All the while, the drumbeat was unremitting, a funereal drone that became louder and louder.

Angus ran back to their makeshift camp to apprise the other men of what they were witnessing, prompting several to approach the wall and observe the spectacle for themselves.

As the army neared their position, it wheeled to the south, away from the road and across the open moor towards Croy. They were so close now that they could see the muddied gaiters of the approaching redcoats, the cannon wheels tilting into the soft earth and the glint from the barrels of over 6,000 muskets. Three columns, each of five battalions, passed by, followed by the bat wagons, bread wagons and sutler's wagons. Amongst them were the women and the wives, some walking, some carried on the carts, dangling their long, muddied skirts from the tailboards. To the rear were the officers' carriages and then more carts carrying luggage in the form of leather chests and crates. The whole procession had taken over an hour to pass, its length so great that the sound of the drums at its head was now fading in their ears.

During its progression, Simon had noticed that a dozen or so wagons in the train had attracted a greater level of security than the rest. They had been piled high with great trunks and had each been guarded by an escort of half a dozen infantrymen, who were unusually accompanied by an officer on horseback. In most cases, another soldier sat next to the waggoner. Some carts were also carrying a gentleman in civilian attire, riding at the front with the waggoner and his military companion.

As the last of the bat wagons passed by his position, Simon's attention was drawn to another cart, bringing up the rear at a much slower pace than the rest. He estimated that it must have trailed the end of the train by at least a hundred yards, and from the look of the rear wheel, which was wobbling uncontrollably on its axle, all was not well with the vehicle.

As with the others he had observed, six soldiers marched by its side. They wore belted plaids of green, black and blue tartan, and blue bonnets bearing red crosses, the insignia of the Earl of Loudon's 64th Highlanders. This was a unit raised by the Campbells and loyal to King George. As in the case of the other carts, next to the waggoner sat a soldier dressed in scarlet frock coat, and next to him, a civilian dressed all in black. To the rear of the wagon rode an officer on a grey mount, again dressed in scarlet frock coat with blue facings, muddy black leather-trimmed riding boots, and a black tricorne pulled low over his brow.

'More Campbells,' Simon muttered under his breath, and as he did so, there was a loud crack followed by the squeal of splitting wood. Evidently, the wagon's rear axle had finally given way. The cart tilted backwards and to the left before settling onto the wet peat, its huge wheel running off at an angle before coming to rest a few yards distant. The officer, whose horse had shied at the din, bawled angrily at the waggoner. The youth who'd been holding the reins leapt from his seat and ran around the cart to inspect the damage, subsequently throwing up his arms in obvious despair. Meanwhile, some of the trunks had slipped backwards and tumbled onto the ground nearby. Ahead, the train rumbled on, whilst the watching clansmen waited to see who would return to assist their stranded comrades.

Twenty minutes on, and the last vehicles in the army's baggage train were now tiny dots in the distance. Strangely, no one had returned, and those men escorting the cart were now busily engaged in some form of repair, whilst the officer looked on from his horse.

Simon had considered his position during this time and a plan had now formed in his mind; a plan born out of the realisation that there was something eminently profitable being carried on that wagon! It would be risky, but the fruits of such an endeavour would, if his suspicions were correct, be substantial. The question was, would they ever get away with it?

2010

Chapter Twelve

Neil locked the car and ambled across the car park, pausing beside a German-registered camper van to admire the radical wave form design of the Culloden Battlefield visitor centre. Built of Caithness stone and clad in local larch, the impressive structure had opened its doors to the public two years before, on the anniversary of the battle. It was now thronged with dozens of tourists, each of whom was entirely incognisant of the events that had occurred a few days previously.

Once through the substantial glass doors, he was greeted, bizarrely, by a kilted Highland soldier of the Jacobite period, equipped with targe and broadsword.

'Welcome to Culloden Battlefield,' the re-enactor announced enthusiastically. 'Tickets can be purchas—'

'I actually have an appointment with Dr Malcolm Breckenridge,' Neil interjected. 'I'm a police officer.'

'Oh, I see. I suppose you've come about that dreadful murder?'

The man swung around and pointed towards an open door behind the reception desk. 'You'll find Malcolm hiding in there.'

'Thanks. Nice outfit, by the way.' Neil grinned and edged

his way around the reception desk. He was intercepted in the doorway by Breckenridge, who'd evidently overheard the Highlander's directions. The doctor was wearing a brightly coloured shirt that peeked out from a baggy sweatshirt, and crumpled grey cords, the bottoms of which sat bunched over well-worn canvas walking boots. Ideal dress for an archaeologist, Neil considered.

The doctor stood impassively, hand outstretched.

'DCI Strachan, good to see you again. Terrible business, these murders. Do you have any leads yet?'

'We're working on it. In fact I'm hoping you may provide me with one or two!'

'Anything I can do to help, just ask away.'

'Well, for starters, I need to try and understand why the male victim ended up here at Culloden, and whether he was connected to the battlefield in any way. Perhaps we could take a stroll out onto the moor, away from intrusive ears?'

'Certainly, I'll just get my jacket.'

Breckenridge turned and disappeared into the office, emerging seconds later carrying a dark green combat jacket.

'Let's go,' he declared, pulling on the jacket so that his wispy hair spilled over the upturned collar like ivy clinging to an old wall.

'How did you become interested in this site particularly?' Neil asked as they strolled down the pathway towards Leanach Cottage.

'Oh, the battles of the Jacobite rebellions have always fascinated me, and this one is arguably the jewel in the crown, for want of a better description. As you know, officially, I'm employed by the Centre for Battlefield Archaeology at the university. I based my master's thesis on Charles Edward Stuart's relatively short campaign, and have since written several books on the subject. The "Forty Five", as it's become known, has developed into something of an obsession,

I'm afraid. So when the opportunity arose to carry on the archaeological work up here, I jumped at it!'

He pulled a small lead ball out of his pocket and handed it to Neil.

'French musket ball, used by the Jacobite infantry. I found it yesterday, lying in the peat, roughly where the Royal Écossais… on the Jacobite side, would have been positioned during the early stages of the battle. They were a Scottish unit in French service.'

He stopped and gestured with his outstretched arm. 'There's still a treasure trove of archaeological material lying beneath this moor, and we find evidence of it every day.'

'I see,' said Neil, who was caressing the smooth lead ball between his thumb and forefinger. 'So tell me about this Well of the Dead. I understand it's the place where the MacGillivray chief, Alexander, was killed during the battle?'

'True enough,' Breckenridge agreed, 'but his position within the Jacobite chain of command on that day was a little more involved, shall we say, than you have just described.'

'How, exactly?'

'The MacGillivrays were an ancient clan who we believe originated in Lochaber, over in the west. Back in the 1200s they sought protection from the chief of the Clan Mackintosh, and the story goes that they followed the Mackintoshes when they eventually returned to their lands in Badenoch, south of here. The MacGillivrays finally settled in the fertile country around Dunmaglass in Strathnairn, always remaining fiercely loyal to the Mackintoshes. Now, fast-forward 500 years to the time of Culloden, when the young Lady Anne Mackintosh, whose seat was just down the road from here at Moy, needed a field commander for her regiment. This was because her husband, the clan chief, had unfortunately pledged his allegiance to the crown. She duly selected Alexander MacGillivray… or

Alasdair Ruadh as he was known amongst his clan… a giant of a man by all accounts, and a fearless warrior.'

'So Cullaird Castle is located smack bang in the middle of MacGillivray country?' Neil interrupted.

'Indeed so,' Breckenridge confirmed. By now the two men had reached the well itself, and were standing respectfully by the gnarled marker stone, staring down at the compressed grass where Duncan Fraser's body had lain a short time before.

After a short pause, Breckenridge resumed his briefing. 'The MacGillivrays and the Mackintoshes were constituents of a wider confederation of clans, the Clan Chattan, known as "the clan of the cat"…'

Neil peered across at Breckenridge, excitement now present in his eyes, but he remained silent.

The archaeologist continued, unperturbed.

'Now the Clan Chattan, once an ancient tribe in its own right, slowly evolved over time through marital alliances and suchlike until it became what some might call a super clan. By the time of Culloden, the Macphersons, the Farquharsons, the MacBeans, the Shaws and the Davidsons, to name but a few, all marched under its banner. So, on the 16th April 1746, Alexander not only led Mackintoshes and MacGillivrays but he also led the entire Clan Chattan Regiment onto the field. On the occasion of the battle, they numbered 500 men, taken mainly from the MacGillivrays, Mackintoshes and MacBeans, mostly non-jurant Protestants, raised by the young Colonel Anne herself.'

He grinned. 'I told you it was involved!'

Neil sucked on his lower lip. 'I see. So I assume Alexander was felled by the redcoats, whilst leading his men during their fateful Highland charge?'

'He was. Contemporary records suggest that his regiment was first to charge. He found himself in the midst of frenzied hand-to-hand combat, and broke through the government front line, hacking down the enemy with his broadsword. By the time he'd reached the second line of redcoats, he'd been critically wounded, and crawled back to this well, where he died, amongst literally piles of his clansmen. They say the water from the spring ran red with blood, and thereafter, this place was known as the Well of the Dead.'

Neil tried to picture the scene so vividly described by Breckenridge.

'One of my colleagues told me Alexander had been buried over the way at Petty Church. Is that true?'

'Yes, that's correct. Reports after the battle suggest that his body and fifty others were thrown into a large pit here on the moor, and there they remained for six weeks, until the government troops moved on. The people of Dunmaglass then returned and dug up the corpses, later reinterring some of them at various churches in the area, amongst them the one at Petty.'

Breckenridge folded his arms, a look of uneasiness spreading across his bearded features.

'What is it?' Neil asked.

'I saw something when I found that body that gave me the creeps, if I'm honest.'

'What exactly?'

'The white handkerchief tied to his arm. You see, the story goes that a local woman found Alexander's body and tied a handkerchief to his arm, so that his fiancée, Elizabeth Campbell of Clunas, might recognise him amidst the field of corpses.' He swallowed hard whilst Neil stared at him in disbelief.

'Good God,' were the only words he could muster. 'And did she find him?'

What relevance this was to a police enquiry he couldn't be sure exactly, but by now he'd been well and truly caught up in the romanticism of the episode.

'So they say,' Breckenridge confirmed with a nod. 'She helped arrange his removal and secret reinterment under the doorstep of Petty Church. Tragically, she only survived him for four months, long enough to ensure that his remains were buried in consecrated ground, before she died at the age of twenty-four, some say of a broken heart.'

A chill ran down Neil's spine, prompting him to move away from the melancholy site upon which they now stood. 'Shall we take a walk back?' he suggested.

They set off towards the warmth of the visitors' centre, passing beneath the lively red flags that tugged at their halyards in the brisk east wind.

'Are you familiar with the Fraser family at Cullaird, Doctor?' Neil asked as they walked.

'I certainly know *of* them, and the castle. That's about it. The castle is known to have been associated with the MacGillivrays since way back, but the genealogical line of the Frasers who live there now... well, that's another matter. You'd have to ask them.'

'From that, I gather you've no personal knowledge of their possible links with the MacGillivrays, or with the Clan Chattan, for that matter?'

'No, I've never had any personal dealings with the family. I can only suggest that if their family association with the castle does go back to the time when it was built, then there must be one, perhaps through marriage.'

'I've seen a portrait of a MacGillivray that had been hanging in one of the rooms of the castle, which may be a clue, perhaps. No doubt, as you say, the family will be able to tell me more.'

'They should be able to. These old families are normally fiercely proud of their ancestry.'

'Did the Clan Fraser itself have any links to those we've been talking about?' Neil glanced up as the first spots of rain dampened his cheeks.

'Not really. They fought under their own banner at Culloden and were one of the larger Highland regiments. They were raised by Simon Fraser, the eleventh Lord Lovat, whose seat was over at Beauly – not far from Strathnairn, I suppose. The Frasers would've charged with Alexander's men at Culloden, and I know they too suffered terrible casualties, including their colonel, Charles, who was effectively murdered whilst he lay wounded on the battlefield. The old Lord Lovat went on the run after the battle and was eventually captured and taken to the Tower of London. Incidentally, he was the last man to be beheaded with an axe on Tower Hill.'

'Interesting. You certainly know your clans!' Neil reflected, duly impressed.

'Sorry, Mr Strachan, it's the historian in me,' Breckenridge replied.

'No, I find the whole subject fascinating. So let's talk cats…'

'You mean, in connection with the Clan Chattan?'

'Yes, I do. They keep popping up in the enquiry, you see…'

'You mean like the one carved on that body?'

'You saw it, then?'

'Couldn't miss it.'

'I assume, from what you said earlier, the cat features on the emblem of the Clan Chattan?'

They were now passing through the vestibule of the visitor centre.

'Come into the office and I'll show you,' Breckenridge suggested, unzipping his jacket.

Neil looked on as the archaeologist went to a low cupboard and retrieved a massive reference work entitled *Encyclopedia of Scottish Clans and Tartans*. He flipped the pages until he reached the section on the Clan Chattan and prodded a large illustration on the page.

'This is the emblem of the Clan Chattan. A wildcat

crouching between sprigs of red whortleberry, a plant found in abundance in the forests of Clan Chattan country. The motto "Touch not the cat bot a glove" is intended to warn off those who might threaten the clan or anyone affiliated to it.'

'I assume the word "bot" means "without"?' Neil deduced.

'Correct. The clan chief had his own coat of arms too. See here.'

'I've seen that coat of arms on the frame in the corner of the MacGillivray portrait I was telling you about. There was another one too, very similar, and a different version of the cat badge on the opposing corner.'

Breckenridge turned more pages until he came to the first page of the MacGillivray section. 'You mean like this one?'

'Yes, that's the one, where the belt encloses the cat, and the motto is simplified to "Touch not this cat".'

'All the clans affiliated to the Clan Chattan would have their own version of the cat emblem and motto. In fact, even the Clan Chattan emblem itself, call it what you will, varied in its design, sometimes incorporating the belted scroll, sometimes the whortleberry. All the affiliated clans shared and wore the whortleberry plant badge too.'

'Plant badge?'

'Badges or emblems, often sprigs of a specific plant, were used to identify members of a particular clan. They were normally worn on the bonnet as a means of identification in battle, like the bunch of white ribbons that formed the white cockade of the Jacobites.'

'Okay. Well it seems our killer was particularly interested in the Clan Chattan version of the emblem. Whenever he came across an example of it in the castle, he practically demolished everything in the vicinity. One doesn't have to be much of a detective to conclude that he was looking for something significant!'

Neil's examination of the illustrations on the page in front of him was cut short when his mobile phone began to vibrate. He retrieved it from his pocket and tapped the call receive button. Holly's voice drifted into his ear.

'Hi, sir, thought you'd want to know we've just had a call from a guy called Edward Craig, a farmworker who works out Culloden way. He saw the TV footage of the police activity at the battlefield. Says he cycles past the entrance every morning on his way to work and seems to think he may have seen the killer and his vehicle.'

Neil looked across at Breckenridge wide-eyed. 'That's good news, Holly. Get over and see Mr Craig now and get a statement from him. I'll see you back at the office later on.'

'Okay, leave it with me. Bye for now.' The line went dead.

'Looks like we've got ourselves a witness,' Neil announced, in anticipation of Breckenridge's next question.

'Excellent,' the doctor extolled, as if Neil had just passed an exam. 'Let's hope you get a breakthrough!'

'Fingers crossed, eh? Look, before I go, I was wondering whether you'd ever seen this symbol before.' Neil plucked a pencil from the pen tidy on the desk, and recreated on a Post-it pad the linear symbol that had been carved into the two victims.

'I saw that too, on the man's body,' said Breckenridge. He shook his head. 'Can't say I've seen it before. If I had to hazard a guess, I'd say a symbol such as this wouldn't look out of place on the wall of a cave.'

'So you reckon it's much older, not connected with the period we've been discussing this morning?'

'I really can't say, Chief Inspector. Ancient symbolism isn't exactly my area of expertise. It may be something only the killer understands, something he created himself.'

Neil looked disappointed. 'You may be right, but thanks anyway. You've certainly clarified the matter relating to the cats!'

'I'm glad I've been of some assistance. How about a cup of coffee?'

'Thanks, but no thanks. I'd better head off and see what our witness has to say.'

Neil half jogged to the car, eager to get back and hear what Holly had gleaned from Mr Edward Craig. But when he breezed into the incident room, Ross Haggarty looked up from his desk, and studied him indifferently.

'She's only just gone out to see him, Neil. It seems he was halfway through milking his cows when she spoke to him initially.'

'Great. I'll go and get some grub, then.'

'Take your time, mate. If she gets the statement I'm hoping she'll get, we won't see her for hours!'

Neil nodded. 'Let's hope so. And less of the "mate", Inspector. It's "sir" to you!'

With that last parting shot, he was gone.

Haggarty had been right. Holly's meeting with Eddie Craig had exceeded three hours, and her skills, when it came to extracting every morsel of information from the cattleman's memory banks, had been sorely tested!

Neil had retreated to his office, and had been busying himself with the routine bureaucracy of a murder enquiry when she poked her head around the door, some time after three o'clock.

'Can I come in, sir?'

'Of course. Tell me about your encounter with Mr Craig.'

Holly settled herself once more into one of the chairs opposite Neil's desk. She was clutching a wad of statement forms, upon which Neil recognised the distinctive flowing longhand that he'd seen on other examples of her work.

'It's all a bit creepy, really. Eddie... that's what he likes to be called… says that he cycles past the battlefield every morning, on his way to work at his brother-in-law's farm at Croy. Around five thirty on the morning of the 16th April, he remembers passing the junction where the approach road to the visitor centre meets the B9006, when he…'

Holly went on to describe Craig's chance encounter with the plaided Highlander in detail. All the while, Neil listened intently, his expression one of abject disbelief. When she had finished, he remained silent for a few seconds, struggling with the concept that what he'd just heard should be the stuff of fiction. But, worryingly, the account appeared to be fact.

'Sir?'

'Aye, sorry, I was just taking it all in. What do you make of this Eddie Craig? He's no… well you know what I mean.'

'I know what you mean, sir, and no, he's definitely reliable. I have no concerns about him at all. He saw this so-called Highlander all right… *and* his bloody sword!'.

'And he saw him getting into a long wheelbase Land Rover Defender?'

'Aye, he's sure about that. They have one on the farm.'

'Colour?'

'Green, he believes.'

'Well that would fit in with the suggestion of fresh tyre tracks at that location.'

'Exactly, and there's a footpath from where those tracks were found, directly across the moor that joins the main path from the visitor centre down to the well. I stopped off and had a look on my way back.'

Holly checked the statement, in case she'd missed anything. 'The only problem is, Craig only saw this man for several seconds, and from a considerable distance. He doesn't feel he'd recognise him facially. So a photofit's probably out of the question.'

'Okay. Well, see if there are any re-enactment societies that specialise in the Jacobite period, anyone who likes dressing up like this. I'll talk to the press officer, see if there's any mileage in getting an artist's impression circulated of this fella.'

Holly got up and gathered up her paperwork. 'How did *your* morning go?'

Neil sat back and folded his arms. 'It seems the cat emblem this nutter's interested in is that of the Clan Chattan.'

He explained the relationship between the federation of clans and their link to the Well of the Dead, concluding with the tragic tale of Alexander MacGillivray and his sweetheart, Elizabeth.

'So that's what the handkerchief around the arm was all about?' Holly shook her head in disbelief.

Neil frowned. 'If I hadn't seen the tattoos on those victims and heard the account Eddie Craig has just given, I just wouldn't believe it. But now I'm afraid I do. There seems little doubt we're dealing with someone who's convinced he's a reincarnation of a Jacobite clansman... and something in that keep over at Cullaird is somehow pushing his buttons...'

He picked up the phone and tapped on the keypad. '... And until we find out *what* exactly, I'm going to crank up the security around the Fraser family.'

Chapter Thirteen

The trudge up the stairs was just long enough to read the long list of text messages displayed on the screen of his phone. Neil deleted them as he went, having replied in the briefest of fashions. Hardie wanted him to call, urgently. Cat wanted him to buy milk on the way home. That made him smile. She'd stopped the milk delivery to the house. Said it was too expensive… and now they were always running out! Then he stopped when he saw a one-liner from Holly. 'Think I've got a lead on the linear tattoo. Cu later. H.'

He tapped out her mobile number as he approached the doorway to the large open-plan office that was home to MEU. A jingle, one that he recognised, rang out from somewhere behind the legion of computer screens populating the brightly lit workplace.

Holly looked up from her desk when he walked through the door.

'Morning. I just texted you,' she informed him.

'I know. I've just seen it. You're in early!'

'I couldn't sleep, so thought I'd get to work trying to identify all the saddos who like dressing up in period costume and playing soldiers.'

'What's all this about the tattoo?'

'I gave the intelligence unit a call, asked them to research that strange symbol with the criss-cross lines. It occurred to me that someone else may have it tattooed on them. You know, perhaps if they were into the same weird pagan stuff as our killer!'

'And?'

'They've come back with something similar, from a record over in Aberdeen. Certainly worth following up though.'

Neil dropped his jacket on a nearby desk and settled into the empty chair next to it.

'Tell me more. What have the clever people in the force intelligence unit come up with?'

Holly swung the PC monitor around so that Neil had a clear view of the face that filled the screen. 'This handsome specimen of a man is Conal Francis Moffett, CRO. Born in 1951, a long-time resident of the "Granite City" and its various penal institutions.'

Neil looked into Moffett's soulless eyes. His reddy-brown hair was all but gone. Only traces of it still clung to the sides of his head, coalescing with the grey that followed his jawline and ringed his chin in the form of a ragged beard. Most prominent was the blue eagle tattoo that adorned his furrowed forehead. The bird was depicted in a launching posture, as if it had been nesting in the convict's brindled eyebrows.

'Looks like he's had a long career in the villainy business,' Neil observed.

'He has,' Holly confirmed, checking the criminal records office data in front of her. 'He has convictions for possession and supply of controlled drugs, assault, and housebreaking. Spent most of his early life in Craiginches Prison. Then he stepped up a level and did a six stretch for robbery in HMP Peterhead from 1996.'

'Huh. They called that place "Scotland's Gulag" once

upon a time,' Neil recalled. 'Even had to deploy the SAS to end a riot and kidnapping there in the late eighties. So what did he do to get six years?'

Holly returned to her screen and read out the modus operandi.

'Did, with another, enter a bookmaker's, assaulted staff, male, with a hammer, and stole cash to the value of £5,000.'

'Did he learn his lesson?' Neil enquired with a wry smile.

'Unfortunately not. He was back in HMP Aberdeen for three years in 2004, for housebreaking again.'

'So what is Mr Moffett's connection with this tattoo?'

Holly produced a photocopy of a Scottish Criminal Records Office descriptive form, submitted by Grampian Police following Moffett's arrest in 2003. 'This tattoo was recorded as being present on his left forearm at the time of arrest. According to prison records, it wasn't there when he was discharged from Peterhead Prison in 2002.'

Neil examined the illustration on the form. It depicted a vertical line from which four parallel horizontal lines projected.

'It's not exactly the same as the one carved into the Frasers' bodies, but, I agree, there are distinct similarities. Perhaps it's some form of underworld symbolism. Did FIU have any ideas?'

'None. It's not a style of tattoo that crops up very often, if ever.'

'Good work, Holly. So where will we find Moffett currently?'

'He lives on his own in a one-bed flat off Victoria Road in Aberdeen. Not surprisingly, he doesn't work, so there's a good chance we'll find him in if we knock on his door early enough.'

'Then we'll pay him a visit tomorrow… combine it with a visit to Alex Brodie in hospital.'

Neil's praise had filled Holly with ebullience. She beamed across at him.

'You certainly know how to give a girl a good time,' she quipped.

Neil picked up his jacket, trying hard not to respond too obviously to Holly's remark. 'Any luck with the re-enactment societies?'

Her demeanour instantly took on a more business like comportment. 'There seem to be several. I'll contact their secretaries… or send out a horseman if necessary!'

This time Neil couldn't resist a sideways grin. 'Just get on with it then, DS Anderson.'

On the stroke of midday, the two detectives were standing in the reception vestibule at the Lochmhor Distillery. The complex was a melange of old and new buildings, fronted by attractive grey stone malting sheds that dated back to the nineteenth century. Today their ageing walls were shrouded in a new growth of Virginia creeper, a curtain of green, interlaced with the remnants of the vivid crimson foliage that had survived from the previous autumn. Behind its antiquated facade and pagoda-style chimneys, a more modern distillery lurked. In its bland prefabricated sheds, wooden casks, filled with whisky, were stacked on towering racks. They were maturing slowly, until such a time, perhaps a decade on, when their contents, known locally as *uisge beatha*, the water of life, would be transferred into Lochmhor's distinctive amber bottles.

'Good morning, or is it afternoon now?' A distinguished-looking man, aged around sixty, burst through an internal door to greet them. 'Sandy Blair… pleased to meet you.'

Having invited Neil and Holly to accompany him to his office, he led them down a corridor, lined by a series of closed doors. Neil observed him from behind, as he marched along expressing his shock at hearing of the events up at the castle. He wore a crumpled grey suit, over the collar of which flowed a mane of grey hair, and he left in his wake the distinctive aroma of a pungent aftershave. Neil formed the impression that Mr Blair was a canny individual, which was surprising really, taking account of the generous salary the Frasers must've been paying him!

The detectives were duly ushered into his plushly appointed office and offered refreshment. Having politely declined, Neil gazed past him through the large double-glazed window.

'Impressive view,' he remarked. 'Allows you to keep an eye on the production process, I suppose?'

Blair looked out onto the cobbled quadrangle, and the large glass-sided distilling shed opposite. 'Aye, those six copper wash stills are on the go day and night.'

His enquiry satisfied, Neil's attention snapped back to the man in front of him. He focussed for a second on his smiling face before asking his next question.

'Do you hail from these parts, then, Mr Blair?'

'Not exactly,' came the softly spoken reply. 'I was brought up near Elgin. When I left school, I did an apprenticeship at the Glenallachie Distillery over in Strathspey. Worked my way up to plant manager and moved across to here in 1980, when Duncan Fraser made me an offer I couldn't refuse.'

'How did you get to know Duncan, then?'

'It's more than a wee bit cliquey up here, amongst the whisky distilling community, I mean. Everyone knows everyone else, you see. I suppose it's only to be expected, being such a specialised industry. If a plant's doing well then managers tend to get poached.'

'And Duncan Fraser *poached* you, did he?'

'Aye, that's about the strength of it.'

'How was your relationship with the Frasers?' Holly asked, not wishing to be sidelined in the conversation.

Blair turned his attention to her and rocked back in his chair. 'I've been here since 1980, as I mentioned. That's thirty years, if my maths are correct. What do you think, Sergeant?'

'Sounds like you got on with them very well, and rewarded them with amazing loyalty. The thing is, Mr Blair, circumstances change… so do relationships, sometimes for the worse.' Holly was a little niggled that the question had been turned back onto her.

Blair reddened slightly. 'Exactly right. Fair point. All I can say is, they've treated me like family during all that time. I watched their kids grow up, and their kids' kids too. In a nutshell, we were very close.'

'Umm, that's what Selina Cope told us,' Neil confirmed. 'What about the staff here? Did they all have such a good relationship with their employer?'

'Pretty much without exception, yes, they did. Some of them have worked here since school, and their parents before them.'

He pondered for a second before qualifying his response. 'I suppose we've had a few disgruntled employees over the years, you know, when we've had to let people go because of downturns in the industry. But I'd never point the finger at anyone as being capable of taking any sort of revenge against the family.'

'All the same,' said Holly. 'We'd like a list of all those staff laid off during the past five years.'

'Aye, of course, no problem. My PA can arrange that for you. It'll be a short list, mind!'

Neil was now admiring the artwork on the walls. 'This may seem a silly question, Mr Blair, but have any of your staff given you the impression that they have particularly strong clan ties?'

Blair laughed. 'No, not the youngsters. I'm not so sure

some of them even know which clan they're affiliated to! Some of the older ones wore the kilt at Christmas parties… and at the summer party the Frasers always held for their staff every year. MacGillivray was always a popular tartan, as I recall. But this is MacGillivray territory around here, so they're all probably interrelated way back, anyway!'

Neil smiled. 'Aye, I know. What about you, Mr Blair? The Clan Blair had its roots down south, did it not?'

'Actually, my affiliation is with the Blairs of Balthayock, down near Blairgowrie. My mother was a Cumming from near Elgin. So I'm something of a foreigner in these parts.'

Neil shook Blair's hand. 'Well you've been very helpful, Mr Blair. If you think of anything that may be of help to us, please give DS Anderson or me a call.'

He placed a business card on Blair's desk, prompting him to scoop it up and read the details. 'I will, Chief Inspector. Don't you worry.'

'So if you could provide us with that list of staff, we'll be off.' Neil stood by the open door and waited for their host to lead the way.

During the short walk to the PA's tiny office, Blair seemed a little agitated, as if he wanted to say something, but couldn't quite raise the courage. When they reached her newly painted door, he said unexpectedly, 'I was wondering whether Selina had mentioned to you what she intended doing with the distillery, now that Duncan's, well, not around.'

Neil gave him a lingering look. 'I don't believe they've considered the issue as yet, Mr Blair. It's a little early to be worrying about such things, don't you think?'

Blair nodded anxiously. 'Of course. How insensitive of me to even think about it. Forgive me, Chief Inspector.'

'Do *you* anticipate them selling the business, Mr Blair? Only it's been in the family for generations. Surely they'd never do such a thing?' Holly was intrigued by his enquiry.

Blair smiled. 'No, probably not, I suppose. It's just that Selina has never really been interested in the distillery, and Alisdair... Well I wouldn't put it past him to close the place down just to spite his father's memory!'

'They didn't really get on that well, did they? We've already picked up on that.'

'No, Duncan wanted him to take on the business, but he preferred to run off to France. I'm sure that wife of his, Simone, was behind it all.'

'Sometimes there are two sides to every story,' Neil interjected.

'Not in this case,' Blair retorted indignantly. 'Alisdair has always been a tricky customer, even I can vouch for that! Still, none of my business, I suppose.'

Neil seemed sceptical. 'That's not entirely true, though, is it? Your job's at stake if they sell. So in a way, it's very much your business.' Neil looked deeply into Blair's steely eyes. 'I assume that's what you're worried about, your position here?'

'No, no, not at all,' the plant manager whimpered. Then he changed tack. 'Well, yes, of course it is, I suppose. I just can't afford to be unemployed, Chief Inspector. My wife has MS, and I have a daughter and grandchild living at home to support. The son-in-law decided he was too young to remain married and have a child, you see. I've also got a son at university, and that's costing me a small fortune.'

He rubbed his brow. 'Sorry to burden you with my problems. But you did ask.'

Neil placed a reassuring hand on his shoulder. 'Things sound a little tough at present. I'm sorry to hear that, Mr Blair. And I don't suppose there are similar positions popping up all the time, are there?'

'I'd give it a while. Then have a chat with Selina. See what comes from that,' Holly suggested.

'Yes, yes, of course, I'll do that,' said Blair. 'Now let's get you that list.'

The narrow road that led away from the distillery to the east twisted its way between low heather-clad hills, still wrapped in their brown winter blanket. By the roadside, the odd wiry birch tree punctuated its vivid green verges. Neil stared into the middle distance seeking out the next bend.

'I do feel sorry for him. Sandy Blair, I mean. He can't be having it easy at present, and now his world's been pitched into uncertainty. Poor bugger.'

'He certainly doesn't have much time for Alisdair Fraser and his lovely wife, Simone,' Holly observed, peering out of the side window.

'I don't blame him, do you? I wasn't too impressed myself!'

Holly looked back at him. 'Aye, I got that impression. You don't think Alisdair disliked his father enough to—'

Neil cut her short. 'They're all on the radar at present, Holly, until we can establish otherwise. Now, have you got those photos Fraser Gunn took of that old portrait of Major MacGillivray?'

'I certainly have. Let's see what Selina can tell us about her illustrious ancestor.'

When they arrived at East Lodge, they found the Copes loading luggage into their car.

'Thinking of leaving us so soon?' Neil quipped.

Selina's head appeared around the side of the Mercedes. 'Oh, it's you, Mr Strachan. No, we're moving up to the castle today. Your people have finally completed their examination of the place, so we thought we'd make a start sorting out my parents' estate. It'll be easier doing the paperwork up there.'

Neil slammed the car door. 'I hope you'll be getting some help.'

'Yes, of course. Nat's taken leave, and Emily's staying up here with us too, so we'll be fine. It'll keep our minds off other things, if you see what I mean?'

She walked around the car and looked searchingly at Neil.

'Nat says there's been a police car permanently stationed at the end of the driveway since yesterday. Anything I should know about?'

Neil shook his head. 'It's just a precaution, really. We believe that whoever broke into the castle and attacked your parents may have been looking for something specific. The thing is, I can't rule out that they may return for a repeat performance, or even seek out members of your family in an attempt to gather information.'

He paused whilst Selina processed what she'd just been told. 'I fully understand that you need to carry on as normal, but now that I know you are heading up to the castle, I'll arrange for some electronic gadgetry to be fitted. A panic button, and our own alarm system, stuff like that. Your two FLOs have been instructed to be around as much as possible, and there will be a uniform presence outside the property at all times. Are you okay with that?'

Selina nodded. 'Of course, thank you. You know I have no intention of staying away from the old place. But perhaps we'll send Emily home, just to be on the safe side.'

'It may be a wise move,' Holly agreed. 'I understand from my colleague Lorna that your brother and cousin have now returned home?'

'Yes, Alisdair and Simone had work commitments, and Alban never likes to be away from Aldo, his partner, for very long. They'll be back for the funerals, though.'

Nathaniel and Emily appeared through the open front door carrying boxes of groceries.

'Morning, Chief Inspector… Sergeant,' Nathaniel greeted them. 'You've heard we're moving out, then?'

'Aye, we won't detain you. Just wanted to ask a couple of questions, if that's okay.'

Selina gestured towards the door. 'Well, please do come in. These two can take the luggage down to the castle. I'll put the kettle on.'

This time Neil and Holly responded in the affirmative and followed her into the lodge.

'How can I help you both?' Selina asked, having perched on the edge of the sofa whilst stirring her tea.

Neil placed a sheet of paper on the coffee table in front of her. On it was drawn the mysterious lined symbol that had featured so prominently in the enquiry.

'Do you recognise this symbol, Selina? Have you ever seen it before?'

Neil studied her reaction as she examined the drawing.

She inhaled deeply and shook her head. 'Haven't a clue what it's supposed to be. Never seen it before. What's the significance of it?'

She looked from one detective to the other, prompting them to exchange glances too, before Neil said softly, 'It's probably best we tell you whilst Emily's not here.'

'Tell me what, exactly?' Selina replied.

'We found this symbol, and a representation of a cat, scratched onto both your parents' bodies, Selina. It's as if the person who attacked them wants to give us a clue.'

Selina looked at them wide-eyed and she could sense the onset of more tears. 'Oh my God,' she gasped, her reply muffled by the mask of her raised hands.

Holly shifted across to the sofa and placed an arm around Selina's shoulders. 'We know this must be terribly distressing, but we need to ask these questions, I'm afraid.'

Selina removed her hands and sat up proudly, sniffing back

the tears. 'Nope, I haven't the slightest clue why someone would have disfigured my parents in this way,' she declared defiantly.

'What about the cat symbol? You told us it had connections to your family.'

Selina accepted a tissue from Holly. 'Yes, it does,' she replied, whilst wiping her nose. 'I spoke to Alban and my brother about the cat emblem above the fireplace, after you'd mentioned it the other day. Apparently it's the ancient emblem of the Clan MacGillivray, not the Frasers, as some may have believed.'

'Aye, I've since discovered that to be the case from an alternative source,' Neil interpolated. 'But how do the MacGillivrays link in to the Frasers?'

'Oh, I see what you're getting at.' Selina got up and went to a small bureau in the next room. She pulled down the flap and extracted a notepad, then returned to the sofa.

'Alban wrote this down for me. It's a bit complicated, I'm afraid, so I'd never have remembered all the details.'

She studied the pages of handwritten notes for a few seconds before looking up.

'Back in the 1650s, one of my ancestors, a man called Lachlan MacGillivray, was gifted the castle by his half-brother Farquhar "Fladhaigh" MacGillivray, who was the clan's sixth chief. Lachlan already farmed the land around the castle, held by him under *tack* or lease granted by Farquhar's father, Alexander, the fifth chief. You see Lachlan was not considered part of Alexander's immediate family. Obviously there had been some controversy, now lost in history, surrounding Lachlan's birth.'

'You mean Lachlan was Alexander's bastard son?' prompted Neil, stony-faced.

'Well, yes, in a word. So the story goes.'

She moved on quickly. 'To cut a long story short, three

generations down the line from Lachlan, the male line died out, when…' she checked her notes again, '… my ancestor, Duncan MacGillivray, had just one child, a daughter called Elizabeth. So, when he committed suicide in 1805, Elizabeth, who'd married a gentleman farmer from Stratherick called John Fraser, inherited the Cullaird estate. Henceforth, our family carried the name "Fraser".'

'Oh, I see,' said Neil. 'Now it all makes sense. So your MacGillivray ancestors must've been related to Colonel Alexander, the guy who fell at the battle of Culloden… at the Well of the Dead?'

'Yes, that's right. He was the *eighth* chief, so would've been—'

'Lachlan's great-nephew,' Holly chipped in.

'Exactly,' said Selina, not entirely sure, but nodding in agreement anyway!

Neil then showed Selina the photo of the damaged portrait of Major Alisdair MacGillivray. 'How does he fit into the family tree?'

Selina studied the photo whilst she spoke. 'Alisdair was Lachlan's eldest son, a colourful character, so Alban tells me. He fought with the Earl of Mar during the earlier Jacobite rebellion in 1715, was taken prisoner and sentenced to death for treason. Then, just before the sentence was carried out, he was released under the provisions of the Indemnity Act, which was passed in 1717. His younger brother Raonull was killed at Culloden.'

'Did Alisdair fight at Culloden?'

'No, he died of fever, up at the castle three years before the battle.'

Neil leaned forward and tapped the photo. 'Now the frame of this portrait carries the emblems of both the MacGillivrays and the Clan Chattan. Is that just because the MacGillivrays were a constituent clan of the Clan Chattan?'

Selina shrugged. 'I suppose so. I've never really examined that frame in any great detail.'

'Okay, enough genealogy for now. We'd better get going and let you complete your move up to the castle.'

He gathered up his papers and got up, prompting Holly to do the same. 'We'll get DC McKirdy to get all the details of our conversation recorded on an additional statement.'

'Okay, I'm available any time.' Selina picked up the empty cups. 'You will catch this bastard, won't you? Tell me you will.'

'You can count on it,' Holly responded, knowing Neil would not commit himself. She glared at him, having been given the 'How can you say that?' look. Neil took the hint, and followed her to the door. He had other things on his mind, namely why had Duncan Fraser ended up dead at the same tristful location, and 264 years after his famed red-haired ancestor had met the same fate? But his spirits had been lifted that afternoon. At least he had now discovered the link between the two MacGillivray men!

Chapter Fourteen

Aberdeen
Thursday 22nd April

Watery, early morning sun struggled above the rooftops of Bucksburn as they entered the outskirts of Aberdeen. It had been a long two-hour drive along the A96 and Neil needed a caffeine boost. His roving eye glimpsed the familiar signboard of a McDonald's restaurant and he broke the silence he'd maintained for the previous twenty minutes.

'Thank God for the big "M". I'll pop in there and get us a coffee.'

'He speaks,' Holly responded, still staring out of the window. 'Latte, no sugar. Thanks.'

Neil scowled back at her but said nothing. He knew he deserved that caustic comment, having been so preoccupied, and for so long!

When he returned with the two styrofoam cups, she waited for him to slip into the driver's seat before asking, 'Feeling better now?'

'Aye, much.' He smiled this time.

'Penny for them.'

'What do you mean?'

'Oh, do spare me the look of puzzlement, *sir*. You've been deep in thought for the last thirty miles.'

Neil grunted and handed her a cup. He hesitated for a second or two, trying to decide whether he wanted to open up to her or not. But he found himself speaking before he could stop himself.

'I'm a wee bit worried about Cat,' he blurted out. 'She told me she'd been to the gym the Monday before last, but I found out she hadn't. It's unlike her to lie like that.'

Holly sipped from her cup whilst studying him at the same time. 'Was it just that one time… she lied to you, I mean?'

'Aye, as far as I know.'

'And how long have you two been together?'

'A good few years now, I suppose.'

Holly shook her head. 'You *suppose*! I bet Cat would know exactly!'

She raised the cup to her lips again, her eyes still very much focussed on his.

'Sorry for asking, but is everything else okay between you?'

He looked at her a little perplexed. 'Aye, of course.'

'Okay, and is your birthday coming up?'

'No. What on earth's that got to do with it?'

'A family member's?'

'Not that I'm aware of. Look, what are you driving at?'

'Well, she might be arranging a surprise for someone. You, perhaps.'

'I don't think so. I suspect there's something else going on. Don't ask me why, I just know her, that's all.'

Holly sighed. 'Well, seeing it from a woman's perspective, something tells me it's not what you think. But it is strange, I grant you that. If you want my advice, I'd ask her straight. Get it out into the open.'

'Aye, I know. I keep telling myself that, but I can't for some reason. It's as if I don't want to know the truth.'

'Och, get over yourself, man. Perhaps you need to know

for her sake. So you can help her sort out whatever's going on.'

He nodded, evidently convinced. 'You're right. I'll speak to her. I know I'm being stupid.'

He smiled at her, but it wasn't a blithe smile. It was more of a polite gesture, acknowledging her support.

He turned the ignition key. 'So where are we heading for?' he asked, now wanting to change the subject.

Holly looked at the road atlas lying open on her lap.

'Next roundabout, turn right down the A90. Then we take Riverside Drive along the side of the Dee, and over the Wellington Road Bridge. Once we're on the other side, ask me again.'

Twenty minutes later, they'd pulled up opposite a row of shopfronts in Victoria Road. The premises they were visiting rose to four storeys above a vacant Indian takeaway, once known proudly as The Bengal Lancer.

Neil got out of the car and looked around him. The properties in the street were older Victorian structures, imposing terraced villas and a church on one side of the wide road, and the row of run-down shops on the other. All were constructed from the traditional grey stone that gave Aberdeen its well-deserved name, 'The Granite City'.

Above the peeling brown fascia board of The Bengal Lancer were a number of narrow windows, their yellowing frames sharing the wall space with a plethora of satellite dishes. Neil looked up, hoping to detect some sign of habitation, but little could be seen beyond the greying nets and weather-soiled glass.

Several loud raps on the shabby front door to the side of the shop front eventually prompted some activity from within. The sound of shuffling feet descending wooden stairs could be heard, before the swollen door was finally tugged open. And there stood Conal Francis Moffett, complete with eagle tattoo, eyeing up the two detectives suspiciously.

'Ah suppose you're the polis?' he enquired in the strongest of Doric dialects.

Neil produced his warrant card, and at the same time, introduced himself and his colleague.

'Can we come in and have a chat, Conal? It's a wee bit chilly out here.'

'Depends, son. What do you want tae blether tae me aboot?'

'We're investigating a murder over in Inverness back on the 15th April, and we think you might be able to help us.'

'Ah havenae done a murder in Inverness, mister. Ah've never gotten over there since ah was a laddie.'

'Okay, Conal. We're not accusing you of anything. We just need your help, that's all.'

Moffett turned and shuffled away into the gloom. 'Best you come in, then. The place is nothin' special, mind.'

He lumbered slowly up the stairs, whilst Neil and Holly followed at a respectable distance, eventually reaching an open doorway on the second-floor landing. On entering Moffett's little world, they – or more accurately their nostrils – were greeted by the putrescent atmosphere of rising damp and decaying food. The hallway was dark and uninviting. Hoary cobwebs hung in clusters between wall and ceiling, very much akin to a tunnel in a ghost train ride.

The sitting room fared little better. It was a cluttered, tawdry little room, filled with the debris of copious drinking sessions and takeaway meals. Moffett swept several empty Special Brew cans from the sofa, and gestured towards it.

'Sit yerselves doon, then.'

Neil's mouth twitched at the edges, revealing his sense of unease. 'Don't worry, Conal. We'll stand, if you don't mind.' He sensed Holly's sigh of relief from behind him.

Moffett's saturnine features lightened momentarily. 'Dinnae want tae get yer expensive suit grubby, eh?'

He handed Neil a crumpled piece of paper that had been lying on a nearby table. It was a charge sheet issued by Grampian Police, Aberdeen City Division. The document outlined a complaint of Breach of the Peace against Moffett, requiring him to appear at the Aberdeen Sheriff Court on 15th April 2010. Crucially, the offence was committed in the early hours of that day, and the time of charging was eight in the morning. Moffett appeared to have a watertight alibi for the break-in at Cullaird Castle. Not that Neil suspected him in the first place. He sensed the man had hardly ever stepped outside of Aberdeen's city limits… except to be committed to prison!

Neil's unease was plain to see. 'No, not at all,' he lied. 'We've just been sitting in the car for hours, that's all. Thanks for letting me see this.'

'Fancy a cuppa tea, then?'

'Sorry?' Neil was becoming more and more exasperated with Moffett's extreme dialect.

'He's asking if we'd like a cup of tea, sir,' Holly interpreted, with a sideways grin that obviously appealed to Moffett's sense of humour.

'No, no, we won't take up too much of your valuable time, Conal.'

Neil urgently needed to get to the point, before the extreme fetidness of the place made him boak.

'We understand that you have a tattoo on your left forearm, a vertical line with four horizontal bars extending from it. Is that right, Conal?'

Moffett contemplated Neil for several seconds before pushing up the sleeve of his grubby grey sweatshirt to reveal the all-important artwork. He pointed at it, looking a little puzzled. 'This one?'

'Aye, that's the one. What does it represent, Conal? I've never seen anything like it before.'

'It's ogham, son. The sign o' the hazel and the letter C for Conal.'

'Ogham?' Holly looked at Neil enquiringly.

Her boss gazed into Moffett's sunken eyes, trying to assess the truthfulness of his answer.

'Ogham? You mean the ancient Celtic alphabet that supposedly originated in Ireland? As I recall, it was adopted by the Picts. You sometimes see it on standing stones. Am I right, Conal?'

'Aye, you are. Each letter represents a sacred tree, and a feelin', like strength or wisdom.'

'I'm impressed,' Holly declared. 'You obviously listened to your history teacher more than I did!'

Neil ignored her little gibe. 'So why get ogham symbols tattooed onto yourself? Are you into all that mystic stuff, Conal?'

'Ah learnt about it when ah was doing time in the Gulag. Liked the idea of an ancient symbol as a tattoo and had it done after my release in 2002.'

'The Gulag… you mean Peterhead Prison?'

'Aye, that's the one.'

Moffett seemed to relish the attention he was getting, and went on to describe how he and his fellow inmates would use the ogham symbols as signatures after punishment had been dished out to other prisoners. They would carve their ogham initials onto the soles of the feet of those singled out for attention. So, whilst they would be painful to walk on for the person concerned, the tattoos would rarely be picked up by the prison authorities. If anyone did complain, then they would get another beating.

'Nice,' Holly remarked. 'So there are ex-cons out there with your ogham symbol carved permanently into their feet?'

'Aye. Some boys wouldnae whack their fags… things like that.'

Neil shook his head. What was this guy saying?

'Some of the inmates wouldn't share their cigarettes… is that it?'

'Aye, aye.'

Neil pulled out the drawing of the symbol tattooed onto the Frasers' bodies. 'Is this from the ogham alphabet, then?'

Moffett examined the drawing, then looked up with a pained expression on his face. 'This mark was on those people who were murdered?'

'That's right,' Neil confirmed. 'Do you recognise it, Conal?'

'Aye, that's the sign o' the heather: the letter U. Ma cellmate at the Gulag used it.'

'And who would that be, Conal?'

'His name was Ualas. Ah dinnae remember his full name. He carved the U ontae the feet of those he beat up. He was the start of the ogham hoojakapiv.'

'So *he* started it all, the feet carving thing?'

'Aye. We called him "the Cat". He had the cat of the Clan Chattan tattooed on his *kist*. Never had the U tattooed on him, though. He just used it on others.'

Neil and Holly's eyes met, their excitement palpable. Ualas… 'the Cat'. Was this the monster they were looking for?

'Where was the tattoo of the cat, Conal?'

'On his *kist*, son… his chest.'

'And why did he have it? Did he have some connection with the clan?'

'Aye, it was his clan. He was always tellin' stories aboot the Chattans.'

'Do you know what happened to him, Conal, this man Ualas?'

Neil found himself speaking slowly and deliberately, as he would to a foreigner, not a kinsman from the land of his birth! The two men lived no more than two hours' drive from each other, but the A96 could've been the Pacific Ocean when it came to language difference. He knew Doric shared its linguistic roots with the Scandinavian countries across the North Sea, and for those Scots who hailed from the west, it could be as challenging to understand as it would be for a southerner. But he'd never come across anyone speaking with such a strong dialect as this before. In fact 'dialect' was perhaps the wrong word. Moffett was speaking an entirely different language!

'No. Ah was released in 2002. He still had a year tae do. Ah never saw him again.'

Moffett looked up at Neil. He looked wan and watery-eyed. Either he'd had a heavy night on the water of life, or his long association with hard drugs was beginning to take its toll.

'Were you and Ualas good pals when you were inside?' Neil asked.

'Aye we were. We had tae be. But he was a hard man. Ah was glad tae see the back o' him.'

'What about family? Did he speak of any?'

'He kept in touch with a sister in Inverness. She came tae visit him at the Gulag.'

'Okay, Conal, we'll leave it there. Don't suppose there's any chance of getting a statement from you about your connection with Ualas?'

'You *are* jokin', Mr Strachan. Ah never give statements tae the polis. And besides, ah dinnae want Ualas comin' after me!'

'I thought not,' Neil smiled. 'Okay, we'll see ourselves out.'

Neil took another lungful of fresh air before getting into the car, but try as he might, the noisome aromas from Moffett's flat still lingered deep within his nasal passages. He looked at his watch. 'Come on, let's get another coffee. I need to quell the stench of that stinking place somehow.'

'Never say no to a coffee,' Holly replied as she got into the car. 'Where to after that?'

'We'll drop into the infirmary and see Alex Brodie. Then I think we'll pay Peterhead Prison a visit whilst we're out this way.'

The visit to Brodie turned out to be a short one. Fifteen minutes after their arrival, Neil's burly red-haired boss was wheeled away for what the nurse referred to as a routine scan.

Brodie had been sitting in a chair next to his bed. His militaristic bearing had not been affected in the slightest, and the knife-edge creases that ran down his pyjama sleeves amused Neil whilst they sat and talked. The man from Stornaway was understandably eager to hear of any progress in the investigation, and interrogated his two colleagues unremittingly, all the while feasting on the grapes they'd bought him in a Tesco Express store on the way to the hospital.

'So what's your next move?' he enquired, delving into the plastic bag for another grape, his eyes fixed on his visitors.

'We're going to drop in to the prison over at Peterhead. See if we can find out who this Ualas character is.'

Neil leaned forward to take a grape, prompting Brodie to pull the bag out of reach. 'Have you no shame, son? They're for a sick man, to aid his recovery, like.'

He looked across at Holly, his expression austere. 'I bet he'd take the pennies off a dead man's eyes. You watch yourself, lassie.' Then he grinned and pushed the bag back towards Neil. 'Just the one mind.'

'So how are you doing, Boss?' Neil asked, whilst holding up the one grape for all to see.

'Och, fine. I'm still a wee bit sore, but that's to be expected. They say they're pleased with my progress, and will be looking to kick me out of here in the next couple of days. Then it's home, and complete rest for a good few weeks, being nagged by she who must be obeyed! So make the most of it… sittin' in my chair, son. Typical, eh? We get a job like this, and I have to let my junior run with it whilst I'm languishing in here with a busted ticker.'

The nurse then arrived with a wheelchair to break up the party. Neil got up and shook Brodie's hand. 'You keep up the good work Alex, and if there's anything you or the family need, give me a call.'

Brodie raised a hand in thanks. 'Aye, that's good of you, son. Now get across to that bloody prison and find out who this bastard is whose carving folk up on our patch.'

Then he was gone. The back of his carrot-tinted head and the immaculately pressed pyjamas were the last enduring memory of their brief visit to the burly islander.

The stark granite walls of HM Prison Peterhead soon came into view as they approached along South Road. Rising above those walls, slate-roofed accommodation blocks predominated, beyond which the grey wind-roiled waters of Peterhead Bay presented a felicitous backdrop to this most austere of Victorian penitentiaries.

The prison officer at the gate examined their warrant cards, and on hearing the reason for their visit, summoned a colleague to escort the two detectives to the administration wing. There, a refined-looking woman called Muriel greeted them and gestured towards the two chairs that stood in front of her desk.

'Do sit down, please,' she requested. Then she perched primly on the chair that stood on her side of the desk. 'So how can we help you, Detective Chief Inspector?'

'We're trying to trace the cellmates of a prisoner who was serving time here in the late nineties, through to 2002. We're hoping you can help.'

Muriel cleared her throat. 'I think we might be able to come up with something.' Then she added mordaciously, 'A little notice is always helpful,' and rose from her perch.

'The officer we spoke to on the phone suggested dropping by wouldn't be a problem,' Holly retorted, taking the wind out of her boss's sails. Neil merely smiled back. The words 'cantankerous bitch' never quite left his mouth. A ventriloquist would've been proud!

'And which inmate would you be interested in?' Muriel enquired haughtily.

'Conal Francis Moffett,' Neil replied bluntly. 'We believe he shared a cell at some stage with a prisoner called Ualas, known amongst his cellmates as "the Cat"?'

Muriel's eyes widened. 'Ualas MacBean, you mean? What's he been up to this time?'

'We're not at all sure he has been up to anything. We're just following up a line of enquiry, that's all.'

'I can tell you now that Moffett and MacBean shared a cell towards the end of their sentences. They were bad news, both of them, and their pal Mungo McQuade...' She broke off. 'Wait here whilst I look out their files,' then she disappeared out of the door.

Her return was heralded by the cadence of marching feet along the corridor. She breezed through the door, pushing it closed behind her, and sat down heavily behind her desk.

'These should provide all the information you need on the three rogues we've been discussing,' she announced, opening each of the three Manila folders positioned in front of her.

Neil slid the files towards him. 'You're very kind. Do you mind if we borrow these for a while?'

'Be my guest, Chief Inspector. If one, or any of them, are up to their old tricks again, they need locking up for good and the key thrown into the bay!'

Chapter Fifteen

At 9.00 am, Neil found himself standing in one of the meeting rooms in the MEU suite. He was gazing down at the enquiring faces that had assembled for the daily Operation Cawdor progress meeting. They sat randomly around the long conference table, coffee mugs in hand, eagerly awaiting his summary of developments during the previous twenty-four hours. Angus Hardie, Ross Haggarty, Holly Anderson and Fraser Gunn sat closest to Neil. Then there were the DSs and the DCs, the FLOs and representatives from the Media Relations Unit and the fiscal's office.

Neil commenced his briefing with an account of his visit to Conal Moffett and the nettlesome meeting with the formidable Muriel at Peterhead Prison.

'I now believe we have ourselves a suspect,' he announced with some pride, and tapped on the large A3 photograph Blu-Tacked to the whiteboard that stood beside him. 'This is *Ualas Diamid MacBean*, sometimes referred to as Wallace, of which Ualas is the Gaelic derivative. He is also known amongst his peers as "the Cat". He was born near Torness in Strathnairn on 12th February 1965, which makes him forty-five years old. MacBean has previous convictions for theft, housebreaking...

into large country houses, and a string of assaults going back to his early teens. In 1991 he was convicted of culpable homicide.'

He paused so that his next disclosure would have maximum impact.

'The victim on that occasion was his own brother, whom he stabbed during a family argument at the family croft, known as Leud Lainn.'

Predictably, a number of shocked sighs effused from around the table, prompting Neil to continue.

'For this offence, MacBean served twelve years in HMP Peterhead. That's where he met Conal Moffett. They both shared a cell with a third party, and all three were persistent thorns in the governor's side. They were, in effect, a three-man Mafia!'

He turned to look at the photograph. MacBean's dark expressionless eyes stared out at the team like those of an alligator seeking its next meal. Tangled red hair, rarely if ever brushed, hung across his pale, leathery brow, not quite reaching the bridge of his flattened nose.

'He was released on licence in 2003, and was housed at a hostel for three months. Then he moved south, and worked on and off as a docker down in Port Glasgow, where he was convicted again in 2006 for a minor assault following a bar brawl. According to DIU, he went to ground shortly afterwards and hasn't been seen since.'

'The term "troglodyte" comes to mind. I bet he's hiding out in a cave somewhere!' Haggarty commented. 'What happened to his ear, for Christ's sake?'

The lobe of MacBean's right ear, partially obscured by strands of the red hair, was ragged and limp.

'It was partly bitten off by another prison inmate during an argument,' Neil explained.

'Jeez, it must've been some argument,' Fraser Gunn added, prompting a ripple of laughter.

'It was,' Neil replied, straight-faced. 'The other guy had ventured to suggest that Bonnie Prince Charlie was homosexual. For that, he spent a week in the prison hospital wing, having been stabbed in the eye with a pencil.'

Haggarty fidgeted about on his less than comfortable plastic seat.

'Quite the Scottish patriot, Mr MacBean, eh?'

'And that's what makes him so interesting in terms of this enquiry,' Neil responded. 'The prison service have told us that he was obsessed with the Jacobite period of Scottish history. He apparently read numerous books on the subject, and sketched scenes from the various events of that period, Culloden and the raising of the Prince's standard at Glenfinnan, to name but a couple. I'm told he plastered them all over the walls of his cell. He was also passionate about his clan ancestry. The MacBeans were… are, one of the component clans of the Clan Chattan federation, together with the MacGillivrays, from whom the Fraser family from Cullaird have descended. So, you see, there are several potential links, albeit historically, between our victims and this creature here.'

There was an uneasy silence, then one of the DSs standing in shadow at the back spoke up.

'So you're looking at the possibility that these killings were not the result of a robbery at the castle, but were clan-related?' He shook his head. 'I thought we'd moved on from all that stuff over 200 years ago!'

Neil shook his head. 'No, I still believe theft or robbery was the primary motive. The search of the keep at Cullaird indicates that, but this clan connection has some significance, I'm sure of it.'

Holly looked around to face her colleagues. 'We believe MacBean was looking for something at the castle, something that may possibly have once belonged to his clan, family, whatever you want to call them. Unfortunately, the Frasers, who were supposed to have been abroad at the time, had returned to Cullaird early because of a family bereavement, and disturbed him. Laura was subsequently killed, and we think Duncan was taken somewhere for further interrogation, before he too was murdered.'

Hardie folded his arms, his response irresolute. 'But surely, we're merely theorising about the clan side of things? There's no real evidence of a clash of the clans, is there?'

Neil shook his head. 'No, there isn't, but the fact that the cat emblem of the Clan Chattan was carved onto his victims does suggest a clan *connection*... at least.'

'It could just be his trademark,' Gunn interjected. 'Some killers like to leave clues as to their identity, to tease the cops hunting them. What about the other strange symbols?'

'I was about to come on to that,' said Neil, a little irritated that Gunn had pre-empted him. 'Conal Moffett has told us that these symbols may relate to the ancient Celtic language of ogham, and that the symbol found on the Frasers' bodies denote the letter U in that alphabet... U for Ualas, as it happens. The letters are also linked to various trees and plants. U is connected to the heather.'

He could see the vacant expressions around the table, and grinned. 'Let me explain,' he proposed. 'Historians believe the ogham language first appeared in Ireland, but in time, it spread to Scotland, and was used by the early Picts. It consists of around twenty characters, simple marks, easily drawn using vertical and cross strokes. There's a theory that the symbols were used as a form of sign language, but that's only one of many suggestions as to their origin.'

Having enlightened his colleagues as to the history and structure of the ogham language, Neil paused to sip his coffee.

Hardie looked concerned. 'If your theory is correct, Neil, there's surely every likelihood that MacBean will have another crack at getting into the castle. What's the current situation with the family and their security?'

'Most of them have gone home, sir. Only Selina Cope and her husband Nathaniel are staying on, primarily to sort out the Frasers' estate. They're adamant that they base themselves at the castle, for convenience, I suppose. So I've arranged for a panic alarm to be installed at the property. There will also be a double-crewed marked vehicle stationed at the gate twenty-four seven for the foreseeable future, certainly whilst the Copes remain in residence. I've also directed that one of the FLOs will be on site there at all times, at least when the family are present.'

'I bet you're popular with the uniform boys, keeping two of their finest standing guard out in the middle of nowhere, ad infinitum,' Haggarty reflected sardonically. His career-long scorn for his front-line colleagues was once again in evidence.

'They're being funded from this operation… on overtime, actually, Ross.' Neil could never understand this form of rivalry. They were all on the same side, or so he thought!

'We've also asked the duty armed response teams and dog units to pay passing attention to the area during their shifts,' Holly added.

'Okay,' said Hardie. 'What about circulating MacBean via the media, getting the public involved in the search? Surely, if it is him, the sooner we take this maniac off the streets, the better.'

Neil nodded in acknowledgement. 'I've been thinking about that. Personally, I think he will disappear completely if we splash his photo over the front pages of every paper. I'm still minded to follow up on our enquiries for the time being, certainly before resorting to that option. I don't believe he's a threat to the general public. This obsession of his is personal, and I'm convinced it relates only to the Frasers and Cullaird Castle.'

'Okay, you're the SIO, Neil. I just hope your assessment is on the mark. We don't want anyone else getting caught in the crossfire.'

Hardie turned to the assistant fiscal. 'Are you okay with keeping the suspect's identity under wraps from the media for the time being?'

'Aye,' the young man agreed. 'I see what Neil is getting at. So I'm content Hugh Jardine will go with it. But any more criminal activity involving this man, and I'm sure he'll be calling for the gloves to come off.'

'Agreed,' Neil acknowledged with a smile, pleased that his opinion had been taken on board.

The DS at the back raised a hand. 'You mentioned Moffett had an alibi, but what do we know about the third cellmate, the one who shared with MacBean? Could he have had any involvement in all this?'

Neil gestured to Holly to answer.

'Good question. As DCI Strachan mentioned earlier, the evidence is that only one offender was present at the scene as far as we can tell. That's not to say others weren't involved, so we'll need to be open-minded to that possibility. To answer your question about the third cellmate, his name was Mungo Hector McQuade, a native of the Drumchapel district of Glasgow. McQuade was doing three years for a football-related glassing involving an Aberdeen fan outside the Pittodrie stadium in 1998—'

The DS interrupted her. 'Do we know where he is now?'

'We believe he resides above an antique shop in Govanhill, a premises called Cathcart Antiques. His flatmate and business partner is a guy called Boyd Eugene Duff, now in his early fifties. He's done a couple of stretches in Barlinnie for theft and reset, amongst other things.'

'Ideal front for fencing stolen goods, an antiques shop,' Haggarty muttered.

'Bet Strathclyde have paid them a few early morning visits over time.'

Another brief, half-hearted ripple of laughter broke out.

'I'm waiting for a call back from a colleague down in Strathclyde, with a view to getting McQuade visited ASAP,' Neil added. His eyes followed Holly, as she circulated antecedent and previous conviction summaries appertaining to the three cellmates around the room.

Having accepted his copies, Fraser Gunn surveyed the mugshot of McQuade's stubbly, desolate face. He was a powerful-looking man, with long slicked-back hair and cold eyes that glared out of the page, as if he'd had a personal grudge against the photographer.

'He looks like he'd be the life and soul of the party at the antique dealers' Christmas convention,' Gunn propounded, slipping a strip of chewing gum into his mouth and grinning at the DC sitting next to him.

The briefing had now reached its natural conclusion. Having fielded the last few questions and listened to the enquiry teams' progress reports, Neil closed the meeting and gathered up his papers.

Bryan Findlay's jowly face then appeared through the departing crowd. 'Got a DI Willie Gemmell from Strathclyde on the phone for you, sur. Says he wants tae talk t'you about Mungo McQuade...'

Cathcart Road was typical of many urban Glasgow thoroughfares. It remained thronged with traffic throughout the day and was used not only as a north-south through route, but also by visitors to the host of small shops and businesses that traded beneath the imposing turn of the century sandstone tenements.

Detective Inspector Willie Gemmell parked at the end

of a bus bay directly opposite Cathcart Antiques. He slowly emerged from his begrimed CID car and squinted across the road towards the seedy-looking antiques shop that bore the full name of Mungo McQuade's little empire: *Cathcart Antiques and Collectibles*.

As he waited for a gap in the traffic, he could just about make out the small sign hanging inside the door, informing passers-by that the shop was open for business. More importantly, Gemmell's restless bloodshot eyes also detected vague signs of movement inside. The seasoned Strathclyde detective had been here before, initially when he was a young DC, investigating a string of housebreakings around Mount Florida and Kings Park. He'd worked out of the Cathcart office then, but now, pushing fifty, he headed up a busy proactive team working out of Craigie Street.

He still enjoyed the work, boshing doors in the early hours and taking out South Glasgow's netherworld when they least expected it. This was especially the case when they were tucked up in bed with their molls, or emerging from drug- and drink-fuelled stupors engendered in the smoke-filled back rooms of Glasgow's seedy bars. It was as if the delivery of justice was all the more rewarding, seeing the shocked, confused looks on the wee bampots' faces when they were dragged out of their holes in handcuffs. But the years of working antisocial hours had definitely taken their toll, and Gemmell's once brooding good looks had given way to the onset of eye bags and a fast-food belly.

An Asian taxi driver, with whom Gemmell was familiar, eventually paused to let him traverse the busy thoroughfare. The detective raised a grateful hand and ambled slowly across the road, resembling an eighties crime lord, his hands plunged deep into the pockets of his three-quarter length leather jacket, his eyes never straying from the shop's dark interior.

The door opened, and a weaselly young man with a guilty

197

countenance squeezed past him. They exchanged looks, prompting the weasel to look down at his feet and scurry away. When the door closed behind him, a bell tinkled somewhere in the bowels of the building, resulting after thirty seconds or so in the appearance of yet another weasel. This one was in his mid fifties, bandy-legged and balding, wearing an overly large polo shirt and faded grey jeans.

'How can ah help you?' he asked, with a gravelly Glaswegian accent.

Gemmell said nothing, but thrust his warrant card out to his front whilst scanning the contents of the shop.

'Och, the polis. Ah didnae recognise you. Ah must be losing ma touch.'

Gemmell eyed him impassively. 'Ah'm looking for Mungo McQuade, pal. Am ah speakin t'him?'

The weasel looked puzzled. His top lip twitched beneath the grey hairs of his straggly moustache.

'No. Ah'm his business partner… name of Boyd Duff. What d'you want with Mungo?'

'Just a wee chat, that's all.'

'Well, he's away, checkin' out a couple of antique fairs down south.'

Gemmell ran his hand in a large arc over the top of the dark oak chest that stood beside him. He stepped back and admired it. 'Nice piece, this. Where d'you get it from, Boyd?'

'Och, dinnae start that. Ah can assure you it's perfectly legit,' Duff growled. 'We got it from a lassie over in Cumbernauld a wee while ago.'

He folded his arms defensively. 'Ah've got the paperwork, if you want tae see it.'

Gemmell smiled. 'Och, no. Ah was just admiring it, that's all. Old, is it?'

'Jacobean, early seventeenth century. Why d'you ask?'

'No reason. It'll no doubt fetch a fair price, then?'

Gemmell slapped his business card down on the top of the chest, as if he were playing a card in a poker game. 'Can you tell your pal Mungo that DI Willie Gemmell, from Craigie Street polis office, was asking for him?'

He turned and looked around nonchalantly. 'And how's business, Boyd? Managing tae keep ya head above water?'

'So-so. Cannae complain,' Duff replied, a tad peevishly.

'That's good tae hear. Tell me, have you ever heard of a fella called Ualas MacBean? Has Mungo ever mentioned him at all?'

Duff glowered back at him, his bald head now noticeably shiny. 'Aye, Ah've heard of him. Mungo served time inside with the laddie... but you know that already, don't you?'

'No flies on you, Boyd. Ah just wondered whether you ever saw him at all... socially, like?'

'Och no, that were a good few year ago. Ah think Mungo said he'd gone down south someplace.'

Gemmell tapped the business card. 'Well, you ask Mungo to give me a wee call, eh?'

He turned and headed towards the door, calling out as he went, 'Who's Pamela, then?'

Duff looked down at the faded blue tattoo, just visible on his parchment-skinned forearm.

'She was ma wife once,' he replied wistfully. The bell tinkled again, and when he looked up the detective had gone.

Duff hurried over to the window and peered out, watching anxiously as Gemmell crossed the road and climbed slowly into his car. Finally content that the coast was clear, he reversed the sign on the door to display the word 'Closed', and turned the key in the lock. He then retraced his steps to the steep staircase behind the counter and climbed the stairs two at a time, turning left at the top and finally reaching the sanctuary of his pokey little office. Once seated behind the rickety desk in the corner, he pushed a pile of assorted paperwork aside and picked up the handset of the old sage-coloured telephone that had been buried beneath. Having timorously rotated the dial a number of times, he waited.

'Mungo, is that you, pal?' There was a pause. 'Ah've just had a visit from the polis. A cocky bastard called DI Gemmell from Craigie Street. Gave me the bloody creeps, he did.'

There was another pause.

'He wanted tae know whether we knew where Ualas MacBean was stayin' just now. He's left you a number tae call. You need tae speak t'him, Mungo. Ah dinnae want him makin' regular visits to the shop.'

Duff then listened to the muffled voice issuing from the earpiece, nodding intermittently.

'Ah know, but you need tae deal with it, ah'm tellin you.' He listened again.

'Aye, you need tae tell him they're on t'him too… Okay?'

Duff gripped the handset so tightly that his knuckles turned white.

'Aye, ah do. Aye. The bastard even started takin' an interest in that friggin' chest. It was as if he knew somethin'. Ah'm no happy aboot this, Mungo… just sort it, eh?'

He dropped the handset back onto its cradle and sat gazing out through the tiny window, his head cradled in the palms of his hands. 'Jesus Christ,' he grumbled under his breath. 'Ah really dinnae need this shite.'

Neil appeared behind Holly's shoulder and stooped over her, checking out the colourful images on her PC screen.

'What the hell is all that stuff?' he asked, his dark eyebrows arching inquisitively.

'Oh, just some bumph about the ogham alphabet and its association with the heather plant. Did you know the Celts and the druids made mead with it? The heather, that is. By all accounts, it was powerful stuff too. Apparently a fungus grows on the leaves of the heather that contains a strong hallucinogenic.'

Neil recoiled. 'Oh, God, no! Don't go advertising that outside of this office, or the happy baccy set'll be out scouring the hills and glens for their next fix!'

'Umm, of course they will,' Holly agreed blithely, still reading. 'And that would surely play havoc with the tourist trade. No bonnie purple heather… whatever next!' She closed down the page and spun her chair around, grinning. 'What did DI Gemmell say, then?'

'He dropped into Cathcart Antiques this afternoon. Boyd Duff was there, but McQuade was away, visiting some antiques fair, apparently. Duff said he knew of MacBean, but that's all.'

Holly looked up at him. 'I know there's a lot of circumstantial stuff connecting MacBean to these murders. I just hope it's not merely coincidence, and we're barking up the wrong tree.'

'No, I don't think so,' Neil reassured her. 'For what it's worth, Gemmell agrees. He reckons Duff was dancing on hot coals when he paid him a visit. No, we're on the right track, Holly. MacBean, Duff, McQuade… they're all involved in this somehow.'

Chapter Sixteen

Cat was a little late leaving the office that day. She'd graciously offered to finish a colleague's outstanding work when the onset of a severe migraine had precipitated her early departure for home.

The working day now finally complete, she emerged through the heavy glass doors into the rush hour drizzle and hurried along Baron Taylor's Street towards the Eastgate Centre and her usual bus stop.

She resembled a heavily laden Sherpa that evening, her gym bag slung casually over one shoulder and an expensive leather shoulder bag over the other. She had no intention of lingering and was focussed solely on her progress along the insalubrious back street that led away from the procurator fiscal's office.

Had she looked about her when she exited those glass doors, she may have caught a glimpse of her partner, observing her progress from the shadowy doorway of a shop front in nearby Church Street.

Neil stood in the semi-darkness, his shoulders hunched against the chill of the misty spring rain. He was reading a text on his phone that Cat had sent him ten minutes earlier… '*Hi, honey. Just leaving work now and off to the gym, see you around eight. Feed yourself from the fridge tonight. C x.'*

It was the first Monday Cat had planned to go to the gym since that day, two weeks before, when she'd lied to him so convincingly. He'd felt wretched all day about his decision to follow her that evening, but it hadn't dissuaded him from embarking upon his current course of action.

The prospect of it had conjured up conflicting emotions. He hated himself for stooping to such depths, yet there was also a profane sense of excitement deep within him, a feeling that tonight all would become clear, and in a sense, he'd even looked forward to it!

His stomach felt distinctly uneasy, the same way he'd felt at his last two promotion boards. *Was he going to come face to face with her secret lover... perhaps someone he knew?* No, his gut instinct was that she would never see someone behind his back. But there was something wrong, something for which she couldn't seek his help for some reason. That was it... or was it just possible there was someone else?

With his level of paranoia now heightened to a new amplitude, he set off along Baron Taylor's Street in pursuit of his partner, who was now marching along some one hundred yards ahead of him.

When she emerged into Academy Street, she halted and looked about her. Neil pulled up too. If she intended going to the gym, she'd turn left and take the short walk to the bus station or to Queensgate. But to his surprise she turned right, and disappeared out of sight. Perhaps she was heading for the Eastgate stop, the one she normally used to travel home. His stomach turned again as he quickened his pace to catch up.

When he too finally reached the junction with Academy Street, his eyes urgently scanned the route she would have taken to get to the bus stop. But there was no sign of her at all.

'Damn,' he muttered to himself, then widened the scope

of his visual search up into Inglis Street. It took him only a few seconds to seek her out. To be fair, it was her long blonde hair that gave her away, as she walked past the opticians he himself often used. He quickened his pace, his eyes fixed on that golden hair. Then something unexpected happened that caused him to halt abruptly. Cat paused and looked over her shoulder, then hurried into the coffee shop on the opposite side of the street.

Neil approached with caution, edging his way along the shopfronts adjoining the opticians. When he drew level with the coffee shop, he peered in through the glass-panelled frontage, fully expecting to witness her making her covert rendezvous.

The place was busy, bodies everywhere, but there she was, alone at the counter speaking with the female barista, purse in hand. He walked on, his heart pounding, mulling over his next move. He found himself standing on Market Brae steps looking back down Inglis Street, from where he had a good view of the coffee shop and its doorway. If she was just picking up a takeaway, then he'd definitely see her leave.

His phone rang at that point, prompting him to dig around frenziedly in his jacket pocket. He answered it, hoping that it wasn't a call back to work.

'You all right?' Holly queried, having detected his lugubrious tone.

'Aye, of course I am. What's up, Holly?'

'Willie Gemmell left a message for you a few minutes ago. Wanted you to call him back at some stage.'

'Ah, look, I'm a wee bit tied up just now. Can you call him back and see what he wants? Let me know if it's anything pressing, eh?'

'Aye, of course. You sure you're okay, sir?'

'Aye, Holly, I'm fine. I'll get back to you as soon as I can. Okay?'

He slid the phone back into his pocket and turned his attention back towards the coffee shop. Cat had not re-emerged. *Surely it didn't take this long to buy a takeaway coffee.* He started walking slowly back down Inglis Street, his anxiety heightened once more. This time he couldn't see her. *Christ, had she come out and he'd missed her?*

He backtracked again, closer to the window this time, fearful that she'd spot him if she was still inside, but there was no other way. He had to locate her.

The place was still heaving, movement everywhere. He almost gave up, resigning himself to the fact that he'd missed her and that his surveillance skills were sadly lacking. So he kept walking, dispiritedly, until the crowded interior had almost slipped out of view. That's when he spotted her, sitting at a small round table, with a large china mug in front of her. More importantly, she was still alone, looking down at a magazine that lay open upon her lap.

Neil walked on, a confused frown now crumpling his features, but at the same time he was strangely relieved.

And so the cycle went on… and on, for over an hour. Neil walked past several times, but by now the level of pedestrian traffic up and down Inglis Street had reduced to such an extent that he was at certain risk of being seen. By now, she'd drained at least two large cups of coffee, and the cups supplied in these establishments were indeed large!

A little after six, she finally re-emerged, just as the staff were locking up. Neil followed her back down to Academy Street, where she crossed the road and disappeared into the bar of the Royal Highland Hotel. *This must be it then*, Neil thought. She must've just been killing time in the coffee shop!

Keeping tabs on her was going to be even more difficult now. He entered the grandiose turn of the century lobby with the irresolute air of a man who'd just strayed into a ladies' toilet. Now surrounded by a melee of tourists and their luggage, he paused and looked around him, hoping to God that she wasn't going to appear out of nowhere.

But again she'd managed, albeit unwittingly, to evade him. He surveyed the majestic, tartan-carpeted staircase, notable as having once inspired the designers of the Titanic, hoping not to see her skipping up to one of the rooms arm in arm with some strange man. But no... mercifully, she wasn't there. He threaded his way back towards the main entrance, only to be challenged by one of the reception staff.

'Can I help you, sir?' the attractive young brunette enquired.

'No, no,' he replied, shaking his head. 'I was just looking for someone. That's all.'

'Have you tried the bar, sir?' came the helpful reply.

The young woman's question prompted him to look over her shoulder through the open doorway, where, to his temporary relief, he spotted her. She was once again sitting alone in mournful silence, sipping from a glass of something that resembled mineral water.

Neil thanked his dark-haired saviour for her help, then found himself a sumptuous Queen Anne armchair from which he could still observe Cat clearly. It was a perfect vantage point, allowing him to merge seamlessly into the assemblage that thronged the lobby.

He waited for a couple of minutes, then powered up his phone and tapped out a text... *Hi. Do u want me to pick u up from the gym? Leaving work in next half hour. N x*

Seconds passed. Then he saw Cat pick up her phone. She paused and then began typing. Her response arrived instantaneously and his phone began to vibrate. He tapped the little yellow envelope and read the message. His heart sank as he digested its content... *Hi. Don't worry. Changing now, then grabbing a quick drink with the girls. C U around 8. X*

Neil puffed his cheeks in disbelief. He returned the phone to his pocket and resumed his vigil.

The scene playing out before Neil's eyes saddened him deeply. Cat sat alone for the next hour or so, periodically sipping her drink between checks of her mobile phone and then her watch. No one joined her and she gave no indication from her body language that she was expecting someone. In fact rarely did she ever look up, let alone search for a face in the crowd, as one would've expected of somebody who was eagerly awaiting the arrival of someone special.

At seven fifteen, she checked her watch again, drained her glass, and got up. Neil responded by leaving his chair, and retreating to a darkened alcove by the staircase. Cat walked past within ten feet of him, clutching her bags and looking crestfallen.

Once in the street, she headed back to the bus stop outside the Eastgate shopping centre and waited with the handful of like-minded home-goers. Neil skirted furtively around behind her and stood inconspicuously by the doors to the centre... watching her every move.

Minutes later, she climbed aboard the service that would take her out to Westhill and home. She never saw Neil, of course... but someone else did. The watcher was being watched, through dark and vacant eyes. They quickly registered the threat, then lowered wearily, like those of a monk about to engage in prayer...

When the tail lights of the bus had disappeared into the distance, Neil broke into a run, back to the CID car he'd left parked in the underground car park across the road.

He caught up with the bus in Culloden Road and overtook it whilst it disgorged some of its passengers at one of the stops near the A9. He then parked up in a side road a short distance from the stop at Woodside Farm Drive where Cat normally alighted.

When the bus finally arrived, there was no sign of her. He jumped out of the car and jogged across to the vehicle, which seemed to be waiting for no apparent reason with the doors still open. He jumped onto the step, still panting from the run. None of the blank faces looking at him from the seats on the bus were Cat's.

'Do you remember a young woman with blonde hair getting off between Academy Street and here?' he enquired of the young male driver.

'Aye, I do, mate. She got off at the last stop, back at Tower Road. Thought it a bit strange, as she usually gets off here.'

'You know her, then?'

'Aye, I see her from time to time, especially in the mornings. I'm often workin' this service.'

'Oh, right, thanks.' Neil turned and hopped off the step.

'She your missus?' the driver called after him with a cheeky smile.

Neil looked back. 'She's my partner, actually.'

'Lucky man y'are, too.' The driver grinned again. Then the doors hissed and closed… Neil's cue to trot back to the car.

He drove back around the residential loop that brought him onto Tower Road, and it wasn't long before he came across Cat, walking slowly along the footpath.

He pulled up and leaned across to open the door for her.

'Didn't you get enough exercise tonight?' he asked with a smile.

She climbed in, straight-faced.

'I needed some fresh air, that's all. I've got a bit of a headache for some reason,' she replied, disregarding his little joke.

'You just finished work?' she asked him.

'Aye. You should've let me pick you up from the leisure centre.'

'No need. I bussed into town with a couple of the girls from the gym.'

'I see. Fair enough,' said Neil, staring ahead and trying to hold it together.

Little else was said during the remainder of the short journey home.

Once inside, Cat opted to have a soak in the bath, having greeted and fed an excited Tam.

Neil was so close to saying something. He was desperate to bring things to a head, and watched from the bedroom door whilst Cat got undressed.

'Cat,' he called out, prompting her to appear in the doorway of the en suite wrapped in a towel.

'Yes, Neil?' she replied.

Just then, his mobile rang. He sighed. 'Nothing. Look, I'd better take this call.'

The moment was lost and she retreated back into the steam, whilst he headed off downstairs.

'I thought you were going to call me back?' Holly made no attempt to hide her irritation.

'Sorry, I got waylaid. Picked up Cat on the way home.' To his chagrin, Neil's excuse was pretty weak, to say the least!

'Oh, right. Have you sorted things out with her then? I sincerely hope so!' This was quickly followed up with, 'Sorry, sir, I'll mind my own business.'

Normally Neil would've agreed with her, but for some reason, tonight he welcomed the support she had afforded him. 'I was just about to talk to Cat, when you called...'

'Oh no, don't use me as a bloody excuse... sir!' Amused by her vexed reply, Neil found himself ginning briefly, primarily to disguise his embarrassment. 'Don't worry, I won't. Sorry... again! So what did DI Gemmell say?'

'He wanted you to know that Mungo McQuade had called him. Apparently he was pretty non-committal. Said he hadn't seen Ualas MacBean for over five years. Thinks he went down south, possibly to work in London.'

'Is that all?'

'He mentioned that McQuade was pretty abrasive. Wasn't at all happy being questioned about his old cellmate. He was asking all sorts of questions…'

'Like what?'

'Stuff like why was *he* being contacted? Was he a suspect? Was Ualas a suspect?'

'Did he say where he was calling from?'

'Somewhere down near Newcastle, at some antiques auction.'

'Anything else?'

'Nope, apart from the fact that DI Gemmell doesn't believe him at all. But I get the impression there are very few people that DI Gemmell believes!'

'Okay, Holly, thanks for that. I'll see you in the morning.'

'Aye, sir, and remember what I said?'

'Sort it! Yes, I remember. Night, Holly.'

Neil poured himself a large tumbler of malt, the twelve-year-old Lochmhor his father had bought him for Christmas. He stretched out onto the sofa and examined the contents of the glass, deep in thought. Tam jumped up next to him and collapsed, content to rest his chocolate head upon his master's thigh and lapse into immediate unconsciousness. Neil stroked the dog's long ears whilst he sipped his whisky. He relived the events of that evening in his mind, desperately trying to make some sense of what he'd seen. Had Cat intended to meet someone? Someone who'd stood her up? Or was she just killing time to avoid going home? She didn't need to stay away on his account, because she knew he was still at work. She must've been stood up, that's why she kept looking at her phone. She was waiting for *him* to text her, but he didn't.

He looked up suddenly. '*Texts…* I need to see her texts,' he mouthed, almost immediately regretting his new-found desire to employ ever more heinous tactics to get to the bottom of the mystery. But his mind was made up. Before confronting her, he needed to explore all avenues that might, just might, provide him with some answers. She may of course have deleted any incriminating messages already, but he needed to check her phone all the same.

Getting the opportunity was not going to be easy. Cat's phone permanently lived amongst the clutter that filled her capacious shoulder bag. A search would be necessary and that would take time. Such opportunities would rarely arise, because the bag was normally located within easy reach of its owner.

He got up and climbed the stairs, hoping that Cat was still in the bath. But no. She was sitting on a stool in the bedroom, drying her hair. The bag stood on the floor next to the bed.

'You okay?' she asked with a smile.

'Err, fine,' Neil mumbled. 'I'm just going to take Tam for a walk.'

'Okay... don't go far... I'm about to start supper.'

Neil nodded and drained the remainder of his whisky. His quest for conclusive evidence of his partner's infidelity would have to wait...

Chapter Seventeen

Inverness
Tuesday 27th April

The kettle began to boil, just as Neil had removed his second round of toast from the toaster. He poured the hot water into his mug, looking forward to his first cup of coffee of the day. In the silence that had now been restored to the kitchen, he could clearly hear the electric shower pump in the bathroom upstairs. Cat always used the bathroom in the morning, so that he could shower in the en suite.

He took a slug of his coffee and looked down into Tam's doleful eyes. The dog was a master of sycophancy when it came to mealtimes!

Leaving the dog munching triumphantly on a piece of buttered toast, Neil bounded up the stairs, two at a time. He found Cat's bag standing by the side of the bed and when he looked inside, he could see her phone lying prominently amongst the contents. He checked behind him and took a deep breath, knowing that he was on the cusp of invading her privacy, something he would never have entertained previously. But things had changed. His sense of righteousness had been temporarily deflected, and aberrance now seemed to be the order of the day.

The jet from the shower was still pounding the glass

screen in the bathroom across the landing, so he had time if he was going to do this. He groaned, somehow frustrated by the situation in which he now found himself. Then he reached into the bag. The phone recovered from standby mode instantaneously and he tapped the text symbol, practically holding his breath.

A list flashed up on the screen, a long list, populated by the names of friends and numerous phone numbers. Many of the names he recognised, but towards the top of the list were half a dozen references to the same mobile telephone number: one he certainly didn't recognise.

He tapped the top message and as he read the content, his eyes began to narrow, drawing his brows arching downward like dark hoods. A blend of shock and anger coursed through him as he read the message again and again.

> *...Hello Cat, sorry I couldn't get to see you tonight. What about later? I'll catch up with you then. Remember what I told you. This is our little secret. But Neil's been keeping an eye on you it seems. That wasn't part of the bargain was it?*

Attached to the text were two photos. One of the front of their house, in which Tam could be clearly seen reposing on the top of the sofa inside the bay window. The second showed *him*, Neil, the previous evening, waiting near the bus stop outside the Eastgate Centre. It was a little grainy as the light was fading and the camera operator had zoomed in on him, but it was definitely him! The text had been received at 21.30 the previous evening.

Neil brought up the next message from the same number.

> *... Hello Cat, I'll try to be at the Leisure Centre tonight, but can't promise anything. It was a shame I've missed you three weeks running. I hope you're not avoiding me. If we don't*

meet soon, I'll have to come and find you… at home maybe.
Xx

This message was timed 17.00, also the previous evening. He tapped on the other texts in succession, a collection of obscene ramblings from someone evidently obsessed with his partner… and very keen that she should keep their communications to herself. Time after time he read, *Don't tell Neil… Neil mustn't learn of our little secret… If you value that cute brown dog, don't tell Neil.*

He thumbed the screen downwards until he came to the first message from the now familiar number. It read, *Sorry about the other night Cat, didn't mean to frighten you. Can we try again? Please don't tell Neil. That would be a big mistake!* The message was dated 08.24 hrs: 31/3/10.

The other night? What was the caller on about? Neil could feel his heartbeat quicken as he pointlessly tried to put an imaginary face to the caller, one that he could pummel remorselessly. He'd been so preoccupied with the texts, he hadn't noticed that the shower had been turned off. Cat's voice caught him completely off guard.

'What are you doing with my phone, Neil?'

He swung about and tossed the phone onto the bed, then glared at her. There was a haunted expression upon his face, as if someone had strapped a bomb to his body.

'I was wondering whether I knew the guy you were meeting up with on gym nights. Seems I don't. Which is just as well, really. He doesn't appear to be your type.'

He stared hard into her blue eyes whilst she tightened the cord on her bathrobe. 'Do you want to tell me what's going on, Cat?'

The blue eyes glistened. Then the first tear tracked down her cheek.

'I haven't been seeing anyone. But you must've discovered that for yourself if you've been following me.'

A silence followed, whilst they both stood and contemplated each other, waiting for the other to speak.

'You should've told me,' Neil finally blurted out.

'I couldn't. He was threatening to do something horrid, to Tam or to the house if I told you.'

She began to sob, standing, head bowed like a naughty schoolgirl who'd been caught out by her teacher. Neil lurched forward and threw his arms around her, stroking her wet hair whilst her tears soaked into his shirt. And there they stood for a full minute, in a silent embrace, whilst Tam sat beside them, looking up longingly, his long, feathery tail swishing to and fro across the carpet.

Neil sat at the kitchen table, thumbing through the texts for a second time. The muscles along his jawline twitched uncontrollably as he scrutinised the words for clues as to the identity of the writer.

'So this was the first text you received from him, on Wednesday 31st March?'

'Aye, that's right.'

Cat sat across from him, cradling a mug of coffee with both hands. She hadn't bothered to brush her hair, allowing it to drape limply across her shoulders. She'd told Neil everything. It had been like a dam opening and she'd wanted to get it all out faster than her mouth could form the words. Neil had listened, but repeatedly interrupted her so that he could clarify the various elements of her story.

It had all started on Monday 29th March, two weeks before that eventful evening when he'd received the phone call from Andrea Maclean.

Cat had gone to the leisure centre out on the west side of the city as usual. It was an ongoing arrangement she'd had with two of her friends, Andrea and Kirsten Graham for over a year. They'd meet up at the centre after work, use the gym at the complex, and having dropped into the bar for a quick drink, they'd travel back to the city centre together on the bus. From there, they'd go their separate ways, as they lived in different areas of Inverness. Cat would catch the service that ran from the Eastgate Centre out to Westhill and eventually home.

On that Monday in March, she'd arrived at the leisure centre as normal, and had walked alone, across the open car park to the entrance. Just as she'd passed some tall bushes that bordered the only secluded section of her route, a voice had called out to her.

'Hello, Cat.'

Standing by a gap in the bushes was a figure, a slightly built male, wearing a hoody, the top of which had been pulled up to conceal his face in shadow. Cat was adamant that the figure was male, and the voice confirmed it. In fact she thought she recognised the voice, but couldn't quite place it. Not that she'd waited to find out. Stupidly, instead of running to the sanctuary of the leisure centre, she'd made off in the opposite direction, back along the lane towards the bus stop. Thankfully, the hoody hadn't followed her and had walked off across car park at a brisk pace.

As she'd sat on the bus back to the city centre, she'd played the voice over and over in her mind, convincing herself that it was none other than that of her young colleague, Jack Guthrie. She was under no illusion that he'd had a crush on her for some time, and although she'd always tried to play things down, he'd unfortunately persisted. Not only that, he was a regular attendee at the gym she used, and only the week before, she'd seen him working out there.

The problem was, Cat knew Guthrie's parents very well. They had been family friends for a number of years and were really nice people. So she hadn't wanted to rock the boat at that stage. Jack, if it was him, hadn't done anything, anyway. He had just said 'Hello', for heaven's sake!

It had been *her* who'd bolted like a frightened sheep, overreacting big time! So she'd decided to let the whole thing drop and had called her friends to say that she'd felt under the weather. And that had been that.

Then on the 31st, she'd been waiting at the bus stop in Westhill whilst on her way to work when she received the first text. The words *please don't tell Neil. That would be a big mistake,* had really worried her, so much so that she'd challenged Guthrie when she arrived at the office. Not surprisingly, he'd robustly denied being anywhere near the leisure centre two days previously, but she'd remained unconvinced.

Then the texts had become more frequent, more threatening, and she'd become confused. No longer was she sure that the culprit was Guthrie, but neither was she convinced that it wasn't! What she did know was that any word to Neil could possibly prompt violent retribution against her home and family, and she couldn't allow that to happen. Silence seemed to be the only policy open to her, and of course, a conscious decision not to go near that damned gym!

'So instead of going to the leisure centre, you've been hanging out in town, killing time?' Neil deduced.

'Only three times,' Cat confirmed, placing her mug on the table. 'The week after seeing him that first time, then again that night you'd been to the dentist, and of course last night.'

'You were wearing your tracksuit the night I'd been to the dentist,' he queried.

'Aye, I know. I changed at work, then went to get some groceries. I had a drink in the cafe at Tescos and then came home.'

Neil shook his head. 'I should've spoken to you earlier.'

'Why didn't you, then?'

'I suppose I just didn't want to know the truth.'

He buried his face in his hands, prompting her to get up

and squat down by his side. She stroked his arm tenderly with one hand, whilst wiping away her tears with the other. 'You know I'd never cheat on you, don't you?'

'I know, I know,' he sighed. 'But how would you have felt in my position? There was always a lingering doubt.'

She nodded thoughtfully. 'Aye, you're right. I'm sorry. I would've probably taken it out on the contents of your wardrobe, and that would've been *before* I discovered the truth. Impulsive, that's me.'

They both laughed, and Tam barked, as if in accord.

'Tell, me,' said Neil. 'Have you ever tried to call this number back?'

The emotion had begun to ebb away, only to be replaced with anger and a determination to find the bastard who'd turned their lives upside down.

'I did once, but got no answer. Then I was too scared to try again.'

Neil selected the number and pressed call.

'It's ringing,' he announced, looking up. But that's all it did: ring and ring. 'It's probably a pay-as-you-go phone, anyway.'

He sat up straight, as if shaking off the cloak of sentimentality that had initially enveloped him. 'Okay, this is what we're going to do. This idiot seems to know who I am. His activities are not necessarily restricted to Monday gym nights either. So tomorrow, I'll get Holly to shadow you on your way home from work and I'll personally keep an eye on Jack Guthrie. Let's see what he gets up to.'

Cat looked concerned. 'You won't do anything silly, will you, Neil? We don't know it's him.'

Neil grinned. 'I'm not a thug, you know. I'm only going to keep an eye on him, that's all.'

'What about today? I'm going to need to leave for work shortly.'

'I will take you to work today… and pick you up. Just give me a call when you're ready. I'm also going to take Tam to my mother's place this morning. Better safe than sorry, eh?'

'Okay, that sounds like a good idea. Look I hope this isn't going to distract you from the case you're working on. It's far more important than some silly stalker!'

'Rubbish. Stalking may be a nuisance to start with, but things can get quickly out of hand if we don't put a stop to it. Besides, there's no way he's going to get away with this!'

'Just don't let this get out of hand and damage your career, Neil. I'd never forgive myself. Can't someone else deal with it?'

'Listen, let's just see how things develop. Yes, I may need to get someone to take this on, but initially I want to make my own enquiries. See if we can't resolve this without getting too many other people involved.'

Neil kissed her, then smiled. 'I may be the boss, but I'm also part of a team… and the team can hold the fort for a couple of hours this morning. I'll take Tam with me. One of the girls in the office can keep an eye on him whilst I do the morning briefing for the Operation Cawdor team. Then I'll head out to Cromarty.'

'Okay, if you insist, Boss.'

'I do,' he reassured her, whilst taking the mugs to the sink.

Cat had then gone off to get dressed, now much relieved. When she returned, Neil was standing by the table. He held up two mobile phones. One was hers, the other was a pay-as-you-go device that Neil kept as a spare.

'I want you to use this phone for the time being,' he said, handing her the battered old flip phone. 'It'll do for a while, so that I can keep yours and monitor any incoming calls or texts. I'll let you know about any important stuff.' He placed the phone on the table. 'Now, don't go giving this number out to anyone at all. I mean *anyone*, understand? Only close family and I will ever call you on this phone, okay?'

Cat nodded. 'Just text back to any of my friends and ask them to call me at home, if you have time.'

'Sure. Will do.'

Cat was duly delivered to work. 'Any problems, just call me... anything at all,' he called through the open window, whilst Tam slunk onto the warm seat that she'd just vacated. 'Oh, and see if you can get hold of Jack's mobile number. On the quiet, like.'

Cat placed her bag on the ground and responded with a mock salute, then headed off towards the office door.

When Holly knocked and walked into Neil's office, he was standing by the window, checking the screen on Cat's mobile phone. Tam was lying nonchalantly on the carpet in front of the desk, his tail flailing wildly.

She dropped down to stroke him. 'Hello, Tam. You're a handsome boy, aren't you?' Then she looked up. 'I assume this *is* the famous Tam?' she asked.

'Aye, and he's got a thing about attractive blondes, so watch yourself.'

Holly stood up abruptly. 'Butter wouldn't melt comes to mind,' she muttered, looking down into the spaniel's excited brown eyes. Then she turned her attention back to Neil, and smiled. 'So I'm an attractive blonde, then, sir?'

Neil lowered himself into his chair, unabashed.

'Without a doubt, Holly,' he declared with a hint of sarcasm.

'Umm, so man and dog in total agreement? I'm flattered.' Holly flushed slightly.

Neil was ferreting about in his in tray. 'The difference between us is... he'd pounce on you as soon as your back was turned. The most you'd get from me is a cup of coffee!'

Holly cleared her throat, the floridity of her face now greatly enhanced.

'Charming,' she croaked.

Neil looked up, smiling. 'Anything to tell me, then?'

Holly knew she was blushing, and could feel the heat radiating from her cheeks.

'I've been speaking to the secretaries of several re-enactment societies that have connections with Culloden Battlefield. There wasn't anything specifically planned for the day Duncan Fraser's body was found, and the description didn't prompt much of a response either, I'm afraid.'

She sat down and placed a folder on the desk. Tam immediately sidled up to her when her hand strayed onto his head. She crossed her legs, and looked a little anxious.

'I did warn you… about him, I mean,' Neil grinned.

Holly blushed again. 'Err, I also mentioned the name Ualas MacBean to them. They knew of a good few MacBeans, but not one called Ualas.'

'Okay, thanks for doing that. I'm not particularly surprised. I don't really see our man as being much of a team player.'

'I've also been speaking to the guy who runs the Strathnairn Local Heritage Group. He was really helpful.'

She pulled a sheet of notes out from the folder. 'He told me that the Clan MacBean has been strongly represented in the Loch Ruthven area for centuries. They lived shoulder to shoulder with the local MacGillivrays for much of that time, there being numerous instances of intermarriage and the like. But here's the interesting bit. He knew all about Ualas's family, who've been crofters in the area for generations. They are believed to be one of the longest surviving bloodlines of the clan. From what he told me, Ualas's father, Diamid, could trace his descendants back to before Culloden.'

She checked her notes again. 'Two of Ualas's ancestors, a James MacBean and his brother Calum, were both killed at Culloden, fighting with the Clan Chattan. Now, James' wife was a woman called Margaret MacGillivray, a cousin of the sixth MacGillivray chief, Farquhar "Fladhaigh" MacGillivray. With me so far?'

'I think so,' Neil confirmed, his brow becoming ever more creased.

'Good. Well, Margaret is reputed to have wet-nursed Alisdair MacGillivray, the guy in the portrait. Remember? She also had a son called Fionn, who was killed at Culloden, fighting side by side with his father and uncle. Now, it seems clan tradition dictated that when a woman wet-nursed a son or grandson of the chief, then her own male progeny were deemed to be brothers to that son or grandson…'

'And your point is, Holly?'

'My point is, sir… that there is a direct family link between Ualas MacBean's ancestry, and that of our victims. Remember what Selina told us about her ancestor Lachlan being great uncle to Alexander MacGillivray of Dunmaglass, who was killed by the Well of the Dead?'

Neil nodded in agreement. 'Okay, and it seems this generation of the MacBeans paid a high price at Culloden. Three of them killed and Margaret robbed of a husband, a son and a brother-in-law. Do you suppose something happened during the battle that has perhaps incited Ualas MacBean to seek some sort of revenge against the MacGillivrays, or Frasers as they now call themselves?'

'Very possibly,' said Holly. 'But what… and why now?'

Neil thumbed his lower lip whilst he mulled over his theory, then looked up. 'Because something has now come to light, only recently, that provides proof of what happened back then… or he's now *aware* that proof exists somewhere within Cullaird Castle.'

'Certainly something to think about,' Holly mused, having got up and backed away towards the door, all the while keeping an eye on the now sleeping spaniel.

'Why have you brought Tam into work, anyway? You know we're supposed to be seeing Selina Cope later?'

'Ah,' Neil uttered, 'that's the other thing I wanted to talk to you about. He pointed to the chair. 'You'd best sit down again.'

'I'm not looking after him for you,' she warned, lowering herself back into the chair. 'Not now that I know he's a sex offender!'

'No, it's nothing like that. I'm taking him over to my mother's after the briefing at nine. I need to speak about a situation that has arisen involving Cat.'

Holly now expected the worst... to hear that she'd left home for some other man – a friend of Neil's, perhaps. But she sat agape as Neil recounted the events of the previous three weeks, and the action he'd taken that morning.

'Jesus, you can't take all this on yourself, Neil. You need to tell Angus Hardie about it.' Then she winced when she realised she'd used his first name unwittingly, but it had obviously passed him by.

He brushed aside her concerns. 'I just want you to record this as an offence of stalking and allocate the enquiry to yourself. Don't worry, I'll do all the legwork. I've got it all in hand for now, and I just want to put a stop to it soonest. But if things become more complicated, I will tell him, you can be sure of that.'

He paused but saw that Holly was unconvinced. 'Look, if he knows, he'll feel obliged to take me off this case. He's struggling to find SIOs as it is, what with Alex off sick and David Chisholm on leave. Who else is going to pick up the reins?'

Holly looked at him deprecatingly. 'I know we're hard pressed, but I'm concerned you might take your eye off the ball, either on this job or whilst you're trying to keep Cat safe. It's so not right.' She shook her head and frowned. 'Why don't you pass it on to one of the divisional staff?'

'Because I don't want it becoming just another file sitting on a pile of other files, and that could be the reality of it. You know that as well as I do!'

He looked hard at her, as if to make his point. Then, when he at last detected a glimmer of empathy, he spoke again.

'I do need your help, Holly. Starting tomorrow night if nothing crops up with Op Cawdor. Can I count on you?'

She looked away towards the window whilst she considered his request, then her mouth widened into a grin and she turned back, her eyes glinting. 'As long as it doesn't involve the dog, okay? And if I feel things are getting out of hand, I'll tell Hardie myself. Deal?'

Neil grinned back. 'It's a deal.'

Holly pulled a pen out of her shirt pocket. 'Then perhaps you'd like to provide me with the details I need for a crime report, sir.'

Chapter Eighteen

The time-ravaged walls of Cullaird Castle glowed in the late morning sunshine, a honey-coloured stone tapestry, exalted by the steel blue sky.

Holly took a few seconds to absorb the scene before climbing out of the car and trudging across to the old oak doorway. She was alone on this visit. Neil had gone off with his dog to Cromarty, delegating her to impart the news to Selina that a suspect had been identified.

'So who is this Ualas MacBean?' Selina had asked, wide-eyed. Holly then explained the possible link to MacBean, whilst she and Nathaniel sat attentively and in silence.

She allowed them a few seconds to process what they'd been told, before asking, 'I know it's probably a silly question, but I don't suppose you've ever heard this man's name before, Selina, even in passing? His family did originate in this part of the world.'

The Copes both shook their heads.

'It's hardly likely, is it? Us knowing a man with a background like his?' Nathaniel remarked bemusedly.

'Well, you never know. Like I said, his family are local to Strathnairn. I wondered whether any of them had worked at the distillery, or on the estate at some stage, perhaps.'

Selina puffed out her cheeks. 'We'll certainly check with the factor and with Sandy Blair, Holly, but the name Ualas MacBean means nothing to me.'

She then offered Holly a biscuit. 'Shortbread?'

Holly politely declined, prompting Selina to return the plate to the table. 'So do you have any idea where this man MacBean is hiding out?'

Holly shook her head. 'No, not right now, I'm afraid, but you can rest assured we're working on it.'

She then changed the subject. 'Does the term ogham mean anything to either of you?'

They looked at each other then turned back to her, vacant looks on both their faces. 'No. What's ogham?' Nathaniel asked.

'It's an ancient Celtic alphabet, each letter of which is supposed to have some sort of spiritual link to a plant or tree. We believe the marks found scratched onto your parents' bodies, the ones Neil showed you the other day, were ogham symbols. In fact, we think they were both the ogham letter U, the letter associated with the heather plant.'

'U for Ualas, I assume?' Nathaniel commented astutely.

'Exactly,' said Holly. 'That's what we think too.'

'This all seems really weird,' said Selina. 'Ogham symbols and cat emblems. I can't think what all this has to do with my parents. It's like something out of the occult... and they were so straight-laced.'

'Well that's what we're paid to find out,' Holly responded, smiling. 'Why don't we talk about something else? How are you getting on with the administration side of things?'

'Slowly,' said Selina munching on a biscuit. 'Nat can't stay on up here indefinitely, so I'm keeping him busy whilst he's in residence. The family solicitor has been very helpful too. We're expecting him to call any time now, as it happens.'

'Then I'll be on my way and let you get on with it. The FLOs are looking after you, I assume?'

Selina swallowed the last of her shortbread. 'Yes, they've been brilliant. No complaints. So have the uniformed officers who've been patrolling around outside. They do like their tea, though!'

'Show me a cop that doesn't.' Holly was on her feet and making her way to the door.

'Let us know if there are any developments,' Selina called after her as she walked over to the car. Holly raised a hand. 'Will do.'

The Copes watched as Holly's Ford Focus receded into a haze of gravel dust.

'I know someone who has an interest in all that old pagan stuff,' she announced lugubriously, and without turning her head.

Nathaniel looked down at her, clearly perplexed. 'Who would that be?' he asked. 'I thought you'd never heard the term ogham before.'

Selina looked back at him. 'I haven't, and it doesn't matter who, Nat. Because there's no way they're involved in all this.'

Holly stopped at the bottom of the driveway, where she had a brief conversation with the two constables sitting in the police car, prominently positioned on the grass verge. Then she followed the narrow road northward, up the hill from Cullaird, that would take her across the sparsely wooded isthmus separating Loch Duntelchaig from the smaller Loch Ceo Glais.

At the junction with the B862, she would've normally turned right and taken the lonely road back to Inverness. But on this occasion she hesitated, looked both ways, and then swung the car around to the left, heading west down to Torness, and to Ualas MacBean's ancestral home.

The hamlet of Torness, if you could call it that, amounted to no more than a handful of small, whitewashed cottages. They stood dispersed amongst the mixed woodland plantations that flourished along the stony banks of the River Farigaig.

Holly had parked by the bridge that spanned the river and stood for a while, looking down into the peaty brown water that rushed, as clear as smoked glass, amongst the glacial detritus that littered its course. It was a peaceful place, Torness, and she could easily imagine the comings and goings of those plaided crofters who'd lived simple lives here, centuries before.

The sound of an engine close by compelled her to look over her shoulder. A work-soiled tractor was rumbling up the road towards her, slowing as it approached the narrow bridge. A massive bale of hay hung impaled upon the vehicle's muddy forks, above which she could just get a glimpse of the figure behind the wheel.

She raised a hand, signalling to the grey-haired driver to stop next to her. He duly obliged and peered down from his lofty cabin.

'Can ah help you, lassie?'

'You might be able to. Would you know where Leud Lainn is?' she asked, squinting into the late morning sun.

'Aye, it's back over the bridge,' he boomed over the drone of the diesel engine. 'Follow the road back a hundred yards or so, and it's up the track to the left.' He then followed up his directions with a warning. 'It's no more than a ruin now, mind.'

Holly waved her thanks, prompting the farmer to nod back as he pumped the accelerator of his blue monster and trundled away down the road.

The track that led up to Leud Lainn, the croft where Ualas MacBean had spent his early life, was steep and potholed. It curved away towards the river she'd been gazing down into only minutes before, which made sense, really. Those early crofters would have, by necessity, built their homesteads close to a suitable water source.

After a short walk, the roofless gables of the MacBeans' old home came into view. The farmer had been right; it was just a ruin. The interior consisted of four walls of loosely packed stone, and a blackened fireplace in which even now, traces of grey ash still resided.

Behind the ruin, the river's relentless babble filled her ears, unseen amongst the small conifers that creaked gently in the breeze. Back along the track, bare heather-clad hills framed the northern horizon. What a penurious existence their suspect must've endured as a child… and latterly as a young man, no doubt.

She took one last look about her and then followed the track back to the road, stooping by a fence post en route to recover the rotten remains of a wooden sign confirming that this was indeed Leud Lainn Croft.

A buzzard circled above her as she walked up the road to the car, mewing as if to announce that a stranger was present in the locale. She watched it for several minutes as it soared above her, maintaining its graceful patrol. Then the familiar sound of the tractor distracted her once again, and she wheeled about to see the old blue beast, now minus the hay bale, pulling up behind her.

This time the engine stuttered and died, and the tawny-haired driver jumped down, brushing hay from his shapeless corduroy trousers.

'Don't often see too many city lassies poking around out here,' he observed casually. 'You an estate agent or somethin'?'

Holly pulled out her warrant card. 'No. You're cold, I'm afraid. Detective Sergeant Holly Anderson, Northern Police Major Enquiry Unit.'

'Polis, eh? Don't see many of you lot out here either. Not since young Ualas MacBean stabbed his brother to death up yonder at that croft you've just been snoopin' around.'

'Funny you should mention Ualas MacBean,' said Holly, beaming. 'He's the reason I was "snoopin' around"… to use your very own words. Perhaps we can have a wee chat. I'm sure your tractor won't get in the way of any motorists for a minute or two!'

'What do you want to talk about, then? Has that bugger Ualas got himself into bother again?'

'Sorry, I didn't catch your name,' said Holly, initially ignoring his question.

'It's Danny Geddes. I run the farm back up the hill there.'

'I can't say for sure, Danny. Did you know Ualas MacBean personally?'

'Aye, we went to school together. Used to knock about a wee bit as laddies.'

'Tell me about the family. I don't know much about them, to be honest.'

Geddes rubbed his stubbly chin and leaned back against the wheel of his tractor.

'What's there to tell? Old Diamid's folks had the croft up there for generations. He was a hard man, was Diamid; a heavy drinker with a nasty temper on him. He'd beat the shite out of the three boys regularly, but never the three girls, thankfully.' He chuckled. 'The old bastard must've had some scruples, I suppose!'

'So there were six kids in all?'

'Aye, that's right. He lost his missus in childbirth, when she had Ualas, back in the mid sixties, as I recall. Diamid never forgave the boy for it. It was he who bore the brunt of his father's vicious tempers.'

'Must've been hard, bringing up six kids alone, though. There couldn't have been much money about.'

'They were pretty poor, sure enough. Diamid worked the croft and did a bit of labouring on the local farms hereabouts. They got benefits too, like.'

Holly pulled out a pack of chewing gum and offered Geddes some. 'What happened to all the kids, then?'

'Och, they all went their separate ways. Ann, the eldest, lives in Inverness, somewhere down Kessock Road, right at the end, looking out towards the bridge.'

'D'you recall which house?'

'There's an old caravan in the front garden. Got the saltire hangin' in the back window. The son stays in it.'

'What about the others, Danny? Do they live locally?'

The farmer's stumpy fingers returned to his jaw again, massaging it as if the gesture would aid his memory. 'Ruth's gone now. Cancer, it was. Died young, she did, poor lassie. Ceit and James... haven't a clue. They went off down south, to Glasgow, I think.'

He eased a stone out from the tread of one of the tractor's tyres, whilst looking down at her. 'Ualas killed Fearghas, of course, back in '91. The story goes... they were all fleein' one night after a session on their heather ale. They started arguing about clan stuff and Ualas ended up stabbing Fearghas five times with a corkscrew.'

Holly winced. 'All over a disagreement about *clan stuff*? What a tragic waste of a life.'

'Aye, you never criticised the MacBeans' lineage. One wrong word, and ye'd be run through. Diamid was the worst and Ualas was no better; a chip off the old block if there ever was one.' He chortled again, briefly. 'They'd always be on about this clan or that clan, and who'd done what at the battles with the English.'

'Tell me more about this heather ale. Sounds like it was potent stuff!'

Holly recalled her online research into the ogham alphabet and the connection to heather mead. Geddes now alluding to the fact that the MacBeans often imbibed the plant-derived drink had certainly not passed her by.

'It *was* potent,' he explained. 'The ale was a traditional drink that dated back to the Picts and beyond. *Leann fraoich*, they called it. Instead of using hops... because they wouldn't grow well in Scotland... they used the heather. The problem was the heather contained a substance that made it almost drug-like. Could send a man off his head, so they say.'

'Really?' she responded, feigning ignorance of the drink's side effects. 'I suppose it must've been like operating a home still, brewing this stuff.'

'Aye it was, true enough. In fact the first whisky came into being almost by mistake, when some of this heather concoction was being warmed over a fire in a clansman's home, many years ago.'

'I never knew that! So what did Ualas do with himself when he wasn't brewing heather ale or serving time in some penal establishment?'

'Och, he did a bit of labouring, a bit of poaching, this and that.' Geddes laughed, a sardonic laugh. 'He worked for my pa for a wee while, until he smacked him with a spade because his hours had been reduced. Did nine months for that little episode, in Porterfield Jail, back in 1985.'

'Do you recall when you last saw any of the MacBeans, Danny?'

Geddes stuffed his hands in his pockets and whistled. 'I saw Ann a couple of months ago, at the retail park out by the airport. The others... well, I havenae seen them for years and years.'

'They never come back to visit the old homestead, then?'

'Well, I've never seen them if they have,' Geddes replied, sporting a smirk that partially revealed several nicotine-stained teeth.

Holly shook his hand. 'Thank you so much for your time, Danny. You'd better move that tractor now, before a policeman comes along and gives you a ticket!'

She grinned as she marched off to her car, leaving the earthy Farmer Geddes staring incredulously at her back, wondering whether she was joking or not!

Kessock Road snaked its way out along a promontory between the River Ness and the Caledonian Canal. Behind low walls and neatly tended front gardens, a long row of plain little houses faced out onto the roadway, all with enviable views across the Beauly Firth towards the Black Isle.

Holly drove along slowly, searching for the saltire-adorned caravan Geddes had told her about. She eventually found it, just before the turning circle at the end of the road, where traffic was directed back towards the city centre.

Skirting around the caravan, she peered in through the small oval window. The vehicle was empty, so she proceeded up to the front door, searching for her warrant card as she went. She'd just located it, deep inside her jacket pocket, when a female voice prompted her to turn about.

'Can I help you, dear?'

A portly, middle-aged woman stood at the gate, holding onto the handles of a pushchair. Her features were verging on austere, an image accentuated by her straight red hair being tightly pulled back, as if to restrict it from having any life of its own.

Holly joined her at the gate and introduced herself.

'Cute wee laddie,' she remarked whilst eyeing the sleeping toddler in the pushchair.

'He's my youngest grandson,' said the woman, more interested in discovering the reason for Holly's presence at her front door. 'Is everything all right?'

Holly smiled at her. 'Aye, of course it is. Would you be Ann MacBean, by any chance?' She then noticed the woman's wedding band. 'Well, once, perhaps!'

'I'm Ann Reid, these days. But aye, I was a MacBean thirty or so year ago.'

'I wanted to ask you about your brother Ualas, Ann. Do you have a minute or two?'

Ann sighed. 'What's he got himself into now?'

'We're just trying to find him, that's all.'

'You'd better come in. I don't want the neighbours listening to this.'

Ann pushed the chair up to the front porch and released the young boy from its clutches. She opened the door and led the way into the sitting room. It was a cluttered little space, littered with toys and filled with a clothes airer, upon which copious amounts of children's clothes were suspended.

Ann sat down and commenced the awkward task of removing her grandson's outer garments. 'I've not seen Ualas for maybe five years,' she declared. 'He was in prison until 2003, for killing our brother, but you must know that already?'

'Aye, I do, Ann. So you've seen him since his release then?'

She nodded. 'When he was released on licence in 2003, he lived in a hostel up the road. He'd visit here regularly and I'd give him his meals, even though my husband didn't approve. But I realised that he'd changed in prison. He was always one to be on the edge of a fight, but he seemed more laid-back when he first came here after his spell inside. He'd found himself casual labouring work out on the farms around Croy, and I really believed he'd turned a corner. Then in the months after his release, he became more and more irrational. He'd not speak when he visited, almost as if he was trapped in his own wee world. I'm sure he was high on drugs half the time, if I'm honest. He kept complaining about burning pains in his arms and legs, but wouldn't go and see a doctor. Then he threatened my son-in-law one time. Over nothing at all, it was. That was it. I told him to go and not come back. He stormed out, not before he'd punched a bloody great hole in the kitchen wall. The day before Hogmanay it was, in 2005. I believe he then went down to Glasgow for a while, worked somewhere on the docks.'

She looked up and smiled weakly. 'That's all I can tell you, Sergeant. I haven't seen or heard from him since, thank God.'

Holly perched herself down on the sofa. 'I was talking to Danny Geddes over at Torness earlier.'

Ann's face lit up. 'Och, I havenae seen Danny for a good while. Is he keeping well? They were good pals, you know, Danny and our Ualas.' Her expression then darkened again. 'So tell me… Why are you looking for my brother?'

Holly explained, leaving out most of the detail, and giving the impression that any link to the Frasers' murders was merely a tenuous one.

Ann raised her eyes to the ceiling and shook her head. 'Oh dear, I hope to God you're wrong, Sergeant. But y'know what, he did have a thing about the folk who lived up at that castle. I remember asking him once what it was all about. All he'd say was they'd let their brothers down when it mattered. He'd never explain fully what he meant. Said I wouldn't understand. I do know there was supposed to be some connection between our family way back, and the people who owned the castle. The truth is, I never paid much attention to the stories my father told us, but Ualas always did. Hung off his every word, more's the pity.'

Holly stroked the little boy's head. 'Are you sure you can't remember anything else about your family's links with the castle, Ann? It may be really important.'

'No, lassie, I'm afraid I cannae. Sorry.'

'What about your brother James, and sister Ceit? Would Ualas get in touch with them, maybe?'

Ann laughed. 'I doubt it. James vowed he'd do the same to Ualas that was meted out to Fearghas if their paths ever crossed again. Which is unlikely, because James lives in Cyprus now.

Even I never hear from him. Ceit lives in Glasgow, and she's got no time for Ualas either. I'll definitely ask her, though.'

Holly felt it was time to call it a day as the wee boy was now becoming increasingly agitated that his grandmother was not giving him her full attention.

'One last question. Did Ualas own any type of motor vehicle last time you saw him?'

'You're joking, surely?' Ann riposted blithely. 'He never passed his driving test, for starters. Not that a small detail like that would stop him, I suppose. But no, he's always blagged a lift from some poor unsuspecting soul, or used the bus when he had the money.'

Holly left Ann Reid to attend to her grandson and drove back along Kessock Road towards the city centre. The wind-ruffled waters of the firth surged up onto the shingle just yards from the roadway, whilst the rising breeze buffeted the small police car, providing confirmation, if any were needed, that this would be a bleak place to live in the depths of winter.

Whilst she drove, a ribbon of thought fed Holly's subconscious. It slowly merged into a patchwork of mental images and spoken words that now convinced her more than ever that Ualas MacBean was indeed their man. That being the case though, she still seriously doubted that he'd acted alone!

More intriguing, though, was his obsession with the inhabitants of Cullaird Castle. His words to his sister resounded through her head time and time again... *'They'd let their brothers down when it mattered.'*

What did he mean? What did Selina Cope's forebears do to let their brothers down?

1746

Chapter Nineteen

Angus Mackintosh shuffled along, bent double so as not to reveal himself to Loudon's men on the roadway below. His master had summoned the ruddy-faced farrier to join him from his position further along the crumbling wall. Simon MacGillivray now spoke in low tones, not wishing to attract the attention of the other men present in the vicinity.

'I have a plan, Angus, but before I execute the scheme, I would value your countenance as my trusted lieutenant.'

Angus grinned. 'Then you have my ear, sir.'

Simon adjusted his position, then leaned across towards Angus so that he wouldn't be overheard.

'We will advance upon that wagon down there and attempt to capture it and its cargo. Are you up for it?'

Angus, his eyes full of trepidation, was about to protest but Simon raised a hand to interrupt his flow.

'Look, you see those chests down there? Well, it doesn't take a six-man escort to protect a colonel's finery, does it? No, there is something far more valuable within those chests, and I am disposed to discover exactly what those contents might be. The cart may also be used to carry the weariest amongst us home to Strathnairn. So what do you say, Angus? I implore that you respond promptly, though.'

Angus contemplated the stricken wagon, alongside which some of the soldiers had been deployed to lift the affected side. At the same time, the waggoner and the man in civilian attire attempted to position the wheel back onto its shaft. Nearby, the soldiers' Brown Bess muskets were stacked neatly in a cone whilst they strained to lift the afflicted vehicle. Only two men remained armed, standing nonchalantly and leaning upon their weapons as they watched the work progress.

'Is it really worth us getting ourselves slain for?' Angus asked, still gazing down at the scene before him.

'We'll be upon them before they know it, and we outnumber them by one, even if old John stays out of the fray. The pickings will be worth it. Trust me.'

'If you are so strongly inclined upon it, then I shall of course follow you, sir.'

'Good,' Simon whispered with a smile. 'Go and tell the others to muster here without delay.'

Angus crept away along the wall, whilst Simon pulled the two Highland dags from his belt and prepared them for firing. These highly decorated, claw-handled steel pistols would normally be discarded, having been discharged during the famed Highland charge. But today, Simon hoped that no such discharge would be necessary.

By the time he'd slung his powder horn back around his neck, he was surrounded by the eleven men who would accompany him on the raid. His briefing was short and succinct. They would advance down the slope until their dags were within range, whereupon he would then challenge the enemy to lay down their arms. He then directed that each man should ensure sufficient spacing from the next, and that any attempt to take up a musket on the part of the government men should be met with a pistol shot. Close-quarter action would be avoided at all costs, unless he directed otherwise.

With a nod of their heads, the little band of warriors slipped out from behind the wall and advanced furtively down the gentle slope towards their quarry. Their stealth was assisted by the dense heather and the absence of loose rock underfoot.

At a point no more than ten yards from the wagon, their presence was betrayed by some small sound that alerted the officer on horseback. He looked back over his shoulder, seeking the source of the distraction, and was greeted with the disconcerting sight of twelve shabbily clad men advancing upon him, some with broadswords drawn and studded targes raised to deflect any attack. Others carried dags at the ready, primed and cocked, their gleaming barrels all aimed in his direction. He wheeled his horse around to face the threat, and drew the gold-hilted sabre that hung at his side.

'Rebels,' he cried. 'Take up your arms, men!'

His words were lost, muffled by the explosion from Angus Mackintosh's long-barrelled dag that sent a lead ball powering towards him. It hissed past the horseman's head, missing the rim of his tricorne by several inches.

The other soldiers stood motionless and immediately raised their hands in surrender. Those still in possession of their muskets promptly dropped them and did the same.

Simon scrambled down to the road and approached the officer, fixing his eyes on him, and signalling that he should dismount.

'Good day to you, sir,' he declared, whilst leaning to bow in a gentlemanly fashion. 'I humbly request that you step down from your mount so that we may converse face to face.'

The officer looked about him, and seeing that his company had chosen not to resist, he nervously pivoted his sword hilt downwards and offered it to Simon in surrender. Once disarmed, he dismounted and stood glaring at the young Highlander.

'What is this about, sir? What is your intention here?'

Simon ignored his enquiry and called across to Angus. 'Round up these treacherous Campbells and ensure they are fully disarmed. Then detain them away from their weapons whilst we conclude our business here.'

He pointed in the direction of Croy. 'One of you lads… keep watch for any horsemen who may return to assist these gentlemen.'

When the clansmen moved in to comply with the request, the soldier who'd been riding with the waggoner drew his sword and lunged forward towards Conal Mackintosh. The burly Highlander sidestepped the thrust and grasped his assailant by the collar of his frock coat, throwing him face first onto the ground. When the muddied soldier rolled over, he found himself staring up at the wavering blade of Conal's broadsword. There was a flurry of laughter from the other Cullaird men, a response that infuriated the redcoat officer. He turned to Simon, his face puce with rage.

'How dare you, sir. You and your unruly band of rebels will surely hang for this misdeed.'

Simon turned his head to face the officer; it was a slow, lingering turn, clearly demonstrating his contempt for such threats. 'And by what name does my judge go by, sir? So that I may l know exactly who pervades my soul with fear and causes me to tremble?' He shook his hand mockingly.

'My name, sir, is Captain Henry Asquith, Paymaster of Barrell's 4th Regiment of Foot.'

'I see. And the little man in his black finery… who would he be?'

The 'little man' himself spoke up. 'I am Mr William Cochrane, the Colonel's Regimental Clerk, and the poor fellow you have sprawled across the ground there is Sergeant William Dunn, the Regimental Paymaster Sergeant.'

'Well, gentlemen, thank you kindly for the introductions. Am I therefore to assume that these here locked chests contain the cash that pays your regiment's salaries?'

Asquith said nothing, preferring to scowl at Simon as he drew his dag and walked across to one of the battered leather chests. There followed another loud report as the pistol discharged, sending a brief plume of smoke issuing from the flintlock's pan. The brass lock disintegrated, leaving the lid of the chest slightly ajar. Simon tucked the dag into his belt and drew his sword, inserting the point under the lid and flipping it back. What he saw caused him to step back in awe. His pale eyes feasted themselves upon the flash of gold that effused from within the chest. It was filled with coins, guineas, half guineas, and even five-guinea pieces. They lay piled to the rim... a quantity of cash that few men living north of Edinburgh would ever see, let alone amass during their lifetime.

'Well, well, Captain Asquith, I do believe that I have never seen such an agreeable sight.'

He pointed his sword in the direction of the other chests that lay upon the wet ground.

'Am I to assume that these coffers contain riches in equal measure?'

Asquith looked down at his feet. 'Some, yes. The remainder contain the regimental silver and some personal belongings pertaining to Lieutenant Colonel Sir Robert Rich, my commanding officer.'

Simon turned to William Cochrane. 'Tell me, Mr Regimental Clerk, sir, what is the total value of your cargo here today?'

Cochrane looked across at Asquith, who, with hands clasped firmly behind his back, continued to stare down at his muddy boots, whilst he teased a stone out of the soil with his left foot.

'I would wager… upwards of twelve hundred guineas,' Cochrane confessed. He looked away, his face clearly displaying the disgust that he felt, having to disclose such a truth.

Simon puffed his cheeks. 'Then we shall do a deal, sir. My friends and I will relieve you of said chests and this here cart to carry them upon. In return, we will offer each of you quarter, and allow you to rejoin your regiments unharmed. You may then personally explain to Lieutenant Colonel Rich why he has nothing from which to sup his port at the end of the day. If he survives that long, of course.'

He paused, before pointing back along the road.

'But first I require that you walk east, back to Nairn. I will leave men posted nearby to ensure that you comply with this condition. If you return this way before sunset, you may find that your days are ended abruptly upon this moor… Understand?'

Cochrane nodded eagerly, then blabbered, 'That sounds eminently reasonable. I thank you, sir. What say you, Asquith?'

Asquith looked up, and raised his arms in a gesture of reluctant acceptance. 'It seems that we have little choice in the matter, and may I enquire who it is who offers us quarter in this charitable fashion?'

Simon smiled and shook his head. 'That is not an enquiry to which I may honour you with a response, sir. You may only know that we are allied to His Royal Highness, Prince Charles Edward Stuart, and that we accept this gracious gesture on his behalf, so that we may continue the struggle to free our homeland from the tyranny inflicted upon us by the House of Hanover.'

Simon turned to the waggoner.

'From where do you hail, my young friend?'

The scrawny youth pulled his bonnet from his head and

clutched it nervously to his front. 'Auldearn, sir, back beyond Nairn.'

'Aye, I know of it. Then return to your home, boy, and accept my apologies for the loss of your cart. Is the wheel now properly repaired?'

'Yes, sir. It should cause you no problem along the way.'

'Good. Now wait with me a moment.'

He turned to Asquith.

'Captain Asquith, you may now commence your march to Nairn. It has been my pleasure to be acquainted with you.'

Asquith scowled again and prepared to climb up onto his mount.

Simon wagged his finger at the Englishman.

'No, no, Captain! The walk will do you good. I will take the horse off your hands.'

Asquith released the reins, his face rigid with barely contained rage. He pointed at Simon. 'You *will* hang for this, you impudent fellow. Mark my words.' He then marched off towards the group of soldiers who were waiting to depart.

Once out of earshot, and content that none of the redcoats were observing him, Simon scooped up several golden guineas from the open chest and pressed them into the young waggoner's muddy hand.

'Secrete these well, boy, and all in your village will be blessed with a cart!' He smiled and patted the youth on the shoulder, then looked on as he turned and jogged away towards the soldiers.

Having watched the dejected little group of crimson-clad men slowly fade into the distant landscape, Simon climbed up onto Asquith's horse and urgently issued instructions to his covey of clansmen. Two were sent up to the wood to collect John Shaw, whilst the remaining group loaded the heavy chests back onto the cart.

It was a little after ten o'clock when they headed off back

towards the dirt road that hugged the Moray coastline to the north of the Culloden Parks.

Simon rode alongside the wagon, which was now carrying all eight chests. Ahead, a small group scouted for government patrols and two men walked some way behind, bringing up their rear.

From his vantage point, Simon could clearly see across the fields that bordered the firth, and out to the Royal Navy ships that lay at anchor beyond. From the south, he thought he could hear the strains of the pipes drifting down from the moor, accompanied by drums beating from somewhere to his rear. He imagined the ragged line of Highlanders, supported by their allied regiments formed up across the ridge beyond. The image was clear in his mind, and for some reason he was drawn to their eyes, straining against cold and fatigue to catch a first glimpse of the men who marched behind the drums, men formed up in faceless ranks of crimson, blue and heaven knows what other colour, whom they must surely engage in the coming hours.

In many ways, he wished that he was with them, standing shoulder to shoulder with the men of Clan Chattan, waiting for the order to charge across the heather and into the enemy lines, where close-quarter combat would be waged amongst the smoke of battle and the screams of the dying. It was an ancient tactic, and one that the Highlanders had used to deadly effect during previous spats with King George's men. But today would be different. The ground underfoot would be treacherous and difficult to run across. Furthermore, they would be hemmed in between the dry stone dykes that flanked their lines, features that the enemy would surely utilise to their advantage. There was also talk of the government infantry battalions being ruthlessly drilled in the use of the bayonet; to thrust at the man attacking their colleague to the right, thereby exploiting the area of his torso unprotected by his heavy targe.

No, this was going to be a disaster and Simon was not prepared to expose his men, his friends, to such pointless carnage.

Conal Mackintosh looked up at him from the waggoner's bench at the head of the cart. He held the reins loose, allowing the powerful dapple-grey mare that was drawing the vehicle to amble along at a leisurely pace.

'Do you not think we should've left men to prevent the Campbells and their officer from turning back, sir?'

Simon looked down at him and grinned. 'Och, no, Conal. I'll wager they'll be more than happy to be marching away from the field of battle with their gizzards intact. Besides, it's not *their* wealth that's been looted, is it?'

Conal chuckled. 'No, that's true enough.' He thought for a moment or two, and then spoke again. 'So now that we have embarked upon this admirable contrivance, what do you see as its eventual outcome? Are we all to become wealthy men?'

'Fear not, young Conal. I will see to it that you and your family are properly provided for. But, sadly, I must disappoint you. The bulk of this hoard will be secreted at Cullaird until we are acquainted with the outcome of today's engagement and its aftermath. Then we will use it as a war chest; to underwrite the ongoing struggle from the safety of our remote glens. From there, we can undertake military operations that are suited to our own strengths, operations that will in time erode the efficiency of a standing army such as that of Cumberland.'

Conal looked sombre. 'Do you foresee defeat today for our forces then, sir?'

'Sadly, Conal, I do. There are many who share my view, including Lord Murray, but regrettably, the Prince has become infatuated by his Irish mentors, and so our influence is much limited. You must trust me that my lust for the fight is as strong as any man's, but a warrior cannot fight with his sword arm tied behind his back, and that is what I fear for this forthcoming engagement. No, Conal, we will fight, but on our own terms and in our own time.'

They travelled along in silence for a while, the sounds of the wind and the squeal of the cart's wooden wheels replacing those of human conversation. Sleet had begun to fall, prompting Simon to wonder how his comrades were faring up on the moor. Whatever was to come, he wished them well.

The journey to Cullaird was around twenty miles from their current location. They struggled on with the wind at their backs, and reached the outskirts of Inverness around one o'clock, the going having been slower than they'd hoped. At the fork with the track that curved away back towards Culloden House and Drumossie Moor, they met a steady stream of pedestrians making their way towards the field where the battle was expected to take place. They were spectators, eager to catch a view of the spectacle when it came: the old, the young, women and children. Simon led the way through the crowd, a little sickened by the macabre nature of their outing. Some folk hurled insults at the little group escorting the cart. *'Yer goin' the wrong way boys,'* and *'What's this? Has German Geordie paid you off or somethin'?'*

The Cullaird men stared ahead, not wishing to provoke the crowd, and not wishing to take the bait, finally leaving them behind. In the quiet that followed, they heard the first cannon shot. Ironically, it was a British three-pounder, captured at Fontenoy and delivered to the Jacobites by the French. Shortly after, another report boomed in the distance. There was a pause, then a much louder fusillade from multiple cannon, the reply from the Royal Artillery's ten guns. And so the Battle of Culloden had begun, the last pitched battle ever to be fought on British soil.

Simon's men clustered around the cart as it clattered through the narrow streets of Inverness. The place seemed almost deserted, with only a few local people going about their business as normal. They fixed the little band of men with surprised glares, as if to question, like those heading out to the moor, why they were not up on the battlefield fighting with their clans.

In the centre of the town, they turned south, onto the Fort Augustus Road. Cullaird... and home, was now less than fifteen miles away.

The light was fading when they sighted the eastern tip of Loch Ruthven, steely grey and nestling between the gentle braes of Strathnairn. The cart track at the head of the loch passed by the tall stone pillars that marked the gateway to Cullaird Castle. Simon wheeled his horse to the right, between the pillars, and proceeded along the avenue of Caledonian pines towards the ancient edifice itself. Several minutes later, the castle came into view, a sturdy L-shaped fortified keep or fortalice, its honey stone walls six feet thick and soaring to over eighty feet high. Each corner was adorned with a small round tower, above which a cluster of chimneys projected from a dark slate roof.

The castle had stood on this site since 1540, originally the home of Duncan Mór, Earl of Strathnairn, and a MacGillivray through marriage. It had later been appropriated by the clan chief in the 1670s and had been granted to his half-brother Lachlan as his family seat. Now it was the home of Lachlan's grandson, Simon, and his attractive wife Meg.

Meg was standing in the open doorway when the cart was drawn up in front of the castle. Her waxen features communicated no sign of emotion as she watched the men arrive. She kept her arms tightly folded, other than to periodically sweep away the long strands of auburn hair that fell across her brow.

Simon climbed down from his horse and marched across

to greet her. He embraced her slender form, but received no reciprocation.

He stood back, surprised. 'Are you not pleased to see me, my love? I am returned to you in one piece, as are these gallant laddies who followed me up to the moor.'

Meg looked him up and down suspiciously.

'You seem muddied but not bloodied,' she observed. 'For that I am grateful, but I have news to impart, of which I suspect you have no knowledge, news that cannot be graced with good cheer.'

Tears beaded in the corners of her guileless green eyes and tracked slowly down her cheeks.

'What is it, lassie? Tell me. Do you have news of the battle?'

She nodded, then threw her arms around him. 'You weren't there, were you? Thank the Lord.'

He nestled his chin into her cool neck, his smile now gone. 'What have you learnt? I must know.'

Meg sniffed back the tears. 'Our boys were struck down like rats, hundreds of them. It seems they stood and waited in line whilst the government grapeshot shredded their limbs, and then when they finally charged, most fell before they reached the redcoats' line. Those that did were cut to pieces by bayonet and sabre. The Chattans fared particularly badly.' She sobbed again whilst he took it all in.

'Who has delivered this news so quickly?'

'One of the farm boys from Dunlichity. He found himself a horse and rode hard from the battlefield but an hour ago.'

Meg looked into his eyes. 'Your cousin Alexander is dead, Simon. So is Gillies MacBean. Fraser of Inverallochie also fell, and Cameron of Lochiel too. His ankles were shattered by canister shot during the charge.'

Simon paled, and his eyes glazed. He tore his bonnet from his head and threw it onto the ground, then squatted next to it, reflecting upon the news.

He looked up at her forlornly. 'And what of the Prince? Is there news of his fate?'

'He was seen being taken from the field by his escort.'

'Unharmed?'

'Aye, as far as I know.'

Meg looked down and placed a comforting hand on his shoulder. 'Where were you, Simon, not to know of this?'

He rose stiffly and placed his hands on her shoulders. 'It is a long story, my love, and I will share it with you all in good time, when we have unloaded these chests and secreted them properly. I knew this day would end like this. There could have been no other outcome, engaging Cumberland's forces up on that wretched moor. I suppose I may feel blessed that I have brought my boys home safe to their families.'

Meg raised her hand and placed it upon his. 'Whatever action you deem necessary to take, you must accomplish now, and with haste, as I fear the redcoats will be sweeping west to apprehend those who were able to flee.'

She turned on her heels, her long skirts swirling about her as she marched away towards the door. Then, suddenly she halted and looked back.

'What is contained in those chests that is *so* important that you forsook your duty to stand in line of battle with your neighbours?'

Simon smiled. 'Gold coin and other treasure, my love, a great quantity of it. So much that we will be able to rise up from this defeat, and continue the struggle from the hills.'

Her eyebrows lifted enquiringly. 'And pray, who is the poor unfortunate who has mislaid such a hoard as this?'

'German Geordie, of course, my love. Who else?'

2010

Chapter Twenty

Cat had been adamant that she was going to catch the bus again that morning.

'I can't rely on you every day, Neil,' she'd protested as she scurried from one room to another, seeking the hairbrush that she'd deposited somewhere and now couldn't find. 'I don't want you getting overprotective, especially now that we've had no contact from that weirdo since Monday.'

Neil followed in her wake, coffee mug in hand. 'That means nothing, Cat. Remember, I want to know if you see anyone you're not happy with, okay? And I mean *anyone!*'

'Message received and understood, Captain,' she replied churlishly, dropping the brush into her bag.

But Neil hadn't finished. 'You know that Holly will be following you home tonight, don't you?'

'Aye, and you're going to follow Jack Guthrie at the same time. Just be a little subtle about it, eh?'

She stopped in her tracks. 'So what does this Holly Anderson look like, Neil? You'll have to introduce me sometime, you know.'

'Tonight is not the time for introductions. In fact it's best you don't know what she looks like. I don't want you giving the game away, trying to spot her in the crowd.'

Cat grinned. 'I'll spot her, don't worry. You lot always stand out like sore thumbs.'

Neil shook his head, prompting a peck on the cheek from her as she opened the front door. 'Don't forget to check on Tam,' she called out as she hurried up the path.

Neil watched her go. He knew that this ostentatious display of courage by Cat was only skin-deep. Both of them were deeply worried, and so now was his mother and his usually unflappable Uncle Euan over in Cromarty.

Cat had to run to catch the bus. It was standing in the bay, waiting, its nearside indicator still blinking as she trotted alongside and jumped up onto the step. Out of breath, she presented her pass to the young man sitting behind the wheel.

'That was close,' he advised, with a toothy grin.

'Aye, it was. Thanks for waiting.'

'No worries,' he responded turning his attention to the road ahead.

Cat had spotted Maureen Cameron sitting immediately behind the driver. She slumped into the seat next to her and they exchanged smiles.

'Haven't seen you for a few days,' Maureen remarked. 'I thought you were sick or something.'

'No, nothing like that.'

Cat leaned towards her fellow passenger and continued her answer in a more hushed tone, conscious of the other passengers sitting around them.

'I've been having a few problems with a nuisance phone caller,' she said, not wishing to go into too much detail. 'Neil's been taking me into work the last couple of days.'

'All right for some, having a copper as a boyfriend,' Maureen joked. 'I wouldn't mind having your man as a bodyguard!'

Cat flushed slightly. 'Well, he's on the case now and seems

to have a few ideas, but personally I doubt whether he'll ever catch the miscreant who's behind these calls.'

'Sounds frightening,' Maureen added. 'You keep your wits about you, lassie.' Then she smiled and tapped the page of the *Hello* magazine that lay open upon her lap.

'Having said that, there are a few hunks in here who could stalk me if they wished.'

'It's not funny, y'know, Maureen,' Cat protested with a frown and a playful punch.

Neil and Holly sat in the staff canteen two floors above the MEU suite, feasting on bacon sandwiches. Neil stopped eating and checked his watch. 'She'll be at work by now. I told her to text me.'

He glanced across at Holly, who was concentrating hard on repacking a wayward rasher of bacon between the two slices of bread she was holding.

'Still happy to follow her home tonight?'

Holly carefully returned the sandwich to the plate and eyed him casually.

'More than happy, sir. Look, I'm sure you'll get a text any time now. Patience is a virtue, they say.'

She picked up the sandwich again and was about to take a bite when Neil's phone buzzed. He picked it up, and read the content of the message that had just arrived. Then he sighed, as if a heavy burden had been lifted from him. 'She got there okay,' he muttered.

Holly swallowed hard. 'Told you so.' She tapped the witness statement lying on the table. 'That's Cat's, I assume?'

'Aye, we did it last night. It covers everything since the night she first encountered that hoody over at the leisure centre.'

Holly slid the document towards her and began reading between sips of coffee.

'So the only suspect is this Jack Guthrie, then?'

'I'm clutching at straws, I know.' Neil sighed. 'But he's been paying Cat a lot of attention lately. It was her who flagged him up in the first place, and I don't particularly like him either, if I'm honest.'

'So that's him definitely in the frame, then,' Holly retorted, straight-faced.

But Neil was adamant. 'Well, I want to have a look at him, whatever.'

Holly shrugged. 'Okay, I'll pick Cat up outside her office and keep an eye on her all the way home. Then perhaps when you get back, you can drop me over to my place?'

'My pleasure. It might take me a wee while to get back from Fortrose, though.'

'No worries. I'll have a snoop about in the vicinity of your house whilst I'm waiting. This guy's obviously done the same, and taken photos of Tam sitting in the window.'

'Aye, I know. I've spoken to the neighbours, by the way. You can tick the house-to-house box on your crime report.'

'Anything from them?'

'Nope, they're all out at work during the day.'

'No geeks with CCTV living in your street, then?'

'This is Westhill, Inverness we're talking about, not Beverley Hills you know!'

'I was just asking. Settle down.'

Neil grunted. 'Sorry. Fair question, I suppose.'

His work phone then rang again. This time it was Adam Carnie, the pathologist.

'Morning, Neil. Got something to get your sleuthing juices going.'

'Oh really, Adam? Tell me more.'

'We've had the toxicology results back on Duncan Fraser, most of which I pretty much expected. The interesting thing is, there were traces of ergot alkaloids present in his blood…'

'Ergot alkaloids… what on earth are they?'

'In policeman-speak, Neil, they're a group of a naturally occurring chemical compounds. They're produced by a variety of organisms, such as plants, fungi, bacteria, and animals. You name it. The type we have found in the samples taken from Duncan Fraser are produced from a fungus of the genus *Claviceps*, which is found mainly on rye and associated grasses.'

'And that is interesting because, Adam…?'

'Well, these alkaloids can cause ergotism in humans. Severe pathological syndromes such as hallucinations, irrational behaviour and suchlike. In fact ergot contains both lysergic acid and ergotamine, the precursor to the drug LSD! Long-term exposure to this type of fungus will really mess you up.' He paused to take a breath. 'Physically it can cause burning sensations in the limbs, gangrene and eventually death. In fact, in the Middle Ages they called it St Anthony's fire, after the monks who tried to treat people suffering from the horrendous effects of ergotism.'

'I'm in danger of becoming confused here,' Neil protested. 'So what are we saying? That Duncan Fraser was some sort of druggie?'

'Well he either consumed the fungus deliberately, as you suggest, for its narcotic effect. On the face of it, that seems a little drastic in this day and age, let alone by a pillar of the local society like him! *Or* he's consumed something unknowingly: grain… wheat, perhaps. Something that's been unwashed and contaminated with ergofungus. Which was quite a common occurrence in days gone by—'

'But not in modern times?' Neil interjected.

'No, of course not. The only other possibility is that the fungus was introduced into his body against his will, but that seems unlikely too. Like I said just now, any harmful effects would only occur after long-term exposure, so there'd seem little point forcing it into him!'

. Neil thought for a moment, then he looked across at Holly, as if something within her had provoked his next question.

'What about heather? Could this ergofungus grow on heather?'

'Without a doubt, dear boy. Have you not heard the words of the poem by Robert Louis Stevenson?'

'Go on. I'm sure you're going to enlighten me, Adam!'

And with that he was off...

From the bonny bells of heather
They brewed a drink long-syne,
Was sweeter far than honey,
Was stronger far than wine.
They brewed it and they drank it,
And lay in a blessed swound
For days and days together
In their dwellings underground...

The line went quiet, although Neil could hear the pathologist's trademark chuckle, somewhere in the background.

'Nice little ditty, eh? You know, heather ale has been consumed in our beloved land for over 2,000 years. In fact the Picts drank it as a magic potion, to give them enhanced courage and the warrior spirit that was so frightening to the Romans.'

'Well, thank you for that rendition, Adam. Very interesting. Holly was telling me all about this heather ale. Apparently our suspect was rather partial to it!'

'Well, there you have it then, Neil. The noose is tightening, eh?'

There was another, louder guffaw, forcing Neil to jerk the phone away from his ear and frown.

'I'll send the full report through to Fraser Gunn. Still a couple of tests to come back, so I'll be in touch.'

Neil thanked the congenial pathologist for his call and slipped the phone back into his pocket. He then related the gist of his conversation with Carnie to Holly.

'Do you know what? I reckon MacBean got Duncan Fraser tanked up on his weird brew, hoping that he'd spill the beans about whatever it is he was searching for in the castle.'

Holly nodded in agreement. 'I think you may be right, but there's something else that's beginning to concern me.'

'What's that?' Neil asked, whilst finishing off his bacon sandwich.

'If this guy Ualas MacBean is regularly getting stuck into a drink that's effectively liquid LSD, then he's potentially one very dangerous character. His sister intimated that he'd possibly been taking drugs when she saw him five years ago. She mentioned too that he'd had burning pains in his arms and legs, so the chances are he's been suffering from this ergotism! Which means he's been on this stuff long-term, so we need to catch up with him before he does any more damage.'

Neil nodded, whilst swallowing the last morsel of sandwich. 'Aye, good point. I'll speak to Hardie and Jardine. I think the time has come to advertise our interest in Ualas Diamid MacBean more actively. Particularly through the media, locally and nationally.'

That afternoon, Neil visited Alex Brodie at his home in Craigton, a small cluster of modern-looking dwellings located high on a hill above the Moray Firth. Neil always liked going there. The views from this hidden corner of the Black Isle were stunning on a good day... or any day, come to that! The Kessock Bridge predominated in the foreground, and the traffic noise was, in Neil's view, the only downside to living in Brodie's detached self-build. But such a disadvantage was, without doubt, eclipsed by the vistas to the south and west, encompassing the blunted snow-covered fells of the Cairngorms, and the jagged peaks away towards Lochaber.

Brodie had been discharged from hospital four days previously, and was sitting on a wooden bench to the front of the property, reading a newspaper. Neil sat down next to his ailing boss and took in the view.

'Good to see you up and about. How's the recovery going, then?'

'The cardiologist says I'm doing surprisingly well... be back behind my desk in no time at all, according to him.'

'In your dreams, you will be...'

Brodie's straight-talking wife, Jill, delivered two mugs of tea, one to each of them.

'He's going nowhere for weeks,' she proclaimed. 'And don't listen to him when he says the doctors have prescribed him malt whisky to thin his blood!'

She disappeared back into the house, whereupon Brodie leaned forward to check the coast was clear. He then reached behind him and produced a small pewter hip flask. With a broad grin, he unscrewed the cap and poured a generous measure into both their mugs.

'She knows bugger all about what's good for me. As Mark Twain once said... "Too much of anything is bad, but too much good whisky is barely enough." Very true!'

He tapped Neil's mug with his own. '*Slàinte*,' he murmured and the two men lapsed into silence, gazing out over the firth.

'How's the manhunt going, then?' Brodie enquired, thirty seconds later.

'Aye, we're making slow progress,' Neil informed him by way of introduction, before briefing him on the enquiry to date.

Brodie supped his fortified tea, listening intently. 'I'm glad you've stepped up security around the victims' family, but I predict that the Divisional Commander will be nippin' at yer heels before long, trying to scale down the cover you've put in place. Just fight your corner, son. Don't roll over when they start pecking away at you about value for money, and crap like that. The bloody phrase galls me. It's over-used management-speak for service on the cheap.'

Neil allowed himself a brief smile. That was rich, coming from the force's number one offender!

Brodie changed tack. 'I remember I was working nights over in Stornaway once. I was a uniformed sergeant then, newly promoted. A bunch of local peat cutters got stuck into that heather mead stuff one night. They almost trashed the town during a two-hour rampage. Two of my boys hospitalised, thousands of pounds of damage... absolute chaos, they caused. When you find that laddie MacBean, you make sure you're prepared for a scrap.'

Their conversation then turned to Holly Anderson.

'How's that lassie Pepper doing, Neil? I meant to ask you why you never allocated her to the FLO team.'

Neil sensed he was in the dock, but was quick to respond.

'She's as sharp as a knife, Alex, and feisty with it. I certainly rate her, and find it easy to bounce ideas off her. No, she's going places, and a chance to get involved in a job like this will do her no harm at all.'

'Umm, I admire your willingness to develop our fledgling stars of tomorrow, but the term "feisty" worries me. You see what I have to put up with in there.' He gestured towards the house, evoking another smile from his junior colleague. Neil wasn't going down that conversational route, though!

'And how's the lovely Cat getting on, whilst we're on the subject of the fairer sex?'

In the seconds between asking the question, and receiving Neil's evasive answer, Brodie must've picked up on a subtle change in the younger man's expression that told him all was not well. He cocked his head to one side. 'You're bullshitting me, son. Let's try again.'

Brodie's inexorable outburst had the desired effect.

'She's got a stalker, Alex.' He heard the words coming out of his mouth, but didn't recall forming them.

Brodie turned to face him. 'She's got a what?'

Neil told him everything. He hadn't planned to, because he knew what was coming.

'You can't run a double murder enquiry *and* investigate a stalking of your own partner. It can't happen, son.'

Neil was, in Brodie's words, more than willing to fight his own corner.

'Look, the only trained SIO I can hand over to is Hardie himself, as things stand. What happens then, if we get another major enquiry? Besides, the stalking may have already run its course. There's been no contact for a while. Holly's overseeing it.'

Brodie's eyes narrowed further. 'Like that's going to happen! And she's working on these murders too. She can't cover both. At the very least, one of the divisional boys should pick it up.'

Neil needed to placate him somehow. 'That's exactly what will happen if things take a turn for the worse. Believe me, it's in hand.'

'It had better be, or I'll speak to Angus Hardie myself.'

Jill appeared from the side gate.

'What's with the raised voices?' she asked, frowning. 'You're supposed to be maintaining a stress-free existence, Alex Brodie. I'll let you off with the whisky escapade…' She held out her hand. '… If you surrender the hip flask to me right now! Yes, I saw you dishing out the nips from the bedroom window.'

Brodie slapped the pewter flask into her hand, muttering under his breath.

'Cat's being stalked, and matey boy here wants to become a one-man bloody police force.'

Jill listened, arms folded. 'He's right, you know,' she deprecated. 'But you're a big boy, Neil, and you'll have to fight your own battles, because this "big boy" isn't getting involved!'

Neil was just about to protest that he was indeed fighting his own battles, when he received a text from Cat confirming her departure from work.

'I've got to go,' he said, getting up and handing Jill his mug. 'Thanks for the advice, both of you.'

'Let me know how you get on,' demanded Brodie, deliberately ignoring his wife's icy glare.

'Will do,' Neil retorted. 'And don't worry, this big boy won't be biting off more than he can chew!'

'You'd better not, son,' were his boss's final words as he paced the short distance to his car.

When Cat left the office in Baron Taylor's Street, she was alone. Holly had been watching from the pub opposite, and waited for her quarry to make some progress along the shadowy wynd, before falling in behind her.

Forty yards away, Neil maintained his position across the street, waiting impatiently for Jack Guthrie to emerge through the same glass doors. It was five minutes before his wish was finally granted, and long after Cat had disappeared from view.

Guthrie was in no hurry. He sauntered along between the parked cars, busily texting someone, obviously not Cat, according to the mobile phone languishing in his pocket. Neither was he exhibiting the behaviour of someone intent on stalking one of his colleagues!

A little further down the street, Neil checked that Cat's phone still contained charge, waiting, and hoping the thing would vibrate in answer to Guthrie's text. But it didn't.

One would've expected Guthrie to turn left towards the bus station when he emerged onto Academy Street, but to

Neil's surprise, the young man turned right... following the same route that Cat had just taken.

Neil quickened his pace, as indeed Guthrie had, having finished tapping out his texts. But disappointment soon followed. Instead of heading towards the bus stop where Cat would have been waiting, Guthrie hurried into Marks & Spencers across the road. Neil watched, whilst he purchased a T-shirt, one he'd obviously preselected, and then resumed his trek back to the main bus station.

Once the young man was safely ensconced aboard his usual bus for Fortrose, Neil finally accepted that he wasn't going anywhere other than home. He returned to his car, which he'd left parked behind the bus station, and sped out into Academy Street. He needed to be sure. No way was he going to be had over by Jack Guthrie. So he edged his way through the late afternoon traffic until he caught up with the bus as it lumbered its way out of the city centre, en route to the Black Isle.

By now, Neil was beginning to suspect that this whole exercise had been a waste of time, and he was to be proved right. Whilst he sat almost opposite the neat, modern bungalow that his target called home, Guthrie opened the white UPVC front door and disappeared inside, slamming it shut behind him.

Holly's experience had been equally disappointing. Cat's journey home had also been uneventful, and the young detective shadowing her could not identify anyone who remotely showed any interest in the tall, attractive blonde. Neil found her hunched against the evening chill, loitering at the end of the road.

'Well, that was a waste of time,' she remarked with some asperity.

'Okay, okay... wind your neck in, Sergeant. It was worth a try, surely?'

'Well, let's try on a Monday next time, shall we, sir? We might possibly get a result then, *and* my cat'll get fed on time!'

Neil felt a little irritated by her ill-tempered demeanour, but decided that he wasn't going to make a big deal of it. He did after all want to keep her onside. Perhaps she was right… she probably was! But if Guthrie, or whoever it was who was following Cat, was stupid enough to operate only on a Monday, knowing that Neil was now involved, he was indeed one cocksure individual!

'Home, then?' Neil enquired, looking across at his colleague.

She glowered at him momentarily, then broke into a smile.

'No, actually. You can take me to your house and introduce me to the woman I've just been following for the last hour… and then open a bottle of red wine to show your gratitude.'

Neil looked shocked. 'Okay. What about your cat?'

'My neighbour's fed him tonight. I was just making a point!'

'Point made, then,' said Neil, turning the car around.

Chapter Twenty-One

The task of winding up the estate of her prematurely deceased parents was never going to be anything but daunting for Selina. But with the help of her lawyer husband, and the family solicitor, they had made some headway, ploughing through the mountain of papers that seemed to be filed away in all corners of the Frasers' five-storey home. In fact, so engrossed had they become, they'd failed to fully appreciate the dwindling levels of food and household supplies that normally populated the cupboards and refrigerated appliances in the basement kitchen. Until, that was, breakfast time on that glorious late spring morning, when the first meal of the day had, through necessity, consisted of leftover cheese and after dinner biscuits, washed down with green tea, purchased on a date that neither of them really wished to dwell upon.

So, before the grandfather clock in the hall had struck nine, the couple had spoken to the FLOs on the phone and had driven out along the driveway, past the two bored-looking police officers stationed at the gate. Their destination was one of the large supermarkets in Inverness, and then lunch, out along the Moray coast somewhere.

By ten o'clock, the marked police car had gone too, back

to Inverness to drop off the second member of the crew, now required for football duty at the Caledonian Stadium, where Inverness Caledonian Thistle had a home game with Dundee.

At 10.20 am precisely, a mud-spattered green Land Rover turned slowly into the driveway and headed up to the castle. A tall man dressed in combat fatigues climbed out and knocked on the low oak door. When there was no reply, he returned to the Land Rover and nodded to the shadowy figure still sitting in the driver's seat. Together they slid an alloy ladder out from the back of the vehicle, and carrying it between them, hurried around to the rear of the building. Minutes later, the jangle of smashing glass sent the flock of finches feasting hungrily on the lawn scattering into the nearby trees.

The two men reappeared, returning the ladder to the Land Rover. The taller of the two men then hurried across to the door and let himself in with a key. With a wave of the hand, he disappeared inside, prompting the other to drive away at speed, churning up a cloud of dust.

The Copes had hoped to lunch at a favourite restaurant inland from the coast near Archiestown. But on their arrival in the car park, they'd been disappointed to find it closed for renovations.

'Bugger,' grumbled Nathaniel, returning to the car. 'We've come all the way out here too. Should've called first, I suppose.'

'Don't worry,' Selina called out. 'There's enough food in this car to feed all of Strathnairn. Look, it's nearly one thirty now: too late to start searching around. Let's go back to Cullaird and I'll cook.'

So they turned the car into the sun and retraced the lonely route back across the wild moorland and to civilization.

Just before three, they turned in between the two stone pillars at the end of the drive. The yellow and blue liveried patrol car was parked on the verge, as it had been when they'd left. Strangely though, it looked empty.

'They've probably gone for a walk. Must be boring just sitting out there all day,' Selina had suggested.

'We'll probably find them prowling about up by the keep,' said Nathaniel, looking left and right for their elusive guardians.

They swept around in front of the castle and came to a halt by the front door.

'You go in, and I'll bring the groceries,' said Nathaniel, climbing stiffly out of the Mercedes.

Selina did as she'd been asked, unlocking the heavy oak door and bobbing down beneath its low lintel, before vanishing into the castle's gloomy interior. Nathaniel proceeded to open the car's tailgate and began unloading the copious quantity of fully laden carrier bags they'd accrued from their shopping expedition.

The scream made him drop the bag he was holding. Liquid yellow yolk flowed from a cardboard egg container over the bag's remaining contents as he bolted for the doorway. He'd just reached the threshold and ducked to run through, when he was body-checked by the powerful frame of a man in a camouflage jacket. The force of the collision winded him momentarily, pitching him backwards onto the gravel. But as he fell, he glanced up into his assailant's eyes; dark, emotionless and surmounted by the odd twisted strand of light-coloured eyebrow. That's all he saw beyond the featureless green balaclava of a face. And now the man was running down the drive, carrying a large canvas holdall in his right hand.

Selina appeared in the doorway, pale and distraught, but unharmed. Nathaniel, relieved to see his wife, lay back for a second, struggling for breath. Then adrenalin began to surge through him, and he sprung to his feet.

'Are you okay?' he called out. She nodded as she tapped

out 999 onto the cordless landline phone. 'See where he goes,' she screamed, 'and find those bloody coppers.'

Nathaniel sprinted off in pursuit, trying to focus on the small mottled green figure that seemed to be diminishing in size as the distance between them opened up. The roadway came into view, and the figure halted, allowing Nathaniel to catch up. He pulled up twenty yards distant, just as the figure looked back at him. Nathaniel stared once again into those dark eyes. They were wide and anxious now, like those of the deer that roamed the hills behind him, peering out through the cutouts in the balaclava, almost willing his pursuer to advance.

But fear and a sense of self-preservation now gripped Nathaniel. What if this camouflaged figure had a weapon? What if he were to end up like his parents-in-law? Then his daughter's face flashed through his mind, a timely cue that the stakes were too high. So he stood his ground, temporising whilst they regarded each other. He could see the still-empty police car parked nearby and looked around him, resigned to the fact that Her Majesty's Constabulary were nowhere to be seen. Lying amongst the heather to his left was a long, grey conifer branch, the thickness of a man's arm. He picked it up and resumed his standoff, wondering how things would now play out.

Almost a minute had passed, probably the longest minute in his life, when the sound of a motor vehicle travelling at speed reached his ears. *Here come the cavalry, thank God*, he thought. But no… it was someone's cavalry, but not his. The green Land Rover screeched to a halt at the end of the driveway and the passenger door flew open. In the blink of an eye they were gone, leaving him alone to contemplate the view across to the silvery expanse of Loch Ruthven.

The adrenalin surge had now begun to subside with an inverse proportionality to the intensification of pain that now flowed through his upper torso. He dropped the branch and staggered cautiously towards the empty police car, nursing his ribs. The passenger door was slightly ajar and he could just hear the burble from the vehicle's main radio set. Still clutching at his aching chest, he threw open the door, mumbling, 'There's never a copper aroun—' But the words had not been fully uttered when he stumbled backwards, an expression of abject horror fixed upon his already pained features.

Lying across the two front seats was a uniformed policeman, his yellow protective jacket soaked in his own blood; its origin, a gaping wound to the back of his head. Nathaniel leaned forward into the car, grimacing at the deep crescent-shaped laceration. It seemed clear, even to a layman such as him, that the officer had been struck from behind with a blunt object, rather than a bladed one. Strands of fair hair crisscrossed the wound, compacted into the congealing jam-like gloop within its ragged edges. His trembling fingers felt for a pulse and to his relief he found one. It was faint, but the man was alive. Further reassurance came in the form of a pitiful whimper, evoking a softly spoken response from the shocked lawyer.

'You just lie still for me and I'll get you some help. Don't worry, you're going to be absolutely fine.'

He grabbed the handset from its cradle on the dashboard, and depressed the transmitter tab.

'Hello, hello… is anyone there? I need some help urgently.'

The speaker crackled back. It was a female voice. 'Unit calling, please identify yourself, over.'

He pressed the transmitter button again. 'My name is Nat Cope. I'm with your officer at Cullaird Castle. He's been attacked and seriously injured. We need an ambulance pronto!'

He released the transmitter, then depressed it again. 'You need to tell DCI Strachan urgently; this is related to your Operation Cawdor.'

There was a short pause, then a response.

'Understood, Mr Cope. Don't worry. Units are on their way to you. Your wife has called us already. Are the persons responsible for this still in the vicinity?'

'No, they made off in a green Land Rover. I didn't get the registration. There were two of them.'

'Okay. Thank you, Mr Cope. I'm arranging an ambulance for my colleague. Is he conscious?'

Nathaniel gave a brief summary of the officer's condition, then reinforced his demand. 'We need that ambulance fast. I don't know how long he can hold on.'

'It's all in hand, sir. Please just stay by the radio.' She then gave Nathaniel some first aid advice, but as it happened there was little more he could do for the policeman at that moment in time.

The minutes ticked by, whilst the policeman groaned and gurgled, and Nathaniel did his best to stem the flow of blood and convince the young man that he was going to survive.

Selina jogged down the driveway to find him. She stood in stunned silence whilst her husband recounted his experience prior to the discovery of the police officer. Eventually she removed her hand from her mouth.

'Is there anything more we can do for him?' she asked.

Nathaniel shook his head. 'He's pretty much lying in the recovery position, and the wound's starting to clot. It's the damage that's been done underneath that concerns me. I just wish that ambulance would get here.'

As if on cue, the steady drone of a powerful aero engine began to drift in on the easterly breeze. A bright yellow helicopter appeared overhead, hovering briefly, before sinking slowly onto a rocky terrace next to the road.

The Copes looked on as the bright yellow Eurocopter, operated by the Scottish Air Ambulance, settled amongst a vortex of swirling dust. Its rotors slowly swished to a halt, but not before two emerald-clad paramedics had leapt out.

They headed straight for the police car, carrying their bulky backpacks with them, a cue for Nathaniel to make way and return to hug his wife.

The pilot also climbed out of the aircraft, having called in their arrival and landing.

'The cops are hot on our heels,' he announced phlegmatically. 'Should see or hear them any time... You two okay?'

'Yes, of course, thank you for asking,' Nathaniel reassured him, still embracing Selina.

The pilot was right. In fact they came from all directions. An armed response vehicle and a dog handler from the direction of Loch Duntelchaig, and two equally garish coloured patrol cars from the opposite end of the lane. The subtle mid afternoon light, the type that photographers so love, had now been replaced by a pulsing blue glare, perpetrated by the strobe bars mounted on the various police vehicles.

From out of this blue effulgence, a burly police sergeant appeared. 'Perhaps we'd better get you both up to the castle,' he suggested. The officer was followed by the dog handler, a ferocious-looking man in his fifties with a balding head but kindly eyes, who was straining to control the long-haired German shepherd that danced excitedly around him.

'He's just happy to be out of the van,' said the now cheerful-looking handler. 'He knows he's going to work.'

'He's a bit late,' Nathaniel replied. 'Those thugs have long gone.'

'We'll put him through the property anyway, if you don't mind. Better to be safe than sorry.'

The four of them returned to the castle, and having established no known persons – or animals – were present in the building, the dog was subsequently unleashed. To the command 'Find him, Ben,' the wolf-like creature screeched with delight and hurtled through the front door.

Of course no one *was* present, and once the disappointed Ben had been reconnected to his leash, the sergeant escorted the Copes through the rooms, offering what sympathy and advice he could. 'Our scenes of crime people are on their way, as are the Operation Cawdor team, so please don't touch anything for the time being.'

'Oh, don't worry,' said Selina sarcastically. 'Our family are old hands at this now.'

She looked away, out through the landing window and watched as the yellow helicopter ascended above the trees, dipped its nose and hurried off towards Raigmore Hospital.

Neil Strachan had been visiting his mother when he got the call. He'd been out for a long walk with Cat and Tam, a rare interlude from the complex and exacting train of events that now seemed to be dominating their lives.

At least Cat's mysterious admirer had been keeping his head down, but now, as he tanked the MG back down the long straight on the A832 towards Davidston, he had more pressing matters to consider. Like what went wrong with the security measures he'd put in place at Cullaird Castle?

He felt his stomach tighten when he saw the police car encircled by scene tape. Its doors were open and two white-suited scene investigators were poring over its interior. A few yards away, the crew of the armed response vehicle stood chatting to another uniformed police officer. Neil waved as he passed, but he didn't stop and continued up the driveway to the castle, his features grimly fixed on the scene ahead.

When he pulled up on the gravel frontage outside the building, a conference was already underway beside several parked police cars. Holly was there with Aili Hughes, one of the FLOs, talking to Fraser Gunn and Lynn Cowan. The dog handler stood a respectable distance away, whilst Ben lay panting at his handler's feet watching the comings and goings with waning interest.

The talking stopped and heads turned when Neil heaved himself out of the little sports car.

'Afternoon, sir. I expect you want to know what's been occurring?'

'I know what's bloody well been occurring,' Neil reacted peevishly. 'This place has been turned over again, and now a colleague's been half beaten to death. What I *want* to know, is how that could happen? Are the Copes okay, Aili?'

'Aye sir, they're fine. Just a bit shaken up, that's all.'

'What about PC Irvine?'

'Critical but stable in the ITU at Raigmore.' Holly was the bearer of the bad news. 'Uniform supervision are dealing with the welfare side of things.'

Neil's tone softened a little. 'I'll drop by the hospital later on. Best you bring me up to speed then, starting with who was or wasn't here when this happened.'

Holly looked at Aili, hoping that she would take the lead.

'I'm waiting.' Neil was checking his mobile phone for a signal.

Aili began to mount her defence. 'Mr and Mrs Cope left just before nine this morning, to go shopping in Inverness. They told me on the phone that they were then going for lunch somewhere and wouldn't be back until after five. So the ARV was asked to pay passing attention, and I decided to stay in the office until they returned. I knew the uniform boys were still here.'

'One of them, not two. So what's all that about?'

'In a word, *football*,' said Holly. 'The duty inspector knew the Copes were out, so reduced the crew out here to one. To be fair, he was pretty strapped for staff.'

'Bet he regrets that now,' Neil snapped.

Holly didn't bother responding.

'Let's take a wee walk around the back,' Gunn suggested, in an attempt to diffuse the tension. 'I need to show you something.'

'Lead on,' said Neil, adjusting the collar of his anorak.

At the rear of the castle, Gunn pointed up to a small mullioned window, no more than twelve feet from the ground. The glass had been knocked out to leave a gaping hole.

'On the face of it, you'd think that was the point of entry. The thing is, I'm not so sure.'

Neil looked up, shading the sun from his eyes with his hand.

'Well, they would've needed a ladder to get up there, and if the Copes disturbed them, why isn't it still *in situ*? They must've removed it once they'd got in, before the Copes returned. Seems a little strange.'

He looked at Gunn, awaiting his response.

'Exactly, Neil. More likely, they removed it after they'd smashed the glass. You see, my theory is *they*... and we now know there were *two* offenders... broke this window, hoping that we'd think they got in this way and then exited through the front door... classic MO. But there's nothing to forensically support an entry through that window. No prints, no fibres on the jagged edges of the remaining window fragments and no footmarks or disturbance to the broken glass inside. In a word, this supposed point of entry is a sham.'

Cowan took up the explanation. 'The grass out here has been in shadow for most of the morning. It's still dewy in places, even now. So we'd expect some damp footprints on the stone floor inside, especially beneath the window. In addition to that, the Copes described the man they disturbed as being well built, which makes me doubt whether he could've got through that small opening. And to have done so without leaving any fibres... well, I just can't believe it.'

'What if the other guy was smaller?' Neil questioned.

Cowan smiled. 'Then my response would be the same. No disturbance inside and nothing at the point of entry. The accomplice would've needed to be no bigger than a leprechaun to get through that window cleanly without leaving a trace. No, in my professional opinion, no one got through that window.'

'Which means they got in with a key,' Neil concluded, his brow creasing in puzzlement. 'There's no other option, short of tunnelling, or being landed on the roof by helicopter!' The little group allowed themselves a chuckle. Iceman was thawing!

'The Copes took the large iron key with them when they left. The door was definitely locked,' Holly added. 'And there is absolutely no evidence of the front door being forced.'

'She's right. They would've needed a battering ram,' said Gunn.

'Like I said, not if *they* had a key,' said Neil. 'The sham point of entry was intended to put us off the scent.'

'You mean this is an inside job; the offenders have connections to the family?' Holly looked at him wide-eyed.

'In essence, yes. They've realised that we would quickly reach such a conclusion if there was no forced entry. Unfortunately, they've underestimated the deductive skills of our forensic colleagues here!'

He placed a congratulatory hand on Gunn's shoulder.

'Okay, let's go inside. Aili, get the dog handler to have a look around the grounds, just in case they've dumped a ladder anywhere.'

The FLO hurried off to brief Ben's handler whilst the others marched in line through the front door.

Neil's first visit was to the basement kitchen, where the Copes were sitting drinking tea with the uniformed sergeant.

'I'm so sorry this has happened again,' he apologised. 'Are you both okay?'

Selina placed the kettle on the Aga. 'We're fine, Chief Inspector, just in shock seeing that poor policeman. We're sorry too. We should've told your colleagues we were coming back early. Would you like some coffee?'

Mugs in hand, they walked from room to room, examining the intruders' latest efforts to find whatever it was they wanted to find. They also listened to Nathaniel's account of his brush with them.

As they walked, it became obvious to Neil that the search had been more thorough this time, as if no stone had been unturned: a search that must've taken some considerable time to complete.

When they reached the master bedroom on the second floor, Gunn motioned the little group towards the small arched doorway providing access to the laird's spy chamber. The door stood open, its bulky iron key still present in the lock.

Inside the room, a white-suited scene investigator was dusting the back of the door for fingerprints.

'Found anything of value?' Gunn enquired.

The pale marbled eyes located between the white hood and the surgical mask swivelled to meet his and the white head shook.

'Only more Marigold marks,' was his muffled reply.

Gunn frowned. 'We won't go into the room while he's working, but as you can see from out here, there is ample evidence in this room to support the theory that our intruders were searching for something that had been securely hidden.'

Neil poked his head into the bare stone-walled chamber. The room's chill found his nose, and he sniffed in response. Several of the heavy oak floorboards within the room had been prised away from the joists.

'They really were going for it this time,' Neil muttered

with a low whistle. 'They must've had some pretty heavy tools to do this. One of which probably ended up cracking PC Irvine's skull.'

He pointed to the wall on the other side of the chamber. 'Did *they* do that?'

'Aye, they did,' Gunn confirmed. 'They probably noticed the mortar missing from around that slab, and tried to get it out, to see what was behind it.'

'What is this room used for now, Selina?' Neil asked.

'Nothing, these days. My father used to keep his fishing gear in here once, but that's all. It's been empty for years. My ancestors used it to keep an eye on what was going on in the great hall below.'

She pointed to a group of round holes in the stonework of the opposite wall. 'Through those small spyholes in the wall over there. Paranoia was rife in those days, it seems.'

When they retreated into the bedroom, Neil gestured towards the large key, still in place in the keyhole.

'I don't recall that being in the lock, last time I looked in this room.'

'You're right,' said Cowan. 'It wasn't.'

'It usually hangs on a hook inside the fireplace, out of sight,' Selina added.

Neil and Holly glanced across at each other. 'Who would've known it was there?' Neil asked.

'Oh, various members of the family, household staff… maintenance people, I suppose.'

'So its location was no great secret, then?'

'No, probably not.'

'What about the key to the front door? Have you managed to compile that list yet?'

Selina shrugged. 'Sorry, I know you've reminded me on several occasions. It's not proving to be the simplest of tasks, I'm afraid! I'm going to have to speak to John, the factor, as soon as I can. I've tried to call him but there's no answer on his daughter's phone number.'

She raised her hands in a gesture of hopelessness. 'I don't really know how many copies are in existence, to be honest. Like I said, Ruth the cleaner certainly has one. She and her husband are the main keyholders, but you already know that. You know I have one, of course, me being the child living closest. There was always one in the back of the door, the one I took with me this morning, and I now recall there was a spare in my father's desk. That's still there. I checked. They're very old keys and pretty bulky, so I can't see there being too many others in existence.'

'Well, I wasn't sure initially, but it looks like someone used a key to get access to the castle whilst you were out this morning.'

Selina looked worried. 'So you're suggesting that whoever got in here today may actually be known to us?'

Neil looked unsure. 'It's possible. Having said that, a key may have been copied or passed onto someone previously. If the security of the keys has never been that tight… well, anything could've happened to one of them. That's why we need that list!'

'I'll redouble my efforts, Chief Inspector, and I'll ask around just in case any of the extended family has got one or has ever had one.'

Their tour of the house concluded, they stood in a huddle by the front door. Holly checked the alarm control box beside the coat hooks. Selina saw her looking and pre-empted her question.

'Yes, I know what you're going to say,' was her discomfited response. 'We forgot to set it before we went out. Sorry again!'

'At least PC Irvine may have heard it and called it in before investigating,' Holly mused.

Neil shot her a troubled glance. 'Aye, that's if he'd been

here when the system had been activated! But, you know what? I have a feeling it was the driver of the Land Rover who dealt with him, whilst the other guy got on with his work up here. They must've already broken in when PC Irvine returned from dropping his colleague off in Inverness.'

He turned to Selina, concern still etched on his face.

'Are you sure you still want to stay out here? In the circumstances, it may be better to stay a little closer to civilisation.'

'Absolutely not,' came the recalcitrant reply. 'I'm not being forced out of my own family home by these loathsome creatures. No, we're staying put. Decision most definitely made.'

She scanned the anxious faces before her, looking from one to the other.

'Surely they won't come back again. They must've looked everywhere for whatever it is they're after, mustn't they?'

'Fair point,' said Holly. 'They were probably in here for several hours on this occasion. Not only that, they were disturbed *again*. If it was me, I'd be giving up by now.'

Neil was not convinced. 'But *you're* not Ualas MacBean, are you?'

Then his features softened as he addressed the Copes.

'I understand your motivation to remain here. We will of course tighten up on our security arrangements and do all we can to catch up with whoever is behind this.'

He gestured towards their car. 'Come on, Holly, I need to get back to town. The duty inspector and I need to have a serious discussion about policing priorities!'

Chapter Twenty-Two

Daviot Wood
6.45 pm, Saturday 1ˢᵗ May

David was waiting for him when he pulled into the car park at Daviot Wood. The popular wayside picnic area was located next to the A9, just to the south of Inverness. At that time of the day, the site was practically deserted, a haven of peace and muted birdsong, where soft evening light permeated the treetops, falling upon the vacant picnic tables that stood scattered amongst the pines.

The tourist information centre, standing prominently by the car park entrance, was now closed, and the occupants of the only other vehicle present were studying a map that had been posted on the wall of the building.

Mack urgently sought a glimpse of David's car. It was not present in the main parking area, so he swung the Land Rover around to the left onto the forestry track that led off into the trees. Just a short distance further along, he found David sitting in his car listening to a CD. He'd parked in a clearing close to the picnic site, but well hidden from the traffic on the A9 that passed nearby.

Mack pulled up directly in front of the shiny-looking saloon, as if to prevent it moving off and escaping. Then he waited impatiently whilst David switched off the music and climbed out. His dark eyes followed the stocky little man as he walked around the front of the Land Rover and opened the passenger door.

'Mind if I come aboard?' David grinned.

'Just get in, will you? Ah haven't got long.'

David hauled himself up onto the running board and slipped in next to Mack. 'So, tell me. Did you have any luck this time?'

'Not much. They came back early again, the daughter and her husband. She disturbed your new pal, whilst he was still in the place.'

David looked across at him disbelievingly. 'You're joking. They were planning to be out all day!'

'So much for his so-called sources, eh?'

'Please tell me they're still breathing and walking. You haven't harmed them, have you?'

'Luckily for you, ah was driving this thing, or the situation may well have played out differently. As it happens, they decided not to take us on. Ah cannae say that for the polisman guarding the gate, though. He really kicked off, so ah had to take drastic steps to put him out of action.'

'How drastic, exactly?'

'Let's just say, if he survives, he's goin' tae have one hell of a headache.' Mack shrugged. 'Still… his choice.'

'Oh, for Christ's sake, this has to stop.' David looked ashen. He peered out through the windscreen, taking it all in, then asked, 'And you found nothing at all? No clues, no nothing?'

'Not a brass razoo. Ah'm just hopin', for your sake, we havnae missed the boat, my friend. My so-called partner in crime says he went over that place with a fine-tooth comb. He even jemmied up the floorboards in some of the rooms. Not a damned thing.'

'Did anyone see the Land Rover? What if they got a look at the number plate?'

'No chance. Trust me, the husband was too far away.'

'Surely the cops will be searching for this thing by now, whatever the case?'

'Dinnae worry, we'll stash it somewhere out of the way until such time we need it again. Perhaps change the plates again too.'

David wasn't so confident. 'I think we need to give up on it. At least we've had a go. There's no other option. The stash must've been found years ago, damn it.'

Mack turned and glared at him.

'Oh, no, ah havenae put ma future on the line just for you to say "give up on it"!' He smirked. 'No, I have a plan, but I'll need someone's help.'

David glared back at him. 'Whose exactly?'

'The daughter's. Up tae now we've been trying tae solve this fucking riddle ourselves. Perhaps it's time we enlisted some more help from the Frasers.'

David shook his head. 'Look, if *we* can't locate that stash, they're not going to be able to, are they? Duncan Fraser wasn't much help, and he lived there. Why would his daughter know any more than he did? Be realistic, man.'

'But neither he, nor she, have seen that letter, have they? So how can you say that? She knows that place better than any of us. She grew up there, so I'm told. Which means, if she's shown the letter and offered a wee inducement, she may come up with the goods, yes?'

'You're mad. She won't have a clue, I tell you. And what do you mean by inducement? Roughing her up I suppose, like her father?'

'We'll do whatever it takes, pal, anything that will focus her pretty little mind on the clues in that letter.'

David nervously rubbed the top of his thighs. '*We* doesn't come into this. You're on your own from now on, Mack.' He paused. 'Tell me you're not going to kidnap Selina Cope?'

Mack's eyes glinted. 'Like ah said, we'll do whatever it takes. Oh, and by the way, our wee mate is on board with it too.'

'Never. I don't believe it.'

'Aye, the persuasion thing worked on him a treat.'

'What do you mean, "worked on him"?'

'Well he's got a lot to lose, hasn't he? One anonymous phone call to the polis, and he'd be finished for good. Would you no agree?'

'But then he'd bring us down with him, surely?'

'Ah, but that's a big call tae make, just to get back at *us*. No, he'll play ball. Ah'm confident things won't get that complicated. He's far too focussed on saving his own sorry skin, believe me.'

Mack leaned across and whispered in David's ear.

'That brings me ontae you. If you want out, that's your business. But don't interfere in mine. Betray me and you'll discover that ah'm a man who holds a grudge for as long as it takes. Remember, even if ah end up inside, ah've still got plenty of wee pals on the outside who'll do ma dirty work for me.'

He sat back and smiled. 'So, if you're planning tae bail out, now's the time tae disappear back into yer wee hole.'

David swallowed hard. 'When are you going to execute this so-called plan of yours? Surely the police will be swarming all over the place from now on. They may even move the family out, to a safe house, perhaps.'

'Aye, ah'd thought of that. We'll have tae wait and see. One thing's for sure, ah intend to let things well and truly settle down before ah make any move. Time's on my side, you see, and our mutual friend will keep me right as tae the future movements of the lovely Selina Cope.'

David had no more to say. He opened the door and slipped out, taking a moment to look back at Mack, whose eyes were following his every move. He gently closed the door of the Land Rover before walking back to the sanctuary of his own car. Once safely inside, he started the engine and waited nervously for his partner in crime to manoeuvre the Land Rover out of his way.

Mack waited, watching David from behind his fly-spattered windscreen. Then, after what seemed to David like an age, he engaged reverse gear and rolled slowly backwards. The saloon flashed past the Land Rover, on towards the car park and out onto the A9. There, it turned to the north, and gained speed, merging into the queue of slow-moving traffic.

David looked in his rear-view mirror, unable to suppress the sensation of nausea rising in his throat. The last thing he wanted to see was that green Land Rover surging up behind him. But it wasn't there, so he began to relax a little. A mile or so to the north, he was relieved to come across a turn-off, and took it, intending to pass under the main road and then to head back south, down towards Aviemore. He negotiated a small roundabout, then took the southbound slip, his mind racing as he ruminated over what to do next. The reality was, there were few options, other than to put as much mileage between himself and Cullaird Castle as possible!

He accelerated back onto the A9, still searching the opposite carriageway for the Land Rover. Then he saw it, heading north at a sedate pace, being overtaken by several other cars. He flashed past it, unseen by Mack, who seemed content to peer out disinterestedly at the traffic ahead of him.

David exhaled deeply, then turned on the CD player and settled back into his seat to consider his position further. By the time he'd reached Moy, his mind was made up. He'd do nothing for the time being. He'd stay out of the way, well out of the way, until he knew that Mack actually intended to carry out his madcap plan. Then he'd have to make a decision. Let things happen, or pass on a warning to the Copes, perhaps. He knew full well that Selina would not be able to provide the information that Mack wanted. The whole thing had got way out of hand, and all he could do now was to take measures to avert a further needless tragedy.

He did still have one card up his sleeve, though. Their 'mutual friend' was as much in *his* pocket as he was in Mack's, and David had no doubt that he could still exert a good deal of influence over him too!

Mack pulled up outside the cabin, slamming the Land Rover door as he got out. He'd been brooding all the way back from his meeting with David, and had expected better things from the wee man. It was *him* after all who'd instigated this quest for the so-called Cullaird hoard. But now, collateral damage had been done and he'd become jittery. The thing was, they needed David on side. It was him who'd lined up a buyer for the hoard, and they'd never get a better deal than the one offered! He shrugged, and with a wild swing of his booted foot, he kicked the door of the cabin open.

There was little furniture present inside, the largest item being a battered leather sofa. He sank into it heavily, releasing a cloud of dust, and began thumbing his chin, mulling over his current position. Then he leapt up and went over to the small chest by the window. A cheap bottle of whisky, half empty, stood next to some binoculars on its ring-marked top. Mack twisted the cap off the bottle and sniffed the contents. When he read the label, his features crumpled. 'What sort of shite have you been drinkin', Ualas? No wonder you preferred that fuckin' heather stuff!' He took a long slug from the bottle, then returned to the sofa, dangling it between his fingers.

He must've sat there for twenty minutes or so, staring vacantly through the open doorway, and supping periodically from the bottle. Then he finally closed his eyes and allowed his head to fall back against the sofa. Something creaked repeatedly elsewhere in the cabin, no doubt due to the draft from the open door. Outside, the forest birds sang in accompaniment, producing a curiously effective refrain that eventually lulled Mack towards unconsciousness. The desire to sleep overwhelmed him, as if he were sliding slowly but surely from a large slippery boulder into a pool of deep, warm water. Then he woke abruptly, the dreamy sensation that had just gripped him instantly snuffed out. The sound of an approaching car engine had him on his feet in a trice. The blade of his stiletto snapped into place as he sought refuge in the shadow of the window.

A large expensive-looking car approached up the track, its tyres snapping the small branches that littered the route in from the outside world. It took him a few seconds to focus his eyes, even from the brief period of sleep he'd just enjoyed. But he was sure now. He'd last seen the highly polished saloon at Daviot Wood an hour and a half previously. It was David's car!

David's rotund form emerged from the vehicle and he stood by the open door, hands thrust deeply into the pockets of his trench coat. He called out. 'Anyone home?'

Mack appeared from the gloomy interior of the cabin, carefully retracting his stiletto blade.

'Not taking any chances, then?' David called over to him.

'Ah wasnae expecting any visitors. Least of all you!'

'I *wasnae* planning to visit myself, to use your phraseology.'

'So why are y'here, then? Ah thought you were heading south, so you could distance yerself from ma little plan.'

David took a few steps towards him. 'Because you need my help to offload the fruits of your labour, should you ever find it, of course. And I still want my share. Let's face it, you wouldn't even be looking if it wasn't for me.'

Mack gestured to him to enter the cabin. David hesitated, then stepped cautiously through the open doorway. He found Mack lounging on the dusty sofa, drinking from the bottle of whisky.

David remained by the door, keen to maintain a means of escape. He lit a cigarette and ejected blue smoke up towards the dusty rafters above his head.

'I started to think about things when I drove away just now. Realised I'm in this up to my neck, anyway: getting MacBean involved, planning the break-in to the castle… you name it. But let's be sure about one thing. I never advocated the killing of the Frasers and I don't wish any harm to befall Selina Cope. That's not why I got involved in this. If your intention is merely to put the frighteners up her, perhaps elicit some ideas as to where we look for the stash, then I'm still in. If you have no intention of her walking away at the end of it, then I'm not. That goes for my buyer too.'

Mack grinned. He got up and handed David the bottle.

'Let's drink tae it, then,' he grunted.

David took a swig, flinched briefly when the vile-tasting spirit found his taste buds, and handed it back, his eyes never leaving Mack's.

'I suggest you lie low now until the end of May. Let things get back to normal. The police will not want to pay for additional security for too long.'

Mack wasn't convinced. 'What if the Copes go home before then? Ah've nae intention of missing the boat, like ah said.'

'Selina Cope won't go home until this whole business is wrapped up and she can bury her parents in the manner they deserve, believe me. She may go down to visit her kids for a few days, but she'll be back. She's got a lot to sort out, including the upkeep of the estate and the future of the distillery. That'll take time, a lot of time.'

Mack slumped back onto the sofa. 'Then we'll wait, my friend. Ah've got ma own business to attend to down in the big city.'

David nodded. 'I'll keep my ear to the ground and advise you when the best opportunity arises to do this thing.'

He leaned over and shook hands. 'I'm glad we're back on track. It would be a shame to ruin a long friendship and squander such a lucrative deal.'

Mack took his hand. 'It would be a shame for you tae hav'tae keep lookin' over ya shoulder too, pal.'

David ignored the comment. 'I'll speak to you-know-who, and explain to him what we intend to do.' Then he gestured in the direction of the hallway that led off from the front room.

'When are you going to dispose of that "package" you left in the back room? It's been there a good while now, and believe me, it's becoming a little unpleasant on the nose.'

Mack's eyes flashed up to meet his. 'Aye, okay, ah said ah would. Ah didnae want tae go drawing attention t'this place unnecessarily though.' Then he winced. 'You're no wrong, though. We'd best do something, rather than keep it in here now the weather's getting warmer.'

David didn't want to enter into any debate on the subject. Not now they'd managed to get things back on an even keel! Once Mack had also assured him that the Land Rover would be hidden and kept off the road for a while, he walked out of the cabin and back to his car, leaving his so-called friend still sprawled on the sofa, watching him go.

When the tail lights of David's car had finally disappeared from view, Mack hauled himself up onto his feet. His features contorted into a wearied grimace as the putrescent smell from the back room once more invaded his nostrils. David had been right. The place was becoming a little whiffy, to say the least!

He made his way along the hallway and unlocked the door at the far end. With one hand protecting his mouth and nose, he entered gingerly. The smell was stronger now, worse than when he'd last entered. Several flies danced around his head as he approached the bed and the 'package' that lay upon it.

He stood back, preparing himself mentally for the task ahead, then stooped to grab a handful of the material that enshrouded the limp figure laid out on the mattress. He heaved the corpse up into a sitting position, then manoeuvred it onto his shoulder before struggling to stand upright. Having eventually succeeded, he edged out of the room and along the hallway to the front door, then staggered around to the side of the cabin to a small timber hut that stood some ten feet away.

Mack halted by the hut's sagging door and gave it a kick. It moved slightly, squealing upon its rusting hinges. Content his burden would not topple from his shoulder, he pushed the door fully open, sensing the soft grey wood against his boot, and moved slowly forward. Once inside, he lowered his cargo into a sitting position on an old trunk at the back of the structure.

Straightening up, he took a step back, not wishing to remain too close to the cadaver, then produced his stiletto, stepping forward again and running the blade down through the soft linen until it fell away to reveal the bloodied form beneath. Its eyes stared out, glazed and dejected, like those of the doleful-looking figures depicted in medieval stained glass.

Mack raised the back of his hand to his mouth and nose, then returned his knife to his pocket. He smiled briefly at the ivory face sitting before him.

'There you go, pal. You just sit there and behave yerself, and we'll be back in no time at all. Then we'll give you a proper send-off. It's the least we can do.'

He pulled the door shut and returned to the cabin, taking one last look around and pausing to pick up the whisky bottle.

'You'll do as refreshment, my son. I've got a long drive ahead of me.'

He locked the outer door to the cabin and returned to the Land Rover, having previously moved it into the trees immediately behind the cabin. Rolled up on the floor between the bench seats in the rear was a large grey tarpaulin. He eased it out through the back door and then went about spreading the heavy weatherproof sheet over the roof of the vehicle, finally anchoring it down by tying it to the rusting chrome bumper bars.

He stood back to admire his work, before making his way across to a battered old Ford Mondeo that had been secreted nearby, its dull black bodywork all but invisible in the shadow cast by the densely planted pines.

He settled himself behind the wheel and raised the whisky bottle to his lips whilst his free hand fumbled for the ignition key.

The engine turned and coughed several times, finally bursting reluctantly into life. Relieved as always that the temperamental old thing had actually started up, Mack eased it out from its tenebrous hiding place and accelerated away towards the forestry track that would take him out of the forest, the initial stage of his long journey south.

Chapter Twenty-Three

The coral-coloured stonework of Crumbathyn glowed in the midday sun. It was a deep pink colour that often inspired tourists to pause and admire the elegant-looking merchant's house on Shore Street. Neil never tired of it either; it was, after all, his childhood home.

But it wasn't the luminescence of the building's Georgian stonework that prevented him from climbing out of the MG. There was something else preying on his mind, something that had worried him since they'd crossed the Kessock Bridge, thirty minutes earlier.

'Are we getting out of this car, or are we just going to sit here admiring the view?' Cat asked, whilst she released her seat belt. Neil blinked, jolted back into the present. He unclipped his belt too. 'Sorry, I was deep in thought about something.'

'Not work, surely? Not today.'

He shook his head vigorously.

'No, just this and that. Nothing important.'

Their exit from the MG was strangely synchronised. Cat then trotted across the road to the front gate, behind which an excited Tam was waiting, his entire rear end swinging from side to side as his tail wagged furiously.

Neil opened the tailgate of the little sports car and heaved a large bag of dog food up into his arms. His expression remained solemn, not because of the weight of the sack, but because of the motorcyclist who'd followed them all the way from the A9, before turning off into Bank Street and heading down to Cromarty's little harbour. Neil hadn't told Cat, of course, but he'd monitored the leather-clad rider's every move through his less than efficient wing mirrors.

He was sure in his own mind that the rider was male, but the robotic figure tailing him at a steady speed hadn't given much away. He did recall the full-face helmet, though, bright blue, atop of which was painted the white saltire cross. He also remembered the reflective visor, upon which the passing trees flickered in momentary semblance.

His flashback was interrupted when Tam thundered across the road and hurled himself at his unsuspecting owner.

'Hello, wee boy, how've ya been?'

Neil dropped the sack and crouched to embrace his excited dog. In the blink of an eye, the sinister-looking biker receded into the nebulous depths of his memory. But as he wrestled with Tam, he attempted to rationalise the sighting. There was only one main route along to Cromarty, so why wouldn't a visiting or resident biker have followed him along its entire length? He told himself that he had to get things into perspective, before the buds of paranoia began to take hold. Then it occurred to him. *If this is how I'm reacting, what on earth must Cat be thinking each time she ventures outside the house?*

Neil followed Tam into the house, where he was embraced by his mother.

'I see you remembered to get me the dog food I asked for yesterday,' Rona Strachan chirped as he headed out to the kitchen.

'Aye, Ma. Service with a smile.'

'How's Tam been behaving himself?' Cat asked from her seat at the kitchen table. 'Not been too demanding, I hope?'

Rona sat down opposite her and poured out three mugs of coffee from a large cafetière.

'You mean, when he's not sleeping with me on my bed, eating me out of house and home and demanding that I throw his tennis ball every time I go into the garden?'

She glanced down at the spaniel, who was now sitting at her feet, looking up at her dutifully.

'Just as well this particular Strachan's no pushover,' she growled. Then she looked up and smiled. 'No, he's been fine, the perfect grandchild!'

Neil shrugged. 'Comments like that will get you nowhere, Ma. You're just going to have to get used to your four-legged grandson for the foreseeable!'

He leaned across the table to select a biscuit from the plate next to the cafetière. 'Where's Uncle Euan? He's usually round here on a Sunday mumping lunch!'

'He's got a bowls match, followed by a reception at the Admiral Napier.'

She was referring to the large white-fronted Georgian hotel located by the harbour, the preferred drinking hole of Neil's venerable ex-policeman uncle.

Neil brayed with laughter. '*Reception*! Piss-up, more like.'

'Aye, well the gentle folk of the bowls club prefer to call it a reception,' Rona declared primly, having furtively passed Tam a Hobnob under the table.

Over lunch, Rona asked whether any progress had been made identifying Cat's 'nuisance admirer', as she preferred to call him.

'Have you had any more texts?' she'd enquired, clearly concerned.

'Not so much as a murmur,' Neil reassured her whilst

refreshing everyone's wine glass. 'No news is good news, I suppose.'

'I've got a feeling he's seen sense at last,' Cat surmised.

'I admire your relaxed approach to all this, my dear, but I know it can't be easy for you... certainly not until you discover once and for all who this wretch really is.'

'The truth is, Ma, we may never know,' Neil added sceptically.

'I suppose not. Perhaps that's not such a bad thing, I suppose, as long as all this nonsense stops.'

She turned to Cat. 'You are of course welcome to come and stay out here with me, if you wish. I know your parents are away, and Neil seems to be working long hours on this terrible murder case across in Strathnairn.'

'Thanks Rona, I appreciate your offer. But it would be really inconvenient for work, and, well, I'd just prefer to be at home for now.'

Cat smiled graciously, having shot Neil a brief glance. 'Are you still okay having Tam for a while, Rona? He's our main concern, until we know for sure this problem's gone away.'

'Of course, dear. I love the wee laddie, and he keeps me company when I'm here on my own.'

'Well, just tell me if it becomes a problem,' said Neil. 'And let me know at once if you see anyone hanging around *here* you don't like the look of.'

Rona frowned and glanced questioningly across at Cat. 'Surely you're not expecting anyone to come all the way out here, to stalk *me*, or a dog? That's a wee bit over the top, don't you think?'

Neil felt a little silly, especially when the scenario was presented in the manner his mother had just done. Cat was also studying him with a degree of disbelief.

'There's not something going on that you're not telling us?' Rona enquired.

'Of course not,' said Neil, the visualisation of the motorcyclist now clear again in his subconscious. 'You just never know, that's all.'

'Well, then, nothing to worry about. Tam will be safe and sound staying here with me.'

The visit concluded with a late afternoon walk along the beach, before Cat and Neil said their goodbyes to Rona and Tam and pointed the MG in the direction of Inverness.

'I hate leaving him behind,' Cat sighed, as they passed through a low tunnel of trees arching casually across the road and left Cromarty behind them.

'I know. So do I. It shouldn't be for long, though, and you know Ma loves having him. At least he's always happy staying there.'

The MG emerged from the shade of the trees into warm early evening sunshine. Neil reached across Cat to the passenger glove box for his sunglasses. As he did so, he caught a glimpse of the mouth of a narrow track to his left. It was known locally as 'The Paye', and ran back down the hill towards the centre of Cromarty.

The Paye was barely wide enough for a four-wheeled vehicle of any size to pass along, but a *two*-wheeled vehicle… well, that was another matter. Standing, waiting, just out of sight of any passing traffic, was just such a vehicle. It was a powerful motorcycle, astride which sat a figure protected by full black leathers… and a blue, saltire-patterned crash helmet.

Neil recoiled into his normal driving position and checked his mirrors. The motorcycle pulled out slowly, very slowly, and dropped in behind them, following at a distance of about a hundred yards.

In the mirror, the blackened visor reflected menacingly back at him. The rider's posture was unchanged. Neil sped up, but the distance between him and the machine remained the same, indicating that the rider was content merely to keep pace with the little MG.

'Hey, watch your speed,' Cat warned, as they took a left-hand bend at a speed at least twenty miles per hour faster than that which she considered to be safe.

The drab granite walls of a cluster of farm buildings flashed past as Neil finally eased his foot off the accelerator. He checked his rear-view mirror again... nothing in sight behind them.

He exhaled, relieved. But the relief was momentary. His anxious eyes jerked right, checking his wing mirror, and there he was, back again, leaning sedately into the bend, still one hundred yards behind them.

Cat had sensed his unease, and looked over her shoulder. 'What's wrong, Neil?' she bellowed over the roar of the slipstream.

Neil hesitated, but he knew he had to provide her with an explanation. He leaned towards her, one eye still on the mirror.

'It's that bike behind us. He followed us into Cromarty earlier today, and now he's back behind us again. I think he's tailing us.'

The news left Cat with a distinctly worried visage.

'Perhaps he lives there or he's returning from a visit to friends. I'm sure it's just a coincidence, for God's sake. Now slow down. You'll kill us.'

Neil glared back at her, disbelieving of her ingenuous assessment of the situation.

From then on, Cat kept her eyes glued to the road ahead. Periodically, they would stray across towards Neil. He didn't know whether it was a display of anger, directed at him, or just an expression of pure terror, but suspected he was right on both counts!

The road dropped down into the little town of Rosemarkie,

and with it came a necessary reduction in speed. The growl of the MG's engine now reverberated off the plain-fronted cottages that stood either side of the main street. They'd slowed significantly and were following half a dozen cars along the main route through the congested town centre. A check in the rear mirror confirmed that the bike was still there, humming along behind them... still one hundred yards back.

Once outside the town, the opportunity to overtake finally presented itself. They had now entered the long straight down towards Fortrose, the Moray Firth glinting across the fields to their left. Neil dropped two gears, and overtook first one, then two of the vehicles ahead of him. The road opened out ahead and he pressed down on the accelerator. Cat was pale, her expression fixed. There was no point in saying anything.

He checked his mirror again, and there it was, its headlamp blazing, its engine at screaming pitch as it overtook the same two cars and fell in behind him again.

Neil slammed on the brakes, reducing the distance between them in seconds. The anonymous visored rider did likewise and the bike slowed. Then, without warning, it surged forward again, its front wheel climbing high into the air. There it remained for fifty or so yards, in a blatant display of rampancy, as if the rider was demonstrating his contempt of Neil's efforts to evade him.

Fortrose now closed in around them, requiring another drop in speed, but Neil had a plan. It was a plan that he'd execute once they'd passed through the town, when the road straightened out again as it hugged the rocky Black Isle shoreline.

As expected, the bike was still there when they left Fortrose, maintaining its speed and distance as before. The A832 now ran alongside the firth for a mile or so, probably its most scenic stretch before reaching the village of Avoch.

Ahead of him, Neil could just make out a lay-by on his

side of the road. It was located opposite the remains of an old corrugated shed, its rusting red roof resembling a homing beacon and contrasting starkly with the green foliage that grew on the embankment beyond.

'Brace yourself,' he warned Cat, 'I'm stopping in this lay-by coming up.'

'Oh no. You're not going to confront him, are you?'

Cat rolled her blue eyes in disbelief.

'Bloody right I am. We need to bring this thing to a close.'

The eastern end of the lay-by had now flashed by them, and Neil applied the brakes hard. The MG squealed, decelerating rapidly, and skidded to a halt at the western end of the pull-in.

He switched off the ignition and checked over his shoulder. The motorcycle reduced speed, in an almost leisurely fashion, and swept into the layby, coming to a standstill some fifty yards behind them.

'Be careful, please. He may have a knife or something,' Cat implored, looking back at the motorbike and its rider.

The road was empty now, and only the gentle lapping of the firth against the rocks beneath them competed with the rhythmic tickover of the bike's throaty engine. The rider made no attempt to dismount, preferring to sit hunched over the black petrol tank, content to observe his prey from a distance.

The standoff continued for a minute or so before Neil asked, 'Have you got your phone with you, Cat?'

She nodded anxiously. 'Of course. Why?'

He handed her the keys to the MG. 'When I get out, I want you to get behind the wheel. If things kick off back there, I want you to make yourself scarce. Call the police and tell them what's happened, but don't stop. Go directly to the police station in Inverness, understand?'

Cat was shaking now (or was it shivering) as a tide of fear swept through her.

'Let's speak to him together,' she stammered. 'Surely we're better off doing that?'

Neil leaned between the seats and produced a long, black Maglite torch.

'No,' he said. 'I'll be fine. Just do as I say.'

He kissed her on the forehead and smiled. 'I may not be James Bond, but I'm no pushover, you know.'

He slowly got out of the car and started to walk back towards the motorcycle, his torch swinging lazily in his right hand.

The rider was sitting erect now, his gloved hands resting insouciantly on the top of his petrol tank, watching and waiting.

Neil estimated that he was both taller and stockier than the rider, and, as he'd just reminded Cat, he would be no pushover! But that didn't stop his heart pounding inside his chest.

At around twenty yards out from the MG, he called out. 'Why don't you turn your engine off, so we can have a wee chat? Come on, let's sort this out here and now.'

There was no response from the faceless rider, so Neil continued to advance warily. A truck passed by, followed by a car, reassuring reminders that he was not alone on that stretch of road. The sinister visored helmet then slowly began to move from side to side, as if to communicate its disappointment at the forthcoming confrontation. Neil was close now. He could clearly see the zip fasteners dangling from the rider's leather suit; the mud compacted onto the bike's front tyre.

Only yards to go, anger began to well up in him, more in disbelief at this bastard's arrogance than anything else. His grip on the Maglite became firmer; the showdown between them now seemed inevitable.

But the rider had other ideas. He dropped back to his riding position, gunned the throttle and kicked the bike into gear. The rear wheel spun furiously as the heavy black machine spun around on its axis, showering Neil with sand and grit. He stopped abruptly in his tracks and raised his free arm to shield his face from the flying debris. As he did so, the bike screamed away, back onto the road, and disappeared in the direction from whence it had come.

Watching the motorbike's profile diminish into the distance, Neil could have sworn the rider was pulling another wheelie. Almost as if he were giving him the finger, a 1000 cc finger!

Climbing back into the MG, he was greeted with a hug from Cat.

'What was that for?' he asked, grinning. She scowled back, a tetchy expression upon her normally serene features. 'I don't know, Neil. Because you don't deserve it!' Her fist appeared from nowhere, like a lunging crab, and punched him hard on the upper arm.

'Ouch. Is that all the thanks I get?' He glared back at her, whilst tapping out the landline number of the MEU office on his mobile phone. It was only then that he realised that the motorbike had not been displaying a registration plate!

Bryan Findlay answered the phone in his usual jocular manner, only to revert to a more punctilious demeanour when he realised his boss was on the other end of the line.

Neil provided him with a summary of the incident involving the mysterious motorcyclist and gave a description of the machine and its rider. He kept it at that, never alluding to the previous incidents involving Cat and requesting that Holly be informed as soon as possible.

His partner, now a little calmer, tried to suppress a grin when it came to the descriptions. Neil's responses had without doubt been a source of amusement!

'It was big and black, that's all I know. I didn't see the make. If I had, I'd have mentioned it… no, I'm not into bloody motorbikes. I haven't a clue.'

It didn't finish there either. '… No, there was definitely no registration plate. No, I didn't *not* see it!'

He ended the call and started the engine. 'Christ, talk about the Spanish Inquisition! Then he tells me he's looking at the resource availability screen in front of him and there are no uncommitted units, well, no units at all, out on the Black Isle currently. Fat lot of good that is!'

They set off at a leisurely pace along the road towards Avoch, Neil's eyes never straying far from his mirrors.

'What *are* they going to do, then?' Cat still seemed a little on edge.

'Circulate the description of the bike and rider force-wide, and tag it for Holly to pick up when she gets back from whatever she's doing. That's about all they can do with the scant information I've just given them!'

When they arrived home, the red light on the answerphone was flashing. It was Holly.

'Got your message, sir. I've updated the crime report. Speak later.'

Neil settled onto the bottom tread of the stairs and called his mother to reinforce his warning about walking around Cromarty with Tam.

Having first established that any motorcyclist seen east of the A9 was ostensibly a suspect and a threat, he tried in vain to recover the situation and reassure her. The realisation was now dawning on him that an isolated incident at the leisure centre, and a few disquieting texts, had now become something far more sinister, something that was affecting and causing angst amongst his entire family.

He picked up the phone again and dialled Holly's number.

'Hello, DS Anderson, MEU,' came her polite reply.

'Hello, Holly. It's Neil Strachan.'

'Oh, hi. Are you both okay?'

Holly was eager to hear the motorcycle story from a first-hand source, and Neil duly obliged.

'That's a bit worrying, the fact that he's prepared to act so brazenly, even when *you're* present!' she remarked.

'I know, and he's had the presence of mind to remove his reg plates from his bike too, cheeky wee bastard.'

'Are you sure the time hasn't come to speak to Angus Hardie about this?'

'No, Holly. Tomorrow is Monday. Cat will be going back to the gym for the first time since the initial incident. Let's see what happens tomorrow. You're going to pick her up in the morning, as planned?'

'Aye, I will, and then again when she leaves work and goes out to the gym.'

'Thanks, Holly. She'll have her gym bag with her tomorrow morning, so anyone watching will know what her intentions are. It's important you stick with her throughout the day, until she gets home from the gym, agreed?'

'Your wish is my command, sir.'

'Right answer, Holly. I'll keep an eye on Guthrie again and will catch up with you afterwards. Thing is, he doesn't have a motorbike as far as I'm aware.'

'His brother does, though,' Cat called out from somewhere upstairs.

'Thanks. Now you tell me… Did you hear that, Holly?'

'I did, sir. So he could still be in the frame, just?'

'Aye, for now. Depends on the type of motorbike. I'm not holding my breath, though!'

'Okay, I'm heading off home now. Fingers crossed we'll get a break tomorrow, eh?'

'I hope so, because things could start to get a little difficult for us if our phantom biker keeps this up. I might end up having to bite the bullet and speak to Angus.'

'We'll find the wee shite before you have to do that, trust me!' Holly reassured him, somewhat unexpectedly.

'You've changed your tune. I hope you're right, Holly.'

'Well, I've met the victim now. I think we'll get on pretty well, Cat and I!'

'Sounds ominous! Look, thanks a lot for your help. You know we both appreciate it.'

There was a brief pause, then Holly said, 'My pleasure,' and the line went dead.

Neil slowly replaced the handset onto its cradle. He could've sworn that his new sergeant had been a little choked up just before she'd ended that call!

Chapter Twenty-Four

Holly had boarded the bus three stops before Cat's. She took a seat towards the rear, hoping for an unobstructed view of all those passengers seated in front of her. The ploy had been partially successful, but the vehicle was almost full by the time it pulled up at the bus shelter in Woodside Farm Drive. Cat was the first of three people to board, gym bag slung casually over her shoulder.

She exchanged pleasantries with the female driver, and then took an aisle seat, four rows from the front. Before sitting down, she scanned the sea of heads for Holly and quickly located her, sitting by the window. Neither woman reacted when their eyes met, so that no observer, not even one with a honed eye would've known they were in any way on familiar terms.

The bus eased away from the stop and gained speed. Holly studied everyone in turn. Only Maureen Cameron showed any real interest in Cat. She was sitting on the opposite side of the bus, and Cat's reaction to her wave bespoke their acquaintance.

Holly's gaze then fell upon another passenger, a young man, casually dressed and in his early thirties. He observed

Cat as she settled herself into her seat and arranged her bags around her. But his interest was short-lived and he returned to his magazine, never looking up again, even when Cat alighted from the bus at the Eastgate Centre.

Holly continued to follow at a respectable distance as Cat made her way along Baron Taylor's Street and through the familiar glass doors providing access to her office. She then continued across Church Street, taking one last look back along the route she'd just walked. No one, nothing, not even a wandering moggy had followed Cat down that street! So she made her way across to the waiting car in Bank Lane and climbed in beside Bryan Findlay.

'Did you enjoy yer wee bus ride this morning, Sarge?' he grinned.

'Just drive, Fin, back to my car please.'

'Of course, m'lady!'

Neil was sitting behind his unusually cluttered desk, drinking coffee with Fraser Gunn and Steve Armsley, when Holly poked her head around the door.

He ushered her in, but his eyes said more than the words he spoke. She was becoming used to Neil's surreptitious mode of communicating whilst in the presence of others.

'Bumped into Cat just now, on her way to work,' she announced, as she lowered herself into the last vacant chair in the office.

'Oh, really? Was she okay?' Neil enquired nonchalantly.

'Aye, fine. Said her morning had been pretty uneventful so far.'

Neil visibly relaxed. 'That's good. I was just discussing this secondary search of Cullaird Castle we've got planned for tomorrow. Steve's kicking off at nine. So we'll go over there before he starts and have a word with the Copes. They know we intend to leave no stone unturned this time… literally!'

'I'm not that hopeful,' Armsley said, leaning over a plan of the building that had been spread across the last vacant space on Neil's desk. 'My guys did a pretty thorough job last time, and short of knocking holes in the walls, there's little else we can physically search.'

'I know,' Neil agreed, 'but I just need to be sure we've done all that we can. You'll be looking into roof voids and under floors this time, yes?'

'Yes, where it's practical to do so, and without causing too much damage, of course. We need to bear in mind that whoever secreted *whatever* it is we're trying to find probably did so without the help of sophisticated equipment, and in a location where they could retrieve it relatively easily.'

He straightened up and massaged his lower back. 'And the size of whatever *it* is also dictates where we look. We're running blind here, guv.'

At that point Angus Hardie appeared in the doorway.

'Got a second, Neil? Just need to run something past you.'

When Neil had left the office, Armsley turned to Holly, a look of concern exaggerating his usual sombre countenance.

'Isn't he getting a little paranoid over this hidden object… document, whatever it is?' he asked. 'I'm pretty sure we would've found whatever it is by now… *if* it was still there!'

'Aye, Steve, I know he tends to get a bee in his bonnet over some things, but you know what? I trust his instinct!'

'She's right,' Gunn chipped in. 'Remember that job over at Glendaig, when those hikers found the skeleton on the beach? He kept on beavering away over there when everyone thought he was wasting his time. Surprise, surprise, he eventually turns up a wartime German sailor who'd been living here under the radar for nearly seventy years.'

'Not to mention the other two corpses hidden in that grave in the churchyard,' Holly added.

309

Armsley raised a conciliatory hand. 'Okay, you've made your point.'

Gunn continued with his defence of the SIO. 'It's the historian in him, Steve. He's probably at his happiest ferreting about with a trowel, digging up the past!'

Holly looked confused. 'I thought it was archaeologists who ferreted about with trowels, Fraser?'

'Aye, it is. They're just a type of historian, though, aren't they?'

Neil re-entered the room and immediately noticed the smug grins on the faces around the desk.

'Have I missed something?' he enquired.

'No, no, we were just discussing the difference between historians and archaeologists,' Holly proclaimed.

'Archaeologists ferret around in dirty trenches searching for things with trowels,' he retorted. 'Historians, on the other hand... well they don't need to get their hands dirty. They delve into the past in an altogether more civilised way, like detectives.'

Neil sat back behind his desk, his eyes drilling into Armsley. 'Which makes me the indefatigable paranoid historian, and you the dirty, ferreting archaeologist, Steve. Partition walls have ears, you know!'

The discomfited PolSA's cheeks promptly turned a florid colour. 'Best I go and find my trowel, then,' he muttered, rising from his chair.

When he had gone, Neil turned to Gunn. 'Any updates on the latest raid at the castle, Fraser?'

'That's what I dropped in to tell you about. We took casts from some more examples of fresh tyre tracks close to where the police car had been parked. Although they were well-worn, we managed to get some of the pattern.'

'What's the verdict, then?'

'Goodyear Wranglers. They're the same as the tracks we found out at the battlefield.'

'Don't tell me. They're a type fitted to Land Rover Defenders, am I right?'

'They are indeed, Neil.'

'Eddie Craig and Nathaniel Cope were not mistaken, then. If we're right about Ualas MacBean, he's driving around in a green Land Rover.'

'Surely not,' said Holly with a wry smile. 'His sister says he doesn't have a licence!'

'Aye, right, I'm sure a driving licence is top of his list of priorities,' said Neil, grinning. 'He seems to have been on his own when Eddie saw him. So if it is him, he doesn't seem that bothered about being caught driving without one! You never know, though. The vehicle may belong to, or perhaps have been driven by, his accomplice.'

'Shame we've got no registration number,' said Holly.

'I've asked the uniform lads to pull over any green Land Rovers they see. You never know, we may get lucky,' Neil propounded. 'Problem is, they will have realised they've been spotted in it, so may dump it.'

'They're pretty common up in this part of the world too,' Holly added.

'Aye, well, it's worth a try. Anything else to report from the scene, Fraser?'

'Not really. Once again, nothing was stolen, as far as we can tell. There are some tooling marks where walls and floors have been worked on, and several areas where we've found Marigold glove marks again.' He shrugged. 'That's about it, I'm afraid. Tell me, have you heard how the injured PC is getting on?'

'Off the critical list last night, but still pretty poorly, though. They've fixed some sort of steel plate onto his skull.'

'Bloody hell! And we thought these guys might be worried about driving around without a licence!'

'Exactly,' said Neil. He tapped the folded newspaper lying

on his desk. 'Let's hope the good old public can provide us with a sighting of these two before they trash someone else's life!'

Five o'clock saw Neil and Holly sitting in Bank Lane again, looking through the CID car's grimy windscreen towards the corner of Baron Taylor's Street.

A steady flow of workers streamed through the glass doors of Number Two, employees of the various organisations that shared the office space within the building.

When Cat appeared, she neither looked left or right, but headed off along her normal route towards Academy Street, where she'd catch the bus to the leisure centre.

Holly fell in behind her, whilst Neil waited for Guthrie to appear. When he finally emerged from the building, Neil turned the car around and made his way back down the narrow road towards the River Ness.

It was a full ten minutes before Guthrie eventually showed up at the bus stop from where he'd catch his bus back to Fortrose. Neil observed unblinkingly, as the young man climbed onto his bus. Then, when it pulled away, he once again eased into the traffic behind it and followed. The journey was very much the same as before, and one that Neil now endured with some degree of indifference.

It ended without incident, outside Guthrie's front door, concluding Neil's second and final foray into Fortrose's residential hinterland.

He pointed the car back in the direction of Inverness, and pulled in by the side of the A832, outside a pair of run-down farm cottages. From there he rang Holly.

'Where are you now?' he asked.

'Following Cat from the bus stop to the leisure centre,' came the panted reply. 'Jeez, your girlfriend walks fast!'

'So all's well, then?'

'Never better. She's on her own, by the way.'

'Aye, I know. Her friends make their own way there on occasions.'

'That's okay, then; probably not a bad thing.'

'I'm on my way back from Fortrose now. Guthrie's back at his parents' place, so I'll head out your way.'

He dropped the phone back onto the passenger's seat, and selected first gear. But then a brief buzzing tone from inside his jacket stopped him in his tracks. It took him a second or two to realise that it was a text alert, emanating from Cat's personal phone.

He pulled up the handbrake and searched the garment frantically for the device, finally withdrawing it from an internal pocket. A yellow envelope icon with the figure one against it languished at the bottom of the home screen, indicating an incoming text. He tapped the icon and read the message. All the while, a deepening frown crept across his face…

Can we meet, Cat? Then I'll leave you alone, I promise. I'll be in the car park of the North Kessock Hotel. Say 7.30 pm, after your gym session. Get a taxi from the leisure centre. Xx

The message had come from the same number as the other texts. Surely it couldn't be Guthrie?

Neil ground his teeth as he thought about what to do next. He looked out at the dilapidated cottages to his left, his eyes fixed and icy, like stones on the bed of a mountain burn. Then he shrugged, and read the message once more, before tapping the reply icon and beginning to type…

Okay, I'll be there at 7.30 sharp. In the bar.

He hit the 'send' button and waited for a response, but none came. So he drove the ten miles to North Kessock, in no particular hurry, and deep in thought.

How would he recognise this guy? Would he turn up on that motorbike? Would it be someone he knew?

The hotel was busy that evening. Couples sat chatting and sipping drinks on the green and white covered veranda, whilst he watched from his car in the small car park opposite. Each and every customer who entered or left the establishment was treated as a potential suspect. The problem was, none of them looked like one. Not to him, anyway.

His watch told him it was just after seven. Less than half an hour to go. He hadn't contacted Holly. He didn't want her to take her eye off the ball. It had even crossed his mind that there may even be two saddos involved in this miscreancy!

He turned to look out across the Beauly Firth. Beyond its muddy weed-strewn foreshore, the water shimmered in the warm evening sun, a pale translucence that reminded him of ruffled silk. It was a welcome interlude, but his eyes soon flashed back to his watch again. Time was dragging, but surely his tormentor would want to be there, *in situ*, before his victim arrived. He squinted as the sun's glare reflected back at him from the hotel windows, then followed the progress of a foursome of twenty-somethings as they skipped playfully along the roadway before disappearing into the bar.

Ten minutes later, and the minute hand on his watch flicked onto the figure six. It was seven thirty, and he hadn't seen anyone during the preceding half hour who could possibly have been the author of the texts. But then who was he kidding? What did a stalker look like, anyway? If he was right, then his quarry may have been in the bar already.

Neil opened the car door and leaned across to pick up Cat's phone... just as it began to buzz again!

He slumped back into his seat when he saw the new text

icon and tapped it hard, a sense of urgency rising within him. The message flashed up instantaneously…

> *Dear, Dear Neil. You didn't think I'd fall for that one did you? I know she's told you about me, and now it seems you have her phone. First you follow her, then you try to impersonate her. You're going to have to try harder than that Mr Plod…*

Neil stared incredulously at the screen, trying to make sense of the message. There were no flies on this guy. He was just toying with them. Neil tapped out a reply…

> *Don't know what you're on about. Come on, let's meet. I'm waiting at the hotel for you. Let's talk…*

There was a short pause before Cat's phone buzzed again…

> *Thanks for getting back Neil. I saw that cute little Samsung thingy she's been using, so let's not play games. By the way, you'd better hurry if you're going to get to the leisure centre in time. You can't protect her from there!*

'You bastard,' Neil growled as he frantically changed out of text mode, and tapped out Cat's phone number. But there was no answer. It did buzz and vibrate deep in the bag that sat at Cat's feet, but she didn't hear it over the background din of the leisure centre bar.

Neil uttered a string of imprecations, whilst he waited for Cat to answer. Then another buzzing sent him fumbling back to the text menu…

> *At least you know now, I'm not that skinny guy with the greasy hair. Remember time is of the essence, Sherlock. Tick Tock…*

Next on the call list was Holly, but this time he was greeted by an engaged tone. Unbeknown to him, his young sergeant was sitting in the foyer of the leisure centre explaining to her adopted older sister, Annabelle, that she couldn't get down to Edinburgh for a shopping weekend any time soon!

More cursing as the phone tumbled into the passenger's seat, and Neil turned the key in the ignition. The wheels of the CID car spun as the vehicle lurched away from its parking space and screamed towards the car park exit. Heads turned inquisitively on the hotel veranda, and looked on with incredulity as the Ford Focus sped away, back towards the A9.

Holly, having concluded her phone call, checked her watch impatiently.

'Come on, Cat. Drink up, luvvie,' she muttered, realising that the time was nudging seven forty. The foyer was quiet now, so she stepped outside to the sweeping approach road that led up to the centre.

All was quiet. Just a couple of young girls were being picked up by their parents in a large black SUV. So she returned to the warmth of the reception area and sat down again.

Her wait finally ended when Cat appeared through some swing doors nearby and hurried past her, bags slung as before over her shoulders. She had left her friends in the bar, making the excuse that Neil was going to pick her up on his way home from work.

When she had left the building, Holly followed, along the approach road and across the car park towards the lane that would take Cat to her bus stop.

Holly deliberately maintained her distance, even though Cat was now walking purposefully towards the car park exit and opening up the gap between them.

Her phone then began to vibrate. 'Holly…'

A male voice interrupted her, a voice just discernable over the laboured whine of a car engine.

'… I think he's there, at the centre. Keep close to her. I'm on my way.'

Then the line went dead.

Holly stuffed the phone into the pocket of her jeans and quickened her pace, rapidly closing the distance with Cat. She urgently scanned the car park, but there was no one nearby, nothing to raise her suspicions.

Without stopping, and with only a brief downward glance, she unclipped the pepper spray cannister from the holder on her belt. But when she looked up again, she'd temporarily lost sight of Cat.

A tall hedge loomed ahead of her. It ran alongside a running track, at an angle to the path she'd been walking along. Cat must've changed direction, and followed the line of the hedge towards the exit gate. Then she heard a scream and began to run. When she rounded the end of the hedge, there was Cat, grappling with a figure dressed in a dark grey hooded fleece. Holly broke into a sprint, her pepper spray in hand and its safety flap now flipped off.

'Stop. Police officer,' she bawled, at the top of her voice, prompting Cat's assailant to straighten up and look back at her. She could just make out a pair of eyes, staring out from the otherwise featureless black face that lurked within the hood, but nothing more. He quickly untangled himself from Cat's flailing limbs and began running towards the car park exit as fast as he could.

Holly slowed as she reached Cat, who was sitting on the grass sobbing. 'You okay, Cat?' she questioned as she passed.

'Aye, I'll be fine. See if you can see where he goes.'

So Holly sped up again, across the remaining parking lots and through the gap in the stone wall that led out into the adjoining lane. From there it was a chase along the long, straight road that skirted the Caledonian Canal.

The hoody was quick, but Holly was younger and fitter. She could sense herself gaining on him as they darted towards the small row of cottages that stood at the junction with the Fort William road. The hoody looked anxiously back at her, very briefly, but long enough to reduce his speed. It was as she'd suspected. He was wearing a balaclava under the hood.

Holly grimaced as she asked more of her tiring legs. The distance lessened until she could hear the hoody's laboured breathing an arm's length ahead of her. She lunged, her right hand latching onto the soft grey material of his jacket.

'Stop, you bastard,' she panted, pulling with all her strength in an effort to bring the figure to a halt. It worked, to an extent. The two of them decelerated to almost a walking pace, but as she continued to pull, she felt herself falling backwards. Then she realised why, when the hooded garment came off in her hand, and the momentum generated by her pulling caused her to crash to the ground.

The figure, who she was now content to describe as male, dressed only in jeans and a black polo shirt, raced off towards the main road. Eventually he pulled off his balaclava when he'd reached a safe distance, revealing short dark hair, but she never saw his face before he turned right and disappeared.

Holly sat in the middle of the road, gasping for breath as her body fought to reduce her oxygen debt. There was no point trying to follow him. Her legs had turned to jelly. The chase was over.

By the time she'd found her way back to where Cat had fallen, Neil had arrived, and was sitting with her in the CID car, a comforting arm wrapped around her shoulders.

'I assume you lost him, then?' Neil snapped, his disappointment clear to see.

Holly glared at him. 'I gave it my best bloody shot,' she complained, still panting.

Neil's anguished expression began to soften. 'I know you did… thanks. Are you okay?'

'Aye, just out of breath, that's all.'

'Did you get a look at him?'

'Only the back of his head. He had a balaclava on initially.'

Neil frowned. 'Not another bloody balaclava!'

Holly turned her attention to Neil's partner. 'Are you okay, Cat? He didn't… well, you know…?'

'Touch me up, you mean? No he didn't, thanks to you turning up when you did.'

'Good. Any injuries?'

Cat managed a weak smile. 'No, I'm fine, thanks. I appreciate you looking out for me. He just came out of nowhere, grabbed me around the neck and pulled me onto the ground. Then you appeared and he ran.'

'Did he say anything to you?' Holly asked.

'Only "Don't make me angry. Don't take me for a fool".'

'Bastard. He's certainly upped the ante tonight!' said Neil.

As they spoke, a marked police car pulled up behind them, followed by a dog unit. Neil got out of the car to speak to the officers who were now hurrying towards them.

'That was a close call,' Cat admitted, wiping her eye with a tissue.

'I know,' Holly agreed, as she massaged Cat's arm compassionately. 'But there is some good news.' She held up the hoody's grey fleece. 'I got a partial look at him, and now we've got his jacket, and possibly his DNA… which could be his undoing!'

Chapter Twenty-Five

'So how long's this been going on?' Fraser Gunn asked deprecatingly. He stood in Neil's office, straight-faced, clutching the evidence bag that contained the grey hooded jacket. Then he ran his finger across the exhibit label. 'HMA/ONE. Holly's exhibit, I see.'

Neil looked up from the pile of expense forms in front of him.

'Aye, Holly's the OIC. She was keeping obs on Cat last night. Almost caught the bastard too.'

'And these would've been unofficial observations, I assume... Does Angus Hardie know about this, Neil?'

'Not yet, Fraser. But seeing that you and everyone else around here knows what happened last night, I suppose I'm going to have to tell him!'

'*I* would if I were you,' Gunn advised, 'before he finds out through the thin blue grapevine. Procrastinating over this, so that you get to oversee both enquiries, is definitely not a good strategy, believe me.'

'Thanks for your advice, Fraser,' Neil replied, piqued by Gunn's unwanted pep talk. 'But you can leave that side of things to me.'

Gunn shrugged. 'That's me told, then.'

He held up the paper bag. 'This will go off to the lab today, together with Cat's clothing. Normally it would take anything up to four weeks, but I've called in a favour, so it'll be fast-tracked.'

'Good. Thanks. How long till we get a result, then?'

'Three days, if you're lucky.'

'Anything else from the scene?'

'Not a thing. Did Holly get a look at him?'

'Not really. Initially he was wearing a balaclava under his hood. He pulled it off when he made his escape, but she only saw the back of his head. She reckons he was in his twenties, just under six feet and slim with darkish hair, possibly gelled.'

'Shame, but we'll get him. Don't you worry.'

'Oh, you can count on that,' said Neil, his face devoid of any emotion.

Gunn headed for the door. 'I just hope it's not *you* that catches up with him first! Still, I'll do all that I can to help.'

'Thanks, Fraser,' said Neil, genuinely thankful. 'And I will speak to Hardie, okay?'

'Your choice, my friend.' Gunn closed the door after himself, but with a force that bordered on a slam!

They took the B851 down to Cullaird that morning. The drive along the lonely single-track road on a clear sunny day was always a pleasure. The route followed the course of the meandering River Nairn as it flowed, clear and sparkling, through expansive green pastures, fringed by low, rounded hills. Those same hills appeared drab and green that day, unremarkable features that didn't warrant a second look, but during the summer months they would abound with large tracts of purple heather, creating an altogether more memorable vista.

'Something tells me this is going to be a waste of time,'

said Neil, as he watched the scenery rush by. 'If the Frasers' ancestors have hidden something in or around that castle, they've done a very good job of doing so. Then again, we may be chasing shadows. There may be nothing there at all.'

Holly kept her eyes on the road. 'Nothing wrong with following up on a well-considered hunch, though. Fraser and I made that clear to Steve Armsley yesterday... especially as it's *your* hunch!'

Neil regarded her cameo-like profile as she drove, touched by her unabashed declaration of support.

'Yes, I know. I appreciate that, Holly. Thanks.'

'Oh yes, I forgot, walls have ears.' She giggled, then turned her head, sensing he was looking at her. 'What?' she asked.

'Nothing.' He looked away, a little embarrassed.

'How's Cat today?' she asked, changing the subject.

'She didn't sleep much last night. Had to give her a wee tot of my best malt.'

'Heaven forbid. You must have been worried! Did it work?'

'Aye, she said it did, for a while at least.'

'I take it she's not gone into work today?' Holly glanced across again. It was an anxious but sincere glance.

'No, Hugh Jardine's given her a few days off. She's staying with her sister, Hannah, at her place, whilst I'm working.'

'She's the air hostie, yes?'

'They call them flight attendants these days, Holly. But aye, that's right. She's off on leave for a week too.'

He paused, then murmured, 'Fingers crossed our man will keep his head down for a while, having had such a close shave with the law.'

He turned slowly to look out of the window once again. Holly could see the tiredness in his eyes and provided only a one-word answer. 'Hopefully,' she said softly, and left him to his thoughts.

Several unmarked police vans stood outside the castle, their rear doors left wide open whilst a bevy of black-overalled search officers busied themselves unloading their equipment. Neil and Holly walked quickly past, en route to the open doorway, just as Steve Armsley poked his head out of the back of one of the vehicles.

'Morning, Steve. Got your trowel with you?' Neil grinned.

'He's so bloody funny,' Armsley muttered, responding to the puzzled expressions present on the faces of his team.

'I'll be out to brief your team in ten minutes,' Neil continued, before disappearing through the doorway.

They found Selina and Nathaniel in the great hall, emptying the contents of a large roll-topped writing bureau.

'God, my parents were hoarders,' Selina divulged, as she walked over to greet them, one hand spread across her brow in a gesture of frustration.

'Still, best not to miss anything important,' Neil replied tactfully.

'So your guys are going to go through the place again today, looking for… whatever. You know what, I think it's been done to death, but hey, you're the experts!'

He shrugged. 'We just want to be sure that we've done the best we can…'

She grinned. 'Short of taking the place to pieces, stone by stone?'

'Sort of.'

Neil saw Selina's smile and responded in kind.

'Okay if they make a start?'

'Of course. Tell them to fill their boots. I'll go down and make some coffee for them.'

Neil followed her down the stairs and went out to brief the search team, whilst Holly remained in the great hall with Nathaniel. Sensing he wanted to carry on with the task he'd set himself, she closed in on the long table next to the fireplace and began a systematic examination of the silver-framed photographs that crowded its highly polished surface. She was studying one of the larger family portraits, notable as one of the few sepia photographs in the display, when Neil and Selina returned, the former carrying a tray loaded with a coffee pot and mugs.

'Ah, that's Great-Grandpa George and Great-Grandma Susan, taken here at the castle in June 1917.'

Selina arranged the contents of the tray upon another low table next to a large leather sofa, liberally adorned with tartan scatter cushions.

'They look very happy, and what a handsome couple,' Holly commented. She gazed into the eyes of the dashing young army officer, dressed in his crumpled uniform, over which a shiny leather Sam Browne belt and shoulder strap were much in evidence.

'They were certainly a colourful pair,' Selina informed her, whilst handing Neil a mug.

'George was a captain in the Royal Flying Corps when that photo was taken. He was home on leave from France. Sadly, it was the last photo ever taken of him. He was killed the day after he returned to the front.'

Holly leaned forward. 'Oh yes, I see the wings on his tunic now. What happened to him, then?'

'During the Battle of Messines, his squadron were ordered by Hugh Trenchard, the general commanding the RFC, to fly low over the German trenches and attack all available targets. Well, not surprisingly, he was shot down and crashed into a German trench, killing him instantly. The Germans gave him a funeral with full military honours, apparently. He was only thirty-two.'

'That's very sad. What about your great-grandmother? She looks very regal in this portrait.' Neil had joined Holly and was sipping his coffee whilst he too looked at the photograph.

Selina reclined onto the sofa. 'Great-Grandma Susan was born in Yorkshire. Her father, Charles Huntsby-MacLean was an Indian civil servant. The family lived for some time in Bengal, where her mother was something of a socialite. Susan's father was serving with the Imperial Civil Service as advisor to Sir Andrew Henderson Leith Fraser. He was the Lieutenant Governor of Bengal at the time. She met George at a ball out there in 1906, when he was stationed briefly in India as a young subaltern on General Kitchener's staff.'

'Shame it all ended when they were so young,' Holly interjected.

'Yes, indeed. Susan had just celebrated her thirtieth birthday when that photo was taken. That's why George had come home on leave, to celebrate it with her.'

'Did she ever marry again?' Neil asked.

'No, she pretty much devoted her life to running this estate and overseeing the distillery, until her two sons, Farquhar and Alisdair, returned from military service after the Second World War.'

'What about George's father or siblings? Surely they were still alive when George was killed?'

'His father was,' Selina confirmed. 'But he died in 1919, two years after his son. George was the only child, so Susan had no choice but to pick up the reins, assisted initially by her mother-in-law, Grace.'

'It must've been a particularly difficult time,' Holly suggested, returning the photo to the table.

'I'm sure it was,' said Selina, gazing nervously up at the ceiling in response to the sound of banging above her head. 'The family almost went bankrupt after George died. There were substantial death duties to pay on his personal fortune and the war had seriously affected the profitability of the distillery. There was also a lack of male workers available to assist Susan and Grace with the day-to-day running of the

Cullaird estate. They had all been conscripted into the armed forces, of course.'

'They obviously managed to get through that difficult period unscathed,' Holly concluded.

'They did, but Susan had to sell off some of the castle's contents to raise the required capital. Some very valuable antiques went to auction: furniture, paintings and so forth.'

'What a shame,' Neil concluded, finally draining his mug. 'I mean, to lose family heirlooms that had been here for what, centuries?' He returned the mug to the tray. 'You have a fascinating family history, Selina. I got the impression from our earlier conversations that you weren't that interested in your ancestry.'

Selina topped up her mug with fresh coffee.

'Not so much those characters from way back. But the more recent generations mean more to me. You know, the members of the family who were actually photographed and spoken about by my parents, and of course living family. I suppose I was more interested because they actually knew them.'

'I see. Well, if you'll excuse us, we'd better go and see how Sergeant Armsley and his team are getting on. We'll leave you to sort out that bureau!'

At that point, Nathaniel spoke for the first time since the discussion about George and Susan Fraser had commenced.

'It's a shame Susan wasn't able to get her hands on a few more of these,' he joked, holding up what looked like a couple of gold coins. 'May have helped her pay off those infernal death duties!'

'What have you got there?' Neil asked. 'Pieces of eight?'

'You're not far off the truth there,' Nathaniel grinned. 'I'm afraid they may actually be stolen property, Chief Inspector.' He looked across at his wife. 'What was the story behind these, Selina? You know better than me.'

She craned her neck to see what he was holding.

'Oh, those old coins. Funnily enough, they were supposed to have belonged to Great-Grandpa George. They were given to him by his father Alisdair on his twenty-first birthday, in accordance with an old family tradition. The story goes that one of our long-lost ancestors came into possession of a large hoard of gold coins during the Jacobite uprising, apparently stolen from the King himself. Supposedly, he brought it back here to Cullaird and buried it somewhere. To this day, its whereabouts have remained a mystery.' She chuckled. 'Those coins were said to have come from the hoard, handed down to the first son of each generation so that the story would never be forgotten. But of course that's exactly what it is: just a story!'

'How do you know it's *just* a story?' Neil questioned, the historian in him instantly being revived.

Selina seemed indifferent to his enquiry. 'Because every generation of this family for the last hundred years has searched high and low for the said hoard, but none has ever found it. Furthermore, there is no documentation or historical evidence at all to support the story, as far as I am aware, so until I see some verification, it will remain a romantic myth – only a myth.'

Neil and Holly joined Nathaniel by the bureau and examined the two coins. They looked as if they'd just been newly minted, shiny gold with no indication of wear or use. Both coins were large, and both bore the wreathed head of King George the Second, a fact confirmed by the inscription around the head. 'They look the same,' Neil remarked, 'except this one is dated 1729, and the other 1746. The same year as Culloden, would you believe?'

'One thing I do know is that they are five-guinea coins,' said Selina.

'Surely these coins *are* evidence of there being a hoard

hidden somewhere, the verification you've been seeking?' Holly suggested.

'Could be, I suppose,' said Nathaniel. 'But as Selina just said, no one has ever found it. These little beauties could've come from anywhere!'

Neil caressed one of the coins in his right hand. 'Have you ever had them valued? They must be worth hundreds, if not thousands of pounds by now.'

Selina draped herself over the back of the sofa, resting her chin on her hands. 'Oh, Daddy possibly did. I don't know. We just see them as family heirlooms, so their value is academic. They are lovely, though, and in such good condition.'

Neil then produced his mobile phone. 'Do you mind if I take a photo of these coins?'

'Fire away,' said Nathaniel.

Neil took close-ups of both sides of each coin. He smiled as he did so, but beneath the jovial facade he was a little irritated. *Why the hell hadn't they mentioned this so-called hoard before? Because now they had a motive. Myth or no myth!*

'Thanks. It's a shame we didn't know of this story about the hoard from the outset,' he said, trying to be diplomatic, but failing, his tone clearly revealing his true feelings on the matter.

'Why?' Selina asked, almost taking offence. 'Like I said, it's just a myth, nothing more.'

Then the realisation dawned upon her. 'Oh, dear God, you don't think…?'

'Actually, yes, I do think,' Neil responded sharply, surprised by her apparent naivety. 'Whether the hoard exists or not, I have a feeling our persistent intruder, Ualas MacBean, or whoever it may be, has found out about it. Now, he wants to find it, and evidently will stop at nothing to do so!'

Selina's hand shot up to cover her mouth. Her shocked eyes met those of her husband, conveying her stupefaction at the concept of a romantic legend being connected to the murders of both her parents.

'It just never occurred to me,' she stammered. 'I'd completely forgotten about the story until you produced those wretched coins, Nat.'

She could feel tears moistening her eyelids and a tightening of her stomach, almost like nausea, as she contemplated this new theory.

'The story of the hoard hasn't been discussed for as long as I can remember. What a fool I've been, not to think of it.'

Her husband joined her on the sofa and wrapped his arm around her.

'Look, I knew about the story too, and it didn't occur to me either. So it's pointless beating yourself up over it, darling.'

He looked across at Neil. 'The chief inspector has to look at all the possibilities, but the hoard theory may have nothing to do with what's happened here.'

Holly sighed, and then mumbled under her breath. 'Bit heavy handed, sir. Good job.'

Her words were just loud enough for Neil to hear, and he glowered back at her as she moved away to help console Selina.

Neil wanted to kick himself for allowing his frustration to get the better of him, and for the insensitivity he'd shown. Damage limitation now seemed appropriate.

'Look, your husband's right, Selina, and in a way, I hope I'm wrong. But as he correctly points out, we have to consider the possibility. At least we know about the story now.'

He smiled limply, avoiding Holly's scowl. Her lips never moved, but her eyes said it all. The phrase 'digging a hole' then came to mind, so he just followed up with, 'I'm just going to have a chat with Sergeant Armsley. Won't be long.' With that, he scurried away, eager to extract himself from the situation.

Armsley was working in an upstairs bedroom, his head and

shoulders obscured by the lintel of a fireplace. When Neil called out, he ducked down and emerged from within the blackened void, a mirror in one hand and a torch in the other. He put the tools down and ran his hand briskly through his grey hair.

'Something up?' he enquired.

'Only that I may now have some idea what you are looking for,' Neil informed him, his face conveying no emotion at all.

'What would that be?'

'A large hoard of gold coins, God knows how big.'

Armsley looked at him bemusedly as he spoke into the microphone of his radio, summoning his team for an update.

Neil then recounted the story of the hoard, whilst they waited for the team to assemble.

'Good of them to tell us,' Armsley grunted. 'We've been looking for cracks in bricks!'

Neil nodded. 'Just don't go whingeing to Holly. She'll swallow you whole, just like she's just done to me. Still, I deserved it… left the room feeling the size of one of the characters from *Toy Story*!'

Armsley grinned. 'Sheriff Woody, no doubt!'

With the team briefed, the operation continued. There had been consensus amongst all parties that the extent of the search within the castle should remain the same, and the latest information would merely be taken into consideration, rather than become a reason for redirecting the entire search area. After all, any such hoard could well have been broken up into smaller segments.

Neil returned to the great hall, where all was now well, and his sergeant unexpectedly greeted him with a warm smile!

Selina's eyes, still glistening from the tears, followed him as he walked across the room. 'I was just saying to Holly here, I'm not really up on the story of the hoard, but I'm sure my cousin Miriam will be able to tell you more. She's a generation older than me, you see.'

'Isn't she on a cruise somewhere?' Neil asked.

'She's back on Thursday, and then she's coming up to stay with me on Sunday so that Nat can go back to work.'

'So you told her about your parents, then?'

'Yes, we eventually decided it was the right thing to do.'

'Okay, we'll have a chat with her then. Thanks.'

He then changed the subject. 'The search is still ongoing, and will be for some time, I'm afraid. They will also be commencing a sweep of the grounds, both within and outside the boundary walls, to check for anything that's been buried.'

'How will they do that?' Nathaniel queried.

'The search supervisor is arranging for some ground-penetrating radar equipment to be brought across. That'll take a while, unfortunately.'

Selina looked glum-faced. 'Sorry I didn't think to tell...'

Neil raised a conciliatory hand. 'No, not at all, I'm sorry I came across in the way I did. Of course we couldn't expect you to have considered a 200-year-old *legend* as a motive for something like this.'

He was still feeling awkward when he and Holly left. She looked straight ahead as they approached the car. '*I* couldn't expect, would've been more appropriate... you know, with an *I*,' Holly chirped.

'I'm sorry? What are you on about?' Neil enquired, clearly confused.

'You said in there, *we* couldn't have expected Selina to consider the legend. *I* didn't expect anything! It had nothing to do with me!'

'Okay, okay, you've made your point. Can we let it drop now?'

'Only if you drive, sir,' she replied with a smile, and threw the car keys over the roof of the car to him.

He took the B862 back to Inverness, the road that hugged the south bank of Loch Ness and latterly the river that fed it. For a long time they sat in silence, Neil apparently deep in thought and Holly busily tapping away on the keys of her phone. Then just before they reached the urban sprawl of Inverness, he spoke for the first time.

'Has the CCTV at the entrance to that haulage yard we've just passed been checked?' he asked.

Holly looked back over her shoulder through the tunnel of trees they'd emerged from.

'Aye, the day Laura Fraser's body was found. Then again after the incident the other day. An action was raised to collect the tape after the latest break-in at the castle. I haven't viewed it, though. DI Haggarty was going to arrange that.'

'Okay. Chase it up, will you? Especially now we have a specific vehicle to look for.'

'Yes, Boss, I'm on to it,' she replied alacritously.

Neil once again fell silent. A medley of thoughts ran wildly around his head like excited dogs playing in a park. Not surprisingly, a state of lassitude was slowly consuming him. Only to be expected, he reasoned, when his personal and professional lives were being plagued in equal measure, by not one, but two competing nemeses!

But there was something else that rendered the throbbing in his temples a tad more bearable. The possibility, however remote, that a fortune in gold coins, stolen from the Hanoverian royal dynasty, still occupied their forgotten hiding place at Cullaird Castle after more than a quarter of a millennium!

Neil recalled the words of his old history tutor many years before. He'd been lecturing about the restoration of episcopacy in Scotland in 1662 and had alluded to the discovery of some priceless handwritten documents in an old merchant's house in Fife. The perfectly preserved artefacts contained scrawled details of sermons written by the rebellious covenanters from around that time. The tutor had heard rumours that the documents were secreted behind the panelling of the main bedchamber, and when others had dismissed the claim, he'd persisted in his search, eventually recovering the papers from a different room. Later, when he and Neil had been discussing the find in the university refectory, the canny old professor had advised him... 'Remember, Neil, my boy, there is no smoke without fire. Whenever we academics hear of such stories, however bedimmed they are by the passage of time, it is often history pleading with us to be uncovered. Never dismiss any rumour, Neil. Never dismiss it...'

The question now occupying Neil's mind was a simple one. Was it possible the Cullaird hoard was pleading to be recovered?

1746

Chapter Twenty-Six

Simon MacGillivray pushed his plate away and sat thoughtfully, listening to the comforting crackle of the nearby fire. He rested his elbows on the time-scarred surface of the old oak table and lowered his chin onto his interlocked fingers. They were sitting in the castle's dingy ground floor kitchen, a space that had been used by the family as an informal dining area for over a hundred years. He wasn't at all hungry, and the meal of oatmeal brose the cook had prepared for his breakfast remained untouched. In fact he'd eaten very little since hearing the reports of the catastrophic defeat at Culloden the previous day.

News had continued to filter through during the night, as local men, some terribly wounded, had found their way home to the tiny, scattered settlements around Strathnairn. Countless word-of-mouth accounts had by now reached the doors of Cullaird Castle, tales of suicidal valour and an inept chain of command. The part-time warriors of the Clan Chattan had led the charge against the crimson ranks of Cumberland's army and had paid a terrible price. Scores of them still lay upon the battlefield, their bodies ravaged by grapeshot, musket ball and bayonet. The names of many of the local crofters, loyal men who'd been the backbone of the community, were now confirmed as being amongst the slain. Some, though, were still missing. Whether they'd managed to flee and were in hiding, or were lying dead or wounded on the battlefield, was anyone's guess.

Meg wiped her wet hands on her apron and sat herself down on the bench next to Simon. 'You must eat something, my love. Your hunger will not bring those laddies home.'

The young laird looked around at her, dewy-eyed.

'Then I must do something that *will* bring them back. I am gratified that I have brought all the men from Cullaird safely home, but until I do something, I fear that despair will continue to surge through me like the cold winter wind. The esteem in which I am held by my clan brothers has doubtless been blemished as a result of my actions, and my disloyalty to the other Chattan men has been unseemly.'

He brought his fist down on the table, startling both Meg and the cook.

'I must return to Drumossie Moor forthwith and assist those neighbours who remain there and may still be located.'

Meg took hold of his forearm and squeezed it. She attempted a smile, but it had faded by the time he looked into her eyes.

'The country between here and the parks of Culloden abound with redcoats and government dragoons. I fear you have come to this decision by way of unsound reasoning, Simon.'

He smiled back at her. 'I am well versed in the unorthodox tactics required to ensure success in such a venture. With a small band of men, I can hopefully avoid the enemy and when the sun has set, search the country close to the field of battle. If it be God's will, we'll surely find some of our wounded and missing, and bring them safely home.'

Meg nodded. 'Then you must go, because I am confident that I can say nothing to dissuade you. Have no misconception, though, I harbour grave reservations as to the wisdom of this plan of yours.'

Simon got up, and slipped his sword strap over his shoulder.

'We must make haste. I will summon the men I returned with and we will depart without delay.'

He delivered a gentle, lingering kiss to the top of Meg's head and marched out of the kitchen, leaving his wife staring haplessly at his discarded plate.

Within two hours, Simon had mustered the eleven men who'd set out with him three days before. Such was their loyalty and respect for him, not one man had failed to answer the call. Only John Shaw was missing. Fatigue, hunger and exposure to the elements had taken their toll on him, and he had now taken to his bed, suffering from what a physician from a later age would call pneumonia.

Meg watched from an upstairs window as the little group of men proceeded down the track towards Loch Ruthven. Sleet still danced upon the chill breeze, tapping incessantly upon the windowpane, behind which she recited a short Gaelic prayer. When the murk had finally enshrouded the clansmen, she turned, wiping away the tear that had settled upon her cheek.

They made good time to the western end of Loch Ruthven, then headed north over the moor to Loch Ceo Glais, reaching the cart track that would take them down to the distant grey expanse of Loch Ness. From there, they would join the military road that ran from Fort Augustus to Inverness, a route that hugged the southern shore of the great loch all the way to the Highland capital. Once on the road, they would need to take great care. This isolated byway had erstwhile been used as a supply line between the two important garrisons, and now that Cumberland's men had reached Inverness, it would no doubt become so again.

By noon they had jogged down the steep, heathery slope that bordered the lonely dirt road. The wind-whipped waters of Scotland's second largest loch now stretched out before them. Its surface was scarred by a legion of whitecaps that surged westward, urged on by the prevailing wind. The men from Cullaird progressed nervously, skirting the edge of the road, and prepared to scatter into the heather should any horsemen appear in the distance. But none came, so they assumed that the government forces were still establishing themselves to the east in Inverness, before venturing out along the lochside.

They stopped briefly for bread and ale by the kirk at Dores, welcome sustenance, lovingly prepared by their wives and carried in sheepskin satchels upon their backs. Then it was onwards again, a rapid but cautious advance to the northeast, past isolated crofts and fields of Highland cattle, until they reached the twin fords before Holm. Here, the waters of Loch Ashie flowed down into Loch Ness. The site was known as a popular watering hole for horsemen, military or otherwise, who wished to refresh their animals before continuing on their journey along General Wade's lonely road. It was here at this very time that a reconnaissance squadron of Kingston's Light Horse had chosen to do exactly that. Twenty or so troopers, dressed in blue frock coats, faced in red, with distinctive buff shoulder belts from which hung their deadly carbines. These, together with sword and pistol, rendered the Duke of Kingston's mounted troops a deadly enemy in any engagement.

Simon crouched by the verge some two hundred yards from the government men. His comrades followed suit behind him, remaining silent whilst their leader assessed the situation.

He glanced back over his shoulder, cagey, like a wildcat caught in the open.

'There are but two options open to us here. We either engage these troopers, who, if my calculations are correct, outnumber us more than two to one...'

'And the second?' whispered Conal Mackintosh.

'We pass around them, through those trees yonder,' Simon replied, pointing at the sparse plantation of pines that grew upon the hillside to the south of the road.

Conal seemed concerned. 'The trees are well-spaced, sir. They offer us little concealment, and once amongst them and sighted by the enemy, we will have no place to flee from a galloping horse.'

Simon grinned. 'Then we must pass by and *not* be sighted, Conal, and if we are, then we must fight it out. Now pass the word back to the others.'

Conal pursed his lips and shrugged. He knew better than to argue with Simon MacGillivray when his mind was made up. The funny thing was, he was usually right! So he shuffled about to apprise his brother of the plan, leaving Simon to observe the troops in the distance, most of whom were chatting and laughing, whilst above them, wisps of white smoke climbed skyward from their clay pipes. In fact they seemed not to have a care in the world, as they stood next to their horses whilst they drank from the ford.

Once all the Cullaird men had been told of the plan, Simon led them across the road and up onto the hillside. At this point there were few trees to shelter them from sight. Miraculously, though, the troopers were too engrossed in conversation to notice the approaching Highlanders.

Simon reached the edge of the plantation first. The ground rose more steeply here, and he moved between the trees gingerly, paying particular attention to the branch debris that carpeted the sloping woodland floor. He paused and checked behind him, and was relieved to see the others progressing with an equal measure of stealth. By now, he had reached a point where several trees had fallen, and a large gap beckoned. He could now look down upon the unsuspecting dragoons, most of whom were still facing the loch and admiring the scenery before them. He felt his heart thumping against his chest and inhaled deeply before heading to the next tree. Finally, he stepped out and made his move. Ten feet and he was there, crouching again whilst his men caught up. Angus Mackintosh was the next to follow his route. He crept out into the open space, and headed towards Simon. Then, *snap*, he stepped heavily on a dry branch that cracked under his weight. One of the blue-coated troopers turned abruptly, the sound having been carried down to him on the gentle breeze. He peered up into the trees and there in front of him, some twenty yards away, was Angus, his faded plaid of red and green Mackintosh tartan silhouetted against the dark hillside. The trooper called out to his comrades. '*Rebels!* Up there in the trees,' and pulled out a pistol from under his frock coat. The other members of Simon's company scattered in panic, running between the pines and up the slope to the daylight that beckoned beyond. Simon remained where he was, still unseen by the soldier. He unslung his French-made musket and hurriedly prepared it for firing. Angus had frozen, though, like a rabbit caught in the light of a lamp. He stood, apparently unable to move, resignation in his eyes as the first lead ball from the soldier's pistol tore through his plaid and into his chest.

Simon lifted the musket to his shoulder and took aim, just as another round, this time from a carbine, passed clean through Angus Mackintosh's left eye. He crumpled and rolled head first down the slope until his progress was finally checked by a blackened tree stump.

Simon pulled the trigger on his weapon, and watched as the soldier who'd fired the shot at his friend dropped to his knees, crying out and clutching at his shoulder. Panting uncontrollably, he discarded the heavy firearm and took off up the slope, zigzagging between the trees in an effort to catch up with his men. The dragoons meanwhile were climbing up onto their mounts, pulling hard on the reins in an effort to control them as they wheeled about, startled by the series of loud shots.

Simon burst out of the trees onto the barren hillside, a moonscape strewn with boulders and random clumps of heather. His men were ahead of him, still climbing, but slowing now as the gradient became steeper and their legs began to tire. There was nowhere to go; they must stand and fight. But only half of them carried muskets and pistols; the others carried only their broadswords and dirks.

'Come back,' he called. 'We must face them here, together, or be shot in our backs.'

The others turned and stared back at him, then one by one they scurried down the slope to where he was standing, a pistol in one hand and his sword in the other.

Those that had them began to prepare their muskets for firing. Conal Mackintosh pulled a paper cartridge out from the leather pouch slung around his neck. He tore the end off with his teeth and spat the sodden paper out whilst half cocking the hammer and pouring some powder into the priming pan. He observed Simon through anxious eyes, not really needing to concentrate on what he was doing.

'Have you seen my brother, sir? I lost him in the wood, and he's not come out.'

Simon's frown gave him his answer. Conal's young face sagged in a momentary response, but he said nothing and returned to the task of loading his musket by pouring the remaining gunpowder down its barrel.

'Make each shot count, boys. You'll only have one chance,' Simon warned the defiant little group.

Each weapon was raised to the shoulder, one by one. Five

in all. Five shots for at least eighteen troopers. The fight would therefore end at close quarters, and no doubt be bloody.

They waited, perched proudly on that wild, treeless hillside, anticipating their fate: twelve gallant warriors enwrapped in the tartans their ancestors had fought in for generations.

It seemed an age, just standing there, the hiss of the wind in their ears and the sting of sleet upon their unshaven faces. Then came the distant thunder of hooves and an explosion of blue and red, as the men of Kingston's Light Horse emerged from the treeline below and charged up the slope towards them.

'Hold your fire... until you see the brass of their buttons, boys.' Simon raised his pistol in readiness. 'Steady, steady... Fire!'

A rapid staccato of musket shots filled the air, wispy white smoke from the firing mechanisms briefly obscuring the Highlanders' faces. The result was disappointing, though. One horse went down, throwing its rider. Another trooper teetered precariously upon his mount before crashing into the heather, his tricorne shredded by a musket ball. But the remaining riders continued their charge, before halting unexpectedly, no more than twenty yards from their enemy. Simon's finger pressed harder on the trigger of his dag as he waited for what came next.

One of the troopers called out above the whinnying of the horses.

'You may surrender now, sir, and I guarantee His Majesty's Forces will grant you quarter. What do you say?'

There was a momentary pause, before Simon bellowed '*Dunmaghlas!*' the war cry of the MacGillivrays, and discharged his pistol at the trooper, killing him instantly. He dropped the dag and charged forward, his broadsword raised in his right hand and his father's dirk in the left. The other Cullaird men also surged forward, repeating the war cry as they went.

344

The government men responded swiftly, running their carbines up to their shoulders on the specially adapted swivels attached to their shoulder belts. A fusillade of shots rang out, dropping all but three of the charging Highlanders. Conal limped on, lead shot imbedded in his thigh, whilst young William MacGillivray remained unharmed. Simon was also wounded in the arm, but continued apace.

'Reminds me of a pheasant shoot back home,' one of the troopers sneered as he dropped his carbine to his side and drew his pistol.

Another round of shots echoed across the hillside, just as the three remaining Highlanders staggered to within ten feet of the horsemen. The lead balls from the dragoons' pistols finally finished the job. Conal fell first, shot through the throat, and lay bleeding out on the heather. Simon took three balls to the chest, but still tottered on, summoning all his remaining strength to raise his sword and thrust at the first trooper to come into range. But he did not reckon upon the man's comrade, who wheeled round behind him and buried his heavy-bladed cavalry sabre deep into his skull. Simon slumped with a defeated sigh and Meg's name on his lips. Young William had also taken several shots to his torso. Shock, and loss of blood, had left him reeling. He seemed disorientated, staggering around in a widening circle, an expression of vacant disbelief upon his blood-spattered face. The will to fight gone, he dropped to his knees and waited for the end. Through the fog of impending unconsciousness, he sensed a horse bearing down upon him. It carried a figure dressed in blue, its arm outstretched. William's glazed eyes followed the figure as it rode around behind him; then there was a *bang*, as darkness descended and the side of his head disintegrated.

The bodies of the Cullaird men lay strewn across the hillside, whilst the men of the Light Horse wandered amongst them, admiring their work. The two that had shown signs of life were run through until their twitching ceased.

'They all finished orf?' their officer, a toff called Cranham from Melton Mowbray, enquired.

'They are, sir,' one of his troopers replied, cleaning the blade of his sabre. 'What shall we do with the corpses?'

'Leave them where they lie. I'll send a cart for them when we have established full control of this road. Evidently the rebels still roam these hills and they must first be subdued.'

The dead troopers were unceremoniously slumped over their horses and led back through the trees to the road. Fearing the arrival of more rebels, their comrades hastily packed up the rest of their belongings and resumed their journey to the Highland capital.

At Cullaird Castle, Meg sat by the roaring fire in the great hall. The light from the various candles that flickered around the room danced upon her cheeks, highlighting the elfin lineament of her face. It was a face reddened by the heat from flames that had just been revitalised by an enormous log.

She looked up from her embroidery and beamed at her two young sons, who were engaged in mock combat with wooden swords nearby.

'You must soon be away to your beds, my handsome laddies. What would your father say if he were here?'

Her words faded away upon hearing footsteps climbing the stone stairway outside. It was her maid Alice, in company with William Shaw, John's eldest son.

Alice announced him. 'Mr William Shaw of Tullich wishes to speak with you, Mistress.'

William stepped forward, removed his bonnet and bade Meg good evening.

She in turn ushered the children out with Alice and beckoned to him to come closer.

'Good evening to you, William. Come and sit yourself down by the fire. Have you ridden all the way from the farm at Tullich?'

'Aye, Madam, I have.'

He approached as requested and sat down on the high-backed oak bench that stood by the hearth. There was an uneasy silence, whilst William adjudged how best to impart his news. The big man clearly found his predicament most awkward, prompting Meg to set her embroidery aside and study him intently.

'Whatever is the matter, William? You look as if you have seen a ghost.' She tilted her head inquisitively. 'How does your father today? Is he showing signs of recovery from the fatigue of his long march?'

William fidgeted with his bonnet and looked up, his demeanour as dark as the Highland night.

'He is dead, Madam. He breathed his last but an hour before I set out for Cullaird.'

Meg gasped, then rose from her chair and joined William on the bench. She took his hand in hers and looked into his sunken eyes.

'I am so terribly sorry, William. Your father was a good and loyal friend to this family. You must tell me if there is anything I can do for your people.'

She smiled weakly, a sad caring smile, but refrained from speaking further as she sensed there was more bad news to come.

William gazed dolefully into her eyes. 'Just before my father died, we received a visit from Allister MacBean. He is my mother's cousin from Dores. Allister heard from the shepherd there, that his dog had found the body of a man in the trees by the side of the Inverness road.' His voice faltered briefly. 'When he enquired further at the location, he discovered the corpses of eleven other men who'd been slain in violent circumstances. Most of them wore the sett of the MacGillivrays.'

Meg recoiled, raising her hands to her mouth in shock. 'My husband departed this morning with eleven men, intending upon that road.'

William probed beneath the folds of his plaid, and produced a dirk.

'This was found upon one of the men, who I am told was dressed as a gentleman.'

He handed it to Meg, his eyes never straying from hers. She took the weapon from him and caressed its blood-stained hilt. Tears pooled around her eyes and clung to her lashes, glittering in the firelight. The dirk was Simon's. She would have recognised it anywhere, with its ornate hilt of carved antler, into which the feline crest of the MacGillivrays had been modelled. It also bore the telltale damage to the blade, a small chip, broken off on the sword of one of General Mackay's dragoons at Killiecrankie.

'Then he is dead,' she sobbed in a half-whisper. 'They are all dead.'

She stared into the hearth, the light from the flames flickering on her dampened cheeks. 'And what of their corpses? Who will bring them home?'

'We will send men out to collect them at first light, Madam. You have my word.'

'Thank you, William.'

He rose stiffly from the bench. 'I will take my leave of you now, Madam, as I have a long ride. But before I go I must recount my father's last words. He urged me to make them known to you.'

'Tell me, William. What did he say?'

He told me to remind you, that upon his death, only you

will have knowledge of the deeds perpetrated by the Cullaird men upon Drumossie Moor, and that you must use or dispose of the proceeds sagaciously and in the best interests of both your family and the Jacobite cause. Then he breathed his last. Are these words meaningful, Madam?'

Meg nodded and patted him on the arm. 'Yes, they are, William. They certainly are.'

'That is reassuring Madam. Then I will bid you good night, if there is such a thing.'

'The like to you too, William. I will pray for your father.'

With a deferential bow, he turned and hurried away, leaving the young widow to her grief and the realisation that now, she alone presided over her husband's plundered fortune. It was a fortune that would provide the Young Pretender with a means of furthering his campaign, but would ostensibly place her immediate clan family in danger of annihilation if its location were discovered. For now, though, she could think only of Simon. Clutching his dirk close to her breast, she wailed and slumped to the cold stone floor in pitiful lament.

2010

Chapter Twenty-Seven

The subject of the email was 'DNA Results Analysis – Hooded fleece garment, Exhibit HMA/ONE. OIC Det Sgt H Anderson'. It had come through from the lab, addressed to Fraser Gunn, who'd copied it to Holly and to the SIO.

Neil inclined across his desk, almost touching the screen, and opened the attachment. He expected the worst, but hoped for the best as far as the results went. His eyes skimmed over the usual scientific waffle, and then his mouth widened into a broad grin. Today 'best' had prevailed!

They'd got something from the hairs deposited on the jacket. Not one trace, but two. Both with a full DNA profile, but only one match on the database. Still, that didn't matter. They had one… and a name to boot!

He slammed his fist down onto the desk, so hard that the small gathering of DCs chatting in the adjacent office looked up, seeking the source of the thud.

Bradley Gordon Mackinnon was the name. Born in 1985. That made him twenty-five. Neil switched screens and typed his criminal record number into both the national and Scottish Criminal Justice Information database. Then he sat back and scanned the results.

Mackinnon's physical description broadly corresponded to that of the male Holly had chased from the leisure centre. He lived in Inverness, with a last known address in Telford Road, and was unemployed when the details had been entered onto the system.

Neil scrolled down the page to the list of his previous convictions. Several assaults were recorded against him, none against females, but all drink-related. He'd received several cautions for cannabis possession, and one for malicious damage. Not exactly an arch-criminal! He scrolled up again. The last involvement with the police in Inverness was in 2006. So he'd been a good boy for several years now.

Neil picked up the phone and spoke to one of the DCs in the local intelligence unit, but his enquiry regarding Mackinnon bore no further fruit. There had been a couple of recent sightings of him whilst in company with other parties known to the police, but that was about it. He thanked the constable, then redialled – Holly this time.

Her voice sung out. 'Hi, sir. So you've seen the email, then?'

'I have. Are you free to pay a wee visit?'

'See you in the car park in five minutes.'

Telford Road was on the other side of town, one of a tight network of residential streets situated on the same narrow strip of land between the River Ness and the Caledonian Canal, not far away from Kessock Road.

The two detectives cruised slowly along the cluttered street, negotiating the parked cars and vans that hugged the kerb line. Homes built in a variety of architectural styles faced out over small gardens, some traditional stone but and ben cottages, and others with more modern facades; bungalows, flats and the like.

'It'll be on your side,' said Neil, braking to allow a mother and child to cross the street ahead of them.

And so it was, a tiny cottage with two dormer windows projecting from a slate roof. The unpainted harled walls were liberally streaked with grime, the result of years of relentless weathering. In fact the grubby white PVC windows and front door seemed to have been the only attempt made to improve the appearance of the property.

They parked around the corner, by a newly built apartment block, and strolled back, continuing past the address so as to get a view along its side elevation and into the rear garden.

Neil had seen something large when they initially drove by, something covered in a green tarpaulin. It was standing several yards back from the metal gate that provided access to the pathway running along the side of the house. He thought he knew what it was, and a closer inspection on foot confirmed it. Poking out from under the heavy covering were two wheels… motorcycle wheels.

'Gets better,' he murmured as he opened the matching gate by the front door. It squealed when he pushed it, but the low bass thud of music emanating from the half-opened upstairs window would've masked any audible warning of their approach. He rapped on the door several times, before the music suddenly ceased and the sound of footsteps on hard flooring could be heard approaching the door. When it opened, a musty aroma was released from the shadowy interior, and there stood a young man in crumpled shirt and jogging pants.

'Aye,' was the one-word greeting.

Neil produced his warrant card from inside his suit jacket.

'DCI Strachan. This is DS Anderson. We're attached to the Northern Police Major Enquiry Unit.' He smiled. 'And who would you be?'

The young man eyed Neil suspiciously. 'Ciaran Lusk. So what's this about?'

'We just wondered if you could help us find someone.'

Neil nodded towards the hallway. 'Could we perhaps come in? Wouldn't want the neighbours talking, would we?'

Lusk stepped aside and gestured to them to enter. Once inside, Neil was close enough to detect the stale smell of liquor on Lusk's breath. He studied his host for a second, there being a vague air of familiarity about him. Lusk stared back, his lank hair compressed to one side like windblown grass, his eyes red from partying and lack of sleep.

'Have we met before, Ciaran?'

Lusk frowned. 'Not unless you drink in the Moray Tavern down in the town.'

'As if,' Neil replied, straight-faced. 'The only occasion I've had the pleasure of being in there was to execute a search warrant.'

Lusk shrugged, not knowing exactly what to say in response. As it happened, Holly gave him an out.

'Heavy session last night, Ciaran?' she asked.

'Aye, a few beers in town. So how is it I can help you?'

'Do you know a Bradley Mackinnon, Ciaran?' Neil was asking the questions again.

'Aye, he shares this place with us. What about him?'

'We want to have a chat with him, that's all. Don't suppose he's in?'

A sardonic smile crept across Lusk's face. 'No, he's not in, mate.'

Neil was becoming irritated by Lusk's petulance. 'So how do we go about finding him then, *mate*?'

The grin was still there. 'Well, first y'll have to get yerself a wee boat.'

Neil's brow crumpled. He stepped forward, his eyes drilling into Lusk's.

'I think it's only fair you should know, Mr Lusk, I got out of the wrong side of the bed this morning. Which means

I'm on a really short fuse, and you've just made it that much shorter. So I recommend you lose the attitude, my friend.'

Holly stepped forward, just in case. Hopefully Neil's judgment wouldn't be clouded by his personal feelings, but she wasn't convinced.

Lusk's grin evaporated, and he swallowed hard. 'He works on a rig… an oil rig in the middle of the North bloody Sea.'

Neil retreated. 'That's better, Ciaran. So when's he due back?'

'Next Monday, the tenth, I think.'

'Do you remember when he left?'

'A couple of days ago, it was. Aye… Wednesday, it was.'

'Umm, he's a lucky laddie, then. My father worked on the rigs. He did two-week stints, sometimes longer. Do you know which company he works for?'

'Some Norwegian outfit called Thomassen-Viking SubSea. They call him here sometimes.'

'Thank you, Ciaran. We'll give them a call.'

He turned to Holly. 'Let's show him the photo.'

'Have you seen this before?' Holly asked, producing an A4-sized photograph of the hooded jacket discarded by Cat's assailant.

Lusk pursed his lips. 'Could be Bradley's, I suppose. Can't be sure, though.'

'Have you seen him wearing one like this?'

'Aye, on occasions.'

Whilst Holly was speaking, Neil was trying to get a view into the small room to the right of the front door, the interior of which was partially visible through the open doorway. Although curtains were pulled across the one window and darkness filled the room, he could see cardboard boxes on the floor, stacked with personal belongings. 'Whose room is that?' Neil asked.

'Bradley's,' came the surly retort.

'Mind if I take a quick peek? Seems like he's packing his things up to leave.'

'Look, I'm not so sure,' Lusk replied hesitantly. 'Don't you need a warrant or something?'

Neil had already manoeuvred around to the side of him, and was now peering into the room.

'No. I'm not searching, just looking,' he asserted, directing his reply into the open space.

When Neil's eyes adjusted to the lack of light, they focussed immediately on the shiny spherical object lying on the floor by the unmade bed. He didn't say anything, but withdrew, smiling.

'So tell me, *is* Mr Mackinnon planning to move on?'

'Aye, he's got a place over in Aberdeen, closer to his work.'

'And how long will he be here when he finishes his latest stint on the rig?' Holly enquired.

'A week or so, until he can get into the new place.'

'I see. Well we'd better make sure we catch him before he goes.'

Neil scanned the hallway as he spoke. His attention then flashed back to Lusk once more. 'You mentioned Bradley shared the place with *us* earlier. So who else lives here?'

'A guy called Luke Reid. He has a room upstairs.'

'And I assume he's out too. Am I right?' Neil's eyes were roving again.

'Aye, he works. Sells double glazing over on the Longman Estate.'

'What about you? Do you work, Ciaran?'

'No, not presently. I'm out lookin'.'

'So when will Luke be back?' Neil was staring straight at Lusk again.

'He works eight to five, six days. Then he comes and goes; spends a lot of time at his girlfriend's place.'

Neil headed for the door. 'Okay, Ciaran, we'll leave it at that for now. If you're speaking to Bradley or Luke, tell them I'm wanting to have a wee chat with them.'

He opened the door and stepped out, leaving a relieved Ciaran Lusk to just nod in acknowledgement.

Neil then stopped in his tracks. 'Och, I almost forgot. Who owns the motorbike, Ciaran?'

'It's Bradley's.'

'Thought so. Mind if I have a peek?'

'S'pose not. It's no mine.'

Neil and Holly walked around to the side of the house, where Neil stooped to lift the green tarpaulin. Underneath was a shiny black Moto Guzzi V7. He checked the rear for a number plate, but there was none.

Then he looked over his shoulder at Lusk, who was watching them from the open doorway.

'Nice bike,' Neil called out. 'What happened to the reg plate?'

'You'll have to ask Bradley,' he replied acrimoniously.

'Don't worry. I will,' Neil replied as he straightened up.

The two detectives exited through the gate and walked back past the front door, just as it was slammed closed.

'Bet his mother's proud of him,' Neil remarked as he searched his pockets for the car keys.

'I thought you were going to give him a smack in there,' Holly remarked when they'd got back into the car.

'Who, me? Course not.' Neil replied, grinning. 'Wouldn't want to dirty my hands on that wee shite.'

He pulled his seat belt across him, and turned the key in the ignition. 'You know, his face seemed strangely familiar to me, for some reason.'

'You probably saw him in the Moray Tavern when you

were executing one of your warrants,' Holly suggested lightheartedly.

The comment passed without response. Neil was still searching his memory for a clue as to where – or indeed *if* – he had come across Lusk before.

They'd travelled to the end of the road when Neil next spoke. 'On the face of it, Mackinnon is looking very much like our stalker. He was here in Inverness at the time, has a big black motorbike with no number plate, and guess what?'

'Go on.'

'There was a shiny blue crash helmet in his room with the saltire adorned across the top… just like the one that maniac who followed us back from Cromarty was wearing.'

'So that's what you saw in that room. I thought you looked pleased with yourself. Did you recognise the bike at all?'

'Not really. The only time I got anywhere near it was when he spun the damned thing around and showered me in muck. But I did register the absence of a number plate.'

Their progress back through town was slow. Neil sat impatiently, tapping on the steering wheel at some red lights in Academy Street.

'It seems strange to me that Mackinnon is doing one-week turnarounds out on the rig… less in fact. I'm pretty sure they do longer than that. We need to make sure, and arrange a return visit the minute he shows up from Aberdeen.'

'I'll get on to it as soon as we get back to the office. Why don't we drop in on Cat at her sister's place and let her know how we got on just now?'

Neil looked impressed. 'Glad to see the investigating officer is eager to keep her victim informed of developments.'

'Would you have expected anything less?'

'No, as it happens.'

He swung right, underneath the Eastgate Centre, and

headed back towards the River Ness and Hannah's plush new apartment in Island Bank Road.

They spent half an hour with Cat, discussing their visit to Ciaran Lusk over a cup of coffee. But Neil was impatient to get back to the office, where he'd arranged a twelve o'clock meeting with Steve Armsley. He wanted an update as to the progress of the search at Cullaird Castle, and he also wanted Holly to make contact with Thomassen-Viking SubSea.

Armsley was waiting for him when he breezed into his office and dropped his phone on the desk.

'So how goes it?' Neil enquired, positioning his swing chair so that he could sit down and face his colleague.

'Not a thing, so far, Boss. We completed the search of the castle just over an hour ago. The only items we found when we looked under the floorboards was a Victorian sixpence and the skeletons of…' Neil's eyes widened and he looked across at him anxiously.

'Wait for it,' Armsley warned. '*Mice*, that's what we found… mice bones!'

'And that's it? You're happy no stone's been left unturned?'

'Ironically, turning the stones in the walls is the one thing we haven't done. If you want that done, then perhaps we're not the best people to ask!' He paused before reinforcing what he'd just said. 'If it's not cemented in, then we've searched it.'

Neil raised his hand. 'Okay, I think we'll draw a line there. But you've checked the underfloor spaces, up the chimneys… you know, the usual hiding places?'

Armsley frowned. It was a long, disapproving frown and Neil got the message. 'Okay, so no pile of treasure tucked away under the floorboards, then?'

'Nope, not where we looked. They're just finishing the radar and metal detector sweep of the grounds, inside and outside the boundary wall, as you asked, but then we'll have done all we can, short of getting a demolition crew in!'

'Thanks for that Steve, and thank your team too.'

'Our pleasure. I'll sign the job off with Ross Haggarty and give you an update when I get final confirmation of the ground survey.'

Holly saw Armsley leave, and the look of disappointment on the SIO's face through the glass partition. She was sitting at her desk, telephone handset clamped between her shoulder and cheek, whilst she tapped rapidly on the keyboard in front of her. She called out to one of the DCs, who was boiling the kettle at the end of the office.

'Make one for the boss, will you? I think he might need a cup.'

The young man gave her the thumbs up and reached up to pull another mug off of the shelf.

The ringtone in her ear was replaced by the voice of a young woman with a distinct but educated Aberdonian dialect.

'Good afternoon. Thomassen-Viking SubSea, Aberdeen office... Jacqui Laidlaw speaking. Can I help you?'

Holly introduced herself, sensing Andrea's surprise at a call from the police.

'I'm trying to locate one of your employees,' she asked. 'Can you help?'

'I'm sure we can,' Jacqui replied politely. 'Can I have a name?'

'Bradley Mackinnon. We believe he's currently working out on one of your offshore rigs.'

'I see. Do we need to get a message to him? It's not bad news, I hope.'

'No, no, we are just trying to establish when he went out to the rig, and his return date.'

'Oh, I see,' said Jacqui. 'If you can hold, I'll speak to

our movements coordinator. She arranges all the helicopter transfers out to the drilling platforms.'

The line went quiet and then a crackling rendition of 'Swan Lake' drifted through the earpiece. Two minutes had elapsed when Jacqui's voice supplanted the mournful melody from Tchaikovsky's ballet.

'Hello, Sergeant Anderson, are you still there?'

'Aye, I am.'

'Sorry to keep you waiting. Yes, we do have a Mr Bradley Mackinnon working for us. He's a roughneck out on our Norse Alpha Field…'

'Sorry, he's a what? Did you say *roughneck*?'

Holly could hear Jacqui giggle down the line.

'Yes, I don't mean he's a thug, or anything like that! Roughnecks are the guys who do all the heavy manual labour on the rigs. It's an oil industry term. My apologies.'

'Oh, I see. Sorry to interrupt you.'

'That's okay. My colleague tells me he flew out to the Norse Viking platform from Dyce Airport on the evening of the 5th May. He's due back on the afternoon of the 10th May. We can arrange for you to speak with him out on the rig, if you'd like.'

'No, it can wait, Jacqui. It's just a routine enquiry, that's all. We'll catch up with him on his return. Thanks, you've been very helpful.'

'No problem. Well, thank you for calling Thomassen-Viking SubSea this afternoon. You have a great day now.'

The phone went dead. Holly gazed momentarily at the handset before dropping it onto its cradle. 'What the hell's she been on?' she muttered under her breath.

Neil was reading through his emails when she tapped on the door.

'Well?' he asked. 'Is our man where he's supposed to be?'

'He certainly is. Ciaran Lusk was spot on with his dates too. Mackinnon's flying back into Dyce on the afternoon of the 10th May.'

'Well then, I stand corrected. Perhaps the Norwegians' health and safety regulations dictate shorter turnaround times for their rig crews.'

'*Roughnecks*,' Holly interjected. 'They're called *roughnecks*!'

Neil grinned. 'Yes, I know. Well, clear your diary for the morning of the 11th May, because we've got a hot date booked with Mr Bradley Gordon Mackinnon!'

'The 11th. Not the 10th?'

'Aye. Keen as I am to meet him, even roughnecks are entitled to their sleep!'

Chapter Twenty-Eight

Culloden
Saturday 8th May

They parted company at the roundabout on the Old Perth Road; Neil in his green MG, heading for Culloden Battlefield, and Holly in the Ford Focus en route to Lochend Haulage on the back road to Foyers.

When Neil arrived at the visitor centre, Malcolm Breckenridge was just visible through a sea of brightly coloured baseball hats. He saw the policeman walk in through the glass doors, and indicated to him that he would be delayed for a couple of minutes. So Neil positioned himself by the reception desk and listened, whilst Breckenridge fielded the last of a series of searching questions from the baseball cap brigade. They eventually traipsed out at the behest of their coach driver, releasing the archaeologist for another, different type of quizzing!

'I came in especially today. Canadians, on a whistle-stop UK battlefield tour,' Breckenridge explained as he guided Neil into his office.

Once seated, he smiled, 'So you're lucky to catch me on a weekend, Chief Inspector. How are your enquiries coming along?'

'Rather slowly,' Neil conceded, 'but something *has* come up that I wanted to run past you.'

'Fire away,' his host retorted. 'I only hope I can help.'

Neil recounted the story of the legendary stolen hoard, hidden at Cullaird Castle, and apparently lost for centuries.

'The details seem to have faded over the passage of time, but I was shown two coins that had allegedly come from the hoard. One was a five-guinea piece dated 1746... the same year as Culloden. Here, let me show you.'

He found the photos he'd taken of the coins on his mobile phone, and passed the device across the desk to Breckenridge.

'Do you think there may be a connection, perhaps to one of the military garrisons up here during the Jacobite rebellion? Something like that?'

Breckenridge studied the photos, pinching them out to see the inscriptions in greater detail. Then he looked up, his eyes glinting like sunlight dancing on water. 'You say these were *stolen* from the *king*?'

'Aye, according to the Copes.'

'I'm not so sure about robbing British military garrisons. To try to do so would've been tantamount to suicide.'

'What, then?'

'The British Army on the march, Chief Inspector. Cumberland's army!'

He fell silent and beamed at Neil, as if wanting to give the detective sufficient time to fully absorb the revelation. 'Because his was the only military force of any significant size, this far north at that time.'

'What? You mean the Jacobites raided one of the Hanoverian encampments en route to Culloden?'

'Not exactly. I'm suggesting they raided Cumberland's supply train whilst the army was en route to Culloden itself! Let me first set the scene. Data is available from documents created at the time, by the Treasury and the Royal Mint, that a great quantity of coin was shipped by the Royal Navy to Aberdeen on 6th April 1746. This was only a short time before the Duke of Cumberland left the city on his march westwards. You see, estimates suggest the average-sized regiments at the time would have been allocated between 1,000 to 3,000 guineas each, to pay their men during a campaign march such as that from Aberdeen to Inverness. This would also cover incidental regimental expenses, such as paying the civilian waggoners, for example. Back then, like now, a paid soldier was a happy soldier. Not only that, but in those days, each man was responsible for the cost of some of his kit and subsistence, unlike today, of course. He needed his pay to cover these expenses. So, you see, it had to be carried, however vulnerable the cargo was.'

Neil eyed him with increasing interest. 'Go on, I'm all ears.'

Breckenridge seemed eager to oblige.

'Now, Cumberland paid his troops whilst he was still in Aberdeen. Military ledgers confirm this. Between then and 16th April there wouldn't have been much time for paying the army. Even if they did, perhaps when they camped at Nairn, much of the cash would still have been carried in the baggage train when they headed out for Culloden and eventually Inverness.'

'So where are you going with this, Doctor?'

He pushed back his chair and stood up. 'Please bear with me, and all will be revealed. Oh, this is very exciting.'

With that he disappeared through the open doorway, leaving Neil looking a little perplexed.

Minutes later he returned, clutching what looked like a photocopy of an old handwritten document.

'Sorry about that. Had to extract this from the archive store.'

He placed the item on the desk and spun it around so Neil could see it properly.

'This is a facsimile copy of a letter, written on the 19th April

1746 by Lord John Murray, colonel of the 43rd Highlanders, The Royal Highland Regiment of Foot. They're probably better known to you as "The Black Watch". One paragraph of this text has been hotly debated by us historians over the years. That's the only reason I remember it so clearly!'

Neil examined the spidery scrawl on the page in front of him.

'The Black Watch were on the government side at Culloden, weren't they?'

'They were indeed, and this chap...' he paused and tapped the document repeatedly, as if to emphasise his excitement, 'was a lifelong career soldier and servant of the crown, eldest son, by his second wife, of the first Duke of Atholl.'

'The Atholls were pretty much divided during the Jacobite uprising, as I recall,' Neil suggested, looking up at him.

'They most certainly were. John's half-brother, Lord George, for one, was a general and much-respected figure on the Jacobite side... a confidante of Prince Charles Edward Stewart, no less. Now this letter is written by Lord John to his half-brother James, who became Second Duke of Atholl, and who was also a Hanoverian supporter, serving in the Duke of Cumberland's army.'

He tapped the document again, this time to specify a paragraph halfway down the page.

Neil followed his finger and read the passage.

... I am uncertain Brother, whether you know of the despoiling of the Duke's Train better than I. A Treasury Cart suffered the wretched misfortune to be stranded near Croy, only to be plundered by those despicable Rebels. They were led by a rufous haired Fellow of gentlemanly standing and clad in the most vivid of setts. Word is circulating amidst our Ranks that Barrell's Regiment of Foot may have lost not only their pecuniary wealth, a Sum exceeding Twelve hundred Guineas,

but their Regimental Silver also. The Duke has desired that
extraordinary attempts be made to recover the spoils of this
deed, and to seek out those Criminals now made infamous by
its accomplishment...

Once Breckenridge was sure that Neil had digested the all-important paragraph, he continued with the explanation.

'The original of this document is kept by the family down in Perthshire. It is the only known record of this event... until now, it seems! Historians have always questioned the reliability of Lord John's account, there being no corroboration elsewhere. But this talk of a hoard, hidden in a castle, deep in Jacobite country... Well, that could change things.'

Neil read the paragraph again, several times.

'Over a thousand guineas and the regimental silverware. That would be worth something today, don't you think?'

Breckenridge beamed. 'Without a doubt. If such a treasure were to be located, the historical significance alone of such a find would be immense.'

'The problem is,' Neil added, 'we've searched that castle high and low, using the most sophisticated kit on the market, and still haven't found anything.'

Breckenridge raised a finger. 'From what you've told me, *someone* thinks it's there! So why start searching now? My guess is, they've come across a compelling clue somewhere.'

'Umm. My thoughts exactly,' Neil concurred.

The archaeologist returned to his chair.

'Like I said, historians have debated the contents of this letter for years. Several names have been put forward for the so-called gentlemanly thief, but never one of the MacGillivrays... or the Frasers from Cullaird, to come to that.'

Neil remained mystified. 'I can't believe this event is only recorded on *one* surviving document. Surely something like this would've been on a par with the Great Train Robbery at the time?'

Breckenridge nodded in agreement. 'Of course, and that's the strange thing about it. There are plenty of documents still in existence from that time, especially those appertaining to Cumberland's Culloden army. But there is no mention of any such heist. Some of my esteemed colleagues have argued that the whole episode was covered up by the Hanoverian government. They wouldn't have wanted the Scots to create another legendary icon to inspire them. You know, someone like Rob Roy MacGregor, who died only eleven years before Culloden, or even William Wallace, come to that. The Georgian establishment would never have encouraged such a thing. These rebellious Highlanders were nothing more than troublesome vermin, in their eyes.'

He raised his finger again, signifying that he had more to say.

'Then there's the alternative school of thought... that such a heist never really took place at all. It was just some silly rumour born out of an insignificant incident that had become hugely embellished over time.'

'You mean, the regimental silverware somehow became temporarily misplaced within the baggage train, but someone suggested it may have been stolen by the rebels?'

'Possibly. It may even have been a cover story to account for someone's neglect! The absence of any other corroborative evidence has tended to render the latter option as the accepted explanation... until now, of course! It seems crazy that the Frasers' story has never become common knowledge.'

Neil contemplated Breckenridge's views momentarily. 'Would *you* want to advertise the fact that a treasure hoard had been buried under your floorboards and risk your home being plundered for it? Keeping the story under wraps was not a bad plan when you consider what has happened during the last couple of weeks!'

'All the more reason to believe that details of the story have somehow been divulged to someone,' Breckenridge theorised.

'That's right,' Neil agreed. 'Either the story of the hoard itself, or clues to its location!'

He sat back and folded his arms. 'So from the content of that letter, written... what? Three days after the battle? We can say that the theft allegedly took place actually on the 16th April.'

'Yes, the letter clearly refers to the army's advance to Culloden, past the village of Croy on the morning of the battle.'

'So, by checking for the names of the then residents of Cullaird Castle on the records of those combatants believed to have been present at Culloden before the battle, we could come up with a suspect?'

Breckenridge didn't seem convinced. He sighed. 'It's not as easy as that, I'm afraid. You are right of course. Establishing who was in residence at the castle at the time will of course provide some clues. Equally, there are modern works available that provide details of many of the Jacobite supporters present on the battlefield that day. The Prince's army, like any other, maintained comprehensive muster rolls, but once it was clear that his campaign had failed, it was not deemed safe to preserve the records of those clansmen, for fear of them being pursued as traitors. So some contemporary records do still exist, but they may not be as accurate as we'd like them to be. In fact, I have no doubt that many participants in the battle, whose names are now all but forgotten, are remembered only through family traditions.'

'Worth a try, though, surely?'

'Of course, but don't hold your breath, Chief Inspector. In fact I've already looked at our own reference material, following our conversation the other day. I'm sorry to say that although there are many MacGillivrays and Frasers included, I can find no reference to those from Cullaird Castle in the muster roll.'

Neil shrugged. 'Of course, if you'd just stolen a wagonload of coins and silver, you'd probably want to make yourself scarce. Taking part in a battle where there was every likelihood you were going to end up dead wouldn't be a priority, would it?'

'Too right,' Breckenridge agreed. 'It would've taken the perpetrators of that crime a day or more to get their haul back to Cullaird. No time for fighting battles, unless they hid the hoard temporarily and went back for it later, which I suggest would be highly unlikely!'

It was now Neil's turn to wag his finger.

'What, return to where we'd refer to today as "behind enemy lines", and then run the gauntlet back again? No, whoever did the deed wasn't present at the battle. That's certainly my view.'

'We are both in agreement, then,' said Breckenridge. 'Of course, the only way we will prove this event ever took place is to find the hoard itself.'

'Or possibly the existence of additional documentary evidence, that may provide a clue to the hoard's current location!'

Whilst Breckenridge digested his last comment, Neil produced the drawing of the ogham symbol again.

'We've now established these symbols carved onto the Frasers' bodies are most probably from the old Pictish alphabet called ogham. Are you familiar with the term, Doctor?'

'I am, Chief Inspector. I have knowledge of its existence, but it's a little outside my sphere of interest I'm afraid. I wouldn't have connected the mutilations on the body I saw with the ogham alphabet.'

'You use the term "mutilations"? I don't believe we've ever

referred to the injuries as mutilations before!' Neil looked confused.

Breckenridge flushed a little and cleared his throat. 'What are you getting at, Chief Inspector?'

Neil looked knowingly at the doctor. 'Tell me, have you told anyone about these so-called mutilations?'

Breckenridge stared blankly at him. 'Umm… I might've mentioned what I'd seen to a friend of mine at some stage.'

'And that friend… He wouldn't be Rodaidh Morton, would he?'

'Well, yes, now you come to mention it. How did you know?'

Neil frowned. 'Call it intuition.' Then he relented. 'Actually, I was looking at the impressive list of donors you have recorded on the ceiling of your cafe, and noticed the name Tordarroch Trout Farm amongst them. Rodaidh also referred to the bodies as having been "mutilated" when I spoke to him. So I put two and two together!'

Breckenridge felt he had to explain himself. 'Well spotted, Chief Inspector. As it happens, I know Rodaidh quite well. I fish the lochs down at Tordarroch on occasions. Rodaidh's a wood carver in his spare time, you see. He specialises in ancient Celtic art; turns out some impressive pieces. We sell some of his work here in the shop.'

'Yes, I know he's a carver.' Neil shook his head. 'I wondered how he'd somehow discovered that the bodies had been "mutilated", to use his phrase. His wife certainly hadn't mentioned it. She hadn't actually seen the marks on Laura Fraser's body.'

'I'm very sorry, Chief Inspector. It's just that the Mortons knew the victims so well, and when I told him that I'd discovered Mr Fraser's body… well, he just wanted to know what I knew, that's all. I shouldn't have said anything, and I hope it hasn't caused embarrassment.'

'No, as it happens, Doctor. I suppose I'm just relieved to know how the information leaked out. But I'd appreciate it if you could treat any future conversations we have in the utmost confidence.'

'Of course, Chief Inspector. Of course. Is there anything else I can help you with?' Breckenridge asked obsequiously.

'Well, I'd appreciate a copy of that letter you showed me just now.'

'Consider it done.'

Breckenridge was up and out of the office in a flash. When he returned, he placed a copy of the letter on the desk in front of Neil, together with a brightly coloured business card bearing an image of a battered old coin.

'I suggest you pay this chap a visit. He's a coin expert, deals in them professionally. He'll be able to provide much more information as to the monetary values of those coins you spoke of. And their origin, no doubt.'

Neil picked up the card and read from it. '*In For a Penny, In For a Pound,* Qualified Numismatist and Coinage Dealers. Prop Mr Paul Lennie, MBNTA. Thanks, Doctor. I'll drop by and have a chat with him.'

Whilst Neil was ensconced in Malcolm Breckenridge's bright air-conditioned office, Holly, on the other hand, had drawn the short straw. She sat, perched on the edge of an ancient-looking swing chair, the upholstery of which harboured stains so ingrained that they could possibly have dated back to the time of Culloden! She wanted to check the backside of her new designer jeans, just in case, but it was out of the question just then, and she knew she'd have to wait until her current task was complete.

In front of her was an equally grubby and somewhat ancient CCTV monitor, and standing at her shoulder was the intimidating bulk of Archibald McAdam. 'Archie', as everyone called him, weighed nearly twenty stone. His bald, pointed scalp and extensive turkey neck had somehow distorted his head into the shape of a rugby ball. It was not a bonnie sight, Holly had concluded as she conversed with the proprietor and – according to the wooden sign on his dust-coated desk – Managing Director of Lochend Haulage Ltd.

He leaned over her, pressing and holding the seek button on the monitor. Their intimacy was almost too much to bear, whilst a strange fragrance that comprised a blend of body odour and fried food hung about him.

'Should no take a minute to find the time period you're wantin', darlin',' he snorted.

'That's most kind, Mr McAdam.'

The tape whirred, as jerky black-and-white images leapt about the dusty screen.

'Och, Archie's the name, darlin'. No need for formalities around here. Right, here we go: 7.30 am, Saturday 1st May. Fill yer boots, wee girl.'

And there she sat for the next two hours, watching the traffic, light as it was, passing the entrance to the haulage yard, occasionally supping from a tannin-stained mug bearing the corporate emblem of the company. As if this wasn't bad enough, the sounds of the managing director's hard, stertorous breathing drifted across incessantly as he tackled a mountain of paperwork.

Holly watched until the time on the monitor showed 5.00 pm. She'd fast-forwarded through periods when there had been no activity on the road outside the yard, and was now as sure as she could be that no Land Rover of the type described had passed that way. She seized the tape anyway, and having thanked Archie for his hospitality and checked quickly that her jeans were not ruined, she climbed back into the CID car, reflecting upon her morning's work. If the two offenders hadn't used the B862 from Inverness to approach Cullaird, then they must've used the only other option available to them, the road down from Daviot. Unless of course, they'd come from the direction of Fort Augustus. She thought for a moment, then dismissed that possibility, at least for the time being. No. Ualas MacBean, if it was him, had connections to the Culloden area, and the road up through Daviot would take him directly to and from the battlefield.

So instead of returning to Inverness, she turned west towards Foyers and then made her way across the green and copper moorland that rose up beyond Loch Duntelchaig. Once past the entrance to Cullaird Castle and the glassy expanse of Loch Ruthven, it was only a few minutes' drive to the junction with the B851. Then the search began in earnest, a potentially fruitless search admittedly... for a CCTV camera!

The route up to the A9 was mainly rural, bordered by scattered dwellings and very little in the way of business premises. She briefly checked the Inverarnie Stores, but they were some distance away from the main road, so she continued on, heading east.

Her quest finally took her across the A9 and onto the eastbound continuation of the B851. The narrow road now threaded its way through gently sloping green fields and scattered woodland towards the battlefield site above the River Nairn.

It was almost time to give up, there being little chance of finding anyone along this lonely route with CCTV cameras covering the roadway. Until, that was, she passed Leanach House, an imposing modern home with detached outbuildings, standing on a slight rise above the road. Immaculately kept lawns ran down to the roadside, where a ranch-style gate guarded the entrance to a sweeping driveway. She passed at speed, but then braked suddenly and reversed. Yes, there it was, a small camera fixed to the gatepost, no doubt providing the owners with a remote means of screening visitors. Holly wasn't holding her breath, but it was worth a try.

The automatic gates opened silently once she'd announced her arrival and presented her warrant card up to the camera. At the top of the drive there were panoramic views down to the river, and when Holly climbed out of the car, she paused to admire the vista before her.

A voice then startled her. 'Can I help you, officer?'

The owner of the property, a silver-haired man in his early sixties, was standing in the open doorway several yards away. Holly turned and smiled. 'Lovely view you have here.'

She made her way purposefully towards the front door, speaking as she went. 'I just wanted to ask about your CCTV camera, Mr ...?'

'Campbell,' the man informed her.

A minute or so later, and she was sitting in Paul Campbell's study, whilst he stood by her side, busily working the wireless mouse next to his desktop computer. It was altogether a more wholesome experience than her previous task!

'We fitted this system after we were burgled last year. Personally, I thought it was a lot of money, but my wife insisted, so here it is. It's certainly good for watching the deer out on the road on summer mornings!'

'You can never be too security-conscious, Mr Campbell. Believe me. So how far back can we go?' Holly asked.

'Oh, thirty days plus. We set our system to motion detection mode, so that extends the recording capacity significantly.'

'By that, I assume you mean the system only records when it detects movement?'

'Aye, that's right. Here we are. Saturday morning, 1st May, 6.00 am.'

What a difference from the museum piece she'd been working with at Lochend Haulage!

'So, just fast-forward here – there are several speeds – until you see something you want to view in real time. Then click here. The camera always picks up the passing traffic, which, as you can appreciate, isn't very heavy. Shouldn't take you long to view the period you are interested in.'

He straightened up. 'I'll leave you to it, then. Call if you need anything.'

Campbell was right. It was quick. She'd covered the period from 6.00 to 7.00 am in the blink of an eye. There were only three passing cars and a tractor between 7.00 and 8.00 am. And what detail: crystal-clear images, to the extent that she could even read registration numbers. The timings were becoming interesting now. Another tractor passed the gate at 8.12 am, a blue-coloured monster with the name *New Holland* emblazoned upon it. Then several private cars and a courier van at 8.40 am. At 8.52, the ranch gates opened inwards, and the Volvo estate she'd seen parked outside the garage departed from the property, turning left towards Culloden. Then before the gates had even begun to close, a dirty green, long wheelbase Land Rover cruised past the gates, heading west!

Holly hit the 'stop' button and rewound to the point when the Volvo had disappeared. There it was again, containing two men: a dark-haired driver and a passenger clad in a camouflaged jacket and some sort of woollen hat. The unfortunate thing was that the registration plate couldn't be seen because of the angle of the camera on the gate.

She mouthed a fierce imprecation, forgetting for a moment where she was. Then she thought… *If they come back the same way then I'll get it, surely.* So to save time, she fast-forwarded the recording through to 3.00 pm. The traffic flow had understandably increased a little during the afternoon, probably tourists, driving back towards the A9 from the battlefield or the famous Clava Cairns.

Then at 4.29 pm, her hunch paid off. The Land Rover returned, travelling eastbound as expected, and this time she got the registration... bingo! To add to her excitement, the passenger was now seated on the same side of the vehicle as the camera, and as if to make her day, he looked straight at it as he passed. Unfortunately, there was some blurring of the face, compounded by the reflection from the window glass, so she couldn't be sure, but the passenger wearing the hat could well have been Ualas MacBean! She froze the footage and stared into the passenger's grainy eyes. *Perhaps the hat was a rolled up balaclava*, she mused.

She called out to Paul Campbell, who appeared thirty seconds later with a golden retriever hot on his heels.

'Find anything?' he asked, patting the dog.

'Oh, yes!' said Holly, beaming. 'Exactly what I was after! Thank you so much.'

Ten minutes later she was climbing back into the Ford Focus, with a newly burnt DVD of the relevant footage clamped tightly within her slender hand.

Chapter Twenty-Nine

Holly checked the Police National Computer on her return to the office at two thirty. She was hoping for a further breakthrough, before disclosing the CCTV footage of the Land Rover to her boss. But now she was sitting back with a bemused expression as she read the record displayed on the screen.

The registration number she had entered had been allocated to a green Land Rover all right, but one owned by the Sutherland Country Club and Hotel, an exclusive resort on the shore of Loch Shin. Interestingly, there was no marker on the record indicating that the vehicle or its number plates had been stolen.

She switched screens and checked the hotel's website, then picked up the phone and called the telephone number shown. The female receptionist immediately transferred her call to the duty manager. He in turn was quick to confirm that the Land Rover in question was still owned by them, but was currently languishing in the workshop of a local garage, having its clutch replaced! The efficient-sounding administrant even supplied the mobile phone number of the garage owner. He also provided Holly with a clue, by explaining that the vehicle was regularly used to convey hotel guests to and from Inverness Airport. So there was every chance the hotel staff had gone to the airport to meet a flight from somewhere, only to have had the vehicle's registration number taken clandestinely, so that cloned plates could be made up for the identical vehicle being used by their suspects. They could then drive around with relative confidence that they wouldn't be pulled over by the police. Even if they were, they would've probably known who owned the vehicle, so at least had a chance to talk their way out of any problems.

Having provided the hotel manager with some advice, and a reference to quote should his staff be stopped in the Land Rover with the genuine plates, she set off along the corridor to find her boss.

Neil was in equally buoyant mood when she entered his office. He eagerly recited the tale of the much-debated letter from Lord John Murray to his half-brother, then handed her the copy to read.

'I'm becoming more and more convinced that the story behind this hoard is one of truth rather than myth. In fact I'm now confident that's what our suspects have been searching for! They've come across some sort of clue, the provenance of which is clearly compelling, and have since been acting on that information.'

He retrieved the letter from Holly and placed it on his desk. 'According to Breckenridge, the monetary value of a stash this size, combined with the historic significance of it, could amount to a substantial fortune.'

Holly's ebullience was more measured. 'But the link between this unsubstantiated historical event and the Fraser family's so-called legend remains conjectural, surely.' Then as an afterthought, she added, 'As encouraging as things may seem?'

'Of course, Holly. That goes without saying,' Neil

admitted, his bubble now well and truly burst. 'But you have to agree, it is a potential motive and could explain what's been going on over at Cullaird, couldn't it?'

'Absolutely. I do, sir.'

'What's that you've got there?' he asked, having spotted the DVD in her hand.

'It's CCTV footage, possibly of Mr MacBean and his accomplice, going to, and returning from their latest outing to Cullaird last Saturday.'

'You're kidding me?' Neil looked stunned. 'Tell me more.'

So she did, whilst he sat in silence, hanging onto her every word. They then watched the footage over and over, whilst Neil compared the images of the passenger to that of Ualas MacBean, from a photo he had on his desk.

'Can't be sure, but it could be him,' he finally concluded. 'Well done you, Holly.'

'Shame about the plates, though, eh?'

'Aah, that's not surprising,' Neil murmured dismissively. 'They'd be fools to drive around in a truck like that with genuine plates on it. Still, false or not, we now have a number to circulate. So if they carry on using them, they're going to ping up on ANPR at some stage.'

The automatic number plate recognition system was a revolutionary crime-fighting tool recently introduced to the far north. So when those vehicles bearing the cloned or genuine registration plates strayed anywhere from the remotest of Highland roads, their presence would theoretically attract prompt attention from the local police! In the case of the hotel staff, it could prove inconvenient, of course. But as far as the two suspects were concerned, their days would, hopefully, be numbered.

'I reckon they're basing themselves somewhere out Culloden way,' Neil continued. 'If it is MacBean, he's come *from* and returned *to* that area. I'll ask the uniform boys to focus their patrols out there, see if we get lucky.'

He removed the disc from his PC tower and patted it gently.

'You get the circulations done. Let's hope the poor devils who use those plates legally don't get hammered. May be worth having a word with them, you know, give them a heads-up.'

'Already have done, sir. They understand fully. A letter of thanks to Mr Watson, the manager, may not go amiss, though.'

'Good idea. I'll get on to it!'

Neil waited until Holly had left the office, then picked up the phone and dialled the number of the chief inspector, operations. Having been reassured by his opposite number in the uniform branch that he would be briefing his patrol officers to intensify the search for the green Land Rover, he called Selina Cope.

There was no answer at the castle, so he tapped out the number of her mobile phone. This time she replied. Her voice seemed distant, and the hum of an engine droned in the background.

'I'm on my way to the railway station in Inverness,' she shouted above the din. 'I'm picking up my cousin Miriam. She wanted to come up today, so managed to get on a flight to Edinburgh.'

'I see,' Neil replied. 'I was hoping to have a chat, but it's not so urgent.'

'Okay… tell you what. I'm dropping Nat off at the airport, then heading into town. Why don't you meet us for tea at the Royal Highland Hotel by the station, say four o'clock? Miriam's train is due in at a quarter to. I'm sure she would like to meet you.'

'Good idea. Four o'clock it is, then. Thanks.'

He replaced the handset, relieved in a way that he didn't have to drive out to Cullaird again.

By three thirty, he'd signed off the last of a pile of overtime claims and was on his way out. He paused by Holly's desk as he passed. 'I'm off for tea with Selina Cope and her cousin,' he announced. 'Want to come?'

'Not really, sir. I'm hoping to get off early tonight. Got a hot date to get ready for.'

Neil stopped pushing his arms into the sleeves of his jacket.

'Really?' he asked. 'I didn't know there was a man in your life currently.'

'There isn't. This guy's my ex. He's just back from Colorado, where he's been working as a ski instructor.'

She smiled weakly. 'We dated when he was working down at Aviemore. Then he got the job abroad and we drifted apart from then on.'

'Colorado's one hell of a distance from sleepy old Aviemore. Still, at least he's not on our books. What's your current score? Two DCs and a DS... who I believe was married?' He raised a questioning eyebrow.

'Aye, well that's all in the past now. For the record, he did say he was divorced, that DS. I wouldn't have gone anywhere near him if I'd known! Anyway, that's enough of my love life. How's Cat doing?'

Her convenient change of tack amused Neil.

'She's fine. The time with her sister has helped, I think. She's back at home now.'

'I assume there have been no more texts from Mr Hoody?'

'Not a squeak. He's probably been spooked, you getting close enough to him to start tearing his clothes off!'

She grinned. 'It's probably awkward, stalking and texting from the middle of the North Sea!'

'Umm, must be. Well you have a good night out with your ski instructor... no going off-piste mind!' Neil glanced over his shoulder, checking her reaction, as he weaved his way between the other DCs' desks to the doorway.

'Don't worry, I'll be good,' she called after him. 'Enjoy your tea.'

He did enjoy his tea as it happened... *and* the selection of small cakes the foreign-sounding waitress had placed before them. He'd caught up with the two women just as they'd emerged from the railway station concourse. They were walking arm in arm, whilst Miriam pulled a large suitcase on wheels.

Now, they sat facing each other in the hotel's comfortable lounge, watching Selina pour tea into their cups from a large silver pot. Neil was becoming quite familiar with the location, having sat outside only a short time before, watching Cat sitting alone whilst she waited for... well, no one, actually!

He was sitting directly across from Miriam Fraser, and although she was easily sixty-five plus, he found her to be more than a little attractive. She had certainly worn well... no doubt the result of a privileged lifestyle since birth. Beneath the short, trendily cut mousy-blonde hair, lurked inquisitive eyes and a character to match. However, the talk had been about *her* since they'd settled down onto the peach-coloured sofas. To be fair she was an easy person to talk about, a woman whose background was positively Cartlandesque!

So far he'd discovered that Miriam's mother, Fenella Cunningham as she was, before her marriage to Selina's Great-Uncle Farquhar, had inherited the imposing Clune House near Dores and its surrounding hunting estate at the end of the war. It was here that Miriam was raised, before attending Ramsay House private girls' school in Edinburgh, and thereafter, a Swiss finishing school near Geneva.

She'd eventually returned to Clune House, and a life plagued by her domineering mother. Things had apparently come to a head when Miriam, with no prior knowledge, had been betrothed to a local landowner and high-flying diplomat called Malcolm Dewar. The row that followed sealed the fate of her relationship with her mother, and so she applied for a job with the BBC's fast-developing television arm. To her surprise – not Neil's – she quickly landed one, as a PA to a wildlife documentary producer. Around that time, her boss was travelling to Africa regularly, particularly the south of the country, during the making of a flagship TV series called *Safari Watch*... and that's when Selina had handed her a cup of tea.

'Oh, thank you, darling,' she purred, charm oozing out of her like holy water. 'I've been yearning for a cup of the brown stuff since I left Waverley.'

'Surely the trains have refreshment facilities on them, Miriam?' Selina suggested, only to be put firmly in her place.

'Oh, Selina dear, you mean from those ghastly little trollies serving tea in paper cups? Heaven forbid!'

Neil leaned forward and selected a square of Battenberg cake. 'You were saying about Africa, Mrs Fraser?'

'*Ms*, darling, *Ms*. I left the *R* behind at the divorce court. But call me Miriam, please.'

'Oh, sorry Miriam.' Neil flushed.

'That's all right, darling. I decided to go back to the maiden name. Didn't want the constant reminder of my ex, and Fraser seemed the better of the two options, I s'pose. I mean... Van Nieuwoudt. What a bloody mouthful.'

'Sounds like you found yourself a South African husband, then,' Neil propounded, as if he didn't already know!

'Spot on, Inspector. No flies on you, eh? Yes, he was—'

Selina finished the phrase for her. '*Boer* by name and *bore* by nature.' She chuckled. 'You don't change, do you?'

Miriam scrunched her face. 'Well, it's true, is it not? Despicable little man, having affairs all over the place.'

Selina winked an eye at Neil. 'Well, one big one, to be exact! But he is a *rich* little man too, though.'

'Yes, dear, I will give him that. I didn't want for much when I was married to him. At least I saw to it that his gold-digging trollop, Elize Kuiper, didn't get any of his wealth, damn her.'

Selina turned to Neil, her glossy lips forming an embarrassed smile.

'Dawie, that's his name, had a ten-year affair with his PA… the trollop, Elize, until Miriam found out! He co-owns a company called Noordhoek Diamonds and Tanzanites with his son Peter.'

'Tanzanites? Aren't they some sort of precious stone?'

'Oh, they're certainly *precious*!' Miriam interjected. 'Tanzanite is a bluey violet-coloured gemstone, found only in northern Tanzania. In its natural state, tanzanite is extremely rare, and is only extracted in the Mererani Hills. Its value, when refined, is astronomic. Hence my ex-husband being very rich indeed.'

'I see, and is he still based in South Africa?'

'Oh yes, he'd never leave the place. He lives in the Clifton area of Capetown, an exclusive waterfront district just outside the city. Mind you, he's rarely there, though. Always travelling around the world collecting his little silver snuff boxes or playing golf. Dawie's more of a sleeping partner in the business these days. Leaves most of the work to Peter. Well, he is nearly seventy, I suppose.'

She selected an éclair from the cake stand on the table.

'Now, enough of my private life. Tell me, Chief Inspector, how close are you to catching this monster who murdered my dear cousin and his wife?'

'We have a suspect, a man called Ualas MacBean. It's just a matter of catching up with him. He's proving to be somewhat elusive at present.'

Selina patted her cousin's knee. 'Mr Strachan reckons this

man MacBean may have found a clue relating to the so-called Cullaird treasure hoard, and now he wants to find it, come hell or high water.'

'There are other considerations,' Neil added. 'We also think this man may have some sort of grudge against your family. From the evidence we've gleaned so far, he seems very keen to advertise the fact that he's taken his revenge for something.'

Miriam shook her head. 'Appalling situation,' she murmured. 'We must do all that we can to bring about the apprehension of this fellow. What can I do to help, Chief Inspector?'

'Well, firstly we're pleased you've come up to stay with Selina, now that Mr Cope has gone down south. But I'm not entirely happy that you're both staying in the castle. I wouldn't be surprised I'm afraid if MacBean, or whoever he's associated with, came back for a third attempt at finishing the job.'

Miriam studied Neil intently. 'But surely you're guarding the place, and you've got alarms fitted to the castle, haven't you?'

'Yes, that's as may be,' he replied glumly, 'but we're dealing with a shrewd operator here, a man who's focussed fully on his objective. I already have an officer in hospital with a cracked skull as a result.'

'No way am I going to move out,' Selina protested. 'That's my family home. I still have work to do there in respect of my parents' estate. I need to be on site.'

'Well said, darling. If Mr Mac… whatever his name is, wants to return, we will be waiting for him.'

Neil raised his hands in frustration. 'At least you know my views on the subject, but of course, I can only advise you.'

'Consider us advised, then,' said Miriam defiantly, tugging at the cashmere scarf that adorned her shoulders.

Selina didn't want to dwell on the subject of residency, so she switched her attention back to Miriam.

'Mr Strachan wanted to know something of the background relating to the hoard. I told him you knew more about these family stories, being a member of the older generation!'

'Charming,' said Miriam, reaching for her teacup. 'Just as well us oldies listened to the tales passed down by our forebears. If we left it to you lot they'd be lost forever!'

She sipped her tea, and pondered the question. Then, to the surprise of her two companions, she slapped the arm of the sofa.

'Right, I think I've got the story right in my head. It all revolves around one of our eighteenth-century ancestors, a swashbuckling fellow by the name of Captain Simon MacGillivray.'

'I don't think I've heard his name mentioned before,' said Neil.

'No, you're right. We only discussed Major Alisdair, the guy in the painting,' Selina confirmed.

Miriam raised a finger in acknowledgement. 'Ah, well there you have it. Simon was Alisdair's son, the oldest child of six. Five girls, although one died at birth, and the one boy. He was well educated during his early years and later became a staunch Jacobite and dedicated Episcopalian. At quite a young age he took over the running of his father's estate. Alisdair was a weak and sickly character, you see. Anyway, when Prince Charles Edward Stewart appeared on the scene in 1745, Simon rallied to the MacGillivray chief's call to arms. He subsequently became a captain in the Clan Chattan Regiment, under the command of his second cousin, Alexander MacGillivray of Dunmaglass.'

She stopped to take a further sip of tea before continuing. 'So when the Jacobite army set off to conquer one and all, Simon and a small group of men from Cullaird went along too. In battle, he was apparently considered a natural soldier, regardless of his inexperience in the role. So much so, that Alexander quickly made him his aide-de-camp.'

Neil, as always, wanted to get to the point. 'So was Simon present at the Battle of Culloden?'

Miriam shook her head. She wasn't going to be rushed. 'Patience, please. All will become clear.'

Neil retracted into the cushions that lay scattered about him. No way was he going to incur her displeasure!

'To answer your question, Mr Strachan, yes and no. The story goes that he and his followers *did* muster with the other Chattan men at the Stone of the Swords up in the forest at Gask. From there they marched to Culloden, early on the day before the battle. But the Duke of Cumberland had no intention of fighting on that day… because it was his birthday, bless him! History tells us that Lord George Murray, the Jacobite general, proposed conducting a night raid on the government army encampment at Nairn—'

'But we know that went disastrously wrong,' Neil interrupted her.

'Correct. So the clansmen, many of them exhausted and hungry, wandered back in the darkness towards their Culloden camp. A good number of them got lost, and some, fed up with their treatment, just disappeared back to their homes.'

'So you're going to tell me that Captain Simon and his men were amongst those who became lost and never returned to fight the battle later that day. Instead they conducted a little raid of their own?'

'Pretty much, Mr Strachan. Whether they were lost or not is unclear, but the story according to my grandfather was that Simon and his men came across a pay wagon with a broken wheel… and hijacked it. Then, instead of returning to the battlefield and being mown down shoulder to shoulder with his clan brothers, he decided to bypass it altogether and take his booty home.'

Neil looked at her in wonderment. 'That's some tale! Almost too good to be true… if I hadn't read about this so-called highjacking in a letter, only a few hours ago!'

'Really! What letter would that be?' Both women looked puzzled.

Neil took out the copy of the letter that Breckenridge had produced, and recounted what the archaeologist had told him.

'That's incredible,' said Selina, having read the letter for the third time. 'So the legend may actually be fact!'

'I'm not surprised. The account passed down through the generations was very detailed,' Miriam pointed out. 'No smoke without fire, and all that!'

She sat back, looking pleased with herself. 'A word of caution, though. This doesn't mean the hoard is still hidden at the castle. Remember that.'

'I agree with you on that score,' Neil replied. 'What I can't understand is how these two accounts, which in effect corroborate each other, have never been married up before!'

'Family secrets are powerful things, Chief Inspector! The details of this one have been well kept, so much so that even Selina knows very little of the finer detail. My father only told me just before he died, and even then, he warned me to keep my mouth shut about the whole affair! He didn't want all and sundry nosing around looking to get rich quick.'

'I understand entirely, but I'm still astounded that the story has never found its way into the public domain,' said Neil. 'So was Simon looking to line his own pockets or what?'

'Oh no,' Miriam asserted. 'He was neither common thief nor coward. But equally, he was no fool. He knew that fighting a battle on that moor would result in disaster. He saw the hoard as the spoils of war, and intended to hide it and use the money to support the furtherance of the Jacobite cause.'

'So what went wrong? What happened to Simon and his men?'

'It took them most of the day to return to Cullaird, and when news reached them at the castle of the devastating defeat at Culloden, they vowed to return to the moor to help recover and arrange burial of their dead comrades. So they set out the next day, but by then the government forces were sweeping westwards, and not surprisingly they came across a troop of dragoons on the road between Fort Augustus and Inverness. Simon and his lads were apparently slaughtered in the ensuing spat. Tragic!'

'My, this story has been kept well under wraps,' Selina remarked. 'I certainly have never heard any of this detail before!'

'Well, dear, Simon only disclosed the location of the hoard to one person, his beloved wife Meg, a Mackintosh girl from Moy. I can only assume she must've told her son, and so the story cascaded down the generations. What I do know is that later generations of the family, starting with my great-great-grandfather, made every effort to restrict the number of people who had knowledge of the story. This was for the reasons I outlined earlier; fear of someone unscrupulous, like this fellow MacBean, doing exactly what has happened now!'

Neil frowned. 'What about the men who must've helped conceal the hoard? I'm surprised they didn't tell their families.'

'These men were fiercely loyal to their leader, landlord... however you wish to interpret their relationship with Captain Simon. It would not have surprised me to learn that they had kept their own counsel even when it came to their own families. As it happened, there would've been only a small window of opportunity to tell anyone, because they were all dead the next day!'

She shrugged. 'Perhaps they did tell someone. We will never know. But one thing I do know. The hoard was never found, and it wasn't through lack of trying.'

Then she turned to Selina. 'You've seen the two five-guinea coins that your father kept?'

'Yes,' Selina replied. 'That's what started all this talk of hoards. Us finding those coins in the bureau.'

'Well, *they* are said to be from the hoard. Initially they were given to Meg, as a gift to hand down, together with the explanation as to their origin, to the eldest son of each generation. I assume the reason for this was to ensure the story of the event never died.'

She thought for a second. 'In fact I do remember my father telling me that Meg was supposed to have left a letter for her son James, telling him where the hoard could be found, should she die unexpectedly. The irony of it was, that's exactly what she did... and before disclosing to him where the wretched letter was!'

'So this letter was never found, then?' Neil asked.

'It would appear not. Of course, it may never have existed in the first place. We can't prove any of this,' Miriam responded resolutely.

Neil raised a cautionary finger. 'Let's suppose then, that this letter *did* exist. Then Meg surely would've hidden it where she could have accessed it relatively easily. I mean, a woman isn't going to start pulling up the floors, or knocking stones out of the walls, is she?'

'I wouldn't have thought so,' said Selina. 'What are you getting at?'

'Well, I would've expected my search team to have found it, if it was, say, tucked up a chimney... something like that.'

'Yes, I see what you're saying, Chief Inspector,' Miriam seemed enthralled.

'I'm just suggesting that the letter may in fact have been thrown out many years ago, unwittingly or otherwise.'

'Surely it would've been read if found, before being discarded by the family,' Selina suggested.

Neil shook his head. 'Not if it wasn't *found*, and ended up being taken out of the castle in something else. A painting or a piece of furniture, perhaps.'

'Oh, I see, and the letter was discovered later, by a stranger.' Selina looked back at him, wide-eyed.

'Yes… like *now*… in 2010.' Neil glanced from one woman to the other, seeking their consensus. 'And it's fallen into someone's hands, together with a big fat clue as to where the hoard was hidden!'

'You mean, like this chap you're searching for?' Miriam concluded.

'Aye, absolutely,' said Neil. 'But the possible finding of the letter doesn't explain the wanton brutality inflicted on your family members, *or* the significance of the Well of the Dead. I still believe there's a secondary motive at play here, not just robbery. And you know what? I think it's to do with an ancient code of honour. The fact that your ancestor, Simon MacGillivray, never took his rightful position on the Jacobite line for that final tragic Highland charge.'

'But why seek vengeance now, after all these years?' Selina asked, looking puzzled.

'Because, Selina, the letter proves that Simon *was* absent. Until then, the whole story was, to use your phrase, "just a legend"! No, we're looking for someone who's prepared not only to commit a high-value robbery, but also to inflict terrible violence upon his victims… as a means of retribution!'

Selina took up the thread. '… Because, not only does he want the hoard, he also wants to avenge his ancestors, for an apparent wrongdoing perpetrated 200 years ago, when *my* ancestor absented himself from the field of battle…'

'Exactly. A battle during which men of his *own* clan, fighting in the same regiment as Simon, were massacred in their droves… the Clan MacBean!'

Chapter Thirty

Monday morning, and Holly was once again driving west across the floodplain of the River Nairn. Her brief was to follow up on Neil's latest theory… that the supposed letter, written and secreted by Meg MacGillivray, was somehow shipped out of Cullaird Castle sometime between April 1746 and May 2010! 'This is crazy,' she mouthed, as she reached over to the passenger's seat for her bottle of mineral water. 'Absolutely crazy!'

Miriam opened the door to her when she arrived at the castle. Selina's hearty cousin looked a little taken aback when she saw Holly, warrant card in hand. 'Goodness, is Her Majesty's Constabulary populated predominantly by women these days? There are two of your colleagues upstairs!'

Holly smiled. 'We're certainly getting our feet under the table more than we used to, Mrs Fraser. We're better value for money than men you see, because we can multitask.'

Miriam warmed to the attractive blonde from the outset, and could see a little of herself in the young detective. She had spirit and a quick wit, something she saw and admired in other modern women, like Selina, and to an extent in her own daughter, Marianne.

The two women commenced the assent of the forty-seven stone steps to the first-floor landing, the hollow echoes of their footfall resounding in their ears.

When Holly reached the top, her eyes focussed naturally upon the leaded lights of the tiny window immediately ahead of her, no doubt because of the bright sunlight flooding through it. But then her attention was diverted to the left, to a tiny portrait in a battered dark wood frame that hung slightly at an angle, two feet from the window.

She paused to get a better look at it, leaning forward as she did so. The portrait was a likeness of a young man with reddy-brown hair tied back with a black ribbon. He was portrayed in a relaxed pose, sitting back on a large rock, a musket supported vertically within the crook of his left arm, whilst he rested the other across the back of a white-coated hound of some description. But it was the great plaid he had wrapped around him that had caught Holly's eye: shades of blue but dominated by the almost orange background.

Miriam looked over her shoulder, sensing that her guest was no longer behind her. She retraced her steps and stood next to Holly, reaching up to straighten the frame.

'We were only talking about him to Chief Inspector Strachan yesterday. His name was Captain Simon MacGillivray, resident here from 1714 to 1746.'

'The tartan's a little on the loud side,' Holly joked. Then, before Miriam could respond, she quoted the line from the letter Neil had shown her two days before. '"Rufous haired fellow of a gentlemanly standing, and clad in the most vivid of setts". Sounds like he could be our Highland Robin Hood!'

'That's one way of putting it,' Miriam agreed, not entirely happy that her ancestor should be compared to an English outlaw. 'He's the chap who allegedly hijacked the Duke of Cumberland's baggage train.' Then, as an afterthought she said, 'The "loud" sett, as you describe it, is the ancient MacGillivray. It *is* rather vivid, if I say so myself.'

They moved on, entering the great hall where Selina was drinking coffee with the two FLOs.

'Coffee, DS Anderson?' Selina asked.

'That's very kind of you,' she responded. 'Black, no sugar.'

Mug in hand, Holly perched upon a richly embroidered footstool.

'DCI Strachan was wondering whether you had any record of the furnishings or contents from the castle that have been sold over the years. I know it's a big ask.'

'I'm sure there would be, somewhere in my father's study.' Then she looked about her before qualifying her remark. 'I haven't noticed anything missing from any of the rooms since my last visit home. In fact, not even from when I was a child, if I'm honest! Most of the contents of this place are family heirlooms, and have been here for generations.'

'So nothing's gone to auction? Perhaps to help with the upkeep of the castle?'

'I don't think so. Certainly not recently.' Selina shook her head.

Holly was persistent. 'Actually, I was thinking more in terms of ninety years ago. You did mention to us on an earlier visit that your great-grandfather's estate attracted heavy death duties at the end of the First World War.'

'Err, yes, it did. But that's going back a bit, isn't it?'

'Not necessarily. Mr Strachan is of the opinion that *any* date is relevant, all the way back to 1746. He's keen that I follow up on all possible lines of enquiry, bless him!' There was more than a hint of sardonicism in her reply.

Miriam returned her empty mug to the tray on the coffee table.

'You are right, dear. I believe Susan, George's wife, had to take drastic action at the time of his death. I actually recall my father complaining bitterly that my grandmother had sold items from the castle without seeking agreement from George's brother and sister. "No bloody Huntsby-Maclean should be selling off the Frasers' property without a Fraser's say-so," the crusty old devil used to say.'

She let forth a little chuckle. 'Then my mother would taunt him, saying, "If you go to meet your maker before me, darling, then it'll be a Cunningham" – that was my mother's maiden name – "who'll be doing the selling... and no other Fraser will be getting a look-in"!'

'Families, eh,' said Selina, shaking her head.

Holly smiled back. 'Do you think it's just possible there may be records of the sale still in existence, Selina?'

'You'll need to give us a chance to have a look in the attic room if we're looking that far back. That's where all the old paperwork is filed away. It's like the National Archive up there, so it may take a while.'

She gestured towards Lorna McKirdy and Aili Hughes. 'Our friendly liaison officers can give us a hand. I'm sure they'd prefer to keep busy!'

'Good idea,' Holly agreed. 'In the meantime, I'll be off up the road to see Mr Blair at the distillery. I don't suppose he or any of the staff there are aware of the story of the hoard, are they?'

Her hosts shook their heads. 'Not that I'm aware of,' said Selina. 'As far as I know, only close family were ever told about it.'

'I can certainly vouch for that,' said Miriam. 'I was only telling Mr Strachan the other day, the story relating to the hoard has always remained a closely guarded family secret. There are very few people alive today who know the whole tale, and *they* would be immediate family... those who are interested, of course!'

'Okay, and what about furnishings? Has anything been

taken from here to the distillery? You know, to furnish offices, something like that.'

Both heads shook again. 'Never, as far as I know.'

Aili then escorted Holly to the front door, but not before the latter had taken a photo of Simon MacGillivray's portrait whilst she passed by. She hesitated and inspected the quality of the image on the screen. 'Umm, that'll do.'

Then, as they descended the stairs, Holly grasped her colleague's arm. 'Make sure you call me, Aili, if you find anything interesting relating to the sale of paintings or furniture from this place.' She hunched her shoulders, as if in desperation. 'In fact let me know about anything sold since Bonnie Prince Charlie was roaming the planet. Anything that could conceivably contain a bloody letter.'

'Will do, Sarge. Looks like we'll have a busy day ahead of us!'

'Well, you can't sit about all day drinking coffee, whilst the rest of us are running around all over the place. That would never do!'

Holly grinned and waved as she walked out to the car. 'Good luck!' she mouthed before climbing in. 'Hope you don't have an allergy to dust!'

Sandy Blair breezed into the reception area of the Lochmhor Distillery. 'Back so soon, Sergeant? And no Mr Strachan today.'

'He's tied up with meetings this morning, so asked me to come and have a wee chat.'

'Come through to my office, then.' Blair held out a welcoming arm.

Halfway along the corridor, beyond the reception area, were two large brass plaques, one commemorating the sacrifice of the twelve Lochmhor employees who lost their lives during the two World Wars. The other listed the Chairmen of the Distillery since its inception in 1872.

Holly stopped to look up at the names. 'So John Fraser set up the distillery back in the Victorian period?'

'Aye, it all started though with his father James, who took on and ran the Cullaird Estate in 1820. He was, by all accounts, a socialite and shrewd businessman. During the Highland potato famine of 1846–47, he kept his workers provisioned and fed when others in this area starved. They in turn worshipped the ground he walked on.'

'I thought the potato famine was restricted to Ireland,' Holly interjected.

'Oh no. The poor Highland crofters suffered from the potato blight too, but to a lesser degree.'

Blair was not one for digressing, and was eager to get on with his story. 'As I was saying, the story goes that one day in 1847, James caught some of his employees using a still on one of the local farms. But instead of preventing its use, he encouraged it, for the benefit of the other estate workers... and of course, himself! From then on, his interest in whisky developed apace, and he came to realise the commercial opportunities of such a venture. He passed on his interest to his son John, but he'd become a career soldier with the Duke of Albany's Highlanders, and spent a great deal of time away from home, mainly in Africa during the Frontier Wars. Then, when John finally left the army and returned home in 1850, he originally confined himself to managing the estate. Until, it seems, he became bored with the humdrum routine of farming and the like. So he rekindled his early interest in the distilling process, realising, like his father, that there was big money to be had from supplying the good stuff to the Victorian gentry. So in 1872, the Lochmhor Distillery was finally born.'

'Very interesting, Mr Blair.' Holly was now scanning the other names inscribed on the plaque, relieved that the biographical histories of James and John Fraser had finally been unravelled. She read from the top to the bottom of the list... Simon Donald Fraser, Alisdair Fraser, Grace Fraser, Susan Fraser... Holly knew all about her! Then there was Farquhar Fraser, and finally Duncan Fraser, whose butchered corpse had been found at the Well of the Dead, two weeks before.

Blair wasn't one for silences! 'It gets very confusing when these old families keep reusing names. Especially with all the Simons and Alisdairs!'

Holly smiled back at him. 'Lead the way, Mr Blair. I wouldn't want to take up too much of your valuable time!'

The sun streamed through the vertical blinds, bathing Blair in a shaft of dusty light, perhaps befittingly in the case of a man about to be interrogated! The glare clearly irritated him, so he sat forward, his hands clasped together on his blotter, nervously awaiting Holly's first question.

'I've already asked Selina about this, but as she's rarely up here, I'll ask you too. Has there been any transfer of items such as furniture or artwork from the castle to the distillery at any time?'

'That's a strange question, Sergeant. Why would the Frasers do such a thing?'

'I don't know. Duncan Fraser had his office here. Perhaps he wanted to personalise it.' She was a little irritated at having her question answered with a question. 'Whatever the reason, can you confirm, yes or no?'

'I'm not aware of any such transfer of items from the castle to here. Everything we have on these premises, including Duncan's office, has been purchased directly from office suppliers, according to need. Our soft furnishings and the few examples of artwork we exhibit were commissioned to complement the theme of our business.'

He gestured towards the large photograph on the wall by

the doorway. It depicted smoke from the distillery's drying kiln, wafting out from its distinctive pagoda chimney against a background of the setting sun.

'Even the cushions on the sofa behind you are covered in our corporate tartan, the Ancient Hunting Fraser.'

'Okay, let's move on. Were you ever made aware of a story that has been handed down through the Frasers' family, suggesting that a hoard of coins was hidden somewhere in or around Cullaird Castle around the time of the Battle of Culloden?'

Blair pursed his lips and shook his head. 'That's news to me,' he replied. Then he grinned. 'Is there any truth in it?'

'We don't know, Mr Blair. We're just following up all lines of enquiry. Would there be any other members of staff here who may have known about such a story?'

Blair shook his head again. 'Well, if you take into account that I'm the longest-serving member of staff here, then I'd suggest that it's unlikely.'

He paused for thought. 'Of course there are staff members here whose parents have worked at the distillery, some for a number of generations, so I can't vouch for them.'

'I don't think we'll make too much of it. It's only a story, after all. I was just interested to know whether it was an open secret, that's all.'

'That certainly doesn't seem to be the case, Sergeant. I've never heard such a story being discussed here. I'll keep my ear to the ground all the same.'

'Thanks. I appreciate that,' Holly responded dismissively.

The phone on Blair's desk then began to burble, interrupting their conversation. He picked it up and announced himself. 'Hello, Selina. How are you…?'

Holly could hear Selina's faint, muffled voice, and gleaned from the conversation that she'd found something interesting that she wanted Holly to see. She was right. When Blair returned the phone to its cradle, he said, 'Selina has found some documentation pertaining to the sale of items from the castle. She asks that you drop by on your way back.'

'In that case, I'll be on my way, Mr Blair.' Thank you for your time today.'

Blair showed Holly out to reception and propped the front door open for her, at which point she stopped and smiled up at him. It was a smile that camouflaged what she had to say next. 'I'd appreciate it if our conversation today, and any other day, remains confidential, Mr Blair. We wouldn't want any talk of hidden hoards going viral, or more importantly, the safety of the Copes being jeopardised as a consequence of any idle gossip amongst your staff.'

Blair smiled back awkwardly as she squeezed past him. 'I fully understand, Sergeant. My lips are sealed.'

Selina, Miriam and Lorna McKirdy were busy sifting through boxes of paperwork in the great hall when Holly arrived back at the castle. She entered the room with Aili Hughes, where dozens of yellowing documents were strewn across the long, polished table.

Selina stopped what she was doing when she saw Holly.

'Thanks for coming back. I thought you'd want to see this.'

She handed Holly a flimsy old document, handwritten in exquisitely neat copperplate.

'It's an inventory, sent to my great-grandmother, Susan Fraser, on 12th October 1918, by James McTeer Auctioneers in Inverness. It itemises twenty lots that went to auction the day before the inventory was dispatched.'

Holly scanned the flamboyant scrawl. 'So these were the items Susan sold off to pay for her husband's death duties?'

The list contained several items of furniture, half a dozen

paintings and various porcelain *objets d'art*. Each item included a concise description and a reserve price, next to which was the sale price. The auction had raised nearly 500 guineas, a large sum in 1918! But it was the items themselves that Holly was interested in. She ran her finger slowly down the list.

The phrase 'nineteenth century' kept appearing. Oil paintings, furniture from the Victorian period, and some from the late Georgian, but nothing that dated to the time of Culloden, until her finger stalled… on lot 18!

She read it out loud…

Rare example of a 17th century Jacobean chest, with classic varying designs of applied geometric mouldings to drawers. Fitted with brass drop handles and escutcheons. Drawers flanked by pilasters of split turned mouldings and standing on stile bun feet. In good original order and good colour. 39" wide by 37" high by 22" deep. Circa 1680.
Reserve price £3 10s 6d. Sold for 4 guineas.

'Everything else post-dates Meg McGillivray. It can only be the chest, surely?' Selina reasoned excitedly.

'Unless someone found the letter elsewhere and re-hid it in one of the later items,' Lorna contended, playing devil's advocate.

'That's not very likely, is it, dear?' Miriam snapped dismissively.

'We may be barking up the wrong tree completely,' said Holly with a sigh.

'Who's to say other items of furniture haven't been sold over the years, long before the 1918 auction? The letter could've been hidden in something else.'

'Very true,' Miriam agreed. 'Of course there's something else that makes this chest a real contender for the so-called "hiding place".'

'What's that, then?' Holly asked.

Miriam produced another elegantly handwritten note.

'Susan Fraser wrote this, noting the details of the items and the locations from which they originated. The chest had been standing in the Laird's chamber upstairs... which, if I'm not mistaken, would've been Meg MacGillivray's bedroom!'

Chapter Thirty-One

A low mist clung to the River Ness that morning, obscuring its fast-moving water as it hurried beneath the Grant Street Bridge towards its convergence with the Beauly Firth. But then it was very early: just after seven when they crossed its low-girdered span towards the little row of shops that lined the street ahead of them.

Neil sat behind the wheel that morning, whilst Holly, still bleary-eyed, apprised him of the developments of the previous day.

'So James McTeer Auctioneers closed down in 1938, then? Not very considerate of them.'

Neil had turned his head towards the pink-sided railway bridge that crossed the river just to the east of their location.

'Why the hell would anyone want to paint a bridge pink?' he uttered, not waiting for Holly to provide him with an answer to his previous comment.

His sergeant didn't respond to his remark about the bridge either, preferring to toy with the ratchet arms of the handcuffs she was holding. Neil, conscious of her silence, shot her an urgent glance.

'When we get there, I'll go to the front door; you keep an

eye on the back. I don't want Mackinnon doing a runner on us if he's there.'

Holly stopped what she was doing. 'I think he'll already be aware of our impending visit by now, don't you? If he *is* our man, I'm not really expecting him to be there.'

'All the same,' Neil reiterated. 'Let's be on our guard.'

Holly looked him hard in the eye. 'Forgive me for thinking that you're almost relishing the prospect of a wee chase when we get there. Tell me you're not going to lose the head when you come face to face with this fella... *are you?*'

'Course not. So long as he behaves himself.'

Holly remained uneasy. The prospect of Neil Strachan meeting the man who'd been stalking his partner for the past month or so filled her with dread. She understood how her boss would be feeling, but his very presence during this visit seemed plain wrong!

They turned left into Lochalsh Road, and then cut through to Telford Road, where Neil parked the car fifty yards short of the shabby little cottage.

Holly dropped the cuffs into her jacket pocket as she climbed out, then followed him towards the property. She took up a position to the side of the house, whilst Neil headed for the front door, clutching the evidence bag that contained the suspect's hooded jacket.

'Motorbike's not here,' she called after him. But he didn't hear what she said. He'd disappeared quickly from view, a man now very much on a mission.

She winced on hearing the series of loud raps on the door. No one could've slept through that, surely! There was silence, followed by a further barrage from Neil's fist. Then she heard Neil's voice.

'Bradley Mackinnon, Ciaran Lusk. Come to the door, please. This is the police. Open up.'

She muttered to herself, 'He's not in. I told you so. The

bike's not here,' all the while observing the overgrown expanse of back garden, just in case. There was more silence, followed by more bangs. She shook her head in disbelief. 'Give it up, will you!'

Then to her surprise, she heard the door being wrenched open and the sound of voices. She hurried back to join Neil at the front of the house, and there, standing in the hallway peering out at him, was a sleepy Bradley Mackinnon!

The young man then switched his attention to her when she appeared at Neil's side.

'Who the hell's this? Am I actually surrounded by the polis, or somethin'?'

'This is my colleague, DS Anderson, Bradley. Look, do you mind if we come in before you catch your death?'

Mackinnon was dressed only in a pair of grey tracksuit bottoms. He stood arms tightly folded against his pale, tattooed torso, shivering in the early morning chill. The detectives waited whilst he considered the proposal, initially standing his ground and running his hand through the tight coating of dark hair that lay compressed upon his scalp. Then he nodded.

'Aye, all right, then. Come in, if you must.'

Once the door was closed behind them, Neil said, 'Do you want to go and put a T-shirt on or something? You're scaring my sergeant here.'

He shrugged, before turning and climbing the stairs. 'How long's this goin' to take?' he mumbled.

'Depends on the answers you give to our questions,' Neil called after him, stony-faced.

When Mackinnon had disappeared from view, Neil pushed open the door at the bottom of the stairs, the one that opened onto the bedroom in which he'd seen the blue and white crash helmet. To his surprise, the room was now all but empty. Just the bed and a couple of tatty pieces of cheap pine furniture remained *in situ*.

Mackinnon reappeared on the landing and dawdled down the stairs, prompting Neil to fire off his first question. 'How come the room down here is empty? I thought it was yours.'

'Then you're mistaken, mister, coz I reside up the stair.'

'Who used that room, then?'

'Ciaran. Why?'

Neil sensed something was amiss. 'When did you get back from Aberdeen, Bradley?'

'Last night. Had a few drinks at the airport after we flew in from the rig, then got a lift back here with a mate. Look, what are you wantin' from me? I havenae done nothin' wrong, as far as I'm aware. I've been stuck out in the North Sea, workin' and sleepin'. That's all you can do out there!'

Holly gazed enquiringly into the young man's eyes. 'We're looking into a case of stalking that culminated in an assault on a young woman at the leisure centre back on the third of this month...'

'Well, that rules me out, lovey. I was away at ma work.'

Holly glowered at him as only she knew how.

'Firstly, I'm not your "lovey", Mr Mackinnon. Secondly, your company have informed us that you didn't fly out to the rig until the evening of the fifth. Your mate Ciaran Lusk also seemed to be of that opinion.'

'Correct,' said Mackinnon confidently, a smirk now present upon his stubbly face. 'What they didn't tell you was that I flew over to the company's training base in Norway on the Sunday before, to attend a two-day firefighting refresher course. I flew back from Stavanger on the afternoon of the fifth and picked up a chopper out to the Norse Viking platform that evening.'

He smiled sarcastically. 'So it seems you've all got your facts wrong, doesn't it?'

Neil turned to Holly, whilst attempting to remain

outwardly insouciant. 'Give the company a ring and check this out, will you?'

Holly sensed the underlying irritability in his voice and wasted no time in complying, slamming the front door behind her.

Neil held up the evidence bag. 'This jacket was discarded by the offender at the scene of the assault. Your DNA was found all over it. Care to explain how that could be the case?'

Mackinnon took a close look at the jacket. 'Aye, I've got a jacket like that.'

He went to the row of coat hooks on the wall behind him and searched through the half a dozen items hanging there.

'It's not here,' he announced. 'I always left it here. Someone must've picked it up in the pub or something.'

'So do you remember leaving it in a pub?'

'No, not exactly.' Mackinnon shook his head slowly, having searched his memory to the best of his ability.

'Did any of your flatmates ever use it when you were away?' Cold realisation was now beginning to dawn on Neil.

'Not that I know of.' Mackinnon had reined in his cocky attitude, now that he'd been confronted with the fact that his own clothing had been found at the scene of a crime.

'Anyone else at home currently?' Neil asked.

'No, Luke's at work.'

'What about Ciaran?'

'Ciaran? Och, he's gone. Left last weekend, apparently.'

'The motorbike that was round by the side of the house… that wasn't yours, was it?'

'Shite, no. I hate the bloody things. The bike was Ciaran's.'

'And the blue crash helmet with the saltire on it. That was his too?'

'Aye, it was.'

Neil felt his heart sink. Lusk had played them for fools… and succeeded!

There was a rap on the door. Holly entered, looking glum. She looked across at Mackinnon waspishly.

'His story checks out. The girls in the office only checked the chopper schedules when I called initially. They didn't realise he'd been out on a training course beforehand. Separate records, apparently.'

'Idiots.' Mackinnon growled, shaking his head in disbelief.

'I don't suppose Ciaran left a forwarding address?' Holly enquired.

'You're joking. He hasn't even paid the rent he owed up to the end of the month.'

'What do you know about him, Bradley? He told us he was out of work.'

Mackinnon looked puzzled. 'That's news to me. He worked on the buses, for Highland Line. He drove for them.'

Then it all fell into place, that vague sense of recognition Neil had experienced when he first saw Lusk. He'd been the bus driver! The guy he'd spoken to on the evening he'd followed Cat, when she'd got off the bus one stop before her normal one. It must've been Lusk who'd taken the photo of him by the doors of the Eastgate Centre that evening, probably whilst he was sitting in his bus at the stop nearby. Neil felt dejected. The slimeball had slipped right through his fingers.

'Did Lusk ever mention the name Cat to you, Bradley? Think hard.'

Mackinnon hesitated, his eyes twitching anxiously. Both cops picked up on it.

'You'd better tell him,' Holly warned. 'You see, Cat's his partner, so this stalking thing is personal. He's going to chew the balls off anyone who's assisted Lusk in any way. You don't want your balls to end up in his porridge tomorrow morn, eh?'

Mackinnon contemplated Neil, who was glaring back at him, his eyes glinting like razors.

'Okay. Ciaran asked me to call her mobile number once. He wanted me to say I was the manager at the bus station. She'd witnessed a minor accident involving his bus one morning, so he said. He took her mobile number so that his boss could call and thank her for offering to be a witness. That's the only involvement I had, honest. He told me he'd met her on the bus and that she was giving him the come-on. He seemed infatuated with her, but didn't want her to think he'd got her number by conning her. My guess is, he wanted to check that she'd given him the right number before calling her himself.'

Holly thought Neil was going to hit him. She grabbed his arm. 'Okay, we'll leave it there. Speak to Luke, and if you hear anything at all about Ciaran Lusk or his whereabouts, call me immediately, eh?'

She handed him her business card before steering Neil out through the front door. He turned back just before Mackinnon closed it behind them. 'And tell Lusk, if you speak to him, I *will* find him, wherever he is. Even if I have to make it my life's work!'

'Come on, sir. Time to go.' Holly tugged at his sleeve again.

Neil didn't speak for several minutes, but she wasn't particularly bothered. She was on the phone doing checks on Ciaran Lusk. Eventually she ended the call and turned her attention back to him. 'Cooled off yet?'

'Aye. I s'pose.'

He continued to look straight ahead, but she could see a grin beginning to develop above his twitching jawline.

'What's so funny?' she asked.

'I hate porridge!'

Holly acknowledged his announcement with a dispassionate nod of the head. 'So what do we know about Mr Lusk?' he asked.

'Not much. No criminal record, just a couple of minor run-ins with Grampian Police. Intel stuff, mainly.'

'That's why he had no record on the DNA database. Whereabouts on Grampian's ground?'

'Central Aberdeen.' She peered out through the windscreen. 'I take it we're heading for the bus depot?'

'Too right we are!'

The Highland Line bus depot in the city centre was a hive of activity at that time of the morning. The operations manager, a rotund, grey-haired little man called Sam Leckie, was nevertheless more than happy to find time to speak to the two detectives.

'Ciaran Lusk, you say? He's no longer employed here, Chief Inspector. He decided to forfeit his job when he failed to turn up on two separate occasions last week. No call, no nothing. I tried to contact him. Even went round to the house, but his mate said he'd left: just packed up and gone.'

Neil smiled resignedly. 'I'm not surprised, Mr Leckie. He knew we'd be knocking on his door too!'

'Oh, I see. Funny, that. He seemed such a nice lad.'

'Do you have any other address for him on record, Mr Leckie?'

'Don't think so. Let's have a look at his file, though.'

He led them into a little office that was attached to the bus garage, a grubby, cluttered space that smelt faintly of diesel oil.

'Here it is,' he said, pulling a battered folder out from the middle drawer of a time-ravaged filing cabinet.

'Ciaran George Lusk.' He examined the contents briefly, then looked up and removed his glasses. 'He worked for us for two years. The only address here is the one in Telford Road.'

He then looked at the copy of his driving licence record. 'There's an address here in Aberdeen, but that's a few years old.'

Neil made a note of it anyway, then asked, 'Do you have the drivers' schedules handy, for the last month or so?'

413

Leckie pulled a heavy ring binder off of the shelf behind his desk. The label on the spine said 'Drivers K to N'.

'Here we are. Ciaran Lusk: driver duties from first of March.'

Neil checked his notebook. 'Can you tell me what he was working on Monday, 29th March?'

Leckie ran his finger down the list. 'He was working an early shift, out on the Culloden, Westhill circuit.'

Neil smiled at Holly. 'Thanks. What about the Mondays after that?'

Leckie looked again, then pursed his lips. 'Looks like he preferred working that route on earlies. He seems to have done a few shift swaps with the other drivers. In fact... he worked the same route on earlies every Monday throughout April...'

'Except on the 26th,' Neil interjected.

Leckie looked surprised. 'Aye, that's right. We were really short of drivers that day, so he had to do his allocated shift, which was a two till ten.'

'I know,' said Neil. 'He was taking photos of me from his bus outside the Eastgate Centre that evening!'

Leckie looked even more nonplussed. 'Really?'

'Aye, *really!*'

'Any other dates I can help you with?'

'What about Sunday 3rd May, and the day after, Monday the 4th?'

'He was on days off, both those days.'

Neil thought for a second. 'And when was the first occasion Lusk failed to turn up for work?'

'He turned up on the Tuesday after those two days off, presumably to clear out his locker. Then failed to show up for two day shifts after that.'

'Thank you, Mr Leckie. You've been really helpful. I don't suppose we can take those sheets with us?'

He pointed to the photo of Lusk, pinned to the inside of the folder. 'And that photo, if you don't mind.'

'Of course. Let me just take a copy of them and then they're all yours.'

'We'll also need a witness statement from you, confirming those dates,' Holly announced, almost as an afterthought.

Leckie smiled. 'Of course, we can do it now if you wish.'

When the two detectives finally emerged from Leckie's office, a small gaggle of uniformed bus crew were standing near the doors to the garage. There were three men and a young dark-haired woman, all enjoying a smoke break and a chat when Holly and Neil strolled over to them.

Holly dealt with the introductions, then asked the first question. 'Do any of you know Ciaran Lusk?'

They all nodded. The elder of the three men dropped his cigarette end onto the ground and twisted his foot onto it.

'He did a runner last week, lassie. If you're wanting a blether with him, you're a wee bit late, I'm afraid.' The others responded with nervous laughter.

'We know he did a runner,' Holly continued, straight-faced. 'I just wondered how you all got on with him.'

The older man seemed to be their spokesperson. 'Aye, he was okay; friendly enough. Kept himself to himself. What's he done, then?'

'We just want to speak to him about an incident we're looking into, that's all,' Neil interjected, irritated by the man's presumptuous reply.

There followed an uneasy silence, before the woman joked, 'He's not been pestering womenfolk again, has he?' The others laughed once more, and a second, bald-headed male then contributed, 'Cos he was a one for the lassies, so he was.'

'What do you mean, exactly, by "one for the lassies"?' Holly enquired.

The woman seemed eager to explain.

'He latched onto me when he started working here. Took me out a couple of times, but he got far too heavy for me, like he was obsessed. I dumped him, but he wouldn't take no for an answer, until I eventually threatened to come and see you lot.'

Holly pulled out her pocket book. 'Do you mind giving me your name? Only, I'd like to get that down in writing, if you're willing, that is?'

The woman looked around at her colleagues, then shrugged.

'Aye, I suppose so. It's Rachel... Rachel Quinn.'

'Well, Rachel, what you've just told us could be very pertinent to our enquiries,' Neil confirmed.

Rachel turned her attention back to her colleagues once more.

'There you go; I told you he was weird,' she announced with a grimace.

'Don't suppose he ever mentioned any places locally he frequented, or may be staying?' Neil continued.

The older man shook his head. 'We knew he was from Aberdeen. Worked as a courier driver over there for a while.'

'Kingcorth,' said the bald man. 'That's where his people stayed. They had a pub there; The Dee Bridge, I think it was called. He never said much else about his life outside work.'

'Like I said, he kept himself to himself,' said the older man.

'Unless you were a *lassie*,' Rachel protested lightheartedly.

Neil handed out copies of his business card to each of the group.

'I'd appreciate a call if you hear anything about him or his whereabouts, day or night.'

They left the little band of drivers gossiping and studying the cards he'd given them, as if they were top-flight tickets to a rock concert.

'Looks like he's moved on,' said Holly as they walked away. 'D'you think he's gone back to Aberdeen?'

'It's possible. I'm not convinced he's moved that far away from here, though. But get a copy of that photo of him across to Grampian Police and ask them to check the address in Kingcorth. That's the one provided on the driving licence counterpart.'

He climbed into the driving seat of the CID car, still speaking. 'And then he can be circulated as wanted!'

Their next port of call was the procurator fiscal's office in Baron Taylor's Street. Cat was sitting at her desk, studying the screen of her computer when they walked in. She looked up, surprised. 'Hi there you two. Not got enough work on?'

They pulled up chairs and waited for her to save the documents she'd been working on.

'I'm intrigued,' she said, sitting back.

'We now know who attacked you the other night,' said Neil, almost under his breath.

Cat looked firstly at him, and then across at Holly. 'Was it this guy, Mackinnon?'

'No, it was his flatmate. The laddie called Ciaran Lusk.'

'But why? Do I know him?' Cat seemed confused.

Neil placed his hand over hers. 'Do you recall speaking to the young man who often drove the bus you travelled on to work every morning?'

Cat thought for a second. 'You mean the young guy with the short, dark spikey hair... quite good looking, very friendly.'

'Aye, well, that was him, Ciaran Lusk,' Holly confirmed. 'He apparently saw you on the bus and became infatuated with you. We've since discovered, he's got previous for it. Surprisingly, he's never appeared on our radar, other than for very minor mischief when he was a kid.'

'Oh my God. I gave him my mobile phone number,' Cat remembered suddenly, now visibly shocked. 'He wanted me to be a witness when a car pulled out in front of the bus and collided with the door. That was weeks ago.'

'We know,' Neil acknowledged. 'Did he ever say anything to you on the bus, anything you considered to be—'

'Inappropriate?' Holly interrupted him.

'No, not really. He did seem overly friendly on occasions, a bit flirty, I suppose. But I never thought anything of it. Some guys are like that, aren't they? Especially the young ones.'

She looked dolefully at Neil. 'Have you arrested him yet?'

Neil shook his head. 'That's the problem. Remember, we went round to his address and spoke to him the other day, looking for his mate, as it happens, and not knowing of course that Lusk was the guy we were really after. We obviously spooked him because he's left his work and gone to ground.'

'Oh no.' Cat covered her mouth with a trembling hand.

'Don't worry,' Holly reassured her. 'We'll catch up with him, now we know who we're looking for.'

'God, I hope so. What if he thinks he's got nothing to lose, now you've discovered that it's him?'

'My guess is, he'll keep a very low profile,' Neil reassured her, not entirely convinced that his assessment was correct, but eager to play down any fears she may be harbouring.

Cat glared at him. 'But you can't be sure, can you?'

'No, we can't,' he said softly. 'We'll just have to adjust our normal routine, until we find him.'

'What sort of life is that going to be, looking over my shoulder everywhere I go?'

Neil patted the top of her hand. 'Nothing much needs to change, but you do need to take care that you're not putting yourself at risk, like being out on your own at night. Simple precautions. You know what I mean?'

'Oh I know what you mean, Neil. I need to watch my back

all day, every day, because some nutter out there is potentially watching my every move.'

Neil tried to remain unfazed. 'Look, I'll pick you up tonight. Then we'll talk about it at home, okay?'

She nodded without saying anything and looked away. It was their cue to leave.

Chapter Thirty-Two

Inverness
Wednesday 12th May

It had been a difficult night. Cat and Neil had sat up into the early hours discussing the predicament in which they now found themselves. Neil had wanted to reassure her, to sound upbeat and be full of optimism that they'd locate Ciaran Lusk without delay. But it was just a facade, beneath which he was worried sick. Cat knew it… she could read him well, having lived with him for so long. He'd spent far too much time discussing the lifestyle changes that would be necessary to ensure her safety. He'd even started the conversation with a request that she go and stay with his mother, not a proposal he'd initially supported when Rona had suggested it herself. Once again she'd declined, citing the complications of commuting to work, but also taking account of Rona's matron-like character, something she knew would irritate her after only a short time. Having said that, they did get on well together for the most part, and if the situation with Lusk was to deteriorate, then she wasn't going to close the door on the idea!

By one o'clock they'd agreed a plan. Cat had finally accepted that she would have to go about her business, whilst exercising a certain degree of caution. Until such time as Lusk was caught, that was, and there was nothing at all she, or Neil, could do about it in the short term.

Hand in hand, they finally climbed the stairs to the bedroom. Cat knew she could sleep in the next morning, having been granted a day off whilst the IT people upgraded the computer equipment in her office. Her partner was not so lucky. He had a meeting with the force press officer at eight o'clock, just before the daily team briefing.

Neil had not slept at all well. His eyes were still heavy with tiredness when he'd conducted the team's morning briefing. Hardie was there again, standing at the back of the room, asking more probing questions about the progress of the Operation Cawdor investigation. Neil quickly picked up on his underlying message. It was true: there was no disguising it. Things had stalled somewhat!

There was a good deal of work going on in the background of course, extensive investigations to trace Ualas MacBean being the main strand of the enquiry. The media coverage had been helpful, and the team had been following up on numerous sightings of the elusive Highlander. Other than that, no real progress had been made on anything else since the development relating to the sale of the Jacobean chest, way back in 1918. Whether or not that could be looked upon as being progress was of course debatable!

What he needed now was a break, and it was whilst he was pouring himself a mug of coffee in the main office that it finally came!

He'd rushed back to his desk, steaming mug in hand, and had picked up the phone whilst lowering himself back into his chair.

The female voice at the end of the line was familiar, and well-educated.

'Good morning, Chief Inspector. So glad I caught you.'

It was Selina Cope and she sounded excited.

'Hello, Selina. What can I do for you?'

'It's more a case of what I can do for you, perhaps. You recall that Jacobean chest we were talking about when Holly was out here on Monday?'

'Aye, sure I do.'

'Well, I believe I've located a photograph of it.'

Neil took a sip of coffee and sat forward attentively, his brain now fully engaged.

'Really?'

Selina gave a little self-gratifying chuckle, then continued with apparent zeal. 'I've been speaking to some of our long-serving staff at the distillery. You know, the people whose families have worked for us for generations, either at the distillery or here at Cullaird. Well, it paid off, because when I mentioned the sale of some of the contents of the castle back in 1918, it struck a chord with a chap whose grandfather worked as a labourer on the estate back then. He has since provided me with a very interesting photograph. It shows the estate workers loading the items onto a McTeers lorry, whilst being supervised by my great-grandmother, of all people.'

'And this photo, does it actually show the chest itself being loaded?' Neil asked.

'Oh yes. It's standing on the ground at the back of the lorry, whilst the paintings are being lifted up by the estate workers for the auctioneer's men to stow. You can see it clearly, and in some detail.'

'That's great,' said Neil. 'Do you have a scanner there?'

'Yes, of course. Miriam's emailing it across to you as we speak.'

Neil checked his inbox with his free hand. Sure enough, there was an email from Laura Fraser's mail address, as if she'd suddenly returned from the dead!

Neil opened the attachment, and there it was, standing as Selina had described, by the tailgate of an old Daimler lorry. A group of men, clad in collarless shirts, tweed waistcoats and oversized floppy caps, their sleeves rolled up, stood between the chest and the lorry, struggling to lift a large painting into the back of the vehicle.

'I've got it,' said Neil. 'You can see all the detail on it. You never know… this photo may help us to locate it.'

'I hope so,' said Selina. 'Look I know it's a long shot. We don't even know whether Meg's letter was ever secreted within it.'

'It's a very big long shot,' Neil acknowledged, 'but I certainly intend to exhaust all avenues of enquiry, however far-fetched!'

The conversation was concluded with a promise that Neil would get the original copy of the photograph collected later that day by one of the FLOs. He then dialled the force press officer's number. Explanations given, the photo of the chest was forwarded to the Media Relations Unit for enhancement and circulation to TV and press at the earliest opportunity. Neil's next call was to his own local television contact, Annie Dunbar, senior correspondent for the popular news show *Highlands Tonight*. It took very little persuasion to elicit a promise from the flirtatious TV personality that the oak chest and the search for its whereabouts would feature as a headline item on the programme that evening.

'My,' she exclaimed in her usual alluringly husky voice. 'They'll soon be making movies about you and your historical mysteries, Neil. What you need is a time-travelling assistant to help you with your investigations… someone like me, perhaps!'

Neil grinned. 'I recall one of my colleagues has already come up with that one,' he replied. 'But think of it, Annie. What if you became stuck in a time where there was no Pinot Grigio?'

She gasped. 'Even worse... Prada and Louis Vuitton may not exist, either. Where would I get my handbags?'

They both laughed. 'Best I stay put in the twenty-first century, then,' she concluded. 'Let me have the photo, and I'll splash it all over tonight's show.'

Neil zoomed in on the sepia image before forwarding it to Annie's email address. He examined the surprising detail visible, particularly in the case of the chest itself, marvelling at the ornately carved decoration on the four pairs of drawers. It was a solid, understated piece, made of rich, dark oak, and typical of the furniture produced during the Jacobean period. Satisfied that he'd seen enough, he attached the image to his email and tapped the send button. 'Over to you, Annie,' he muttered.

Just before midday, he parked the CID car directly outside the quaint little premises of Mr Paul Lennie, MBNTA. Behind the shop window and its internal security grill was an impressive display of coins and medals, thoughtfully mounted on baize-covered display racks. Neil studied the display briefly, before opening the half-glazed door and pausing to admire the innovative name of Lennie's business engraved into the smoked glass. 'In For a Penny, In For a Pound'. *What a great name for a coin dealer*, he thought as he ventured into the musty interior.

A distant bell rang out, somewhere to the rear of the cramped little shop. Then, almost immediately, a short dumpy man in his early sixties appeared, a tight-lipped smile evident beneath his neatly cropped moustache.

'Mr Lennie?' Neil enquired, his attention drawn to the garish bow tie that sprouted from beneath the man's out of vogue sleeveless pullover.

'That is me,' Lennie replied formally, his small button eyes urgently searching his visitor for clues as to his identity.

Neil quickly put the little man out of his misery, and followed up his introduction with a brief explanation as to the reason for his visit. Lennie relaxed a little, finally content that he was not about to be detained for receiving stolen goods or indeed to suffer some other such hideous fate.

'Do you have these coins with you?' Lennie asked, his voice tremulous, like that of a man about to go to the gallows.

'No, I don't, unfortunately, but I do have some really good photos of them on my mobile phone.'

He produced the device and scrolled through the saved photographs with his thumb. Having skipped through a series of six taken of Tam playing in a small burn during a recent walk, he finally came across those of the two coins.

'Here they are,' he announced, handing the phone to Lennie. The numismatist promptly balanced a pair of half-moon spectacles on the end of his broad nose, then pored over the images from a range of just a few inches. There was silence for ten seconds or so before he raised his eyes above the smudged lenses and eyed the policeman with suspicion.

'And you've actually seen these coins?' he asked. 'These… these people just plucked them out of a drawer, you say?'

'Aye, that's about the sum of it. They're supposed to be part of a hoard that was secreted at or near to the premises back in the mid 1700s. Why do you ask?'

Lennie puffed out his cheeks and scrutinised the photos again, pinching them out so that he could examine the coins in greater detail.

'These coins are extremely rare, and in this almost mint condition, I would value them at well over £10,000 each. If there was a largish hoard of these little fellas still in existence, then we could be talking umpteen million in today's market.'

He selected the first of the photos again. 'This one with the old king's head, dated 1746, has a Lima mark, here, you see.' He pointed to the tiny word inscribed under the monarch's bust.

425

Neil frowned. 'What does this Lima mark mean, then?'

'A year before the Battle of Culloden, in 1745, a great prize of silver coin had been seized in the North Atlantic by two British privateers, the *Duke* and the *Prince Frederick*... so the story goes... from two French treasure ships that had sailed from Peru. The booty, consisting mainly of pieces of eight bearing the Lima mint mark, was unloaded at Bristol and hauled, in forty-five carts, no less, up to the Royal Mint in London. It was subsequently requested that coins minted from this treasure bear the name "Lima" to celebrate the exploit.'

Neil was impressed by the little man's level of knowledge.

'Fascinating stuff. And the other example... what can you tell me about that one?'

Lennie switched images to the gold coin dated 1729.

'This one has EIC inscribed under the laureate bust of King George II. The letters refer to the East India Company, who supplied the gold to the Royal Mint. Again, it's extremely rare, and in this condition, would be worth £10,000 upwards.'

He handed the phone back to Neil. 'This is very exciting, and should this hoard theory prove to be true, someone could end up very rich indeed.'

Neil returned the phone to his pocket. 'So 1,200 guineas' worth of these coins at today's prices...'

'We're looking at millions, Mr Strachan. Five million plus pounds. And that's a conservative estimate.'

Neil could sense butterflies in his stomach. Five million was certainly some motive for a robbery. Add to that the value of any regimental silver, and of course the historical significance of any such hoard, and the sky would be the limit when it came to value. Then he wondered how a thief would ever dispose of such an acquisition. It was surely a treasure that history would render priceless!

He thanked Lennie for his assistance and having acknowledged his offer of further help if required, he left the little shop, relieved to be once again out in the strong sunshine. He buried his hands into his pockets and walked the short distance back to the car, the words 'five million plus pounds' still ringing in his ears.

He was just inserting the ignition key into the lock when the mobile in his jacket pocket hummed. It took him a second to realise that it wasn't his work phone; it was Cat's. He pulled it out and tapped the screen, the butterflies having returned to his stomach once more. The new text icon came up. He pressed again, his face paling when he read the words on the screen.

Hello Inspector. Ciaran Lusk here. We met the other day. I know you'll be monitoring this phone still. How foolish of me to become bedevilled by a mantrap, such is your Cat, unfortunately a woman so closely connected to the forces of law and order. No doubt my liberty will be short-lived, so I've one last surprise to bestow upon her, but at a time of my choosing of course.

Neil swallowed hard, fury and fear rising within him in equal measure. The form of wording used in the message seemed strangely incongruous when he recalled his earlier conversation with Lusk. There was a Jekyll and Hyde element to it. A sinister transition from lowly bus driver to Ripper-like fiend!

He tapped out a reply on the keypad. It came from the heart rather than the head, and when he'd pressed send, he immediately regretted it.

I'll warn you only this once, Lusk. Stay well clear of Cat. Lay a finger upon her, and you're a dead man. That's a promise.

He waited for a minute or two, but no reply was forthcoming. He threw the phone onto the seat next to him, ground the car into gear and sped off across town, heading for home.

When he threw the front door open and called out, there was silence. He called Cat's name repeatedly as he ran from room to room, but there was no response; nothing. Next, he took to the stairs, two at a time, and frantically searched the bedrooms. All were empty, so he thundered downstairs again and made for the kitchen, almost losing his footing on the wooden floor in the hallway. Then, as he entered the kitchen, he saw her, or to be more accurate her silhouette behind the glass in the back door. It opened slowly, and she walked in carrying an empty laundry basket.

'Oh hi, I wasn't expecting you,' she grinned. 'Some of your socks are going to have to go in the bin; I'm not mending them... what's the matter? You look as if you've seen a ghost.'

He threw his arms around her and hugged her tight.

'Ummm,' she gasped, trying to catch her breath. 'I think I could get used to these little surprise visits.'

He released her, but still grasped her shoulders. 'Lusk's texted me on your phone. He's up to something. "One last surprise," he said.'

Cat's smile drained away. 'Let me see,' she demanded.

She'd raised the back of her hand to her mouth by the time she'd finished reading the message, her shock plain to see.

'What are we going to do now?'

'First, I want you to go and pack some things. You're going to my mother's place, at least until your parents come home from Italy.'

She didn't argue, but ran upstairs, whilst Neil rang his mother in Cromarty to warn her of their impending arrival.

'I think I'll get your Uncle Euan to move in with us for a few days,' Rona proposed before they ended their conversation.

'Good idea,' Neil agreed, before hanging up.

He then rang Holly Anderson.

'Oh my God, what on earth is this saddo up to? Is there anything you want me to do?' she asked.

'Not immediately. Just make sure everyone knows where I am, and perhaps you'd better get Angus Hardie to call me, soonest.'

'I think that's probably a good idea,' Holly sighed. 'If only to safeguard your career!'

'My career's the last thing on my mind just now, Holly. Look, I'll catch up with you when I get back from Cromarty.'

Cat came down the stairs, putting on her jacket. 'Can you bring my bag down? Only it's a little heavy.'

Neil somehow managed to smile. 'I expected nothing less. It won't be forever, you know.'

He squeezed her arm and headed off upstairs. 'Wait for me in the car. I'll be out shortly.'

Cat was on the phone to Hugh Jardine when he finally appeared, having heaved her bag into the boot.

'What did he say?' Neil asked when she finally ended the call.

'Oh, he was fine... very concerned, which was nice of him. He's given me a week's compassionate leave. Just wants me to keep him updated.'

They pulled out onto Tower Road and headed back towards town.

'At least Tam will be pleased to see me,' she quipped.

Neil looked straight ahead, checking out a cyclist who was waiting to emerge from the next junction. 'Aye, I'm missing the wee fella too. Still, hopefully we'll liken this to nothing more than a bad dream very soon.'

'It'll never be that,' she corrected him. 'I wish it *was* just a horrible dream.'

He looked across at her this time, just as they passed the junction with Tower Brae on their right. He completely missed the motorcyclist sitting out of sight, a little way down the lane.

When they had passed by, the rider snapped down the

tinted visor on his blue and white saltire-emblazoned crash helmet and joined the line of traffic behind them.

Rona Strachan met them at the gate when they arrived at Crumbathyn. She placed a comforting arm around Cat, looked up the street both ways, and then ushered her inside, whilst Neil followed with the holdall.

'I hope you're going to find this beast of a man very soon,' Rona demanded, before he'd closed the front door behind him. Tam skidded to a halt, shaking with excitement, prompting Neil to squat down and gave him a hug.

'Good to see you, wee boy. Enjoying your holiday in Cromarty?'

He looked up at his mother. 'We're doing all we can, Ma. He'll put a foot wrong sooner or later, believe me.'

'Aye, that he will.' Great-Uncle Euan's lean form appeared in the doorway, pipe in hand. 'They all make mistakes in the end.'

The retired policeman greeted Cat affectionately. 'You're safe now, lassie. Auld Euan's here to protect you!'

Neil shook his head. His uncle's sense of humour had certainly not deserted him! 'Just be wary when you're out and about, will you? And let me know if you have any concerns about anything.'

He ruffled the blonde highlights on the spaniel's head, then issued a further warning. 'And no heroics, Uncle Euan! In the unlikely event Lusk turns up here, just lock the doors and dial 999… please.'

'Aye, don't you worry yerself, son,' Euan assured him, wishing that he'd hidden the old polished walnut truncheon that now resided beneath his chair in the sitting room!

As it happened, he needn't have concerned himself, because Rona led them along the hallway to the cluttered but homely kitchen where she'd prepared a pot of coffee.

'Are you going to be all right, son, staying at home on your own?'

She looked concerned as she poured coffee into each of four mugs.

'Aye, of course Ma. I need to be close to my work. It's Cat I'm worried about.'

'Well, don't you worry about her. Catriona will be fine with us.'

Cat blushed. 'Thank you, Rona. I appreciate you having me at short notice like this.'

'Hush, lassie. You're family, for heaven's sake.'

Her eyes flashed meaningfully across to her son. His response was to take a sip of his coffee and change the subject. The verbal punch had found its mark!

'You still happy to have Tam too, Ma?'

'Aye, he's no bother at all.' Rona smiled. 'Just as well I'm an easy touch when it comes to dogs! Top-up?'

Neil declined her offer of more coffee. He'd never intended to stay long. So having said his affectionate goodbyes, he was soon back on the road and heading towards Inverness.

His work phone rang just before he reached the A9, prompting him to pull into a convenient layby. Angus Hardie seemed concerned.

'Neil, Holly's told me about this stalking situation involving your partner. I wish you'd told me earlier, you know.'

'Aye, I'm sorry, sir. I didn't think it would get to this.'

'You'd better bring me up to speed. Where is Cat now? Is she okay?'

Neil explained all, whilst Hardie listened in silence.

'That's about it,' said Neil in conclusion. 'Now you know everything.'

There was a pause before Hardie spoke again. 'Right. Well, I can't have my SIO in a double murder enquiry distracted by personal issues, Neil. You do appreciate that?'

'Of course, sir.'

'Then perhaps it would be best if you concentrated on supporting Cat, and I oversee Op Cawdor.'

'I can assure you I'm more than happy to carry on running Op Cawdor,' Neil responded immediately. 'Holly was overseeing the stalking, but perhaps on reflection it's best if I hand it over to the Divisional CID.'

'Bloody right it is, Neil. Holly can't do both, either. She's attached to Operation Cawdor, just like you are. Now, if you can assure me that you can carry on as SIO and let the local boys deal with the stalking, then we have a deal, but I'll be keeping a close eye on both enquiries, mind you.'

'Understood, sir. I'll brief the Divisional DI as soon as I get back.'

'That's agreed, then. But if this arrangement doesn't work out, I need you to tell me. Understood?'

'Absolutely, sir.'

Hardie's tone softened. 'It goes without saying: anything we can do to support you, just say. I know this is a difficult time for you both.'

'Thank you, sir. I appreciate that. I'm happy Cat's now with my family, at least.'

'Good, but just for safe measure, we'll get a panic alarm installed at your mother's place.'

Hardie's avuncular response put him at ease.

'Okay, sir. That would be reassuring.'

'No problem. I'll speak with you tomorrow. And don't worry. We'll catch up with this guy Lusk in no time at all.'

The line went dead. Neil sat staring through the windscreen at the oncoming traffic. He felt relieved, but also a little discomfited by the veiled dressing-down he'd just received from Hardie. He knew his judgement had been questionable. Holly had rightly warned him that he was on precarious ground, running Operation Cawdor *and* pursuing

Lusk at the same time. But, then again, it wasn't that close to home for them, was it? He started the engine, wondering if he would ever fully be able to honour the deal he'd just made with his boss!

Chapter Thirty-Three

Cullaird Castle
Thursday 13ᵗʰ May

Miriam Fraser was on her way back to the castle. It had been a glorious spring morning and she'd decided to take herself off for a long walk along the banks of Loch Ruthven. Spring was always a good time to enjoy the birdlife around the loch, especially the rare Slavonian grebes that had arrived during late March in time for their breeding season. Miriam had been lucky enough to get several glimpses of the attractive tufted birds as they swam casually upon the glassy surface of the loch, riding the endless succession of wavelets that agitated the dark water. She'd been out for over an hour and was now sauntering back along the driveway, sunhat in one hand, binoculars in the other, closing her eyes periodically and enjoying the warmth of the sun on her face.

Fifty yards short of the castle's wrought-iron gates, she heard the crunch of tyres on the track behind her.

A dark blue Mercedes saloon drew up next to her, and the driver's window lowered with a faint hum. Behind it was the smiling face of her ex-husband, Dawie Van Nieuwoudt.

'Don't look so surprised,' he vociferated, his brown eyes peeking out from behind well-developed eye bags, like muddy water glinting from a newly dug trench.

'What do you expect?' she retorted. 'I thought you were down in Cape Town, adding to your millions.'

'I had some business in Amsterdam so thought I would drop in before flying back home from Heathrow. I intend it to be a visit of condolence. I shan't stay long.'

He gestured towards the passenger seat. 'Why don't you get in?' As if to reinforce his offer, he leaned across and pushed the passenger side door open.

Miriam considered his proposition briefly, before making her way around the front of the car and climbing into the passenger seat.

'I assume Marianne told you about Laura and Duncan?'

'Yes, she called me the other day. Told me you were up here with Selina.'

'How long exactly *are* you intending to stay, Dawie?'

'Only tonight, if you'll have me. My flight out is on Sunday. I need to get back to the office for next week.'

'The tanzanite business is thriving down on the Cape then, I take it?'

'Can't complain,' he replied, selecting 'Drive' on the gear shift.

When they pulled up outside the castle, Selina appeared through the doorway. She too looked shocked when she saw Miriam and Dawie emerge from the vehicle. 'Good God, Dawie…'

He walked purposefully across to her and gave her a hug.

'I'm so very sorry, my dear. Words fail me.' Then he stepped back and grasped her by the shoulders. 'How on earth are you coping with such a terrible tragedy?'

'I'm okay, Dawie. Thanks for asking. Look, you'd better come in.' There was little warmth in her invitation.

'Have you got any bags to bring in?' Miriam called out.

'Only a couple of small ones. Don't worry. I'll get them

later. Right now, I could murder a cup of tea after that drive from Aberdeen.'

They made their way along the corridor to the kitchen, where Van Nieuwoudt leaned his portly form against the worktop and regarded Selina as she put the kettle on.

'I have to say, you're looking particularly well, Selina. It's been a long time.'

Selina smiled back at him. 'It has. I was still a teenager when we last met, remember?'

'Indeed you were. How time flies.'

'So what's going on in your life, Dawie? What are the kids up to?'

'Oh, Marianne's living in Durban with her husband. She's a tennis coach, earning a good living too. She broke the terrible news about your parents to me a few days ago. I've been travelling around a bit, you see. Peter helps me run the family business back home. He's forty now; still living the playboy life. Doesn't want to settle down yet.'

'Apple doesn't fall far from the tree, then.' Miriam strolled into the kitchen and placed her binoculars on the table.

Van Nieuwoudt ignored her, but folded his arms defensively.

'How's Nat and the children?'

'They're fine, thanks. Nat's just gone back down south to look after Fergus and Emily. They're both studying at Marlborough College. Doing really well.'

She paused to pour hot water into some mugs. 'Emily's planning to go to uni next year; wants to become a vet.'

They sat around the table, each accepting one of the mugs from Selina. Then the telephone rang upstairs somewhere.

Selina looked across to where the wall phone usually hung. 'Damn. I must've left the handset upstairs.'

'Don't worry, I'll get it,' said Miriam. 'You two can continue to get acquainted.' She left the room, mug in hand, humming as she went. Van Nieuwoudt watched her go. Then he remarked surreptitiously, 'It's good to see her again.'

Selina smiled politely. 'I'm sure the feeling's mutual.'

'I fear not, but I only have myself to blame for that.' He sighed. 'Enough of this soppiness. Now I hope you don't mind me asking. How is the police investigation progressing? Do they have any idea who committed these terrible crimes?'

'They seem to have a name in mind. Some guy called Ualas MacBean… a real nutcase by all accounts! He's a local man from Strathnairn, into some sort of weird pagan symbolism… stuff like that.'

'So why would this chap want to attack Laura and Duncan? What's the link?'

'The detective in charge thinks he may be searching for a lost hoard of coins. It's all very strange. He seems to be some sort of deranged myth chaser, obsessed by something that isn't there! That's if the detective is right, of course, and I'm not entirely convinced.'

'You don't seem to have much faith in this so-called detective.'

Selina blew into her mug, dispersing the steam that rose from the hot tea.

'Oh no, don't get me wrong. He's very businesslike, very thorough. It's just that all the links to this man MacBean are circumstantial. That's all. I have to ask myself whether his theory is a just a bit too far-fetched.'

'So what do *you* think happened?'

'I'm inclined to think it could have been just a robbery that went wrong. If I'm honest, I haven't a clue!'

'Do you think there could be any truth behind this theory about a hoard?'

'Possibly. I've heard the story, but then sometimes my instinct tells me the motive is probably far more straightforward than that.'

Van Nieuwoudt frowned. 'But my dear, why then would they leave your father's body out on Culloden Moor like that? The whole thing is, as you say, most weird.'

He looked at her, his face blank.

Then it dawned upon her. 'Oh, of course you don't know the whole story, do you?'

She proceeded to brief him in detail as to the events surrounding her parents' murders. Van Nieuwoudt listened, his face paling by the second.

'My God, who could do such a thing? I can't believe it. I just hope they catch the swine as soon as they can.'

By now, Selina wanted to change the subject. 'I'll make up the bed in the blue room on the second floor. You should be comfortable in there.'

Van Nieuwoudt bowed his head in appreciation. 'You're very kind, my dear. I'm so sorry I didn't call sooner, and give you some more notice.'

He turned to Miriam, who'd just returned from taking the phone call. 'I tried your number down in London before I left Cape Town, but the answerphone kept kicking in. I was hoping to persuade you to put me up down there, the night before my flight home from Heathrow on Sunday.'

'Well, you're out of luck, darling,' she smiled. 'You'll just have to spend a tiny part of your fortune on a hotel room.'

Selina grinned. The tension between them was not unexpected. Miriam had provided her with all the sordid details about her colourful ex-husband. She recalled the brief memoir Miriam had provided to Neil Strachan five days earlier. But there was more to their tempestuous relationship than that! Van Nieuwoudt had had numerous relationships as a young man. He was first engaged to a beautiful young woman called Liani De Beer. He was then twenty-four, she twenty-two. In 1965, Liani was killed in a riding accident, a tragedy that he himself witnessed. It was an event that had understandably haunted him for months. Then on a flight back to Cape Town from Johannesburg in May 1967, he met Miriam Fraser, then twenty-three, who was on a work assignment with a female colleague. He was charming and attentive, spending time wining and dining the two young women and showing them around the attractions of the Cape Province. Then he'd followed her back to Scotland, to her parents' home at Clune House in the September of that year, and had stayed for a month. Whilst there, he had travelled around, conducting business in London and Amsterdam, before returning to Dores for the festive season. During that Christmas break he had proposed to the besotted Miriam, and the couple were married in July 1968 at Ruthven Church. They had then returned to South Africa and Dawie's large oceanfront house in the exclusive community of Clifton. Miriam had lived a charmed existence at Clifton, lunching with friends and bringing up the children, whilst her husband spent weeks away on business. Miriam loved the pampered lifestyle, seduced by the wealth she'd married into, but the relationship was short-lived. In 1983, she discovered that Van Nieuwoudt had been having a long-term affair with his devoted secretary, Elize Kuiper. So, they'd divorced in 1985 and Miriam returned to London without her two children, who were by then settled into good schools. They in turn were bitter that their mother had tipped their worlds upside down, and felt that Miriam should have forgiven their father... who, as it happened, spoilt them rotten!

Miriam, on the other hand, had wrought revenge upon her husband in a way that only she could. She'd confronted Elize, and played her an audio tape she'd covertly recorded of her conversation with Van Nieuwoudt when she found out about the affair. In it, he told his wife that Elize meant nothing to him; that there was no depth to her, and that he deemed her to be just a plaything when he was away from home and had only her for company. Elize promptly ended her relationship with Van Nieuwoudt and for a time, he too became extremely bitter towards his ex-wife.

Since their divorce he'd had a couple of short relationships, none of which had stood the test of time, and so had immersed himself in his business and the social life that came with it.

As the years progressed, the couple rekindled their relationship to some extent, mainly through the efforts of their children. They would meet up periodically in both London and South Africa, an arrangement that had worked well up until then. Van Nieuwoudt had once again warmed to Miriam, and she had to him, but was far more reluctant to show it! Selina had been shocked to learn that on occasions the couple had even shared a bed... usually after too much wine, Miriam had been at pains to add!

'Well, you don't need to spend any of your fortune here,' Selina asserted, whilst glaring at her cousin.

'You're most gracious, my dear. Perhaps if you'd excuse me, I'll get my bags out of the car and freshen up.'

'That's fine,' said Selina. 'There's an en suite in your room. Call when you come back in, and I'll show you the way.'

When he had gone, she gathered up the empty mugs. Looking down at Miriam, she said, 'You're so rude to him. Don't tell me you're not pleased to see him, just a wee bit?'

Miriam pouted. 'Oh, I suppose I am. A lot of water has passed under the bridge since 1985.'

'There you are, then. It was good of him to detour out here and drop in to see us.'

Miriam got up, suitably rebuked. 'I'll show him up to his room, if you like.'

Selina smiled. 'That would be nice. There are clean towels in the drawer under the bed.'

Van Nieuwoudt was leaning into the car, searching for his BlackBerry, when he heard another car approach from behind him. The doors slammed and he heard the footfall of two pairs of feet approaching on the gravel.

'Good morning,' said the male voice, with an educated Scots accent.

Van Nieuwoudt recoiled from the car to find himself looking up at a handsome young man in a grey suit with dark wavy hair and rimless spectacles. He was accompanied by an attractive redhead. A hand shot out, containing a police warrant card. 'Detective Chief Inspector Neil Strachan. This is Detective Constable Lorna McKirdy.'

Van Nieuwoudt wiped his hand on his trousers and shook Neil's.

'Dawie Van Nieuwoudt, Miriam's ex-husband. Pleased to meet you both.'

'Ah, yes, from South Africa. I've heard about you, Mr Van Nieuwoudt.'

'Nothing bad, I hope?'

Neil smiled knowingly. 'Not that I can recall,' he replied.

The South African walked around to the car's open boot. 'I was just getting my bags,' he announced, and heaved one of the leather holdalls out into the daylight.

'I wasn't aware you were coming over to join the family,' said Neil, assisting with the other holdall.

'No, I'm afraid I turned up unannounced. I've been in Amsterdam for the last couple of days. Thought I'd stop off here on my way down to Glasgow tomorrow.'

'Where have you travelled from today, then?'

'Oh, Dyce Airport, Aberdeen. Picked up a hire car and've just driven across.'

Neil nodded towards the sticker on the back window of the Mercedes. 'Aye, I can see that.'

Van Nieuwoudt followed his gaze. The sticker on the rear window of the car read 'SpeedyCar Vehicle Rentals'.

He grinned. 'That's why you're a detective and I'm not,' he quipped.

'Here, let me help you,' said Neil, concerned by the stocky little man's ruddy complexion and apparent breathlessness.

'Thank you. I appreciate that.'

The two men walked towards the front door, each carrying an item of baggage whilst Lorna followed behind them.

Van Nieuwoudt looked back at Neil as they passed through the doorway.

'Terrible business, these murders, Chief Inspector. I was just asking Selina whether you had made any progress with the investigation.'

Neil's response was non-committal. 'We're getting there. These things can take time.'

He set the bag down in the hallway. 'I was just coming to tell Selina about a TV appeal we've made. Is she upstairs?'

'No, she was last in the kitchen with Miriam.'

'Right. Let's go and join them, shall we?'

Thirty minutes later, the two police officers were leaving, having consumed a cup of tea and brought Selina up to date with the progress of the enquiry.

As he passed the blue Mercedes, Neil stopped to view the car hire sticker on the window. 'Umm... 0141. That's a Glasgow phone code.'

'Probably their head office number?' Lorna offered up.

Neil gave her a wry smile. 'Maybe, but one thing I do know. They don't have an office at Dyce. I've used the car hire facilities there often enough. Then, of course, you'd expect someone travelling into Aberdeen to have ABZ destination tags on their bags... not South African Airways: GLA via LHR... Glasgow via London Heathrow.'

'Looks like he wants to keep his travel plans to himself,' Lorna suggested. 'Could they not be old tags?'

'Possible, but not at all likely. He wouldn't take the time to remove the most recent tags and leave old ones in place. That doesn't make any sense at all. I'm not so sure the airline would've allowed him to retain the old tags on his baggage, either.'

He settled into the driver's seat and checked his mobile phone. 'Got a signal, just,' he said and dialled the incident room number.

Ross Haggarty answered his call. 'Hello Neil. Holly's been trying to get hold of you. That appeal that went out on the TV yesterday... well, it looks like it was a good call. Some lady living down in the central belt has called in saying she recognises the piece of furniture. Sold an identical chest just a few weeks ago.'

'Are we arranging for someone to go and see her?'

'All sorted. Strathclyde are getting a statement this evening.'

'Good. I'll catch up with Holly later. Now I need someone to make a couple of calls for me, Ross. Firstly to a car hire company in Glasgow called SpeedyCar. I need to know how long a Mr Dawie Van Nieuwoudt has been hiring a blue Mercedes saloon for, and where he hired it from.'

'Let's have the details, then.'

Neil provided Haggarty with the telephone number and the registration number of the Mercedes.

'Anything else, Master?'

'There is, as it happens. Can you confirm what background checks we've done on this South African fella, Dawie Van Nieuwoudt?'

There was a pause whilst Haggarty entered the details onto his system.

'Right... let's see. His name appears in a number of statements. All family background stuff. Usual UK criminal records and intelligence checks have been run. He comes back no trace across the board.'

'Okay, can you call Cape Town, preferably the airport police? The time difference is only an hour. See if they have anything on him as regards travel history and suchlike.'

'Your wish is my command, Neil. I'll get back to you.'

When Neil arrived back at the MEU suite, it was lunchtime and the main office was empty. He hung his jacket on the hook behind his office door and made his way across to the coffee maker, hoping to find a clean mug.

'Ah, you're back.'

Neil turned to see Holly walking through the door. She had a piece of paper in her hand. 'Got a few things to update you on.'

'Fire away,' said Neil, fitting a new paper filter into the machine.

'Divisional CID rang with an update on Lusk. No one's seen him in Aberdeen for months. The good news is, one of his old bus company colleagues has called in to report a sighting of him out on the A9 two days ago.'

'So he hasn't left our area completely, then?'

'Seems not, if it was him. He may just be visiting, though.'

'Okay. Any other good news?'

'DI Haggarty asked me to call that car hire company down in Glasgow—'

'I thought *he* was going to do that?'

Holly looked at him wittingly, but remained silent. Neil smiled meekly in acknowledgement. 'Got tied up, did he?'

'Spot on! Anyway, I spoke to a nice young man who confirmed that the Mercedes was hired out to Mr Van Nieuwoudt on 28th April. He picked it up at Glasgow Airport,

444

and gave a UK contact address as The Hampden Terrace Hotel, Mount Florida, Glasgow.'

'So he's been here all this time. I wonder what he's been up to? Can you—'

She raised a hand. 'Already done. He booked a superior room there from the night of the 28th through to next Sunday, the 16th May. I'm told he has been sleeping there each night, as far as the staff can tell, so if he's just been over to Amsterdam, it was a very quick visit indeed!'

Neil switched on the coffee maker and turned to face her. 'Interesting. Not a man for telling the whole truth, then?'

'It gets better,' said Holly, checking the piece of paper again. 'He was only here a short while ago. Arrived on Saturday 3rd April, and stayed through until Thursday 22nd April. Same room, and everything. So I went back to the car hire people. He even hired the same model of Mercedes... but silver on the first occasion.'

'Good work, Holly. Don't suppose Ross asked you to call South Africa, did he?'

'Aye, he did, as it happens. I spoke to a really laid-back-sounding guy with the airport police at Cape Town. Warrant Officer Mokoena was his name. He said he'd do some digging and get back to us. Don't know when, though. On the plus side, he did invite me over to stay! Wanted to show me around the Cape vineyards.'

'Are you going?'

'Too busy making phone calls for you at present, sir. Later, perhaps!'

Neil smiled. 'I hear the old oak chest may have been located too?'

'Aye, maybe. So you probably know Strathclyde are getting a statement from the woman who recognised it, a Mrs Elizabeth Patterson in Cumbernauld.'

He poured coffee into two mugs and offered her one. 'I

didn't know about the Cumbernauld connection. Looks like we might be getting somewhere at last… Coffee?'

Holly accepted the mug and sat down behind one of the vacant desks.

'Do you really believe this man, Van Nieuwoudt, is somehow connected to this job?'

'I don't know, but he seems to have been here on all the pertinent dates. Then he pops up out of the blue and tells me wee fibs about his travel arrangements. Says he's just arrived into Aberdeen from Amsterdam when, actually, all the evidence suggests he's driven up the road from Glasgow. Now call me old-fashioned…'

Holly raised the mug to her lips with both hands, but hesitated before drinking. 'You're right, there's definitely something not quite right about him. I look forward to hearing what my prospective South African tour guide has to say!'

Chapter Thirty-Four

It was Friday evening, and Neil had worked later than usual, intending to join his team for a drink before heading out to Cromarty to see Cat. They'd been waiting for a call back from Cape Town since first thing, but had given up on the possibility that they'd get one until the following day, if at all!

The office was unusually quiet, and so he'd taken the opportunity to clear the overdue routine paperwork that was once more spilling over the sides of his in tray. He was still enjoying the serenity of his surroundings, when the sudden warble from his desk phone startled him.

'Hello, DCI Strachan?'

The South African voice was clipped and precise.

'Good evening to you, Chief Inspector. Warrant Officer Johan Mokoena, South African Police Service, speaking.'

Neil slouched across his desk, telephone handset clamped to his ear.

'Good evening to you, Warrant Officer Mokoena. Thanks for getting back to me. Have you managed to find out anything about this man Dawie Van Nieuwoudt?'

'Yes, sir, certain things. Firstly, I must apologise for the delay in returning your call, but I needed to speak to our detective branch in the city.'

'That's okay. So what can you tell me about him?'

Neil wasn't in the mood for idle chit-chat. He picked up a pen and positioned a pad of Post-its in front of him so that he could take notes.

'Mr Van Nieuwoudt is well known amongst the business fraternity in Cape Town, sir. You may know that he runs a very successful diamond and tanzanite trading company, Noordhoek Diamonds and Tanzanites, with his son Peter. The company has been trading for many years.'

'Aye, I was aware of its existence.'

'Well, the detectives in our Organised Crime Branch have been interested in this company for some time, mainly in relation to Mr Van Nieuwoudt junior's client base, some of whom appear to be heavily involved in large-scale criminal activity and drug smuggling within South Africa. The company also has links to governments engaged in the blood diamond trade, so it seems there is much intelligence-gathering activity going on.'

'Is that it, then? Nothing directly related to Dawie Van Nieuwoudt himself?'

'No, that's pretty much it, I'm afraid. The father is regarded more as a pillar of the local community than a businessman of ill repute. Neither Mr Van Nieuwoudt senior nor his son have any criminal convictions here in South Africa. Let us say, they always appear to be one step ahead of the law!'

'What about associates abroad? Do you have any intelligence on his international business connections?'

Mokoena seemed a little irritated. 'This man deals with many people across the world, sir, many of whom are of no interest to the authorities here. We do have some names on our databases, but they relate to criminal groups in this country… People who would not be of interest to your investigation, sir.'

He paused, before continuing. 'I can email you a list of these names if you would like.'

'That would be helpful, thanks. So we're saying he's a little shady, but that's all, then?'

'That is the case as I see it, sir.'

'Okay, Warrant Officer. Thanks again for taking the time to call.'

'My pleasure, sir. I particularly liked speaking with your colleague Miss Anderson. I should very much like to meet her, should she wish to visit Cape Town.'

Neil removed the handset from his ear and stared at it with incredulity. Then he heard the South African's voice again.

'Oh, I should mention that I spoke to our immigration colleagues here at the airport. Their records correspond to those you already possess in terms of Mr Van Nieuwoudt's recent visits to the United Kingdom. He does travel regularly to destinations in the USA and in Europe, particularly Amsterdam. The immigration department did also provide me with the name of an inbound UK passenger who'd stated that he was visiting Van Nieuwoudt at his Clifton address. He told the immigration officer that he was a friend of Mr Van Nieuwoudt's and was intending to stay for approximately one week... for leisure purposes, according to the landing card.'

'And that visitor would be...?'

'A Mr Mungo Hector McQuade, sir. From Glasgow. His date of birth is...'

Neil interrupted. 'Oh, I know Mr McQuade's date of birth, Warrant Officer! So when did this visit take place?'

'In 2008, sir, and there was a previous recorded visit in 2006.'

'Thank you, Warrant Officer. You've been very helpful!'

The phone call was concluded with an assurance that he'd pass on Mokoena's best wishes to Holly. Neil tapped his pen on the notepad.

'Well, well,' he murmured to himself. 'Some people form the strangest of friendships! South African diamond merchant and Glasgow slimeball.'

The mist was slowly clearing, and a picture emerging. A picture linking Ualas MacBean through McQuade to the current-day Frasers. He couldn't be sure about Van Nieuwoudt, but was now convinced that McQuade was involved up to his ears in the crimes that had been perpetrated at Cullaird Castle. The chances were that *he'd* been MacBean's partner in crime during the break-ins... old cellmates working together once again!

As if on cue, Bryan Findlay knocked and entered the office.

'Scanned statement just arrived from Cumbernauld, sur. That of a Mrs Elizabeth Jayne Patterson; makes interesting reading, it does.'

He placed the two-page document on the desk in front of Neil and turned to walk out, but not before adding, 'I've given DI Haggarty a copy for inputting on the system. Enjoy!'

Neil picked up the statement. 'Thanks, Fin. Took their time.'

His eyes raced across the document, eager to digest the content. Mrs Patterson was a middle-aged council clerk living quietly with her husband in the North Lanarkshire town, sixteen miles north-east of Glasgow city centre. According to her testimony, an identical chest was auctioned at Mulvaney Street Furniture Auctions in Glasgow, sometime in the 1970s. It was purchased by her father, a Mr John Erskine from Stirling, who in turn gave it to his daughter when he moved into residential care in 1988. Mrs Patterson had sold the chest to a firm of Glasgow antique dealers, who'd been touring the area of Cumbernauld, cold-calling, sometime towards the end of March 2010. The two men had been seeking stock to purchase, particularly old furniture.

Then came the showstopper! The purchaser, who'd

provided Mrs Patterson with a receipt on headed paper, was none other than Cathcart Antiques, Cathcart Road, Govanhill, Glasgow… the dubious little empire of Boyd Eugene Duff and Mungo Hector McQuade!

As Neil reread the statement for the third time, Findlay, together with two other DCs walked past the open door.

'Bet you're a happy man this evening, sur? Will you be joining us up the road for a couple of drams?'

'Aye, just coming. I'll catch you up, boys.'

Neil gathered up his jacket and car keys. He wanted to detain McQuade right away, but he didn't have enough to make the phone call. Damn it, Elizabeth Patterson may have made a mistake. It might not even be the very same chest that Susan Fraser had sold all those years ago! No, more work was needed to confirm the link. He needed something a little more substantial, and tomorrow was another day.

He slipped his arms into the sleeves of his jacket, only to become aware of the vibrations emanating from the inside pocket. It was Cat's mobile phone again.

The text that flashed up on the screen when he tapped on the envelope icon sent a chill down his spine. He'd only been thinking about Ciaran Lusk minutes beforehand, and how elusive he'd been since leaving the Telford Road address. But now it seemed he was back, and as arrogant and minacious as ever! He read the message again…

Good Evening Neil. Late finish tonight? Cat must be missing you, stranded out here on the Black Isle. Just as well she has me close by!

Neil checked the phone number. He started to tap out the digits, but then hesitated, before putting the phone down and running out of the office.

Findlay and his colleagues were standing outside the glass

doors of the reception lobby, waiting for another detective constable to join them. They interrupted their conversation and looked round when they saw Neil hurrying down the stairs, two at a time.

'Everything okay, sur?' Findlay asked as Neil threw open the main door.

'Not really, Fin. Look, can I use your phone?'

'Sure you can,' said the DC, handing it over with a puzzled look on his face.

'Thanks, Fin. Won't be a moment,' Neil panted.

He stepped out of earshot and entered Lusk's number again, not really expecting to have any luck with someone else's phone. He heard the ringtone at the other end of the line, and then to his utter surprise, Lusk's voice answered.

'Hello. Who's this?'

'Where the hell are you, Lusk? We need to sort this out.'

The young man from Aberdeen seemed to have been caught a little off guard.

'Chief Inspector Strachan! Well done. I didn't recognise that number you've just called from. One of your colleague's, is it?'

'It doesn't matter whose number it is. You need to tell me where you are. We need to talk. It can't go on, Ciaran.'

Lusk sniggered. 'Oh, but it can, Neil. All the while I want it to. Look, I hope you're not trying to trace this call with all that hi-tech jiggery-pokery you cops have at your disposal are you?'

'Of course I'm not tracing the call,' Neil spouted between clenched teeth. 'Look, you're piling up grief for yourself, Ciaran. You need to stop this, before things get out of hand. Come in and let's put an end to this. You know it makes sense, eh?'

There was another muffled laugh at the other end of the line, then silence. It was more of a reluctance to speak on Lusk's part, not a silence, intrinsically. Neil could hear faint voices in the background, and then the chink of glass against glass quite close to Lusk's phone.

He then spoke again. 'How's Cat getting on with the in-laws? Ah, but they're not in-laws, are they? Not until you make an honest woman of her. Until then, she's a free agent, I s'pose?'

He was enjoying himself, having sensed the desperation in Neil's voice.

'I *will* catch up with you, Lusk. You know that's a given, don't you?'

'Of that I have no doubt, Neil. But don't deny me a wee bit of fun before the long arm of the law finally taps me on the shoulder.'

There was yet another chuckle, then silence again. It was another productive silence, if you could call it that, a silence that was Lusk's undoing.

Neil heard a young woman's voice drift through the earpiece. She was obviously located very close to Lusk. 'Can I get you anything else at all, darlin'?'

The thing was, it was a voice he recognised. He'd gone to school with that voice, kissed the lips from which it had emanated... behind the bike sheds when they were fifteen! The voice was that of Robena Kennedy, who now worked behind the bar at the Admiral Napier Hotel in Cromarty.

Lusk's voice flowed out of the handset again. 'Anyway, circumstances could change as far as Cat's concerned, eh, Neil? It's all to play for. The clock's ticking, mate. Must go now... good to chat.'

The line went dead. Neil marched back to where his colleagues were standing.

'Thanks, Fin,' he said as he handed the phone back. 'Sorry, I can't make that drink just now. Later, perhaps.' Then he ran towards the car park and his MG. He ground his teeth angrily whilst he pondered his next move. His watch told him that it was coming up for seven o'clock, so he needed to get his skates on.

He approached the little sports car with his phone pressed to his ear. Rona Strachan's number rang and rang. There was no answer. Next on the list was the mobile he'd given to Cat. This time he got an automated message from that annoying bloody woman who seemed to revel in the knowledge that 'the person you're calling is unavailable right now'. Then, to his annoyance, she advised, 'Please try again later'!

They must be out walking Tam. God knows where Euan was. He dropped into the driver's seat of the MG and fired up the engine. His first port of call would be the Admiral Napier Hotel. Next, he rang the operations room and spoke to the supervising sergeant, requesting backup at the hotel.

There was concern in the sergeant's voice when he reported, 'We've got no units available out on the Black Isle at present. I'll divert a traffic unit from Dingwall and let the OIC know what's going on.' As an afterthought he then advised, 'Look, don't put yourself at risk, sir. Wait until the uniforms arrive, will you?' But Neil had gone. He was speeding down the slip road onto the A9 and heading towards the blinking red anti-collision lights on the Kessock Bridge.

By 7.20 pm, he was passing the turning to Rosemarkie Golf Club. He picked up the phone again and called Cat. This time she answered. He didn't have time for niceties.

'Hi. Where are you?'

'Outside your Auntie Jean's in Burnside Place. We're walking the dog.'

'Is Jean there?'

'Aye. We're talking to her now. She's gardening.'

'Listen to me. You need to go inside with her, lock the doors and wait there until I get in touch. I'll explain later.'

'What on earth's going on, Neil?' Then she realised. 'It's Lusk, isn't it? He's coming to Cromarty.'

'He's not *coming*, Cat, he's *there*. So just do as I say. If anyone knocks the door, or you're concerned about anything, dial 999.'

'Okay. Where are you?' But the signal had faded. He'd gone.

The Admiral Napier Hotel was an imposing Georgian structure, dominating the harbour front in Cromarty. It had stood there since the 1790s, and had once been the comfortable home of a rich grain trader. Neil knew it well, having frequented the establishment regularly with his friends, before and during his university days.

He parked around the corner and approached the hotel cautiously on foot, hoping to find Lusk's motorcycle either in the car park or to the front of the premises. But he was disappointed; there was no such vehicle to be seen. So he entered the establishment through the side door and made his way into the lounge area. There were a number of drinkers clustered around the pine-clad bar, and several couples, probably tourists, sat huddled at the tables by the windows, consuming bar meals. Ciaran Lusk, however, was nowhere to be seen.

Neil spotted Robena, wiping down a table in an alcove near the bar and hurried over to her, the urgency of the situation still uppermost in his mind.

She sensed his presence and turned around, a little taken aback.

'Oh, hi stranger.' She beamed seductively at him, her dimpled cheeks a little flushed from the effort of her labours. He smiled back, momentarily recalling their once intimate relationship.

'Hello Robbie. Look, I'm trying to find a young dark-haired guy called Ciaran Lusk. I believe he may have been drinking in here less than an hour ago.'

She nodded. 'Aye, I know who you mean. He's not long moved into the area; rides around on a big black motorbike.'

'That'll be him,' said Neil, a little relieved that she'd at least remembered him.

She draped the tea towel she'd been using over her shoulder, and brushed her dark fringe away from her eyes. 'He left about twenty minutes ago, so you're too late to cadge a drink off him!'

'Bugger.' Neil looked at her anxiously. 'Don't suppose you know where he's living, do you?'

She folded her arms and gazed up at him wide-eyed. 'Are you suggesting that I ask all the menfolk who come in here where they live, Neil Strachan?'

'You asked *me*,' he added, his expression sombre.

She sensed the urgency in his voice, realising this was Neil the policeman asking, not her ex-boyfriend from long ago.

'He's renting a room down in the Little Vennel, top end. Said he was here to help a mate with a building job, then was heading off on his travels again.' She frowned. 'Will he be wishing I never told you that?'

Neil was already heading for the door. He looked over his shoulder. 'He'll be wishing he'd never been born when I catch up with him! Thanks for the info. I'll drop in for a drink sometime.' Then, as an afterthought, he called over to her, 'Oh, and when the uniform boys finally turn up, tell them where I've gone!'

'Don't bring Cat, then… when you drop in for that drink!' she called after him, but her words faded to nothing as the door slammed closed.

The Little Vennel ran from Church Street down to the waterfront at Shore Street, a mere stone's throw from his mother's house, Crumbathyn.

It was no more than an alleyway, in which several white-fronted fishermen's cottages faced out onto a long, rough

456

stone wall that marked the boundary of another of Cromarty's towering Georgian residences.

Neil parked in Shore Street and walked the short distance into the Little Vennel. He then progressed up the slight incline, keeping close to the harled walls of the old cottages, so as not to provide his prey with an early sighting of him. Eventually, his view slowly opened out all the way up to Church Street, and there in front of him, halfway along, was the Moto Guzzi V7, propped up on its stand outside a low terraced cottage, its window surrounds and rainwater goods painted a garish blue.

Neil edged closer to the wall and advanced until he reached the first window of the property. He peeked in, but it was shrouded by grubby nets. There was no sign of movement through the translucent material, so he moved on to the door. There he waited, having placed his ear against the cracked wood. He could now hear the faint drone of music from within. Someone was definitely at home!

Taking a deep breath, he knocked on the door several times, in a rhythm that suggested a friendly, if not familiar, visitor. Seconds later, he heard footsteps. Then the door opened, and there was Lusk, dressed in white T-shirt, faded blue jeans and calf-length motorcycle boots.

'Hello, Ciaran. I think we need to have that chat, don't you?' Neil growled, as he placed a foot over the threshold of the doorway.

Lusk stared at him disbelievingly, his face now a deathly shade of pale.

'In your fucking dreams,' he bawled, and threw the door forward with all his strength onto the policeman's right foot. Neil swore repeatedly, as a terrible pain engulfed his toes, but his foot had done its job and the door failed to close. Lusk didn't wait for another attempt, but turned tail and ran back through the small sitting room before disappearing into the kitchen. By the time the stars had faded from before Neil's eyes, he was gone.

Adrenalin now came to his rescue and Neil soon felt able to move again. So he hobbled through the house into the cluttered little kitchen, where the back door stood open. When he finally emerged into the tiny back garden, he saw Lusk sitting astride the high wall that bordered the rear of the property. The young man grinned down at him, as if having just won a great victory, then he dropped down the other side and disappeared from view once again.

Neil, his ease of mobility returning rapidly, reached the wall in a few strides and threw himself onto it. He pulled himself over, scuffing his fingers on the rough, lichen-encrusted stonework in the process, then dropped into the garden on the other side. He was just in time to see Lusk vaulting the little wrought-iron gate at the end of the garden and then turning left onto Church Street. Lusk looked back, visibly concerned now. He'd really not expected the pursuit to have continued after the initial door slamming!

When Neil emerged onto the roadway, his quarry was nowhere to be seen. He looked left and right, hands on hips and breathing heavily. 'Where are you, you slimy little bastard?' he panted.

As if in answer to his question, a small casement window opened with a squeal from beneath the dormered gable of the house opposite. A white-haired lady squeezed her head through the gap and shouted to him.

'He went down the Little Vennel, Neil. A couple of seconds ago.'

Neil raised his hand in thanks, and started to run. 'Do you know me?' he called out to her as he passed beneath her window.

'No,' she replied, 'but the laddie who jumped that gate just a few seconds before you did. He referred to you as "effing

Neil Strachan". I might be wrong, but you look like the good guy to me!'

'I am, most definitely,' Neil panted. 'Thanks.'

Buoyed by the public-spiritedness of the old lady, he sprinted away and turned left, back into the Little Vennel, where Lusk was sitting astride his motorbike and turning the ignition key. The bike's engine coughed and turned over several times but, frustratingly for its rider, wouldn't fire initially. All the while, Neil closed in at a speed he would never have thought possible just three minutes before!

He was only a few short yards away when the engine finally barked into life. Lusk selected first gear and the machine started to move, but not before Neil had grasped a handful of his T-shirt. The acceleration qualities of the bike proved to be Lusk's saviour, however, and it powered away, leaving Neil staggering hopelessly behind it, fighting to maintain his balance. He looked on despairingly, as the machine reached the junction with Shore Street, turned right and finally disappeared from view. The helmetless fugitive had made good his escape!

Neil panted uncontrollably as he considered his next move. It was conceivable that Lusk could turn back into Church Street a little further along Shore Street, and skirt around him. So he waited and listened, expecting the drone of the motorcycle to intensify to his right. There was no mistaking the high-pitched whine of the bike's engine as it raced along Cromarty's ancient streets, but it didn't return as Neil had predicted. Instead, it faded away to the east... towards South Sutor, and what the locals often referred to as 'The Guns'.

Lusk had played right into his hands. The chase was still on!

Chapter Thirty-Five

Standing either side of the slender portal to the Cromarty Firth were two towering headlands. The sheer cliffs forming their seaward flanks rose to over one hundred metres, standing guard against the relentless onslaught of the North Sea. These headlands were known as 'The Sutors'. So called as they were said to resemble a couple of shoemakers – *souters* in the old Scots language – bent over their lasts.

The headland to the south was accessed by a winding, single-track road that once served an important coastal artillery battery. The battery, officially known as South Sutor Fort, was built to protect the Royal Navy's considerable assets, stationed in and around the firth during the two world wars.

Neil was now back in the MG, and was heading up that narrow road at a speed that some would say was verging on the unsafe. As he climbed higher, between the expansive fields that sloped gently down to the blue-grey waters of the firth, his view opened out. There was still no sign of Lusk. He had, after all, acquired something of a head start, but Neil remained confident, hoping that his quarry had followed the road right to its end.

He braked heavily, having reached a fork in the road. The

track to the left led down the hill to a small white house; the one to the right, on to the fort. Neil weighed up his options. No, Lusk wouldn't go left; he'd stick to the public road, hoping that it was a means of escape. So he jabbed the accelerator again and the little sports car growled away, churning up a cloud of dust from its gleaming spoked wheels. The lane then permeated a small wood, through which a strip of grass had become a feature along its crumbling centre line, attesting to the route's general lack of use. The last of the evening sunlight danced through the trees onto the windscreen, briefly frustrating Neil's visual awareness, before the leafy canopy receded behind him and he found himself once more beneath the lava-red sky. He negotiated a gentle right-hand bend and then the road opened out onto a rudimentary car park, in essence no more than a large sandy lay-by.

To his left was the opposing headland of North Sutor, at the base of which foaming breakers crashed against its precipitous cliffs. Once more Neil braked heavily, his local knowledge reminding him that he was near the end of the road. A little further on, he would reach a metal farm gate that prevented access to the fort, unless on foot. The only other route available was a deeply rutted farm track that climbed away up the hill, providing passage for agricultural vehicles to the fields above.

As he coasted around that last bend, the gate came into view, and there, directly in front of it was Ciaran Lusk, sitting astride the Moto Guzzi. The lay-by was behind him now, and Neil knew that Lusk was trapped. Not even a motorbike could get past him on this narrow stretch of track. So he decided to stop and approach on foot. When the throb of the MG's engine had died away, he leaned forward and slowly opened the glove compartment. Inside was a retractable baton and a set of handcuffs. Thrusting the handcuffs into the pocket of his jacket and secreting the baton up its sleeve, he eased himself out of the car, and began the slow walk towards Lusk.

'It's over, Ciaran,' he called out. 'Let's make this as easy as possible, eh?'

Neil's eyes never deviated from the figure in front of him. For the first time Lusk looked scared, as if an alarm bell had been set off deep inside of him.

When the distance between the two men had reduced to no more than twenty yards, Lusk raised a cautionary hand. 'Stay back there and we'll talk,' he temporised.

Neil stopped. 'The time for talking is over, Ciaran. You're coming back with me.'

'What, in that thing?' Lusk gestured towards the MG and laughed.

'If necessary... although I've got backup on its way to provide you with a more comfortable ride, if that's what's worrying you!'

Well, it was partially true. Hopefully, his uniformed colleagues would be trawling around the streets of Cromarty by now, trying to find him. Unfortunately there was no mobile signal up on the headland. He'd tried to make a call before, whilst walking Tam several months earlier.

'You know what?' Lusk called out. 'I don't think your pals have the faintest idea where you are. I think it's just you and me up here. And you're expecting me to just walk over to your wee car there and get in?'

Neil didn't answer. Lusk's recalcitrance was beginning to annoy him. So he started to advance again, comforted by the cold steel that pressed against his arm.

'You're coming with me to my "wee car", and that's a promise. Whether you get there on your feet or your arse is down to you, Ciaran.'

The grin disappeared from Lusk's face, his bluff called. He hopped deftly off the bike and pushed the heavy machine over into Neil's path, then scaled the gate and sprinted away down the track towards the red, rusting roofs of the old military establishment.

Neil leaned over the bike and recovered the keys that had mercifully been left in the ignition. Then, unruffled by Lusk's apparent escape, he climbed over the gate and trotted down the slope after him. As a precaution, he let the baton slip down from within his sleeve, and he racked it to full length, all the while keeping the distant figure firmly in his sights.

He soon found himself in the heart of the fort, if one could call it that. To refer to this small cluster of buildings as a 'fort' was something of a misnomer. There was no defensive wall, nothing like that: just an assortment of long-abandoned structures... some of concrete, some of brick. There were accommodation huts for the Royal Navy personnel who served there, stores and two large coastal artillery emplacements that once contained the large 6-inch guns protecting the narrow entrance to the Cromarty Firth. Some way from the nucleus of the fort, out of sight, beneath the cliffs, and built on small grassy stacks, were two concrete searchlight towers. These remote structures, built in 1939, were once accessible by a stepped path that clung to the cliff face, a path that had long since crumbled into the sea.

Lusk had now disappeared, prompting Neil to halt when he came to the first group of buildings. One of these was a long shed-like affair, with a pitched corrugated roof and pale concrete walls stained by the ravages of wild winter weather. It was once the fire command post, the bustling nerve centre of the fort.

Neil tried the doors, but they were either locked or seized: one of the two. He then turned his attention to the bunker-like structure standing next to it. The windows of this building were heavily shuttered, there being no means of entry, so he retraced his steps and advanced down the track.

The eastern sky was even darker now, evoking a shimmering purple hue upon the wide expanse of sea ahead of him. A solitary ship, characterised as a tiny black dot, tracked north along the horizon, the only visible sign of life present beyond the cliffs. All around him, the incessant evening birdsong still persisted... small comfort in his present situation, but comfort all the same!

Ahead of him, as the track curved away to the left, two other small bunkers came into view. They had probably been air raid shelters in an earlier life, with ventilation pipes on the roof and blast-protected entrances. Both were fully secured so he continued down the hill, his right hand wrapping ever tighter around the shaft of the baton.

His progress was then stalled by the appearance of a locked gate, either side of which stood a high metal fence, supported by razor-topped steel stakes. Its purpose was presumably to dissuade explorers from venturing further into the site, and reaching the dangerous cliffs beyond. He looked around him. Had Lusk been able to venture beyond this point? Surely not. Neil walked along the fence, his eyes scanning the substantial wire mesh. Surely no one could've scaled an obstacle such as this! But no, they probably didn't need to. Twenty feet from the gate, at ground level, he found a small gap where the mesh had been peeled back. Fortunately, it was just big enough for him to squeeze through.

From here, the track had become overgrown with nettles and suchlike, so much so that the original concrete surface had become almost obscured. It now veered sharply to the right, as if into a grassy cutting, then back again, emerging into the business end of the site, where the two brick built gun emplacements stood. These empty brick-lined pits, now the home of nothing other than assorted litter and rampant growing ivy, served as poignant reminders of the threat posed to Britain's coastline more than half a century before.

The gun emplacements were surrounded by other, smaller structures, chiefly stores once used by the Royal Artillery, and nearby was the all-important magazine escape shaft.

Neil tried the door, but it had seized completely due to heavy rusting. He skirted around it, to what looked like a narrow stairway encased between concrete walls, and above which a rusting crane stanchion stood eerily abandoned. It was then that he sensed movement on the stairway, and so he squinted into the advancing gloom to make out what it was.

Lusk's head had appeared above its concrete threshold, swivelling left and right, as if seeking out his pursuer. When he finally spotted the policeman, he turned tail and disappeared down the concrete steps, gingerly negotiating the debris that lay cluttered at the bottom. Neil followed, turning left at the foot of the steps and heading towards the heavy steel doors that stood ajar at the end of the passageway.

Unbeknown to him, this was once the entrance to the battery's main magazine, long since emptied of its heavy shells and goodness knows what other forms of ordnance that were once stored there. But the function of the chamber was of no relevance. He was more interested in the sound of the feet he could hear scurrying away into the darkness.

Resting the tip of the baton on his shoulder, he moved forward, stopping only to retrieve his mobile phone and activate its small light. Hoping the battery would not let him down, he advanced warily and soon found himself at a crossroads where two low passageways headed off to the left and right, one either side of the steel doors. Choosing the left-hand passage, he stooped down and hurried on into the void. The passageway curved to the right, as if taking him in a large circuitous route around the central chamber. Then he passed an even smaller tunnel leading away to his left, to where he could just make out the outline of a rusty ladder, presumably an escape shaft.

Deciding to stay with the main passage, he hurried on, eventually, as he'd surmised, emerging back into the main tunnel by the large steel doors. He stopped and listened. There was nothing, just the sound of water dripping somewhere behind him.

'Damn,' he murmured. 'Lost the bastard.'

He turned about to shine his light back into the void he'd just emerged from. Suddenly from behind him, there was a rush of feet, and then he felt a significant force thrust into his back, sending him crashing down onto his knees. The sound of the footsteps rapidly diminished as they raced up the concrete steps, back towards the narrow strip of darkening sky.

Neil heaved himself to his feet and gave chase, just getting a glimpse of the white-clad figure disappearing again at the top of the steps.

When he emerged into the dusk, he spotted Lusk racing down the grassy track towards the cliffs.

'You're fast running out of places to hide, my friend,' he mouthed as he took up the chase once again.

The grassy cap to the cliff top dipped steeply away, before finally becoming a sheer wall of rock, heavily mottled with the guano of countless generations of seabirds. Lusk had followed the fading line of the path that had originally led down to the two searchlight towers. He'd now reached the cliff edge, where once the grassy path had been replaced by crudely carved steps. But he'd not realised that the route had long since become impassable due to the incessant march of coastal erosion.

It was, as Neil had assured him thirty minutes earlier, all over! Ciaran Lusk stood stock-still, wide-eyed and frantic as Neil's darkened form appeared above him. The policeman edged forward, his baton grasped tightly in his right hand, slowly closing down the last few square yards of personal space that now represented Lusk's liberty. He stopped at the top of the old steps, just beyond arm's length of his quarry and rested the tip of the baton on his shoulder again, as if in readiness to strike.

They now stood and faced each other, so close that Neil could see the beads of sweat on the young man's brow. Conversely, Lusk could see the fury burning in Neil's eyes.

Lusk was first to break the silence. 'So we've come to the end of the road, then. I suppose this is where you beat the crap out of me with that thing and push me over the edge.'

He glanced down to the foreshore far below, where the incoming breakers hissed and exploded amongst the rocks.

Neil stepped forward, his expression blank and utterly soulless. 'Turn around,' he ordered.

Lusk was suddenly consumed with fear. 'No way! Have you gone crazy, man?'

Neil's eyes continued to drill into Lusk's, feeding on his fear.

'Turn around... now!' he bellowed.

This time Lusk reluctantly complied, trembling as he did so. He sensed Neil approach, and he closed his eyes, hoping it would be over quickly. Then strong hands grasped his wrists, pulling them roughly together behind his back. Neil's face appeared behind his right ear.

'Last chance, Ciaran. You can jump now and end it all, or you can leave *me* to conclude the business between us. Your choice, *mate*.'

'For Christ's sake.' Lusk could feel the warm trickle of urine running down his leg.

Neil's head slowly receded from his peripheral vision. 'Seems like you want to play it my way,' he whispered.

Lusk closed his eyes, expecting the final shove, but instead, he felt the chill of cold steel against his skin and the successive clicks of the handcuffs' ratchet arms as they tightened around his wrists. Then he felt Neil's hand probe inside the rear pocket of his jeans.

'I think I'll keep hold of this,' he muttered, removing the young man's mobile phone. 'You won't be needing it for a while!'

Neil spun Lusk around and marched him away from the edge.

'Ciaran George Lusk, I'm detaining you in connection with an assault on Catriona Duncan and for stalking her between 29th March of this year and today's date.'

He reeled off the usual caution, and then steered his prisoner back along the track. 'Come on, Ciaran, put your best foot forward. I'm hungry and I've missed my tea!'

Lusk stumbled along in silence and when his pace faltered, he was reminded of the fact with a painful twist of the handcuffs against his wrists.

When they reached the final section of the track that led back to the farm gate, Neil was relieved to see two uniformed police officers, clad in reflective vests, walking towards them. Further back, the same dog handler who'd attended Cullaird Castle two weeks before was lifting the hairy form of Ben, the German shepherd, over the gate.

'You're a sight for sore eyes, boys. Thought I was going to have to transport Mr Lusk here in the MG.'

The taller of the two policemen accepted Lusk into his custody. 'We were getting a wee bit worried, sir, not knowing where you were heading. Been like a treasure hunt trying to catch up with you!'

Lusk raised his head and smiled weakly. 'So much for your so-called back up!'

The tall policeman led him away. 'Hush yer mouth, sonny,' he warned. 'You'll have plenty of time to talk later… into a tape recorder.'

Neil watched them go, then called out, 'Best you cover your seats, boys. He's pissed himself.'

Now content, he turned to the second policeman. 'How

did you find me up here?' he asked, as they followed their colleague up the hill.

'Miss Kennedy at the hotel told us you'd gone down to the Little Vennel, so we had a cruise around but couldn't find you. Then this old lady poked her head out of her window. Told us she'd seen a bonnie looking dark-haired man called Neil chasing another, younger man, but he'd escaped on a motorbike. She thought she'd heard it in the distance roaring off up to The Guns.'

'I'm going to have to buy her a large box of chocolates. I should've called in before coming up here; the mobile signal's no good out on the headland. I'm afraid the adrenalin surge seems to have got the better of me. Well, that's my excuse, anyway!'

The policeman gave him one of those looks, as if to say 'You bloody well should have called in'. But he preferred to exercise respect when reproving his senior officer.

'Aye, I know how one's judgement can be affected when the adrenalin's been flowing. Especially in your case. I don't know how you managed to keep your hands off the cocky wee shite!'

Having thanked the dog handler, who remained behind to arrange recovery of the motorbike, Neil followed the tail lamps of the Volvo patrol car down the lane towards the twinkling lights of Cromarty. Lusk was being taken to the custody suite in Inverness, where the Divisional CID would interview and process him. Neil had no desire to set eyes on him again, but had promised to drop in later and provide a witness statement once he'd spoken to Cat and given her the good news.

He pulled up outside Burnside Cottage and turned off the engine, relieved that it was all over. He'd stopped in a lay-by on Shore Street five minutes earlier and called in to update the control room as to his immediate plans, now that he was back in Cromarty. He had also texted Holly and had received a brief reply: *Thank God... Maverick!*

Now he sat in quiet reflection, enjoying the silence and cogitating on how things could've ended up, deep in those gloomy passageways beneath the old fort, or out on the edge of that cliff twenty minutes earlier.

He'd always berated those TV cops who'd gone where angels feared to tread, usually alone, and without anyone knowing where they were. Of course, in the end the cavalry always turned up, just a little too late to see any action! And that's exactly what had just happened. He grinned briefly, but then a sense of reality surged back through him. There could be no argument, no excuse. He'd put himself unnecessarily at risk, and gums would be beating in all the usual places when word got out!

The curtains twitched in the window to the left of the front door, and light flooded out onto the MG. His Auntie Jean, Rona's eldest sister, peered out, before retreating and allowing the heavy drapes to flop back into place. Seconds later, as he was climbing out of the car, Cat opened the front door and ran out, followed by a frantic Tam. She threw her arms around him and planted a lingering kiss on his lips, then leaned back and scowled at him.

'We've been worried sick about you. Where the hell have you been? I've been calling you.'

He put his arm around her. 'Let's go in, and I'll explain all.'

He then stooped to hug Tam, who, without warning, sprung up into his arms. He stroked the dog's head as they entered the cottage. 'It's all right, laddie. Dad's back in one piece.'

The sitting room at Burnside Cottage was tiny, beneath a low ceiling. It was comfortably appointed with chintzy soft furnishings, so typical of many old properties. Jean sat next to Cat on the sofa, whilst Rona examined Neil's injured foot. She pulled no punches, which was only to be expected from a district nurse of her generation.

'You've broken your big toe, son, although an X-ray at Raigmore will be needed to confirm it. The nail will fall off any time from now and you can expect the bruise of all bruises! It's not going to be pretty, and it's going to hurt for days. Best thing I can do his bind it to the other toe for the time being; keep it immobilised.'

'You've been so lucky tonight,' said Cat. 'Fancy going after Lusk on your own like that. What were you thinking, Neil?'

He smiled meekly, then winced when Rona commenced her bandaging. 'Look… what's done is done. The opportunity arose to finally catch up with him and I took it. It's over now.'

Jean, always the diplomat, patted Cat's knee. 'He's right, lassie. All's well that ends well. That despicable creature will be off the streets now, at least for a while.'

'Is that the case, Neil? What will happen to him?' Cat still looked worried.

'He'll appear before the Sherriff Court tomorrow morning, all being well, and then be remanded in custody. He can expect to be locked up for a wee while in the longer term. That's the best we can hope for!'

'So what are your plans now, Neil?' his aunt enquired.

'I'll go back to Inverness and do a statement for the investigating officers. Then I need to wrap up a few things in the office.'

'After which, you'll go and get that foot looked at, just in case there's anything else broken in there,' Cat demanded.

'Aye, Cat, I will. Best you stay where you are tonight and I'll pick you both up in the morning.'

'Sounds sensible,' said Rona. 'You won't get out of A & E until the early hours on a Friday night!'

Neil looked at his watch. 'It's nine thirty now. I'd better get my skates on.'

Cat got up. 'Come on. I'll see you out to the car.'

Having said their goodbyes, Cat leaned into the open window of the MG. 'You know I really appreciate what you did to catch Lusk, don't you? It's just that loving someone sometimes means you get angry with them when they put themselves at risk like that.'

Neil smiled. 'I know you were only play-acting to impress those two old worriers! You can show me just how much you appreciate my efforts tomorrow!'

He kissed her, avoiding the mock punch and wound up the window. Outside, he could still hear her muffled voice when he started the engine.

'Don't push it, Chief Inspector,' she called out when he pulled away from outside the cottage.

As he drove up to Church Street, he could still see her in the red glow of his tail lights, waving furiously with one hand and holding onto Tam's collar with the other. It evoked a warm feeling deep within him, probably the first time in quite a while. All in all, the day had ended well.

With his personal life back on track, he could now turn his full attention to Operation Cawdor at last, and hopefully be able to elicit a positive outcome for the Frasers... if that could ever be the case after what they had been through!

He sat back and accelerated out onto the lonely road back to Fortrose, having no idea that his day was about to become even longer – much longer.

Chapter Thirty-Six

Cullaird Castle
9 pm, Friday 14ᵗʰ May

Selina Cope had just come off the phone to her husband and children. She stretched out on one of the leather sofas in the great hall and toyed with the stem of her wine glass.

'I'm really missing them all down south, you know,' she revealed. 'In fact, I feel I want to go home now, if I'm honest.'

Miriam looked up from her magazine. 'I don't blame you at all, dear. Still, someone's got to be up here on the spot whilst this investigation continues. Then there's your parents' affairs, and the future of the distillery to sort out. It's just a pity that your brother can't come over and take his fair share of the burden.'

'He actually called earlier today, whilst you were saying your goodbyes to Dawie. He's offered to come over next weekend and lend a hand with anything that needs doing.'

'That's good of him!' Miriam replied sardonically.

'Alisdair does have his restaurant to think about. He can't just up and leave, Miriam.'

'Still, it's a bit much, leaving you to do it all! Is he bringing Simone with him?'

'Haven't a clue. He said he'd let me know.'

Not wishing to discuss her brother any longer, she changed the subject.

'It was nice seeing Dawie after all these years. Do you have any plans to meet up with him again any time soon?'

'Not immediately. A little and not often is my rule of thumb when it comes to seeing Dawie.'

Her mouth then twisted into a self-conscious smile. 'The toad paid me a visit during the night, you know.'

Selina sat up, a look of surprise on her face. 'What, he… you know?'

'Exactly. Incorrigible little man.'

'And you turfed him out, of course?'

Miriam smiled again. 'Umm… No, not immediately.'

Selina shook her head. 'Miriam, you never fail to shock. So has a spark been rekindled there or something?'

'Oh no, dear. Single women like me, of a certain age… well, we have needs, you know. And when the opportunity arises, it would be a shame not to take it. Well, that's my excuse, and I'm sticking to it!'

'So, how did he leave it with you? Did he say he'd call?'

'He acted rather strangely, to be honest. Seemed a little desperate.'

'In what way desperate?'

'Last night when we were err… you know… together, he repeatedly advocated that I go down to Glasgow with him. Wanted to spend more time with me before he flew home. Very un-Dawielike.'

'Sounds wildly romantic to me. Why didn't you want to take him up on it?'

Miriam closed the magazine. 'I have not the slightest intention of taking up where we left off, my dear. I enjoy my independence too much. Besides, I will never be convinced that his interest stops with me. A leopard never changes its spots, you know.'

Selina took a sip from her glass. 'So had he got the message, or did he try to persuade you again this morning?'

'Oh yes, he was all but pleading with me. Left me a little unsettled, if I'm honest.'

'Why's that? He was just being nice, bless him.'

'No, Selina, I'm convinced he had a sinister motive. It's just a feeling I have.'

'Oh Miriam, you're becoming neurotic. More wine?'

'No, dear, you finish it. My bath beckons.' Miriam looked at her watch. 'Nine fifteen… I'm late.' She got up and straightened the heavy tweed skirt she was wearing.

'Cocoa, before bed?' Selina asked.

'Of course, my dear. I'll ring down when I'm ready.' She was referring to the old bell call system that still operated throughout the castle. It was in fact an anachronism that still performed a useful function on occasions!

Just then Lorna McKirdy appeared in the doorway. She'd been working on her laptop down in the kitchen.

'Sorry to disturb you both. I'm away home now. Aili will be over in the morning. The two constables down at the gate will keep an eye on things overnight.'

'That's fine,' Selina replied, swinging her legs down from the sofa. 'Then I'll go down to the kitchen and boil up some milk for our cocoa.'

Picking up her empty wine glass, she said, 'I'll come down with you; see you out.'

The two women tripped down the stairs, whilst Miriam went off to have her bath. In the hallway, they parted company, Lorna leaving by the front door and Selina, having locked it after her, making her way to the kitchen.

Less than two minutes after Lorna had passed through it, there were several bangs on the old oak door. Selina hurried along and called out from behind it. 'Who's there?'

The voice that answered was familiar and reassuring. 'It's only me, Lorna. I'm afraid the battery's dead in my car. I'll need to make alternative arrangements to get back to Inverness.'

Selina slid back the heavy bolts and opened the door.

The young detective constable stood there looking a little embarrassed. 'Sorry about this. I'll need to call up and get someone to come out and collect me. Would you mind if I used your landline?'

'Of course not,' said Selina, ushering her in and along the corridor to the kitchen.

When Lorna concluded her call, she turned to Selina, who was stirring milk on the stove. 'Unfortunately it's Friday night. Everyone's rushed off their feet. They're going to be a good while, I'm afraid. Look, I'm really sorry about this.'

Selina stopped stirring and smiled. 'Why don't you get your colleagues at the end of the drive to take you home? It would take them less than an hour, there and back.'

'Good God, no! It would be more than my life's worth. DCI Strachan has decreed that there will be a uniform presence here at all times.'

Selina approached her and rubbed her arm affectionately. 'Look, they'll be back in no time, and we're staying in a castle, for God's sake. No one's going to get in here when that door's locked and bolted... even with a key! Besides, we've got the panic alarm, and people locally we can call upon in an emergency.'

Lorna nodded. 'I suppose, put like that. As long as you're sure.'

Selina grinned. 'I am. Trust me. No one will ever know!'

And so it was. The patrol car stationed at the gate was summonsed to attend the castle. Following a series of protestations from the two young constables crewing the vehicle, they finally acquiesced and their passenger opened the back door. Lorna waved as she climbed in, prompting Selina to reciprocate, before she finally disappeared inside. Once again, the heavy key was turned in the lock and the bolts slid into place. She turned back towards the kitchen, but then realised that she'd left the panic alarm unit upstairs on the coffee table.

Not wishing then and there to climb the two steep flights of stairs to retrieve it, she continued along towards the chapel and turned left for the kitchen.

Less than a minute later, she was back in front of the Aga, standing over the saucepan, stirring the milk for the cocoa and chuckling to herself. Fancy Miriam admitting that her ex-husband, the man she always loved to berate, had snuck into her bed the previous night!

When the milk boiled, she made herself a drink, not prepared to wait for Miriam to ring her little bell. She then settled down at the table and immersed herself in a newly purchased magazine.

More than fifteen minutes must have passed when the phone on the wall began to ring, inducing her to cry out in surprise. Surely, it was getting a bit late for phone calls!

She crossed to the arched stone pillar onto which the device was mounted and lifted the receiver. 'Hello. Ruthven 521664.' She always announced the number. It was something her mother had taught her to do as a child.

There was a silence, during which she thought she could hear passing traffic. Indeed, from the acoustics around the transmitter, she was convinced that the call had originated from a payphone.

A man's voice, gravelly and with a broad Glaswegian accent, drifted through the earpiece. 'Who's this?'

Selina immediately became irritated by the man's lack of politeness.

'Never mind who I am. Who's speaking, please?' she replied curtly, thinking this was one of those wrong number calls.

There was a pause, then the man spoke again. 'Are you Selina Cope?'

Selina, becoming increasingly annoyed, snapped back. 'Who's asking?'

The voice said, 'Look, lady, don't mess me about. If you

are Selina Cope, then ah'd advise you tae leave that castle of yours on the hurry-up. Oh, and you'd better take your cousin Miriam with you.'

Selina couldn't believe what she was hearing. 'Why are you telling me this? Who are you?'

'Never mind who ah am, Selina. Just go now. This is nae joke.'

'So what's going to happen if I don't?'

'Yer worst nightmare, that's what!'

A chill ran down Selina's spine. 'Are you Ualas MacBean? Tell me if you are.'

'Like ah said, lassie, it doesnae matter who ah am. You're wastin' time talkin' tae me, so ah suggest you get movin'.'

The phone line went dead and was replaced with the dialling tone.

Selina swallowed hard. Should she act now? Would it be dangerous to go outside? Yes, perhaps this was a trick. There was no way they were going outside. She picked up the phone again and dialled 999. The female operator responded immediately. 'Emergency... which service, please?'

Selina gulped, her mouth suddenly very dry. 'Police... quickly, please.'

After a second or two, another young female voice came on the line. 'Northern Police... can I help you, caller?'

Selina blurted out what had just happened, quoting, as she'd been told to, Operation Cawdor.

The call taker could be heard typing, then she said calmly... 'And to confirm, there's one other person in the property with you?'

'Yes, that's right, my cousin Miriam Fraser.'

'Okay. Now have you looked outside... through a window, I mean?'

'No, I haven't had the chance to. I've only just put the wretched phone down from speaking to him.'

'Okay, Mrs Cope, try to keep calm. I'll get the officers down by the gate to come up and see you. Is DC McKirdy still there?'

Selina hesitated, not wishing to get her young guardians into any bother with their bosses. But there was nothing for it; she had to be honest.

'Err, no, she's just gone home… with the two officers who were down by the gate!'

There was a silence at the other end of the line.

'I see… right. How long ago did they leave?'

'About twenty minutes back, I suppose.'

'Please bear with me, Mrs Cope. I'll try and get hold of them.'

Thirty agonising seconds passed, then the female voice came back on the line.

'I've tried to contact them, but unfortunately I'm getting no response. They may be travelling through a radio black spot, of which there are many out there in Strathnairn. I've dispatched another unit to you, but they're some way off. Now, can you confirm that the doors are properly secured?'

'Yes. We've only one, and there's no way anyone's getting through that. Not without a battering ram, anyway!'

'Good. Now whilst I'm on the line, can you go and have a look out through the windows? See if you can see anyone hanging around the property.'

'I will, but this *is* a castle, it'll take me a while.'

'That's fine. I'll be here.'

Selina raced upstairs to the first floor. She met Miriam on the landing, emerging from the spiral staircase that descended from the upper floors.

'What on earth's wrong, dear? You're looking very pasty.' She grinned. 'You haven't come face to face with the grey lady have you? Not Lady Agnes and that scent of hers, the bog myrtle?'

479

Selina ran from one window in the great hall to the other, straining to see out into the darkness.

'This is no joke, Miriam. I've just had a phone call from some strange man telling us to leave the castle immediately.'

'Oh my God.' Miriam headed for the panic button, still lying on the coffee table.

'It's okay, I've already called the police and they're on their way.'

'What about the two officers down at the gate?'

'They've taken Lorna home because her car wouldn't start. My suggestion… unfortunately!'

Selina ran past her cousin and hurtled down the stone stairs. Miriam followed, hot on her heels. 'Well, that was a good move! Did you see anything out there?'

'No, not a thing. It's getting dark.'

As they passed the front door, Miriam paused to check that it was locked and bolted. Selina was already back in the kitchen, speaking on the phone.

'I've checked outside. I can't see anything, but the light's going, so I may've missed something.'

'Okay,' said the call-taker with the annoyingly calm voice. 'Our people are heading down through Dores as we speak.'

'Dores is miles away,' Selina protested.

'Like I said, Mrs Cope, we'll be with you in no time at all. I suggest you stay where you are, and don't open the door to *anyone* until we arrive. The officers' names are Murdoch and Walker, but ask to see their warrant cards before allowing them entry. They will be in uniform and in a marked patrol car.'

Selina relaxed a little. 'Okay,' she said. 'I suppose we should be safe, ensconced in a keep with walls two feet thick!'

The call-taker could be heard tittering in the background. 'My thoughts exactly!' Then she reverted to her more professional comportment. 'Is there anyone nearby, someone you could call to come and be with you?'

'Not really,' Selina replied. 'It's pretty isolated out here.'

'Right, well sit tight, then. I can tell you that we've paged DCI Strachan. He still appears to be on duty this evening.'

'That's great. Thank you for your help.'

'Not at all. I'll call back shortly to check that you're both okay.'

Selina replaced the handset. She thought about what the woman had just said.

'I wonder whether Sandy Blair is still anywhere nearby. He told me this morning that he needed to drop in and see one of the staff on the evening shift at the distillery.'

'It's worth a try, I suppose,' Miriam agreed.

So Selina called the landline number for the distillery, but as she would've expected, the number rang and rang until the answerphone activated. Next, on the off-chance, she tried Sandy's mobile phone. To her amazement, he answered.

'Hello Selina, this is a surprise. Is everything okay?'

'Not really, Sandy. We could do with some male company.'

Selina recounted the story of the sinister phone call for the second time. Then she added, 'Where are you, Sandy? Anywhere near us?'

'I'm heading home on the 851 up through Balnafoich. Look, I'll turn around and come back to you. I'll be about fifteen minutes, but at least I'll probably get to you before the police do. They're heading up through Dores, you say?'

'Yes, last we heard.'

'Right, see you shortly.' The phone went dead.

Selina managed a smile. 'Sandy was still on his way home, thank God. He'd not got as far as the A9, so he's turning around and coming back.'

'Looks like we've got it covered, then; men coming from all directions,' Miriam reassured her. 'Shall I make that cocoa now? Sandy might like some too.'

'Well, you do that, and I'll pop up and find some headache tablets. I've got a stinker just come on.'

'I'm not surprised, getting a call like that,' said Miriam.

Selina disappeared along the corridor, leaving her cousin to mull over what had happened. She'd only been gone a couple of minutes when the phone rang again. Miriam picked it up. 'Hello, who's that?'

The line crackled and she sensed someone was trying to speak, but it was no good. The signal was too poor. She spoke into the handset. 'Is that you, Sandy?'

There was still no answer, so she returned the phone to its cradle.

It seemed that no time at all had passed when she heard the sound of Sandy's car on the gravel outside. Then she heard the crunch of his footsteps on that same gravel. The windows in the old vaulted kitchen were high on the walls; too high to see through. There were two of them; one at the front and one at the rear, the latter being the window the intruders had damaged a fortnight before. They were no use at all, other than to provide a small amount of light when the sun was out. So Miriam hurried along the passageway to the entrance vestibule, marvelling at the speed of Sandy's response as it could only have been a few minutes since that unsuccessful call of his. She slid back the bolts on the old oak door, then heaved it open.

'Sandy, thank God you're…'

Miriam would later describe to the police the faceless apparition that confronted her when she'd opened that door. 'Faceless' because *it*, or *he* – she knew it was male – wore a black ribbed ski mask.

The only description she could provide above his neckline was that of the two staring eyes that bore into her as he stepped over the threshold and propelled her backwards along the passageway towards the chapel door. Before she could scream, he'd turned her around and placed a large rubber-gloved hand over her mouth. That's when she fainted.

Funnily enough, it wasn't the ski mask or the gloves that had frightened her the most, it was the *breacan-an-feileadh,* the great belted plaid wrapped about him. Great swirls of loose tartan cloth, secured around the waist by a wide leather belt and then draped unceremoniously over his shoulder. The sett was the red, blue and beige of the ancient MacBean. She recognised it instantly from books on the subject she'd marvelled at as a girl. From its folds hung a basket-hilted broadsword, secured in a leather scabbard. The great sword extended to beyond his bare white knees, to the green tartan hose that contained his powerful calves. Yes, this was indeed an apparition from a time long gone, an apparition of the most malevolent kind!

Selina was on her way downstairs from the second floor. She'd initially delayed her return to the kitchen, having stopped off in the great hall to check her laptop for new emails. She heard the sound of a vehicle on the gravel below, and she too had assumed that it was Sandy arriving. When she turned onto the last flight of stairs that ran down to the main doorway, she stopped. There was no one there, only the void where the door stood open. She could see no vehicle from her viewpoint, ten feet above the door, just the semi-darkness and the gravel directly outside. She advanced, more warily now, and called out.

'Miriam… Sandy… Are you there?'

No one replied, so she continued to the doorway and peered out. To her surprise, Sandy's grey Audi was not parked outside as she would've expected. But there was a green Land Rover Defender, an old one, with an F suffix!

Puzzled, she turned back, only to be confronted by the faceless Highlander who'd been standing behind her. She screamed, frozen to the spot, impelling him to lurch forward and grab her arms. She found the courage to raise her knee to his groin, but her assault had no effect; the power of her strike was absorbed by the thick robe of tartan.

'Who are you?' she screamed. 'Why are you doing this?'

He remained silent, his strong arms now turning her so that he was almost hugging her from behind. There was a mustiness about him, the smell of cloth that had been stored whilst damp, but strangely, she also detected an altogether more pleasant fragrance, something vaguely familiar. It was a strange combination, a sensory cocktail that just didn't add up.

Her struggling quickly sapped her strength, and slowly she sagged, almost accepting of her fate. The Highlander must've sensed his victory too, because he chose that time to thrust her forward and out into the twilight.

She struggled to maintain her footing as they approached the open rear door of the Land Rover, and then she found herself being lifted and bundled in. She now lay face down, terrified of what would come next. The sound of tape ripping was what came next, then duct tape being applied to her mouth and pressed into place. Her shrieking continued, albeit muffled now, whilst the sticky material was subsequently wrapped tightly around her ankles. Then she lay still, exhausted, whimpering and utterly defeated.

What happened next amounted to an unexpected act of kindness. The plaided figure climbed in and lifted her onto one of the metal benches that lined either side of the vehicle's rear compartment. She sighed, relieved to be sitting upright again, and looked up into the direful eyes of her captor. He responded by taping her wrists and then raising a finger to the only other exposed area of his face, his lips. She nodded vigorously, acknowledging his unspoken command to be silent, then closed her eyes as he gently placed a soft eye mask over her head, the type secured by elastic that airlines provided on long-haul flights. With her ability to see now removed, she listened as he jumped out through the open door and slammed it closed. Then she heard the door being locked from the outside and him making his way around to the driver's door. Almost immediately, they were on the move, trundling down the driveway, braking slightly, presumably when they reached the road, and then there was a left turn.

The Highlander had completed his kidnap with only a minute or so to spare. Having just reached the gated entrance to the car park at the Loch Ruthven Nature Reserve, he checked his wing mirror and saw behind him a pulsing blue strobe light shimmering across the still surface of the loch. The cavalry had arrived at last, but too late for Selina Cope.

The creaking and groaning of the old Land Rover seemed unrelenting as it jumped about on the single-track road. But the vehicle's back-jarring dance upon its uneven surface was having an altogether unexpected effect. The eye mask was quite loose, and with every vertical motion of the Land Rover, the mask slipped downwards slightly. After a mile or so, the material had reached a point just below Selina's upper eyelids and she could just see a little of her surroundings. The interior of the vehicle was now dark, and she knew the driver would've had difficulty seeing anything else but a silhouetted form sitting behind him. So she edged along the bench, slowly getting closer to him; all the while flexing her wrists and ankles with all the strength she could muster. The effect was minimal, but she could detect a lessening of the tension in the tape. So much so, that she could at last begin to move the extremities of those limbs secured by the sticky bonds. There was no way she'd be able to escape, but was adamant that she was going to find out exactly who this monster was! So the exercise continued, bit by bit, until she was confident that she could stand up unaided. It was then a matter of timing, making her move and acting quickly when the opportunity arose.

That opportunity eventually came when they reached a long, straight section of road that sounded as if it had been recently resurfaced. The only stretch of the route she could recall as having just been repaired to that extent was a section of the B851 that crossed the River Farigaig, just beyond Aberarder.

When they jumped over a hump in the road and dropped down the other side, she knew she was right; they'd just crossed the little stone bridge over the river, and were heading southwest towards Fort Augustus. She took a deep breath and hoisted herself up onto her feet so that she was facing the front of the vehicle. Then she shuffled along towards the driver as fast as she could. Unwittingly, he then made a decision that aided her progress immensely. Through his rear-view mirror, he saw what she was doing and braked firmly. This had the effect of propelling Selina towards him at an even greater rate, until she collided with the back of his seat. Her knees buckled and she began to fall, but not before she could raise her arms upwards and outwards, frantically searching for his head and its woolly covering.

She found it with relative ease and clenched her fists around the material, pulling it up towards the top of his head with all her might. Then she forced herself to fall backwards into the well of the vehicle. Crashing onto the metal floor, she realised that she'd been successful and the ski mask was still in her hands... she'd pulled it off completely!

Lying on her back, she instantly regretted her actions and dreaded the fate that would now befall her. By now the eye mask had slipped even further, to a point where its upper rim hugged her nose. She looked up at the Land Rover's roof and pondered, *At least I'll look my killer in the eye!* So she tilted her head forward and allowed her eyes to focus on the figure looking back at her from the driver's seat, the man who'd so brutally stolen her liberty, and she stared straight into his baleful eyes.

If anyone had told her at that moment that it was possible for someone to feel their own blood run cold, then she would've agreed with them wholeheartedly. The sight that greeted her, the face that glared back at her, cameoed against the late evening sky, could not be mistaken. Anger now replaced fear. Wonderment replaced conjecture. She gasped in astonishment.

'Oh my God, it's you! What on earth have you done to my family?'

Chapter Thirty-Seven

Cullaird Castle
10.30 pm, Friday 14ᵗʰ May

Neil had picked up the answerphone message around ten past ten, five minutes after the first police unit had arrived at Cullaird. The two constables had found Miriam Fraser behind the half-closed door of the castle's tiny chapel. Miraculously she had not been seriously injured, but did have a nasty gash to her head. She was now sitting in the back of a paramedic ambulance being attended to by its sympathetic crew.

Meanwhile, the SIO of Operation Cawdor was pacing up and down the incident room in Inverness whilst Ross Haggarty sat glum-faced by the phone. He was eagerly awaiting an update from Holly Anderson, who was well on her way to the scene.

'What the hell were they thinking? Especially after that last debacle. Believe me, I'll have their hides when I catch up with them.' Neil stopped next to Haggarty's desk and shot him an angry glance. 'Tell me, am I wrong… to expect people to do their bloody jobs?'

Haggarty smiled weakly. 'Of course not. They were instructed to provide an uninterrupted presence there, and they have failed to do so. I think they know what's coming to them! But you can appreciate the situation they were in. Any other time, and they would've been back before anyone knew it.'

Neil continued to parade up and down. 'It's just not good enough. Christ, *I* would've taken her home if she'd called me.'

Haggarty refreshed his PC screen. 'Lorna was hardly going to do that, was she? Look, she's a good officer, but she's fouled up on this occasion. It's been two weeks since that last break-in, after all.'

Neil threw his arms up in frustration. 'I'm amazed you can be so charitable. I only hope nothing happens to Selina Cope, that's all. If it does, all three of them can kiss their careers goodbye.'

He slumped into a chair opposite Haggarty's desk. 'I knew we should've been pushier about moving the Copes out of that damned castle,' he muttered. 'This is my worst nightmare.'

'No use crying over spilt milk, Neil. You did try after all. If people want to stay in their own homes, what can you do?'

'It's so typical, though. The three idiots had only just gone when this happened.'

Haggarty pulled a rogue hair out of his coffee mug. 'That doesn't look like one of mine.'

Then he looked up, and delivered a killer blow. 'Just think, Neil, this could've kicked off whilst you were doing your own thing, playing Indiana Jones up on South Sutor! You know, whilst we're on the subject of "doing our own thing".'

Neil looked back at him long and hard, initially lost for words. 'Yeah, I s'pose. Point taken.' Then, as if to have the last word, he added, 'Thankfully that's one less worry to contend with, and at least I got the chance to do a statement for the CID boys.'

Haggarty had fired his broadside, and was now checking the surface of his coffee for more hairs before taking another sip.

'Why do you think they've taken her? It's not as if she lived at the castle, after all. Seems a bit desperate if they're just conducting a fishing expedition, and think she may provide them with a clue as to where the hoard is located.'

Neil sighed. 'I've a feeling they've seen the TV appeal about the oak chest and have assumed that the surviving family may have had some knowledge of where the letter was hidden. And if they knew that, then they may have been aware of its contents. I guess this is a way of finding out exactly what they do know, one way or the other.'

'Perhaps,' Haggarty agreed. 'It's possible, I suppose.' He wasn't convinced, though.

A uniformed chief inspector walked purposefully into the room at that point. 'I've actioned all your initial tasks, Neil. We've got points on all the arterial routes out of the area. A9 up at Tore, and down at Daviot. A96 at the retail park roundabout, and the A82 by the Tomnahurich canal bridge. The Land Rover's been circulated to all our units and to surrounding forces. Your witness is sure it was a long wheelbase Land Rover?'

'Aye, Miriam Fraser got a glimpse when she opened the front door. I'm sure she's not mistaken. It's too much of a coincidence, what with the other sightings. What's happening with the availability of air support, should we need it?'

'The Strathclyde chopper's en route to us and the air ambulance is on standby out at the airport. I've also contacted the RAF at Lossiemouth. Their SAR chopper is at our disposal if needed.'

'Good, so how long do you think this call trace is going to take, Ross?'

Haggarty pursed his lips. 'We should hear any time, I stressed how urgent it was.'

The uniformed officer turned about. 'I'll leave you to it then, get back to running my side of things.'

Neil was just about to throw in a caustic comment about 'running his side of things', then bit his lip. One of his own had been equally culpable, after all!

On reaching the doorway, his colleague announced, 'What a night for this to happen, on a Friday just when the bars are kicking out!' Then he looked back over his shoulder. 'Oh, and by the way, Angus Hardie's just parked his car outside.'

'Thanks, Gordon. I'll keep you posted as things develop.'

The phone then rang and Haggarty scooped it up. He listened briefly, then picked up a pen and jotted down a few notes with his free hand. It was obviously the result of the phone trace. Finally, having thanked the caller, he replaced the handset.

'That was the control room. The call was made from a TK in Cathcart Road, Glasgow, at its junction with Preston Street. The call was timed at 21.47 hours.'

Neil folded his arms. 'Cathcart Road, eh? McQuade and Duff were behind that call. Of that I have no doubt.'

'But why give the warning, then?' Haggarty asked.

'Because MacBean's gone rogue, probably, and now they're panicking. That's my theory, anyway. Has someone been dispatched to secure the phone box?'

'Aye, Strathclyde are on their way.'

'Okay, thanks.' Neil checked the contacts page on his mobile and then raised it to his ear.

'Is DI Gemmell around, please? It's DCI Strachan, Northern MEU.'

There was a short delay, then Neil spoke again. 'That's good news. I'll await his call… thanks very much.'

He allowed himself a brief smile. 'Willie Gemmell's picked up on the TK enquiry, and he's gone out to supervise things.'

He'd no sooner put the phone down, when it rang again. This time it was Holly Anderson. Haggarty picked up and handed the phone to Neil.

'What's the story so far, Holly?'

'Miriam Fraser is okay. Suffering from shock and a gash to the head, but otherwise no serious injuries.'

'Did someone hit her, then, to cause the head injury?'

'No, the paramedics are of the opinion she hit her head when she fainted.'

'Okay, tell me more.'

'It appears Selina received a phone call just after nine forty-five, from a male with a strong, possibly Glaswegian accent, telling the women to leave immediately. Selina called the police just afterwards, and then, whilst they were waiting for us to arrive, she called Sandy Blair.'

Neil frowned. 'Sandy Blair... why him?'

'According to Miriam, he'd told Selina earlier today that he was working late this evening. Had to deal with some sort of personnel issue at the distillery. Anyway, he was on his way home and said he'd turn around and come back.'

'And did he?'

'Yes, apparently. He turned up a short while after the uniform boys. They told him they had everything covered and sent him away again.'

'Right, so what happened after Selina had made the calls?'

Holly then explained how Miriam had remained alone in the kitchen, and had heard the sound of the vehicle she believed to be Sandy Blair's.

'So she opened the door, and there was this plaided Highlander wearing a ski mask, right?'

'Aye, spot on. He frogmarched her into the chapel, and that was it. She fainted, fell and banged her head. She doesn't remember anything else until the PC found her and roused her.'

'Any other disruption to the interior of the place?'

'No, sir, I believe all the action occurred within sight of the front door. Fraser Gunn's just arrived, so he'll hopefully be able to tell us more.'

'Okay, Holly. Stay where you are. I'll join you as soon as I can.'

Angus Hardie was now standing silently behind him, waiting for him to terminate the call.

'Everything under control, Neil?'

'Aye, sir, it's early days. I'm just getting up to speed myself.'

'Perhaps we'd better adjourn to your office, so that you can brief me, without interruption, as to how this godforsaken mess occurred.'

'Of course, sir.'

Neil got up and led the way, picking up his jacket as he went. Once out in the corridor, Hardie spoke again. 'I hear you've already had some excitement tonight?'

'Aye, just a little! Still, that wee problem appears to have been sorted now.'

Hardie frowned. 'Lucky for you. This could've kicked off whilst you were running around the countryside over on the Black Isle. Still, it was a good result. Is Cat okay?'

Neil frowned in vexation at the latest referral to his lucky timing.

'Aye, fine, sir.'

'Good, so at last I've got my SIO back and running on all cylinders, eh? Unlike some, it would seem!'

'Yes, unfortunately. Ross and I were just discussing that.'

They reached the door of Neil's office. 'Please, come in… take a seat, sir.'

Neil quickly completed his briefing, and to his palpable relief, Hardie seemed more intent on discussing the matter in hand than the disciplinary issues involving Lorna McKirdy and her two uniformed colleagues! He then checked the live incident log on his computer screen, whilst Hardie took himself off to call the chief constable and prepare himself for the long night ahead.

Neil's mobile buzzed again, and this time it was DI Willie Gemmell down in Glasgow.

'Hi Neil, it all seems to be kicking off up there in the sticks, eh?'

'Aye, you could say that, Willie. Where are you now?'

Gemmell was standing in Cathcart Road, outside a late-night convenience store. He was watching a team of white-suited scene investigators poring over the telephone kiosk on the corner of Preston Street. Neil's voice seemed a little distant, so he turned his back to the street and poked a finger into his other ear so as to muffle the sound of the passing traffic.

'We're still at the TK from where the call was made. Nothing much of use forensically so far, but ah do have some news that will interest you.'

'Go on.'

'Ah've just been intae the convenience store along from the TK. They've got a CCTV system running outside. Looks like it's caught our two suspects returning to their car after they made the call.'

'Two of them! Can you ID them?'

'Aye, one of them. Ah dinnae recognise the other guy, though.'

'Don't tell me... McQuade was one of them?'

'Afraid not, Boss. Sorry tae disappoint you, but one of them was that wee bugger, Boyd Duff.'

'Ah ha. Next best thing, then! What did the other one look like?'

'Short, late middle age, dumpy, dark hair. He was driving a dark-coloured Mercedes. Hang on, ah've got the reg here.'

Neil listened to the registration number being read out, but already knew who it was!

'That second male is a South African. Name of Dawie Van Nieuwoudt. He has ties to the victims' family and to McQuade.'

'Result, then. So what are your instructions, Boss?'

'Van Nieuwoudt is staying at the Hampden Terrace Hotel. I think it's time we picked him up and had a wee look in his room... and car. The clock's ticking on this one, Willie.'

'Aye, ah know that. What about Duff? D'you want him lifted too?'

'Aye, him and McQuade, if they're home. We also need to have a good look at that seedy little shop of theirs, and the flat above it.'

Gemmell smiled. It was a self-gratifying smile that Neil would have appreciated if he'd seen it.

'It will be my pleasure, sur. God knows what we'll stumble across in that wee den of thieves!'

Hampden Terrace comprised a long row of beige-stoned Victorian villas, so typical of the buildings that graced many of the inner suburbs of Glasgow. To approach them, a sloping access road climbed away from the main thoroughfare of Prospecthill Road. Several of the three-storey townhouses had been converted into small boutique hotels, one of which was the establishment currently accommodating Dawie Van Nieuwoudt.

Gemmell and a small team of four detectives edged along the iron railings that bordered the frontages of the properties. The street lamps afforded an amber glow upon their approach route, but dark pools of shadow from the substantial trees that lined the roadway also provided cover from view to anyone wishing to remain unseen from above.

Van Nieuwoudt's blue Mercedes was parked a little way along from the hotel, and Gemmell dispatched two of his group to secure and guard it until he could provide them with the keys.

The three remaining team members slipped through the

glass-fronted doors to the hotel, where Gemmell explained the reason for their visit to the duty manager. She was a smart blonde woman in her forties who spoke with a faint Eastern European accent, and appeared eager to help.

'Follow me please, gentlemen,' she requested. 'He's staying up in our executive suite, room thirty-two.'

Led by the woman, whose shapely rear swung seductively from side to side as they climbed the stairs, they continued their furtive approach, finally arriving outside the ornately moulded door of room thirty-two.

'I trust you will not be damaging the door tonight?' the manager, now known to be called Mariela, asked in a clipped tone. 'I *can* arrange for a master key, should you need it.'

'No, not tonight, lassie,' Gemmell whispered with a grin. 'Unless of course, yer guest wishes tae ignore us and barricades the door. Now, if you could knock and announce yourself, we'll do the rest, okay?'

Mariela waited until the police officers were out of sight of the spyhole fitted to the middle of the door, and then knocked as requested.

'Hello, Mr Van Nieuwoudt. It's Mariela, the duty hotel manager. Could I have a word, please?'

Gemmell could hear the chain being removed from the other side of the door and then the latch being lifted. The door opened and there stood Dawie Van Nieuwoudt in his shirtsleeves, newspaper in hand. He was just about to speak when Gemmell and his team surged through the doorway, warrant cards held aloft, to the cries of, 'Police officers... turn around, please, Mr Van Nieuwoudt.' The South African was far too shocked to resist, and spun around, discomfited and wide-eyed.

Handcuffs were ratcheted in place whilst Gemmell read him his rights. 'Dawie Van Nieuwoudt, ah'm detaining you under the provisions of the Criminal Procedure (Scotland)

Act 1995, because I suspect you of being concerned in the murders of Laura and Duncan Fraser…'

Van Nieuwoudt listened carefully to the caution and the reasons for his arrest, then spoke for the first time.

'This is preposterous. How dare you just burst in here? I have nothing to say to you until I speak to my lawyer.'

Gemmell noted his reply. 'Suit yerself, Mr Van Nieuwoudt. Now, we're going tae have a wee look around yer room. Want tae tell us where t'look?'

Van Nieuwoudt looked around at the detectives. 'Where's your warrant?' he asked morosely.

'Ah dinnae actually need one in urgent circumstances such as these, ma wee friend. There's also such a thing as "common law" in this bonnie land of ours. Allows us do all sorts of stuff, but we'll let your lawyer explain all about that! Besides, the kind lady out there invited us in.'

And so the search commenced. Gemmell began by rummaging through the suitcase that lay open in the corner of the room. As he did so, he looked nonchalantly across at the South African. 'That's an unusual name… Dawie. Is it a nickname, short for something?'

'It's the Afrikaans version of David,' said Van Nieuwoudt, straight-faced.

'Aah, is that right?' Gemmell had moved on from the case, and was now focussing his attention on a nearby table. To his undisguised delight, it didn't take long to come up with what he was looking for!

A Manila folder lay on the table, partially hidden beneath a pile of magazines, next to which stood a half-consumed glass of whisky and an unlit cigar. Gemmell picked up the folder and opened it. Inside were a number of photographs of Cullaird Castle, its driveway and views taken of the roadway outside the castle, facing both directions.

Gemmell sat down by the window and removed the

remaining contents from the folder. He glanced up at Van Nieuwoudt, who was standing by the door with one of the detectives. The South African raised his eyes to the ceiling when the contents of the folder were spilt out across the table, the hopelessness of his situation now dawning upon him.

Gemmell held up an A4-sized photograph of a dilapidated wooden cabin that looked as if it was located deep within a forest of towering pines. Around it were stacks of logs and greying tree trunks lying sedately on their sides amongst a variety of human-generated rubbish.

'Is this where you're holding her, Dawie? Selina Cope, I mean. I suggest you cooperate, ma friend, before anything bad happens tae that lassie.'

Van Nieuwoudt scowled. 'Like I said, I've nothing to say until I speak to a lawyer.'

'As you wish, Dawie. On your head be it.'

He selected another document, a map of Strathnairn, showing the roads running across from Cullaird to the area north of Culloden Battlefield highlighted in lime-coloured marker pen. The line ended with a red star deep within Culloden Forest. Gemmell asked again, 'Is this red mark where the wooden cabin is located? Is that where she is, Dawie?'

Van Nieuwoudt remained silent.

'Damn you,' Gemmell muttered under his breath. He continued to rummage through more photos, some taken of the interior of the castle, and finally one of an old oak chest with four deep drawers, upon which was carved the most exquisite scrolling. The image was attached to a sheet of paper with a metal paper clip. Gemmell slipped the clip off and examined the paper beneath. It was in fact a photocopy of an old letter, a very old letter indeed, in which the words were scrawled thinly across the page like fine scratches. The ink was patchy in some places and smudged in others, but it was just about readable. Gemmell stepped across to the standard lamp that stood nearby and held the letter close, so that he could decipher it. As he read the words, he suddenly realised its significance. It was the clue to the location of the Cullaird hoard, the letter from Meg MacGillivray to her son James…

Cullaird, April 20th
1746

My Dearest Son, James

That you now read these words, bespeaks of my departure from this life. I must now impart upon you, matters relevant to the continued prosperity of this noble house. Matters that only now shall I Suffer you as my eldest Son to become acquainted. Tis for you alone my love, to determine how you may act upon this knowledge, once attained.

Forgive me also, for I am minded to speak in a tongue that I am assured only you will conceive, so that the content of this text may remain safe from all others. So then, look not to the cat of our people, but to that of our Chattan brothers, now unseen by those in its proximity. Heed too, the place where flames do seldom burn that will reveal its sacred locus. Only then, will you safely discover the cell into which your father's legacy is entrusted. Through this means, the patriots that follow our dear Prince may long continue the struggle against Hanover's barbarous house.

Your father's rencounter at Holm, with Dragoons sent by ther darling Cumberland to kill all who oppose his present Majestie, left me with sole knowing of his deeds.

I therefore pray that you precipitate to this Hiding Place and dispose of its contents in a manner that you deem wise and in keeping with his memorie.

I am, my Deerest Son, ever your most loving and affectionate Mother.

Meg

Gemmell read it, and read it again, then turned to Van Nieuwoudt.

'So this is it, then, the letter ah was told about... the one that's responsible for the deaths of two innocent people and now the kidnapping of their daughter.'

He detected a glimmer of surprise in Van Nieuwoudt's eyes, a slight twitch, nothing you could put your finger on.

'You dinnae know, do you? You and yer friend Duff were clearly worried that it was on the cards, but you've nae idea what's happened up at Cullaird tonight?'

Van Nieuwoudt's features had become tight and red, as if he'd sustained a serious case of sunburn. He was desperate to speak, but just shook his head.

Gemmell pressed him further. 'Do you not want tae know what's happened t'your ex-wife and Selina?'

Again the South African's answer was unhelpful. 'I have no comment to make on that score, I'm afraid.'

Gemmell gestured towards his female colleague, and handed her the map that hopefully provided the location of the cabin in Culloden Forest.

'Take this outside, will you? And call Inverness. Make sure they know what's on this map, so they can locate the place and check it oot. Tell them ah'll call DCI Strachan when ah get back tae the office.'

The young woman took the map and left the room, leaving Gemmell to continue the search.

It was a task that didn't take too long, and the little group were soon parading through the front door of the hotel. Van Nieuwoudt, in handcuffs, walked behind Gemmell, who was carrying a clutch of plastic evidence bags containing the contents of the Manila folder. Bringing up the rear was a female detective carrying more bags, containing a laptop, a mobile phone and a pair of muddy shoes.

They met the two officers who'd been searching the

Mercedes walking back towards them empty-handed. 'Nothing in the car, sur. It's as clean as a whistle, but we've arranged tae get it recovered,' said the older of the two.

'Okay,' Gemmell replied. 'We're taking our wee friend back t'the station. You can stay here and wait for the recovery truck.'

Minutes later, they were heading north up Cathcart Road. Just another set of headlights preventing the late-night revellers from staggering across the road.

Willie Gemmell sat in his office, telephone clamped to his ear.

'Is that you, Neil?'

'Aye, got any news?'

'Van Nieuwoudt's in custody, but refusing tae talk t'anyone until he's spoken with his solicitor.'

'Bugger!'

'Ah know, but we have some stuff here from his hotel room. You're really goin' tae want to see this stuff!'

'Go on, then. Put me out of my misery.'

Gemmell described the documents he had spread out across his desk in their respective clear plastic bags.

'Ah'm goin tae scan these into our system and get them up t'you right away. You need tae find that cabin soonest. Had any luck yet?'

'Aye, I've got someone working on it right now, from the description your DC gave us. What about Duff? Any news of him?'

'We've been round tae the shop. There was no reply. The flat upstairs is in darkness, so it looks like they're out and about somewhere. Ah've circulated both their vehicles locally, and one of ma team is sitting up on the premises whilst we jack up a warrant.'

'That's great, Willie. Can't thank you enough. I look forward to seeing those documents you have.'

'Ah'm ontae it now, and ah'll get an early chat in with Van Nieuwoudt when his brief turns up. But dinnae count yer chickens with him. He's a cool customer, that one!'

'Thanks, Willie. I'll be in touch, mate.'

Neil came off the phone, his brain still processing all the new information that had just been passed to him. But it was the map showing the location of the cabin that excited him most. Now, they had to find it and get out there fast!

He saw from the steadily expanding incident log on his screen, which additional dog handlers and armed response units were rendezvousing in the car park three floors beneath him. Steve Armsley, the police search advisor, was on his way in, as were a couple of force negotiators.

He then called Holly and informed her of the arrest and seizures in Glasgow, directing that she return to headquarters soonest, leaving a uniformed sergeant to manage the scene at the castle. His next port of call was the incident room, where Haggarty and several DCs were examining a large-scale Ordnance Survey map of the Moray coast.

'Any ideas how we get to this cabin?' he asked, joining them at the table.

Haggarty tapped the map on the green, shaded area of Culloden Forest. 'Just here,' he said. 'Between Balloch and High Wood. There is some sort of structure shown at the convergence of these three forestry tracks.'

Neil went to the nearest computer screen and logged in. The email from Gemmell was sitting in his inbox, together with a number of attachments. He opened the one titled 'Map' and compared the image in front of him with the map on the table.

'That's got to be it,' he announced. He snatched up the map, and headed for the door. 'Ring downstairs, Ross. I want a meeting with the unit supervisors in the foyer in five minutes. And call Holly Anderson. Tell her to meet me at the entrance to the battlefield.'

Haggarty picked up the phone and grinned. 'Looks like it's all coming together,' he told the DC standing next to him. 'Just as well for him! Better give Holly a call. She won't want to miss all the action!'

Chapter Thirty-Eight

Constables Joe McVeigh and Paul Swinney had been crew partners for three years. Both officers were fast approaching retirement, but nevertheless still enjoyed the buzz of uniform patrol work. Tonight, as on any night shift, they sat attentively in their marked Toyota SUV, patiently watching the diminishing flow of traffic heading north up the A9. The two Tayside officers were drinking coffee from a Thermos flask that Swinney's wife had prepared for them, while waiting for something suitable to pull over. But the options this far north at Pitlochry, just before midnight, were becoming few and far between. The fifth truck had just passed by, rocking the Toyota in its slipstream, and prompting McVeigh to curse its driver repeatedly.

'Bloody trucks. I nearly spilt my coffee.'

He checked his watch. 'Come on, Paul, let's call it a day. We should go and have a punt around the village.'

Swinney swallowed the last of his coffee and screwed the cup back onto the flask.

'Aye, fair dos.' He returned the flask to the bag behind his seat and went to put the vehicle into gear. That was when the old-style Volkswagen Golf shot past them, doing eighty plus!

The two officers perked up instantly, and as the police vehicle screeched away from its hiding place, they strained to maintain a view of the tiny red tail lights that were fast receding into the distance. Swinney had his foot to the floor, urging the Toyota to gain speed quickly, whilst the Volkswagen seemed to be getting further and further away from them.

McVeigh flipped the strobe switch, instantly bathing the spindly conifers either side of the road in a pulsing blue glow. It was a gamble. Either the driver of the Volkswagen would see the blue lights behind him and slow up, or, if he had something to hide, he'd put his foot down and that would be it.

The road now curved gently to the right and then to the left, allowing for protracted high-speed driving, and out there in the Highland wilderness there was plenty of road ahead to catch up on, so they continued the chase with ample exuberance!

After a mile or so, it became obvious that the distance between them was at last diminishing. The red lights became progressively brighter until, just before a blue sign advising of the proximity of 'Lay-by 41', the Volkswagen's nearside indicator began to flash. It then slowed progressively and pulled off the carriageway into the layby and stopped. Swinney brought the police car to a halt close behind it and switched on the roof lamps that now illuminated the car in brilliant white light. They watched the single occupant slowly emerge and stand by the driver's door, as if he were patiently awaiting his fate. So McVeigh pulled on his cap and got out too, leaving his colleague to grab the handset of the main radio, and request a check on the registration plate.

The scrawny little man who'd been driving the Volkswagen greeted the policeman nervously. 'Evenin', officer. Everythin' okay?'

'We were a wee bit concerned at the speed you were doing back there. You do know there's a speed limit of sixty on this stretch of the road?'

'Of course, sorry. Ah was just in a hurry tae get up the road tae Inverness, and it being so quiet… well, ah pushed it a bit.'

'You were certainly doing that! And your name is, sir?'

'Boyd Duff, officer.'

'And this is your own vehicle, Mr Duff?'

'Aye, of course.'

McVeigh walked slowly around the car, directing the beam of his Maglite torch into its dark interior. 'Do you live in Inverness, Mr Duff?'

'No, away down in Glasgow. Ah'm visiting a friend o' mine.'

'Bit late to be travelling up to see friends, is it not?'

'No, not really. It's a short notice thing, y'see.'

The door of the Toyota slammed behind them and Swinney approached the two men.

'Everything okay with the vehicle?' McVeigh enquired.

'Aye, no problem at all. Owner's down as a Mr Boyd Eugene Duff. Is that you?'

Swinney walked up to Duff, who'd lowered his guard a little, expecting no more than words of advice regarding his speeding. He knew these local police cars didn't have on board speed detection equipment fitted, so it was unlikely these cops would take things any further!

'Aye, that's me, officer.'

He was shocked, as was McVeigh, when Swinney, who was somewhat larger than Duff, grabbed his arm firmly and turned him so that he found himself pressed up against the Volkswagen's bodywork.

'Only problem is, Mr Duff, you're wanted in connection with the murders of a Mr Duncan and a Mrs Laura Fraser up near Inverness on or abouts the 15th April.' He snapped on a pair of handcuffs and turned Duff back towards him. 'So we're detaining you in connection with those murders and taking you up to Inverness, understand?'

Duff understood, all right. 'You cannae do this, you fucking hawfwit. This is ridiculous. I havenae murdered anyone.'

He tried to pull away from the officer and kicked out. 'You'll regret this, pal. Ma lawyer will pish all over yous.'

The resistance only lasted for a few seconds. Boyd was searched and unceremoniously led away to the police car, whimpering as the handcuffs bit deeper into his wrists.

Once they were on the road again, McVeigh turned to his colleague. 'Unusual, us havin' to go up to Inverness, Paul. It'll leave no cover on our ground.'

McVeigh nodded. 'I know, but it sounds like they're run off their feet up the road. Some woman's been kidnapped. It's all connected to this business our new friend's involved with, apparently. They're sending a car up from Perth to cover us.'

Duff couldn't help but overhear their conversation.

'Did you say a woman's been kidnapped?' He looked even more troubled now.

'Aye. Something you want to tell us, Boyd, like who did it?'

'Ah havenae a scooby as tae who's done it, pal.'

'Well you've got an hour and a half to think about it. Now sit quietly and behave yerself, understood?'

It was just after midnight when Neil received news of Boyd Duff's arrest. He was sitting in a CID car just inside the entrance to Culloden Battlefield, waiting for Holly, who'd called him to say that she was five minutes away. There was only one seat left in the car. Steve Armsley and Bryan Findlay occupied the other two. Behind them were two marked armed response vehicles, and last in line was a dog unit, specialising in firearms support.

They sat there in silence, waiting, whilst vapour from the vehicle's exhaust pipe slowly dispersed into the clear night air around them.

'Come, on Holly. Get a move on, will you?' Neil checked his watch again. Then, as if on cue, another CID car pulled into the driveway and came to a halt. Holly clambered out and jogged across to her boss's vehicle, dropping into the back seat with a prolonged sigh. 'Sorry to keep you all waiting.'

Neil turned the ignition key. 'Okay, let's get this show on the road.'

He called up the ARV team leader on his phone. 'Over to you, Greg. Lead the way.'

The ARVs pulled around to the head of the convoy and moved off. Neil fell in behind, with the dog unit once again taking up the rear. They headed north along Culloden Road until the small white signpost to Feabuie appeared in the light of the ARV's headlamps. Then it was a right turn onto a narrow lane, followed by what appeared to be an endless drive through the darkness into Culloden Forest. They eventually passed under a stone railway bridge, at which point Armsley, who had the Ordnance Survey map on his lap, broke the silence for the first time since they'd set off.

'I can see where we are now. Should be a forestry track off to the left, shortly.'

He was right. The ARVs turned onto a much rougher stony route, that led into the forest proper. As they probed deeper into the plantation, the forest's canopy closed in above them, blotting out the cloudless star-strewn sky. The ARV immediately ahead of them veered left, sending up a cloud of dust. Then it was another left, onto a straighter section of the route.

Holly sniffed the pine-laden air through the open window. 'I hope he knows where he's going,' she remarked anxiously.

'Yep, he's going the right way.' Armsley's head bobbed up and down as he alternated his view between the map and the route ahead. 'The target premises should be dead ahead, about one hundred yards.'

Seconds later the lead vehicle's brake lights came on.

Neil pulled up behind and turned off the engine. The ARV sergeant and his three constables were already out, checking their weapons.

'Ready when you are, sir,' the sergeant confirmed, tightening the support strap on his Heckler & Koch carbine.

Neil waited for the dog handler to fall in behind them. The massive German shepherd strained excitedly against his leash, panting hard and keen to do his job in support of the men in black.

'Off you go, then. We'll stay back, out of your way.'

The unarmed officers had donned body armour too, not knowing exactly what they may encounter when they eventually reached the cabin.

So they began their approach, moving silently between the trees. Only the shrieks of the nocturnal forest animals and the odd crunch of a twig breaking underfoot interrupted the silence. The dark shapes of the firearms officers were just visible through the darkness... enough to see the sergeant's arm go up when they first spied the black outline of the cabin. Neil instinctively dropped down onto his haunches. His nostrils twitched, sensing the faint aroma of distant smoke. He sniffed a second time. Yes, there it was again. Something had been burning nearby. Findlay whispered to him from somewhere to his right. 'D'you smell smoke, sur?'

'Aye, I do Fin. Perhaps the stove's on in the cabin.'

He could hear low voices ahead as the men with the guns conversed via their dedicated intercoms system and moved into containment positions. They were using the established practice of colour coding to describe the layout of the cabin.

The sergeant had positioned himself by a tree, from where he had a view of the front of the building. 'Foxtrot One... I have the white and red sides. Three openings on white; two windows either side of a central doorway. No openings on red.'

'Roger. Foxtrot Two... black side now in sight; two windows, no doors. Small shed ten feet behind the property, red side. Over.'

'Foxtrot Three... I have white and green. No openings on green.'

'Foxtrot Four... I have the black side and the shed.'

The sergeant spoke again. 'Roger. Call going in now. Stand by.'

His voice boomed through the chill air causing the roosting birds to scatter above them and the police dog to bark repeatedly.

'Armed police... Come out through the front door now, with your hands raised.' There was no response. The cabin stood defiantly in the darkness, as if toying with the gunmen. The sergeant called out again.

'I say again... You are surrounded by armed police officers. Come out through the front door with your hands raised. You will not be harmed if you comply with my instructions.'

Again there was no response. They waited for several minutes. Then there was more chatter between the firearms officers. Slowly, two of them emerged from cover and scurried across to the front door, crouching as they went. They were followed by the dog handler. There was a crash, accompanied by the sound of splintering wood. Torches came on as the door was kicked in, followed by a further warning from the dog handler. Soon after, the excited animal raced inside. Seconds passed until the dog re-emerged and was secured by its handler. Then the armed officers crowded inside. Neil and his companions watched from the safety of the trees as beams of white light flashed around the interior of the cabin. Then the internal lights came on, and the black-clad policemen could be seen through the windows, moving around and conducting a further search. The detectives waited until the sergeant eventually appeared at the doorway of the cabin and beckoned to them to join him.

'Everything all right in there, Greg?'

'Aye, no sign of anyone in the cabin. Sorry, sir, your hostage isn't here, but you'll be wanting to see what the boys have found in that shed around the back!'

Neil and Holly made their way gingerly around the side of the cabin to where two of the constables were standing by the door of the shed. It stood ajar, and now the smell of smoke was noticeably stronger.

'What have you found?' Neil asked as he approached.

'See for yourselves, folks,' came the black-helmeted officer's taut reply.

So Neil turned on his torch and shone it through the doorway. The structure had obviously been used as a woodsman's tool store at one time, but it wasn't the rusting contents that made him step back in horror. It was the charred remains of the male corpse, dressed in a kilted plaid, that was sitting on the old tea chest at the back of the shed.

Neil blinked. 'Good God! Thanks for the warning, guys!'

He directed the torch beam back onto the corpse. The decaying red-haired cadaver stared back at him, an expression of shock frozen onto its lifeless face. In the foreground, a succession of flies flew back and forth through the narrow beam of light.

Under the dead man's gaping mouth, a deeply incised wound extended around his throat, from which a crusty red-brown bloodstain extended downward onto his linen shirt.

'I can smell him now,' Holly gasped, now standing by Neil's shoulder. 'The smell of the smoke must've masked it initially.'

'Looks like he's been dead for a while,' the firearms officer added.

Neil played the beam onto the floor of the shed. 'That's what caused the burning smell,' he said, gazing down at the blackened wood around the entrance to the doorway.

'Someone's tried to burn this shed and the corpse inside it.'

He leaned in and ran his hand down the doorframe. 'The wood's damp. It was never going to catch light without using an accelerant.' He then pulled a pair of latex gloves out of his pocket and slipped them on.

'What are you going to do?' Holly asked.

'I just want to confirm the identity of the corpse,' he replied as he stepped cautiously into the shed. Holly winced as her boss moved some of the lank red hair away from the corpse's right ear, then with a forefinger, pulled the front of the blood-soaked shirt away from the neck to reveal the chest beneath.

'As I thought,' he confirmed, backing out through the door and swatting away more flies. 'This is Ualas MacBean. He's got the damaged right ear and the Clan Chattan cat tattooed onto his chest.'

He turned to Holly, his features disconsolate. 'Looks like he's been dead for several weeks. Which prompts the question, who's taken Selina Cope?'

He removed the gloves and thought for a second. 'In fact I've got a horrible feeling we've just eliminated our prime suspect for the Frasers' murders too!'

'Mungo McQuade must have her, then?' Holly had raised a hand to her mouth, now that the smell had found its way deep into her nostrils.

Neil nodded. 'He's got to be the best bet. We seem to be running out of options.'

They walked back to the front of the cabin, where the firearms sergeant was talking to Steve Armsley.

'We've now got another crime scene on our hands, and our theory as to who was responsible for the Frasers' deaths may have just been blown out of the water.'

'So I hear,' said Armsley. 'Come and have a look in here. It's seriously weird!'

Neil and Holly followed the search advisor into the cabin. The lights were all on now, illuminating what could only be described as a macabre shrine to the Jacobite warrior. The walls were adorned with weaponry that would've been commonplace upon the field of Culloden, the centrepiece being an arrangement of broadswords suspended together in a circular pattern, their blades interlocking to form a starlike display. The basket hilts on these swords varied in design: intricate eighteenth-century workmanship that one could only stand and admire. Elsewhere on the wall hung a variety of war axes, some furnished with prolongations in the line of the shaft and hammers or spikes on the backs of the blades. One such example, known as the Jedburgh Staff, was a long-handled axe with a crescentic blade and a rear-facing spike. Neil himself recognised the axe displayed next to it; the vicious-looking Lochaber Axe with its elongated blade, rounded at the upper end, and with a hook on the end of the staff.

Holly shivered as she walked around, studying the artefacts. 'Are these genuine?' she asked.

'Some of them, without a doubt,' Armsley replied. 'Some look like copies, though.'

The display covered all the walls, and at the end of the room a whole wall was devoted to a display of Highland targes. The targe was a crude shield, constructed of wood, usually fir, over which a covering of leather was stretched for the front and a piece of hide, often of calfskin, with a stuffing for the back.

A brass boss occupied the centre of many of these examples, some of which were fitted with spikes, screwed into sockets at the base of the boss. Their ornamentation matched their efficiency, many being decorated with intricate studwork and engraving.

'These are fine works of art, I have to say,' Neil commented as he moved from one to the other before heading into the next room.

A double bed was present in the second room, upon which a stained and sagging mattress resided. Lengths of twine were attached to each of the bedstead pillars, and a filthy pillow lay on the floor. The only other item of furniture in the room was an old wooden chair in the corner.

'Someone's been held in here,' said Neil, as he approached the bed. He squatted and examined the surface of the mattress, using the light from his torch to enhance the illuminance of the room's dingy ceiling light.

'Can't see any blonde hairs,' he announced before turning his attention to the pillow. He rose stiffly. 'No sign of Selina having been here, but there are some grey hairs on the pillow. Could be Duncan Fraser's.'

There was another empty room next door, and then a rudimentary kitchen with a sink and wooden drainer. A dresser stood against the far wall, and a table beneath the begrimed window. Lying on the table and drainer were piles of decaying heather, the only sign of any form of activity having recently taken place in this most depressing of rooms.

'Looks like he was preparing his heather brew in here before someone cut his throat,' Holly deduced as she re-entered the sitting room. She stopped in the hallway to look at the fading watercolours that hung on the wall. One depicted a Highlander in full fighting garb, and the other, a clearing in a forest into which a shaft of sunlight picked out a small standing stone. Clustered around it, a group of old Highlanders were conversing and sharpening their swords on its craggy surfaces. Intrigued, she moved closer to inspect the artwork and the signature in the bottom corner, but she couldn't make it out. Eager to get out of this house of horrors, she moved on, back to the doorway where Findlay was waiting.

'I've updated Ops room with the latest, Sarge. They're getting a forensic team together, but have asked us to hold the fort.'

Holly grinned back at him. 'It's not going to take much to secure this scene, way out here in the enchanted bloody forest.'

Neil appeared behind them. 'What's that about an enchanted forest?'

'Oh, nothing. Just discussing how we secure the scene here.'

'Well, as of now we leave things be for Fraser Gunn and his team. I'm going to release one of the ARVs. The other will remain, just in case someone comes back here.'

He turned his attention to the veteran detective constable. 'I'd appreciate it if you could stay here with them, Fin.'

'Fine, sur. I can do that. Didnae have anything else planned tonight, other than a wee visit to ma bed.'

Neil smiled wistfully. 'I know what you mean, Fin. Perhaps tomorrow night, eh?' Then he turned and beckoned to Holly. 'We'll head back to the office and regroup.'

The mood in the CID car was one of quiet contemplation during the drive out of the forest. Whether or not it was an opportunity to reflect upon recent events, or a conscious decision on the part of his passengers to allow Neil to concentrate on the drive along the deeply rutted track was anyone's guess.

Holly spoke first as they emerged from the trees and were once again greeted by the blue-black expanse of the night sky.

'D'you suppose someone's playing copycat, wearing all that old costume when they abducted Selina Cope?'

Neil glanced across at her, his face a shade of pale green from the glow of the dashboard instruments. 'I suspect someone wants us to think Ualas MacBean was responsible for the two murders, and didn't plan on us finding *their* hideout and *his* body intact.'

'And we wouldn't have, if that fire had taken hold,' Armsley contributed from the back.

'Exactly,' said Neil. 'Clearly Dawie Van Nieuwoudt is involved in this up to his slimy little armpits, but it's my guess that he's the puppetmaster, not the puppet. No, my money's on Mungo McQuade still. He's a lifelong criminal with a violent past. He has to be our man.'

'You never know,' Holly interjected. 'MacBean still could've committed the murders over at Cullaird, on behalf of the others, then was murdered himself because he was no longer useful to them.'

'Fair point, but I doubt it, having seen that corpse,' Neil replied. 'Adam Carnie will hopefully be able to confirm whether or not that was possible. As things stand currently, any number of combinations are possible.'

The conversation ceased again when they turned back onto the Culloden Road. Then, just before they reached the B9006, Holly suddenly turned to Neil. 'You don't think he would've taken her to that place on the battlefield, the Well of the Dead, do you?'

Neil eased off the power and cruised up to the junction. A pair of headlights were approaching from the Inverness direction, giving him time to think.

'Why would he take her there *now*, for God's sake? He hasn't had her that long. I assume he'll want to get some information out of her first, before he disposes of her.'

Holly clearly didn't subscribe to that theory. 'He's had her for over three hours… and he took her father there, whoever "he" is! Perhaps he intends questioning her there and then disposing of her *in situ*.'

Neil reconsidered Holly's theory for a second or two whilst he turned right towards Inverness… and the battlefield.

Armsley's voice drifted through from the back seat. 'It can't do any harm checking. We're just about to pass the site now.'

Neil knew they were right. He just didn't want to waste a second focussing on a blind alley.

'Okay, you have a point. Let's take a look whilst we're here.'

He braked heavily and swept into the long driveway that led up to the battlefield visitor centre, the very location from where they'd departed in convoy a short time before.

Chapter Thirty-Nine

Culloden Battlefield
12.35 am, Saturday 15ᵗʰ May

They passed Holly's car on the way up to the visitor centre. It stood forlornly where she'd left it, next to the grass verge, twenty yards from the entrance. To the south, the moon shimmered over Beinn Bhuidhe Mhor, as cold and distant as the owl that announced their arrival.

Neil turned right when they reached the main car park entrance. Not surprisingly, it was empty... or so they thought, until the headlamp beams swept around onto the bodywork of a grubby-looking black saloon car.

'Courting couple?' Neil suggested. 'It's a Friday night, after all.'

Holly looked across at him, nonplussed. 'I sure as hell wouldn't be doing my courting in this car park,' she offered up. 'It's got to be one of the spookiest places on earth!'

Neil grinned and brought the CID car to a halt some distance away from the other vehicle. The three officers climbed out and switched on their Maglites. There was no suggestion of anyone being present in the car, so they cautiously approached it, only to discover that it was indeed empty. There was a sleeping bag unravelled on the back seat, together with a hastily discarded anorak and a map.

'Someone's sleeping rough,' said Holly, shining her torch into the passenger side footwell, which was cluttered with drinks cans and discarded food wrappers.

'Where are they, then?' Neil retorted, panning the car park with his torch.

'Call of nature, perhaps?'

Armsley was standing at the rear of what had now been identified as an ageing Ford Mondeo. He had his phone pressed to his ear and was speaking in hushed tones to the control room, checking the Mondeo's registration number.

'Are you sure?' Neil heard him say.

'What is it?' he asked.

Armsley walked over to him and almost whispered, 'There's no trace of a current owner for this vehicle. But the intelligence cell down the road have come across a sighting report that refers to it being stopped whilst being driven by a Mungo McQuade six months ago.'

'Call it in, Steve. Get that ARV, and the dog handler, to turn around and rendezvous with us here. Tell them... no blue lights.' He then joined Holly, who was trying to open the boot. 'No joy,' she informed him. 'It's all locked up.'

'Look, this car's been used by McQuade. I don't know where he is, or if it was him who drove it here, but one thing's for sure, we're going to wait until the ARV and the dog unit return. Then we'll go out onto the field and have a look.'

The three of them were in total agreement. The prospect of searching the moor, knowing there was a possibility that McQuade, armed with God knows what, was on the loose, chilled their souls. So they returned to their own vehicle and waited in the darkness, willing their colleagues to appear. As it happened the two firearms officers and their canine support team had not even reached the A9, and so the beams from their headlights were seen approaching the car park only six minutes later.

The team huddled together briefly behind the armed response vehicle, forming a plan of action. They then set out onto the darkened battlefield, this time with the dog handler in the front. He was flanked by the two armed officers whilst the detectives brought up the rear. Neil felt distinctly uneasy as his eyes struggled to penetrate the darkness, seeking out any movement or sound in the vicinity. But there was none, only the breeze ruffling the clumps of heather that bordered the path and the crunch of their footfall, which seemed inordinately loud as they advanced into the moor's marshy interior.

In the distance the sound of an aero engine hung in the night air. Then, a flashing red anti-collision light appeared in the sky to the north of them. It moved rapidly towards their location from the direction of Inverness Airport, only a couple of miles distant, until it reached a point just ahead of their position. They could make out the outline of the helicopter now, and looked up as it halted in its tracks, its twin engines whining as it hovered high overhead. Armsley had inserted an earpiece from his personal radio and had switched channels to the Strathclyde helicopter's radio frequency. He was now talking to the crew, shouting instructions over the din of the powerful engines. In response, the helicopter's Nitesun searchlight suddenly flooded the battlefield with thirty million candlepower of brilliant white light. They were close to the line of red flags now, the position of the government front line at the time of the battle, and just yards from the well.

Armsley edged closer to Neil and shouted over the din… 'Looks like we've got another body, according to the chopper crew, sir. At the Well of the Dead!'

They approached the little ring of boulders and its prominent stone marker, heavy hearted, dreading their first sight of Selina Cope's blonde hair and preparing themselves for this, the second gruesome ordeal of the evening. As they climbed the slight incline to the marker stone, they could see the outline of the body lying to its right.

Neil groaned and shook his head in disbelief. 'I don't believe this,' he muttered. Then a thought struck him. Maybe he was wrong, but the prone form ahead of him seemed a little big for the petite Selina Cope. When he finally halted at the corpse's feet, he discovered that his assessment had been spot on. This was not the body of Selina Cope, as he'd supposed. This was a very dead Mungo McQuade!

Holly stood by his side. 'Good God, I wasn't expecting this,' she bellowed, also trying to compete with the helicopter's engines, and all the while sweeping her long blonde hair back from her eyes.

'Nor was I,' Neil shouted back, stooping to view the body.

McQuade had been slain with a bladed weapon. That much was certain. His head had become partially detached at the base of the neck, without doubt the result of a powerful strike. The blood loss from this attack had been catastrophic. Most of the ten or so pints that had once filled his veins now soaked the front of his clothing and the grass beneath his limp form.

'Much of this blood is only partially clotted,' Neil observed. He placed the back of his hand against the dead man's cheek. 'He's still warm too. I reckon he's not long been dead.'

He straightened up. 'Steve, get the chopper to do a search of the vicinity with their FLIR. The armed guys and the dog can coordinate with them on the ground. We'll look after things here.'

Armsley stepped away, raising a thumb in acknowledgement. He then began to yell once more into his radio. The response from the helicopter was immediate and the Nitesun snapped off, plunging the officers on the ground into darkness. The aircraft then banked away to the north, its forward-looking infra-red camera scanning the wild moorland for any heat signature that might indicate the presence of a suspect.

Now that the engine note had faded, Neil pulled out his mobile phone and called Angus Hardie. Not surprisingly, the detective superintendent wasn't entirely happy when he received the news that his patch was fast becoming strewn with violently dispatched corpses. To make things worse, they were corpses that had once represented two of their prime suspects!

'So we're back where we started, Neil? With a killer on the loose whose identity is completely unknown, and the body count rising by the hour.'

'Aye, sir, it's not going our way at present, but we do have Van Nieuwoudt and Boyd Duff in custody. I'm still convinced we're on the right track.'

'Well, I certainly hope so, because I'd describe our situation at present as being parked in a siding, Neil! I'll try and sort out another forensic team… if I can find one not committed elsewhere. This is the third major crime scene of the night… so far!'

Neil shared his boss's frustration, and dreaded to think how Alex Brodie would've reacted. News like this would most likely have brought on another heart attack, had he not still been off sick recovering from the first one!

'So where do we go from here?' Holly asked dejectedly.

Neil looked at his watch. 'Well, I'm going back to Inverness. The boss wants an urgent update meeting. Then I'll have an initial chat with Boyd Duff when he arrives. I'd like both of you to remain here until back up arrives. Then, Holly, go back to the cabin. You've got your own transport. Have a better look around when the forensic team get there. I'm pretty sure that place can provide us with a few more clues as to who is behind this.'

'Aye, will do, sir. God knows how long we'll be waiting here, though.'

'I'll call in an hour, see how things are progressing.' Neil switched on his torch and hurried off up the path towards the car park. The helicopter was hovering over the main road now, and he could just make out torch beams, presumably from the firearms officers, somewhere near the fence line directly beneath it.

Holly had only been waiting forty minutes, when the sound of multiple footsteps had been heard approaching from the direction of the car park. The little group was led by a uniformed sergeant from Nairn. He and the group of constables with him had been working on a local public order initiative, which was supposed to have continued until two in the morning. But, to their obvious frustration, they had been redeployed to Operation Cawdor with immediate effect. A small forensic team, already dressed in their white coveralls, followed the officers, laden down with their equipment and several arc lights.

'You're a sight for sore eyes,' Holly declared.

The sergeant zipped his fleece up to his chin. 'Didn't expect to end up out here tonight. Still, all hands to the pump, eh?'

Holly handed over the scene log she'd commenced. 'Hopefully you'll still get home before the sun comes up… if you're lucky!'

'Aye, unless you find any other bloody corpses tonight. Excuse the pun! Seriously, though, is that a possibility?'

Holly pursed her lips. She didn't really have the faintest idea what would happen in the coming hours, days… weeks even! How could she?

The sergeant read her expression. 'Thought so. You haven't got a clue who's behind all this, have you? Call yourselves detectives!'

Holly wasn't going to take that lying down! 'We're currently experiencing a few difficulties because all our suspects appear to be deceased or in custody, as of approximately an hour ago! Still, we've got the live ones to interview, and three crime scenes to examine. So you let me get off and do something constructive, whilst you and your little helpers stand here in the darkness and have a good whinge!'

She looked glumly over her shoulder, as she and Armsley walked away.

'Coz if *we're* not up to the job description, everyone's going to be working around the clock… and that includes you lot! Think on that.'

Fraser Gunn had just arrived at the other scene, deep in Culloden Forest. He was now standing by the tool shed that currently housed Ualas MacBean's putrescent corpse, and was deep in conversation with Adam Carnie. They both looked around when Holly and Steve Armsley pulled up behind the last in a line of police vehicles now in attendance.

Here too, arc lights had been set up around the site, bathing it in refulgent white light that also projected long pencil-like shadows across the forest floor. High above this surreal woodland scene, the treetops moaned and creaked in subtle accompaniment, as if they too wished to contribute to the eerie atmosphere now present in this remote sanguinary place.

'Neil Strachan gone sick yet?' was Gunn's opening gambit.

'I wouldn't blame him, after the evening he's had.' Holly was quick to defend her boss.

'Aye, nor would I. Ross Haggarty told me his first adventure this evening was up on the Sutors, chasing the wee scrote who's been stalking his other half.'

'That's right, Fraser, so he wants to get home soonest… and so do I. Can you therefore provide me with any information that may be of some assistance to our enquiry?' She was in no mood for banter.

'Ooh, touchy,' came the sarcastic reply.

'I'm tired, Fraser, that's all.'

Carnie, although weary himself from having been called out from his bed, recognised the need for a much-needed injection of professionalism.

'What I can tell you, Holly, is that Mr MacBean has been dead for at least four weeks, maybe a little longer. Cause of death was massive blood loss, having had his throat cut from behind. I don't suppose that comes as much of a surprise to you, does it? Interesting thing is the obliquity of the cut is from high on the right side, tailing off low on the left side of the neck, indicating to me that the killer was probably left-handed, the same as the killer of Laura Fraser. Now, I've had a quick look at Mr MacBean's hands, and from the callouses present on the inside of his right palm, I would suggest that he had engaged in heavy physical work over a substantial period. The absence of said callouses on the left hand, suggests—'

'He was right-handed,' Holly interjected.

'Exactly. So my guess is, he wasn't responsible for the murders of Laura and Duncan Fraser.'

'You say his throat had been cut from behind. So he was definitely killed elsewhere, then?' Holly reasoned.

'Without a doubt, lassie. The lack of bloodstaining both in here and in the cabin itself suggests he was merely stored here. Unless of course, his killer has been most thorough when it came to cleaning up after himself.'

Holly nodded towards the cabin. 'Have you seen the state of that place?'

Carnie smiled. 'You have read my mind!'

'Thanks, Doc, that's useful.' She turned to Gunn, whose ebullience had diminished somewhat.

'Can you add anything to that, Fraser?'

Gunn folded his arms defensively. 'We've lifted a number of grey hairs from the mattress in the bedroom. Possibly Duncan Fraser's, but DNA testing will confirm that. No blonde ones, so no indication the daughter has been kept here.'

'Aye, we'd pretty much worked that out for ourselves, Fraser.'

'We've already lifted a number of fingerprints from all over the site. There are also a few blood spatters on the wall next to the bed and around the sink.'

'Okay, what about the burn marks on the shed? Other than the fact that the fire was set not long before we arrived initially.'

'We've taken samples to test for accelerant, but to be honest I don't think there was any. Hence the failure of the fire to take hold. It was obviously a rush job.'

'Okay, that it?'

'Give us a chance, Holly! We haven't been here long.'

'Time is not on our side, Fraser. There's a good chance whoever's got Selina Cope has just partially decapitated Mungo McQuade!'

'Aye, we heard. You may also be interested to know that we've found some faint tyre tracks, similar to those we discovered across at Cullaird. You may've noticed too, that there's sawdust everywhere around the outside of the cabin. My guess is Duncan Fraser was laid on the ground here before being loaded into a vehicle, hence the sawdust being found in his hair during the PM. It'll take more time to examine this site properly, though.'

'Like I said, that's something Selina Cope doesn't have… time, Fraser. So I won't detain you from your labours a moment longer! Mind if I have another poke around inside the cabin? The boss has requested that I take a closer look now that you're here.'

Gunn pulled the hood of his all-in-one suit up over his

bony skull. 'Aye, in view of the circumstances, I'm agreeable, but only if you suit up and follow the instructions of my staff when you're in there.'

They walked across to Gunn's van, where she was supplied with a forensic suit and coverings for her shoes.

'How did things go at the castle?' she asked, whilst she struggled to get her small hands into a pair of latex gloves.

'Not much for us there, to be honest,' said Gunn, his expression still humourless. 'All the action took place just inside the front door. There were a few clothing fibres caught in the grain of the chapel door, but other than that, nothing, except for those tyre impressions in the gravel outside. They're the same width as all the others. Looks like our Land Rover again.'

'I know. Miriam Fraser saw the bloody thing,' said Holly, shaking her head. 'I can't believe we haven't located that vehicle yet. Every police officer in Scotland must be looking for it now.'

Having completed the suiting-up ritual, she placed a comforting hand on Gunn's arm. 'Sorry I was a bit snappy just now. It's been a long day. For what it's worth, Neil Strachan's had an even longer one. In fact it's turned into a perfect storm as far as he's concerned! To make things worse, he's got Hardie on his back now, but he's doing all he can.'

'You know me. I was just trying to lighten things up a bit.' He smiled a weak, half-hearted smile as they parted company and she walked away towards the door of the cabin.

Holly waved to Adam Carnie who was now re-entering the shed to continue his examination of MacBean's remains. She felt for him too. He had yet another corpse waiting for him up the road!

Now hooded and masked, she entered the cabin for a second time and looked around her at the now familiar array of weaponry displayed on the wall. Forensic officers were hard at work in each of the rooms. Their kit was strewn across the bare wooden floor and tripods stood in various locations: some with lamps mounted on them, others with cameras. Threading her way carefully, like a slalom canoeist, between the obstacles, she perused the walls once more. The old weapons hung there undisturbed and liberally coated in dust. Nothing had changed. Nothing new caught her eye. So having been given a thumbs up to search further, she concentrated on the furniture closer to the floor. A sofa stood against the longest wall, an old leather affair draped in a threadbare tartan throw. She checked the underside of the cloth, and carefully probed down the sides of the cushions. Her gloved fingers emerged covered in crumbs: the stale remnants of many years of snacking by the occupant no doubt! Next, she knelt down and tipped the sofa back. As expected, other than thick dust, there was nothing, so she moved onto the small chest of drawers at the end of the room. Opening the drawers one by one, she carefully removed their contents. Much of it was rubbish... old newspapers, a well-thumbed volume of Robert Burns's poems, sweet papers and a box of matches. But in the bottom drawer there were several maps, the one most clearly visible being a hand-drawn plan of the area around the battlefield. Holly called one of the forensic officers across, who videorecorded the find *in situ*. One by one the maps were then removed, individually photographed and bagged until they came across a floor plan, which, although not titled, was clearly that of Cullaird Castle.

'Well, well. Fancy finding this all the way out here!' Holly mused, slipping it into a new bag.

At the bottom of the drawer was one remaining document – well, four to be exact. Stapled printouts from a local heritage website entitled *Clach an Airm – A Short Story*. On the front page was a black-and-white photograph of a standing stone located in a forest clearing. Underneath was an account, told through the eyes of a fictional witness, of the gathering of hundreds of the local clansmen on the morning prior to the Battle of Culloden. Their names were familiar: MacGillivray, MacBean, Mackintosh... all local men from Strathnairn who had come together to form one regiment, the Clan Chattan. It was a moving story, documenting their march from the gathering at the stone to the field of battle, and then later in the day, the survivors' sad return, their numbers much depleted following the disastrous action fought on the moor.

Holly bit her lip, immersed in thought. She then walked across to the watercolour she'd noticed earlier on the wall in the hallway. There was no doubt. The stones were one and the same: the Clach an Airm. Dropping the printout and the maps into evidence bags, she resumed her search.

There was little else to find, so she moved on to the bedrooms. The first, the one containing the bed, was still a hive of activity. She knew her presence would not be welcomed by the scenes of crime officers working in there, so she entered the second bedroom, if you could call it that. It was, after all, empty. She turned slowly around, not wanting to miss anything, but there was nothing to miss. It was as if this had once been someone's home, but had now been cleared of all but a few of that resident's personal effects: the weapons on the wall, a few pictures and some assorted papers.

The kitchen dresser still contained some cutlery and an assortment of chipped mugs and dusty plates. The drawers were empty except for several unopened packs of yellow Marigold rubber gloves... as worn by the intruder during his visits to Cullaird Castle! Holly left them *in situ* and explained the significance of the find to one of the grim-faced team working next door in the bedroom. Not wishing to alienate Gunn's colleagues any further by disrupting their systematic and methodical search of the property, Holly decided to call it a day. She stepped out into the darkness and made her way back towards the line of parked vehicles, eventually finding Gunn drinking from a flask at the rear of his van.

'First one since teatime,' he proclaimed, anticipating a sarcastic comment from the young woman.

'You get it down you,' she encouraged supportively. 'You're at least entitled to a cup of tea!'

She waved the evidence bags. 'I need to retain this stuff, Fraser. It could help us to trace the whereabouts of Selina Cope.'

'Fair enough. The guys have photographed and logged them, I assume?'

'Aye, they have, *in situ* and on the top of the chest.'

'Okay, they're all yours, then. Just keep them in the bags if you can.'

Holly peeled herself out of the forensic suit and headed for her car.

'Good luck,' Gunn called after her. She turned and waved. They were sorely in need of some of it!

Once out on the main road, she pulled over and called Neil's mobile phone. There was no answer, so she tried the incident room. One of the DCs answered, his mouth still filled with the remnants of a half-chewed sandwich.

'I'll wait until you've finished your supper,' Holly growled, her irritation clear.

'Sorry, Sarge,' came the obsequious reply. 'I was just grabbing a bite to eat.'

'Okay... just as well it wasn't a member of the public. Where's the boss?

'He's gone over to the custody suite. This guy Duff's just arrived from Pitlochry.'

'Okay, I'm on my way back. Call the suite and get a message to him. Tell him I might have an idea where Selina Cope *may* have been taken.'

The voice at the end of the line was fully attentive now. 'Right, Sarge. I'll get onto them now. The boss could do with some good news. You should've seen the face on him when he came out of his meeting with Mr Hardie!'

Chapter Forty

Holly had travelled no more than a mile when her phone rang. She pulled over into a bus lay-by and scooped up the device from the empty passenger seat. It was Neil Strachan, returning her call.

'Hello, Holly. What's this about having an idea where Selina's being held?'

'It's just a thought, but do you remember that painting on the wall in the cabin, the one of the standing stone in the forest clearing with the sunlight shining on it?'

'Aye, I vaguely recall taking a peek at it as I walked past.'

'Well, I found some papers in a drawer in that chest. The one in the room with all the weapons on the walls.'

She went on to describe what she'd found, whilst Neil listened in silence. When she'd finished, he answered with a question. 'So MacBean had an interest in some standing stone over in Strathnairn. What makes you think Selina's been taken there?'

'Because, like you, I think whoever is holding her wants to give us the impression that MacBean is responsible for what's been going on at Cullaird. You know, by wearing all the old clothes, dumping bodies at the Well of the Dead... that sort of thing. So if MacBean would've possibly taken Selina to the standing stone, an iconic location for the Clan Chattan, then why wouldn't our mystery man want to follow his lead?'

Neil sat on one of the wooden benches in the reception area of the custody suite. He rubbed his forehead in an attempt to alleviate the burgeoning headache that was now vexing him. 'So you're working on the assumption that our kidnapper doesn't suspect that we have found and identified MacBean's body at the cabin?'

'Exactly. Why would he? And even if he did believe that we'd found the cabin, he may well think his attempt at cremation had actually worked—'

Neil finished off her sentence. '… In the hope that we may never discover that MacBean was dead, merely that he'd based himself there at some stage, but had since disappeared, abroad maybe.'

'That's right, and what better place to take and dump your hostage, than out into the middle of a forest somewhere? It's a place that we'd immediately link to Ualas MacBean's forest cabin, and his beloved clan… if we ever found it, of course!'

'I suppose, as you say, us eventually coming across the stuff about the standing stone out at the cabin *would* further implicate MacBean, especially if we found Selina nearby. But it would depend on us not being able to identify the burnt remains as MacBean's.'

'Agreed,' said Holly. 'But you know what? I don't think our suspect was contemplating us finding that cabin so soon, if at all. My guess is we'd eventually be fed a clue that would've led us to the stone at some stage, irrespective of whether we'd found the cabin or not. And we'd merely make the link between suspect and the significance of the stone when we were.'

A chill suddenly ran down Neil's spine, prompting him to think out loud. 'It's hardly a scenario in which you'd expect to find a live victim, is it?'

'No, it's not,' Holly replied glumly.

'That printout. Does it give a location?'

'Not really. It mentions Gask, Strathnairn. Somewhere surrounded by dense forestation.'

'Remind me what the stone was called.'

'Clach an Airm.' Holly then spelt out the words.

Neil's command of Gaelic was minimal. He could decipher some of the words, from knowledge built up during his study of ancient Scottish historical sites as part of his degree course. He cogitated the words. *Clach* meant 'stone'. *An* was easy. It was 'the' in Gaelic. *Airm*, he recalled, was the Gaelic word for 'weapon'. Stone of the Weapons! The phrase seemed familiar to him, and he was sure that someone had referred to the area of Gask earlier during the enquiry. Then it came to him. It had been Miriam Fraser, during her explanation of Captain Simon MacGillivray's movements prior to the Battle of Culloden. She'd mentioned during their teatime chat at The Royal Highland Hotel that MacGillivray and his men had mustered at the Stone of the Swords, in the forest at Gask.

Holly had been waiting for a response. 'Sir, are you there?'

'Aye, I'm here. Look… *Clach an Airm*, loosely translated, means Stone of the Swords, or Weapons.' He quickly recounted Miriam's story before asking… 'Where's Miriam now?'

'At Raigmore Hospital, having her head stitched. The paramedics thought they'd probably keep her in for observations.'

'Okay, get over there now and see whether she can tell you exactly where this stone is. Whatever the case, we need to locate it and quickly. It may even be on the OS map.'

'Has Duff arrived yet?'

'They're in the vehicle bay now. I'm going to get a quick chat in with him. See what he can tell us, if indeed he's prepared to say anything.'

Neil was returning the phone to his pocket when Duff was brought into the reception area by the two Tayside officers. He looked on whilst the custody officer behind the reception desk informed him of his rights and completed the booking-in process.

Neil tried to sum up the little man with the bandy legs and large protruding ears. He was certainly behaving himself, which was a start. The long journey up the A9 had no doubt provided him with the opportunity to reflect upon his current situation. Duff raised his arms, submitting to a rub-down search, then signed for his rights and property.

'Cell two,' the custody officer directed without looking up from his computer screen. A custody assistant duly stepped forward to escort him to his new accommodation.

Neil got up at this juncture. 'Actually, I'll have him in with me in the interview room.'

The custody officer looked up. 'As you wish, sir.' He nodded to the assistant. 'Take Mr Duff to the interview room, please.'

Neil followed behind, having been given the briefest of inquisitorial glances by Duff.

The Glaswegian was seated, arms folded defensively, when Neil placed his file of papers on the table.

'Welcome to Inverness, Mr Duff. I'm DCI Strachan.'

'Pleased tae meet you, Mr Strachan. Perhaps you can tell me why ah'm sittin' here, because ah'm no murderer.'

Neil ignored the question. 'We'll get started just as soon as my colleague arrives.' He sat down and placed two audio cassette tapes on the table next to him, then looked around when the door opened. A young, fresh-faced detective constable walked in and sat down, apologising for the delay in his arrival.

Duff frowned. 'Christ, laddie, are you old enough tae be on solids yet?'

The DC grinned back. 'Solid enough, Mr Duff.'

Neil suppressed any indication of amusement and fed the tapes into the machine before commencing the formal introductions. At the end of his speech, he smiled across at Duff.

'You've elected not to have any legal representation at this interview, Mr Duff. Can you confirm this for the purpose of the tape?'

'Aye, that's true. Ah havenae done nothin' wrong, so ah dinnae need a brief, do ah?' He shrugged. 'Not the now, anyways.'

'Okay then, let me explain why you're here.'

Neil outlined the circumstances of the murders of Laura and Duncan Fraser, and concluded by disclosing that Ualas MacBean's remains had just been discovered out in Culloden Forest. The response to this news was clear for anyone to see. Duff averted his gaze towards the wall and swallowed hard, then looked back at the interviewers.

'So do you have any evidence that suggests ah was involved in any of this, Chief Inspector Strachan?'

Neil sidestepped the question. 'Were you involved in any of this, Boyd?'

'Ah dinnae have a clue who these people are, Chief Inspector. Look, ah think y'might be wasting yer time just now.'

Neil leaned across the table and glared menacingly at Duff.

'What concerns me, Boyd, is that you're now wasting *my* time.'

He plucked a still photograph from the folder in front of him. It had been taken from the CCTV footage seized in Cathcart Road earlier that evening. He placed it on the table, directly in front of Duff, and tapped it with his finger. 'Who were you calling from this TK just after nine thirty tonight, Boyd?'

The scornful expression that had initially characterised the little man from Glasgow had now been replaced with one of surprise. His skin reddened and he ran a tremulous hand over his shiny scalp.

'Where did you get that? There's nae CCTV camera that covers the street near there.'

Neil pressed home his advantage, having tolerated Duff's time-wasting for long enough.

'I know, Boyd, but the camera in the shop across the road does!' He paused long enough for his response to sink in, then continued with his questions. 'You called Selina Cope at Cullaird Castle, up here in Strathnairn, didn't you, Boyd? She's the daughter of the couple who were brutally murdered a month ago. But you already know that, don't you? You warned her to get out of the castle, but she didn't, and now she's been kidnapped. So you can appreciate we're very worried, and you know what, Boyd? If she comes to any harm at all, then you'll find yourself looking at a longer spell behind bars than you could ever contemplate.'

Duff looked up from the photograph and bit his lower lip whilst he formulated an answer. 'Look, ah've had nothing tae do with any kidnapping. Ah dinnae know who's taken her, honest. Ah havenae got a clue.'

Neil changed tack. 'Tell me about this man, the one you were with when you made the call.'

'His name is Dawie Van Nieuwoudt. He's a friend of ma business partner, Mungo McQuade.'

His voice was faltering, the hopelessness of his situation beginning to permeate through his subconsciousness. There was little doubt they were going to hang him out to dry!

Neil probed further. 'So why didn't Dawie make the call? It was *his* wife who was staying at the castle, after all?'

'He didnae want anyone to recognise his voice. He's South African, for Christ's sake.'

537

'Just what I thought,' said Neil. 'Let's get back to your friend Mungo. Where is he tonight?'

'Ah havenae got a scooby. He came up this way to see a friend yesterday.'

'And that's why you were on your way up here tonight, Boyd? To find Mungo and stop him carrying out this kidnapping. I'm right, aren't I?'

Duff temporised, shaking his head and glowering at Neil.

Neil tried from a different angle. 'So where do you think Mungo might be, right now, Boyd? Tell me.'

'Ah dinnae know. Honest, pal,' Duff answered huskily.

'Shall I tell you where he is, Boyd?'

Duff's eyes met Neil's and the two men studied each other, a bemused expression once again present upon Duff's now rubicund features.

'Dinnae tell me… the fuckin' eejit's in here, locked up? Typical.'

Neil's colleague, who had remained silent throughout the interview, now regarded his boss apprehensively. But Neil's eyes were still fixed on Duff, like a boxer who was about to land a fatal punch.

'He's lying out on Culloden Battlefield, practically decapitated. We think the culprit was a broadsword.' Then he sat back and folded his arms, as would a victorious chess player who'd just declared 'checkmate'!

The little man's eyes glazed over and then he began to visibly shake. 'Yer lyin',' he retorted angrily. 'Ah just dinnae believe you.'

Neil pulled out his mobile phone. 'I can show you a photograph if you wish, Boyd? It's not pretty.'

Duff raised a trembling hand, rejecting the offer. His eyes were glistening now. 'You're a cold-hearted bastard for a young laddie,' he muttered. 'All right, son, ah'll tell you what ah know. You seem to be holdin' all the cards, after all. But first let me repeat what ah said before… Ah've no killed anyone! Ah'm not goin' doon for no murders, understand?'

Holly had diverted into Raigmore Hospital and was now sitting with Miriam in a curtained-off bay in the busy accident and emergency department. Miriam had received six stitches to her head wound and was sitting with Aili Hughes when the detective sergeant had walked in.

'How are you feeling, Miriam?'

'I'm afraid I've got a bit of a headache, but I'll survive, dear.'

She ran her hand over the bloodied collar of her blouse. 'Looks like this will have to go in the bin. Still, enough about me. Have you any idea where Selina's been taken yet?'

'Sorry, no news as yet, but we're pulling out all the stops, believe me.'

'I'm sure you are, dear. I wish I could help but it looks like they're going to keep me in here overnight. They think I may have concussion after the fall.'

Holly then took Miriam's hand and smiled. 'I need to make you aware of some developments this evening. This might come as a bit of a shock…'

Miriam sat open-mouthed for several seconds, trying to take it all in. In the five or so hours since Selina had been taken, both prime suspects in the case had been found brutally murdered, and her ex-husband had been arrested in connection with the killings of her beloved cousin and his wife.

'This is unbelievable,' she gasped, bravely holding back the tears. 'I know Dawie could be something of a rogue, but I would never have believed he was capable of anything like this. Where is he now?'

'He's being held down in Glasgow for the time being. We'll send an escort down for him as soon as we can.'

Miriam pulled out a bloodstained handkerchief and dabbed her eye.

'Well, he deserves all he gets. That's all I can say on the matter. Is that why you came in to see me? To tell me all this?'

Holly released her hand and pulled the document relating to the Clach an Airm out of her bag.

'I wanted to keep you updated, of course, but I also need to ask you about this.'

She handed the plastic bag to Miriam. 'I believe you mentioned this standing stone to Mr Strachan when he was having tea with you in town the other day? You referred to it as the Stone of the Swords.'

Miriam scanned the document and its title. 'Ah yes, dear. That's right, it's the Clach an Airm. The Gaelic title had escaped me.'

'Can you tell me exactly where the stone is located, Mrs Fraser? It may save us some time. We think whoever has got Selina may possibly have taken her there.'

Miriam contemplated Holly's question briefly, then shook her head. 'I know it's deep in the forest somewhere, down on the Gask Plantation, near Loch Caulan. There's no path to it. You'd get to it through the woods, alongside the B861, the back road from Tombreck into Inverness.'

'Thanks, that's very helpful. We'll have a look at the map.'

Holly returned the exhibit to her bag and got up. 'We'll keep you posted as soon as we know anything.'

She broke into a trot across the car park, wanting to get back to the office as soon as possible, where hopefully she would be able to pinpoint the location of the Stone of the Swords. But she was unsure of her theory. It was, after all, one hell of a long shot. What if they were heading down a blind alley? It would all be down to her. It didn't bear thinking about! Neil had placed his confidence in her. Hardie would chew him up if he got it wrong, and where would that leave

Selina Cope? She climbed into the car and clamped her eyes shut, preferring to eliminate such thoughts from her mind.

Neil was wrapping up his interview with Boyd Duff. He'd switched the tape recorder off at three fifteen, and was now gathering up his papers whilst his young colleague had ventured out to get Duff a cup of tea.

The little man sat in silence, his head bowed, whilst he reflected upon his now hopeless situation.

Neil paused in the open doorway. 'We'll talk some more later on, Boyd. In the meantime, I'd get my head down if I were you.'

'There's nae much more tae talk aboot,' Duff stuttered. Neil stepped aside to allow the custody assistant to enter. 'We'll see about that,' he said as he disappeared into the brightly lit corridor.

Holly was back in the main office when he returned to the MEU suite and spilled the folder and tape cassettes onto his desk. She walked in with a large-scale Ordnance Survey map of Strathnairn and a printout from the website of the Royal Commission on the Ancient and Historical Monuments of Scotland.

'I've found it,' she announced, with as much enthusiasm as she could muster at that late hour. 'They've even placed a pin marker on the map.'

She unravelled the OS map and tapped on a red mark she'd penned on a green, shaded area at the south-western extremity of Drumossie Moor. It highlighted the words *Clach an Airm*, written in the distinctive font that denoted an ancient monument. 'It's here, in the forest between the B861 and Loch Caulan, just as Miriam explained. I should've looked here first.'

'Good work, Holly. But don't beat yourself up over it.

There are ancient sites marked like this all over the Highlands. You could've looked all day and missed it. No, speaking to Miriam was definitely worthwhile.'

He picked up the phone and spoke to the force operations room. 'I'm going to need the ARV and the dog unit back here at headquarters. I have another task for them.' He listened to the reply, then said, 'Okay, but it needs to be on the hurry-up. We'll wait for them in the car park.' There was more chatter from the other end, then Neil reeled off the grid reference from the map, pinpointing the Clach an Airm. 'Pass this on to the Air Support Unit. We're also going to need their FLIR capability.'

He put the phone down, then got up and beckoned to Holly as he gathered up his jacket and phone. 'Let's go. I need to update Angus Hardie on the way.'

The detective superintendent wasn't entirely convinced that they'd find Selina Cope at the Clach an Airm, but neither was he prepared to rubbish the idea. Preferring to play it safe, he reluctantly accepted that the location should be checked and eliminated.

'I'm not going to commit any more resources to search that area for the time being,' he'd told them. At least not until there was concrete evidence to support the theory that the offender and victim were currently in the vicinity of Gask and its extensive forest. Neil was happy with that. Five of them and a helicopter were sufficient to check out the location initially. Even he wasn't convinced. But to dismiss Holly's suggestion out of hand, and then be proved wrong, was not an outcome he was prepared to contemplate!

'So what was the outcome of your chat with Boyd Duff?' Holly asked as they skipped down the stairs.

'He's cleared up a number of things, but he's adamant he doesn't know who's got Selina, and you know what, I'm inclined to believe him. He was backed into a corner, was our

Mr Duff, and being the little weasel he is, there was no way he was going to be implicated in any more of this than was absolutely necessary!'

A marked patrol car pulled into the car park just as they were getting into the CID vehicle. It was crewed by two constables from Inverness Police Station.

'Mr Hardie's asked us to join you on your little expedition out to Gask, sir. My partner here lives out that way. Thought he might be able to provide some local knowledge.'

'All assistance is very welcome,' Neil admitted. 'Have they told you what we're doing?'

'Aye, sir, they have. There's a standing stone located in the Gask Plantation that we need to check out regarding this missing woman from Cullaird.'

Neil nodded. 'That's about the extent of it. We just need to wait for the ARV and a dog handler to join us, before we head off.'

They got into the car, glad to be out of the early morning chill. 'You were telling me about your interview with Duff,' Holly reminded him. 'Exactly what did he say?'

Neil turned to face her. 'Where shall I start?'

And so the story was told. Not surprisingly, Dawie Van Nieuwoudt regularly travelled to Scotland around the time he was married to Miriam. On one such occasion in 1980, he'd taken himself off to an antiques fair in Perth, and it was there that the South African had met Mungo McQuade and Boyd Duff. The two Glaswegians had been selling items at the event, and Van Nieuwoudt had spotted a Cape silver snuff box on their stall that had once belonged to a Scottish soldier of the Boer War. Van Nieuwoudt was, it seemed, a prolific collector of Cape silverware, and had purchased the item to add to his extensive collection. McQuade had told him that they often picked up similar items, brought back by soldiers returning home from the South African conflict, and had offered to make contact when they obtained further examples. So they'd exchanged business cards and had kept in touch over the years, culminating in an offer from Dawie to visit him in South Africa in 2006. The invitation was ostensibly a thank-you gesture, for acting as his 'agent' in the UK. The two men had subsequently formed a loose friendship, resulting in McQuade making a further visit to South Africa in 2008.

At this stage, Holly had interjected. 'So it was only McQuade who became friendly with Van Nieuwoudt. Not Duff?'

'That's right. Duff said he didn't really like the man. Considered him to be an "arrogant wee bawbag", to use his own words.'

'Charming. What about Miriam? Did she ever get to meet McQuade or Duff?'

'It seems not. She never had an interest in antiques, so never went with him when he was out hunting for them. Then of course they divorced in '85, so there was little chance of their paths crossing from then on.'

'Okay. Sorry to interrupt.'

Neil went on to explain that at the beginning of April, the pair of antiques dealers had been touring the outlying areas of Glasgow, canvassing door to door for potential purchases. They'd been offered the old chest by Elizabeth Patterson in Cumbernauld, and had immediately seen its potential resale value. So they'd ripped her off, having made a rock-bottom offer for the item, and had taken it back to their shop in Cathcart Road.

Neil grinned. 'Ironically, they haven't been able to offload it, so it's still languishing there now!'

Holly twisted the top off of a bottle of mineral water. 'So I assume they examined it and found this letter, yes?'

'Exactly. It was still nailed to the underside of one of the drawers. Had been there since 1746!'

'Go on. I'm intrigued!'

She listened whilst Neil went on to explain that McQuade had seen the name of Cullaird Castle written at the head of Meg MacGillivray's letter, and had immediately thought of Dawie Van Nieuwoudt. So a phone call had been made, initially to ask the South African whether he'd be interested in buying the chest. Apparently, McQuade and Duff had not at that stage understood the significance of the letter as a clue to the whereabouts of a lost fortune! Van Nieuwoudt had become very excited when he heard about the letter, recounting the story of the lost hoard and its potential current-day value if it was located. He'd disclosed that Duncan Fraser had mentioned the hoard during his brief connection with the family, and evidently he'd always believed that it *was* still hidden somewhere. Van Nieuwoudt had then travelled to Scotland without further ado and had met with McQuade and Duff to discuss whether it would be feasible for them to get into the castle and recover the hoard. Van Nieuwoudt remembered that the Frasers went across to their holiday home in Grand Cayman during the month of April. He'd confirmed this with a family contact, who also had a key to the castle. So a plan was forged to get in and search the place whilst it was empty.

'Hang on.' Holly raised a hand as if confused. 'Who exactly was going to get in, and where does Ualas MacBean fit into all this?'

'I was just coming on to that,' said Neil, his eyes swivelling away towards the entrance of the car park, in the hope that their back up would soon arrive.

He turned back to his colleague and continued with the story. 'Van Nieuwoudt gave assurances that the family contact would, for whatever reason, assist them when it came to getting into the castle. Both he and that contact, understandably, were worried that *we*, the police, might end up knocking on their doors. So Van Nieuwoudt told McQuade that he'd have to come up with some way of ensuring that no suspicion would fall on any of them.'

'He certainly had it all planned out, then,' Holly mused.

'Aye, that's where MacBean comes into play,' said Neil. 'McQuade recalled from his time in prison with MacBean that he was from the Strathnairn area. Better still, the guy was obsessed with all things Jacobite. But, even more importantly, he was always banging on in prison about the MacGillivrays of Cullaird, and how they'd let down the parent clan at Culloden, the Clan Chattan.'

Holly gestured with her bottle of water. 'So they set him up as the fall guy. Fed us a trail of clues that would put him fair and square in the frame for the break-in and the murders.' She shook her head. 'Clever, if it worked... and initially it did!'

'Aye, that's right. McQuade knew where MacBean was living... as a hermit somewhere in Culloden Forest... so that he could spend his days amongst the spirits of his long-dead ancestors, apparently! It appears he spent most of his time in some sort of parallel world, addicted to his heather brews... ales, whatever you want to call them, so much so he'd completely lost the plot. The ideal patsy, eh? Totally unstable mentally, history of housebreaking, and estranged from just about everyone he ever knew. So they – that's McQuade and Van Nieuwoudt – went up to Inverness and paid MacBean a visit, apparently so that Van Nieuwoudt could meet him for himself, like a kind of bizarre audition, I suppose.'

'And then they killed him?' Holly interjected.

'Well, that came as news to Duff. He says he had no idea that killing him was part of the plan. But yes, I think they killed him quite early on, intending to remove any trace of him by burning the corpse. So we'd be out there looking for him until the end of time, convinced from the evidence that he was responsible for the break-in and murders at Cullaird Castle!'

'To what extent do you think Duff really is implicated in all this?' Holly asked.

'He says he knew about the plan to break into the castle, and to frame Ualas MacBean for it, but that was all. He never took part in any of it himself, or any of the killings, and stayed well out of the way.'

'Do you believe him? He clearly knew about the Frasers being murdered. And why was he driving up here tonight?'

'To answer your first question… yes, he knew. He says *they*… that's McQuade and *whoever*, had no intention of killing the couple initially, but when they were confronted by the Frasers unexpectedly, things got out of hand. As we know, Laura and Duncan returned home unannounced, to attend the funeral of Laura's brother. According to Duff, news of this change of plan never reached the ears of the insider who's been helping Van Nieuwoudt and his pals.'

Neil checked his watch, then carried on.

'Duff was coming up here tonight to try and talk McQuade out of kidnapping Selina. Van Nieuwoudt had tried earlier, on the phone, but had failed. According to Duff, his business partner had become obsessed with finding the hoard. It was McQuade's idea to have a second go at getting into the castle, the day Selina and Nathaniel disturbed the guy in the ski mask. Then, when he found out the chest had been featured on TV, he became convinced that for that to happen, Selina must've had knowledge of Meg MacGillivray's letter. I'm not entirely convinced by his sense of logic, but whatever the case, he decided that kidnapping and interrogating her was worth a go. One last desperate attempt to solve the mystery, so to speak.'

'You're saying Duff and Van Nieuwoudt were unsupportive of McQuade's activities, following the Frasers' murders?'

'Aye, very much so, according to Duff.'

At that point the ARV hastened into the car park with the dog unit close behind it.

'Thank God for that,' Neil sighed, as he climbed out of the car and went to speak with the new arrivals.

Holly watched through the windscreen as Neil pointed and gesticulated before returning and slipping into the driver's seat. Then, for the second time that night, they sped out onto the deserted roads of the Highland capital, and headed south towards Culduthel and the B861.

Chapter Forty-One

Gask

3.45 am, Saturday 15th May

'Did you mention the Clach an Airm to Duff?' Holly enquired as they turned left at a roundabout on the outskirts of the city.

'Aye, I did,' Neil responded. 'He just looked at me blankly. He genuinely didn't have a clue what I was on about.'

She glanced into the nearside wing mirror, checking that the headlights of the two other police vehicles were still behind them. The local unit was leading the way, up the hill and along the B861 towards their final destination.

'I do hope we're not wasting our time,' she said, eyeing Neil briefly and seeking further reassurance.

'We'll soon find out, Holly. Hey, can you think of a better place to look? They could be anywhere in the Highlands.'

He checked his rear-view mirror, for the same reason Holly had, seconds before.

'If the intention is to make us think that MacBean is responsible for all this, what better place to take a hostage and hold her? Or God forbid, dump her body.'

'Do you think it *is* feasible that whoever's got Selina hasn't realised that we've found the cabin and identified Ualas MacBean's remains?'

Neil smiled. 'I'd be very surprised if he had, unless he's been creeping around that forest since we arrived at the cabin. No, having killed McQuade, and setting that shed alight, he had no immediate plans to return to the area. It would be too dangerous. No, he'll be wanting to put some distance between himself and Culloden Moor! As you said yourself, why would he go back there? No, let's assume your theory is correct, otherwise there'd be little point him coming all the way out here.'

'Well, clan links aside, it's certainly a remote, out-of-the-way place. There would be no chance of him being disturbed at such a location.'

She fell silent for a second or two. 'I wonder who *he* is!'

Neil shrugged. 'As things stand, your guess is as good as mine!'

Behind them, the distant lights of Inverness were becoming pinpricks of flickering amber. The road was curving through open moorland now, the altitude accentuating the strength of the easterly breeze.

'It may be May,' said Neil, 'but I wouldn't want to spend the night up here!'

He pointed through the windscreen towards the flashing red beacon that had appeared in the night sky to their left. Beyond it, streaks of purple-blue were appearing close to the eastern horizon... the first vestiges of a new dawn.

'There's the chopper... ours, I hope!'

The aircraft roared overhead and settled into a holding pattern above the little convoy of police vehicles, confirming its identity beyond any doubt.

A mile or so further on and the barren landscape was replaced by the first tree plantations, initially to their left, and then all around them as they hurried on into the darkness.

'Can't be far now,' Holly suggested, switching on her torch momentarily and checking the map.

Her prediction was proved correct, when the police car ahead of them slowed and pulled into a muddy lay-by that defined the mouth of a forestry track. The passenger got out and walked back to them. He pointed across to the dense curtain of firs that lined the opposite side of the road.

'You can get to the stone through those woods, sir. It's a bit of a walk, I'm afraid, especially in this darkness.'

'Is there any other way in?'

'There's a farm track off to the left, about half a mile further on. It leads down towards Loch Caulan. But you'd still have a trek through the woods from there.'

'We'll go in from here, then. You take the track to the loch, so we've got it covered from both sides.'

'Fair enough, sir,' he acknowledged, and trotted back to his own car.

The other officers were already out and preparing themselves for the search. The now delirious police dog was being harnessed up and attached to his tracking line, whilst the two firearms officers were donning weatherproof jackets over their body armour. The shorter of the two, a boyish-looking sergeant with chiselled features and a sparse beard, stuffed his map into his trouser pocket and led the way across the road. Neil followed, tightening the Velcro tabs on his own body armour. The sergeant stepped over the low fence. 'Let's do this as per our normal operating procedures, sir. Dog out front, us in close support… if you can bring up the rear.'

'Suits me. Just did the same thing out at the battlefield,' said Neil, gazing up through the canopy of trees at the helicopter, which was hovering high above them.

The dog led them off through the trees, charging across the forest floor and away into the night. After a few minutes they switched on their torches, as the presence of the helicopter had already negated any prospect of stealth. It had probably been a good decision, because the ground beneath their feet was not only uneven but strewn with the trunks of numerous trees, no doubt felled during recent winter storms. Neil could hear the firearms officers communicating in low tones with the helicopter as they pressed forward. It was from this source that news came, confirming that the local officers had reached the other side of the woodland and were awaiting further instructions. They'd found no vehicles on the track up to their current position and were now at the northern edge of the plantation.

Ten minutes in and there was no sign of the standing stone. There were trees though, thousands of them, their uppermost boughs creaking eerily above the officers' heads, whilst twigs cracked and snapped noisily beneath their feet. An owl hooted somewhere in the near vicinity, prompting the German shepherd to halt momentarily and sniff the damp air before charging on.

Suddenly, the firearms men swung to their left and raised their carbines to their shoulders, indicating the presence of something or someone ahead of them.

'Heat source thirty yards ahead,' the young sergeant whispered. The detectives followed in their wake, straining to see through the darkness, until a pair of eyes reflected in their torch beams.

'Shit, what's that?' Holly gasped. The guns were lowered again, when those same eyes turned slowly away and then disappeared.

'Sika deer,' the sergeant called back, grinning.

So the little group swung around again, resuming their initial course towards the recorded location of the Clach an Airm. A further ten or so minutes ticked by as they probed further into the plantation, until the dog handler stopped once more. The sergeant stepped back to stand by Neil's side.

'Chopper's picked up two more heat sources ahead and to the left. Could be more deer, though,' he whispered. 'Still, we'll check it out.'

They closed up on the dog handler and advanced, gingerly now, trying to minimise the sounds emanating from their footfall. The carbines had torches mounted on them, and it was the beams from these weapons that probed furthest into the darkness, warning them of the clearing ahead, and then, at last, highlighting the stumpy grey stone that projected at a slight angle from the grassy mound around it.

Neil heard the sergeant respond to the helicopter. 'Roger that, skirting round to the right.'

Whilst the second officer panned his weapon around to their left, searching for the other heart source, Neil and Holly followed his colleague and the dog handler. Another, narrower face of the standing stone gradually came into view, against which sat the slumped and inanimate form of a human being.

The dog sensed the presence of the figure and began to bark. Then in an instant the helicopter's Nitesun device spilled harsh white light onto the scene, illuminating the clearing in an ethereal glow that highlighted every detail of the Stone of the Swords.

Against it, her head dipped and her mouth taped, lay Selina Cope. Her arms and ankles had been bound, whilst strands of her blonde hair had fallen unceremoniously across her eyes, like strokes from an artist's brush. Miraculously, she was alive. Her face, by its very expression, spoke of her total fear, whilst her eyes stared out at the approaching police officers, darting from one to the other as if seeking to confirm that they would pose her no threat. Holly ran forward and dropped down next to the terrified woman. She eased the duct tape away from her mouth and cradled her head against her shoulder. Selina began to sob uncontrollably as Holly reassured her that she was safe now, but then she pulled back abruptly, her head striking the rocky face of the standing stone. She looked left and right, desperately scouring the darkness beyond the Nitesun's beam.

'He's out there,' she stammered. 'He's still there somewhere.'

Neil joined Holly at Selina's side, assisting her to release the petrified hostage's bonds, whilst the two firearms officers scanned the area about them, chatting to the helicopter crew and confirming that Selina Cope had been found alive.

'Who's out there, Selina? Who brought you here?' Neil asked gently.

She opened her mouth several times, trying to speak between sobs, but the words wouldn't come out.

Neil asked again. 'Take it easy, Selina. Try and tell us.'

The firearms officer to his right then called out aggressively, his voice rising above the whine of the helicopter.

'You there. Stand still… armed police. Stand still, I say.'

Neil, shocked by the sudden outburst, quickly rose to his feet and peered around the edge of the stone. Twenty yards from them, by the tree line and half obscured in darkness, stood a tall, powerful-looking figure dressed in a heavy kilted plaid. His right hand was protected within the basket hilt of the broadsword that hung limply by his side, whilst a red dot danced upon the heavy material draped across his chest, confirmation that the carbine's sights had locked onto its target. The firearms sergeant, content that his colleague had the figure in his sights, drew his black and yellow taser electroshock device and raised it at arm's length. Behind him, the police dog strained on its leash, snarling incessantly now, as the sergeant ordered the figure to step forward into the light.

And so Sandy Blair emerged from the darkness, squinting into the glare of the Nitesun.

Neil couldn't help himself. 'Jesus, I don't believe it.'

He looked back at Holly, who was now standing just behind him.

Blair halted at the edge of the trees, having seen the red dot that had settled on his plaid.

'Drop the sword, now,' the sergeant ordered. 'Do as I say and you'll come to no harm.'

Blair raised his eyes slowly, a vacant smile now present upon his otherwise taut features. He clearly had no intention of complying with the command.

He called out, 'This must've been the last place you would've expected to meet up with me in the middle of the night, Chief Inspector?'

Neil positioned himself so that he was standing shoulder to shoulder with the firearms sergeant.

'I don't understand, Sandy. You've worked for the Frasers for years. You're all but family, for heaven's sake.'

Blair took several steps forward, prompting the two firearms officers to tense up and check their aim.

'There are some things you have no knowledge of, Chief Inspector. Things that forced me into this position through my own damned stupidity.'

'Why don't you put that sword down, and then we can talk, Sandy? Believe me, I want to hear what you have to say.'

Blair grinned back at him. 'No can do, I'm afraid. You see, the sword is my insurance policy. It's the one thing I possess that will ensure this hellish mess ends as I want it to. I know that may be difficult for you to understand.'

'Try me,' Neil retorted.

'Selina never knew, you know. None of the family did. It was between Duncan and me.'

'What was, Sandy?'

Blair rested the blade of the sword on his shoulder. 'You may as well know; it'll be the only time I get to tell you.' He sighed. 'I'd been stealing from the business you see, over five years, to be exact. I was sending cases of the Lochmhor malt... the twenty-eight-year-old Distiller's Choice... out to a contact in Hong Kong. It was top-end stuff: £200 a bottle. Even with a discount, he was paying me handsomely for it. Until, that is, your colleagues over there raided his warehouse and found some of it amongst all the other stuff he'd been illegally importing from Europe. I suppose we'd call it smuggling, wouldn't we? Duncan took the phone call at the distillery. It was Sod's Law, of course. I was on leave and he was covering for me. Otherwise, I would've buried the whole thing. But it all came out, as you'd expect. That was two years ago.'

'But why, Sandy? Why risk a secure position like yours, presumably with a big salary to go with it?'

'Because sometimes, Chief Inspector, the salary's just not big enough. I believe I told you my wife has MS?'

'Aye, I do recall you mentioning it, Sandy.'

'Well, she's had it for some time. It's been getting steadily worse. There was a treatment available in the States that may have helped her. So I promised her I'd raise the money, not that she'd wanted me to. We had a daughter and grandson at home with us too. My daughter's marriage had broken up, you see. And to top it all, I had a son at university and an astronomic mortgage on interest-only terms. The pressure on me was immense, financially.'

'I can understand that, Sandy. So you thought the sideline with the whisky was the way out?'

Blair nodded. 'Aye, it certainly helped to some degree. My wife finally got her treatment at least. Not that it worked in the long term. Anyway, I explained my predicament to Duncan, told him everything, and pleaded for my job. He said he'd think on it. Then he came back to me with a proposal. That I could keep the job, on the understanding that I paid back what I'd taken. So there were to be no pay rises, no bonuses, and an amount would be deducted from my salary each month. I was grateful, I suppose. But, not surprisingly, the money worries just got worse. Duncan didn't care, you see. He told me that my financial difficulties were my problem.'

Neil gestured to the sergeant to relax his aim, so he reluctantly lowered his taser.

'Who else knew about all this, Sandy?'

'No one at all. It was between Duncan and me… that was the deal. But Duncan had warned me that if I defaulted on my payments, the whole thing would become public knowledge.'

Neil raised his hands questioningly. 'So how did you end up getting involved in all this business with Van Nieuwoudt and McQuade?'

Blair shook his head. Neil could see him more clearly now in the light of the Nitesun. He looked tired and drawn. His grey hair, normally neat and well-styled, thrashed around in the strengthening breeze that now blew in through the swaying firs.

'I'd met Dawie Van Nieuwoudt when he was married to Miriam. We got on very well from the outset. He liked to come across to the distillery for a blether when he was over from Cape Town. So, some time after all the nonsense with Duncan had raised its head, I stupidly contacted Dawie and asked him for a loan. I told him everything. He was never a great fan of Duncan's, you see. I thought he may help me, just to spite him. Anyway, he turned me down. All that wealth, and he turned me down.'

Blair paused to reflect upon his disappointment. 'So life just carried on. Me struggling to make ends meet, becoming more desperate as each day passed. The irony was, that my financial situation at home had improved a little. My wife had received her treatment, but her condition was steadily deteriorating anyway. My daughter had moved out and got a job, but my debt to Duncan Fraser was crippling me.'

'Sounds horrendous,' Neil stepped forward. 'Look, give me the sword, Sandy. This is no place to stand and talk.'

'I'd prefer it if you conversed from here, sir,' the sergeant mouthed in a low tone.

Neil nodded in acknowledgement of the advice but remained where he was. 'Come on, Sandy, it's the best way.'

Blair slid the sword from his shoulder and presented it defensively. 'Please, Chief Inspector, don't come any closer. We can talk perfectly well from where we are.'

Neil took a step back. 'Whatever you say, Sandy. You were telling me how you became involved in all this.'

Blair seemed eager to talk, as if it was something of a release from his inner turmoil.

'Aye, well, I got a call from Dawie out of the blue. Must've been the beginning of April, some while after I'd first contacted him for the loan. He said he had a proposal to put to me, a plan that would pay off all my debts and set me up for life. His friend, who was an antique dealer, had bought this old chest that once belonged to the Frasers. He'd found a letter hidden in it, from one of the family's ancestors, that provided a clue to the hiding place of a great hoard of coin and silverware that had been secreted at Cullaird since the 1700s. As it happened, I'd heard of the hoard, and always thought it was no more than a romantic legend. But when he explained things in detail, my mind was changed. The condition was this: to earn my share, I had to get into Cullaird Castle and search for said hoard with this mate of his.'

'By "mate", I assume you mean Mungo McQuade?'

'Aye, that's him. Well, initially I refused, tempted as I was, until Dawie threatened to do the same as Duncan had. To disclose my secret to all and sundry if I didn't assist him in his little venture and provide the key to the castle. I was a keyholder for the place, you see. Until Duncan decided my services in that regard were no longer required. The thing is, he never asked for the key back!'

Blair laughed. 'I'm not surprised they didn't realise. Security wasn't a priority for the Frasers!'

He had no wish to talk about the keys, though, preferring to return to the story of his involvement in the break-in.

'So, like I was saying, in the end I had no choice. We

planned to do the search whilst the Frasers were away on their annual holiday in the Cayman Islands. You can imagine my horror when we walked in and there they were, home early because Laura's brother, Myles, had died suddenly. They'd only got back the night before, so I didn't know.'

Neil pointed towards Blair's sword arm. 'It wasn't you who killed Laura though, was it? Or Duncan and Ualas MacBean, come to that. You're right-handed.'

'Correct, Chief Inspector. Mungo went upstairs and found Laura in the bedroom. She laid into him with a golf club, then chased him into the great hall. That was where he stabbed her, with a dirk he'd taken with him. I didn't even know he had it. Duncan came out of the kitchen, so I restrained him. I didn't know what to do. Then Mungo appeared, covered in blood, and put a knife into him too. He stopped struggling, but wasn't dead, so we took him with us. Mungo wanted to interrogate him, you see.'

'And did he?'

'Aye, he did. Tortured the poor devil for hours. We took him to this old wooden cabin out in the back of beyond. I wanted nothing to do with it, so left him to it. There was no point me taking on McQuade. He would've killed me too. Anyway, the whole thing made me physically sick. Mungo came out eventually, wiping his hands on a towel. Said Duncan had refused to tell him anything, so he'd finished him off with a Lochaber axe, of all things. One that had been hanging on the wall of the cabin as an ornament.'

Blair was visibly disturbed, having recounted the story of the killings. He dropped to his haunches, the sword standing to his front, against which he leaned.

He tugged nervously at the plaid that draped over his shoulder. 'The following morning, on the anniversary of the battle, I was told to dress up in this garb and take Duncan's body out to the Well of the Dead and dump it.'

He looked up. 'What have I become? I sometimes think I'm going to wake up and it'll all have been just a bad dream.'

'So why all the Highland garb, then, Sandy?'

Neil knew why, but wanted *him* to explain the connection with Ualas MacBean.

Blair let out another long sigh. 'Mungo was in Peterhead Prison with this nutcase called Ualas MacBean. MacBean was obsessed with the Jacobites, Bonnie Prince Charlie and the like. His family were from Strathnairn, and coincidentally, he seemed to have a grudge against the Frasers' predecessors... MacGillivrays they were then. Anyway, MacBean was convinced that his ancestors had been let down at Culloden, because the MacGillivrays of Cullaird had not turned up for the battle. He'd also heard the story of the hoard, handed down through the generations of his family, and had always believed that the reason for the MacGillivrays' absence was their decision to line their pockets with the proceeds of this great hoard they'd stolen from somewhere. Anyway, when this laddie MacBean left prison, he rented a cabin in the forest and lived there like a hermit, whilst his brain became slowly addled by the strange concoctions he made from the heather... some sort of ancient mead he was making.'

Neil interrupted him. 'You mean the same cabin out in Culloden Forest to which you took Duncan Fraser?'

Blair's eyes narrowed when he heard Neil mention the location.

'Aye, that's the one. You found it, then.' He hesitated and took a deep breath. 'Well, Ualas lived there as an old Highlander would've done. He dressed like one, he collected old weapons and hung them on his walls, and he even roamed the forest talking to his dead ancestors. Weird guy, he was. Dawie and Mungo's plan from the outset was to fit him up for the break-in at the castle. But they had to extend that to the murders too, when everything started to go wrong. Ualas had a history of breaking into country houses, and even killed his own brother, so he was the perfect scapegoat! He was such a loner, you see. No one had any contact with him, not even his family. Of course I was so bloody naïve. I had no idea that Mungo and Dawie planned to dispose of him too, from the very beginning, even before the first break-in.'

'I know,' Neil confirmed. 'We found his body in a shed at the cabin a few hours ago.'

Blair looked surprised and then shook his head. 'Mungo was supposed to have burnt his remains earlier tonight, dispose of the poor wretch completely, so that he could forever remain the prime suspect, one that could never be found or brought to book!'

'McQuade obviously tried to set the shed alight, but the wood was damp, so the fire went out,' Neil explained.

'Not so clever then, was he?' Blair replied with a smirk. He then looked up at the hovering helicopter. 'You won't need him for much longer. The sky's getting lighter.'

The firearms sergeant looked across at Neil, as if in agreement. 'He's right. The chopper will need to refuel shortly, sir. We need to finish this soon.'

Neil glared at him. 'We need to keep talking. I don't want anyone hurt if I can avoid it. If the helicopter has to go, so be it. We can see Blair well enough now.'

The sergeant shrugged and turned his attention back to his target, whilst speaking into his mouthpiece and requesting that the helicopter remain on station for a few more minutes.

Neil called out, 'So, you were coerced by McQuade and Van Nieuwoudt to step into MacBean's shoes and dress like him, so when – or if –you were seen in the Highland garb by any witnesses, we would naturally assume it was him?'

'In a nutshell, yes. We were of similar height and build, I suppose, so I was the most suitable candidate.' He laughed.

'I even wore a wig of red hair and a blue bonnet when I took Duncan out onto the battlefield. They'd thought of everything!'

Neil folded his arms. 'So it seems. You certainly had us fooled for a while! When and where was Ualas killed, then?'

'Mungo arranged a meeting with Ualas back on the 5th of April, so that Dawie and I could be introduced to him. It was like he was being interviewed as a prospective partner in the whole affair. We met up in a clearing in the forest by another standing stone. Ualas called it "the Stone of the Massacre of the Officers". Anyway, Dawie was happy with what he saw, so we walked back to the Land Rover and left Mungo to do the deed. Needless to say, I had not the slightest clue that they'd planned such a thing! Mungo cut his throat with the same dirk he used on the Frasers. Then he stored him at the cabin, intending to burn the shed and everything else when we were done. Dawie wasn't happy about starting fires initially, in case we somehow drew attention to the site.'

Blair rose up stiffly and leaned on the sword again. 'When the first break-in went wrong, Mungo and Dawie wanted to try again. That's when Nathaniel and Selina caught me there. Mungo had gone off in the Land Rover, and luckily picked me up just in time. Before you ask, by the way, it was Mungo who attacked the policeman, not me.'

'That doesn't surprise me in the slightest,' Neil mused. 'So where's the Land Rover now then, Sandy?'

'I left it up a track behind the distillery. I took Selina there initially from the castle, then transferred her into the boot of my car. I changed clothes temporarily and went back to Cullaird in my own car. Miriam was expecting me to turn up like a knight in shining armour, so I didn't want to disappoint her. Fortunately your uniformed colleagues promptly sent me away. Said they had everything in hand. So I left them to it and made my way out to towards the cabin, to meet Mungo.'

The sergeant spoke again. 'The chopper's heading off, sir. The observer tells me they're now running on vapour.'

Neil nodded. He looked round to see Selina hunched up against Holly. She looked awful, and although she had Holly's jacket draped around her shoulders, she was still shivering. He knew the sergeant was right. They had to finish this soon and get Selina out of the forest. But he also knew that he needed to keep Blair talking... if there was any chance of procuring his surrender by peaceful means.

The Nitesun was switched off, plunging the forest back into its natural shadowy state. There was sufficient light to see clearly now, whilst the putty-like sky, visible above the treetops, heralded the long night's end. The helicopter finally banked away to the east, its navigation lights pulsing brightly against its blue underbelly. The silence that followed was strangely welcome, with only the frustrated whimpering of the German shepherd now audible over the hiss of the breeze.

Neil couldn't believe that Blair had had the temerity to take Selina back to the castle in the boot of his car! However, he didn't wish to dwell on that.

'You say you headed out to the cabin, Sandy. Did you ever get there?'

'No, as it happens... I drove around for a good while, trying to get my head straight.'

'Before you met Mungo out on the battlefield, is that right?'

'So you've been there too? You found the bastard, I take it?'

'Yes, we have, Sandy. Why did you kill him?'

Blair looked up wistfully, then refocussed on Neil. 'It was him who wanted to take Selina in the first place. Everyone else was happy to call it a day, even Dawie. Mungo roped me in with a promise that this was the last time we'd try to find that damned hoard. I had little option, to be fair. The threat of being outed still hung over me. I said I'd do it so long as no one got hurt, but he wanted to have a go at getting something out of her at the cabin. She'd managed to pull my mask off on the way to the distillery, so I knew it was all over for me. I only had two options, as I saw it. To kill her, or release her and accept the consequences. I called Mungo and told him that I wasn't taking her to the cabin, so that he could mutilate her like he'd done to her father. I made it clear that she was staying with me. He seemed to accept what I was saying. Said he would dispose of Ualas's remains at the cabin and then meet up with me. He wanted to discuss the situation, you see. So, stupidly, I agreed to meet and talk with him on open ground, at the well.'

'I gather it wasn't a friendly chat,' Neil surmised, straight-faced.

Blair shook his head in response. 'The conversation started off all right. I'd left Selina in the car whilst we talked. I'd become confused by then, you see. I didn't know what to do for the best. He insisted that we kill her once he'd questioned her, and then leave her out here. I suppose Mungo thought Ualas's remains would've been well and truly burnt by then, so it could all still be safely blamed onto him once again.'

He then digressed a little. 'Ualas loved this place, apparently. He'd told Mungo about the Clach an Airm whilst they were cellmates in prison; that he could sense the presence of his ancestors here. So for him it seemed to have great spiritual significance. Anyway, the plan I initially agreed to was to leave Selina here, but alive. It would serve the same purpose in terms of the link to Ualas, you see.'

'But everything changed when Selina pulled your mask off, right?'

'Aye, without a doubt. Like I said, I knew it would all be over then... if she lived, of course. Anyway, we argued, but he was adamant, so he pushed past me, intending to go and get

Selina and take her with him... out here, I presume. Then he would've killed her and all would be okay in his eyes.'

He shook his head, anger rising in him; anger directed at himself.

'I panicked. All I had with me was this damned sword, so I aimed high. I knew I'd kill him. That's what I wanted...'

His features crumpled as he struggled with the enormity of what he'd done. Then he spun around, responding to the sound of a branch snapping behind him. Two more black-clad firearms officers had taken up position twenty yards away, their Heckler & Koch carbines peeking out from behind the cover afforded by the trunks of the fir trees.

Blair turned back to face Neil. 'Looks like you've done me up like a kipper, Mr Strachan. I'm not going to walk away from here, am I?'

Neil took another step forward, ignoring the sergeant's concerned frown.

'Of course you are, Sandy. Just place the sword on the ground and walk slowly towards us. Do as my colleagues tell you and everything will be fine. Then we can walk out of here together and continue this conversation in more civilised surroundings. What do you say?'

Blair observed Neil protractedly, as if trying to weigh up the genuineness of his offer. Then, cautiously, he stooped and placed the broadsword on the ground, his eyes never straying from Neil's. He hesitated, before slowly standing upright and raising his hands as if in surrender. Neil relaxed a little, sensing that they were close to resolving the situation.

'Okay, Sandy, that's great. Just do as you're told, yes?'

Blair nodded, and the sergeant called out, 'Walk towards me Sandy, very slowly now. Keep those hands in the air. I'll tell you when to stop.'

Blair went to take a step. At the same time, Selina, who'd been sitting quietly with Holly behind the Clach an

565

Airm, suddenly broke free from the detective's embrace and appeared next to Neil in a flash. She stood, shaking visibly, her pallid cheeks streaked by tears.

'You disgraceful waste of bloody space, Sandy Blair,' she screamed. 'Do you know what you've fucking well done? You've destroyed my family, that's what you've done. *They* might be giving you a way out, but I won't. I'll haunt you for the rest of time, you evil, conniving bastard.'

Holly had restrained her by now, and was struggling to steer the distraught woman back behind the stone. The damage had been done, though. Blair stopped in his tracks, dropped down and picked up the sword, then gestured with it nervously.

'She's right, of course. There's no escape from what I've done. I brought her out here so that I could mull over my options. But, like I said, once she'd pulled that mask off, they were pretty much limited to killing her. I suppose that's what I would've done. Anything to protect my family from what is about to rain down upon them.'

The firearms officers sensed the change in his demeanour and tensed up. From behind the sights of his taser, the sergeant called out again. 'Don't be silly, Sandy. She's just upset. Now put the sword down.'

Blair laughed. 'Silly? Is that all I am? I don't think even my family would be as gracious as that. No, this nightmare ends here. Selina has made me see sense. It has to be, for Anne and the kids' sakes.'

The tension was now palpable, with all parties on edge.

'Jesus Christ, what is he going to do?' Neil realised that he was grinding his teeth and consciously tried to stop. The dog began to bark again, whilst the sound of Selina's sobs drifted up towards him above Holly's gentle, reassuring tones. He called out in desperation. 'Come on, Sandy. What can I do to persuade you to put that sword down?'

566

'Nothing,' Blair called back. 'Implication in four murders and a kidnapping... They'll throw away the key and sentence my family to a lifetime of shame. No, I can only ask that you assist me in my deliverance from this nightmare.'

He raised the sword threateningly above his head and began to advance steadily towards the police officers. His actions were met with a stream of frenzied warnings from the men aiming guns at him, but he marched on. The red dot once again quivered restlessly upon his plaided chest, whilst the desperate commands of 'Stop now' and 'Drop the sword' were repeated over and over. Blair looked down. He knew what the dot meant; to him it represented a source of relief from his incubus and so he continued undaunted. His eyes now flickered like those of a man walking upwind of a blizzard, as if anticipating the shots that would bring him down. But still he came, and at ten yards, the taser to Neil's left crackled as the two dart-like barbs launched towards their target. Neil could see the conductive wires shimmer as they rocketed across the once peaceful forest clearing, and he also saw them drop to the ground as the electrodes collided with the dense material of Blair's plaid and bounced off. Instead of delivering the expected powerful electric shock that would incapacitate most men, the taser had failed to provide the one non-fatal opportunity to stop Blair in his tracks. The sergeant had dropped the taser and had drawn his nine-millimetre Glock pistol. Blair ran forward, then let out a high-pitched cry, much the same as those charging Highlanders would've done as they approached the muskets of the redcoat line at Culloden. Neil knew what was coming and closed his eyes. Bang, bang, then a pause and then another double tap from the Glock. Blair crashed headlong onto the ground, a neat grouping of four smouldering black holes present upon the drab tartan plaid that draped across him.

The firearms men rushed forward to administer first aid.

Neil followed behind, knowing that there was no hope. The sergeant looked up, having checked Blair's inert body for signs of life. He shook his head. 'He's gone, I'm afraid.'

He got up and looked down at the corpse, visibly shaken. 'You hear of these instances of suicide by cop, but you never think you'd be in that situation some day!'

They all stood there in silence, gazing down at Blair's lifeless body. Even the police dog had sensed the finality of the situation and had fallen silent. But for the forest birds; the events of the previous hour meant absolutely nothing at all and so they sung like they always did, to herald the beginning of the new day.

Chapter Forty-Two

Miriam looked rather pale when they walked into the hospital room to inform her that Selina had been found safe and well. She sat up in bed, propped up against a stack of pillows, enjoying her first cup of tea of the day. Outside, a uniformed constable stood attentively, knowing that the SIO was sitting in the room behind him.

'Good morning, Miriam. How's the head?' Neil pulled up a chair for Holly and then one for himself.

'It's fine, Chief Inspector, just a scratch. I should've been back at Cullaird, awaiting news of Selina.'

'Well, there's good news on that score. We didn't want to wake you earlier. The staff nurse said you were well away.'

'They gave me a sleeping pill. First time in my life. Never again. Anyway tell me your news. I assume from both your demeanours she's okay?'

'Selina's fine. She's downstairs being assessed, but they're pretty sure she has no physical injuries other than the odd bruise.'

He offered Miriam, then Holly, a mint, before popping one into his own mouth. 'We found her at that place you told me about, out on the Gask Plantation. The Stone of the Swords.'

'Goodness, Chief Inspector, Sergeant Anderson thought that she may have been taken there! But she never really explained why.'

Neil patted the back of her hand. 'It's a bit of a long story. Suffice to say there were a few clues found at a woodsman's cabin that Ualas MacBean was using in Culloden Forest. It was a hunch, really.' He certainly wasn't going to admit how desperate and wild that hunch was! 'There is some other news too. It's going to come as a bit of a shock, I'm afraid. Her kidnapper was Sandy Blair. Unfortunately he's been shot by our firearms officers and didn't survive.'

Miriam raised a trembling hand to her mouth. 'Oh my God. Why?' were the only words she could utter.

Neil explained how he'd become indebted to Duncan Fraser, following the theft of the whisky, and how he'd then become involved with her ex-husband. Miriam sat in silence, wide-eyed and hanging onto his every word. When he eventually fell silent, she turned her head and looked out through the window onto the car park below.

'Words fail me. Sandy was so close to the family, and for so many years. They thought the world of him. How on earth could he have got involved with all this killing?'

Neil nodded. 'I know, but it just goes to show... relationships are not always what they seem.'

'You're most definitely right on that score, Chief Inspector. I had no idea that this... this terrible situation had arisen between him and Duncan. And then he goes and deliberately gets himself killed. How could he? Poor Anne and the children... and the grandchildren!'

Neil shrugged. 'You know what, I recall Ronnie Biggs, the great train robber, once said, "There's a difference between criminals and crooks. Crooks steal. Criminals blow some guy's brains out. I'm a crook." I think Sandy always saw himself as a crook. He could just about live with that. But this morning in the forest, well, Selina's words made him realise that maybe he'd crossed the line to being a criminal, and *that* he couldn't live with.'

Miriam sipped her tea. 'Why in heaven's name did he take her to that stone in the forest? She knew it was him by then, didn't she? There was no way he could just leave her there alive, was there?'

'It doesn't bear thinking about, Miriam. I have a feeling he still couldn't make his mind up as to what he should do. He had no idea we'd found and identified MacBean at that stage, so he still believed he had one option left... to kill her, so that we'd blame MacBean. But like I said, I'm inclined to think that he was struggling with the prospect of sacrificing Selina, even though to have done so would've possibly given him an out, and the prospect of a normal future with his family. He may even have got away with it, had we not discovered the cabin in the forest and MacBean's remains a little too early on. Of course, once we caught up with him and he knew that was the case, his options became limited to one: arrest, and a life behind bars.'

'Or to end things as he did. I cannot believe he was that ruthless.'

'That's exactly my point, Miriam. Perhaps he wasn't, and that's why things *did* end the way they did.'

'So what happens now, Chief Inspector?'

'We've got your ex-husband and Boyd Duff in custody. They will be interviewed over the next couple of days and then charges will be preferred against them.'

He got up and returned the chair to its original position under the window. 'We'll be over to Cullaird to get a statement from you in due course. DC Hughes will stay here with you, and will get you home when the doctors are happy to release you.'

'Thank you, Chief Inspector. I will of course remain here

until Selina is released too. Does Nat know she's been found?'

'Yes, of course. He was driving up overnight once he'd taken the kids to his sister's in Salisbury.'

At that point, the door opened and Selina walked in with Aili Hughes. She still had Holly's jacket wrapped around her shoulders, and looked wan and tired. On seeing her cousin though, her eyes lit up. 'Miriam, are you all right?'

She rushed across to the older woman and embraced her.

'Yes, yes, I'm fine, dear. It's you that I'm worried about.'

'They've discharged me. No physical scars, apparently.'

Selina looked across at Neil. 'I'm so sorry about my outburst in the forest earlier. I don't know what came over me. Fear and anger all at the same time, I suppose. I just boiled over. Now I have to take responsibility for Sandy's death. And you were just beginning to get through to him.'

Neil pulled up the chair he'd just vacated and gestured to Selina to sit down. 'Your reaction was understandable, Selina, taking account of what you've been through during the last month, not to mention last night! It's just one of those things, I'm afraid. Sandy Blair was the master of his own fate. It didn't need to be like that.'

Selina wiped away a tear. 'You know, the worst of it was… I had convinced myself it was someone else, not Sandy, who was responsible for all this.'

'Who?' Holly asked, intrigued.

'Rodaidh Morton, would you believe?' She laughed then. 'I know it's a terrible thing to admit. Part of me knew it could never have been him, I suppose. But the more I thought about it, the more I suspected him. He had access to a key; he dabbles in all that pagan stuff…'

'He'll tell you that Celtic knotwork is far removed from the earlier ogham form of symbolism,' Neil corrected her, not wishing to admit that he himself had considered the cleaner's husband a possible suspect at one stage. That was until a dozen or more trout fishermen had ruled him out on each occasion that the castle was broken into.

Selina didn't wish to expound her theory any further. 'Yes, it was silly of me. I was thinking irrationally at the time.'

She patted Miriam's hand. 'Nat's on his way here from Cullaird. He'll take us home when you're allowed to go.'

'I just need to see the doctor and then we should be on our way, dear. They only kept me in because they thought I might have concussion.'

Neil winked at Holly, then made for the door. 'We'll drop by and discuss statements later on, if that's okay?'

Selina smiled and sighed. 'That's fine. I feel safe now for the first time in a month. Believe me, it's a great sensation, so the paperwork doesn't worry me at all. Best get it over and done with.'

She removed the jacket and handed it back to Holly.

'No, please keep it,' Holly insisted with characteristic blitheness.

'No, it's fine, really. Nat's bringing me one and it's a little hot in here. Thanks all the same.'

Having taken their leave, Neil and Holly strolled down the corridor to the lifts. 'Selina seems to be coping better than I thought,' Holly observed.

Neil held the lift door open for her. 'She's probably still running on adrenalin. When everything settles down, it'll probably hit her big time.'

'Aye, and you must be still running on adrenalin too, after the night you've had?'

Neil grinned. 'Nothing a shower and a cooked breakfast won't put right! Look, I'm going to give Cat a call. I'll see you at the car.'

They parted company in reception. Neil called Cat and updated her briefly on the night's events. She'd just got out of bed, but immediately sensed the languor in his voice.

'Can't you go home and get your head down for a few hours?' she enquired solicitously.

He laughed. 'I wish I could, but we've got two people in custody, several crime scenes to manage, and a host of other things to do. No, I'll be fine. Just wanted to let you know what had happened.'

'I'll be home with Tam later this morning. Is that okay with you?'

'Oh, I think so. I'm looking forward to a little bit of normality, if I'm honest.'

'Oh, so am I,' Cat agreed, her voice weighted with a sense of longing. 'So you get off and do what you've got to do, and I'll see you tonight sometime... Love you.'

Neil stepped out into the fresh air, a gratifying smile now fixed firmly upon his tired features. He returned the phone to his pocket and followed the walkway out to the car park. When he eventually opened the car door, he found his sergeant fast asleep in the passenger seat, her head slumped against the window. He had no intention of disturbing her and eased himself quietly into the driver's seat beside her.

Angus Hardie was waiting patiently in his office when Neil threw open the door and walked in.

'Oh, morning, sir. Wasn't expecting to see you here.'

'Ah well, there you go, Neil. I can still muster some of my old staying power when I need to!' He smiled. 'I'm hardly going to just disappear after a night like that, am I?'

He got up and opened the door. 'Let's go and get a coffee. Then you can bring me up to speed on things. There's also something else I want to discuss with you.'

They stood in the small kitchen at the end of the corridor. Hardie insisted on making the coffee, whilst Neil briefed him on the latest developments in the Cullaird case.

'You've done a great job, Neil. Thanks a lot. I have to say, I was more than a little sceptical about this Stone of the Swords place. It seemed a hell of a long shot, rushing off down there and exploring a forest that size in the dark!'

'Aye, it was certainly a long shot, I have to admit that. Holly just had a hunch when she saw the painting in the cabin, and then found some paperwork also relating to the Clach an Airm. She was rightly of the opinion that whoever abducted Selina Cope may have believed that they'd covered their tracks by burning MacBean's remains. So he could still be set up as the fall guy. Hence the intention to dump her at one of MacBean's favourite locations. What better place to hide a hostage, anyway? In normal circumstances we'd never have gone there in a month of Sundays.'

'Well, it was a good call as SIO, whatever the case, and full marks to young Holly too.' Hardie handed a mug to Neil.

'Credit where credit's due. It was all down to her,' said Neil. 'I wasn't convinced we should go out there either.'

'Aye, but all credit to you, you did! I must seek Holly out, though, and congratulate her.' Hardie stirred his coffee and dropped the spoon in the sink. 'I've arranged for Van Nieuwoudt to be brought up here ASAP. He should be leaving Glasgow before midday. DI Gemmell tells me he's keeping strictly to the "no comment" routine. In the meantime, I suggest you get off for an hour or two and grab yourself something to eat. I'm sure you and Holly will want to have a crack at him when he arrives!'

'Aye, of course, sir. That goes without saying.'

Hardie cradled his mug against his chest. 'The chief's asked me to pass on his thanks. I think he's somewhat relieved to know that this trail of carnage has at last come to an end. Shame that Blair embarked upon the course of action he did. But, from what you say, he was most candid with his admissions before he did so.'

'He was, sir. Luckily Holly had the presence of mind to record the conversation on her mobile phone. The recording comes across as a little distant, but will no doubt be of assistance.'

'Good. Any further support needed, just let me know. I'll be around. The ACC's coming in at 10.30 to discuss the fatal shooting enquiry.' He then leaned back against the wall. 'Now then, on to other things.'

Neil felt his chest tighten. Where was this going?

'Oh, right, sir. Is this about Lorna McKirdy and the two uniformed officers?'

Hardie smiled at him, putting him at ease. 'Not at all. I'm hoping I can leave the disciplinary issues relevant to their indiscretions to you and your uniformed counterpart in the operations department.'

'Yes, of course. I was hoping you'd say that.'

'Just don't be too lenient with them, Neil. The implications of their actions could well have been catastrophic!'

'I know, sir. You can rest assured I will be anything but lenient!'

'Good! Now, as I was saying, on to other matters. I was going to mention this on Friday, but things were getting a little hectic by then, so I decided to leave it. Alex Brodie will shortly be signed off to return to work on light duties. The thing is, he's intimated to me that he has an interest in taking up the vacancy as head of the Professional Standards Department when it comes up shortly. Between you and me, I think this heart attack has scared him a little, forced him to reassess his work-life balance. The PSD role will be a little less pressured. More regular hours, weekends off, etc.... which will leave me with a DCI vacancy to fill. The chief and I were wondering whether you'd be interested in taking on the role permanently.'

He observed Neil closely, awaiting a reaction.

'Err, well that's very kind of you to think of me, sir. Will the role not be advertised?'

'Trust me, Neil. I've been doing my homework. It's a matter of who is qualified and available. The general consensus is that I'm looking at the best candidate!'

'I see. In that case…'

'No need to make any decisions just yet. It's merely a heads-up, that's all. More important things to attend to right now.'

Hardie washed his cup and placed it back in the wall cupboard. 'Have a think about it and let me know, eh? Nothing will happen for at least a couple of weeks.'

He squeezed Neil's arm, then left him pondering over the surprise offer and marched off down the corridor, whistling.

By eleven o'clock, Neil had been home and showered, cooked himself a breakfast, the size of which would've made Cat cringe, and was now back behind the wheel of the Ford Focus CID car, heading down the B851 towards Cullaird.

Holly sat beside him, now refreshed from what she had described as a power nap, albeit a two-hour one!

'I could've taken this statement from Selina,' she protested. 'Surely you've got better things to do?'

'Not really. The escort for Van Nieuwoudt has only just left. It seems the custody officer down there was adamant he needed to get his full period of rest before travelling. Anyway, I personally want to hear Selina's account of what happened. Not that I'm saying you'd miss anything out from the statement.'

'That's reassuring,' Holly muttered, almost to herself.

When they pulled up outside the castle, Nathaniel Cope emerged from the doorway and walked purposefully out to meet them. He shook hands firmly with both officers.

'Thank you both so much for what you've done. I can't tell you what it was like driving up here last night, not knowing what had happened to Selina.'

'I can imagine,' said Neil. 'Thank God it's all over now. How is she doing?'

'She's okay, just relieved to be home and in one piece.'

'Is she still happy to speak to us so soon?'

'Oh yes, of course. Best get it all recorded whilst it's fresh in her mind.'

Minutes later they were settling down in the great hall, clustered around a coffee table, upon which sat the usual tray with mugs and a plate of biscuits.

Selina sat on the sofa, her legs curled up beneath her. She still looked tired, but a bath and change of clothes had certainly had the desired effect, much as it had for Neil. Miriam sat next to her, holding her hand firmly.

Holly rested a garish pink clipboard on her lap. 'If we could just go through the events of last night, so that I can take some notes… Then we'll get onto the statement proper.'

Selina took a deep breath and then began to recount the events of the previous evening. She explained how she'd seen Blair behind her in the hallway, wearing the Highland garb and the menacing black ski mask, how he'd manhandled her to the Land Rover and then driven to the yard behind the Lochmhor Distillery. Then she'd recounted how, on the way, she'd pulled off his mask and the shock and anger that had been present on his face.

'I thought he was going to kill me there and then,' she stammered, the recollection not surprisingly evoking all sorts of emotions.

But fortunately, he'd settled down, as if now resigned to his fate, and had warned her to do as she was told, in which case she wouldn't be harmed. Blair had transferred her from the Land Rover to the boot of his car. After that, all she'd remembered was blackness, and the motion of the vehicle as she was driven about during the period immediately after her incarceration.

She then told them how she remembered hearing the sound of the gravel when the car was driven up to the castle.

'I thought we'd returned to the castle,' she remarked. 'I'd recognise that sound anywhere. Then I heard distant voices, so I tried to make a noise and attract someone's attention, but the bastard had taped my mouth.'

Holly leaned forward to pick up her coffee mug. 'I can't believe he actually took you with him when he returned to the castle to speak to the police! He told us he'd changed his clothes too, and then back again afterwards. Incredible!'

Neil looked across at Holly. 'I wonder why he took such a risk.'

'I think it was because he'd arranged to meet his "friend", as he called him, and time was marching on,' Selina explained. 'He needed to show his face at Cullaird, or questions would most certainly have been asked.'

'So when was the next time you were allowed out of the boot, then?' Holly asked, furiously scribbling on her pad.

'It was out by the Clach an Airm. I remember him driving down an uneven track and secreting the car near a boat shed next to a small loch. He got me out and removed the tape from my mouth. I asked where we were, but he told me it wasn't important. Have you found his car, by the way?'

Neil nodded. 'Aye, we have. It was parked down at the very end of an access track to Loch Caulan. Funnily enough, two of my officers had driven down that track, but didn't go right to the end initially. The Land Rover has also been found, in the forestry plantation behind the distillery. We already knew it had false number plates on it, but it now transpires the vehicle itself had been stolen, from a Forestry Commission compound down by Loch Lomond. No doubt Mungo McQuade was responsible for that!'

'Can you carry on with your account now?' Holly asked, not wishing to digress.

Selina massaged her temples. 'There's not much more to tell. Sandy sat me down against the stone. Told me how lucky I'd been because his friend would've really hurt me, and would probably have ended up killing me. He asked me whether I knew anything about the so-called hoard of coins. I told him I didn't even believe there was one, but certainly had no idea of its location if it did exist. He seemed relieved in a way... when I confirmed that. Then he said he needed to clear his head. He had decisions to make. I asked him what he meant by "decisions". He just said, "How we end this."

'I was really scared then. I asked him to release me and promised that I'd keep my mouth shut about everything. But he just laughed. He told me he'd known me long enough to realise that that was never going to happen! Then I recall asking him whether he planned to kill me. He seemed to think that one of us was going to have to die that night. He just hadn't decided which one at that stage. He suggested that this could all have been avoided if I hadn't pulled his mask off. Then he told me to stay exactly where I was and he went off into the trees. He was gone for ages. The next thing I remember is the torch beams and you guys arriving.'

She began to sniff back the tears, prompting Nathaniel to join her on the sofa. She rested her head upon the arm he had wrapped around her.

'Seeing those torch beams was probably the best moment in my life... after marrying you of course, darling.'

He smiled back at her and her sobbing morphed into a spluttered laugh.

'Did Sandy—' Holly stopped in mid sentence, because Neil had begun asking a question at exactly the same moment. She glared at him, and he raised a conciliatory palm, remembering that the art of delegation was a management tool he still needed to work on. Nevertheless he continued to speak… because he was the boss!

'I was just going to say… did Sandy at any time talk about his rift with your father? Before we arrived on the scene, I mean?'

'No, never. It was only when he came out with it to you that I became aware of it. Up until then, I merely thought he had conspired with his friend to try and locate the hoard, and had killed my parents in the process. The fact that he'd been a welcome guest in our family home for so many years, but was ripping my father off behind his back, just got to me.'

'Okay, Selina. I'm going to let Holly get on with your statement without butting in again. Mustn't upset my staff, if I know what's good for me! Do you mind if I take myself off and have a wander around the grounds? I could do with some fresh air if I'm honest.'

Selina smiled at him. It was a smile that communicated how grateful she was, but without having uttered a word. 'That's fine. Be my guest.'

Neil got up, prompting a similar response from Holly.

'See you later, then,' he murmured, and made his way out to the stairwell.

Chapter Forty-Three

The breeze had stiffened to near gale-force since they had arrived at Cullaird. The upper branches of the trees that stood on the small knoll to the east of the castle swayed and creaked, prompting Neil to stop and look up. The words of Meg McGillivray, in her letter to her son, echoed around his head again and again... *look not to the cat of our people, but to that of our Chattan brothers, now unseen by those in its proximity.*

He walked on, through an iron gate and along a grassy path that ran down to the fast-flowing burn that drained into nearby Loch Ruthven. There he found an old wooden garden seat, and, thankful for the opportunity to enjoy the surroundings, he sat down and allowed his eyes to close. The words of the old letter still filled his head, slowly fading away until unconsciousness enveloped him.

He woke with a start and checked his watch, thinking he'd merely dozed off for a few seconds. But to his astonishment, he discovered that he'd been asleep for more than forty minutes! Jumping up, he hastily retraced his steps back towards the castle. It wasn't long before he was repeating Meg's words once again, over and over, trying to make sense of the age-old clue. Was she referring to something inscribed on the castle walls? Some inscription that had eroded with age?

He doubled back and made his way slowly around the base of the building, running his hand thoughtfully over the undulations in the uneven stonework. At a point halfway along each elevation, he stood back and gazed upward, seeking any man-made blemish, inscription or mark that might fit the bill. But there was none present, nothing at all. Then of course there was the other part of the clue... *heed too the place where flames do seldom burn*. Surely that would indicate the location was somewhere inside the castle: a disused fireplace, perhaps.

They've even got me obsessed with this bloody myth now, he cogitated as he turned around and admired the view back towards the shadowy slopes of Stac Na Cathaig.

The castle was surrounded by beautifully manicured lawns that ran down to recently renovated dry stone walls. These rugged, traditionally built structures marked the outermost boundary of the property, forming a rough square.

Neil wandered down to the north-east corner of the wall, to where it angled away at roughly ninety degrees. He rested his back against the stones and peeled off the wrapper from a strip of chewing gum. Fatigue had begun to wash over him again, so he closed his eyes, allowing the north-easterly wind to cool their tired lids. Enjoying the moment, his mind strayed from the conundrum he'd been obsessing over. He slipped the mint-flavoured confection into his mouth and began to chew. Then suddenly, they were wide open again, frantically searching for the pockets of his jacket. He pulled the crumpled photocopy of Meg's old letter out of one of them and ran his eyes over the italicised script. There it was. He thought he'd seen it when he first read the letter the previous evening, but he'd been too busy to realise its significance then. It was the word 'sacred' that had flashed into his mind. Surely a word like that could only have been used to refer to a place worthy of religious veneration. Why else would anyone use it?

Letter in hand, he marched across the sloping lawn and around to the front door. Once inside he turned left and headed for the chapel. The tiny place of worship seemed more like a tunnel than a conventional space, in which its low, vaulted ceiling merged seamlessly with its vertical walls. At one end, behind the small altar, was an alcove, into which a long, narrow window was inserted. Its translucent glass was the only source of natural daylight in this smallest of holy places. Close to the altar were two rows of antiquated, dark wood pews, and behind them an oak chest, similar to the one that had harboured Meg MacGillivray's long-lost letter. Resting on the chest's deeply scored top was a vase containing fresh white flowers, either side of which were photographs of Laura and Duncan Fraser.

Neil stepped forward and sat quietly at the end of one of the old pews. He looked down at the flagstones beneath his feet, then leaned out over the elaborately carved pew end, examining the floor around him. The flags looked as solid as a rock; heavy grey slabs that had been cemented firmly in place, who knows when. Frustratingly, there were no signs of any disturbance to the flooring, nothing at all.

He read the letter again, not knowing why exactly, because he'd consigned the words to memory by now. *Heed too, the place where flames do seldom burn…* He gazed up at the ceiling, smooth-plastered and shiny in the dim light. Then he scanned the walls for anything unusual. Other than two small candleholders shaped like thistles, mounted either side of the altar, there was very little else on the walls to speak of. To his left was a small hanging tapestry depicting what appeared to be a scene from a centuries-old religious service somewhere in the Highlands. Then it dawned upon him that the location portrayed was the very same chapel in which he was sitting, with its low, arched roof and narrow window at one end.

Several women, dressed in long, flowing tartan skirts, and with shawls wrapped about their shoulders, were clustered around the altar. An elderly priest, white-haired and severe-looking, was presiding over the sacred drama of the Eucharistic liturgy. It was a gloomy affair, illuminated only by the two candles that flickered upon the altar top.

Neil got up and moved closer to the tapestry, so that he could study it in more detail. He marvelled at the intricate needlework, especially the reds and oranges that made up the swirling candle flames... *flames*... That was it... of course! It had come to him at last. He looked back at the small altar that stood several feet behind him. Its top was decorated with a simple wooden Celtic cross and two sallow-coloured candles set into heavy silver holders. The burnt wax from the candles had fully solidified; long, hardened runs of the stuff, that now clung to their smooth white shafts. They were symbolic ornaments, no doubt rarely utilised... candles from which *flames seldom burnt!*

Keen to temper his excitement, he crouched down before the altar and lifted the embroidered white cloth that adorned its heavy oak carcass. The table beneath was a sturdy structure that was generations old and bore the many blemishes of time. He pushed against it with all his might, until it began to edge backwards, squealing as it slid over the undulations in the giant flagstones. Directly beneath the spot on which it had been standing, he discovered a smaller stone with a small iron ring set into its upper face. More importantly, it was loosely set into the floor, not cemented like the others.

Neil took hold of the ring and pulled with all his strength. The slab slowly rose up out of the floor, only to reveal another one underneath.

'Damn!' Neil murmured, as he eased the top stone up onto its side. To his dismay, he realised that the underlying slab was firmly cemented into place. But then his mood changed. He could see the whole extent of the lower slab now. He ran his hand over it and detected an unevenness at its centre, ridges buried in years of dust. He brushed away the detritus to reveal a faintly discernable engraving, badly worn, but mercifully still just visible. It was a representation of a cat, crouching within a sprig of leaves or something similar. Beneath it, although badly eroded, was a partially readable inscription that Neil had no trouble interpreting… *Touch not the catt bot a glove*. It was the Clan Chattan motto, the one referred to in Meg MacGillivray's letter… *look not to the cat of our people, but to that of our Chattan brothers, unseen by those in its proximity.*

Neil eased the top flag back into place, then rose stiffly to his feet and stood back, wiping the dust from his hands and gazing down euphorically.

'Bingo!' he declared in self-celebration. But then it occurred to him that the lower slab, the one that would provide access to any subterranean vault, was far too small to get anything large or heavy through it. A human could just about squeeze through, yes. But chests or large sacks of money… no way!

Selina was reading over her statement when he marched purposefully into the great hall. Miriam looked over her shoulder at him. 'Goodness, my dear, you've been a while. And, if I'm not mistaken, you also look like the cat that's just got to the cream!'

Neil smiled. 'I may just have,' he replied as he settled into one of the armchairs.

'Are you happy with the statement, Selina?' Holly ignored him, keen to stick to the matters at hand.

'Yes, I think that's covered everything succinctly,' she said. 'Where do I sign?'

'Under the declaration and at the end of each page,' said Holly, offering her a pen.

Once the document had been endorsed and safely inserted into Holly's folder, Neil deemed it safe to speak.

'I've just been looking in the chapel, at the tapestry on the wall… the one depicting the priest offering the women Communion. Is it a portrayal of an event that took place in that very chapel, do you know?'

'Yes, it is,' Miriam retorted. 'The picture features one of our ancestors, Lady Agnes MacGillivray of Cullaird. She's the woman taking Communion from the local priest, a man called Thomas MacPhail. The story goes, according to my father, that sometime during the mid 1600s, the castle was besieged by the Clan Cameron, whose lands were over to the west in Lochaber. There had been a long-standing feud between our two families, one that had existed for around 300 years. Anyway, Agnes's husband, Alexander, hid all the women and children of the family in a vault under the chapel floor until the danger had passed. The siege went on for three weeks, until other men from the Clan Chattan federation arrived and sent the Camerons packing. But, during that time, the only occasions on which the women came up from their shelter was for Communion on a Sunday.'

'I see,' said Neil. 'I believe I've located the entrance to that chamber, under the altar.'

Miriam looked a little surprised. 'You mean the loose slab with the ring in it?'

'Aye, that's the one. There's another slab beneath it, but that's well and truly cemented in.'

'That's right. Selina's grandfather, Alisdair, had that done back in the seventies.'

Selina now interjected. 'Before you get too excited, Chief Inspector, I think we should explain that the chamber beneath the chapel was thoroughly checked out by surveyors back then, because my grandfather, bless him, was worried that the chapel floor was unsafe and would cave in at any time. Why, I cannot fathom, because it had been there for centuries, hewn out of solid rock.' She paused for a second before continuing. 'We told your Sergeant Armsley all about the chamber when he was searching the chapel. He seemed happy at the time, especially when he knew it had been checked out only forty years ago and the entrance had been cemented in.'

Miriam picked up on the story. 'I would tend to use the expression "chamber" rather loosely, because it was in fact part of a passageway that ran underground to a point approximately one hundred yards beyond the walls of the castle. It wasn't entirely uncommon in those days to have secret chambers and escape routes, especially when your neighbours were so intent upon attacking your home!'

'So *was* it unsafe, then? The passageway, I mean,' Neil asked.

Selina shrugged. 'I believe my grandfather was advised to seal up the entrance, just to be on the safe side. Sorry to disappoint you, but I think we would've known if they'd found the so-called hoard down there whilst they were checking the place out.'

'Did the surveyors examine the entire passageway, then?' Neil wasn't giving up.

Now Selina was grinning, amused by his doggedness. 'Don't quote me on this, but I recall they went back along the tunnel until they came across a point where it was already bricked up. It must've been our Victorian ancestors who were responsible for that. Apparently there had been a significant collapse beyond that point down towards its exit. Of course that was some way out from the castle walls, so didn't fall within the scope of their survey.'

Neil frowned. 'Do you, by any chance, have any idea where the passageway came up in the grounds?'

Miriam was also intrigued by his persistence. 'I could show you. There's a flattish-shaped stone in the field beyond the boundary wall to mark the entrance. It looks more like a naturally deposited glacial boulder than one manually positioned there. No one's had the stone up or been down the passage from that end for well over a hundred years. I was told you can only get a few yards until you come up against a wall of stone and earth.'

'So why didn't Agnes and her family escape through the passage and get away when the Camerons attacked the castle all those years before?' Holly's curiosity had also been aroused by now.

'Because they would've popped up right in the middle of the Camerons' encampment,' said Miriam, smiling. 'They were effectively trapped inside the walls of the castle!'

Holly shook her head. 'They were that close? The Camerons, I mean.'

'According to the story that's been handed down, yes,' Miriam confirmed.

'Seems there's no end to the romantic tales connected to this place!' Holly concluded.

'Oh, we've got it all here,' said Selina, grinning. 'Secret passageways, spying chambers, ghosts… you name it!'

Ten minutes later, and the little group were clustered around a large flat slab that lay in the field behind the castle. It was much larger than the flagstone that had covered the passageway entrance in the chapel. Neil and Nathaniel attempted to move it, but their efforts met with little success.

Neil wiped the dirt from his hands. 'You say no one's been down there for more than a century, Miriam? How many years would "more than a century" mean, exactly? Any idea?'

Miriam pursed her lips whilst she thought about the question. 'I don't really know. It may even be longer… possibly not since the early 1800s. There's been no reason to. Especially when you can only progress a few yards.'

Neil rested his foot on the stone and looked at Selina enquiringly. 'Would you be averse to some sort of archaeological survey being carried out of the passageway at some stage? From both ends, I mean. I know Steve Armsley was made aware of the chamber during the search, but he hadn't seen the clues in Meg MacGillivray's letter back then. On reflection, I really do believe this passageway is worthy of further examination.'

Selina and Miriam looked at each other. 'Of course. The letter changes everything, and what a fascinating document it is! This all sounds rather exciting,' said Nathaniel, adjusting the angle of his tweed cap so as to shade his eyes from the sun.

'Well, I'm okay with it, but it might be a little hazardous,' said Selina. 'And as long as you don't expect *me* to go down there! Like I said, I really don't think you will find anything.'

Neil nodded. 'You may very well be right, but the clues in the letter do possibly suggest a connection with the tunnel. It's surely worth a look?'

'I agree,' said Miriam. 'Let's face it: we don't *really* know what's down there, do we? Particularly beyond that bricked-up section.'

'Who would be able to do such a survey… safely, I mean?' Selina asked.

Neil seemed relieved that she was supportive of the idea.

'I'd have to make some enquiries, but I know a man who could possibly help us.'

'In that case, I'll leave it to you then, I suppose Nat's right. It *would* be quite exciting. A bit like something out of an old Enid Blyton novel!'

'You don't really think that the hoard is still down in that tunnel?' Holly asked incredulously. They were back in the car, speeding along the B851 towards Inverness.

'Not in the section of the tunnel that runs out from beneath the chapel, no. The surveyors in the 1970s would've located it, without a doubt. I'm more interested in the section beyond the point where the tunnel is bricked up, down towards the roof fall. No one seems to know much about that section.'

'But wouldn't the men who did the bricking up all those years ago have recovered anything worth taking, before they sealed it up once and for all?'

'Well, we'll soon find out, won't we?'

'Sorry, sir, I think you're barking up the wrong tree here!' said Holly.

'Just indulge me,' Neil replied, beaming.

Dawie Van Nieuwoudt and his escort had just left Glasgow when Neil and Holly arrived back at police headquarters. Boyd Duff was now consulting with his solicitor, so any further interviews were some way off.

The two detectives had taken the opportunity to visit the canteen and grab some lunch. Neil finished his sandwich quickly and called Cat. She had now arrived home, and he'd wanted to inform her that Ciaran Lusk had been charged with assault and stalking and would appear at the Sheriff Court on the following Monday.

'What's likely to happen to him?' Cat had asked.

'Depends,' Neil replied. 'He doesn't have much of a criminal history, but in the circumstances, he's looking at some well-earned time behind bars. That's for sure!'

'Well, that's something, at least. Now, when can I expect you home tonight?'

'It's hard to say. We've got some interviews to do. I could be late, I'm afraid.'

'Looks like I'll be cooking for one, then. Still, at least it's all drawing to a close now,' said Cat with a sigh.

'Aye, I've just one thing left to do, once the policing bit is done.'

'What's that?'

'I need to find out what happened to that hoard of coins I told you about.'

Cat laughed. 'And you think *you* can achieve what generations of Frasers couldn't? Is it really your problem, anyway?' She paused for a second. 'Silly question, I suppose. That's the biggest challenge of all as far as you're concerned, isn't it? Locating the proceeds of a 300-year-old robbery!'

Neil ignored her little jibe. 'The thing is, we could be quite close to finding something.' He went on to tell her about the passageway under the castle and the link to the tiny chapel.

'Surely you don't think it's still there? Half the population of Strathnairn's probably been through that tunnel at some stage, if what the Copes say is correct.'

'Got to give it a go, Cat. Otherwise we'll never know, will we?'

'Well, I wish you good luck. I only hope no one gets hurt down in that tunnel whilst engaged on some wild goose chase!'

Neil frowned. 'Look, I've got to go. I'll call you later.'

He frowned as he placed the handset back on its cradle. 'Wild goose chase, indeed.'

His next call was to the Culloden Battlefield visitor centre. Malcolm Breckenridge was not available, but the pleasant young lady who answered the phone helpfully passed on his mobile phone number. Neil tapped it out impatiently and listened for the ringtone. Instead of a response from Breckenridge himself, he got an answerphone message.

'Malcolm here. Sorry, I'm a bit tied up at present. Leave your number and I'll get back to you soonest. Bye.'

'Bugger. Where is he when you need him?' He cleared his throat, then spoke after the bleep.

'Dr Breckenridge... Neil Strachan here. I need to discuss the hoard of coins we spoke about. There's been a development down at Cullaird, and I'll need your help...'

Neil had hardly put the handset down and taken a bite from the sandwich Holly had just delivered to him, when the phone burbled in response.

'Hello, Chief Inspector. It's Malcolm Breckenridge. Sorry I couldn't answer. Just paying for some plants at the garden centre. How can I help you?'

Neil explained to the archaeologist what he'd learnt that morning at Cullaird Castle.

'The thing is, I've got the go ahead to open up that tunnel. It could be a one-off opportunity that might provide a clue to where the hoard was hidden. I'm not at all sure what else we may find down there, and it could be a bit hazardous!'

'Leave that side of things to me, Chief Inspector. I can think of a few members of my team back at Glasgow who'd relish the thought of exploring an old passageway like that. I also have colleagues down at the National Museum of Scotland who may be interested. Especially if there's the slightest chance of finding something of that significance!'

'Good. If you can get back to me with a date, I'll inform the Copes.'

'Sounds like a plan, Chief Inspector.'

'Look, *Neil* will do. Less of a mouthful! I'll let you get back to your plants, then!'

'Okay, speak soon then... Neil!'

Holly peeled back the top slice of bread from her sandwich and examined its meagre filling.

'I don't think they've heard of the term "value for money" down in that canteen.' She looked up. 'I hope you know what you're doing, sir. Could be a little embarrassing if all they find down there is rat droppings!'

'I have broad shoulders,' Neil reassured her. 'And

archaeologists are used to disappointment, you know. They experience it all the time!'

Holly sat back and screwed up the serviette she'd been using. 'You know, Miriam told me an interesting thing whilst you were playing Indiana Jones down in that chapel. Apparently Dawie Van Nieuwoudt visited Cullaird regularly, early on during their marriage. He knew about the story of the hoard back then and seemed intrigued by the prospect of there being a stash of coins hidden somewhere in the castle. She was saying that he often wandered around the place searching for some clue or researching the family archives. She also confirmed that he'd seen the two coins that Nathaniel Cope showed us and had been very interested in them. The funny thing was, Selina then said that *she'd* mentioned the hoard to him when he'd first arrived out of the blue, but he'd not alluded to having any knowledge of it... strange, that! Of course, Selina wouldn't have known that he had knowledge of the story. She was less than six years old when he first started visiting the castle. Interestingly enough, Miriam wasn't present during that conversation the other day, so couldn't challenge him on it.'

Neil tossed the sandwich wrapper into the wastepaper bin. 'It's frustrating how everything falls into place when you start to revisit earlier events. Shame we can't see into the future sometimes.'

'Aye, true enough,' Holly replied. 'I also asked Miriam about Van Nieuwoudt's relationship with the Frasers, you know, before they split up.'

'And?'

'And it was amicable enough. But Dawie fell out with Farquhar, Miriam's father, sometime prior to their divorce, after a very public family row about his gambling and philandering. He was told to leave by Alisdair, her uncle, from a Christmas party at the castle in 1984. According to her, he never returned. Farquhar's lawyers dealt with the divorce proceedings a year later, in 1985.'

'Got all that in statement form?'

'Aye, Aili's sorting it.'

DC Findlay appeared in the doorway of the canteen. When he spotted his boss sitting by the window, he made his way over and pulled up a chair.

'Van Nieuwoudt's arrived at the custody suite, sur. He's speaking with his brief.'

Neil picked up his paperwork. 'Good. We'll make our way over there, then, and let battle commence!'

Chapter Forty-Four

Malcolm Breckenridge had already arrived when Neil and Holly drove through the stone-pillared gateway to the old keep. He was standing with a group of men by the main doorway, talking to Selina and Nathaniel.

'Jeez, they've certainly come prepared,' Holly remarked, eyeing up the little band of hard-hatted archaeologists clustered around the Copes. 'They look more like a cave rescue team than a bunch of academics.'

Breckenridge marched across to them as they climbed out of the car.

'Good to see you again, Chief Inspector... I mean *Neil.*'

Neil shook his hand and looked up towards the large grey clouds that were lumbering like giant, shapeless fleeces across the otherwise blue sky.

'I don't think it's going to stay fine for long,' he commented.

'Well it won't affect us, not where we're going,' said Breckenridge cheerfully. 'Come and meet my colleagues.'

Neil exchanged pleasantries with Selina and Nathaniel before being introduced to the men in the hard hats. He passed from one to another, like a celebrity being introduced to opposing soccer teams just before the cup final. Breckenridge was eager to get on, so at least the pleasantries were expedited to some extent!

'This is Doctor Jeff Barber and his colleague Doctor Trevor Parry from the Battlefield Archaeology faculty at Glasgow. Paul and Daniel here are postgraduate students at the centre. They're always happy to climb into the smallest holes in the furtherance of historical research.'

'We'll send them down the tunnel first, then,' Barber joked. 'Postgrads are always expendable!'

Breckenridge moved onto the last two, more distinguished-looking men, standing apart from the group.

'And this is Professor Ray Lomas and Doctor Andy Sturrock from the National Museum of Scotland, down in Edinburgh.'

'Pleased to meet you,' said Neil, shaking each of their hands in turn. 'I hope I haven't got you up here on a wild goose chase.' (Cat's words immediately came to mind!)

'Don't worry, Neil. The negative experiences make the successes all the more satisfying,' Lomas reassured him.

Neil then felt a tap on the shoulder. He swung about to find Breckenridge offering him a set of grey overalls and a hard hat with a lamp attachment.

'I take it you'll be joining us down in the bowels of this magnificent structure?' he asked.

Neil took the items from him. 'Thanks. I'd be delighted,' he replied.

'Good. What about your colleague here? Would she like to accompany us too?'

Holly gestured towards the overalls. 'Not my colour, I'm afraid. I think I'll stay up here where the air's sweeter and the coffee's hotter. Thanks all the same.'

'I'll come down with you,' said Nathaniel. 'As family representative, so to speak.'

'Of course. Glad to have another pair of hands,' said Breckenridge. 'Wait here. I'll get you some kit.'

Once Neil and Nathaniel had climbed into their overalls, fitted knee and elbow pads and donned their hard hats, the group split up. Barber, Lomas and the postgrads headed out to the field behind the castle, and the external exit to the passageway. Those remaining followed Nathaniel into the building and down the hallway to the chapel. Barber and Breckenridge both carried two-way radios, the latter's crackling into life whilst they edged the altar table back away from the entrance to the passageway.

'Hello... Jeff to Malcolm... Do you read me?'

'Loud and clear, Jeff. Just lifting the entrance slab now. Over.'

'Received. Likewise this end. It's going to take some serious effort. Over.'

'Good luck to you. Over.'

Neil beamed. 'Your radio discipline is better than ours. I'm very impressed.'

Breckenridge responded with an awkward simper, whilst tapping his foot on the loose flagstone that Neil had found during his previous visit. 'Right, let's get this thing up and out of the way.'

Nathaniel helped Neil to lift it to one side, whilst Breckenridge and Parry got to work with the cement around the underlying slab. The rhythmic clanging of bolsters began to echo around the chapel, as the archaeologists, now wearing safety glasses, busily chipped away at the rock-hard mortar.

After five minutes, Breckenridge paused briefly to catch his breath. 'Phew, they did a good job when they sealed this one,' he declared before resuming work.

It took nearly thirty minutes to remove all the mortar from around the stone. Their success was borne out when it finally began to wobble freely when handled. Parry took a number of still photographs of the scene, then swapped to his video camera.

'It all needs to be recorded,' he explained.

The lower slab was far heavier than the flagstone above it, and it took the remaining three men, armed with two long iron bars, some time and effort to lever it upwards. When it slowly began to rise, a black, foetid void was revealed beneath. The men winced as the musty aroma of stale air reached their nostrils, but undeterred, they continued with the lift until the heavy mass of granite was eased away from its resting place. Now, at last, the full extent of the opening could be viewed. It was considerably smaller than the slab that had covered it, but just sufficient to allow a man of ample build to squeeze through into the chamber beneath.

The three women, who'd been standing well back, now moved forward and peered down into the hole.

Holly pinched the end of her nose. 'What a stench. I bet Enid Blyton didn't mention that in her novels!'

Selina chuckled. 'Very funny.' Then she turned to Breckenridge, who was now on his hands and knees and leaning into the chamber's inky interior. 'What can you see, Doctor?'

Breckenridge switched on his flashlight and shone it down into the darkness. 'A rocky floor, approximately eight feet down.'

He lowered his head further into the opening, and panned the torch beam around the roughly hewn walls beneath him. 'I can see the entrance to the passageway proper. Other than that the area is completely empty. Not a sausage in here, folks!'

Miriam groaned, prompting Neil to pat her on the shoulder. 'It's early days yet,' he smiled. 'Have faith!'

Breckenridge then removed a small telescopic ladder from its canvas coverall and extended it to its full length before feeding one end into the void. He fitted a surgical mask over his mouth and nose and switched on the lamp fitted to his hard hat.

'Once more unto the breach, dear friends, as Shakespeare once said.'

He climbed onto the ladder and slipped down into the darkness, finally disappearing from sight. His voice soon echoed up from below. 'As I thought, definitely nothing in here except rock and dust… It's safe for you to come down now.'

Neil climbed down next, followed by Nathaniel and then, finally, Trevor Parry. Neil stood for a second, taking in his new environment and allowing his eyes to adjust to the gloom. The light from his headgear flashed around him, its beam colliding with those from his companions' lamps, and casting long shadows across the crudely hewn rock walls. The chamber measured approximately twelve feet square, and had been fashioned from the volcanic pedestal upon which the castle was built. Green slime streaked the walls and, somewhere in the distance, he could hear water dripping.

Next, he scanned the uneven floor for anything, anything at all. But Breckenridge had been right. There was nothing. It was as if the depressing little chamber had been thoroughly scoured of its past. Neil imagined the scene, three and a half centuries before. The tartan-clad women and their children huddled around the damp walls, their only source of light being the odd candle, and trying desperately to keep warm whilst the hostilities between the Camerons and the Clan Chattan raged above their heads.

'Ready to move on into the passage proper, then?' Breckenridge was eager to go further.

'Aye, lead the way, Malcolm,' Parry responded.

'Good luck,' Miriam called out from above. 'Do take care, please.'

Breckenridge advanced carefully through the crudely

carved opening into the passage. 'Watch your step. It's very uneven,' he warned his companions.

The walls seemed to close in on them as they progressed, and the chill was palpable now, enough to force Neil to wrap his fingers around the end of his nose in an effort to warm it up.

'At least the smell's subsided, now the place has been opened up,' he commented.

'Yes, thank heavens,' Nathaniel agreed, close on his heels. 'It's a touch cold down here, though.'

Breckenridge's radio burst into life just then. Neil's stomach tightened as the suddenness of the transmission jolted his senses.

'Hello, Malcolm. Jeff here. Over.'

'Go ahead.'

'We're finally in at the other end. Took an enormous effort to get that bloody slab away.'

'What can you see?'

'Not a lot… just rock. Oh, and we've picked up a small brass button. Looks quite old; possibly Georgian.'

'How far in are you?'

'Five yards or so. Moving on now.'

'Okay. Keep us posted. Over.'

'Will do.' The echoing stopped and the silence returned.

They'd certainly done better than their colleagues, now having progressed some fifteen yards from the entrance chamber. Their torch beams continued to scour the walls and floor for something of interest, but there was still nothing: not even a discarded button at this end of the tunnel! The obvious absence of any link with the past resulted in a quickening of their pace, perhaps a sign of their mounting frustration. It wasn't long, though, before the radio crackled again.

'Malcolm… Jeff here. We've now reached the limit of our ingress. Massive roof fall, I'm afraid. We've got no idea how extensive it is beyond where we are. Long and the short of it is… we're going no further today. Sorry. Over.'

'Received that, Jeff. Stay put for a bit. We'll give you a shout when we reach the limit of *our* progress. Stand by.'

Breckenridge looked over his shoulder. 'Bit of a shame, that. But it's pretty much what we were expecting, I guess.'

Having received confirmation of the roof fall, he moved on, paying particular attention now to the rocky ceiling above him. Neil was looking up too, checking for cracks and fissures in the rock, and listening for the sound of anything falling from above.

Nathaniel's calming voice then echoed behind him. 'It's stayed up this long. I can't see it falling in on us now.'

'All the same, no harm in being cautious.' Neil was still looking up, when Breckenridge announced, 'Brick wall up ahead, folks. Think we're coming to the end, I'm afraid.'

When they finally reached the wall, Parry moved to the head of the column and examined the still richly coloured brickwork. 'I'd say that this was mid-eighteenth-century hand-moulded bricks; pinks, browns and greys. I've seen similar examples in local farmhouses of the period.'

'Selina seemed to think that her Victorian predecessors were responsible for this work,' said Neil.

'No, this is far earlier than that: mid to late 1700s, in my opinion,' Parry replied.

'So this wall could have been put up just after Culloden, then,' Nathaniel contributed.

'Very likely,' said Parry, running his hand over the old brickwork.

Breckenridge rubbed his chin. 'Is it possible that after the hoard was hidden down here, the roof collapsed behind it, and for some reason it was subsequently bricked up from this end?'

'But why?' said Neil. 'Why brick it up, so you can't get to it?'

'What's to stop you knocking a wall down when you want your money?' Nathaniel reasoned.

'It's possible, I suppose,' Neil agreed. 'What do you think, Malcolm?'

'I think we should remove some bricks and have a look through to the other side. That's what I think we should do.'

They hurried back along the passage and up the ladder to where the women were still waiting. Neil apprised them of the age of the wall, whilst Parry and Breckenridge returned to their cars to collect more tools.

'I had no idea the brickwork in the passage was put up that early,' said Selina. 'I suppose that puts a whole new perspective on things.'

Miriam's eyes sparkled. 'Could it be that they bricked up the hoard as a way of keeping it safe from prying eyes? After the roof fall the other end, I mean.'

'Surely it would be a risky thing to do, leaving the hoard down there with the roof so unstable,' said Holly.

Neil took off his hat and ran his fingers through his sweat-dampened hair.

'But what if they brought the roof down deliberately, so that the entrance from the field was well and truly secured? Then bricked up this end, so that access could be gained only when they so desired. All they needed was a few large hammers, or a ram of sorts, something like that.'

Holly nodded. 'Ingenious, if you're right. It's a shame we will never really know what happened.'

The two archaeologists returned, laden with sledgehammers and bolsters.

'Back to work, then!' said Breckenridge as he climbed down the ladder and accepted the tools from Parry.

Having made a further assessment of the wall, the experts decided to remove a number of bricks close to the floor and in the centre of the structure. The lime mortar was then painstakingly chipped away from the header of the first small brick, until it became loose and could be eased out. Breckenridge handed it to Parry. Then lying on his belly, he shone his torch through the hole. For a second he said nothing, then came a gasp.

'What is it?' said Neil excitedly. 'What can you see?'

Breckenridge scrambled to his feet. He was beaming. 'It's a single-skinned wall, just like we thought; just one course of bricks. I can see beyond it, to the rubble from the roof fall, about ten yards further along the tunnel.'

Then he grabbed Neil's sleeve and swallowed hard. 'I can also see a number of large wooden chests, heavy-looking things. Look for yourself.'

Neil almost fell onto the floor, pressing the button on his Maglite as he went. He could see clearly into the area behind the wall, and to the huge pile of rock debris beyond. Then, as he panned the beam around, there they were... one, two, three large wooden chests: each braced with iron, and dome-topped. They lay about, scattered randomly around the small chamber. Elation began to surge through him and he now had an inkling as to how Howard Carter and Lord Carnarvon must've felt when they finally discovered the tomb of Tutankhamun!

He leapt up, so that Nathaniel and Parry could each take their turn.

'Do you think it's just possible we could've struck lucky?' he suggested, shaking hands with Breckenridge.

'Well, unless those chests are a figment of our imaginations, then we've struck something,' the archaeologist replied, still grinning.

The bricks came out easily once the first gap had been made. But they took no chances, treating the old wall like cut glass and repeatedly checking the integrity of the brickwork above the ever-widening threshold into the past!

Whilst they worked, the team at the other end of the tunnel called again for an update. Breckenridge gave them the good news, which generated a muffled cheer from the handset.

'They seem happy,' Nathaniel remarked as he slid another brick out and handed it to Parry, who was stacking them neatly behind him.

'Let's hope we can give them some better news when we get in there,' said Neil.

It took about twenty minutes to create a large enough hole for a man to safely squeeze through on his stomach. Breckenridge checked above and around the hole for cracks or weakness, then turned back to the others.

'Seems sound enough. I don't want to remove any more bricks than absolutely necessary, so sorry about the size of the hole.' He looked around at the little group. 'So, who's going to go through first? One of us will have to remain here, though… just in case!'

He patted Neil's arm. 'Do you want to be the first through? You did kick this all off in the first place, after all.'

Neil nodded. 'I'm up for it. But what about you, Nat? You're family.'

Nathaniel placed his hand on Neil's shoulder. 'The good doctor's right. This is your baby, Neil. You go through first.'

'Okay, then,' Neil concurred. 'If you're sure.'

'Right, that's agreed then. I'll stay here, until you're all out,' said Parry.

Armed with a torch, Neil dropped down, first to his knees, and then onto his belly. Using his forearms to propel himself, he eased his body through the small gap and into the newly discovered chamber. Sensing his feet were at last clear of the wall, he stood up and brushed himself down.

'You okay in there?' Breckenridge called out.

'Aye, no problem.' He looked up and shone his torch onto the rock above his head. 'The roof looks sound enough in here.'

'Good. Go and put us out of our misery, then. See if you can open the chests.'

'Okay. Cross everything, including your fingers!'

'Let me know if you need any tools,' Breckenridge advised him.

Neil selected the chest nearest to him. He approached it with caution, as if expecting it to suddenly come alive. A sense of anxiety gripped the pit of his stomach as he traced his finger over the faint letters, inscribed in gold leaf on the heavy lid… *G2R*, it read: the royal cypher of King George the Second.

On closer examination, the massive chest appeared to be made of wood and covered in leather with decorative close-nailed brass studding to the top and sides. The container was also accoutred with solid brass carrying handles and brass corner guards, befitting of a royal treasury chest! To the front, the all-important lock and lifting ring were also forged in brass, and looked as if they were in perfect condition. Until, that was, Neil noticed the damage beneath the lock; leverage marks, where someone had obviously prised open the lid at some stage. With a bit of luck, the thing would be unlocked, he predicted. So, he took a deep breath and grasped the sides of the lid. The senseless desire not to corrupt the integrity of this giant artefact had to be overcome, so he slowly began to lift it, swallowing hard as he did so. As the gap widened, he expected his eyes to feast on the glint of gold within. But he was sorely disappointed; the chest was completely empty, its only resident a tiny spider that scampered nervously across its base.

'Have you found anything yet?' The call came from the other side of the hole.

'The first chest is empty,' Neil called out. 'There's evidence of it being forced open at some stage. I'll check the others.'

There was a scrambling from behind him and the light from a torch appeared through the hole in the wall. It was Breckenridge, followed by Nathaniel.

'We'll give you a hand. How many chests are there?'

'I count eight, unless there's any under the rubble from the roof fall.'

'Unlikely,' said Breckenridge, adjusting the lamp on his hat. 'They all seem to be clustered around this end, immediately behind the brick wall.'

Each man selected another chest and urgently checked inside.

'This one's empty,' Breckenridge announced.

'This one too,' said Nathaniel.

'Damn and blast,' Neil growled. 'Same here.'

The next three provided similar disappointment. Not so much as a brass farthing graced the interior of any of them.

Nathaniel wandered across to the last of the eight chests, a dejected look present on his face.

'Might as well check the last one,' he muttered.

'Be my guest,' said Neil, leaning on the lid of the receptacle he'd just opened. 'Looks like we're 260 years too late!'

Nathaniel eased up the lid of the last chest. Its dry brass hinges squealed as it angled back until fully open.

His torch beam probed the void within it.

'Empty as well,' he reported. Then he directed his Maglite into the corners of the chest so that he could see properly.

'Hang on... what's this?' He leaned in and brought out a loosely rolled sheet of yellowing paper, its age no doubt considerable. Also in his hand was a gold coin, its shine muted by dust and time.

His companions were clustered around him in a trice.

'It's exactly the same as the coins we've got upstairs,' Nathaniel declared with some excitement. 'A five-guinea piece, dated 1729. It was jammed behind the corner brace inside.'

Neil took it from him. 'It's got the East India Company mark, the EIC, just like the others. You're looking at ten grand's worth there, Nat!'

Breckenridge, however, was more interested in the delicate roll of paper, which he had unravelled and was now examining under the light of his torch.

'I think this letter finally resolves the mystery of the hoard. Come and have a look.'

Neil and Nathaniel joined him and peered over his shoulder at the spidery scrawl of the Second Earl of Albemarle...

Edinburgh Sepr 12ᵗʰ 1746

Sir,

I received today with infinite satisfaction your most welcome letter, informing me that the bullion recently plundered from His Royall Highness, The Duke of Cumberland's forces in Moray on April 16ᵗʰ has happily been located.

The news of Mistress MacGillivray's wise and courageous decision to deliver the spoils of her late husband's misdeed, is most agreeable.

Tis unfortunate that this poor woman should, as you state, unwittingly inherit the proceeds of so audacious an act as was ever committed, and would I suspect otherwise, she could surely expect the noose. I am, however indebted to you sir, my staff having received excellent hospitality and attention to ther comfort whilst in repose at your home during recent inspections around the north. For these reasons alone, I am favourably disposed to accept the truthfulness of the lady's account and wish to assure both yourself and her, that once all such monies are returned to His Majesty's custody, then nothing more shall be said of this matter and no judicial proceedings will be due.

Please advise your good friend, if you are able, that I have ordered a company of Guises Regt, under Captain Yorke, to proceed with all haste to Cullaird Tower from the garrison at Fort Augustus. Once in receipt of all that is owed, then a

copy of this letter will be duly supplied as confirmation of my
goodwill in this matter.
    I trust this meets with your full expectations.

I am with the greatest regard
Sr
Your most obedient humble servant

Albemarle

Sir John Grieve. Balvonie House, Inverness

Neil let out a low whistle. 'So Meg MacGillivray returned all the money to the government, in exchange for immunity from any form of punishment. I find that astonishing, bearing in mind the family's Jacobite sympathies. The gold contained in these chests would've probably been sufficient to fund a further rebellion!'

Breckenridge shook his head. 'Perhaps the burden of what her husband had done proved too much for her to bear. Let's not forget, the government forces were sweeping through northern Scotland after Culloden, hell-bent on wiping out the Highland way of life and its very culture once and for all. Can you imagine what would've happened if they'd discovered by some other means what had been hidden here?'

Neil grunted in agreement. 'Meg and her family would probably have ended up on the end of a rope, just like Albemarle mentioned in his letter. I wouldn't have been surprised if the castle had been burnt to the ground too. No, I agree with you Malcolm. She obviously gave it up to protect her family and home.'

Nathaniel pointed to the names at the bottom of the letter.

'So who was this guy Albemarle, then? And Sir John Grieve? Have you heard of him?'

Breckenridge provided the answer. 'William Keppel, the 2nd Earl of Albemarle was a well-respected soldier, and an officer in the Coldsteam Guards. His family were very much part of the Hanoverian royal family's inner circle. He commanded the government front line at Culloden and succeeded the Duke of Cumberland as Commander-in-Chief of British Forces in North Britain in the July of 1746. As you can imagine, he was a very powerful man. Ruthless too. Meg was a very lucky woman, thanks to the mediation skills of this chap Grieve!'

Breckenridge then pointed to the stamp at the foot of the page. 'See here, the three escallops within the belted escroll. This was Albemarle's personal stamp.'

'And Grieve... what about him?'

'I've heard the name. He was something of a socialite, a rich landowner who owned large tracts of land south of Loch Ness. We know he enjoyed good working relationships with both the government representatives in the Highlands and the local clan chiefs; a natural diplomat, seemingly. For some reason he's spoken up for Meg. It seems they were well acquainted and she may have approached him to act as intermediary when it came to returning the stolen cash. I'll have to do some more digging in relation to him, I'm afraid.'

'So it looks like we're done here, then,' said Neil with a hint of disappointment.

'Yep, I do believe we are. If Mrs Cope is happy, we'll retain the letter here for further research and perhaps public display in due course. That's if she is agreeable, of course. There may even be some way we can remove the chests at a later stage... you never know. One thing's for sure: we can't underestimate the historical importance of these artefacts and the story behind them, treasure or no treasure.'

'I'm sure that won't be a problem,' said Nathaniel, still clutching the coin.

'At least you're a little bit richer, having come down here,' said Neil, heading back to the hole in the wall.

Nathaniel tucked the coin into his pocket. 'I've got an idea as to what we will do with this little beauty. I'll have to discuss it with Selina, though.'

Neil decided not to pursue the matter. He dropped down by the wall and was about to lower himself onto his stomach so that he could squeeze through the hole. As he did so, his torch beam picked up something further along the wall, something cream-coloured. He shuffled along to investigate and came across two old hessian sacks, both empty and partially perished.

'They must've used these to get the coins out of here,' he surmised when Breckenridge joined him.

'Very likely. You know what? I now think the roof must've fallen in naturally. I can't see them wishing to make unnecessary work for themselves when it came to removing the chests. My guess is they brought them in through the tunnel from the outside. There's no way they carried them down through the chapel floor. The roof must've collapsed sometime between the April and September of that year, so they had to remove the cash in sacks. Then for whatever reason, probably to prevent anyone getting closer to the roof fall, they bricked up the tunnel... and the empty chests.'

'Thereby drawing a line under the saga of the theft once and for all,' Nathaniel contributed.

'I don't think you're far from the truth there, Nat,' Neil agreed. 'Of course they may also have wanted to prevent anyone else finding the chests, empty or not. Secreting such items with the king's cipher emblazoned upon them may well have been misinterpreted by both Jacobites and government troops!'

He crawled back to the hole in the wall and gestured to Nathaniel to exit first.

'Best we get out of here and give your wife the good... or bad news, whichever way you want to spin it!'

With that, they clambered back into the main tunnel. One by one, the loose bricks were carefully replaced, until the abandoned pay chests, once the cherished property of His Majesty's Fourth Regiment of Foot, finally vanished from view...

Epilogue

Selina Cope stood hunched against the icy December blast, her chin buried into the folds of a grey cashmere scarf. Her breath turned to vapour, chilled by the near gale that prowled down the Royal Mile. To the west, above the imposing chimney stacks of grey Georgian tenements, the sky had begun to fade from crisp blue to a deep apricot. It was mid afternoon, and Selina stood arm in arm with her cousin Miriam at the main doorway to Edinburgh's High Court. Nathaniel lingered behind the two women, relieved that it was all over at last.

The trial had lasted for more than three weeks, but the jury had returned a verdict in less than three hours... guilty on all counts. Conspiracy to murder Ualas Diamid MacBean and conspiracy to commit theft by housebreaking had been the primary charges for which he'd been found guilty. Those relating to the murders of Laura and Duncan Fraser had been thrown out. There'd been a couple of other lesser offences dealt with too, but the long and the short of it was a sentence of eighteen years for Dawie Van Nieuwoudt.

Boyd Duff had appeared in the same court the week before, but had been cleared of any direct involvement in the offences committed by Mungo McQuade and his partners in crime. He had, however, been imprisoned for two years for a number of unconnected matters.

A small cluster of press photographers had been waiting for them when they emerged onto the street. They urgently snapped away with their cameras, until Nathaniel finally managed to usher the women away to the refuge of a coffee shop in nearby St Giles Street. They'd been sitting, waiting to be served for a minute or so, when Neil Strachan walked in and joined them.

'The press guys told me you'd sought refuge in here,' he announced with a grin.

'I'm surprised they haven't come in to join us,' Selina muttered discontentedly. 'Still, I suppose they're only doing their job.'

Neil took off his overcoat and pulled up a chair, just as the young waitress arrived to take their order.

'What can I get you, please?' she asked politely.

They all made their choice and the girl scurried away towards the servery, still writing on her notepad.

'What did you make of the verdict?' Neil asked, looking at each of them in turn.

Selina just managed a smile. 'I suppose justice has finally been done. Eighteen years before the possibility of parole is a long time for a man on the verge of turning seventy. I wouldn't be surprised if he died in prison.'

Miriam let out a little snort. 'The bastard deserves everything he gets. I think he got off lightly, if you ask me. It should've been life, meaning life!'

'Well, his advocate successfully argued that he hadn't been instrumental in the murders of Laura and Duncan. It was only ever supposed to have been a break-in whilst they were away on holiday. The jury accepted that it was McQuade who'd acted alone in escalating the whole thing to murder.'

'Do you believe Dawie's story, then, Chief Inspector?' Miriam was shaking her head.

'I think we have to. The notes we found in his hotel room, and all the other evidence, such as his conversations with Boyd Duff, leave us little option.'

Miriam wasn't convinced. 'But he also denied having any involvement in the death of Ualas MacBean. That turned out to be a lie, didn't it? When the content of those text messages from him to McQuade came out in court, you should've seen his face!'

'Aye, I did,' said Neil. 'I can't believe he didn't realise we could retrieve them!'

'And Duff,' said Nathaniel. 'Are we really expected to believe he knew nothing of all this?'

'Oh, he knew about the plan to break into the castle, all right. But as the judge explained to the jury in his summing up, knowledge alone does not constitute involvement in the plan itself.'

'All the same...' Miriam wasn't convinced on that score either.

'Look, if the evidence isn't there, it isn't there,' said Selina. 'He did, after all, call to warn us, and had tried to talk some sense into McQuade. Let's put it all behind us now. McQuade can't hurt us any more, and Sandy Blair... well, his fall from grace was more a tragedy than anything else.'

'For what it's worth, I do believe Duff's account,' Neil interjected. 'He's a small-time villain from the seventies and eighties. Murder and kidnapping are out of his league.'

The waitress then returned and delivered a tray of coffees to the table, prompting a change of direction in the conversation.

'I hear you've been promoted to Detective Chief Inspector on a permanent basis. Congratulations, Mr Strachan.' Selina sipped her coffee, her eyes raised to meet his.

'Thank you.' Neil seemed a little embarrassed. The timing

of his promotion hadn't been the best, and he wanted to make it clear that it hadn't been on the back of the enquiry into the Frasers' murders.

'I have to say, I didn't expect the promotion, but my boss has been ill, and has since moved to another job. It left a vacancy that urgently needed filling.'

'I'm sure there was a little more to it than that, Chief Inspector. You did a fine job back in May, and so did that young detective sergeant of yours. How is she, by the way?'

'Oh, Holly's fine. She wanted to accompany me down here for the sentencing, but unfortunately she's got another trial running over in Aberdeen.'

'Well, pass our good wishes on to her, will you?'

'I certainly will, Selina. Thank you.'

Nathaniel finished his coffee. 'We'd better make tracks over to the station, or we'll miss our train back to Inverness.'

They all got up and headed to the door. Neil followed, just behind Nathaniel. 'You mentioned when we were down in that passageway under the chapel that you had an idea as to what you wanted to do with the five-guinea piece we found in that old chest. Did the idea come to fruition?'

Nathaniel looked back at him. 'It did, yes. We gave it to Sandy Blair's widow. Selina was very keen to make the gesture too. She still feels very guilty about her outburst out at Gask that night. Between you and me, she will always bear a little of the responsibility for Sandy's death. Anne, Sandy's wife, was understandably devastated by what had happened, and her financial situation was a little tight, to say the least. She sold the coin to the National Museum for a tidy sum. It's on display there now with two of the pay chests that we found that day. There's another one on view at the Culloden visitor centre too.'

'Aye, I'd heard you finally managed to get them out.'

Nathaniel smiled. 'It was a pig of a job. We had to take up

more of the chapel floor, but we figured it was worth it, and in the interests of preserving the story for all. Something I'm sure you'd appreciate, Neil, being something of a historian!'

'I most certainly do. And there was some story attached to those pay chests, after all!'

He placed a hand on Nathaniel's shoulder. 'That was a very charitable thing to do… parting company with that coin, I mean.'

'Well, let's face it, we're not short of a quid or two! Anne's needs were far more pressing than ours. She didn't deserve all the bad press her family received following Selina's abduction and the disclosure of Sandy's involvement in the other murders.'

They emerged into the fast-approaching dusk and walked along towards the New Steps, which would take them down to Market Street, and subsequently, Waverley Station.

Neil stopped to say goodbye. 'My car's parked just a little further on, so we'll need to part company here.'

He shook hands with each of them in turn. 'I hope you can move on, now that the trial's finally over. Do you have any plans for the castle?'

'Oh yes,' said Selina, her grey eyes glinting. 'We're moving back to live there permanently. Nat will still be able to do some consultancy work for his company, and we'll run the distillery together… with the help of our new manager, I hasten to add!'

'And I'm going to live there with them,' Miriam added, sporting a wide grin. 'Now the kids are off their hands, they'll be rattling around that place, and they'll never use six bedrooms all at once!'

'Wow. I wasn't expecting news like that,' Neil exclaimed. 'All I can say is, good luck to you all.'

'Thank you for everything, Chief Inspector.' Selina unexpectedly stepped forward and embraced him, planting a firm kiss on his cheek.

'Drop by if you're passing Cullaird,' she called out as the little group skipped down the steps.

Neil watched and waved, until the three heads had disappeared from view, then he turned and walked back towards his car. At the rear of the High Court, a private prison van stood waiting with its side door slid back and its engine ticking quietly over. Then, just as he passed by, the heavy doors to the court swung open and out walked a prison officer carrying a property bag. Handcuffed to him was a dejected-looking Dawie Van Nieuwoudt, still wearing his smart grey suit. His head was bowed, his demeanour acquiescent, as he stepped up into the vehicle. Neil stopped in his tracks and looked on, concluding that the South African had aged visibly during the five long months he'd spent on remand.

When Van Nieuwoudt reached the top of the vehicle's steps, he paused, and for a few short seconds the two men's eyes met, before he was ushered inside.

There had been no discernable expression upon his face, just a vagueness, and a realisation perhaps that his final destination that day would be home for the remainder of his twilight years.

Neil continued his walk down towards Bank Street, and the endless stream of red tail lights that flowed around the corner in front of him. He glanced up at the tiny windows of the prison van as it passed slowly by, but there were no faces pressed against the glass, just the reflection from the internal lights at the Bank of Scotland across the road.

He pulled out his mobile phone and dialled Cat's number, only to be greeted by the cheerful tones of her answerphone message. After the tone, he spoke softly. 'Hi darlin'. I'm all done here and I'm on my way home. See you in three hours…'

Author's Note

The Battle of Culloden took place on a desolate expanse of Drumossie Moor, east of Inverness on 16th April 1746. It was the last pitched battle ever to be fought on British soil, and without a doubt, one of the bloodiest.

A popular myth abounds that the only belligerents on that tragic day were the English and the Scots. In truth, this was anything but the case. Whilst the royal army, commanded by King George the Second's youngest son, Prince William Augustus, Duke of Cumberland, did comprise many notable English regiments, there were a number of Scottish units allied to their cause. These were notably the 2/1st (Royal) Regiment, ('The Royal Scots'), the oldest regiment in the British Army; Campbell's 21st (Royal Scots Fusiliers) Regiment and the 43rd Highlanders, better known today as The Black Watch. It is interesting to note that one of the captains serving in this regiment was Aeneas Mackintosh, Laird of the Clan Mackintosh. His young wife, Lady Anne, raised a regiment from that clan, together with other local men from Strathnairn, such as the MacGillivrays, MacBeans and Shaws in support of the Jacobites. Together they were known as the Clan Chattan, and were led at Culloden by Alexander MacGillivray of Dunmaglass, who fell mortally wounded at the Well of the Dead.

Similarly, the Jacobite army was by no means an exclusively

Highland force. It included Englishmen, serving with the Manchester Regiment, Irishmen with the Irish Picquets and the Frenchmen of the Royal Écossais. Add to the overall mix small contingents of Hessians, Austrians, Ulstermen and Dutchmen, to name but a few, and one can appreciate that this final clash of the Jacobite rebellion was indeed a truly muddled affair, based upon the ideals and political affiliations of a number of diverse groups and nations.

The battle itself is best remembered for the famous charge of the Highland clans. Those who took part were gallant but often ill-disciplined warriors, many of whom were merely crofters or farmers. They were lightly armed and pitched against a well-drilled professional army, supported by artillery and cavalry. The Highlanders fell in their hundreds, victims not only of the well-ordered redcoats, but also the inept, short-sighted tactics of some of their own commanders.

An officer in the government front line summed up the carnage…

Making a dreadful huzza and even crying 'Run ye dogs',
they (the Jacobites) broke in between the grenadiers of Barrel
and Monro; but these had given their fire according to the
general direction, and then parried them with their screwed
bayonets. The two cannon on that division were so well
served, that when within two yards of them they received a
full discharge of cartridge shot, which made a dreadful havoc;
and those who crowded into the opening received a full fire
from the centre of Bligh's regiment, which still increased the
number of slain.

The course of the battle is fully documented elsewhere, but perhaps the above reminiscence epitomises the scale of the slaughter on that sleet-shrouded moor.

Culloden was indeed a tragedy, but it was also the iconic

culmination of a nine-month-long popular uprising that had threatened the very existence of the Hanoverian monarchy.

Before the battle, in early April 1746, Cumberland had marched his army from Aberdeen along the Moray coast, camping at Nairn on the night before the final confrontation. Whilst the government forces celebrated the Duke's twenty-fifth birthday, the Jacobites hatched a plan to attack their camp during the night. The attempt, alluded to in the story above, failed miserably, resulting in widespread desertions and general chaos. The following day, those clansmen who had found their way back to Culloden faced their enemy with empty stomachs and without any proper rest. It was a recipe for disaster!

References to the government army's baggage train, and in particular the carriage of army pay during the period, is in the main historically accurate, as far as can be researched. The robbing of that baggage train, referred to earlier in the book, is of course fictional. I am not aware of any such incident occurring during the Jacobite campaign, but one such attempt was apparently made during the American War of Independence (1775–1783).

The approximate current-day value of George the Second coinage referred to in the book is generally correct at the time of writing, especially in respect of those items that are Lima or EIC marked, and presented in extremely fine condition.

All the main characters portrayed in the book, both historical and those from the present day, are of course entirely fictional. Passing references to genuine historical figures such as Lord George Murray, Alexander MacGillivray of Dunmaglass, and other notable characters from the Jacobite period have been included for reasons of historical context.

The ancestral seat of the Fraser family, Cullaird Castle, does not exist, although its layout and appearance is historically accurate and is based upon a similar structure with which I'm extremely familiar, located in rural Perthshire.

References to locations around Cullaird Castle, namely Strathnairn, Inverness and Culloden, are in the main geographically accurate.

The Clach an Airm stone does exist within the Gask Plantation in Strathnairn. It is documented as a being a rallying point for the Clan Chattan, prior to their final march to Culloden Moor.

I have also, as far as possible, attempted to accurately reflect the policing and judicial processes that would be followed in a case such as that featured in this book. Any technical inaccuracies are my responsibility alone, and will only have been included so as to suit the plot.

Acknowledgements

Once again, I have relied heavily upon online resources during the research for this book. However, I am indebted to the authors of those works mentioned in the bibliography section below for the detailed insights they have provided into the period leading up to, during and immediately after the Battle of Culloden.

Equally, I am thankful for the wealth of information available at the Culloden Battlefield Visitor Centre, where the moving account of this iconic episode in British history is all but brought to life. It has been my many visits to this haunting location that has without doubt inspired me to base this novel on the events that surrounded the battle.

I am also deeply indebted to Mr Ian Bailey, Curator of the Adjutant General's Corps Museum, Winchester, for his time, patience and valuable assistance, by providing numerous copies of historic documents relating to the subject of army pay, and also allowing me to inspect a number of valuable exhibits from the Jacobite period that are displayed in the museum.

My thanks go to Mr William Forbes, whose moving account on the Strathnairn Heritage Society website of the activity that took place at the Clach an Airm stone on the fateful day before the Battle of Culloden, perfectly evokes the sense of history that pervades the place.

As always, I am eternally grateful to my immediate family for their support throughout this project, especially my wife, Rose, who, amongst other things, has accompanied me on my travels around the remote byways of Strathnairn and on many occasions, the windswept Culloden Battlefield, during my research for this book.

Lastly, my thanks go to all my friends, and to those readers of my first novel, *The Drumbeater*, many of whom I've never met, who have encouraged me to get on and write this, my second offering. In doing so, they have been a huge source of motivation, without whom I may never have completed this undertaking!

Clive Allan 2016

Bibliography

Allison, Hugh G, *Culloden Tales*, 2007.
Craig, Maggie, *Bare-Arsed Banditti: The Men of the '45*, 2009.
Pollard, Tony, *Culloden: The History and Archaeology of the Last Clan Battle*, 2009.
Prebble, John, *Culloden*, 1961.
Reid, Stuart, *Cumberland's Culloden Army 1745–46*, 2012.